A SONG
IN THE
DAYLIGHT

A SONG
IN THE
DAYLIGHT

PAULLINA SIMONS

wm

WILLIAM MORROW
An Imprint of HarperCollins*Publishers*

The Society of Authors as the Literary Representatives of the Estate of Virginia Woolf

HarperCollins books may be purchased for educational, business, or sales promotional use. For information, please e-mail the Special Markets Department at SPsales@harpercollins.com.

Originally published as A Song in the Daylight in Great Britain in 2009 by HarperCollins Publishers

FIRST U.S. EDITION

Library of Congress Cataloging-in-Publication Data has been applied for.

ISBN 978-0-06-244437-0

18 19 20 21 22   DIX/LSC   10 9 8 7 6 5 4 3 2

. . . Do not lose heart . . . Outward man is perishing, yet inward man is being renewed day by day . . . We do not look at the things which are seen, but at the things which are not seen. For the things which are seen are temporary, but the things which are not seen are eternal.

2 Corinthians 4:16–1

To Sara Belk, a mother,
a thespian, a theologian,
a friend, a woman extraordinaire

Prologue

Friday Night (Almost)
Like Any Other

"Yes, it's mainly desert lands, nothing but dry creeks," Doug was saying, relaying to Jared his torrid experience in the Australian bush, "but when it rains five hundred miles away, you get an astonishing twenty feet of water pouring through the arid lake beds and salty playas. Doesn't happen very often, though, the deluge. And even when it does, it quickly evaporates. The stasis is earth, waterless and scorched."

"Hmm," Jared muttered, impatient fingers tapping on the desk. He wanted to get back to their conversation about the Yankees' middle relief pitching. But Doug had recently come back from a trip to the Australian outback and for weeks straight had insisted on telling Jared *all* about it.

Jared had had a busy afternoon of capitalization meetings before the long Memorial Day weekend, and at 3:30, his assistant said that Emily had called and needed him to call back *right away*. He was going to, but he got swamped with a Tokyo call, an emergency round-up about a possible bankruptcy filing for one of their affiliates, a Hong Kong call, and finally the usual Friday-night banter from Doug, when at 4:45 the phone rang again.

"Dad!"

"Oh, sorry, Em. I'm snowed under. What's up?" He motioned Doug not to leave; he had one more thing to add to their revolving argument about the Yankees' dire pitching prospects.

"What's *up*," Emily said with all stridency, "is I have a volleyball game today at five and Mom is not home to drive me!"

"Volleyball game *when*?" Jared's hand with the index finger out was still raised.

"In fifteen minutes," said Emily, apparently through her teeth. "And did I mention Mom's not home to drive me?"

"Where is she?" Jared was waving to Doug, to say *wait*.

"Dad? Are you even listening? I don't *know* where she is. I've been calling you since 3:30!"

"I'm sure Mom will be right back, Em. Isn't Michelangelo with her?"

"I thought he was, but Tara just brought him home."

"Who's Tara?"

Emily drew a long breath. "Our neighbor two doors down. Our neighbor for *seven* years."

"Oh, yeah."

"Apparently he had a playdate with Jen and Jess. So here we *all* are, except for Mom—who's not here. I don't know if I've mentioned it, but I have a MEET in fifteen minutes."

Jared's finger was still up for Doug, *just one minute*. "Call her cell."

"Dad, do you think I didn't call her five thousand times before I called you? And then Asher helpfully found her cell phone ringing on her makeup table in the bedroom."

"She didn't take her cell phone?" Jared put his finger down, and stared at his desk, instead of at the casually sitting Doug Grant.

"Correct."

"Well, how far could she have gone?" Jared said. "You know Mom never carries any cash on her."

"Dad!"

"All right." He shook his head. "I'm leaving. I'll be home in thirty minutes."

"I've got to be at the game in fifteen!"

"Can't you call a friend on the team? Have another mom drive you?"

"*Another* mom?"

"Or wait for me. I can't blink myself home, Emily. Either you wait for me, or you call someone else." Jared didn't know any of his daughter's friends by name. "I'm sure your mom will be right back."

"Back from where? Both her cars are in the drive!" Emily slammed down the phone.

Jared got up. "Sorry, Douglas. We'll finish this another time."

"Everything okay?"

"It's fine." He sighed. "Melodrama. Teenagers. Everything has to be done on *their* time." He was throwing his newspapers away as he talked; he stuffed his laptop into his leather bag, plus three annual reports in case he had time to work over the three-day weekend. "Larissa's not home to drive Emily to the game so, you know, major crisis."

"Can't wait for my girls to become cranky teenagers," said Doug. He had two toddlers.

"I don't want you to have the last word. But the Yankees are doomed without middle rotation pitching. When you're over on Monday for the barbecue, I'll explain it more thoroughly. Bring dessert." Jared grinned. "And bathing suits for Kate and the girls. We're firing up the pool."

"I'd love to, mate," said Doug with an Aussie flourish in his New Jersey twang. "You know I like nothing more than to hammer home why you're deluded about the Yanks. They're getting old! They have too many injuries! They can't hit! But I can't do it. The wife and I are going away for the weekend. Our fifth anniversary." Doug raised his eyebrows. "Atlantic City."

"Ah." Jared nodded. "Good for you. Stay away from the tables."

"Don't worry, Kate hates to gamble. I'll be lucky if I get an hour for blackjack. By the way, I've noticed that Jan is much better lately. What'd you say to her? She's sober every day, seems like. Nice work."

Jared shrugged. That last successful chat with Jan was months ago. But he couldn't talk about it now; he had to run.

They shook hands, wished each other a fine weekend. Jared said he would see Doug bright and early on Tuesday morning.

Forty-five traffic-y and frustrating minutes later he walked into his house. Emily had missed her game and was sitting at the kitchen table crying. Asher was in the den watching TV and Michelangelo was coloring on the floor near the dog. As Jared looked closer, he saw his younger son wasn't coloring near the dog, he was coloring *the* dog. Taking the markers (were these even washable?) away from the boy, he patted Emily's back.

She bucked away from his hand like a wild horse. "Don't touch me! Where's Mom?"

"I don't know," said Jared. "I just got home. But don't be mad at me. I'm sorry you missed your game."

"You should've called me back, Dad. I called you so many times."

"I was at work. I was busy." Jared felt a stab of guilt. He *was* at work, and he was busy part of the time, but really, he could've called back an hour earlier, and didn't. Larissa took care of home things; he never had to worry.

He called Maggie. "She's not with me, Jared," said Maggie. "I haven't seen since Tuesday. Maybe with Bo? Evelyn? Or call my husband. He's working late tonight. Researching materialism or immortality or something. On a Friday night, too." She scoffed mildly. "Maybe she's at the theater. *Saint Joan* opens next week. They've been rehearsing every day."

"Materialism and immortality, they're not one and the same?" Jared said jokingly before hanging up.

"Nah, I haven't seen your wife, man," said Ezra when Jared reached him. "She didn't come in today for rehearsals. Which is disturbing since not only do we open next Thursday but we finally did the run-through without the epilogue, as she expressly wanted, and she wasn't even here for it. What be up?"

"Did she call?"

"Didn't. Maybe she's gone out?"

"Yeah, with someone who has a car."

"Weird," said Ezra. "But I did have lunch with her two days ago, and have you noticed your wife's lost a *ton* of weight?"

"You think?" Jared had lost interest in the conversation. "She keeps denying it."

"Oh, yes. Who are you going to believe, me or your lying eyes, she says." Ezra grunted. "Hey, listen, Lar and Maggie are doing a beer run tomorrow afternoon for Monday's party, but are we still on for tomorrow night?"

"Of course. Let me find her first, though, 'kay?"

"Like I said, she's melted away." Ezra chuckled. "She's disappeared before our very eyes."

"Till tomorrow, dude. She can't have lost *that* much weight."

Jared called Bo, who hadn't spoken to Larissa since the week before. Evelyn finally picked up. "I'm bathing all five kids at once, Jared," she said. "I can't leave them for long. What's up?" She hadn't heard from Larissa since her birthday in April. This surprised Jared. Larissa always made an effort to keep in touch with Evelyn, her college friend.

Six o'clock became seven.

The kids were hungry. Jared ordered pizza from Nina's, then sat in the kitchen with them while they ate. For some reason he had lost his appetite. Finally he went upstairs to get changed, put on shorts, a T-shirt; he opened the bathroom, he opened her closet. Everything was neat, orderly, put away. On the bed were seven of his white shirts, still in sheaths of dry cleaner plastic; according to the ticket, picked up for him by her just this morning. The house was quiet. He looked inside Larissa's closet again. Peculiarly, he looked inside her jewelry box. What was he looking for? She had many beautiful things. He ambled around the bedroom. Bed was made, patted down, hospital-cornered; clothes were in the closet; shoes in their boxes; books on the shelves. Diamond earrings he gave her for their fifteenth wedding anniversary, which she loved and never went anywhere special without. Everything was in its place.

Everything except Larissa.

PART ONE
THE STONEMASON

How small of all that human hearts endure,
That part which laws or kings can cause or cure.

Samuel Johnson

Chapter One

1

Things Trains Bring

One sunny afternoon, on the dot of 12:45, from west to the east, after all the leaves had gone and the ground was frozen, into the concrete well of the Summit train station a shiny, stainless, steel-and-blue locomotive rolled in, the doors opened, and a smatter of people alighted.

Train tracks run through Summit, wind through it like the everflowing Passaic River. The station itself is brick and mortar, well kept, maintained by well-to-do people in a well-to-do town. You buy your ticket in a little office with white sash windows and red flowers on the sills, where a woman who wanted to retire ten years ago glares at you from behind the glass and her glasses as she sullenly sells you a one-way to Venice or a round trip to visit your lonely mother in Piermont.

To get to the train, you have to walk down forty concrete steps to the embankment where the train arrives and swishes open its doors for a few minutes. Neither the train nor the tracks can be seen from the road. Clearly this was the intent of the designers. Perhaps so that traffic wouldn't crawl to a stop in a town of twenty thousand

people every twenty minutes. But another reason could be that
the train tracks, unlike a river, were not deemed by the architects
and engineers to be aesthetically pleasing and were deliberately
hidden below the cobblestoned street, remaining invisible to the
town except for a small white-and-black RR sign on Maple Street,
pointing *that* way. You could live your whole life in Summit, New
Jersey, and not ever know your town had a train station that took
people away—and brought people in.

And yet it did bring people in, every day, and this day also.

Today it discharged a friendly woman with a baby carriage, an
older woman with a wheeled suitcase, and a young man in a leather
jacket.

The young man strolled out clacking the pavement with the
metal heels of his black riding boots, looked around, squinted,
pulled down his sunglasses and whistled for the conductor to
open the oversize hold compartment, from which he rolled out a
motorcycle.

"Some bike you got there," the conductor said. "Like a stallion.
But why'd you store it when you could've ridden it cross country?"

"Bike'd be stolen in five seconds." The young man grinned.
"And I'd be robbed and killed." He had a crooked smile, frizzy hair,
stubble.

"Robbed for what?" the conductor muttered. "After they had
your bike, what would they want with you?"

"They'd have to kill me to separate me from the bike."

"Ah." The conductor shrugged. "But I thought you was headed
to Maplewood?"

"I am. This isn't it?"

"No. It's Summit. D'you hear me calling it out?"

"Nah. I was sleeping. Damn." He smiled unperturbed. "How far
to Maplewood?"

"Six miles. You wanna get back on?"

The young man shook his head.

"Or two minutes on that thing." The conductor tipped his cap
enviously. "All aboard!" The train pulled away.

The biker was left standing on the platform, breathing in the freezing air, steadying his bike, the ratty duffel between his legs. He was hungry. He was thirsty. He decided to drive around town for a few minutes, get a bite to eat, relax, and then head to Maplewood. It would've been better had he come in the spring, like he'd planned. Still. *Fates, all kneel before ye*.

He got his bike up to the street on an elevator. After driving around the sleepy subdued Summit and not finding any place he wanted to stop, he looked instead for a road where he could open up the bike for a bit. It was real cold, too cold for him in the long term, but he was happy to be out and about. He wanted a sandwich. On Route 124, he raced at seventy for a few seconds, already out of Summit and in another bare-treed town. "WELCOME TO MADISON." He saw a large supermarket, an empty parking lot. "Grand Opening," the sign read, "Drive-through Pharmacy, Starbucks, Fresh Sushi Daily." *That's* the ticket, the young man thought. A box of raw tuna won't be as good as Maui tuna, but still, a box, maybe two, and five minutes in the saddle under the winter sun in the empty lot. He'd been on the trains too long. He needed air.

2
Che

We are never alone for a moment. We are deceived into loneliness, into solitude, by our pride, by our pretensions. And yet all Che wanted was a child of her own. To never be alone again. She wanted to be renewed by childbirth, and yet it looked like that was *never* going to happen. Forget the biological clock. The boyfriend was the problem.

On the outskirts of south Manila, through the wildly populated isthmus between two warm-water bays, on the edge of a rice field in Parañaque, near Moonwalk, in a thatched hut amid a thousand other thatched huts, at the end of a long afternoon when the palm trees still dripped from the monsoon that had drenched the huts and the mud roads and made going out difficult, near a window and a mirror, a petite Filipino woman sat at a desk dressed in hiking boots, army fatigues, a pink scarf, red lips, tattoos, ebony hair spiked up and streaked white, cigarette dangling, ash falling, and scribbled a letter.

Larissa,

My one true friend, please come and visit your old best friend Che. I'll teach you how to make rice pudding and patties. I'll give you excellent cheap wine. I'll introduce you to Father Emilio and to Lorenzo, if we're still together, God help me. I can't believe last

time I saw you was before you were ever pregnant. I like the last
picture you sent, though I don't think you're right, that your boy
looks like an angel. His eyes are too mischievous. He looks like
he rules your house. And angels don't look like that, like kings.
I should know. Lorenzo looks like that, and he's definitely not an
angel.

What Che didn't write to Larissa, but which was the impetus for
the letter and the slight anxiety underneath the placid epistolary
demeanor, was that the night before, Che thrashed herself awake
from a terrible black vision in which she saw Larissa in a yellow
dress, walking away, while Che was running, calling, *Larissa,*
Larissa . . . Finally out of breath she caught up with her fair friend
and grabbed her by the arm. Larissa spun around. Her face was
pallid and wizened, more like the face of a flightless bird long dead.
Che cried out, and then Larissa spoke, not in her voice, but a dead
stranger's voice. She said, "Che, what if everything in your life had
turned to ashes?"

Che could only shake her head.

"Everything," Larissa repeated. "Every good thing, every terrible
thing just burned to the ground?"

No, Che mouthed.

"What if there was nothing left?"

That's impossible, Che wanted to say. There is always something
left. She reached out. Always.

But Larissa, like fine wet sand, shivered and dissolved to the
earth, a small damp heap of blackened shavings.

Che screamed—in the dream, in real life. For a long time she
couldn't get back to sleep and, because of that, today was exhausted.
Nothing in Larissa's previous letter gave Che any indication that
everything was not, as always, joyous. The dream was incongruous.
Che couldn't put it out of her heart.

The door swung open, and a young swarthy Filipino man stood
at the jamb, his hand on his impatient hip. He was attired like her,
freaky clothes and rips and rags. He had a look on him of a thing

untamed. "What are you doing?" he said. "We're going to be late. We're starting in a half-hour."

"I'll be right there," said Che, turning her gaze away from his brooding face down to the white paper with roses on it. It was Epiphany today. So they were protesting. That's what they were, Che and Lorenzo: professional protesters. For every major holiday and every major feast day, for every international visit and every small item of government policy, for every break in the political climate or even just the status quo, Che and Lorenzo protested. They worked for a company of subcontracted protesters. Whenever there was a demonstration that needed an increase in numbers, they were hired to paint the placards and then walk the streets and shout. "No More War! Separation of Church and State! No American bases! No Blood for Oil! Green Today and Every Day! Fur is Wrong! War is Wrong! Crossing Picket Lines is Wrong! No New Taxes!"

For this Che was paid, poorly. But then she didn't need much. When she needed extra money, she worked for Father Emilio. The nuns grew the fruit, and she sold it at a morning street market in Parañaque, shouting. "Peaches! Ripe, Excellent! Pears! Fresh, Succulent! Tomatoes, from the Vine! Mangoes, in Season!" Che was an excellent shouter, ripe and fresh from the vine and always in season.

> *Amiga, thank you for the box of Nutella jars you sent me. It has nothing organic in it, right? So it'll last me a good long time. Like Oreos. You and Nutella is what I miss the most. Can you send me a little of yourself too, in a box? Sorry this is so short. We have a "God is Dead!" demonstration in thirty minutes. Lorenzo is waiting.*

When she wrote his name, *Lorenzo*, something hot ran through her insides, from the center of her brain through her lungs and heart, through her abdomen, down to where children might come from, in other people, though *clearly*, not in her.

"Che!"

How endearing he was when he shouted for her. Not her Christian name, Claire, that would be too conventional, but Che, a non-conformist shortening of her last name, Cherengue.

"I'm coming. Just . . ." She pondered. "One more word. One more sentence, Lorenzo. Wait." After all, how long have I been waiting for you? A long time, right?

Maybe one day you can come. I know it's hard to leave the kids. You can tell them it's for a good cause. They know how much their mommy likes hopeless causes, the more hopeless the better.

Don't worry about me. I know you think I'm doing crazy work, but these are just rumors of danger, of violence. Like you, I'm living exactly the life I chose. (Almost.) A little anti-God demonstration never hurt anyone. God will forgive me, right? He knows what's in my heart. Last week I went to a pro-war demonstration. The anti-war people set us on fire. I mean, really on fire. Poured gasoline onto the street and lit a match. I'm fine, not a scratch on me. Dear Jesus. It's not the work, it's Lorenzo that's giving me agita. You don't know how lucky you are, not having to think about all this B#$%&!t. This is what we used to obsess about when we were in junior high. So how is it that you've got a hubby and three kids and I'm still obsessing about it? You're living your happily ever after, but, Larissa, am I hopeless?

"Coming, Lorenzo!" Che hurried out of the bedroom. Hear those bells ringing? How could you not? They're as loud as the bells of Notre Dame. The bells of impending non-motherhood.

3

Maggie and Ezra

"This longing for immortality, Maggie," said Ezra, as the DeSwanns got ready in the morning, "don't you think it's a bit compulsive? Consuming? A little like mental illness? Do you think Larissa bothers with this?"

This was said in response to Maggie's informing him that in addition to her other numberless interests, she was now enrolling in an art class.

"What are you talking about, Ezra? It's not for immortality. It's for fun." She snorted. "So I can teach my kids to paint." By kids Maggie didn't mean her own son who was fifteen and way past painting, but the pre-schoolers she taught three mornings a week at the local church day school.

Ezra shook his head. "Thank goodness you're just trying to ruin other people's children. Larissa doesn't bother yearning for the impossible."

"How do you know? I thought you said we all yearn for the impossible? Make up your mind." She scrunched up her wet, curly hair.

Ezra continued to struggle with his bow tie. "Do what *I* do to make life more fun," he said. "Read. Try to understand the workings of the universe." He had just last week become the head of the

English Department at Pingry, the tony private prep school in Short Hills, after the previous department head had *finally* retired, at seventy-seven.

"You are the most miserable son of a bitch I know," said Maggie. "Why in the world would I want to be like you?"

"I will become happy once I understand."

"Tell me, Professor Smarty-pants—all that reading, doing you any good? Happy yet?"

"Who can tell?" said Ezra. "What is happiness anyway?"

Maggie laughed. "See, unlike you, I already believe in my own immortality. I just want to make the flesh have a little more fun. Would you prefer I paint or take a lover?"

With amusement, Ezra glanced at her. "I believe it's a false choice, Mrs. DeSwann," he said. "Do what you like, of course." He changed the subject. "Did you know," he said, "that if there were one fewer electron in the hydrogen atom, one less negative charge, nothing we know would exist? Not us, not the universe, not the galaxies, nothing."

"Huh," said Maggie, straightening out the collar on his white shirt; 7:30 in the morning and he was already looking so disheveled. His brown shirts never matched his taupe jackets, and he frequently wore maroon or green pants that matched nothing. He was *so* eccentric, she couldn't believe he was hers. Yet Larissa perversely *adored* him and thought Maggie married well, so he must be worth keeping. Or did Larissa think that Ezra had married well?

"By the way," said Ezra, "I need to talk to Larissa about a very important matter."

"Every quantum thing with you is an important matter."

"Yes. But this . . ." He shrugged her off. "Denise is leaving for maternity as soon as *Othello* opens. And we have no one to direct our spring play. I'm hoping Larissa will be interested."

"I dunno. Once, perhaps."

Ezra seemed surprised. "I think she'll be over the moon. This is what she's been waiting for."

"You think she's been *waiting?*" Maggie chuckled.

"You're wrong. Besides, I've already recommended her to the headmaster."

"Without talking to her first?" Maggie tapped Ezra scoldingly on his head.

"Theater is her life."

"*Was.*"

"You don't know everything, Margaret. You're off the mark." But he became flummoxed, as if Larissa's potential refusal was the last thing he expected. "She'll say yes. And she'll be excellent."

"Compared to Denise, our cat would be excellent. What a *disaster* that has been. She should direct *The Poseidon Adventure.*" Maggie shook her head, then remembered something. "Speaking of disasters, we're having an ice cream party today. Except three of my kids are allergic to peanut butter, and I got notes yesterday asking if the vanilla ice cream was made with peanut oil. Turn to me." She redid Ezra's fire-red bow tie to go with his wine-colored jacket and green slacks.

"The parents are asking the wrong question," Ezra said.

"Of course they are!" Maggie laughed, kissing him on the cheek. "If the vanilla ice cream had one less electron in it, it wouldn't be here at all, right? The question they should be asking is not about peanut oil. It's about the existence of vanilla ice cream."

"Ah," said Ezra, "you're mocking me." His eyes twinkled at her.

"Not mocking. Teasing." Her eyes twinkled at him.

"Confound them completely by telling them vanilla ice cream is made not with peanut oil but peanut butter." They both laughed. "Tell them Margaret, that if the gods are indifferent to us, then that leaves us free to be indifferent to the gods. If there is no immortality, we have so much less to worry about. Paint, don't paint. Read, don't read. Direct spring plays. Vanilla ice cream, peanut butter. It's all good, Curly. Do whatever you like without thought to consequence. Tell your worried mothers that. I'm going to tell Larissa that. That's what I'm learning from Epicurus. Let's go. We're late."

"As usual. You should be thanking God I'm taking up painting and not the piano," said Maggie, grabbing her bag and heading downstairs. "Pam has suddenly and inexplicably started playing the piano at the age of forty-four. It cost her husband thirty thousand dollars—so far—for an upright that doesn't offend her delicate hearing. But, Ezra, riddle me this, Batman . . ." Maggie got into their old Subaru and cranked the keys in the ignition, while her husband leaned into the window to peck her goodbye. "What if the gods aren't indifferent to us?"

4

Jared

Jared walked in, as usual, to an internal crisis. Well, why not? It was Monday. Crisis was a reaction to Mondays. There was no crisis on Wednesdays, Thursdays, even Tuesdays. Only right before a weekend, to sour things a bit, and right after, to let you know no one wanted to be back at work. This particular Monday, Jan showed up to the morning meeting smelling distinctly *not* of a double latte.

It was one thing for Jan to be incapacitated at 9:30 on a Monday, but Jared had an analyst meeting to run, which involved fifteen sober individuals. And there was Jan, belligerent, inappropriate and loud, interrupting measured voices.

After the aborted meeting, Jared called Jan into his office. His space at the Newark headquarters had a great view of New York City from floor-to-ceiling windows. Unfortunately they were always behind him, and the only time he allowed himself a glance at the Big Apple skyline was when he called Larissa. He would whirl his chair around and chat to her, dreaming of Sunday brunches at the Plaza, the violinist and the pianist playing Chopin's Nocturnes. Just thinking about the music trilling in his ears made him want oysters and waffles. He shook his head to rid himself of melodies and wives.

"Jan, it's like this," he said. "I'm not going to accuse you, and you will have nothing to deny. We've been through this before; the company has been more than lenient. It's paid for your rehab—

twice—and has given you three warnings instead of two, and put you on probation four times, not three. I don't have to remind you that you're still on probation. Which means, if you're caught drinking on the job—again—you can and will be fired summarily, no more warnings, no more meetings, no more rehab."

"But I'm not drinking on the job," said Jan. "I don't know what you're talking about." She was thirtysomething, a single mother of two boys, almost well-dressed if you didn't notice the fraying around the edges, the shirt not quite tucked in, the strap of one Mary Jane unbuckled, the hair not washed this morning. She was in a cavalcade of certain destruction and her breath was stinking up his paneled office, yet she sat saying she wasn't drinking on the job.

"I didn't accuse you of anything," said Jared. "But if I can smell it, other people can smell it, including Larry Fredoso, the CEO. If I can tell you're not acting normal on a Monday morning, other people can, too."

They eyeballed each other, with hostility and resignation.

Jared lowered his voice. "I can smell it."

"I didn't have any carbohydrates this morning," Jan suddenly said. "That's why my breath is bad."

"Your breath isn't bad! It smells like vodka."

"Well, must be the Dayquil," she mumbled. "I haven't been feeling well. I don't know what's wrong with me."

Not feeling well. She'd been wired, jumpy, loud, straining to listen, to comprehend; she'd been leaving ostentatiously early with no explanation or defense. "The signs are everywhere," Jared said. "There are no more chances." He paused. "I want to help you save your job. For your kids. Who else do they have to depend on? You're all they got."

"That's right," she said. "I'm all they got."

"Right. So the responsibility is greater, not less, when it's all on your shoulders."

Jan muttered something he didn't hear, that sounded like perhaps too much responsibility on her sagging shoulders, and then asked if she was being dismissed. He didn't know what she meant.

Dismissed permanently? Or just out of his office? Jared turned away to the window so he wouldn't see her stumbling out. After sitting for a few minutes, he dialed home. He wanted to talk to the mother of his own kids.

The phone rang and rang.

5

Larissa

I want to be neither in pain nor terror, Larissa thought, her palms flat against the pane of wintry glass. *That* is the imperative of my existence: neither, nor.

The day Larissa's life ended, she didn't even know it. The day it ended she was wearing sweatpants. And not Juicy Couture sweatpants, snug and velour, with satin accents, maybe a little heart appliqué on the buttocks area, embroidered in gold silk with little sparkly crystals to make a married woman's rear-end moonlight as a young filly's: maidenly not matronly. No. She was wearing her should've-been-thrown-away-ten-years-ago faded gray sweats, frayed at the hem, baggy, worn to paper thin since college, when you either wore sweatpants or were naked and having sex.

Two months ago in November, *before* Thanksgiving, it snowed. Ice cotton fell out of the sky, ruining all her plans for a bike ride, a walk, a stroll to the store. The coats were still deep in the attic, the gloves, the hats, the galoshes far away.

But the dog was happy. Galloping like an overjoyed beast through the backyard, Riot brought back in her teeth one of Emily's stuffed cats, muddied, blackened, thoroughly mangled.

Snow in November. Didn't bode well for the winter ahead in land-locked Summit. That was the one bad thing about living here. Sometimes out of the sky came ice and didn't stop until late March.

New Yorkers were lucky: they were closer to the water. Water tempered everything.

Oh yes, and when she and Jared lived in a walk-up in Hoboken, with two babies, an old car with no muffler, and one tiny paycheck, it didn't snow? It snowed like they were in the Ninth Circle of Hell. *And* they had no money. It doesn't snow only on the well-to-do, Larissa, she muttered to herself, limping to the storage room to get some book boxes. And all things being equal, better to be on a golf course in swank Summit than in a tenement in Hoboken. She used Jared's tape gun to fix a half-dozen book boxes and then hobbled over to the bookshelves in her master bedroom, her glance toward the windows.

She pressed her face to the Arctic windowpane, her silent house behind her. Every day some form of freezing rain fell from the sky. Yesterday, warm weather came and turned all to slush, until today, when a freakish gale made it twenty below and a hockey rink. The coiffed blonde chick on the six o'clock news last night forecast that it would feel like forty below. Apparently not good for wet faces. And Larissa's face every time she went outside was wet, because for some reason when the chill sun caught her eye, she would start to weep.

∾ৄ৾

The kids had barely got off to school in the morning. That was true for most mornings. By 7:00, Jared was already up and shaved and showering, all hummy and spring-steppy. So cheery. Damn him. Larissa opened the doors to the children's bedrooms, made some noise to get up, stumbled downstairs, put the cereal bowls out, let Riot out, the dog bounding outside into the cold, full of exuberance for the day ahead. Everyone should be a dog. But Larissa's kids, usually spectacularly unobservant, grumbled about how glum it was outside, and freezing, and refused to leave their cozy beds. Larissa almost let them stay home. What's one day? What are they going to miss? The atomic weight of magnesium? The three branches of government? They should be so lucky as to learn that. Asher spent

the entire seventh grade social studies on American History and
didn't read a word of the Constitution. Not a word. He couldn't tell
her what Plymouth Rock was, or the Pilgrims. Or *Mayflower*.

Except Emily had a science quiz, and Asher a clay project on the
Egyptians, and Michelangelo his beloved art class. So she cajoled
them into rising, herself dreaming of falling back into the down
quilts after they left for school.

Would it all be different had she let her children stay home that
gray day? Even the inscrutable atoms moving doggedly on their
inexorable path through the universe were occasionally given to
unexplained and random swerves—jumps and diversions from the
steady path, unpredictable yet permanent. Was letting her children
stay home a break in the pattern of the atom? Or was sending them
to school the break? There was no way to know.

They got ready for school.

The next forty minutes, a litany of supplication. "Asher, take
your glasses from the bathroom." "Em, remember your cello."
"Michelangelo, drink your milk." "Asher, brush your hair." "Em, I
don't know where your shoes are. Probably where you left them."
"Michelangelo, drink your milk, we *have* to go." "Asher, take your
Egyptian pyramid. Yes, the thing we were working on all weekend,
that one." They named him Asher because it meant happy. The
placid boy looked like his mother, tall and lean with a steady gaze.
"Asher, have a yogurt."

"I hate yogurt, Mom. It's disgusting."

"Since when? You used to love yogurt."

"Yeah, and I used to suck my thumb. Things change, Mom."

"No, you can't have a cookie. Have applesauce. Emily, so put on
a different pair of shoes. You must have another pair or two, don't
you?" Emily looked like her dad, but with a round face and pixie
bangs. "Michelangelo! Finish your cereal." They broke the mold to
make their youngest son with his mystifying blond curly mop of hair
and the most unaccommodating demeanor. "Riot! Stop jumping!"

Jared was long gone. Then the two older younglings were
running through the wind, running up the long narrow street for

the middle school bus at the corner of Bellevue and Summit. It was a three-minute Olympian sprint, for which they left precisely ninety seconds. Like Larissa said, getting to school was a (perhaps not such a minor) miracle. She herself limped down the driveway with Michelangelo in tow, though without a scarf or gloves (the absence of which would dub her a bad mother in the parents' lounge, which she fortunately didn't frequent). She drove him the mile and a half to Lincoln Elementary, parked and limped alongside him, holding his small cold hand.

The crossing guard asked her how her leg was. "Getting better finally?"

"Yes, thanks." Though it wasn't, not at all. That it was her left leg and not her right was the only good thing you could say about it. Otherwise she wouldn't be able to drive.

Michelangelo was only ten minutes late. "Oh, good morning, Michael. So nice of you to stop by," said the passing principal, and he turned, smiled impishly at his wan, waving mother, and gunned it down the hall even though he wasn't supposed to gun.

It was in the hours between the missed Pledge of Allegiance and the afternoon food foraging that Larissa stood with her freshly made cardboard boxes near the windows where she put on her makeup. The leg was still too sore to stand on for long even after four weeks. Her bedroom faced the front of the house, and past the tall bare oaks she could see the rolling sloping hills of the golf course, and beyond them the highway, and the mall. The view so convenient: beauty and utility, both natural *and* man-made. Larissa placed her palm on the cold window, to feel the life outside.

Stepping away, she glanced at her books. They'd been freshly dusted and stood spines out and shiny. Ernestina was meticulous. In three hours she and her team of two licked the house clean. *Muy limpio.* The books were never dusty. There was never a speck on them.

Or, for that matter, a dog's ear.

Larissa had forty tall shelves of books in her house, not including those of her children, not including those of her husband. One for every year of her life. Twenty-four shelves held books she'd already read. The other sixteen . . .

In her bedroom, four shelves housed just the books she was *meaning* to read. They had to be cast into categories finally, into a hierarchy of value, like castes of Punjabis, so it would be easier to know in what order *not* to read them. There was the non-fiction subsection, itself separated into memoirs, general interest, religion and philosophy. There was a section of commercial fiction, enough for the next two years. There was serious hardcover fiction she was planning on not reading in the next three. It had been four, five years since she'd touched a book on these shelves. She bought the books and cataloged them like an efficient librarian, hoping that someday she would have the time, find the time. Her house was impeccable and the children were in school and the husband would have dinner tonight, and clean white ironed shirts, and every project would be on time, and each drawer organized. How was she ever going to find the time to open *One Hundred Years of Solitude*, the annotated *Lolita*, *The Executioner's Song*?

But on the plus side, there were no miscellaneous drawers in Larissa's house! The bed was made like the presidential four-poster at the Ritz-Carlton. All five beds in the house. Beautifully made.

The books had no hope of being read. Jared, because he thought he was *so* funny, called it her non-reading list. The only books she attempted to read were the ones that came fresh in a UPS box to her red front door. She thanked Dominick, the UPS man, glanced over his head to the golf course across the narrow street, past the oaks, the manicured lawns like a valley, and then slammed shut the door and opened the cardboard box, efficiently discarding it to stay neat and on top of things. First she placed the book on her side of the bed where it had a slim chance of being opened. If it fell off the bed onto the treadmill, its chances weakened considerably, because on the treadmill the newly arrived books became covered by gossip magazines, by *People*, by *Entertainment Weekly* (though *EW* had a *lot* of words in it, didn't it?); they became covered by used eye-makeup remover pads and discarded bras, by shirts and socks, cardigans, often earrings, sometimes headphones, three pairs of them, and printed pages of nonsense off the Internet on the latest current event she pretended she might catch up on under her Ralph Lauren quilt. Her side of the bed was the only place in the house where chaos reigned.

So today, Larissa took firm charge of the last unruly vestige of her ordered life. Book by book, shelf by shelf, she worked her way from top to bottom, placing the books inside boxes that would be donated to St. Paul's Thrift Shop in Summit.

Had she read *Lord of the Flies* by William Golding? Through books I can be someone else, she thought. She didn't need to read books about it; it was *Lord of the Flies* every night in her house. When reading books, she wanted to be far removed from herself.

Fear of Flying by Erica Jong? No; too much sex. It would just rile her up, inflame her unnecessarily.

Birdsong by Sebastian Faulks? Love! World War I! She knew nothing about the latter; it was perfect. It was also a little *too* removed. Reluctantly she dropped it in the box, recalling with a twinge of regret that that was why she had bought the book in the first place—so she could read about something she knew nothing about.

Lonesome Dove? Too Texan. Once she wanted to read it. But once she wanted to read everything.

Mrs. Dalloway by Virginia Woolf? Wait, she'd read that! How did *that* end up here? She was almost sure she'd read it. There was a line in it she kept coming back to. She devoted herself to that line until it was carved into her memory. But today, as she sat on the floor and leafed through the book, Larissa couldn't even remember what the line was *about*, much less the actual words. All she recalled was that it had meaning, and now she couldn't recall a word of it, a whiff of it. Disgusted, she threw the book in the box, and then the thumb of her memory ran over *I Am Legend* by Richard Matheson. Jared loved that book when he was young(er).

The phone rang; she didn't answer. The doorbell rang. Two men were delivering a dishwasher. She had to leave her book project half completed and babysit Chris the installer and his non-speaking companion, who shook their heads at her dicey kitchen cabinets and said the new machine might not fit without tearing up the floor. "But we're jacks of all trades," hefty Chris said with a smile. "We know what we're doing."

She smiled wanly.

She didn't want to go out today. Hobbling down to the basement, she opened the freezer to see if there was any dubious forgotten meat she could defrost. Maybe they could go vegetarian tonight, fettuccine Alfredo. With bacon bits. Almost vegetarian, that is, if you didn't count the chunks of smoked pig. She could mask the lack of food with garlic bread, except she didn't have any bread. Or garlic. Or bacon bits.

The stainless-steel, smart-wash, nine-cycle machine with sanitized rinse and heated dry hadn't arrived until noon. By the time the crack installers left—without tearing up her floor—it was almost one. She had planned to take a shower before she went out, but now there was no time. She had to pick up Michelangelo from school at 2:40. Besides, to have a shower, she needed Jared to tape her casted leg inside a plastic bag. She didn't think asking Chris and his buddy, the jacks of all trades, to help a naked woman with a broken leg get into the shower was such a swell idea or qualified under one of the trades they were jacks of.

Though truth be told, if she had a choice, she'd rather have two unshaved strangers help her naked into the shower than stagger to King's unpainted and unwashed.

6

King's, Ye Olde Market

But the husband needed to eat. And the children! What about the children? King's was overrun. The entire population of Summit seemed to be clamoring for the tiny parking lot behind King's, 20,000 cars trying to fit into 200 spaces. She sat for exactly three seconds waiting to make the right into the concrete madness where every Escalade was honking at every Range Rover, every woman, her windows down, yelling at another, "Are you leaving?"

Larissa revved the engine. She'd find another supermarket. She could just see herself getting knocked down by the crazy fur-clad lady in a green Hummer.

Trouble was, she didn't know where else to go because she *always* went to King's on Main. It was seven minutes from her house, two lights and a right, and had all the things she needed. The no hassle was important. Larissa worked very hard to make her life hassle-free, which is why the cast on the leg cast a pall on her sunny life. Was the broken leg the atom swerving its own way?

She decided to drive down Main Street to Madison, the next small town over past Chatham, which had no supermarket, to find a store. It was only thirteen minutes away.

Over lunch last week at Neiman's Café, Maggie had asked her, "If you could be any person in the world, who would you be?" and

Larissa had answered one question with two: "Forever? Or just for a little while?"

"Does it make a difference?"

"Yes," Larissa said. "If it's just for a little while, I'd like to be a hundred different people. If it's forever, then no one. I don't want anyone else's life forever."

They'd spent the rest of the blissful lunch thinking of who they'd like to be. Someone else other than us, Larissa concluded, because I want to know what it's like to live a life as far away from my own as possible, and Maggie said, "Larissa, you *are* living a life as far away from your own as possible."

Maggie was right. Summit was already someone else's life, Larissa thought as she drove, gaping at the little shops along the hectic business district, looking for a supermarket. She could've easily become a professional protester with Che, maybe gone to the Philippines with her. Larissa was far removed from her very self. Maybe that's why she wasn't reading.

Oh, excuses, excuses. As many as the day was long.

She had asked Jared if he would want to be someone else, and he said cheerfully without a moment's thought: Robert Neville in *I Am Legend*. Larissa thought it was *such* an odd thing for her husband to wish for. "Completely alone in the world," Jared explained, "trying to eke out a meager survival, hoping to stay alive till daylight because bad things that wanted to suck out your soul came for you in the night. I would want to be a vampire hunter. With silver in my pocket. *Just for one day*." And then he mad-jigged in his underwear through the bedroom.

On her left Larissa spied a "Grand Opening" sign for a Super Stop&Shop. She smiled (because Asher called the chain Stupid Stop&Shop) and flicked on her turn signal, waiting patiently for the oncoming traffic to pass.

This lot was spacious and empty. She parked over by the griffin trees. Through the chain link fence in front of her lay a small local cemetery. Tall granite tombstones were haphazardly laid out in the slushy ground, black on white. As she climbed out of her shiny Escalade, Larissa remembered! Not all of it, not even the gist of it, but the heart of it, the Dalloway quote. Something about Thursday, Friday, Saturday, and then: ". . . that it must end; and no one in the whole world would know how she had loved it all."

7

Burial Grounds

She needed to buy only a few things; why was she still stumbling around the store thirty-five minutes later? After school today, Asher had an orthodontist appointment *and* a guitar lesson. And Emily had cello and voice. How did Larissa allow the last few minutes of her afternoon to be sucked up by aisles of self-rising flours and Cajun spices and new milk bones for Riot, by mozzarella cheese and new yogurt with antibiotic properties, which apparently she couldn't live without? There were only three cashiers working, and one of them was *incredibly* slow. Larissa's ankle felt sore, swollen. She couldn't even muster a tight smile for the chronologically impaired cashier who looked all of twelve and didn't smile much herself.

"Cash back?"

"What?" Larissa's teeth were jammed together.

"Would you like some cash back?"

"No. No, thank you." I'd like thirty minutes of my life back.

A full *fifty* minutes after she walked through Stop&Shop's automatic doors, Larissa slid out of the automatic doors, leaning on the grocery cart for support. It was cold, and her coat was unbuttoned. Her capri-style sweats fit over the boot-cast but also bared her good ankle. She had forgotten the scarf, the gloves. What might it be like to stick her wet tongue on the metal handles of the cart, she wondered, as she pushed it slowly across the parking lot. And what if her tongue got stuck? She and Che used to do that when they were kids. The image of herself—nearly forty, limping, freezing cold, coat opened, shirt too thin, six bags of food in front of her, on a sub-zero January weekday, her wet tongue crazy-glued to the steel handlebars—made Larissa laugh.

Her face still bearing the lines of the smile, she inched past a young man sitting astride a shiny flash motorcycle, about to pull a helmet over his ears. He wore the motorcycle. Black leather jacket, jeans, black boots. The helmet was metallic silver, to *not* match the burnt yellow and black of the bike. He smiled at her.

"What's so funny?" he asked.

Larissa looked for her car. Flustered by her idiotic thoughts and her vapid grin, she tried to cover it up with a shrug, and a "Oh, nothing," grimace now frozen on her face, morphing into a polite stranger nod. He spoke again. "Need help?" He pointed to her cast.

"I'm fine." She averted her gaze, not for any reason other than she tried not to make prolonged eye contact with young male strangers, especially young male strangers wearing bikes and jeans and boots and shiny helmets. "Thanks, anyway."

He got off his bike and came toward her.

"How long in a cast?"

"Uh—about four weeks, I guess."

"You broke it at Christmastime?" He whistled. "Bad luck. How'd you do it? Skiing?"

"Skiing? No. I don't ski. I just—it's silly." She still wasn't looking at him, but she did slow down. Not stopped—just slowed down. "I tripped coming out of the hairdresser's."

Now *he* laughed. "You tripped coming out of the *hairdresser's*? That's rich."

"Well, I didn't think so at the time."

"That *is* worth laughing about."

"Really?" she said noncommittally, wanting to breathe into her cold hands. "That's not why—" God! She stopped walking.

"I've noticed," he said with a teasing air of formality, "one thing about women based upon years of careful observation . . ."

"*Years?*" Larissa muttered, drawing attention to his youth. "Really."

His chuckle was easy. "Yes, really. I grew up with a mother, a grandmother, and two older sisters. As I was saying. After years of observation, I've concluded that women take great care with their hair."

Larissa forgot for a moment how cold she was. "You don't *say*."

The boy refused to be baited. "Even in the neon supermarket on a Monday afternoon, women take more care with their hair than with any other part of their appearance." He spoke of it like he was reading poetry, like it was his life's philosophy, while Larissa wanted suddenly to button her coat so he wouldn't catch a glimpse of her frumpy sweats. He spoke of hair the way Ezra spoke about the metaphysical reality of the soul!

"The hair is always clean," he continued, "it's styled, moussed, gelled. Women *think* about hair. No one just gets out of the shower in their empty house and towel dries."

"What did you say?" She squinted. Empty house? "Not even *you?*" His hair was sticking out every which way till Sunday. He took off his helmet to show her his kinky helmet head, thin brown-blond hair frizzing in all directions.

"Yeah, okay, me," he said cheerfully. "But not women."

"I don't agree."

"No? You don't think about what to put in it, how to curl it, thin it, thicken it, style it, shape it? How to put it up, how to braid it?" He pointed to an older woman pushing her cart past them through the thick cold. "Take a look," he said. "She's wearing a sheepskin rug for a coat, and her husband's loafers, but her hair is blown dry and immaculate and shining! No makeup, but the hair is perfect. Like the Werewolf, baby."

Werewolf! Larissa stared at him, wondering at what point to take offense and at what point to laugh. His eyes were merry. He clearly thought he was being clever. "I don't mean it as a criticism," he assured her. "I mean it as a compliment. Hair rules the world."

Okay, she'll play on this cold Monday. Why not?

"Hair and shoes," she said.

"Yes!" he heartily agreed. "Everything in the middle, you can pretty much not waste your time or money on."

It was true. Did anyone care that she spent twenty-seven bucks on Chanel mascara instead of six bucks on Maybelline?

She didn't say anything, just squinted in the sunlight. He put the helmet back on his head. In the few seconds of silence that passed between them, Larissa's mind traveled from hair to boots, from mascara to jeans and in between belts and necklaces saw the other thing that both men and women noticed. Probably third after hair and shoes.

The swell between the breasts. Cleavage.

"I'll tell you a little secret," he said. "Men never notice shoes."

"Some men."

"Not straight men."

She laughed. "So not shoes but hair?"

"Yes," he said. "Hair we notice."

And breasts. She hoped the sunlight would keep him out of the expression in her eyes. But he said nothing—in that pointed way people say nothing when they're thinking about things that can't be said.

"Jewelry?" She was fishing for other things in the water.

"If it's sparkly, come-hither jewelry, yes."

Come-hither jewelry! Now *she* said nothing in that pointed way people say nothing when they're thinking about things that can't be said.

He inclined his head toward her; Larissa inclined her body away and pushed her cart forward. "Well, have a great day."

"You sure you don't need help?" Stepping away from his bike, he put his hand on her shopping cart. Was he allowed to do that? Wasn't that like putting your hands on someone's pregnant belly?

Against some sort of Super Stupid food shopping etiquette? "I'll help you put your 12-pack of Diet Coke into your car. You far?"

"No, no." *No, no* was to the help, not the far. He wasn't listening, already pushing, as she walked next to him, slow. Before she found the unlock button on her key ring, a thought flashed: is he safe? What if he's one of those . . . I don't know. Didn't she hear about them? Men who abducted girls from parking lots?

And did what with them?

Plus he wasn't a man.

Plus she wasn't a girl.

He looked exotic, his brown eyes slanted, his cheekbones wide and high, almost Asian. He looked sweet and scruffy. Who would abduct *her* from a parking lot? And, more important, why?

And even more important, how did she feel about being abducted?

And was that a rhetorical question?

And furthermore, how come all these thoughts, impressions, fears, anxieties, reactions, flashed in her head before her next blink, like a dream that seems to take hours but is just a couple of seconds before the alarm goes off? Why so much thinking?

And was *that* a rhetorical question?

She lifted the back hatch and he said with a whistle, "Awesome Escalade. All spec'ed out." Like he knew.

It took him all of twenty seconds to load her groceries into her luxury utility vehicle. Slamming the liftgate shut, he smiled. "You okay now?"

"Of course, yes." She was okay before, but didn't say that. It sounded rude.

He began to walk back to his bike. "Have a good one. And stay away from hairdressers," he added advisedly. "It's not like you need it."

When Larissa got home, she left her bags in the car, left her purse in the car, crashed through the house from back door to the front, limped to the full-length mirror in the entry hall and stood square in front of it.

She wore a lichen parka, old gray sweats, a taupe torn top. She had not a shred of makeup on her face, and her pale hair was unwashed a day and unbrushed since two hours ago. Her lips were chapped from the cold, her cheeks slightly flushed and splotchy.

Whatever could he *possibly* mean? She stood in front of the mirror for an eternal minute until she startled herself back into life, and rushed out, Quasimodo-style, to pick up her youngest child from school.

8

99 Red Balloons

While Michelangelo cut and pasted for school, and munched his cup of dry Cheerios, a string cheese, a cookie, a glass of milk, and a fruit cup, Larissa puttered around, looking inside her freezer, realizing belatedly that she hadn't bought meat. Now she was searching for some ground beef she could hastily defrost for a casserole or a pie. Maybe she could leave Michelangelo with the two oldest; they should be home any minute—

And there they were. The back door slammed, the backpacks thumped to the floor, shoes flew off. They bounded into the kitchen, opened the fridge and . . . "There's nothing to eat in this house," said Emily, slamming the refrigerator door. "Mom, we gotta go. Last week we were almost late to my lesson and I don't want to be almost late again."

"Okay, honey," said Larissa. "I'll hurry with dinner, so you won't be almost late again."

First was cello. Then karate for Michelangelo and guitar for Asher. Mondays were busy.

"Track is starting next month," said Asher from the back. "I'm joining."

"Is that before or after karate? Is that before or after band?"

"It's *with*, Mom."

"Is that before or after the orthodontist at five tonight?"

"With, Mom. With."

Ezra had called when she was out, saying he needed to talk to her, but when she called back *he* was out and Maggie was cryptic on the phone, saying only that he would talk to Larissa Saturday night at dinner.

When Jared got home, he took one look at her and said jokingly, "Oh, hon, don't get all gussied up on my account." Her plain face, her unsmiling mouth didn't deter him from kissing her, tickling her, from heartily eating the hamburger pie she made, from taking the garbage out, and getting the poster board for Asher's project on hooligans, from looking at the eight boxes taped and stacked against the bedroom wall and saying, "Whoa. Whoa right there. What in the world have you been doing? Is that why you didn't answer the phone all day?"

And then it was night and everyone was asleep, everyone but Larissa, who sat in bed, with a *People* magazine in her lap, staring at her peacefully sleeping husband, the vampire hunter, and the carousel spinning round and round in her head was *it will soon be gone and no one will ever know how much she had loved it all*.

Chapter Two

1

Things Which Are Seen

The external life is all Larissa knows, most of the time. She married the man she fell in love with in college. She loved him because her friends were either hippie potheads like Che, or sesquipedalian book chewers like Ezra, but Jared had the unbeatable combination of being both, plus he was a baseball jock. There was something so adorably sporty and cerebral about him. He wore baseball caps and black-rimmed glasses and pitched until his arm gave out, but couldn't live without baseball, so he got a job teaching English and coaching Little League, and then, according to Ezra, completely sold out and got an MBA, instead of the long-planned PhD in *fin de siècle* American Lit, but the difference between the two terminal degrees meant that Larissa and Jared weren't broke anymore, and Ezra and Maggie were.

They bought a gray-colored sprawling colonial farmhouse on Bellevue Avenue on a raised corner lot overlooking the golf course, the kind of house that dreams are made on, the house of twelve gables and white-painted windows adorned with black shutters.

Through the pathways and the nooks thirty clay pots sprouted red flowers summer and winter—pansies, impatiens, poinsettia.

Larissa and Jared owned sleek flatscreen televisions and the latest stereo equipment. In the game room, they had a pool table, a ping-pong table, and an air hockey table; in the backyard, a heated pool and a Jacuzzi. Their closets were organized by two professional closet organizers (how was *that* for a job description), and three times a year a file organizer came over to assess their files. Jared paid the bills. He drove a Lexus SUV, she her Escalade. Their appliances were stainless steel and there was marble in their bathrooms. The floors were parquet, the countertops granite, the lights recessed and on dimmers. The sixty windows that were professionally cleaned four times a year were trimmed in white wood to match the crown mouldings.

She lived a mile away from Summit's Main Street, and five minutes drive from the upscale Mall at Short Hills, with Saks, Bloomies, Nordstrom, Neiman Marcus and Macy's. It had valet parking, sushi and cappuccino, a glass ceiling, and every store worth shopping in.

The children, who were once little and required all her time, were now older and required slightly more. Emily had been the perfect child at eleven, playing championship volleyball and all-state cello, but now at nearly fourteen was exhibiting three of the five signs of demonic possession. The flying off the handle at absolutely nothing. You couldn't say *anything* to her without her interpreting it the wrong way and bursting into tears. The taking of great offense at *everything*. The disagreeing with *everything*. She had become so transparent that recently Larissa had started asking her the exact opposite of what she wanted. "Wear a jacket, it's freezing out." "No, I'm fine. It's not that cold, *Mom*." "Em, don't wear a coat today, it's supposed to be warm." "Are you kidding me? You want me to *freeze* to death?"

Michelangelo had manifest gifts of artistic ability. A note from his first grade teacher read: *I think he is showing real promise*. He drew a donkey in geometric shapes, even the tail. Kandinsky by a six-year-old. Or was it just his name that fooled his parents into delusions of gifts? Che was wrong about that boy. He might not have *been* an angel, with his obdurate nature and single-minded pursuit of his own interests, but he sure *looked* like an angel. He had a cherubic halo of blond curly hair and the sweetest face.

No one was particularly sure what Asher did. Today he played guitar, yesterday took karate, tomorrow would run track. Or maybe not. Asher spent every day just being in it, and when it came to New Year's resolutions he was the one who could never think of anything to write because he would say, "I don't want to change anything. I have a perfect life." He was the one who a month ago, at almost thirteen, refused to make a Christmas list because, as he chipperly put it, "I really don't want that much." He wanted one thing: an electric miniscooter. If Larissa and Jared could have, they would've gotten him the scooter in every color available, black, lime, lilac and pink. Here, we couldn't decide which color to get for you, have all four of them, Merry Christmas, darling. The blood of angels flowed through Asher's veins. *He* should've been named Angel.

Jared maintained Asher resembled Larissa in temperament and looks. But Larissa knew: only in looks. Emily, on the other hand, wanted nothing to do with being in any way like her mother, perming her hair, coloring it blue. Larissa was usually impeccably put together; Emily made a point of looking like hardcore indie Seattle grunge. Larissa didn't play any musical instruments, Emily did. Larissa loved theater, Emily hated it. Larissa frowned for Emily's sake, but shrugged for everyone else's. If that's rebellion, I'll take it, she said. I'd rather blue hair than grandchildren.

Larissa wished Che could know her children. She missed Che. They grew up together in Piermont, had known each other since they were three or four. Larissa loved Che's mother, a funny little lady who smoked a ton and cooked great. They were always broke, but somehow Mrs. Cherengue found the money to ship Che's dad's body back to Manila. The mother and daughter flew to the Philippines for the funeral. That was *fifteen* years ago. Larissa was

barely pregnant with Emily. She was devastated and sore for years.
How could you leave me, Che? What about us living parallel
lives? What about us seeing each other every day? What about our
friendship?

But Che remained in Manila ("It feels a little bit like home, Lar,
what can I say?"), and then her mother got sick and died. Larissa
cried after she heard. Larissa's own mother, Barbara Connelly, said,
"I hope you're going to cry like this when *I* kick the bucket." That
comment went pointedly unanswered.

Che had already met Lorenzo by the time her mother died. So
now she lived in Parañaque, without her mother, hiring out her
passionate protesting, waiting for Lorenzo to propose and give her a
baby, not necessarily in that order.

*Che came to the house one morning. I'm in trouble, Lar. I'm in deep
deep trouble. Larissa was a senior, Che a junior. Seventeen, sixteen,
going on too adult. I'm pregnant.*

No. Are you sure?

I'm positive.

Oh, please no. Are you sure?

*I'm completely positive. I'm two weeks late. I'm never late. What am
I going to do?*

Don't worry. We'll fix it. Whatever happens.

No, you don't understand.

I do. It's bad. But it'll be okay.

*Lar, it's the single worst thing that can happen to me. Honestly. What
am I going to tell my mother? She'll kill me.*

*No. Your mother? Never. She's a sweetheart. And why would you
tell her?*

Oh, Larissa. My family is not your family. I tell my mother things.

No, not this. Especially not this.

Well, what am I going to do? She's going to have to know eventually.

*Why? I'm serious. Why will she have to know? We'll go to Planned
Parenthood. They'll help us. You'll see. Your mom will never have to
know.*

Planned Parenthood costs money.

Don't worry. I'll . . . I'll help you. But we have to go there quick. Get a test.

Lar, a test? And then what? I can't have . . . I can't do it. Don't you understand? I'm not like you. I'm Catholic. I can't do it.

Well, what are you going to do? You gonna be Catholic, or you gonna be smart?

Why can't I be both?

Choose, Che.

I can't. All I know is I can't have this baby. But also, I can't not have this baby.

That's what I'm saying. I'll get the money together.

How much you think it's going to be?

Over three hundred dollars.

Che cried. Where am I going to get that kind of money?

I'll give it to you. I have it. I have it saved up.

How am I going to pay you back?

Don't worry.

How did you save that much money?

Little by little. Dollar by dollar. Took me four years.

Oh, Larissa.

It's okay. That's what it's for. I didn't know what I was saving for. But I knew I would need it for something.

I can't take your money.

To save yourself?

Save myself for the short term, burn in hell for eternity.

Che, you're not going to burn in hell. Who told you this? Larissa appraised Che, contemplated her. I didn't know you and Maury went that far, she finally said.

Che wouldn't look at Larissa. We didn't. With a fake-casual shrug at Larissa's startled face. Oh, last month, during spring break, remember Nuño?

No, I don't remember Nuño!

Yeah, me neither. It wasn't meant to be. Just a fun few hours.

Maury was Che's boyfriend, her high school sweetheart. They were going to the junior prom next month. Yet there it was.

Oh.

I know. I told you it's no good.

You can't tell this to your mother, Che. You can never tell her.

She'll know.

She won't.

God will know, said Che, bending over her hands, on the stoop of Larissa's quiet Piermont house. They were going to be late for school half an hour ago. It was a sunny morning.

You'll be fine, said Larissa. You'll be okay. You'll see. You can't have a baby at sixteen. That's all there is to it. There'll be plenty of time to have a baby. But we've got big plans after high school, after college. We're going to travel the world. We're going to go live in Rome and teach English as a second language. Then Greece. We're going to become tour guides in France, remember?

I remember. But Che was slumped into a fetal position, her backpack on the concrete steps next to her. She looked like a backpack herself, dark and small and curled up. Larissa sat down next to her, patting her back. How could Che have been so careless when she knew what it would mean? When the decision was utterly unbearable, how could she not have taken every precaution and then some? They went to school. And Larissa carried her books, and laughed in the hall, and pretended that everything was as it always was. Only Che's pallid face by the lockers in between periods was Larissa's ruthless reminder that nothing was the same.

Later they went to New York University together, where Larissa, a theater major, met Ezra and Evelyn and Jared, while Che, an undeclared major, got busy with her causes: saving the spotted owl, saving the whale—and then her dad had a heart attack and died, and she left the U.S. for good. The girls never did get to Rome or Greece or become tour guides in France.

Nowadays, without Che, Larissa had lunch with Maggie most Tuesdays, and twice a month saw her friend Bo, who worked at the Met in the city, and once a month on Thursdays she drove to Hoboken to visit Evelyn, whom she loved and envied. Occasionally she took a walk with Tara down the street, who, though married with two kids, always seemed lonely. Larissa walked, while Tara talked, and it suited them both. On Fridays, after she had her nails done and her eyebrows waxed with her young nail friend Fran Finklestein, Larissa would write Che a short note, like a diary entry, gingerly holding the pen with her painted nails. She told Che of Maggie and Ezra, of Evelyn and her five children, of Bo and her hypochondriac mother and her layabout boyfriend. Bo was the only one working in that household and lately it had been driving her crazy. Che was far away and liked to hear news from home.

When the mail came, Larissa would leaf through the catalogs and the magazines standing over the island in her kitchen. She didn't read sitting down anymore. She didn't have time. There was always the next thing, and the next. The phone was always ringing. Evelyn called to ask her what she thought of Marilynne Robinson's new book (which Larissa hadn't read, but pretended she was really into because Evelyn was so smart and intimidated Larissa).

Evelyn and Malcolm didn't watch TV in Hoboken. They didn't even have a TV! They had two couches, a chair, and a fireplace. And a low long table on which to set the tea cups and wine glasses and the books they were reading. Whenever she and Jared went over, all they did was sit and talk about books. Larissa often held Evelyn up to Jared, who said, "Do you think it's because they live in Hoboken that they don't have a television? We lived in Hoboken, we had a TV." And, "What do you want to do, Lar, you want to get rid of the TV? Propose it, I'll say yes."

Evelyn homeschooled her kids. It was incongruous that she had the time, could find the time, could do it. "What do you want to do, Lar?" said Jared. "You want to homeschool our kids? Propose it, I'll say yes."

"You're impossible when you get self-righteous," said Larissa.

She envied Evelyn the abilities that Larissa didn't even know how to begin to begin to have. It was all Larissa could do to keep her house organized. Evelyn's house was a lot less organized, but she *homeschooled* her kids! Evelyn also had twenty-four hours in her day, right? How come she had time to homeschool five children *and* read Marilynne Robinson?

"TV never goes on," Evelyn explained with a smile.

"Well, I know. But you've got *five* kids."

"They go to bed. Eventually." When Evelyn smiled, Larissa always felt better about everything. Evelyn had a light-up smile.

In the summertime, most Jerseyites rented a house on the shore by the ocean. But Larissa and Jared didn't want to be like everybody else. They bought a lake house in the middle of rural Pennsylvania, two and half hours from anywhere, on Lingertots Pond in the woods, and Larissa went there with the kids for the summer. First year Michelangelo was old enough to speak, he called the place Lillypond, and it stuck. Jared drove out on Thursday nights and stayed through Sunday. At the end of August they went on family vacations, last year to Mount Rushmore, the year before to California and Disneyland. They took hiking vacations and camping vacations. They fished and rock climbed. They went to the Maine Coast and to the Rockies, to the Grand Canyon and Key West. For their anniversary last June, Jared took Larissa to Las Vegas. This was all in the six years since Michelangelo was born. Until he came, they had no money and went nowhere. The boy said he brought his family good luck. Since they lived on a street that was shaped like a horseshoe, they believed it.

As for family before her own family, Larissa had three much older brothers who were sharply ambitious and successful, executive vice-presidents, sales directors and school chancellors. They fiercely competed with one another, but Larissa had no one to compete with. She had neither exceeded nor subverted anyone's expectations. Nothing was expected of her. Her parents unconditionally supported her in every crazy endeavor of her heart. Violin playing? Sure. Punk rock phase with Sid Vicious posters and temporary tattoos that looked real? But of course! At twenty, when she met Jared, her hair was still laced with hot pink. During their more intimate moments Jared still called her his hot pink girl. Which was sexy when she recalled it through the pulsing place inside her that remembered things.

Theater was the thing Larissa thought about when there was

nothing else to think about. *If I could pray to move, prayers would move me; but I am constant as the Northern Star.* She had Mark Antony's agony over Caesar's murder carved into her heart. *"For Brutus is an honorable man; so are they all, all honorable men."* She recited Desdemona's death while she washed the dishes. *"Kill me tomorrow, but let me live tonight but half an hour . . ."* This was why she painted stage sets for the theater department at Pingry. So that a few times a week, she could still hear unbroken voices shout the bard. *If love be rough with you, be rough with love!*

She was thoughtful, non-aggressive, not much of a nag, liked jewelry and cooking utensils, therefore was easy to buy for, unlike her friend Maggie, who for all her many virtues was impossible to buy for.

That was Larissa Stark. Constant as the North Star.

2

Othello

On Saturday night Larissa made a pitcher of Margaritas with Triple Sec, Cointreau *and* Grand Marnier and thus liquefied, the four of them played Scruples, the game that challenged everyone's idea of what was right, a game of moral dilemmas, everyone's hated favorite, all conundrummy ambiguity chased down the gullet by hard liquor.

"I don't want to play," declared Jared. "I want to have some superficial laughs. I don't want to delve into the complexities of my psyche, or anyone else's psyche for that matter. Why can't we be like regular people, and just talk baseball free-agency trades?"

He was voted down. The children remained clean and well-behaved (aside from three whines and a stomp from Emily, and silence from the adolescent and sullen Dylan, Maggie and Ezra's son), and nothing broke and nothing burned. Larissa, her cast still on, wore a green, form-fitting jersey sweater and tailored black slacks, her hair loosely piled, her makeup deceptively light. She served Brie in puff pastry, a chicken paprika with pappardelle, a bacon salad with her own dressing, and a rum baba for dessert, also homemade. They drank red wine, and chased it down with shots of Reposado, following it with Margaritas. On the stereo, Glenn Gould played Bach like only Gould could play him—exquisitely—his six Partitas (especially BWV 830) imprinted on Larissa's soul so clearly she could almost play them herself, if only she had a piano, and could play. The fires were on in all three fireplaces, and when the kids ran to the playroom for ping-pong and G-rated board games, the adults were able to talk while the house sparkled, and outside a light dusting of snow fell quietly on the tall bare oaks and the frozen ground.

The question that seemed to come up in Scruples a lot came up. Larissa personally thought it was the *only* question the game of Scruples ever asked. It was the only question they got mired in, despite the Triple Sec. *"You see your best friend's wife making out with another man. Do you tell?"* Last time they played it with Evelyn and Malcolm, and that question came up, Evelyn had told Larissa she and Malcolm didn't talk for four days afterward.

Last time they played with Bo and Jonny, Jonny's nonchalant response to this stupid question ("Of course you don't tell. That's the guy code.") so infuriated Bo, they had to take a break from the relationship. Which was difficult considering they continued to live together in an apartment that belonged to Jonny.

When the card was flipped over and read this Saturday night, Ezra and Maggie laughed, Larissa groaned, and Jared said, "You know what I'm going to do from now on? Give a different answer each time it's asked, to drive you all crazy and maybe next time we can just play Risk."

"What do you mean *from now on?*" said Maggie. "That's what you always do."

"Jared," Larissa said to her husband, "just answer the dumb question."

"No," said Jared. "The entreaty is clear. Do not end marriages, cause family rifts, or destroy friendships by revealing something totally inappropriate. And that's by the guys who designed the game!"

Larissa sipped her drink, the salt on the rim deliciously swelling her lime mouth. "Jared's right. We should heed their rules. Besides," she added, "I think we're overlooking the obvious. How come the only one not in any trouble is the actual adulterer? It's all about the friends, the secrets, the obligations to the friendship. What about the obligations to the marriage?"

"Yeah, but that's too obvious," replied Jared. "That's why it's not a Scruples question. It's not even an ethical dilemma."

"It *is* a question, however," Ezra said. "A question, among many others," he added pointedly, "that a certain Larissa is refusing to answer. She's doing that a lot tonight. Not answering questions."

"Oh, calm down, Ezra," said Larissa. "Have another drink."

"Are you a relativist or an absolutist, Larissa?" asked Maggie.

"Well, it depends," Larissa replied to the laughter of everyone, and she laughed herself, though she couldn't quite tell what was so funny.

"All right, Miss I-absolutely-shouldn't-have-made-my-'ritas-so-strong," said Ezra, looking up at Larissa who was busy squeezing more lime into what was left of his drink. "Can we talk about business for a sec? Don't avoid me."

Larissa pulled out a card. "Let's play Invent a Question of Scruples instead," she said.

"Fine," agreed Ezra. "But I ask first."

Larissa had two Margaritas and six partitas in her. She smiled, unafraid, tipping her glass in a toast. "What's your question?"

"Denise goes on maternity leave after *Othello*. That's *next* month."

This was all he said, like a riddle.

"Is this part of Invent a Question?" Larissa wanted to know. "Denise goes on maternity leave. But she's ambivalent about the baby, being forty-four and a first-time mom. I believe Denise's feelings are justified. She doesn't seem very maternal. You're asking if should I try to dissuade her from having the child and stay on as director?"

"Larissa."

"Yes, Ezra?"

"Stop being deliberately obtuse."

"How am I obtuse?" She loved her Saturday nights with her friends. They were like family.

"Why do you make me tell it to you twice? You know I want you to become the new director for the Pingry Theater Department."

Larissa swayed while sitting down. She and Jared exchanged a brief but conflicted look.

She painted background murals. She was the set decorator. Which described her life at home too. And every once in a while, when she was working, she'd hear in the nuance of the rehearsals of the sixteen-year-old's interpretation of *Othello* something that would catch her ear, and she'd clear her throat and say quietly, but loud enough so that Moor of Venice could hear: "Try it again, Linus, but this time with the emphasis on *must* as in, '*And yet she* must *die, else she'll betray more men.*'"

The paint she used for the sets sometimes needed to be thinned with turps, which gave her a vicious, delicious headache, because secretly she loved the smell even as she suffered, and she listened more intently to the last act as she stirred the paint, the black and white to make a stormy gray, and waited for the thickened paint to thin so she could paint the walls behind Desdemona's bed, on which lay the fifteen-year-old siren Tiffany from Chatham, still in braces but with a Coach purse, straight from the Swim Club, waiting for her lover in the form of Linus from Summit in Birkenstocks to persuade himself of her unthinkable, of his unthinkable.

"That death's unnatural that kills for loving.
Alas, why gnaw you so your nether lip?
Some bloody passion shakes your very frame:
These are portents; but yet I hope, I hope,
They do not point on me."

"Do you *ever* plan to answer me?" Ezra demanded.

"Yes." Larissa picked up another Scruples card. "Ezra, would you be willing to eat a bowl of live crickets for $40,000?"

⚘

"Lar," Jared said, "if you want it, you should take it."

"Want what?" she said innocently. They were getting undressed.

"Come on. Seriously."

But she had too much to drink for seriously. She fell on the bed in her black bra and underwear, her hair loose, her made-up eyes half closing. Pulling up her casted leg, she motioned for Jared with her index finger, and he fell on top of her, in his clothes, also having had a little too much to drink.

"We'll work out the kids," he muttered, kissing her. "Take the job. You know Ezra will be thrilled."

"What, I'm now accepting work to make Ezra happy?" Her arms flung around him.

"No, to make *you* happy." They nestled, rumbled to an inebriated rhythm of a married Saturday night with nowhere to go on Sunday morning.

"I'm happy," she said. "Don't worry about me."

"I know how much you used to love it. Directing."

"Yes." Her eyes remained closed. The true unspoken inquiry hung in the air, the real issue, the only one worth having an answer to, the thirsty dilemma at the crux of each human heart: *How is it best for me to live?*

Soon Larissa would be asleep. She felt herself drifting, even as excitement built up in her from the feel of Jared's body on top of her, from the smell of his liquored-up breath, from his lips on her lips, on her throat. "I'll think about it," she said. It was like a placeholder to end the conversation. I'll think about it meant she would endeavor never to give it another thought. Theatrically she moaned. Jared forgot about theater, as she hoped he would.

3
Aisle 12

The cast came off a few days later and Larissa limped with a walking stick to her car, like Uriah Heep—like her grandmother who had died aged ninety-eight—and then drove to Pingry and finished painting the backdrop for Desdemona's death. She went to the library, got some books for Asher's school project on Abraham Lincoln, and then dropped by Nee Dells to see if there were any new boots (there weren't), afterward stopping at Panera Bakery in Madison to get a mozzarella and pepper baguette and chicken noodle soup. After finishing lunch, she still had an hour left before Michelangelo. This day and every day was punctuated by the regimen of her children. When she was a kid, all she and Che wanted was to be free of school; little did Larissa realize that she'd never be free of it, that morning, afternoon and night, the homework, the projects, the notes home, the agenda books, the signatures on tests, the packed lunches, the bought lunches, the chaperones and the school trips, the exams and the #2 pencils, the rulers and compasses and looseleaf paper, the parent-teacher conferences, all of it, wasn't just twelve years of her life. No. It was the *rest* of her life, the better part of the better part of her life. Sure, eventually it stopped, but when it stopped, you stopped too. Larissa would be over fifty when the last child would graduate high school, and who said it would be over by then? Who said that her daughter wouldn't be back home, living as a single mother in the room upstairs, and suddenly it was playgroup and kindergarten and first grade again, and Larissa would be sixty, picking up her grandkids from school, still looking at her watch, saying, two hours left, one hour left, thirty minutes left.

How could Ezra not see how impossible it was for her to take on theater, too? What did mothers who worked outside the home do? Did their bodies also shift slightly downward, as if some perverse internal clock was ringing its alarm at them—it's 2:30. It's 3:00, it's school bus time. Every day. Every year. Whatever it was they were doing, did they also lift their heads from their desks and acknowledge that while they were in their cubicles, their children were getting off the bus to come home to a house where their mothers weren't?

Larissa wouldn't have her life any other way. She would not pay someone else to take care of her kids to rehearse plays with other people's children whose mothers were working.

Today she had an hour. Not enough time to choose, edit, cast and direct a play for spring. It was bitterly cold. She drove to Stop&Shop instead. She went because she needed detergent. Jared needed tissues for his office and some chewy caramels for his candy jar. Asher needed posterboard and glue, and Michelangelo colored pencils (of course he did). Emily needed her own shampoo because the family's Pantene Smooth and Sleek just wouldn't do. Larissa parked by the cemetery again, hurrying in from the cold.

She was scheduled like a mother. Every minute of her life was accounted for.

Every minute, except for the present one after Panera's and before Michelangelo's bus.

⌒⌒⌒

She was getting laundry detergent in aisle 12 when she heard his voice.

"Hey, what are you doing here," he said, like a voiceover narrative track, "in the laundry aisle?"

He was pushing his own cart, in which he had nothing but three containers of sushi and some dried almonds. She switched her gaze from his cart to him.

"Um—getting laundry?" Why did he smile like that was amusing? "Family's run out." She got that in there. Family.

Larissa wasn't trying to be coy. She wasn't trying to be much of anything. She actually *was* shopping for her family.

"How's your ankle?"

"Good," she replied. "Cast came off."

"I see that. Feeling better?"

"Meh." She stood awkwardly next to the fabric softener. The aisle smelled faintly of fake lavender. Best to go get some food now.

Larissa got some softener just in case, since she was standing right next to it. Got big containers, two of them, so she wouldn't have to come back to aisle 12 anytime soon, and also to show him that she had a family that needed giant amounts of fabric softener because she was a good mother and softened their laundered clothes. He rolled his cart down the aisle beside her. He wore torn jeans, brown boots, brown leather. His hair didn't look brushed. He looked underfed in that skinny young guy way when they can't keep the weight on no matter what they do.

"You ride in this weather?" she asked him. "That's crazy."

"Yeah. It *is* pretty crazy. I'm not used to it." He pointed to his splotched face. "I get windburn."

Her mother taught her to be polite so Larissa said she couldn't tell. But where was he from that he wasn't used to it? One winter in Jersey and you pretty much knew what to expect. She didn't ask.

When she turned to aisle 13, to the frozen section and the bread, he turned, too. She didn't need any frozen food. She bought some anyway. Frozen hash browns, frozen broccoli, ice cream. And some frozen pizza since that's what they were having for dinner tonight. They got in line, he right behind her. Outside in the stinging sunshine, he asked where she was parked and they both saw she was parked close to his bike.

"You're like me," he said. "You don't want to forget where you left your transportation." His fingerless gloves clutched the paper bag full of sushi.

"Can't imagine you'd forget where you parked *that*," Larissa said. "I don't know much about motorcycles." Risk-averse and proud of it. "But it looks nice."

He looked amused. "Well, you're right. It *is* a nice bike. It's a Ducati Sportclassic."

Her face didn't change; she couldn't even fake being impressed. "You bought it new?"

"Nah, it's too expensive. It was my old man's. He left it when he died."

"Oh." She studied him. "Sorry."

"Yeah, but," he said, "look at the bike." He raised his eyebrows and smiled, slightly ironically, but maybe not. Slightly ruefully, but maybe not.

He helped her again, the heavy detergent, the fabric softeners, the 12-pack of Diet Coke. "Someone drinks a lot of soda in your house," he remarked. "All that carbon dioxide is terrible for your metabolism."

"What?"

"Oh, yeah. It slows down your Krebs cycle to a crawl. It interferes with the enzyme that receives the oxygen molecule. Terrible if you're trying to lose weight. What, you didn't know?"

"I didn't know," she said slowly, frowning at him. "How do *you* know?"

"Ninth grade bio." Instead of frowning, he smiled. "Not that *you* should care about losing weight," he said. "See ya. Keep warm."

"Yeah, you too." She wanted to ask him his name, but didn't dare. *Ninth* grade bio!

Bo called as soon as Larissa got home. "My life is being slowly destroyed," she said. "Today she told me she was going blind. Blind! I said, Mother, have you tried your glasses? They're right on the nightstand. Oh God. I'm leaving work early today to take her to the eye doctor. Can I come over first?"

"How can you not?" said Larissa. She liked Bo, who was stately and attractive and deliberate in her movements, but what she liked best about Bo was that she could hide herself in the fray of Bo's graceful self-absorption.

4

"Moisten Your Head with Lubricant"

"Do you *refuse* to give me an answer?" said Ezra incredulously, cornering her in the kitchen after another January week had passed. Her oatmeal chocolate chip cookies would burn if she didn't take them out *right now*.

"Ezra, excuse me." Oven mitts on, Larissa opened the oven door. Damn. Overdone by two minutes.

He sighed behind her. "I thought you were going to think about it."

"I *have* thought about it." She took out a clanging metal cookie rack.

"Well, think some more. Think until you give me the answer I want."

Giggling, she started to scrape the cookies onto a cooling rack. "I can't do it. I don't have the time."

"What the hell are you talking about? You have from eight till two each and every day to dedicate to the unfailing pursuit of theatrical excellence."

"Only in your limited and one-dimensional world," said Larissa, "do I have nothing to do from eight till two."

"Lar," said Jared, pouring drinks and always ready to instigate, "tell our friends how long it takes you to get out of the house."

Larissa stayed quiet!

"How long?" said Ezra. "Thirty minutes?"

"Thirty?" said Jared, raising his eyebrows. "Tell him, Lar."

After veal shank and rice with corn, and everyone full and relaxed at the table, Larissa told them.

Did this seem unreasonable?

Brushing teeth, etc.	5 minutes
Shower	15 minutes
Drying	5 minutes
Drying smaller parts, like ears	5 minutes
Lotioning	10 minutes
Makeup	20 minutes
Getting dressed	10 minutes
Hair	30 minutes
Jewelry	5 minutes
Misc tasks, e.g., shoes, purse	10 minutes
Total:	1 hour, 55 minutes

"That's without dawdling, making coffee, or doing a single thing for any of the kids," Larissa finished.

"Is this a joke?"

"I don't see what's so funny."

Ezra stammered. "Jared, you allow this?"

"I don't *allow* it, that's just how long it takes." Jared gazed at Larissa.

"But it takes *me* fifteen minutes!"

"Ezra," Larissa said calmly, "I've seen you spend longer in the bathroom when you have company."

Ezra whirled to Maggie. "How long does it take me?"

"Fifteen minutes," replied Maggie.

"I shave, five minutes, shower, five minutes, I put on my clothes, five more minutes. Done."

"Yeah. So? What does your business have to do with my business?"

"You weren't always like this. You weren't like this in college!"

"In college, Ezra? We walked around in the same pair of jeans for weeks! We were theater hippies. We prided ourselves on not washing. Things have changed."

"Clearly."

They all tried that Saturday night to make Larissa more efficient at getting beautiful so she could become a drama director for Pingry.

"Why do you *have* to put lotion on?"

"You want me to have scaly skin, Ezra? Like a snake?"

"I don't care either way, but you won't be scaly."

"I will be. My husband likes touching soft skin."

All inebriated eyes turned from wine to the husband.

"I do like the soft skin," admitted the sheepish, grinning husband, his shaggy gray-brown hair falling over his forehead, his hand reaching out to stroke Larissa's cheek.

"Why can't you let your hair dry naturally?" suggested Ezra. "You'll cut thirty minutes right there."

"Because I will look a fright." Larissa suddenly remembered the bike dude's disquisition on women and hair, and became uncomfortable, in her own home, recalling laughing with a stranger in a parking lot.

"You can't possibly," said Maggie. "You would look beautiful no matter what. Your hair looks so pretty now."

"Took me forty-five minutes. Thirty to blow dry and fifteen more to get it into a bun that looks casually messy." Larissa gracefully moved on from the freeform poetry of hair. "Why do you *want* me to be dry, disheveled, down?"

"Because I want you to direct the spring play," said Ezra. "Why do you spend five minutes on jewelry? You don't need jewelry to go to the supermarket, do you?"

"More than anywhere else," Larissa replied. "Obviously you've never been to the supermarket. Do you know how many times I hear, I like your necklace, your earrings, your bracelet?"

"No, how many?" asked Jared, poking her, his eyes glinting.

Pinching Jared's arm, Larissa went on. "How many times I hear, where did you get that beautiful necklace and I say I got it from Jean. Is that what you want, Ezra? Frump me up and run Jean's business out of Summit? Besides," she continued, on a pleasant, non-defensive roll, "Jared buys me my jewelry. You want me not to wear his lovely gifts? Some wife I am."

"You don't wear *everything* I buy for you," Jared said with a wink.

Stop it, she mouthed to him, winking back. It was Saturday night, after all, and Larissa had a fair amount of liquid Eros in her.

They worked on her the rest of the evening. Here in her external present life, the minutia of hairspray was scrutinized: should she spritz once or twice, and why moisturizer *and* foundation, while in her other past life, one evening she and Maggie and Ezra, and Evelyn and Malcolm, and even Jared, had spent 1 hour, 55 minutes figuring out why Psalm 23 sounded so sublime in its King Jamesian rendition but so much less so in successive, though (possibly) more accurate versions.

One version read: *You moisten my head with lubricant* instead of, *You anoint my head with oil.*

"*Moisten?* Who says that? It sounds . . . I don't know," Larissa had said with distaste she was unable to hide. "Slightly sexual."

Ezra had chuckled, adjusting his red plaid blazer. "Well, in the original Hebrew, the word had no sacramental connotations," he said. "The words were *lubricate with pleasure*."

"*You lubricate my head with pleasure?*" Larissa had said incredulously. "That's better than *anoint*?"

"No, quite right," agreed Ezra. "Which is why we use *moisten*."

So Larissa could conclude now in the fullness of time that in the end all philosophical discussions, past and present, were about lotion.

"I *anoint* my body with oil," Larissa said to Ezra and Maggie this evening.

"You *what?*"

It was pleasant to sit, to chat. There was no denying the delights of her subzero freezer and canyon-capacity washing machine and her funny loquacious friends. It was only when she stood at her books and touched the spines of the unread memoirs and comedies before she boxed them all to be donated, it was only when she was saying no to Ezra for something so outlandishly magical as to live on the stage, that Larissa fleetingly thought that though she looked so rad in her glad rags, perhaps the books weren't getting read and *Othello* wasn't getting directed by her because she was taking 1 hour, 55 minutes to moisten her head with lubricant.

5

Between Childhood Friends

Larissa, you look great, let's go.

Just one more coat of mascara, Che.

No, seriously, let's go. My mom won't let me go out with you if she sees you with globs of makeup.

It's your prom. She'll let you.

Come on, enough. You've been at this for an hour.

No, I haven't. And it's the prom!

I know. But we'll miss the whole thing if you don't hurry up. Look, you're not even dressed yet.

Che . . . why don't you want to talk about the other thing?

Put on the corsage and let's go.

I need the dress on first.

So put it on.

Che . . .

Larissa, I don't want to talk about the other thing.

But we have to do something.

I'm hoping it will just go away.

By itself?

With God's help.

Oh, Che.

Look, I know. But I can't deal with it, okay.

But you're not alone. I'll help you. I'm here. I'll go with you.

I'm not ready.

Why don't you want to go, at least get the test?

Because then I'll have to deal with it.

You don't want to wait too long . . .

What does it matter?

Because up to thirteen weeks costs three hundred bucks, but after thirteen is six hundred.

How do you know this? Che squinted at her friend.

Casually Larissa shrugged, standing in front of the mirror in her black bra and high heels, her young legs impossibly long like marshland reeds. I looked into it.

Why does it cost more?

I don't know.

Oh, didn't look into that part? Che paused. *Maybe because there's more to scrape out?*

Che . . . come on.

Okay. Like I said, let's not talk about it. It's prom night. Are you done yet?

Che . . . don't be afraid. I'm here. I'm always here for you.

Larissa, you can't help me with this.

I can. I will. I am.

No. Don't you understand? I can't do what I know I must do. I must do it, but I can't do it. Quite a pickle, isn't it? Enough lipstick. You look like a streetwalker in daylight. Wipe it off before my mother comes in. You want her to like you, don't you? Get dressed.

Well, you can't have a baby, Che.

Shh!

You can't.

There's a lot I can't do.

You want my advice?

No. I know your advice. But you're not me. You're not my mother's daughter. You're your mother's daughter.

We're not telling your mother.

I'm still her daughter. I'm still Filipino. I'm still Catholic. I'm still what I am. Telling her, not telling her, won't change any of those things. Won't change the truth of things, Larissa, no matter if it's three hundred dollars or six thousand.

Except I don't have six hundred dollars. I have three-fifty.

Okay. I won't need it.

Oh, Che.

And Che cried again, in her silk blue gown, her white orchid corsage, her waterproof mascara enduring, but streaks remaining in her foundation when the doorbell rang, and her mother yelled that their young men were here.

All right, Ma. Stop shouting, We're not deaf.

Please. Just take the test.

What good will it do?

Let's go to Planned Parenthood.

What good will it do?

You'll talk to someone.

What good will it do?

So what are you going to do, have that baby?

I can't have it.

Exactly.

I can't do the other thing either.

How are you going to explain it to Maury?

I can't explain it.

Exactly.

Right. Are you going downstairs in your bra or are you finally going to put some clothes on? Che wiped her face, wiped the blush and foundation off her wet cheeks, straightened up, pretended to smile.

How many weeks are you late now?

Eight, mouthed Che, in terror, into Larissa's sinking heart.

❧

Dear Che,

Why did you return the money order I sent you? Come on, it's like a birthday gift certificate. I'd send you stuff but besides Nutella

I don't know what else you need. And anyway, how much Nutella can a girl eat? Please. I'm resending the money order, happy birthday, merry Christmas. Accept. Please.

Why are you worried about me? I should be worried about you. Everything is good here. Same as always. Nothing to report. I'm not aggrieved. I'm whole, not wanting. My temperature is as always climate-controlled, why are you anxious about me?

Larissa stopped writing. She couldn't put into words what she was feeling. Highway 24 ran between the golf course and the shopping mall. Golf course—beauty. Shopping mall—luxury. But between them one hundred and twenty feet of concrete, and cars whizzing by.

Where were they going? East, they were headed to New York. But the other way, west. Where were *they* headed? Pennsylvania? Ohio, to visit relatives? Or somewhere farther? Farther where? Kansas? Colorado? California? Where after that? She would listen to the cars, racing as if rushing, hurrying along, hastening away, faster, faster away, out of New Jersey, beyond, far, away, and gone.

It got to be so that every time Larissa opened her front door, every time she got into her ivory Escalade or walked down the driveway to get the mail, or opened the windows, or stood briefly to take in the view from the slope of her property, all she heard was the madlong rush of cars.

Che, I know you'll think I'm crazy for wondering this, but though I think you're nuts for having that awful protesting job, sometimes I wonder what it's like to be you. To have your life. What is it like to worry about Lorenzo, to sleep late if you want to, or get up early, or have your own schedule? I read your letters with such fascination. Human beings are perverse, aren't they?

I sometimes wonder how your day breaks down into its many hours.

You know I'd love to come. Michelangelo won't spare me. But I think the rest of them can take me or leave me. Especially Emily. She's becoming so snotty. The hormones are going straight to her mouth. She can't say anything to me without her hand on her hip like a kettle. Remember when we were the same way with our mothers? I miss you so much. Whenever I think of you, I picture us only as kids. You're the only one who knows me from back then.

⌒⌒⌒

Dear Larissa,

I've decided to keep your Christmas gift. Thank you. I want to get a manicure and buy new sneakers but I think I'll just pay my three months' back rent, if it's all the same to you.

You want to know about my day? Okay, I'll tell you about yesterday. What you do is, you take yesterday and multiply it by 365, and you'll get the picture.

I woke up at seven, because the outdoor market was opening at eight, and I had to go get the fruit baskets from Father Emilio. I got to him by 7:30, but he made me go to Mass first, which is okay, but Lorenzo and I have been fighting so much I didn't think I deserved communion for all the nasty things I kept yelling, but when I told Father Emilio this, he said that was my pride talking. He said to me, "You're going to keep yourself away from God's sacrament because you think you're not perfect? When do you think you'll ever be perfect enough, sinless enough, to receive the Eucharist?" So . . . I went to Mass, and felt a little better about things, and then carried thirteen bushels, one by one, of mangoes and tomatoes and pears and spent till noon selling them, and when I got back home, having made a thousand pesos, I found Lorenzo still sleeping! And you know, we're so broke, and he needs to work, ride a rickshaw in Manila, which he hates to do, so instead he goes out drinking with his derelict radical buddies and then sleeps till noon, and, like I said, we haven't paid the rent for three months, living hand to mouth (without the rent).

We had a fight that lasted till one, but then made up nicely, till two, and he got hungry, so we went to San Agustin and had lunch with Father Emilio and his orphans, for free, and then made copies of our leaflets at the mission because Father Emilio lets me use the copier, for free, and afterward went to Manila City Hall Square and distributed them at a joint rally with the Manila Police and the Philippines Motorcycle Association in support of our current president. Imagine us in a joint rally with the police. It ended peacefully at 6:30, and we met up with some friends and went out drinking but I left because I didn't want to hang out with his loser friends, and besides, I was three days late and wanted to take a pregnancy test. The test cost me 750 pesos. It was negative. I took it at 9:00 p.m., and then cried until Lorenzo returned at eleven, too drunk to care that we weren't having a baby, but he did get blazing mad that I spent 750 pesos on a stupid test. Oh, to think that once upon a time, I avoided the test like the Black Death, and now I spend money I don't have to take it randomly throughout the month, just in case.

So . . . we had another fight, this time till well after midnight, when the neighbors finally called the police because it was getting ugly, and the cops we had rallied with wanted to arrest Lorenzo, but I said no. After they left, I left too, and went to sleep in one of the rooms at the orphanage. Father Emilio keeps telling me that I can come and live with him. He doesn't have enough hands to take care of the kids. But I said being around so many unwanted children would make me feel even worse about my life, if that's possible, because here I am, wanting a baby, and unable to have one. Lorenzo came to get me at three, and we lay in the twin bed together, and had sex under God's eyes at San Agustin. I wondered if Father would still think I was worthy of communion. To test him, I came to him this morning, and challenged him with the truth of last night. And you know what he said? God never turns away from you. He is longing for your heart, Che. Yours and Lorenzo's.

I give up on that Father Emilio.

So that was my day.

What do you think?

Want to trade?

6

Loose Change

At the breakfast island, Asher said, "Mom, if you and Dad got divorced, *we* would decide who to go live with."

"No, you wouldn't, Ash," said Larissa. "Mom and Dad would decide."

"Are you getting divorced?" Michelangelo kept eating his Frosted Flakes.

"No, buddy. Eat quick. We gotta jet."

"Well, I'll go with *you*," Asher declared, though no one asked. "You yell less."

"Are you *kidding*?" said Emily. "Mom has *such* a temper. No, we should go with Dad."

Michelangelo hugged his mother around the middle. "You and Daddy aren't getting divorced, right?" Still kept on with that soggy cereal, though.

"No, sweetums," said Larissa, running her fingers through his tangly gold curls.

"Mom," said Asher, "if you and Dad both died, like, tomorrow, who would we go to live with? Uncle Jimmy?" Larissa's brother Jimmy lived in Detroit.

"Uncle Jimmy has no room," said Larissa, getting some pretzels and a drink into a paper bag for Michelangelo's snack. "Besides, he knows nothing of kids. What about Grandma?" She said that with negative conviction. She said it while shaking her head behind the question, no, no.

"Yeah, I guess." Asher was thoughtful. "Maybe Florida with Grandpa?"

"We should go to school, that's where we should go," said Larissa.

"Yeah!" said Michelangelo. "Grandpa. I want to go to Grandpa." Michelangelo loved Jared's dad more than anyone else in the world. Drawings of Grandpa in his golf cart popped up all over Larissa's house.

"Oh, but how would we get there? We have no money for a plane ticket." Asher turned to his mother. "Mom, can you give me cash for all the gifts cards I got for Christmas? I have, like, two hundred dollars. I'll be able to buy a plane ticket then."

"But what about me?" wailed Michelangelo. "*I* don't have two hundred dollars."

"Let's look around the house for loose change," said Asher. "Let's start now. We'll get enough for a plane ticket by the time they're dead."

"How about if you start your search for loose change right after school," said Larissa. "Okey-doke?"

"We're going to miss the bus," said Emily. "Let's go, Ash. Mom, I can't find my sneakers. I have gym today."

She couldn't find them for ten minutes. They missed the bus. She had to borrow her mother's footwear, but when she moved her backpack off the floor, there were the sneakers, cleverly hidden underneath. An exasperated Larissa drove them all to school. "Maybe a little less discussion about my death, and we'd all be more punctual."

"No, I don't think so, Mom," said Asher. "I believe the two are unrelated."

"Go to school. Learn something."

Michelangelo was late for his spelling test. Asher forgot his clarinet, *and* his glasses. Emily "forgot" her coat, though it was ten degrees below zero.

To recuperate from the morning, Larissa spent the early

afternoon walking the mall with Maggie. She didn't think it counted as a calorie burner, though, shuffling along at their creaky middle-aged pace.

"Larissa, you know that Ezra is *shocked* you're not genuflecting at his feet for offering you the drama director job."

They were strolling, looking indifferently through the store displays.

"Mags, I know. But he doesn't understand things anymore."

"He says you've changed."

"I haven't changed. I'm exactly the same. My life has changed. I can't just la-di-dah and take on a huge commitment like a theater director job."

"He says you did it in Hoboken when the kids were babies."

"Believe it or not they required less! And I was thirteen years younger. I was still entertaining the unsustainable hope that stage was going to be my life. That's over and done with. I can't be memorizing, chewing pencils, rehearsing, on the phone, getting involved with parents and students. It'll consume me. Just like before. I barely have enough time to be a chauffeur. The kids need me for twenty different things in the afternoon. I have a husband who works twelve hours a day and who likes his food hot. What does he care if his wife is engaged in minutia of play rehearsals? Which scene to cut? Who's going to play Desdemona? He just wants his steak on the table. And I understand that. But look, I'm still there. Ezra knows I can't be far from it. I do the sets, I sew the costumes. I run the lines. Honest, that's enough for me." She turned her face away to the Tumi flagship store windows.

They bought things they didn't need, like bras and hoodies. They were roped into some Dead Sea scrub, for seventy dollars!—"Made from Dead Sea Scrolls, I'm sure," said Maggie—and were deciding on lunch at California Pizza Kitchen or their beloved Neiman's Café, which had the most exquisite monkey bread with strawberry butter, when Larissa spotted the Ducati dude from Stop&Shop strolling toward them with a male friend. They were talking, lightly laughing; they acknowledged the women not at all but for a polite

half-second glance, except as they were passing, the Ducati dude
tipped his baseball cap at Larissa, his head tilting and his mouth
stretching in a casual but unmistakable white-teeth smile.

Barely exhaling, Larissa looked away from his face, casting her
gaze down to his faded ripped jeans, his worn boots. His friend was
neat, ironed blue Dockers, a white shirt. Not him.

"Who was *that?*" Maggie asked absent-mindedly as they glided
past, and Larissa, picking up on the absent-minded, decided to play
deaf, a trick she had learned from her kids. She ignored the question
hoping it would hang in the air and be gone.

"Lar! Who *was* that?"

Didn't work that time. "I've no idea," said Larissa. "He must've
mistook me for someone else."

"Get out."

"Yes."

"No way."

"Yes way. Maybe he was saying hello to you."

"Larissa!"

"Okay, I'm joking. What, you don't know him?"

"Larissa!"

"I don't know him either. What can I tell you?"

"Does he go to school with Emily?"

"Emily? Why would you say that?" Larissa got defensive.

"What are you getting all huffy for? He must know you from
somewhere."

"Who's huffy? But why Emily? And he doesn't. Just a mistake.
But he looks much too old to know anyone like Emily."

"I didn't say *like* Emily. I said *actual* Emily."

"No. How silly. Well, what did we decide on? Neiman's?"

They strolled on.

"You better watch out," Larissa said, "or I'll tell Ezra how you
brushed your hair for twenty minutes at my house because we were
going to be valeted by Manuel at Saks."

"First of all," Maggie said officiously, bending her unruly red mop in Larissa's direction, "you know perfectly well that Ezra wouldn't care if Manuel and I went at it doggie-style in the parking lot. Of all things Ezra is, he is *not* Othello. Second of all, that wasn't Manuel but Esteban. Manuel was off today. Third of all, I never brush my hair, and if your hair were curly, you'd know that. Poor Michelangelo. How he must suffer under your hand if you think you can brush his hair. And fourth of all, Manuel says to me '*Vaya con Dios*' every time he brings me my car. That's a man who deserves special attention."

"Does Ezra know this?"

"Ezra loves my little friends."

Why did Larissa lie?

Why would she need to?

Flushed inside and out, she walked on, stifling the urge to turn around. For some reason she felt he might've turned around too. The whole thing made her jerkily uncomfortable, as if ants were crawling on her skin. And what's more—the ants kept on crawling, worrying the circle around the loop of the question, or was it around the pinpoint of the answer? Why would Larissa *need* to lie to Maggie about such a minor detail? Why didn't she just say, oh, he helped me with my groceries? Took pity on a woman with a broken leg. And yet she didn't. She hid it. Hid herself. Hid him. Why?

At lunch they discussed Bo, her current pervasive, unsolvable problems (discussed blissfully because they weren't their problems), and Maggie's new love of painting ("Are you good, Mags?" "No, I'm terrible. But completely obsessed.") and about Ezra's lack of understanding of same.

"For all his bookishness, Ezra can be pretty dense about stuff," agreed Larissa. "Don't forget to tell him," she added, "that he should brush up on his Ecclesiastes." She hadn't been a drama teacher for nothing. "*For in much wisdom, there is much grief, and he who increases knowledge, also increases sorrow.*"

෨൶ඁ

To Jared in the morning, Larissa said, "I found a new market. Stop&Shop in Madison. They give out tasters all over the store, their meats are great, and their fruit is good."

"Tasters, wonderful," he said, kissing her. "I'm pleased for you. I know how much you like supermarkets. Go get us something nice."

There.

She went food-shopping with the full approval of her husband.

The ground was hard like pavement, the grass in slumber. She bundled herself into a maroon cashmere Juicy tracksuit, she fussed with her hair, and drove to Stop&Shop. Before she left, she put moisturizer on, because who in their right mind would go out into that blistering January without protection for their face? She wasn't as young as she used to be. She had to protect her skin. She had to put foundation on. Then a little blush because in the winter she looked so pale. A little mascara to not feel so plain. Mascara, like a mask for the eyes. Lipstick to brighten those winter lips. Deodorant was a must. So was perfume. Perfume because when Jared came home, it had lived on her skin and he said she smelled good. She put on Creed's Virgin Island Water to go to the supermarket for Jared so he could nuzzle when he came home and tell her she smelled like summer coconut and lime.

Produce first, then tea, then sugar, then diet soda (again!). It was for hubby. She herself had stopped drinking it: didn't want her metabolism to slow. With her ankle still slightly throbbing, she bought some chicken, some ground sirloin, a Cornish hen, cast a look of revolt at the calves' liver, and made her way to the paper aisle.

"Would you like me to get those down for you?" a voice said behind her.

He was next to her, smiling, looking up at the 6-pack of paper towels she'd been trying to pull off the top shelf.

"Please," she said, lightly smiling back. "I guess it helps to be tall."

"Well, you're no slouch in the tall department." He pulled them down with one arm. "Just not quite tall enough."

She *was* quite tall for a woman. Five-eight in her bare feet. He wore his leather jacket, an aviator scarf, ripped jeans again, old boots. His smile was clean, shiny, like he was thinking of a joke, of something witty to say.

"So what were you doing at the mall the other day?" he asked. "I said hello; didn't you recognize me?"

That was witty? "Shopping. What were *you* doing at the mall?" She ignored the other, unanswerable bits of his question.

"Hanging out with my buddy Gil. He says I need some new clothes if I'm going to make an impression on my new bosses. So reluctantly I got myself a white shirt."

"Oh, yeah?" Should she ask? Well, why not? They were just making small talk in the supermarket. She picked up a box of light bulbs, casual. "Where are you working?" She hoped he wouldn't say Baskin-Robbins.

He pointed in some nebulous direction. "At the Jag dealership down the street. But that's later in the day. Two mornings a week I got another job."

"Oh, yeah?"

"At John Cortese in Summit. I'm a stonemason."

"Stonemason." She pondered the definition of that. Mason . . . was that Latin for to build, to make?

"I'm excellent with irregular blue stone," he said. "Also concrete pavers. Any kind of stonework, really. Do you need anything done at your home?"

"Um—no. But thanks."

"A patio? Some landscaping walls? A walkway?"

"Thanks, we're all set."

"I'm saving up," he said with a jerky kid-like shrug. "Hence two jobs." He grinned. "I have this dream of starting my own business."

He was saving money! He was responsible. He had dreams! He was ambitious. He had actual skills. He was hard-working. And he wasn't in school.

He worked with stone? That might explain his skinny, hard-looking body. The light bulbs nearly fell out of her hands and broke.

Her question was: *did* one lay bricks in January? Wasn't it a seasonal thing? I mean, today was twenty below zero with the wind chill howling it down another ten degrees. Did one lay pavers outside in Short Hills in January?

And the point of the doubt was what? That he was lying about being a stonemason? His real job was a hedge fund manager and he didn't want her to know? Or maybe his real job was a senior in high school and he didn't want her to know. Maybe she could bring him home, get him some milk and cookies and send him to the den to play video games with Asher.

"Much call for stone work in the wintertime?"

"Not really," he admitted. "I'm part time till the summer. Mostly I'm at the Jag place." He grinned. He was so friendly, so cute. So harmless. He would be a very good bag boy right here at Stop&Shop. And then he could help her take the groceries to her car.

"You must be glad the cast's off," he said. "Think of how many accidents could be avoided if only women would stay away from hairdressers. And the husbands would save so much money."

"Yes," said Larissa, "but we'd have roots and be ugly."

"Not you." He paused, as if for colorizing effect on her spousal skin. "That looks like your natural hair," he elaborated.

"Yeah, the best natural hair money can buy."

"Worth every broken bone," he said, tipping his invisible hat. "Hey, are you in the market for a new car? Because we have some beautiful models coming in next week."

"A *Jaguar*?" Larissa shook her head with an incredulous titter. "I don't think so."

"You sure?" He was smiling.

She squinted at him. It occurred to her that they'd been standing entirely too long, standing, not moving, standing, not shopping. Their carts were touching, his against hers, kind of bucked up, backed up. His front to her back. "Are you shilling for work in the supermarket?" Larissa asked. "Drumming up business in the produce aisle? First stonework, now Jags?"

"First of all, we're in plastic and paper, and I don't know what you mean. Just asking. Making small talk."

"We're not in the market for a car. But thank you."

"Well, if you change your mind and do come in, don't forget to ask for me. Here's my card." Proudly he pulled out a stack of them from his pocket and handed her one. He *was* shilling!

Gingerly she took one, glancing at the name. "KAI PASSANI. SALES REPRESENTATIVE."

"*Kay?*" She'd never heard that before. "What kind of name is that?"

"Well, mine for starters. And it's not *Kay*. It's Kai. Rhymes with guy."

"Oh, of course." She nearly stammered.

He had mercy on her. "Hawaiian."

"Passani's Hawaiian?"

"French. My old man was French. And Vietnamese."

That explained the striking, non-Jersey nature of his appearance. "Your mom is Hawaiian?"

"We lived in Hawaii. Is that the same thing? She's actually from Canada, I think."

"You lived in Hawaii? Lucky you."

"Nah. Rock island fever from the time I could crawl." He half shrugged, half shuddered. "Glad I'm out." He looked so casual when he spoke about a place so extraordinary. And she glimpsed that he *was* exotic, though on the surface, without that second glance, he looked almost ordinary. Unthreateningly friendly, unmenacingly young, just a kid on a motorbike, with jeans and boots and kinky hair, not especially well-kept, a little out of place in her part of the world. He had an amiable smile, a relaxed manner. But there was something else too, behind the dancing eyes and the straight spine. A peculiar way his attention was laser-focused on the supposedly slapdash chatter with her.

"Glad you're out in *Jersey?*" She bestowed him with her most skeptical face.

"Especially in Jersey." His eyes scrunched up. He tucked his wiry hair behind his ears. "Bruce Springsteen made me love it. And what is *your* name, miss?"

"Larissa. And it's Mrs."

"Hmm," he said, nodding in approval. "You look like a Larissa."

They did not shake hands, he didn't extend his, as if he had read Emily Post and knew that a young man did not offer his hand to a married woman unless she offered hers first. And Larissa, who *had* read Emily Post, did not presume for a second to extend her hand to him. In fact, Emily Post said you're supposed to just wave or say hi when you're introduced to children.

"Do I?" What did a Larissa look like?

"Yes. There's something elegant and feminine about that name. Straight-haired."

She looked into her cart. His low-frequency voice kept fooling her. His was not a child's voice with that timbre, that out-of-state elocution. She didn't know what to do next. The awkwardness!

She decided to pass him, the wheels of her cart screeching a bit, and as she was flush with him, her shoulder to his chest, distinctly and unmistakably she heard him inhale. As she passed by him, he drew in a soft breath; why?

"Is that you?" he asked. "Coconut and lime?"

She didn't look up from her paper towels. "I guess. Vestige of summer."

"Yeah. Like a drink. With a little umbrella." He smiled, nodding. "Nice."

Larissa didn't want to make a crack, to ask if he was old enough to drink. "So what kind of business are you thinking about going into?"

He rolled alongside her to the tissues. "I want to run sightseeing tours."

"Where, in New York?"

"Nah. Right here."

"In *Jersey?*"

"Sure."

"In *Summit?*"

"Why not? I get one tour bus to start, one of those 1930s National Park open utility vehicles. I show the travelers the Short Hills Mall, a decent attraction. I show them Deserted Village. That's a whole day right there. The Great Swamp. What an adventure, especially if it rains in the marshes. Then we move to the snowy valleys and the skiing slopes. The factories. The outlet shops. The Jersey Turnpike. The amusement park. The Atlantic. Lots to see. We finish in Atlantic City on a blackjack run. I make them pay me first, though."

Larissa couldn't help herself, she laughed. And he laughed too.

"You're joking, right?"

"No, I'm dead serious." His eyes were so merry.

"I have to go. Excuse me."

He moved his cart out of her way, let her pass. "See ya, Mrs. Larissa."

And she, without looking at him again, forcefully pushed her cart forward, and in a business-like manner clopped toward the milk and honey.

7

Ezra's Boredom

Larissa, I told my mother.

You what?

I had to. I was losing my mind.

You told your mother? Why?

I needed help.

I told you I would help you.

I needed a different kind of help, Larissa. I needed counsel.

I gave you counsel.

I needed . . . different counsel. You're my only friend. I love you. But you're not hearing me.

Oh, for Pete's sake. Why would you tell your mother?

Because there are things you don't understand.

What are you talking about? I understand everything.

No.

Che, you just don't want to listen to me. That's not the same as me not understanding.

It is. I don't want to listen to you because you don't understand.

Che, you're sixteen years old and still in high school!

I know.

You think I don't know how hard this is?

No, I don't think you do. I think you would do what had to be done and wouldn't lose a minute's sleep over it.

Because I knew it had to be done!

I also know this. But I just can't do it. You can. Not me.

Holy cow. What did your mother say? Oh, I can't even imagine.

She cried. Then she prayed. For, like, three hours. Then she cried some more. She refused to talk to me until we went to church. Then she still refused to talk to me. She just kept crying. I said I know how you feel, Ma.

Larissa was now the one with her head in her hands, curled over a desk in her room.

My mother said she couldn't believe I would be so reckless.

I told you that, too.

I know. You're both right. Doesn't help me much, though.

Did she say anything helpful?

She said she didn't know I was being bad when I was out—she thought I was a good girl. She was so upset. How could I have been so careless with my one life, she kept repeating.

I said that to you, too. But how is that helpful?

She beat her hands against her chest. Did you do that? I said to her, Ma, what are you so upset about? This is about me, about my plans. You should have thought about plans before, not after, she said.

Okay, Ma, I said. I made a mistake. I was dumb. Can't I be smart now?

It was too late for smart, she told me. Now it was time for action. Che bowed her head. *My dad is semi-retired. Ma said he would take his retirement early and watch the baby while I finished school.*

Che, no. Oh, my goodness. No. Don't you count at all? What about you?

She said I could still go to college and leave the baby with them. They would help me.

But you'd never be free, said Larissa with fear and emptiness.

Ma said life is a bitch, Claire. Should've thought of that earlier. Now it's too late.

It's never too late. That's the beauty of it. You make a little mistake, and three hundred bucks later everything can still go back to how it was before.

Che bowed her head.

It's not too late!

My mother wouldn't even discuss the other thing.

Why did you have to tell your mother?

If this happened to you, wouldn't you tell your mother?

Never, said Larissa. And who says it hasn't happened to me?

Now it was Che's turn to gape at her friend.

Just kidding, Larissa said. But even if it did, I'd never tell my mother.

Che stared at Larissa. Larissa stared at Che. You have to think about it harder, Larissa said. Think about your life. It's your life, not your mom's, not your dad's. Yours. You only have the one. Is this what you want?

No, said Che.

You're sixteen! It was a mistake. Everybody makes mistakes. You're allowed one do-over.

Who said?

Oh, come on.

The baby is not going to get a do-over, though.

Yes, but you are. It'll be like it was before. Nothing will be any different.

Larissa, come on, you don't really believe that, do you?

With all my heart.

The whole universe will be different, said Che.

No, it won't. And you'll have your whole life to have another baby. Please.

Che kept staring at Larissa. You don't think it's wrong, Larissa, that a baby be sacrificed so I can live as I like?

You'll have another baby!

You didn't answer my question, Larissa.

❧

"Ezra," Larissa asked her friend on Saturday night, "why do we sit here every week and regurgitate the same old questions on the unfathomable workings of the bottomless universe? Are we really trying to figure it out? Or do you think we're bored?"

Why did she sound hopeful? Did she *want* Ezra to be bored? Ezra, who had an opinion on every subject, who could debate good and evil with the devil himself, could talk to an engineer about bridges and to a scientist about quantum mechanics. Economists had to defend the margin of low supply side against him and Ayn Rand her objectivism and Christians their faith in the Triune nature of God and the nominal reasons behind the Great Schism. He was a linguist, a scholar, he loved movies and semiotics. He knew the differences between communism, socialism and collectivism, and could ask you fifteen questions about evolutionary theory for which you had no answer, not a single one. He could recite the Bill of Rights from the heart, knew the Declaration of Independence, and most of Shakespeare's sonnets. *By heart.* His favorite writers were Dante and Donne. ("That's because he hasn't read past the Ds," quipped Jared.) He thought *Paradise Lost* was the greatest work of literature in the English language. He spoke fluent French. No one could out-argue him. Ezra watched movies like Aronofsky's *Pi* and said it was his favorite film of all time. To defy classification he also said *Bachelor Party* was his favorite film of all time. Larissa loved Ezra. He defied classification.

Could this Ezra be bored?

He looked slightly liquid, funny, completely engaged. "Yes," he said cheerfully. "I'm bored."

"Oh, Ezra, stop it," said Maggie, laying down her letters. "You're not bored in the slightest. All you do is stir up trouble. Stop it. It's your turn. You're losing, darling, you're last at Scrabble, Professor Bored. You have 80 points, while your uneducated wife and her over-theatrical though under-ambitious best friend have 120 and 113 points respectively. It's your turn, sweetheart, the great conversationalist."

Ezra put down his letters. *Colloquy* was his word. Bingo, plus 50 points, with Q on triple letter. Ezra was no longer last. Maggie snorted in annoyance. Glancing sideways at a laughing Larissa, Ezra put his hand inside the letter bag. "All we think about is ourselves, Larissa. This breeds boredom. And unhappiness. We become like sharks, always needing to keep moving or we die."

"Ezra," Larissa, said, "but last week you told me and Evelyn and Malcolm that we needed to think *more* of ourselves, remember?"

Ezra drew a blank look, and Maggie laughed. "I told you, Lar, he is nothing but a sophist," she said. "Advocating only for the position you don't happen to hold on this particular evening. Don't listen to anything he says, darling."

"I can't imagine myself saying this," said a defensive Ezra. "Since I think we're spilling out of our ears. We are stuffed to the gills with ourselves."

"Last week you said we were unknowable!"

"Yes? And how is that incompatible with what I'm saying tonight?"

"I'm not unknowable to myself," bristled Larissa.

"You sure about that, Lar?"

"Positive."

"Describe yourself in five phrases."

"Fine. Um. I am a mother. I am a wife. I am a set decorator. I am a good cook. I am a lover of books." She said the last one sheepishly.

Ezra drew a laugh. "No, Larissa. Not who you are. *What* you are."

Less certainly she said, "I am neat. I am orderly. I am meticulous."

"Ah," said Ezra. "Three different words to say the same tedious thing."

"I am motherly. And wiferly. I'm a planner." She thought. "I am well-dressed."

He nodded. "One more. But make it a good one."

Larissa was still thinking. She was still thinking. It wasn't fair. It was hard to describe yourself in five phrases.

"But you just said you knew yourself better than you know anything," Ezra said. "Why should it be hard at all? Just think of the five most important things about you. You can name five things about a lion, can't you? Or a chimp?"

Spending her days swirling red paint around on the sets of school plays. Larissa, the Jackson Pollock of high school productions of *Guys and Dolls*. Theater hadn't even made the cut. How could *that* be? The children hadn't made it. Love. Yearning. Contentment. None of it.

"Get rid of one of the neat freak traits," Ezra said, "and you'll have more room for painting."

But Larissa felt it still wouldn't get to the bottom of things. The bottom of who she was.

Ezra clapped in delight. "It's easier after ten minutes of nominal research to talk for an hour about anabolic metabolism than it is to talk with any degree of authority about yourself, even though you've been stuck with yourself your whole damn life. Clearly you're not thinking enough about yourself, Larissa," he concluded, stretching out his hand with the emptied Margarita glass. "See, you think you're bored because your glass is overflowing," he said, "but what if it had tipped over and is empty and you don't even know it?"

8

A Birthday Gift

And then one night, Jared said to Larissa after dinner, with a big smile, "Whose birthday is coming up?"

"What are you smiling about? I'm cancelling all birthdays this year."

"Just the opposite. We need to celebrate like we're twenty."

"We'll have to start early." Larissa stabbed at her empty plate. "You're asleep by ten. Did you always fall asleep by ten when you were twenty?"

"Actually, yes. I don't know if you've noticed after knowing me for twenty years, but I'm a morning person. But seriously, you want to hear what I'm thinking of for a present for one very good wife?"

"Which part of cancelling the birthday didn't we understand?"

The kids had just dispersed, though loudly and not far, and husband and wife had a few precious minutes to themselves.

Jared stared at her with his "are you finished" stare. She smiled. "I don't need anything. I already have everything."

"And Ezra told us what he thinks of that," Jared exclaimed happily. "He would prefer we had nothing—like in college. So what do you get a woman who has everything but who's turning a very young 4–0?"

"Diamonds?"

"Nah, you have those. I was thinking more along the lines of," said Jared, with a dramatic tone and expression, "a new car."

She stared at him dumbstruck. "A new *what*?"

"A new car! Something snazzy. A sports thing. A two-seater. Not a mom car. A Larissa car." He beamed. "A Beamer? A Merc?"

"A Jaguar . . . ?" she intoned dully.

"Well . . . I was thinking more of something sturdy and German-made."

"Like a VW?"

"No! Sturdy but snazzy. But sure, a Jag if you want."

"I thought the British built Jags." She couldn't think of anything else to say.

"Not anymore; long ago sold out to a Ford division in Michigan. Pricey. But a good idea." He nodded agreeably. "They have some fine-looking sports cars. And they keep almost half their value. There's a new dealership that opened on Main Street in Madison. Why don't you go there next week, see if there's anything you like, and then I can come in, swoop in at the end, check it out with the checkbook?" Jared's straight light hair was in a shaggy mop, he looked healthy, happy, still in a dark gray suit, pleased with himself. Leaning over, he kissed her. "But pick yourself something nice. Something babelicious."

"Yes, except at twenty we were riding rusted bicycles, not Jags," Larissa said, getting up from the table, the dirty plate in her hands, the silverware, the cup, the soiled napkin. "That's the irony. When you're young and want to ride a flash motorcycle, you can hardly afford it, and by the time you can afford it, you look ridiculous on it."

The kids were playing pool in the den, even the six-year-old. Larissa hoped he wouldn't stab his older brother with a pool cue.

"I'm quite happy with my Escalade, Jared," she went on. "It'd be a waste of money. Honest. I don't need a new car."

"Yes, you do. And don't be a spoilsport. What else am I going to get you?"

"A vacation? Hawaii, maybe?"

"Hmm. Hawaii's a good idea. But you know, with the kids . . . we'll need a vacation after that vacation. Besides," he added glibly, "a vacation is over in seven days. But a Jag you have forever."

~⊙~

So this became Larissa's life internal: talking herself *out* of going to the Jag dealership. She didn't want a new car. She'd be satisfied with a BMW. Except Jared told her that Doug Grant thought a Jag would be finer than any other car except maybe a Porsche.

"What, Doug is now a car expert?" She brightened. "But a Porsche might be nice."

"Off the table. Too expensive."

"I'm not sure about Doug's opinion," she said. "I'm going to ask Ezra."

"Ezra!" Jared loosened his tie. "You're going to ask a man who drives a twelve-year-old Subaru wagon with a hatchback that doesn't open what kind of luxury car he thinks *you* should get?"

"Ezra is very smart. Do you deny that?"

"He's an idiot about cars!" Just to prove his point, Jared got Ezra on the phone despite Larissa's protestations that dinner was about to achieve room temperature. "Ez, it's me. My wife wants to know what kind of sports car *you* think *I* should buy her for her birthday."

Larissa was violently rolling her eyes while Jared was nodding into the phone. "Exactly. My point entirely. Thanks, man. See you Saturday." He hung up. "Do you want to know what Ezra said?"

"I can't tell you how much I don't care."

Jared laughed. "But you wanted to ask him! He told me. Would you like to hear?"

"Suddenly, no."

On Friday, Larissa asked Fran's opinion, her twentysomething friend with whom she did only one thing—sit at the nail salon. Finklestein liked the beautiful things in life, though she was a part-time receptionist at a Midtown-based news agency and had no actual money. The girl was single, young, hip and didn't fit in with

Larissa's other friends. Her singlehood and youth dazzled Larissa; Finklestein was what a Republican looked like to a Democrat: unfathomable. This time over a latte, flash Fran denounced Larissa's false dilemma by administering a brutal piece of advice. Any sports car would do, Fran said dismissively. Pick the one that will please you the most.

The ever-practical Maggie tried to talk her out of the car entirely. She didn't share Ezra's risible indifference to the question. Always thrifty, Maggie deemed such a purchase an unnecessary extravagance.

Larissa couldn't talk to Bo about something so trivial as buying a car when Bo was living in a two-bedroom apartment with her unhinged mother and freelance Jonny, who'd been looking for a long-term gig for *three* years. Bo spent her days on the sixth floor of the Met during lunchtime, ambling through neo-Impressionist floral displays from South America and dreaming of a different life. Talking to Bo about Jaguars was as absurd as talking to Michelangelo about it, who saw a brochure his father had brought home and said, "Ooh, nice blue car without a top, Mommy, but how you gonna fit your whole family in there?"

～∽∽∽～

Che didn't come to school, one day, two. She didn't pick up the phone either. Larissa walked to her house after school. She was on half-days; soon she would graduate, summer, then college! But Larissa's daydreams of impending adulthood had faded recently in the face of Che's trauma.

Che's mother let her in, curt, impersonal. It wasn't like her. Che's mother loved Larissa. She's upstairs, was all she said.

Che was on her bed, face down.

Why is your mother mad at me?

She's not mad.

Why did she give me the evil eye? Larissa thought about it. Oh, no. Did you tell her I wanted you not to have it?

Che nodded.

Thanks a lot, girlfriend.

She asked me. What is Larissa advising you to do? So I told her.

But what's happened? Larissa perched on the edge of the bed, touching Che's heaving back. What else could've happened?

I'm not pregnant anymore, said Che in a dead voice.

Larissa's heart jumped, flew up into the summer sky. Oh, Che! That's wonderful!

Che didn't seem to think so.

How do you know?

I'm bleeding.

So you were never pregnant? I told you, you should've taken that test.

Che rose from the bed, her face red, her eyes swollen. Don't you see? she said. I know my body. I was ten weeks late. You think that's normal? Now I'm bleeding out like my jugular's been cut. She put her face in her hands.

Larissa patted her friend, tried to soothe her. No, it's good. It's so much better this way. The impossible decision was taken out of your hands. It's the greatest day.

Almost like God intervening, said Che.

I guess, said Larissa. You were lucky. You were given a reprieve, a second chance. Now you can live your life right, learn from this, do things differently in the future. I don't understand why you're so upset.

What if God, like my mom, was disappointed in me? That's what it feels like. He said, you're not ready to be a mother. You're not ready for this child.

That's absolutely true.

In my free-falling blood I feel His disappointment.

That's silly. He helped you out. Took matters into his own hands. Oh, if only every time it were so easy! How sweet life would be.

But Che was inconsolable. I did this to myself, she said. I should have had to live with the consequences.

You narrowly escaped a harrowing future. How can you be upset?

A baby is not harrowing.

At sixteen? Come on, clean yourself up. Let's go to town, hang out. I told some people I'd meet them at Jerry's Ices.

Larissa lay down on the twin bed, next to Che. Come on, girlfriend, she whispered, putting her arm around Che's sobbing body. No worries now. We're golden. Every little thing's gonna be all right.

❧

Larissa wrote to Che, mentioning the Jag as a postscript, omitting the real reason for her agonizing.

Che wrote back.

Larissa, why so much commotion over a small matter? I feel like there's something you're not telling me. To bring up a car in an occasional letter? It's a car. You didn't finish telling me why Bo doesn't throw Jonny out or move out herself. Since when do you care so much about what you drive? Buy or not buy. I'm forty next year too, you know. You're worried about a car, and my mother couldn't live long enough for me to have a baby. Soon I'm not going to live long enough for me to have a baby. I'm sending you a recent picture of Lorenzo. Tell me if you think he's worth it. Send me a recent picture of the Jag. I'll tell you if the car is worth it.

Larissa read newspapers, magazines, to keep ahead of the times, but being versed in current events made her *more* anxious, not less. The only news out there was that everything was going to hell, spinning out of control.

She wrote to Che about this. There was mental illness, homelessness, robberies, random shootings, sometimes all related, Larissa wrote. Shark attacks, poison oak epidemics, rabies. Seventy-year-old women giving birth, severed heads abandoned outside newsrooms. There were bombings and threats to peace. Is peace just an illusion? she asked Che. Will the Jaguar bring me an illusion of peace?

"That's a philosophical question, Larissa," replied Ezra, while she was still waiting on Che's reply. "The question is, will the Jaguar bring you something tangible? Is it a desire for something you don't have? If so, what is it? And after you get it, will that be it, or will there be something else you want that you don't have? Is it the quest you're after, not the object?"

"How about," said Jared, "the car is gorgeous—she'll turn all heads while driving it?"

"She turns all heads anyway," said Maggie, looking admiringly at Larissa, in jeans and a red silky top, with a bit of décolletage and red lipstick.

"Hardly," Larissa said, embellishing her embarrassment and turning to Ezra.

"I know, Larissa, that you read Ecclesiastes only because you had to, to get a pass/fail in your philosophy course in college," said Ezra, "which is not the same thing as *understanding* Ecclesiastes, but nonetheless, it will do you well right about now to remember what he said."

Larissa stared at him vacantly.

"All is vanity," said Ezra. "To buy, not to buy. To eat, to shop, to hire women to clean your house, to not clean it. *All* is vexation of spirit, except union with God. *All* is vanity."

"So buy the Jag, then?" said Jared.

༄ৎৎৎ

Che wrote back.

> *Larissa,*
>   *Here is your real answer, the one Father Emilio gave me when I asked him. You shall hear of wars and rumors of wars. See that ye not be troubled. For all these things must come to pass but the end is not yet.*
>   *For nation shall rise against nation, and kingdom against kingdom. There shall be famines and pestilences and earthquakes in diverse places.*
>   *All these are just the beginnings of sorrows. Because iniquity shall abound, the love of many shall wax cold.*

Lorenzo's love is waxing cold, Larissa. And I'm still without a baby. All these years I have been living in poverty, and I don't mean the money kind. I'm so far from what I want.

Please don't be far from what you want.

I wish for a baby more than anything. I desperately want a little girl so I could raise her to make all the mistakes I made, only start younger.

You are a wonderful person. You don't drive anyone crazy like Lorenzo. Get the car.

Would it be nice to have a Jag, rather than live amid unclaimed wishes yet unwished for?

But what if you knew that the car would lead you to penury and destitution, the things Che speaks of, writes about, feels, lives? What would you do then?

But you don't know.

But what if you did?

But you don't.

And if you did?

But . . . you don't.

And . . . if you did?

~~~

The whole thing filled Larissa with shame. She even threw out the business card Kai had given her, which was the most shameful thing of all. How ridiculous that was. How ridiculous she was.

But now what?

What would she wear to a Jag dealership? She couldn't go in sweats. But she couldn't go too dressed up.

She couldn't go.

The eternal moral order was the real question, the Aztec gold buried like a treasure in the hills of Mexico. Was there such a thing, and was Larissa turning her back on it?

Kai Passani. The first time she said his name out loud to herself, she turned red like she'd accidentally cursed in front of the children. Peeking into the magnifying mirror, she stared at her flushed face, her glassy eyes.

His name was Hawaiian. Kai. She looked it up. In Hawaiian, it meant the ocean. Ocean, as in bottomless?

Oh, what was wrong with her!

Passani. "From the Champagne region of France." The urban legend goes that the monk who discovered the sparkling wine ran to his Benedictine brother with the cry, *"J'ai goûté des étoiles!"* I'm tasting stars.

Kai Passani.

~✿~

To save herself from the Jaguar, Larissa replaced all thought of it with Gucci. Gucci, Chanel, Zanotti, Dior. She bought herself a pair of reading glasses that replaced the need for reading. All she needed was the blue Swarovsky-clad Versaces; she didn't need to read *A Life* by Elia Kazan. The reading glasses just had to sit on her face, like graceful jewels. Burberry, not Brontë. Gucci not Dante. Chanel not Charlotte. Prada not Pound.

To go to the library (with her kids) she put on Libretto. The mall required a different ensemble, as did the supermarket, which is why she didn't like to combine her outings, because she was inevitably dressed wrong for all but one of them. To the mall in summer she wore Betsey Johnson dresses and Marc Jacobs sandals. In the winter, tight Marciano jeans and lowheeled boots (the lower the heel, the more expensive the boot, as in counterattack).

Kids' winter concerts? Fur and (very) high-heeled boots. Ball games? Caps and jeans and jerseys, so affected, so designer.

Food-shopping required only mini-skirts and cowboy boots, possibly Frye.

And she blow-dried her hair. Damn that Kai. She left it long, very straight and hippie-like, an illusion of casual chic. She haphazardly highlighted it, an illusion of being outside and sunstreaked. She wore taupe makeup, to make it seem like she wasn't wearing any, like she had just rolled out of bed and into her car. She got dressed up for everything. Except that one day when she left the house in sweats and a cast.

The question was, and truly this was the profound question that demanded an answer: what to wear to a Jag dealership to go look at a sports car you don't need and don't want, just so you can be looked at by the dancing eyes of a vivid kid on a motorbike?

Ezra would say it was a false choice. It wasn't about what to wear. "It has nothing to do with the car," he kept repeating. "It has to do with what the car represents. The car tells you, and therefore the whole world, where you are in life. That's what it means. It's a long way from the fifth-floor walk-up. But a long way up or a long way down?" Ezra paused for maximum effect. "Every time you drive to the supermarket, do you want to know how far you are from Hoboken? Do you want everyone else to know too? As Walker Percy says, we live in a deranged age, more deranged than usual, because in spite of great scientific and technological advances, man has not the faintest idea who he is, or where he is going. We live stifling in our souls all questions about the meaning of our own life, and life in general. So the real question is, Larissa, will this car help you discover who you are and where you're going?"

To go or not to go.

Chapter Three

1

0–60 in 4.9 Seconds

"Mrs. Stark!" Kai was in a white shirt and tie, neat, and beaming. "How nice of you to drop by. To what do we owe this pleasure?"

Larissa had walked through the doors fifteen minutes earlier and asked the receptionist for a salesperson to help her, and the receptionist, a chirpy young thing named Crystal, tried to hook her up with a Gary, and Larissa said, actually I was looking for Kai, and Crystal said, no, no, he's busy today. Gary is very good, and has a lot more experience, he'll be glad to help you. Larissa frowned. Was she wearing too much or too little? Under her brown suede jacket, she wore jeans, high-heeled Fryes and a simple maroon sweater. Her makeup was light (20 minutes), her hair casual (40 minutes). "If he's not available today, I'll make an appointment and come back." She said this while glancing around the spotless cream-colored dealership. It was eleven on a Monday morning, and there was no one on the floor except the salesmen, the receptionist, and the business people. She was the only customer. Crystal said Monday was Kai's day off, so he wasn't even supposed to be in, and tomorrow he was all booked. "I don't think he'll have enough time to take care of you properly, Mrs. . . . ?"

"Stark. Larissa Stark. Please let him know I'm here, and if he's too busy, he'll direct me to someone else."

Finally Crystal, out of excuses (WTF?) rang Kai's extension, and in three seconds he was at the center of the showroom beaming at her.

He even shook her hand gently, Emily Post notwithstanding, because in front of other people it was easy to be polite. Hand out, her hand in. His was wiry and warm, hers fashionable and cool, the pink nails freshly buffed.

"I'm interested in finding out a little bit about your sports models," she said, mock laid-back like her hair. "Not to purchase. Just to shop around."

"Of course. No one comes in here *ready* to purchase."

"But Crystal here," Larissa continued calmly, "tells me today might not be a good day for you. I can always come back."

"No, today is perfect," said Kai, throwing the flustered Crystal a quizzical look. "I'll stay as long as I need to take care of my customers, Crystal, you know that. Come." He guided Larissa with his fanned-out hand on the back of her suede.

He showed her two models on the floor, a sedan and a white coupe. She didn't like either. "Is that the price tag?" she said, astonished.

Glancing at her with a "How much did you think a Jag cost?" expression, he put on his leather jacket and out they stepped into the windy bitterness to look at the models on the lot. She found a tiny sporty thing she thought looked kinda cool, and Kai said, "Oh, sure, you *would* pick that one."

"I didn't pick it. I don't like the color." It was Metallic Indigo.

"We can either get you a discount on the color you don't want or for full price any color you prefer straight from the factory."

"Discount on something I don't want?" Larissa smiled. "Kai, you drive a hard bargain."

"Thanks. That's my specialty. You can't say no." He grinned

back. He was well groomed today, respectable with his thin black tie, his white shirt and unripped, ironed jeans. His unruly longish hair was gelled off his forehead and moussed back, neat, presentable. He looked older.

"You're all cleaned up," she said.

"The other me is my motorcycle-chic costume." He laughed. "This is my take people's money costume."

"You're right, the shirt should be ironed for that."

"Even the jeans," he said.

She wanted to ask who ironed his jeans, but of course didn't. Larissa walked around the car, her hand on it, to feel the lines, to touch the cold glass. Too cold. She put her gloves on. "What's so special about this one?"

"This is the XKR supercharged sports convertible. Our most expensive model."

"Really?" She studied it with slightly more interest. "What else is great about it? Can't be the color."

Handing her a pair of keys, he opened the driver door. "Get in and see for yourself."

"I'm driving?"

"Well, I could drive, but what would the point be? I'm not buying it."

"I'm not buying it either." She got behind the wheel. Car smelled new and leathery. "What's the interior color? It's a nice combo."

"Isn't it, though? Color of the leather is caramel. The dashboard accents are burl."

"Burl? What the heck kind of color is burl?" She touched the smooth pebbly leopard-looking dashboard with her fingers.

"This color."

Gingerly Larissa drove out onto Main Street. She was going twenty miles an hour. "Drives nice in traffic," she said after a silence. "Stops at red lights. Makes lefts. Signals work. It shifts from park to drive almost as if it has an automatic transmission."

Kai blinked at her. "You're making fun of my sales pitch that I haven't had a chance to make yet?"

"I'm not making fun. It actually does do all these things. I'm not being ironic."

"Ironic, no. Mocking, yes."

"Mocking, no. Questioning, yes. As in, what's here that's worth somebody's annual salary?"

"Four hundred and twenty horsepower. Tell you what. Make a left at the college and drive till you hit the open road. Glenside Avenue runs around the Watchung Reservation on the way to Deserted Village. Let's go see what this baby can do."

"It brakes beautifully."

"All righty now."

"And the seatbelts work. No, it's excellent. Your best, you say? Clearly a superior model."

"Didn't you notice how everybody on Main Street was eyeballing you?"

"What, you think it's the car?" Larissa chuckled. "You think they were impressed with the way a Jag sat five minutes at a red light?"

"Maybe they were just admiring the driver. Make a left here and go straight for a mile."

"Oh! It goes straight so well!" They drove in unruffled silence. She resisted the urge to glance at her eyes in the rearview mirror, to catch a glimpse of herself after he said people might be eyeballing her. Also resisted the urge to comment on how noticeably straight up he was sitting, with Buddha-like tranquility, his entire back flush and composed against the seat.

"This model has a supercharged 420 horsepower 4.2 liter engine. Do you have any idea what that means?"

"Um—no?"

"You can't imagine power like this. It's like a rocket."

"You want me to demonstrate its rocket-like qualities on Glenside?"

"It's an empty road. And clearly, until you do, you will not cease the snarky comments."

"Oh, no, those will continue." Glenside, which ran in a long straight line along the edge of the protected national wildlife reservation, was deserted. No main streets ran through it, no exits to shopping areas, no gas stations, no small towns. It had the forest on the right and forest on the left. The sun was shining.

"Not too far," Larissa said, stepping on the gas. The car soared forward.

"As far as you want."

～～⌒～

They were gone forty minutes. Maybe forty-five.

"So . . . what do you think?" He was grinning at her after she slowed down to get on the Interstate. *Slowed down* to get on the Interstate.

"It's nice," she said noncommittally.

"Don't pretend. Car's incredible," Kai said. "Handles beautifully. Has great power."

She revved up, smoking a Mercedes 550SL in the right lane. "Yes."

"The XKR goes from 0 to 60 in 4.9 seconds."

The snark had gone. Rockets couldn't be as fast as this. He was right. It was unbelievable. Like nothing she'd ever driven.

"You might not need this much power," said Kai, as Larissa gripped the leather-clad wheel with her leather-clad hands. "It's more money than the regular XK. Which is also a very fine car at 300 horsepower, and it may be all the power you need. Did I mention it's less money?"

"Some salesman you are." Larissa sped to eighty. Then ninety.

"Slow down, this isn't Glenside. You don't want to get a ticket," Kai said. "I know. I've gotten two."

Reluctantly she slowed down. "How fast were you going?" she asked.

"Buck twenty. The cops weren't happy. I just went to court for it. Ticket cost me a week's pay."

She slowed down some more. "You're probably right. I don't need this much power."

"Right." He paused. "Though it's great for getting on the highway. You never have to worry."

"That's good, not having to worry," said Larissa. "I like to not worry. But I never go on the highway. Do I really need a supercharged Jag convertible to drive to Stop&Shop?"

"You tell me," said Kai.

When they were almost at the dealership parking lot, Larissa was surprised to discover it was after one.

"I have to run," she said. "But I like it. I like it very much."

"Yes," was all he said. "I thought you might."

She didn't know what to say next. Does she call him? Does he call her? Does she fill out a sheet with her details on it? Does she shake his hand? Does she say how this is going to end, or say, I'll talk to my husband, maybe call back in a couple of days. What *does* she do?

"I'm starved," he said. "Drive on to Stop&Shop. I'll buy us some sushi."

"They sell sushi you can eat at Stop&Shop?" This surprised her.

"It's not bad. It's fresh. The sushi chef knows me. Makes me an excellent rainbow roll. You like sushi?"

Larissa didn't want to say she'd never eaten sushi. She hesitated. "Come," he said. "We'll get you a tuna roll. You like avocado and cucumber? You like spicy?"

"It's the raw fish I have a problem with," she said to him. "Make it medium well, and I'll eat it."

Kai laughed. "Regular stand-up today, aren't we?"

She parked, and they walked in together through the automatic doors, she first. As it should be, she thought. *Age before beauty.* In the back of the store, she met Al, a friendly wide bald Japanese man with a thick accent and an even thicker goatee. She didn't understand him at all, but he and Kai spoke a secret language. Kai asked him for something while Al nodded and smiled. "It really is surprisingly good here," Kai said while they waited. "Good enough for a Maui boy who ate sushi before he drank milk."

She hurried off to buy some sirloin for dinner.

Kai paid for the sushi, they walked out, and got inside the Jaguar, where he turned up the heat and the radio. "I can't believe you've never had sushi," he said, opening up her plastic container. "Do you like wasabi?"

"I might if I knew what it was."

"What about soy sauce? Do you know what *that* is?"

"Oh, who's the comedian now?" She watched him skeptically as he used chopsticks to spread a little green paste over one of the sushi balls or rolls or whatever the heck it was, then deftly pick it up with the chopsticks and . . .

Well, it wasn't like the sushi was on a fork. He couldn't hand her the chopsticks. Once embarked on a course of action, they had no choice but to see it through; it was a good thing he was so unselfconscious. He brought the chopsticks with the sushi to her, she leaned forward, and put the whole roll in her mouth.

"Well?" He was excited. "What do you think?"

Her eyes teared up from the spice. "What *is* that? It's going right to my nose."

He laughed. "That's the wasabi. It's Japanese horseradish. Good?"

"Well, sure." She swallowed. "If you think eating Vicks VapoRub is good, then yeah, absolutely."

He handed her the plastic tray, and she put her own wasabi on the sushi, just a drop, not a teaspoon. It was marginally better. She couldn't believe she was eating raw fish. Forty years and never once. Now suddenly in a Jag, with chopsticks.

"On Maui," Kai said, eating happily, drinking his Coke, "there was a place near our apartment where the guy caught the tuna in the morning and made the sushi for me two hours later. It was *most* outrageous. I lived on tuna morning, noon, and night. Then one day, Charlie, the guy who owned the joint, asked me to go fishing with him, and I got all excited, until we went out in his boat at dawn and I saw the size of the tuna. Mamma mia! I thought tuna were tiny little fish, you know, big enough to fit into a 6-oz can."

He laughed. "But they were like whales! Three times the size of our boat. I said to him, Charlie, you bastard, you tricked me. He was laughing so hard he peed himself. I couldn't catch a thing, they scared the shit out of me, excuse my French."

"If you're expecting plankton and you get whale, yeah, I can see how that might have an impact."

"But good, right?"

"It's not bad."

"There's a place nearby in Madison, they make really good special roll. Crab, salmon, tuna, avocado, cucumber, and a spicy sauce. Pretty awesome."

"I bet." She was busy trying to gingerly carry the large roll between two wooden sticks to her mouth before it fell.

"If you buy the car, I'll take you there for lunch as a thank you. You'll love it."

"Well, you're very kind. But no thanks will be necessary."

They sat facing the gravestones and had their sushi out of plastic containers with the car running and the classical jazz station playing Nina Simone singing, "*If He Changed My Name*."

"I hope you don't have ice cream in the back," he said when they were done eating.

"No ice cream today. Just meat." Damn, they'd had steak last night. She pulled out of the parking lot. They were a minute away from the dealership. She had to jet. It was after two, and Michelangelo was getting out in a half-hour.

"So you love the car?"

She pulled into the Jag lot, to the front, put the car in park, idled.

"I love it. But I have to go."

"Come back tomorrow," Kai said. "I'm here in the morning. I can show you two other models. The flagship of our line, the XJR."

"Is the flagship a convertible?"

"No, a sedan."

Larissa pursed her lips. Sedans were so middle-age.

He smiled. "Okay. Only quad tailpipes with polished chrome for you."

Quad tailpipes? What would Jared think of that? "The heated leather seats might come in handy."

"Oh, for sure. And the leather is hand-selected."

"What other kind would I ever want, Mr. Passani?"

"Exactly." He grabbed the brown paper bag of empty sushi boxes. "But that's not why you buy a Jag, Miss Stark."

"No," she said, "you buy it for the body-colored spoiler and the four tailpipes with bright finishes. And it's *Mrs.*"

His smile was wide. "So you're going to stop by tomorrow?"

For some reason he wasn't getting out of the car.

"Kai, I really have to run. I've got to pick up my son from school." Still not moving.

She looked at him. He looked at her. "Um, car's not yet yours, *Mrs.* Stark," he said, keeping the teasing grin away. "Would you like me to walk you to your own vehicle?"

"Oh God!" Larissa flipped off the ignition. "Sorry." Idiot.

"Feels like yours, though, doesn't it?" They both got out. He did walk her to the Escalade, even shook her hand gently. "Almost like you already own it."

༄

Larissa came back the next morning. When he saw her, Kai Cheshire-grinned. She couldn't help it. She smiled back.

"I don't want to see another car," she said. "I want you to show me what colors you have on the one I drove. Besides burl."

Kai got her a coffee and they sat and talked at his desk, in full view of the rest of the dealership, chatted for an hour about luxury packages and sound options, about the convertible cover, wheel coverings, rich high-gloss burl walnut. She noticed he had a battered paperback on his desk: *The Sorrows of Young Werther*.

Of all the books! "You're reading that?"

He nodded. "*Re*reading it. Werther is so wretched and self-pitying, I love it."

"Well, he *is* pining. That's what happens to pining people."

"Pining *and* self-pitying," said Kai. "Such attractive qualities in a man." He pitched his baritone an octave higher. "'Oh, why did my greatest joy turn into my greatest misery? Wah.'"

"Mmm." Larissa tried not to smile. Kai clearly thought he was being clever and amusing. "Then how come all the girls think he is a dashing romantic hero?"

"Who? Not the girl he's pining for. And in real life, the girls wouldn't come within a mile of him. Girls hate a whiner."

"Well," said Larissa, "perhaps you're right. Otherwise, we wouldn't have Werther's sorrows." She stared away into his desk. He read. Why did that impress her? She didn't want him to see that she was impressed; he might find it condescending. But reading *Werther*! Honestly. About a young man who falls desperately in love with a married woman and kills himself when he realizes he will never have her for his own. Blood rushed to her fingertips. Her fingertips blushed!

"So you like to read?" she asked slowly, sharply regretting giving away eight boxes of her unread books.

"Yeah, I inhale books," he replied. "So much better when you don't read for school, don't you think? Everything I read for school I hated. But I can't hate a book now. I find something to like in all of them."

"You have a favorite?"

"Nah. I'm on a German run at the moment. I finished, *The Tin Drum*, then *Faust*, now this."

Larissa said nothing.

"Do you want to take the car out one more time? I want you to be sure." Kai twirled the key on a ring around his finger.

"I'm pretty sure," she said. Pause. "Okay, one more time."

Afterward they got sushi by the cemetery.

That evening Larissa searched and found her old copy of *Werther* and reread it in one anxious gulp (*why* was he reading that?), and the next day went to the bookstore and bought copies of some of the books she had recently donated, making sure they were all distributed among the shelves before Jared came home and had a chance to comment on the oddity of giving away books one week only to buy the same ones again the next.

∽⫯◡⫯∽

On Saturday afternoon, Larissa returned with Jared. The dealership was busier than it had been during the week.

Jared and Kai shook hands. Kai seemed taller, if only because of his narrow lanky build. Maybe it was the biker boots he was wearing. *Werther* had disappeared, replaced with a dog-eared *Confessions of Felix Krull*. Larissa kept her gaze firmly on the desk, and on Jared's shoulder, or his chin, or the windows outside, on anything but the two men eyeing each other over Kai's desk.

"Ah," said Jared, pointing to the book. "Felix Krull, the confidence man. I read that a long time ago. How are you enjoying that?"

"It's pretty good," replied Kai. "It's witty. I especially like Felix's identification with Hermes, here, of course, in his capacity as the god of thieves."

"Yes." Jared studied Kai. Larissa studied the desk. "How does the management feel about you reading a book at the dealership about the god of thieves?"

"Lucky for me," said Kai, serious, sober, untwinkly, with a short polite nod, "the management is somewhat unfamiliar with the later works of Thomas Mann. Otherwise you're right, I'd be in real trouble." He took the keys from the hooks on the wall. "Shall we?"

While Jared test-drove the two-seater convertible with Kai, Larissa remained in Kai's cubicle, her eyes on *Felix Krull*, thinking of Werther and his poetic longings, and also about Krull's shock at discovering how in much of all that he came into contact with, reality was an illusion and illusion reality. Snow was on the ground, they probably wouldn't go far. It was too slippery to drive fast. Would Kai take Jared to Glenside? She wondered what they would talk about. Would Kai be chatty funny, like he was with her?

They were gone ten minutes. "I like the car," Jared said to her when he returned. "I *love* the car." She jumped up, excited. Kai went behind his desk to take a phone call. Jared pulled her away to the showroom. "Not at *all* sure about the salesman," he said quietly. "Has he been giving you the business?"

"No, of course not," Larissa said, taken aback. "Why would you say that?"

"I dunno. Something about him. A vibe I get."

"He's a salesman, Jared," Larissa said. "This is what they do. They try to sell us something we don't want at a price we don't want to pay."

When he considered her, she said quickly, either misunderstanding him or not wanting to understand, "I do want the car, I do. Pricey, though, huh?"

"Forget that. If he's such a fine salesman, let me ask you, why didn't he say a single thing to me?"

"When you say not a thing . . ."

"I mean not a word. A syllable."

Larissa quietly chewed her lip. "You mean he didn't mention the revolutionary aluminum body construction?"

"Oddly, no. And that might've been a good thing to mention. If you're actually trying to sell the damn thing." Jared stood close. "We can go somewhere else. We don't have to get it here." He glanced over at Kai behind the desk.

Larissa tapped Jared to get his attention. "We can. But why? I like the car. Why don't we talk to Chad, the finance guy? He's Irish. Let's see if the numbers add up."

"Oh, is that synonymous with good business sense, those two things? Irish and finance?"

They were in the middle of the dealership, talking in hushed spousal tones. Jared wasn't dressed for success today; on Saturdays he was all about the comfortable jeans and sweatshirts. He hadn't shaved, his hair was shaggy. Larissa wished he were more formal. Might make negotiating easier. She didn't want Jared to get squeezed. "We can go somewhere else if you want," she said in a resigned voice.

"You want to?" Why did he sound so hopeful?

"Look, I said from the beginning I didn't want the car. You're the one who insisted. Now that I found one I like, you're getting cold feet. Why put me through that? Just get me a necklace or something. Take me out to dinner."

His hand went on her arm, on her shoulder. He drew her near. "You're right," he said. "I don't need my horse sense here."

"No, just a little sense."

"I don't even know what it is."

"Is it something he said?"

"No! I told you. It's all the things he didn't say. He acted like he didn't even have to sell me on it."

"And because of that you think he's giving you the business?"

"Well, why else would he be sitting in that car as if it's already a done deal?"

"I don't know, Jared."

"Revolutionary construction my ass. Okay, let me go try to talk to him. You think maybe he doesn't speak English? Can't be that; he was waxing all English major on me with that *Felix Krull* bullshit. Hermes, the god of thieves. The arrogance." Jared snorted. "Wait a few minutes, okay?"

"You want me with you? For moral support?"

He squeezed her. "Let me deal with him my own way. I'll be five minutes."

Jared returned to Kai's desk while Larissa sat inside the snow-white sedan on the showroom floor and anxiously played with the controls. But the two men seemed to be actually speaking this time. Kai was measured, extremely still in his body, no twitching, jerking, no gratuitous movement of any kind, not even the drumming on the desk with a pencil. Just his mouth moved. They weren't five minutes, more like forty-five. Back and forth, Kai getting up, coming back.

"Larissa," Jared finally called out to her, "what color were you thinking of?"

She slammed shut the white door and walked across the

hush-hush cappuccino carpet over to Kai's metal desk. She liked the sterility of the dealership. Cars were shiny, no dirt, no oil, no exhaust, no fumes, no black smoke. Just a glossy pristine hunk of steel. "I haven't decided yet," she said. "I was looking at the green. Also porcelain."

"You didn't like the indigo blue in the lot? He says he can give us a discount on it."

Larissa didn't like the way Jared said *he* while referring to the man sitting across the narrow desk from him. Emily Post declared that rather rude. And it wasn't like Jared; it was out of character for him, the mildest of men. Larissa made a dedicated effort not to glance at Kai to acknowledge either her husband's incivility, or the familiarity of the topic of the car color between them. For that would imply that she and Kai chatted quite freely, perhaps even had raw fish together while sitting in a parked car listening to Nina Simone. "I would prefer not to have the blue," she said, her mouth tightening.

Kai and Jared leaned over the desk, studying the colors in the brochure while she stood over them. "What about Winter Gold?" said Kai.

"I was *just* about to say that," said Jared. "Winter Gold goes with your coloring, Lar."

She leaned over to contemplate. The color was darker than porcelain. More metallic ash. It matched her hair color. Gold and taupe blended in alchemy.

"Okay," she agreed. She didn't know what it was, but it was true, Kai did not act with Jared in the same friendly and amiable way he acted with her. Jared himself was clipped and cold, and Larissa didn't know what came first, whether the clipped Jared resulted in the silent Kai, or vice versa, or perhaps simultaneously, but all she knew was that both men behaved as they weren't, instead of as they were. Which made Larissa wonder if she were behaving as she wasn't, instead of as she was. Was she more silent herself? Jared was so sharply on guard. This was *such* a bad idea in hindsight. Getting the car, that is.

"You're going to have to do better than that on the price," Jared said stiffly to Kai.

"Look, I've gone back and forth three times already. I'm trying to get you the best deal. Your wife likes the car."

"It's not about how my wife feels about it. It's about getting the best deal possible for your customers."

"Fine. Let me talk to Chad one more time."

"No." Jared stood up. "Where is this Chad? I'll talk to him myself."

"Be my guest," said Kai coolly, also getting up. "I'll take you to him." He strode out from behind his desk. "Coming?" That was to Larissa.

"Coming?" Jared whispered in an irritated mimic, poking her in the back.

Jared talked to Chad for over an hour negotiating the terms, while Larissa sat and chafed in the adjacent chair. The kids had been alone *all* day. The whole Saturday. She would barely have enough time to cook dinner before Ezra, Maggie and Dylan came over. Emily must be going nuts. She never liked to be left to babysit, she was always on the phone or the computer. She liked to get paid, just didn't like to do the work. Poor Michelangelo, the sweet boy alone with that cranky Emily. Dylan should babysit him. He was much nicer. Or even Asher, if he weren't so easily distractable and liable to forget he even had a little brother in the house.

"Larissa?"

"Oh, what, sorry?" She hadn't been paying attention. She had been catching, through the semi-private partitions, the desks, the chairs, a glimpse of the tailored white shirt, the pressed jeans, the hand on the phone, the back turned to the dealership, wild hair slicked down.

"Chad wants to know if you're interested in the advanced technology package?"

"A *what*?"

"A navigation system."

"No, thank you."

"You sure?"

"Absolutely." She didn't want to spend a minute thinking about it. She tuned out but after a few minutes something in the conversation between the two men brought her back. Jared was asking Chad about Kai.

"Is he on the up and up?" Jared lowered his voice. "Seems awful young to be selling cars of this caliber."

"This is what we all thought," said Chad, also lowering his voice. "He's new. Still on probation. But he's impeccable. Punctual, hard-working, never a bit of trouble. And he's been salesman of the month both months he's been here."

"He's only been here two months!"

"Exactly. And let me tell you, the runner-up sold one car. Kai sold *seven*."

"Seven?" Jared whistled. "Seven altogether?"

"No. Seven in one month. Yours will be eight."

"No . . ."

"Eight this month, five last month. That's over a million dollars to this dealership."

"Wow." Jared glanced over the cars to the cubicle where Kai stood working the phone, with an expression of surprised and grudging respect, as if for some reason Jared didn't want Kai to be a successful salesman. "What's his secret? How does he do it?"

"No one knows. He's a bit of a loner, keeps to himself. Perhaps he's got great closing game?" Chad grinned affably at Larissa. "How did he close it with you?"

Larissa shrugged. "He showed me a beautiful car. I was won over. What's so hard about that?"

"Yeah. It does help that the cars are nice." Chad pointed to a middle-aged man behind the business office counter. "But Gary over there, our senior salesman, with us twenty years, with us as long as Kai's been alive, sells the same merchandise. Yet, he can't move 'em."

Oh dear God, he was twenty!

"Must be the youth," said Jared.

Larissa looked down deeply into her lap, her fingertips not flushed this time but draining of blood.

"Must be." Chad leaned forward. "You know what I think? Kai just won't take no for an answer. If he sees a potential sale, he will not quit. But he also doesn't waste time on those who're just window-shopping. Maybe that's his gift. He can instantly tell the browsers from the buyers."

Now Jared shrugged. "He seemed shifty. Like he was trying to get one over on me."

"He wasn't, though. You saw. He's a superb closer. He's got end game."

"No, I know. The price was fair. With all those options and packages, I was afraid we were getting snowed." Which was ironic, for how you can be snowed when the party doing the snowing wasn't doing any talking? "But Kelley Blue Book said good price. I'm satisfied." Relaxed, Jared smiled at Larissa.

"It's a great car, darling," said Larissa, glancing at her watch, forcing a toothy smile. "What wife wouldn't want a 420-horsepower Jag convertible?"

They signed off on the terms of the lien, the amount of the down payment, the interest rate, the taxes and delivery charges. Before he left, Jared shook Chad's hand. He did not seek out Kai, nor seek out his hand to shake. He didn't even nod in his direction as he was leaving.

2

Winter Gold

Othello was sold out for all three performances. On Saturday night they brought the kids, sat in the second row, admired the actors, the well-rendered words, the superb set decoration. Michelangelo told his mother that she had painted a beautiful death scene.

Jared, leaning into Larissa, sitting by his side, said during the intermission, "I know that Shakespeare must have considered Desdemona and Othello's marriage a good one, noble and decent and all that, but what if, I mean, wouldn't it be funny if Desdemona actually *did* sleep with Cassio?"

"Dad's right. This play is not appropriate for children, Mother," said Emily, leaning over Michelangelo. "You should not have brought him."

"She shouldn't have brought *you*," said Michelangelo, shoving away his sister.

"Perhaps Emily is right," Jared said. "This play is not appropriate for adults *or* children."

"What kind of a tragedy would it be if Desdemona was righteously killed?" asked Larissa. "This is like the things Leroy says when he wants to revise the script by 'improving' Shakespeare's words."

"Who the hell is Leroy?"

"You know. Leroy." She pointed. "Standing with the script in his hand on the other side of Fred."

"Who the hell is Fred?"

"Oh, darling, I told you about Fred." Larissa sighed. "You never listen to me. He's the annoying one, the theater department head wannabe next to the stage director wannabe."

"You have to be more specific than that, Lar." Laughing, Jared put his arm around her. "Hey, why can't it still be a tragedy?" He kissed her temple. "To love, to be betrayed. That's not tragic?"

"Not for Shakespeare. It's par for the course."

Asher leaned over his father. "When is this over? I *really* have to go home."

"It'll be over when everybody is dead, son. That's how you'll know it's over." Jared turned to Larissa. "What's the spring play?"

"No one's decided yet," said Larissa as the curtain rose. "Much to Ezra's torment, Leroy thinks it'll be up to him."

"Hmm," Jared said. "*You* should be the director. You can drive to work in your little gold Jag. So zexy. When's it coming?"

"I don't know. Two weeks?"

"Did he say he was going to call you when it was in?"

"He didn't say. I assume someone will call."

"Usually the salesman calls."

"Well, I guess then he'll call."

"He hasn't called yet?"

"Jared, no, he hasn't called. You know how you know? I'm not driving a little gold Jag."

"Hmm. I guess. God, he was so pretentious," whispered Jared. "Reading *Felix Krull*. Who does he think he is?"

"Who are you talking about?" Larissa said mock-tiredly, amazed at Jared's visceral inexplicable hostility to Kai's stoic silence in one ten-minute car ride.

Act III began. Enter Cassio and some musicians. "*Masters play here. I will content your pains.*"

❧

At the end of February, the Jag came in. A momentous occasion like that deserved Jared taking time off work, but he was busy restructuring the fixed retirement instruments department and couldn't. Larissa had to wait, but she did drive over in the afternoon to take a look at it.

"Winter Gold is nice, ey?" Kai said, beaming to a beaming Larissa, who put both palms on the hood, both forearms on the hood. It was magnificent. She wanted to lie down on it. She wanted to sleep inside it.

"Certainly better than the blue," she said, wishing she could drive it off the lot that very second. She settled for tuna and rice in the Escalade with Kai from 1:25 until 1:55.

After dinner Jared drove Larissa to the dealership. The release paperwork was signed for the plates and the temporary registration. The keys were exchanged and keyless combinations revealed. The car was so spanking, even Jared shook Kai's hand! Larissa kept saying thank you. There was a lot to be grateful for. The Jaguar brought Jared and Kai together! Maybe they could be friends. Perhaps Kai could come over in the summer, reseal the walkway from the garage to the front door, and then have a frosty glass of freshly squeezed lemonade in her kitchen.

"So all is forgiven, darling?" Larissa said quietly and teasingly to Jared, while Kai went inside to grab the second set of keys. The situation was so diffused, she could even tease!

"I don't know what you're talking about," Jared said. And then louder, when Kai returned. "The color is fantastic. Perfect for Larissa." And Kai agreed. Winter Gold was perfect for Larissa.

He showed her things: how to put the top down, how to adjust the power seat, control the automatic climate buttons, work the stereo and the menu buttons. They spent forty minutes in the car, him patiently explaining, while Jared sat in his Lexus tapping his fingers. "Lar, ready to go?" he asked, finally getting out and walking over to the Jag window. "It's getting late."

"Just a few more minutes, honey," said Larissa. "I have to figure out when to use the third gear." She looked at Jared brightly. "You can go home, if you want. I'll follow you in, like, five minutes." .

Jared looked from Kai to Larissa and back again. "If it's really going to be five minutes, I'll wait," he said.

Finally they left, Larissa as excited as a boy with trains on Christmas morning. She drove her Winter Gold Jaguar twenty miles an hour down Main Street with Jared behind her in his Lexus, honking at her to hurry it along. There was no putting down the top, since it was drizzling freezing slush. When she got home and pulled the car into the garage, she took out a roll of paper towels, went out and started drying the car by hand. Jared laughed at her.

"The children all want a ride, Lar," he said. "Better keep that paper towel roll handy." Since the car was a two-seater, she had to take them one by one, though Michelangelo made do with the tiny back seat, scrunched up, and went along with both Emily and Asher.

"Mom, that is the *coolest* car I've ever seen," Asher said. "I want you to drive me to guitar in it every week."

"Yes, but we'll have to get another mother with another car to drive the other two children to their activities, won't we?" said Larissa. "We won't all fit in this one."

Jared put his foot down. "This is not a mother car," he said. "This is a Larissa car, okay, guys? When you want a mother, she drives you in the Escalade. Larissa drives the Jag. Got it?"

That Saturday night they invited themselves to Maggie and Ezra's just so Larissa could drive her Jag. Even the unflappable Ezra looked impressed.

"Happy now?" Ezra said, walking around the car, patting its trunk and windows.

"Delirious. But careful. You'll scratch it with your ring."

"Why would I scratch your car with my wedding ring?" said Ezra, taking his hands off it. "So has the Jag provided you with all the answers?"

"Give it time, Ezra. I've only had it two days."

"What about the theater, Larissa? You've been thinking about it a lot longer than two days. I'm about to offer the job to Leroy."

"Don't threaten me with Leroy, Ezra. Offer him the job if you want." She paused. "He is a fine man and a single dad. Don't let his theatrical incompetence stand in your way."

"Come inside." Ezra prodded her away from the Jag. "I will ply you full of liquor and terrorize you with stories of Leroy. Do you remember how he decided to change the ending of *Hamlet*? He thought Hamlet shouldn't die in the end, but rather learn the error of his ways and be redeemed with pompous self-discovery?"

"Ezra!"

"What about when Desdemona and Othello kissed and made up at the end? And Juliet woke up just in time to stay Romeo's hand."

"All right, enough."

"Caesar lives!"

"Ezra!"

"The people forgive Antony and Cleopatra for their decadent ways!"

"We're leaving."

"Ivan Ilyich gets better!"

"Well, how can it be called *The Death of Ivan Ilyich* then?" said an exasperated Larissa.

"My point exactly. Only you can save us from Leroy, Larissa."

"I said no."

"Come inside. Drink till you say yes."

"That's how she got three children, Ez," piped up Jared, pulling a reluctant Larissa away from the Jag. All she wanted to do was ride it on the open road.

But not alone.

❦

After the first time of sitting in a car and eating sushi, an illusory world was established in which it was possible for Larissa to sit with Kai, first in her cream SUV and now in her Jaguar, in the middle of a bright day parked near a chain-link fence separating the parking lot from the cemetery and, without looking at each other, eat raw seafood.

His age was the most ridiculous thing, and upsetting to her at first, but almost immediately the knowledge that he was not even in the flush of young adulthood—but at the end of adolescence, at the very beginning of the beginning of the rest of his life—liberated her from worry. Fretting about propriety had vanished and was replaced by an amused banter, a cheerful demeanor and a guiltless heart. Since any acknowledgment of his maleness and her femaleness in terms approaching equality either of body or of spirit was beyond the realm of possibility (his being *twenty* and all), having a quick lunch with him was pushed beyond the realm of anxiety. It was just a way to pass a few minutes in the afternoon, nothing more, and Larissa thought no more of it. No further justifications were needed. When she recalled her weeks-long agonizing over going to the dealership to look at a car, she was embarrassed at her own silliness. How overwrought! It was outlandish to be concerned about such trivial things. Illusion versus reality. The reality was, he was a boy barely out of high school and needed to have lunch in the afternoon. She was a grown woman with three children and a busy life who needed to have lunch in the afternoon. End of story. Jeepers.

They sat in her Jag as the breeze rustled her hair and blew their napkins around, and the sound of the road was like a soundtrack of her life. Police sirens, honkings, cars pulling in and out, wheels screeching, life buzzing on, while they sat facing tombstones laid out amid slushy grounds and bare trees, not yet greening, not yet budding. The temperature rose, and once in the middle of March it got to sixty-six degrees! Larissa didn't wear a coat, just a blouse with a denim jacket over it and jeans. This is what she wore now in these afternoons of her life. Jeans. Because jeans were the wardrobe of the young.

They rolled down their windows, she turned on the CD player, they listened to the Doors and Minnie Riperton. She discovered Kai knew by heart some of Jim Morrison's poetry. She was surprised by that; often he would do that: say things that surprised her. "Huh. Impressive," she said when he told her that the grand highway was crowded with searchers and leavers.

"Jim Morrison or me?" He blinked cheerfully.

She didn't have an answer, and he didn't want one. "I know a *lot* of Morrison," he said. "There was a point in my life when *The American Night* was all I read. *Wonderland Avenue* used to be my favorite book."

"Used to be?"

"Yeah . . . I'm less interested in that heroin culture now." He stuffed his empty plastic containers into the paper bag and refused to say more. "Still a good book, though. Have you read it?"

"No."

"It's by Danny Sugerman," he said, and the next day brought her a copy, all weathered and frayed. "You can borrow it," he said, "but careful, okay, it's a first print edition."

"You shouldn't give it to me, then. I'm apt to leave it somewhere."

"Like where?"

She took it. "Did you want to *be* like Morrison?"

"Nah. In Hawaii, we're more mellow. But Morrison rocks. Just listen to his lyrics, to his voice. I was more into Mahalo music, ukulele riffs, island chants, you know?"

She didn't know. She wanted to hear more of Morrison's poetry.

"I liked that he wanted to expand the bounds of his reality," said Kai, "expand it beyond all limits trying to find the sacred. You know how that can be?"

She wasn't sure she did but she wanted to hear more Morrison through Kai's lips.

3

Perpetual Change

Larissa knew she might be in a spot of trouble when Maggie called about lunch the following week and Larissa lied. Actually lied. Said she was busy. A doctor's appointment, blah blah, couldn't make it, and Maggie said, how long is this doctor's appointment, I'll meet you after, and Larissa said, no it's in Morristown, and this doctor always runs late, and Maggie took no for an answer, rescheduling for Wednesday from noon to two, and Larissa didn't know how or what to say to Kai, because to say she was busy tomorrow was ridiculous! But to say nothing might mean—would mean—that he'd be waiting for her, and she couldn't just not show up.

What would Emily Post say about the etiquette on that one?

Dear Abby:

I have this problem. For forty minutes a day I sit in my car with a young man not my husband and we have lunch. We talk about the most trivial nonsense, we are barely acquaintances, but we do this nearly every day. Tomorrow I can't make it. I don't know if it's appropriate to tell him I can't make it. I don't want it to seem like there's an obligation or like I owe him an explanation, because clearly I do not. Yet to not show up seems odd.

Dear Abby:

Yesterday afternoon, a young man not my husband held open for me the door of the car he sold me, and as I got in, I inhaled to smell him.

Question: Should I now try to smell random men on the streets of my sleepy little town to prove to myself that it was an aberration and that sometimes this is what women of a certain age do? Smell male strangers?

⇛⇝

She was eating tuna and cucumber, he a rainbow roll with eel and salmon. His hair was especially kinky today, covering much of his face.

"Masonry is hard work," he was saying. "But I love being outdoors all day in the summer. Selling Jags is actually harder work for me."

"So quit."

"I'd be a fool to quit a job where I make so much money." He waved his hand in the air. "Ah. Everything is hard. In its own way."

Larissa thought about her day, of sushi lunches and painting theater sets and ice cream and homework, and shopping, and slowness. A little baking, a little shopping, a little housework. Was that hard, too? In its own way?

Chewing her lip, she said nothing, glancing at his cracked young hands holding the chopsticks, as she listened to Yes on the radio, on low, but unmistakably serenading her about *perpetual change* . . . the world in their hands, the moon, the stars; the impending disaster gazing down on them, thought forward to April, to summer. What to do? It's just a boy I see, an illusion in front of me . . .

"So what happened to your dad?"

Kai stiffened slightly. With a thin smile he turned his head to her. "Nah, I don't want to talk about my dad, you know? We weren't close, he was . . . Papa was a rolling stone. Every day I worry someone is going to walk through the dealership door and say he's my half-brother. My old man was into some bad shit, and my mom and grandma raised us on their own. He disappeared; then I heard he went to jail for possession. A little while ago he popped around again. I was his only son."

Larissa said nothing.

"He disappeared again, like a magic act. We figured he probably went back to his two wives, his three mistresses; that's what my mother said. But we heard he was sick and in the hospital. Then he died. Left me the bike. I do love my bike."

"I'm sorry he got sick," Larissa said.

"That's okay. People get sick. We have bodies, and our bodies aren't perfect. Nothing is perfect. Even our souls aren't perfect."

So true. But still. "Did you get to see him before he died?"

Kai emitted a short laugh, an exhale. "For someone who didn't want to talk about it, I sure am talking a lot about it." He took a sip of Coke. "Yeah. My sisters and I went to the hospital to see him. Even my mother went." He stopped. "The Catholic nun who did rounds carried a guitar with her along with the Bible, and once she came into my dad's room and sat with us and asked if he wanted to hear something. Well, he couldn't talk anymore, he was slipping in and out of consciousness, but Melissa, my older sister, said his favorite song when she was growing up was 'King of the Road'. Do you know it? Roger Miller?"

Larissa shook her head.

And Kai sang it to her. Just a little, his head bobbing from side to side; it was a lilting melody, he carried a cheerful tune . . . *"Two hours of pushing broom buys an eight-by-twelve four-bit room . . ."* and then broke off and said, "Well, this nun chick, I've never heard anyone sing and play the guitar like her, not even Roger Miller. It was unbelievable. And my dad, even though he couldn't speak, and the doctors said he couldn't hear or see or understand anything anymore, he lay there, and you could almost swear his misty eyes were twitching in rhythm to the tune. My sisters said I was crazy. But he heard every word. The nun told me privately that the last thing to go on a man is his hearing; the dying hear everything, and I knew she was right. I asked her if she knew where he was headed because he hadn't been a very good man, certainly not a good father, which is the thing that affected me most when I was younger, not having a dad. And do you know what she told me?"

Larissa twitched, misty-eyed herself, to the rhythm of Kai's words. "No, what did she say?"

"She said, well, you say he's no good, but look, all his kids are sitting here with him, and his ex-wife, your mother, was here with him. You're angry for the way he treated her, but you're here, and she is here. There are some people who die completely alone, no kids, no friends, nobody at the end of their life. So you know, maybe your old man wasn't all bad."

A short pause followed before Larissa breathed in and said, "Look at the time." It was after two. They'd been sitting for over an hour.

∿⌘∾

Next day. That's how she moved now. Lunch hour, from one to two Monday to Friday. Housewives and bikers, women and men, mothers and sons, actors and singers, salesmen, masons, shoppers and sinners, lunch hour from one to two, all welcome.

"So where's your mom now, your sisters?"

"Still in Hawaii."

"Oh." Why did that make her happy? Him being here without his family. "What are you doing in Jersey? Seems a long way to go to work at a car dealership."

"Yeah. But a friend of mine moved out here from Maui. So I followed him."

"Is that your mall buddy, Gil?"

"Yeah. And his roomie. They go to Rutgers, live in Maplewood. Initially I came to bunk with them till I got a gig. But it just so happened that I got a gig right away, so I got my own crib."

"Where?" She didn't mean to sound so high-pitched. But she felt high-pitched.

"A few blocks away." He was calm in response. He was always calm. "I can walk to work."

"Maplewood's a nice town," Larissa said, in a more even tone. It didn't seem quite right for college kids. It was more a family town. Like Summit. "Your friends like it?"

Kai cleared his throat. "Unfortunately my buddy Gil was arrested a while back dealing dope on campus. So he's temporarily out of commission."

"For how long?"

"Three to seven. Chance of parole in eighteen months."

"Geez. Three to seven seems steep."

"I think," said Kai, "it might not have been his first offense."

"Oh."

"The guy had to pay his tuition somehow. Parents got divorced and there were no funds to be had, and yet—well, you know how it is."

Just thinking about how it was got Larissa all flushed, because Kai said, "Is this making you uncomfortable? The drugs? That's not my scene."

"No, I was just . . . the food went down wrong." His age was supposed to be the liberating thing! The thing that made everything else so easy-peasy lemon-squeezy. Almost like sitting with one of her drama students, having a chat in the breeze. Why did thinking of his friends dealing drugs to pay for their college tuition make her feel so twisted up inside? Could it be because her own college experience of dope and crazy protesting friends was twenty years ago? His lifetime ago.

"Madison is a great small town," Kai said. "Don't you think?"

She wasn't sure. "Like Hawaii?"

"Nah. Too many transients in Hawaii. Too many vacationers. Nothing is permanent there. This good stable life is so strange. So exotic."

"*This* life is exotic?" Larissa repeated in a flat tone. What was he talking about!

"Honestly, you'd be hard-pressed to find a town as quaint and cute as Madison. I'm not saying I want to live here forever. I want to see the world. But to settle down? To raise a family? There is no better place. Really."

"If you say so. But it's not exotic, Kai. It's just not. It's too normal to be exotic."

"See, to me, the normal is the exotic."

"Do you know what's exotic? The Philippines. My best friend lives near Manila; she's always asking me to go visit her."

"Why don't you?"

"Well, I can't just pick up and go."

"Why not?"

"What's my family going to do?"

"Oh, they'll manage for a few weeks, won't they?"

"I don't think they will."

"Go," Kai said. "Have you ever gone anywhere on your own?"

Larissa was actually scared to go. She didn't know how to say that. She was scared of malaria, of dengue fever, of the horrid water; Che's stories of never being able to drink the water without boiling it first filled her with dread. That's why the children couldn't come with her. She was scared for their safety. And for her own, though she wouldn't confess that to Kai, who didn't seem the type to be easily spooked, riding around on a speed-demon bike and having friends who were in prison. Besides, her best friend lived in Manila and was not afflicted, other than with childlessness, so it may have been in Larissa's head. But then, much of life was in her head. Didn't make it any less real.

Time to go.

Next.

Next.

Next.

Why did she sit? She didn't know. All she knew was that she sat with him for a few fine merry moments, and then it was over. Which was a good way to describe many things you did that didn't involve routine or work. For a few fine moments, Maggie painted, Emily played volleyball, Evelyn sipped her wine and read her books,

Tara walked and complained. Jared played basketball with Asher in the front drive. Ezra read tomes on existential materialism. Larissa dreamed of the joyous moments of a spring play from high school, intoning, "*I do love nothing in the world so well as you. Is not that strange?*" Except all those other things didn't involve pushing open the closed door that in red block letters read, DANGER: LIVE ELECTRIC CURRENT. ENTER AT OWN RISK.

4

Waiting for Godot

"You don't do theater anymore?"

"What makes you say that? I do. I just . . ." Larissa broke off. "I do." Just not like before. "I was director of the theater department at a private school in Hoboken for many years."

He grunted. "You don't say."

Oh, why, why did she have to say *many*. Since when did hated pride come before puffed-up vanity? She'd rather be young and talentless than impress him with how many long years she'd been director of a theater department at a school where he could've tried out for a school play. "I once belonged to a theater troupe called The Great Swamp Revue. We were excellent." When he chuckled, she, encouraged, asked, "Are you interested in theater?"

"Nah," he said. "I was always more of a music guy."

"Music, really?" Mental note to thyself: less about self and theater. Nothing more tedious than a woman basking in the deluded glory of former theater days, convinced she is the center of the universe.

"What, you don't believe me?"

"Of course I do. What do you play?"

"A little of everything. Guitar. Harmonica. Drums. In Hawaii every boy plays the ukulele, so I did too. So how come you don't do theater anymore? No time?"

She nodded; indeed there was no time. "I barely have time to paint the sets these days."

"You went from director to set decorator?"

"Less stress," she said almost without a beat.

He smiled. "Kids seem like a lot of stress to me."

This was where the whole thing became so bogus. You just knew it was bogus.

"Hey," he said suddenly, "ever been on a bike?"

"What, a bicycle?" A *bicycle built for two*. "Sure, who hasn't? Many times. You?"

He laughed. "Are you being funny?"

She didn't know. She didn't know if she was being funny.

He pointed out of her Jag to his Ducati. "I brought my bike today. Want to go for a ride?"

Larissa couldn't remember the last time she became this flustered. Not looking at him, hemming, hawing, she said, "No, thank you, but, uh, maybe another time. Seems too cold anyway. Well, it actually is cold. Windy. I don't know how you do it, I mean, it must be even colder on the bike. And look at the breeze, it's nippy. It's like a squall." Her cheeks were burning as she ruffled her napkins, stuffing them into the brown bag. "Maggie, my friend," she said, just throwing it out there, "is taking me to lunch tomorrow."

"The curly one from the mall?" Kai opened the car door and got out, leaning in. "You two have fun." His face was smiling at her, his small brown eyes dancing, his kinky hair blowing about; he had a manner about him of boyish sweetness, of youthful pride, of innocent joy when he said, "There's nothing like being on a bike, going fast. You sure you don't want a spin?"

She shook her head mutely.

She tried to think of something that might be like being on a Ducati going fast, in spring, with the wind in her hair, but couldn't.

∽✼∽

On Thursday Kai wasn't at Stop&Shop. One o'clock, 1:30. She bought paper towels and cereal, wandered the aisles, paid, sat in the car until two.

Friday he wasn't there either. Larissa didn't know what to make of it.

One thing for sure, whatever she couldn't make of it, she spent all weekend not making anything of it. Every conscious minute, she spent getting her mind away from it.

The report cards arrived in the mail. They weren't good. Emily's was okay, but Asher was doing dismally in English, and Michelangelo couldn't spell. Larissa pretended to deal with it, and on Saturday night she and Jared went over to Maggie and Ezra's for dinner and games, and the only person who noticed that things were not all square with her was Ezra, who said, to no one in particular, "Boy, is Lar ever in her own world. What are you thinking, Lar? Illuminate us."

"I'm fine, Ezra. What do you mean?"

"Are you thinking of accepting the job? Because Leroy wants to stage *Waiting for Godot* for the spring play. I'm going to shoot myself."

"*Waiting for Godot*, good play. Good choice," Larissa said.

"A nihilist two-person play? For spring!" shouted an aggrieved Ezra.

She came out of it a little. "Uh, no, it's terrible. Impossible. Put your foot down, tell him he can't."

"What's wrong with you? Why would you say it's a good idea?"

"How was your doctor's appointment?" asked Maggie. "I forgot to ask on Wednesday."

"What doctor's appointment?"

"Yeah, what doctor's appointment?" asked Jared. He was shuffling cards, trying to teach them how to play blackjack since they were planning a trip to Atlantic City for Memorial Day weekend. But it wasn't taking. They were readers, not mathematicians.

"She went to the doctor on Tuesday," Maggie said.

"She did?" Jared glanced at Larissa. "You did?"

"I'm fine," she said. "Just the dermatologist."

"Ooooh!" said Maggie. "Dermatologist. Lar is getting Botox! No wonder she looks to be in the first flush of youth."

"Do I?" Larissa asked quietly.

"No wonder you kept asking me how young you looked. Now I know your secret. How much does he charge?"

"No Botox, Mags, sorry," Larissa said, "just a routine check-up of moles and things."

They discussed this for an inordinately long time. Moles and cancers, what they were supposed to look like, what they morphed into, the signs of danger, where the moles appeared, the suddenness and yet the inevitability of bad news coming upon you (that was Ezra—of course!) and then what you did with that bad news. No one wanted to play cards anymore. Everybody knew someone who had melanoma on their back, basal cell on their face, squamous cell on their arms.

The irony of this conversation did not go unremarked upon by Jared, who in the car on the way home said, "Larissa, you didn't think that was odd, talking about moles at such excruciating length?"

"No, why? Did you?"

He coughed. "You and I both know you haven't got a single blemish on that body of yours, not a single mark of any kind, not even a childhood scar!" Jared chuckled. "Waxing all poetic about non-existent moles. You're hilarious. So why'd you blow Maggie off?"

She chuckled too, sheepishly. He leaned over and kissed her at the red light. "You're so funny. Why don't you just tell her you don't want to hang out all the time? Tell her you're reading. It wouldn't even be a lie. You *are* actually reading nowadays."

"Yes." Larissa's gaze focused on the road.

Saturday passed and Sunday too, and then Monday came, and she drove her Jag to Stop&Shop.

Kai wasn't there. Not there on Monday, his day off from work, when he always showed up and they did their weekly shopping together.

Larissa didn't know what to think. She hung around thirty minutes on Monday, ten on Tuesday, and then Wednesday morning came and she looked at herself in the hall mirror, at her straight highlighted hair, her sensible brown eyes, her long arms, slender fingers, her body, trim from walking, from downward-dog yoga poses, everything still slim, still in proportion. She thought about a manicure with Fran, maybe a mommy-and-daughter day in the city with Emily, just the girls. She thought about organizing a fundraiser for the spring play, she thought ahead to planning the Hawaii trip in August and whether they should take an extra day for Memorial Day Atlantic City weekend.

Larissa thought of writing to Che, telling her she'd been eating kinilaw for two months, and she ruminated on packing up all her winter sweaters and taking out her summer shirts. But what she really contemplated was never ever ever going to Stop&Shop again, and the knot inside her for a brief moment was untied and loose of anxiety, like dangling threads. Clear of everything.

She would go back to King's. Sure it was crowded and the aisles were narrow, and the parking lot was tiny, but her leg wasn't broken anymore, and to celebrate, she got on the treadmill for thirty minutes and watched a talk show and then showered, and cleaned her bedroom, and got dressed, and made coffee and sat in the kitchen for five minutes, ten minutes, planning dinner and vacation, with *Love's Labors Lost* opened to the page that said, *The blood of youth burns not with such excess as gravity's revolt to wantonness.* And in her head, brutal words swirled about like blood-on-snow candy canes. What are you doing here? What do you want? Is it music? We can play music. But you want more. You want something and someone new. You want ecstasy.

She bolted from the island, got into her car and drove to Stop&Shop.

He wasn't there.

This time Larissa waited an hour, as if saying goodbye. She sat in the parking lot, overlooking the graveyard, eating sushi and listening to Chet Baker singing "These Foolish Things" that made his heart a dancer, and wondered about spring, and whether she needed new shoes, new sandals, perhaps. A girl always needed new sandals for spring. At two she drove to pick up Michelangelo, and sat quietly in the parking lot at her son's school. So close to the end, to the beginning. So close to the middle, which implied just as much ahead as there had been behind. And yet close to absolutely nothing.

5

The Navigation System

On Thursday Larissa called the Jag dealership to schedule an appointment for service. "Have you had the car for three months, Mrs. Stark?" Brian, the service manager, intoned into the receiver. He had a seedy voice.

"Um, no," she stammered. "But I think the oil might be low."

"Has the oil light gone on?"

"No, but the car's making a funny noise at higher speeds, like a rattling noise."

"What kind of speeds?"

"I don't know. Seventy?"

"Hmm. Okay. Bring it in tomorrow, we'll check it out."

When Larissa hung up she wondered if there was a way they could tell that she'd never taken the car on the highway, had never gone above fifty in it; that it was smooth as silk—all the way to fifty. How high was self-immolation-by-lying-to-service-station-flacks on the list of venial things human beings were taught not to do?

On Friday she brought the Jag into the shop. She looked for Kai's amber bike, but couldn't catch a pumpkin glimpse of it. Brian, a tall, scrawny man with thin greasy hair, shook his head. "We're busy before the weekend," he said. "You really had to bring it in early. I told you to bring it in by eight, and here it is, nearly ten. Can you leave it till Monday?"

Not to have her car for the weekend? But then she'd have to explain to Jared that there was something wrong with it, and Jared knew about cars, he might get upset, go in, or call. Might demand another car. Perhaps cancel the deal. So much scrutiny. Too much.

"No," she said. "I can't leave it, we're going away. Please, can you try for today?"

"Miss, I don't know." She loved it when they called her *miss*— her, a wife, a mother.

She tried cajoling, using the voice she used on her children. "Come on. Maybe it's nothing. Just a simple oil change."

Brian looked into the monitor. "Car brand new, factory-delivered four weeks ago. I don't think it's the oil. Who sold you this car? Kai?"

That's all she needed, an in. "Yes. Is he here? Maybe he can help?"

"Nah, he's not. Besides he's not a mechanic."

"Yes, but I have a technical question for him. I lost the card with the keyless entry code."

"I can get you that. I'll have to call the factory."

"And," Larissa continued, "I wanted to see if he could order me a navigation system."

"A nav? Really? Well, I can do that for you. He's not here anyway."

"Will he be back on Monday?"

"Dunno." Brian wasn't looking at her as he typed up her order on the computer. "He had a funeral or something. Had to fly back to Hawaii, I think. We don't know if he'll be back. He just left abruptly."

A funeral!

"Don't worry. I'll help you." Brian grinned. "I do this stuff. Kai just sells the vehicle. All the after-sale service, I do. Sign right here. I'll call you in the afternoon. Do you need a ride?"

"I kind of do, yeah."

"Hmm. Lemme see." Brian paged Gary, the other salesman, who

gave Larissa a ride home. On the way they barely talked. Except for the words she couldn't help.

"So what happened to my salesman?"

"Who? Kai? No one knows. He took personal leave. Our manager asked him when he was coming back and he said he didn't know."

"*Is* he coming back?"

"The way he left, we don't think so."

"Did he clear his desk?"

"Never had anything there to begin with." Gary shrugged as he drove. "Weird guy. But a good salesman, I'll give him that. Very good." He smiled. "The ladies liked him."

"Did they?"

"Yeah. He could really turn on the charm when he wanted to."

"Huh," said Larissa, staring straight ahead at Springfield Avenue. She enjoyed the grilled cheese sandwiches at the Summit Diner. Maybe she could go back to having them. "I didn't see much of that. Neither did my husband. Make the next right on Summit."

Gary laughed. "No, the husbands never saw much good in him, that's true."

What was she going to do? After she was dropped off, she rushed to Michelangelo's school; she was the mystery reader that afternoon and had plumb forgot.

Of course the car was fine. "I can find nothing wrong with it, miss," said Brian when he called later. "You gonna come pick it up?" She thought about asking Maggie to drive her to the dealership, but didn't want it to get back to Jared that there might be a problem with the car. Gary came to pick up her and Michelangelo, and Larissa had to pay a hundred and thirty dollars to Brian for doing nothing.

Afterward she took Michelangelo for ice cream at Ricky's. The boy had yum-yum bubble gum and she a crazy chocolate; they sat at one of the outdoor tables and licked their cones and chatted. It was an unseasonable sixty-four degrees, sunny, windy. Michelangelo talked about *Jumanji*, the book his mother had picked to read to his class. He didn't understand why so many kids were scared by it, because he wasn't scared at all, and he watched the movie like thirty-one times. Well, you are a good brave boy, Larissa said, licking her crazy chocolate through clenched teeth, through a tight throat.

He might not be coming back. That was something she wasn't ready to get used to, the suddenness of it. Sitting next to Michelangelo in his blue camo pants, dripping melting bubble gum ice cream on them and licking his fingers, Larissa watched her son for a while with her arm on his back. Kai wouldn't leave his bike behind. She was sure of that. He wouldn't leave his Ducati Sportclassic behind.

But what if he didn't leave it?

On the one hand, such a welcome breath of liberation.

On the other, emptiness that felt like pale death.

⋘⋙

Monday morning she met Maggie for a quick coffee before her play meeting at ten. They discussed Dylan, who was demanding drums for his birthday, and Maggie, usually indulgent, this time was terrified. "Drums, Larissa. Do you understand?"

Larissa understood. Drums were loud.

"No one else in the house will be able to live."

"There's no one else in the house."

"Ezra likes it quiet so he can read."

"Frankly a little less reading . . . perhaps drums are exactly what you need."

"Don't joke, it's not funny."

"You'll be fine. Put Dylan in the basement."

"The basement is where our whole life is! Our pool table is there. Our air hockey. My treadmill. I know I never go on it, but it's still there. My washer and dryer."

"So don't get the drums."

"He says he can't live without them."

"We say that about a lot of things."

"*He* doesn't."

"So? He'll learn not to be able to live without something else."

"Hah."

"Seriously, divert him. When Michelangelo wants a lollipop three minutes before dinner, I don't give in. I give him a crayon instead."

"I hope your child doesn't suck on too many of those," said Maggie. "Because how long can you fool a six-year-old? Soon he'll figure out a crayon is not a very tasty substitute. Dylan is sixteen. He can't be talked out of things that easily."

"Easily? You have *met* Michelangelo, right?" Larissa got up. "So offer Dylan something else. I gotta go. Creative meeting with your husband and Leroy."

Maggie laughed. "Ah, yes. *Waiting for Godot*. Ezra is treating this like a Shakespearean tragedy in and of itself."

"Isn't it?" Larissa was wearing jeans, a jeans jacket, a white T-shirt, a bandanna around her hair.

"Who's going to take you seriously at this meeting?" said Maggie. "You look twelve."

Why did she beam? It was too late for that.

6

Much Ado About Nothing

A tensely waiting Ezra pulled her aside as soon as she entered the school lobby. "I *have* to talk to you," he said.

"What's up?"

"Not here. My office."

"No."

"No, we can't go to my office?"

"No to whatever it is you want to ask me in it."

They walked speedily down the hall and into Ezra's comfortable, chaotic, book-lined chambers. It must be nice to be head of the department.

She fell into his visitor chair. "Whazzup?"

"I'm not asking you anymore. I'm begging you. You have to save us."

"Ezra, I told you a thousand times. I've thought about it. I talked to Jared about it. To you. To Maggie. To Bo. I've written to Che about it."

"How *is* our little professional protester?"

"Not pregnant. But I'm talked out."

"Will you *hear* me out?"

"Ezra, you got Leroy. What's wrong with him?" She smirked. "Besides wanting to stage a two-man play for spring?"

"Leroy said he'd prefer not to do it," admitted Ezra. "His kid is failing math."

"So you want me to do it so *my* kids will fail math? My kid is already failing English!"

"They're honor students!"

"Not Asher. Not Michelangelo. He glues all day. Can't get far in life with glue, Ezra."

"Bring him. Bring them both. I'll tutor them."

"You'll tutor Michelangelo." Larissa looked down into her hands with incredulity. "Tutor him in what? Obstinacy? Sculpture?"

"We'll pay you."

"Jared works his ass off all week. We can't both be away from the kids."

"You won't be away. Studies have shown that children benefit from seeing their parents be successful at something other than parenting."

Larissa stared at him. "Are you making this crap up?"

"Yes."

She laughed. "Ez, what am I supposed to do when Emily has cello in Chatham, and Asher a track meet in Maplewood, and I'm in Short Hills in the afternoon directing *Godot*? You haven't thought this through."

"I have, too. We'll rehearse on Saturdays. And *please*, not *Godot*."

Larissa said nothing. Ezra took that as encouragement.

"It's just for two, three months. Play goes on in June. If you don't want to continue next fall, we'll get someone else. I promise. Denise will come back."

"Denise is going to leave her baby and come back?"

Straightening his red tie, Ezra adjusted his falling-down crooked glasses, beaming at her. "We have a deal?"

Larissa shook her head. "Ez, do you remember how the parents hated me at the Hudson School?"

"No, they loved you. But a little diplomacy here at Pingry wouldn't kill you."

"It's either the play or diplomacy."

Ezra nearly clapped. "So we're set? Auditions are next week."

"How can that be? We haven't chosen a play yet! Or should we stick with Leroy's terrific suggestion? *In an instant it all will vanish and we'll be alone once more in the midst of nothingness.* What, that's not inspiring enough for spring?" Larissa smiled. This diversion for her . . . it was ideal. It would take her mind off things, help her get back on track.

"Lar," Ezra said, helping her up from the chair, "let's go and announce the good news and choose a play. Try to think of something appropriate."

"How much time do I have?"

Ezra looked at his watch. "Can you think while we walk down the hall?" He pulled her up by her elbow. "Hurry. Meeting started fifteen minutes ago."

"How can the meeting have started? We're not there!"

"Come on," he said prodding her out. "Fret as you walk."

"Ezra, you've gotten very demanding since you've become department head." Picking up her purse, she took out a lipstick. "I liked you better absent-minded and lackadaisical." Without a mirror, she applied a shade of pink beige to her lips.

"We don't have an hour fifty-five, Larissa," Ezra said, watching her.

She didn't want him to know she was grateful. She wanted him to think she was grudging. Otherwise, how to explain her sudden exhilaration?

But no matter how welcome the distraction, the everyday stress of theater, the demand of it made her anxious even as she rushed down the sunlit hallway. "What if I can't do it, Ez? What if it's just too much for me?"

"You'll be fabulous. We don't want someone who never reaches. You always reach, Larissa. For places other people can't go. That's why we need you."

"Plus you're desperate."

"That, too."

They stopped at the double doors of the conference room. He looked her over before they came in. "So how come today of all days you're dressed to go ride the go-karts?"

"Because I thought I was coming in as the set decorator," Larissa rejoined, opening the doors. "This is what painters wear."

~

Inside the conference room, buoyed with black coffee and a sense of his own importance, Leroy, though having relinquished the coveted position of director, clearly did so resentfully. His first action after they all sat down and got some water was to distribute to each of the eight seated people copies of *Godot*, and embark on a long sermon punctuated by no periods on why it was the greatest play of this or any century.

Larissa could tell that there were some people at the table who did not think a set decorator was qualified to be a director, despite Ezra's excited recital of Larissa's credentials: theater and English double major at NYU, summer stock theater (the Great Swamp Revue and Jersey Footlight Players) director of the acclaimed theater department at the Hudson School. Larissa could tell neither Leroy nor Fred, Ezra's assistant, was impressed.

"Leroy," Larissa said in her no-nonsense voice, palms down on the table, her manner sober, "I appreciate your recommendation, and we can all agree to the quality of *Godot*, but we need a different direction. Something more lighthearted. I was thinking of a Shakespearean comedy."

Leroy had no intention of giving up. "*Godot* is a comedy."

"Well, yes. A tragicomedy. But *Godot* is wrong for spring, with all due respect. The air of bleak existentialism as read mostly by a cast of two, with a set of one scraggly tree is not the joyful experience most children and parents associate with a spring production. I'm thinking of something more inclusive and multi-parted. A little funnier, a little less angst-ridden." She smiled amiably at him. He did not return the smile. Ezra, though, smiled exquisitely at Larissa.

For the next *ninety minutes*, Larissa, Ezra, Fred, Leroy, Sheila

Meade, Vanessa (Sheila's assistant), Vincent (Leroy's), and David, the line reader, pounded out the possibilities. Leroy shot everything down. *As You Like It* was not funny enough ("certainly not as funny as *Godot*"), *Midsummer* had too much confusing dialogue, and *Much Ado* was too long. ("*Godot*, on the other hand, is brilliant, funny, deceptively short, and will be simple to stage and direct.")

Larissa kept quiet. Ezra had to prod her. "Well, Larissa, you're the director," he said. "What do *you* think?"

"Choosing a play is a collaboration," Leroy announced haughtily.

"Yes, but the director has final say," Ezra pointed out. "Lar, what say you?"

"We all have to agree so we can throw our support behind it," Leroy announced, with Vincent nodding next to him.

Larissa suddenly realized it was nearing one! She had to go. Knowing that time was running short tensed her into silence. She had to get into her car *right now* and drive away.

Wait. Wasn't she going to forget about Stop&Shop? Wasn't that the purpose of all this? Wasn't she freed from the constraints of the supermarket parking lot? Accept the position of director, straighten out, back on the rails.

If she left now, she would barely make it there for one.

She felt fourteen pairs of eyes on her as if they expected her to decide; at the very least to speak. "Okay, here's what I think," Larissa said. She was out of time. "*As You like It* is meant to be performed outside. We can do it inside, but it won't be as good, and outside is impossible." She tried not to sound impatient or hurried. "I suggest *Comedy of Errors*. It takes place in one day, serious subjects such as death by hanging and slavery are pushed aside for the sake of the joke, and all action is physical rather than internal, which makes it easier to rehearse and execute successfully." She fell silent, waiting for them to agree. From Leroy's barely suppressed sneers, Larissa guessed he was not a fan of *The Comedy of Errors*. Sheila said she preferred to do *As You Like It*. Twenty-six-year-old Vanessa, who was trying on theater for size before she fled into the world of fashion design, agreed with her boss. Vincent agreed with his.

Young Vincent painted sets with her, so Larissa was miffed at his backstabbing, while Fred, who worked with Ezra, fancied himself smarter than anyone (including his boss) and therefore had to have an opposite opinion on everything just to prove his intellectual superiority. David, the line reader, thought because he read lines with the kids, he was qualified to make staging decisions. Ezra was, as always, bemused. Noncommittal, but bemused.

Well, whatever. At one time, back in college, in Hoboken, theater consumed Larissa. Being on the stage herself, what power! But that was over ten years ago. Dionysus was not her god anymore. Oh, sure, if you gave in to him, surrendered yourself to his charms, he would make you good, he would make you great. But it was a Faustian deal you made with him. And while Larissa accepted Ezra's offer, she accepted it for her own reasons and was not about to dance with Dionysus again. She just didn't care that much anymore.

"Why not *Tempest?*" Leroy suggested sourly.

"Maybe *Taming of the Shrew?*" Fred piped up. Oh, so he was unhappily married, Larissa thought, him and his bow ties and French berets. He certainly looked unhappily something.

"*Tempest* is too long," Larissa said.

"So?"

"Leroy, but you were just lauding the brevity of *Godot*. Now you don't care how long the proposed play is. Plus," she continued evenly, "*Tempest* is complicated, it's hard to memorize and stage." She turned to Fred. "As for *Shrew*, we put it on three years ago last fall."

"I don't think that's true." Just to be contrary!

Larissa was quiet. "I painted the sets. I know. Vinnie might recall it." She glared at him. "He painted the sets with me. Remember, Vinnie?"

A sheepish Vincent barely nodded, hoping Leroy and Fred wouldn't see him agreeing with her!

Larissa exchanged an impatient glance with Ezra, that reluctant-to-intervene people-watcher. "Fred, I don't understand what the issue is. What's wrong with *Comedy of Errors?*"

"What's wrong with *Much Ado About Nothing?*" he countered. "We didn't stage *that* three years ago, did we?"

"I still think *Tempest* is a good idea," Leroy weighed in. "It's not an actual tragedy, you know."

"I know," Larissa drew out. "Do you really want to stage it?"

"Let's say yes."

"Can I ask you, Leroy, why are you so suddenly adamant about *The Tempest*? In my hands I'm still holding the play you were adamant about an hour ago."

"Well, if I can't have the one I really want . . ."

Vinnie and Sheila and Fred nodded in assent.

Ezra finally spoke. "How do we feel about *Much Ado?*"

Leroy first looked at Larissa, as if to gauge her imminent reaction. Then he said, "I like it. It's a fine choice."

"What do you think, Lar?"

Now he speaks! "It's fine for *fifteen*-year-olds?" said Larissa. "On the one hand we have *Comedy of Errors*, 122 pages, light, external, easy to set, funny, just right for spring. On the other we have *Much Ado About Nothing*, about betrayal, shame, humiliation, infidelity, death, itself only one bad performance away from becoming a tragedy."

"That's what makes it so rich and rewarding," said Leroy.

"According to you, Larissa, every comedy in Shakespeare is a breath away from becoming a tragedy," said Fred.

"And not just in Shakespeare," muttered Larissa.

"Okay, then how about *Midsummer Night's Dream?*" interjected Ezra as the situation was about to become untenable. (About to?)

"*Midsummer Night's Dream*," repeated Larissa in a slow voice, (poorly) hiding her supreme irritation, "deals with lovelorn triangulating. It's too adult to be performed by fifteen-year-olds. Then again . . ." She didn't even have to glance at her watch. She knew it was one o'clock. Getting up, she grabbed her denim suede purse off the back of the chair.

"You're leaving?" said Ezra. "But we haven't finished."

"You're right," Larissa said. "But you know my opinion. Discuss amongst yourselves. Tell me tomorrow what you've decided."

"Should we do a casting call this afternoon?" asked David the line reader, already thinking ahead.

"Choose the play first."

"Larissa . . ." That was Ezra.

"I really have to go, guys. Honest, I have no dog in this fight. It's the end of March, the play opens in June, that'll be barely eight weeks after auditions to rehearse. Not a lot of time. Whatever you decide, I'm fine."

Ezra followed her to the double doors.

"Lar, what are you doing?" he said quietly. "They think you're storming out."

"Aren't I?" She patted him on the sleeve, "Make nice with them, as only you can."

"We have to have a decision!"

"Am I the director, or are you? Or is Fred? Or perhaps Leroy wants to direct from the sidelines. I hear there's a play he's just dying to do," she added with a brisk smile, pleased with herself. She waved *Godot* in front of Ezra.

"Stop it."

"Gotcha. Well, I'm going to tell you how it's going to work." She placed her implacable hand on the metal bar, ready to push open the doors and sprint. "If you want me to be the director, I have final say. That's how it works. What play we do, whom we cast, how we stage it, what I cut. *I* decide." She nodded in Fred and Leroy's direction. "No devil's advocate arguments from the peanut gallery."

"Fine. Decide."

"I'm going to torture you and give you what you want. *Much Ado About Nothing*. Betrayal, shame, humiliation. In spring. I'll see you." She blew him a teasing kiss and ran down the hall in her Frye boots. Ran. From Pingry to Stop&Shop was 5.2 miles and twelve minutes if she made *all* the lights and there was no traffic. She made no lights, and there was a mob of traffic. She made it in nine minutes anyway.

He wasn't there.

Granted, it was 1:20 and perhaps he had come and gone, but then it was 1:30, then 1:40 and he wasn't there. Larissa bought some steak for dinner, potatoes, frozen corn, peanut butter—1:50—cereal, coffee, sugar, tea, dry dog food—1:55—and then reluctantly went to stand in the express line and listened to a heavy, sour woman (perhaps Fred's spouse?) behind her say, "Looks like you have more than twelve items there, dearie." And Larissa said, "All righty, I'll play." Normally, she wouldn't have done it, but this is what happened when small inflammations festered into giant sores. "Let's count together. One, two, three, four, five, six, seven, eight, nine, ten, eleven, twelve—look at that! Exactly twelve." Larissa gave the embarrassed woman a cold stare. "Unless of course, you want to count each of the steaks as a separate piece. But we might have to count your six English muffins individually, and then where would we be?"

The woman mumbled something about the sign saying TWELVE OR LESS.

"Yes, and I've got one of those. Twelve. See?" Harrumphing to the cashier, Larissa pushed her items down the conveyor belt.

"Cash back?"

"No," Larissa barked to the register girl. "Just the receipt, please."

Still steaming, she bagged, paid and without a backward glance of smug contemptuous self-satisfaction pushed her cart outside. She was almost at her car when a voice behind her said, "Boy, you really showed her."

She whirled around, swirled around like a tornado on boots, and in front of her Kai stood, looking worn and pale, unshaven, scraggly, unwell and sad, holding a coffee and a brown paper bag in his hands.

"Hey," she said, her heart thumping, her voice shaking a little. Damn! Larissa hated that old witch even more for forcing her to be unlikeable when he was nearby. "Everything okay?" What to say? What to *say*! "Haven't seen you in a while."

"Yeah . . . I had . . ." He bowed his head. "I know," he said, without looking up. "You have time to grab a bite?"

It was 2:07. Larissa had exactly seven minutes to grab a bite, and then she stood a thirty percent chance of being five minutes late to pick up Michelangelo. She wished that once, just *once* . . .

"Hang on," she said. "Let me call my friend." While he waited, Larissa called Donna, whose kids were walkers, asking her to please keep Michelangelo for ten minutes because she was running "a tiny bit" behind. Though she and Larissa had spoken barely two words the whole year, Donna was gracious. She and her own kids were headed to the playground. Could she take Michelangelo with them? "Oh, he'd love that. Thank you so much. I owe you one . . ."

Larissa turned to Kai. She stood dumbly in the parking lot, and her steak in the Jersey sun was going to reach room temperature, oh, in say, fifteen minutes, just long enough for her to get home and throw it out.

"Did you already eat?" he said, holding his brown bag in his hands. "We can split my sushi if you want."

"No," she said. "I'm okay." It was unseemly to say she was starving. As if she had uncontrollable appetites. She stayed composed in front of him, the way she was with everyone, the line lady and Leroy notwithstanding.

They had nowhere to go but her car. So they went and sat in her car.

"Is everything okay?" she said, turning on the engine and staring ahead at her comforting tombstones. Was it her imagination, or had some new ones popped up? She could swear there were more gray markers in the ground than last week.

"It's fine," he said curtly. After a silence that seemed to Larissa like someone stopping playing the piano because he couldn't figure out what the next note was, Kai continued, "You know—everything is not fine, but I really can't talk about it, so . . ."

"I understand." She wanted to tell him that Brian and Gary already mentioned a funeral, but there was no good way of explaining her reasons for dropping by his dealership when he wasn't there, and talking about him to not one but two men. She was silent because she herself couldn't figure out what the next note was.

"Everything okay at work?"

"I guess. Monday's my day off," he said, taking a gulp of coffee, then another, and staring at his open and untouched container of sushi.

Who had died? Was it his mother? He looked pale enough for it to be his mother. A friend of his? He had mentioned that he had to leave Hawaii because of stuff. Could this have something to do with that? Larissa was idly curious, slightly concerned, but mostly shamelessly relieved that he was back. A funeral in Hawaii seemed a long dry spell away from her current pool of calm water.

"How's the weather been here?"

Talk about small talk. "It's been pretty good," she replied. "A little chilly. It rained all weekend. What about Hawaii?"

"Same old, same old," he said. "Never changes. Eighty. Sunny. Windy in the afternoon."

"Sounds fantastic."

"I guess."

Oh, so now he didn't want to chit-chat even about the weather. They sat. The music played low, Alice Cooper, the Ramones.

Could she here deny the story that is printed in her blood? Leonato says to Friar Francis in *Much Ado*. Love conquered all, despite one's best intentions. What a lesson it would be for her young charges. Larissa had to go. She didn't want Michelangelo to worry.

"I just wanted to say I'm sorry." What she wanted was to touch him.

"For what?"

She said nothing. He said nothing. Then he groaned, in small restrained anguish. "Larissa," Kai said. The way he said it, her name had a din to it, like a song of the summer swallows, something deep that rolled off his tongue.

The name was a caress. *Larissa*, he caressed her with her own name. The rest of what he said was insignificant.

"It's not that I don't want to tell you. But trust me that the story is worse and more tawdry than you imagine, and there will be nothing for you to feel but pity, and the reason I don't want to tell you is because I don't particularly want your pity. Can you understand?" He didn't look away from her as he spoke. "It will seem like I'm trying to manipulate you with tragedy. And I don't want to do that."

"I understand. Don't worry. Just . . . take care of yourself."

"I might eventually tell you," he said.

"Eventually? Why not now, said the undertaker."

Kai half smiled, half didn't. "Funny. But I won't ever *feel* like telling you." He looked wretched when he said it.

"Does it have anything to do with why you left Hawaii in the first place?"

"Everything." He took his empty can, his uneaten sushi, opened the door. "Nice to see you again," he said.

"Yes, you too."

That was positively breaking the courtesy barrier! Larissa thought as she drove to pick up Michelangelo, the fingers gripping the wheel trembling from the tension.

7

Explanation of the Navigation

Next morning at 9:30 the phone rang. She was getting ready to drive to Pingry and debated not picking up, but the caller ID said, "Madison Jaguar Dealer". With all due haste she picked up.

"Larissa?" Kai said. Again!

"Yes, hello," she said. It set her blood coursing, his calling her house, like breaking and entering.

"Um, Brian just told me that your navigation system is in," he said. There was an amused glint to his voice. "Now, correct me if I'm wrong but I didn't know you needed a navigation system."

"I didn't think I did," said Larissa. "But it turns out I do."

"Do you remember me trying to sell it to you?"

"Yes. But I didn't know I needed it then."

"I see. Okey-dokey. When can you bring in the Jag so we can install it?"

"When is good?" She had to order twenty-five copies of the play and write up the audition notice. That would take some time, probably most of the morning.

"Now is good."

"Now?" Not twenty-four hours as director and already the play was interfering adversely in her life! She should've never accepted. Oh, hell. She would call Ezra, make nice, ask Sheila to order the books, and she'd write the casting notice this afternoon. What was one more day? "Yes, okay," she said to Kai in an even voice. "I'll bring it in."

"Thirty minutes?"

In twenty-eight Larissa was at the dealership. She brought her car to the back, walked through the service door, filled out some paperwork, signed on the dotted line, gave her credit card (what would Jared say when he found out that she bought a navigation system she didn't need for $2900?) and took her receipt.

"Nav will be ready this afternoon," said Brian. "You want one of my guys to give you a ride home?"

"No, that's okay, I'm fine today," Larissa said, keeping it succinct, her face impassive like her voice. She smiled.

Brian didn't even glance at her. She liked hiding behind the polite words. Everything so smooth, normal, even keel, not a prob, nothing to see here, folks, just passing through, like all wives who have work done on their cars. She strolled through the dealership, smiled at the idle business office guys, barely acknowledged Crystal, the snippy receptionist, and made her way to Kai's desk, where he was looking into a computer, drinking coffee and on the phone. Nodding to her, he pointed to the chair in front of him. She perched and waited. He was on the phone five minutes or more, searching for a car for a prospective client. The phone rang for him half a dozen times. The receptionist walked over to mouth to him there was another phone call waiting and he pantomimed to her to take a message. When he hung up, he faced her. "How you doing?"

"I'm good. You?"

"Busy like a bee. Dropped off your car?"

"Yep. Brian said it'd be ready this afternoon."

"For sure."

"If you're too busy, Brian said he can have one of his guys give me a ride home . . ."

Kai shook his head. "I *am* one of his guys." He grinned. "You ready?" He was less pale today. He took his keys. "I'll be back in ten," he called out to the business office crew, who were gawking at them in a way Larissa didn't appreciate.

"It's not you," Kai said. "They just love giving me a hard time."
He led her outside and around the corner. "I'm parked over here.
They keep torturing me that I never give the men a ride home."

"Is that true?"

Outside was warm and sunny. It was promising to be a good
spring. The Ducati was parked on the side of the white building.

"Perhaps," he replied with a shrug. "I admit I don't often have
men on the back of my bike behind me."

She looked at it. He looked at her.

"We're going on the bike?"

"It's the only wheels I got." He looked her over. She was wearing
jeans, boots, a leather jacket. She was certainly dressed for the bike.
He hopped on first, handing her his helmet. "You take it. I only
have the one."

It felt too loose on her head, and she couldn't get the strap
under her chin to close. Kai had to climb off the bike to help her.
Adjusting the helmet with both hands, he put his fingers under her
chin to clip the buckle shut. His face, tilted close and near her chin,
was clean-shaven, smiley, friendly. His breath smelled of coffee. "It's
going to mess up your hair," he said. "But you don't mind, right? You
hardly think about hair."

"Har-de-har-har."

He was back on the bike. "Hop on, and hold on," he said. "That's
the most important thing."

"The hopping, or the holding?"

"The holding."

She hopped on, like onto a horse, one leg over, the other in the
stirrup. She'd never been on a horse or a bike. She wanted to ask
him what she was supposed to hold on to; nothing to hold on to but
the rider and his leather. Larissa grabbed the sides of Kai's jacket.
Her knees were flanking his denim-clad legs. It was weird, too close,
inappropriate. She would never hop on the back of Gary's bike, or
Brian's, with his unwashed hair.

"You gotta hold on," Kai yelled to her, revving up the engine.
"Once I push off, you'll go flying if you don't grab on tighter."

"Well, don't push off, okay? Go very slow."

He pulled out onto Main Street and zoomed down the road. "Go slower!" she squealed, the wind whipping her hair under the helmet. She wasn't sure he could hear her.

"If I go any slower," he yelled back, "we'll lose our balance and fall off."

"God, why does it seem like a jet plane?" she said when he had stopped at a red light.

In response, he revved the idling engine. "Tell me where you live again."

She directed him as best she could with the road over his shoulder. She smelled the leather of his jacket. Not wanting him to ride through Summit where the owner of the Summit Diner and Ricky's Candy knew her, where all the gas station attendants, candy sellers, ice cream makers, shoe purveyors, dry cleaners could wave hi to her strapped to the back of a black and lava-bright Ducati Sportclassic, Larissa took him instead on a roundabout route, down Route 24 service road, avoiding town. She wasn't doing anything wrong, and yet she didn't want to ride through Summit with his helmet on her head. Because there was no difference in the *appearance* of things between wrong and right. Both looked exactly the same. A young man in a leather jacket and jeans, whizzing through a small suburban almost greening town on his flame Ducati, while a long-haired woman of a certain age, married with three children, a possible member of the Women's Junior League of New Jersey, was astride the back of his bike, both hands gripping his waist, her face close to his back, close to his jacket.

On the open road, he accelerated. She gasped for breath. For a moment Larissa saw herself from the heavens, from the blue sky, saw herself as the birds saw her, on the back of a bike behind a young man, her hair in a swirl, riding fast, near fresh April. The sensation of speed, of being unable to catch her breath, of danger, of exhilaration, of fear mingled with spring and sunshine, of the undeniable life-yell of Wow, made her miss her right turn on Summit and in a mile, or three, she had to nudge him to turn around. Another blazing moment behind his back.

Finally Kai turned onto Bellevue, coasted down the gentle slope, and Larissa saw herself once again as she was, not as she wished she might be, because he pulled into the driveway of her gray, black-shuttered house.

"You all right?" He eased to a stop behind her Escalade.

She got off the bike, took off his helmet. "Sure," she said, her face flushed from the speed, the wind.

Taking the helmet from her, Kai smiled infectiously. "There's nothing like it, is there? Maybe some other time I can take you behind town, near the Watchung reservation and the Deserted Village. Like we did with your Jag. I can burn some serious rubber on that road. The Ducati's nothin' but engine."

"See, the problem with you is you think *that's* a plus."

He laughed. "I'll call you when the nav's installed."

"If I'm not here, just leave a message."

"You want me to call you on your cell?"

"Oh. Uh—" A stutter. "Yeah. Sure." And just like that she gave him her cell number.

Her back was to the house, but she saw him eyeing it, top to bottom, the skyscraper trees, the ebony shutters, the volume, the breadth of it, taking it all in, the fresh gray paint and the red tulips lining the paved walk, the manicured sloping lawns, the decorative lamp posts. "So this is where you live." He whistled. "Wow."

"Thanks. We didn't always live here."

"I imagine not. You have to earn a lot of pennies to live in a place like this."

She assented silently.

"What does your husband do again?"

"He's the CFO of Prudential Securities."

Kai whistled again. "He must be pretty proud to live here."

Again she silently nodded. "He says the only way he's ever leaving this house is when they carry him out of it feet first."

Kai blinked approvingly. "And what about you?"

There was a second's pause. "Yes, me too, of course," she said quickly. "Where could you possibly go from here?"

"And, more important, why would you want to?" Kai started up his bike, revved his engine. "Listen to how secluded it is. My bike sounds like an airplane with the echo off the golf course. Hey, is that your mall across the highway?" Lightly he laughed. "That's *sweeeet*. Seeing the shopping possibilities from your sparkling windows." He raised his gloved hand in a goodbye. "I'll call when it's ready, 'kay?"

In the silence of her Bellevue life, Larissa heard his bike gunning it up the road away on Summit Avenue as she walked up her driveway and let herself into the empty house. Then she sat in her kitchen and waited. Not waited, just . . . sat in her house, clean, spic-and-span, at the island, cup of coffee in her hands, and tried to catch a glimpse of herself in the black granite, seeing only the glimpse of herself on a motorcycle at forty. She should go let Riot in from the backyard. She should start up the computer and compose the casting call notice. She should call Ezra. She should take the Escalade and drive to Pingry and order the books. She should . . .

The phone rang. It was Maggie: would Larissa like to grab some lunch? Instantly Larissa agreed. Anything to get her mind off things. She met Maggie in the parking lot of Neiman's.

"What, no Jag today?" Maggie's hair was colored, curly, dark red. She looked good after having recently been under the weather; she was even sporting some light makeup.

"Nah, the kids have stuff in the afternoon," replied Larissa, prodding her friend away from the truck. "Come on, I'm starved."

"I heard you're courting trouble," Maggie said, all twinkly and ironic, as they sat down in the checkered café.

"What do you mean?" Why did Larissa sound so shrill when she asked? Neiman's Café was empty. It was just the two of them and seven waiters.

"Ezra told me how you got into Leroy's grill and into Fred's. Well done."

Calm down, Larissa.

"So why'd you finally agree to do it?"

"Because your husband begged like a pauper. He didn't know how else to stop Leroy."

"No one can stop Leroy."

"Thank God differential equations are too hard for a ten-year-old." Larissa ordered squash soup and a Waldorf salad with grilled chicken. Maggie got a Neiman's sampler. While Maggie was ordering, Larissa surreptitiously glanced into her purse, to make sure the cell phone was on ring and not on silent.

"But are you really going to do *Much Ado About Nothing?*" Maggie shook her head.

"Yes, that's my compromise. Apparently I have to compromise. I wanted the airy *Comedy of Errors*. But no. I had seven naysayers. They insisted on something other than what I wanted. Well, fine. They got their way."

"But see, Ezra said Leroy and Fred don't want to do *Much Ado* anymore."

Larissa laughed deliciously. "Oh, they don't want to *do* it anymore! As I suspected. Then why'd they suggest it?"

"They said just to put something out there."

The monkey bread came; the girls dug in.

"I knew it," she said. "All that yackety-yak just to be contrary. Well, too late. And too bad. We're doing it."

They spent the rest of lunch talking about Bo, whose boyfriend, Jonny, was close to getting a job, and about Ezra, who was so overworked, with his three classes, running the English department and overseeing the theater department that the other day he actually forgot the name of his only child. "And I mean, forgot, Lar. He blanked at Dylan, as if he couldn't understand why this cranky drummer boy was in his house."

As they were paying, Larissa's cell phone rang. The caller ID read *Passani, K.*

"Hello?" Was he calling her from his cell phone and not from work?

"Hi. It's Kai."

"Hey." She fought the impulse to turn her back to Maggie so she wouldn't have to talk to him with her face showing.

"Car's ready," he said. "Are you going to be able to pick it up? I know school must be letting out soon."

"Yeah . . . and I'll have my son with me." She nodded to the waiter, to Maggie, to give her the receipt to sign, to leave a tip, to take her credit card, to close her purse, to get up, push the chair back, all the while on the phone with him.

"Well, look, how about I bring the car, and you two can give me a ride back. That okay?"

"That's okay." What else could she do? There was no way she could leave the car at the dealership overnight. What would she tell Jared? "On second thought, let me leave it overnight. I'll pick it up tomorrow. The kids have . . . things this afternoon."

"You sure? You don't need it?"

"I have my truck."

"Well, fine. I'll bring it to you in the morning then?"

She was about to say fine, all this with Maggie watching, listening—to everything! But then remembered she blew off theater today, and she couldn't not show up again tomorrow. "I've got stuff to do in the morning. Noon?"

They agreed he would bring the car to her house at noon. He had a good phone voice. Of course he did. Of course he would.

Larissa hung up without saying anything, Maggie's gaze interfering with her inane courtesies.

"Who was that?"

"Jag dealership." How nice and passive! "They installed a nav system."

"What do you need one of those for? Where do you go? Can't find your way to the mall, Lar?"

"Oh, *funny* today, Mags."

With the check paid, they traipsed across the black-and-white tiled floor.

"You didn't tell me your car was in the shop."

"It's not like it's *in* the shop. Nothing's wrong with it."

"So why didn't you tell me about the nav earlier when I asked where your car was?"

Larissa sped up. If she wasn't able to answer Maggie's questions, how in the world was she going to answer Jared's?

∞⌒∞

"You bought *what?*" said Jared, setting down his dinner fork, which signaled the heightened level of his commitment to the conversation.

Larissa shrugged—her most nonchalant shrug. "The car was supposed to come with it. We got a model without it. But it's *supposed* to have it."

Jared was silent. "Larissa, it's not what the car is supposed to have. It's not whether or not you need it."

"What is it then?" she said casually, her pleasant face on, the smile at her lips.

"It's that you would, could, spend three thousand dollars of our money without even bringing it up in a five-second conversation first."

"I know. I'm sorry about that. Honest, that was a mistake on my part. It was an impulse buy. I'd gone in for service, and then ordered it on the spot without even asking Brian how much it cost. I thought it would only be a few hundred bucks. By the time they installed it and I paid for it, I was as shocked as you, believe me, but I was already in for a penny."

"Three hundred thousand pennies."

"I know."

"Do you have the receipt?"

"I do. It's in my bag. You want to see it?"

"I don't want to *see* it, but I do need it for our records." His eyes were on her, not blinking. "Who did you buy it from?"

"What?"

"Who did you order the system from?"

"Brian, I told you."

"Who's Brian?"

"The service guy in the back."

"Not Chad?" He paused. "Not Kai?"

"Never got to the front of the dealership, honey. I'm really sorry." She smiled sweetly. "Jared, I know it's a lot of money to spend all at once, but strictly speaking, what's the difference between spending it all in one gulp, and buying four or five pairs of shoes or boots, which I do all the time without calling you up on the phone, interrupting your board meetings, saying, sweetie, I saw this awesome pair of Gucci's; do you mind?"

To Jared's credit, he mulled that one over. "The difference," he said at last, "is of degree. It's too much, it seems out of the ordinary."

He was right. That's what it was. Out of the ordinary.

⟳⟲

Larissa rushed to Pingry in the morning to sit with Sheila and Leroy and line by line edit *Much Ado* down to high school production size, chewing the pencil between her teeth, mindful of the time, ten, eleven, nearly noon.

"I gotta run, guys," she finally said.

"But we're not done!"

"Can you finish up? You have some very good ideas. Just a couple of things: Sheila, don't cut too many of Don Pedro's lines; he is after all the conscience of the play. And Leroy, same goes for Benedick, who is the hero. Even in a comedy that role is given some prominence."

"Um, did I cut something you didn't want me to?" asked Leroy, sensing a rebuke.

"I'm thinking you should probably keep the line when Benedick says, *All hearts in love speak their own tongue*," Larissa said with a smile, counting out the beats before she could bound out of doors. "But otherwise you're doing great. See you tomorrow." *My merry day isn't long enough despite what Shakespeare says*, she thought, seeking comfort in math, 5.2 miles in twelve splendid minutes.

She was a few minutes past crisp and windy March noon when

she found her Jag in the drive, but Kai not in it. Did he leave already? She saw the back gate by the garage ajar and when she walked around the side of the house to the back, she found Kai chasing Riot all over her yard.

"He was barking at me," Kai said, running up to her, panting. "I petted him, but he clearly had other things in mind. Not a very ferocious dog, is he?"

"No, *she* isn't," said Larissa. "She is a mashed potato. She would show you to the good silver if we had any."

"Come on," he said, even the whites of his teeth teasing her, "you must, in that house. What's her name anyway?"

"Riot. Like you, we thought she was a boy."

Riot was bumping Kai's knees with her head, having brought the three-foot stick back. Kai wrested it away, threw it for her, and then chased her across the yard, yelling, "Riot! Give it! Give it back!" It was Riot's favorite game. Pretending to fetch the stick and then being chased by a human for it. She could play it all day. How did Kai instinctively know this? Seeing him run after her dog in her back yard, like a carefree kid, filled Larissa with a troubling heaviness on this blustery day, like the new leaves were clogging up the drains of her heart.

"Hey, you want a lemonade?" Did she even have lemonade?

"How about ice water?"

She left him with Riot and went into her kitchen. As she fixed him a glass, she watched him from the window. There was such young joy in his movements.

He came in flushed and perspiring. "What am I going to do with my shirt?" he said. "I look like I've been rolling in it."

He took the drink from her hands, gulped it down, chewed the ice. "We never had a dog," he said. "We lived in an apartment; hard to keep a dog in the apartment. But I love dogs."

"Clearly they also enjoy your company." Riot was standing on her back paws at the door, banging on the screen with her front paws, as if to say, *Get back out here, wimp.*

"What a great dog." Kai drummed on the counter, looking around Larissa's kitchen.

She stood in her quiet house, around her clean black granite and white cabinets and watched him get his work face back. He was usually so composed; now suddenly he was panting. There was something vulnerably undeniably human about it.

"Well, the nav looks pretty good. Have you seen it?"

"No, I came straight in the back."

"You want me to show you how to use it?"

"Sure."

"Come," he said. "Because I've got to start heading back. I have an appointment at one. What time is it?"

"Twelve-thirty."

"Yeah, I gotta run. Normally I don't schedule anything for lunch, but this is a sure sale, the widowed sixty-year-old man wants to buy a Jag for his thirty-year-old girlfriend."

"Isn't that a bit of an overkill?"

Kai grinned naughtily. "How else," he said, "is he going to get her to sleep with him?"

And in the afternoon Larissa stood in front of the mirror in the front hall, staring severely into her face, into her eyes, while the ice cream melted in the plastic bags, still in the trunk of her Jag. A small thing that might eventually be noticed by the discerning youngest members of her family, those who enjoyed eating ice cream. Mom, they might say, why does the ice cream always taste like it's been melted and refrozen? Why are you bringing home melted ice cream? How long is the drive from King's, Mom? Isn't it just four minutes? Does ice cream melt this fast? What are you doing with your afternoons that you need to keep standing in front of the mirror while our precious ice cream turns to heavy cream?

One thing Larissa did not do as the ice cream pooled on her Jaguar floor was write to Che. *Dear Che, help me.* How do I extricate myself from this awful thing I'm falling into, a thing made geometrically more awful by the stark truth of it: I don't even write you this so-called letter asking for instructions on self-extrication. I rationalize it away like a college grad, a slightly mocking adult who can reason. I say, how in the world is Che going to help *me*? She can't even help herself with Lorenzo. That's what I *say*. But the real reason I can't write to you is because I don't want to, and that's worse even than sitting in the car, the knowledge of my unashamed and actualized self. I *know* that all I want is for one o'clock to come, to be upon me faster, so I can see his face, so I can hear his laughing, teasing voice speak to me I don't even know of what—masonry? Luxury cars? Funerals? I don't know. I don't care. I barely listen. Sitting next to him is what I listen to. The leather and Dial soap and denim smell of him in my car, twenty, unmarried, childless. When I look at him, I'm not in the middle of my life but at the very beginning, one of the Great Swamp Revue traveling Jersey in search of a stage, a joke, a performance, something real amid the illusion, or is it an illusion amid all things real? The Jersey Footlight Players is what I am part of again, putting on quite a show on that stage that's the driver seat of my Winter Gold Jag, and that's the sordid *why* I haven't written you since February. I'm afraid that in my shallow words you will hear the profound truth of what's happening to me. I'm drawing away from you as I'm drawing nearer the black chasm that's got him in it, slowly realizing, reluctantly admitting that he is the only thing I want.

8

Auditing Safeguards

The navigation purchase did not ease its way into Jared's full comprehension over the next few days, and on Saturday night, when they had gathered with their friends for dinner at the house, Jared brought it up again.

Maggie immediately exclaimed, "Jared! That's what I said to her! Explain yourself, Larissa, to your friends and your husband. It makes no sense."

"Why *do* you need a nav system, Lar?" asked Ezra.

"It. Was. An. Impulse. Buy." Larissa shot Jared a look that she hoped conveyed that if he wanted a woman tonight it would have to be one other than his wife.

"I understand," said Ezra. "But it's like you listening to someone else's stage direction. It's just so out of character."

"Perhaps I'm playing a different character."

She and Jared had a fight instead of sex that Saturday night. Larissa was upset with him for embarrassing her, and he said, "Embarrassing *you*? Well, let me ask you, how do you think I feel when Ezra says to me earlier tonight, hey man, can't believe your wife finally agreed to direct the spring play?"

"So? You're *embarrassed* by that?"

"Not by that!" he shouted. Jared never shouted. "But you never told *me*."

Why did she look so surprised by this? As if she hadn't realized she hadn't told him. "It just happened, Jared. It wasn't like I was keeping it from you. It happened two days ago. Three."

"It happened on Monday, and today is Saturday—night—and this is the first conversation you and I are having about it."

"If you can call this a conversation."

"It's more words than we've had about it for a week!"

"A couple of days!"

"Stop it, Larissa. I know when I'm being bullshitted."

"Jared, you were home late on Monday, on Tuesday we had Emily's cello, on Wednesday, I don't even know. I wasn't hiding it." She stammered a little, then recovered.

"Did it slip your mind?"

"Yes. It slipped my mind. What's the big deal?"

"Larissa, what's the big *deal*? It's only been the sole topic of conversation between you and Ezra the past two months."

"Come on, not the sole topic . . ."

"Ezra didn't tell it to me like it was news," Jared said. "He mentioned it to me, as in, isn't it great that Larissa is doing this. Why would you not tell me?"

"I forgot!"

"You forgot? Like you forgot to tell me about the nav system?"

"Oh, cut it out! Just stop it. I didn't tell you because I thought you'd be upset, okay? We had decided I wouldn't take the position, and then I did."

"So which is it, Larissa? Did it slip your mind, or did you deliberately not tell me? Let's not mix up the lamest of your excuses."

She breathed in and out deeply, like she was training for a scene. "You're upset."

"You're so observant. Why didn't you talk to me about it first?"

"You told me to take the play if I wanted to! Remember? Those were your words. Take it if you want, Lar. Now suddenly I have to call you on Monday morning about it!"

"You could've told me Monday night, no?"

"No! Leroy was about to cast auditions for *Godot*! It was an emergency."

"What does that have to do with Monday night?"

"Immediate action was required."

"Immediate action, yes. But immediate secrecy?"

"Oh, for God's sake! What are you more upset by, Jared? That I agreed to do it, or that I didn't tell you?"

"So many things I can't name them all."

"Which one would you like to deal with first?"

"None of them, Larissa. Not a single fucking one." And then a second later: "How about this one? Why would you keep these things a secret from me?"

"How can it be a secret? I was the one who told you!"

"Not about the play."

"No," she conceded. "But about the nav."

"Oh, so now we're parsing our secrecy, are we?"

"Oh God!"

"And you could hardly keep the nav hidden, could you?"

"I had no intention of keeping it hidden!"

"Your car," Jared continued, "was not in the garage when I came home. You had to 'splain that one somehow. And now you're going to be spending all your time at Pingry. What do you intend to do with our children?"

"Do not be so melodramatic. I have Sheila, I have Leroy. Fred, Ezra. I have my line reader. We'll be fine."

"Fine and dandy. You'll know how to get to Pingry. You'll have your navigation system, won't you?"

❧

Without resolution Jared was confounded all Sunday. He felt as if there was a piece of the puzzle he was missing, but he didn't know what the piece was. He didn't even know there had been a puzzle! Now suddenly there were missing pieces in it. What was the thing that grated on him, in the scheme of things, in the whole tapestry? He didn't care if Larissa decided to direct a play. If it worked out, great. And he didn't really care about the nav system, though he certainly didn't think it was money well spent. But if she wanted it, then she should have it. No, there was something else niggling him, feeling not right to him. Was it something about Larissa, something about her boots? No. Her jeans? No. Her made-up face, her styled hair? Her smile, the details of the hastily prepared dinner, of Michelangelo's drawing lying on the floor in the mud room instead of being hung up on the fridge? Something wasn't quite right . . . like a razor blade in Jell-O.

But then on Monday, Prudential's second quarter results showed a drop in revenue of twelve percent, and Jared spent the day going over every department's budget after a directive to cut costs by a commensurate twelve percent; the conservation of assets required his direct participation in every facet of revenues, expenditures, and payroll and took his every available brain molecule. To implement the short-range goal of resolving the unknowable mystery that was his complicated yet complete marriage to Larissa required strategy and planning, but all week he developed projects and programs that lowered the operating costs of a multi-billion-dollar business. Analyzing cash flow and pinpointing weak investment product lines took all his time and his mental resources. A week passed.

The second week was all about the auditing safeguards. With the personal tax liability deadline looming, he stayed at work till seven or eight at night to enact guidelines that would make an audit by the Treasury Department not frightening but welcome. He welcomed the transparency of a more streamlined organization, the diversification of the company's assets into other ventures around New Jersey that masked some of the heavy tax burden the company was carrying. This was no small undertaking. And no one knew New Jersey's financial regulatory statutes better than Jared. The company depended on him and he would not let them down. By the time the crisis at work was averted—by him—and costs were brought under control, he tried once again to reach for the bug that had niggled him, but it was gone. And at home, Larissa was her old smiling, cooking, pleasant self, the kids were dressed, homework was done, chores, TV, everything ticked along smoothly. It was just an aberration, Jared said to himself, after she had apologized yet again for forgetting to tell him about the play, about the stupid navigation. He had been anxious about other things and took it out on her. Filled with remorse, he had bought her something extra beautiful for her birthday on April 4, a white gold necklace with her name etched in diamonds. "Does this mean we have to give the car back?" she said. "Because technically you already gave me a birthday present."

Three weeks later on a glittering Saturday night in late April he drove her in her Jag to a belated celebration dinner in New York. Maggie, Ezra, Evelyn, Malcolm, Bo and Jonny met up with them. They reserved a round table in the middle of Union Square Café like knights of the Algonquin. It was a raucous, loud evening, and it wouldn't be a get-together between old friends if there weren't a passionate altercation about one thing or another. This time it was about altruism. But before altruism, Ezra proclaimed that Larissa was doing a bang-up job with *Much Ado*; once again, another tinge of remorse for Jared. There he was yelling at her, while the kids at home and at school adored her. He made a mental note to be nicer to her, to cut her some slack. Look how beautiful she was, with the diamond necklace, her face young and gleaming, laughing at some stupid thing Ezra said, or Malcolm, quoting verbatim from Shakespeare, her long hair shiny, silky, all of her shiny, silky. She didn't look forty, that was for sure, as her melodious soft alto sang counterpoint to the tune of Ezra's argumentative reasoned tenor.

"Is that what you want to be?" Ezra was saying. "An altruist? You don't believe you have any right to exist for your own sake, for the sake of existing? Must you only find value in your own existence by becoming a slave to someone else's? Why is everything about self-sacrifice? You are not an animal, Larissa, why are you acting like a burnt offering? And why do I suspect you're just being a devil's advocate? Don't smile. I know I'm right. What about *you*? Have you got no intrinsic value of your own? No worth inherent to you simply by the virtue of your own existence?"

Malcolm intervened. Malcolm loved to intervene. He had a mustache that he twirled, a disagreeable gesture that was very good for intervening. "But, Ezra," said Malcolm, twirling the fervent brown 'stache, making Larissa laugh from across the table, "Ezra, you're talking nonsense, no?"

"No!"

"Wait." Malcolm took the hand away from his face to raise it patiently to an excited Ezra. "You *have* to help other people. We are a community, this is what makes us a civilization."

"Oh, please. Community is just a way for people to judge you. Doesn't it matter what else you've done? You could've created the wireless radio. The wheel. The guy who spends all his time watching rabbits mate, you think he's doing it for civilization? Or the guy who sits in a dank room pining after his dead child and writes a bitter treatise on the randomness of the beginning of life, changing the course of civilization—why didn't they tell him to serve in a soup kitchen? The man thought organic matter could grow from inorganic things! Do we judge him? Civilization has always moved forward on the backs and with the sweat of those who recognized their internal needs as equally worthy of the community's needs. *More* worthy."

"Why can't you do both?" Maggie piped up.

"That's a woman's answer," said Ezra, looking at his wife with frank affection.

"Why can't you do neither?" asked Larissa.

Ezra laughed. "That's a Romantic's answer," he replied. "Is that what you are?"

"A woman *can* do both," Maggie persisted.

"A woman can't!" Ezra exclaimed. "From ancient times, the woman has made the choice that subservience for the greater good is more important than her own interests. You know this to be true, for biological reasons, for sociological reasons. Which is why women are to be found almost nowhere in the progress of civilization. Women defend the status quo. The nest. The offspring. Women have given themselves over to this purpose."

"Yet without women all life would come to a grinding halt."

"I'm not saying you don't serve a purpose, Mary-Margaret," Ezra said solemnly.

"Women have made a *choice* to do this, to take care of their young!" Maggie said. "Because it is for the ultimate good of mankind—so that bastards like you could spend all their time reading idiotic books and playing with your test tubes." Maggie scored major points with the two women at the table.

"Yes," said Ezra with amusement. "It *is* for the good of mankind. But what about the good of the woman?"

"Yes, for the good of her, too, Ezra," said Evelyn. "Larissa and I were discussing this just the other day, right, Larissa?"

"Right, Ev."

"*Women are saved through childbirth*," said Evelyn, smiling, with Larissa blinklessly nodding.

"Exactly," said Ezra. "But you know why they can be saved? Because someone else hunts and gathers. Someone has to get up each morning, slog to work, deal with people he doesn't like, do crap things, answer to crap bosses, make boring phone calls, attend numbing meetings. Right, Jared?"

"I know you love to mock what I do, Professor," said Jared, "but I run the finances of a company that has global assets totaling $485 billion." Malcolm whistled. Evelyn looked at him impressed. Maggie glared at Ezra with a "pwned!" expression. Bo glared at her Jonny as if to say, why can't you get a damned job, even as a dishwasher? Only Larissa was playing with the umbrella in her Sangria and didn't look up. "We have thirty-five thousand employees," continued Jared. "That's a lot of men and women I pay who hunt and gather for their families. I'm not even talking about all the money instruments we offer so an English teacher like you can put Dylan through college. That's got to be worth something, isn't it, Ezra?"

"It is," Ezra assented. "Because of that, your wife is home. Larissa bakes, which smells good and tastes delicious. She takes care of your offspring, most of whom I assume you love because they do not bang the drums at two in the morning. Larissa, tell us—to take care of things you love, is there slog in that?"

"There is no slog, Ezra," agreed Larissa, drink thoroughly stirred.

"But, Ezra," said Maggie, "you were just arguing that the woman is a more pathetic creature than man because she lives to serve other people. Yet you paint man as also serving, except serving those he doesn't love. So who's got the better life?"

"Without a doubt, the woman," said Ezra, and they all laughed. Voices calmed down, emotions ran slower, Jared poured more red wine, the music overhead switched to reggae jazz, quite the combo. When Jared glanced at Larissa sitting on his right, the smile was frozen on her porcelain face, her white teeth as if in a lion's grimace, her made-up eyes glazed by—drink? And then she spoke in a non-sequitur. She said: *"We can do it on a sunny floor . . . Roll on our backs screaming with mirth, glad in the guilt of our madness."*

Ezra and Malcolm looked at her blankly, but Jonny went ooooh, ain't Lar so fly quoting Morrison, because Jonny was a music freak and knew everything, and Evelyn responded by quoting Chesterton, and then Walker Percy. They had been talking about the angst of life, or perhaps the emptiness of living only for yourself, or what it meant to be a working man, a working woman, to be parents . . . and suddenly the little bug Jared had been searching for crawled out from wherever it was hiding, on Jim Morrison's back, dragging the navigation system and the play and the secrets with it, because in the twenty years he had known Larissa, she had never quoted Morrison. Ever. And tonight, *voilà*, a whole punctuation-ridden sentence, like a bawdy limerick, straight from the Lizard King's mouth. Were The Doors and Shakespeare in any way related? But he couldn't ask because the moment had passed. The waiter brought the cake, and it was her birthday celebration, after all—he didn't want to seem churlish—and in the car Larissa slept, having drunk too much, and Jared drove home with the radio on, and of course, what else playing . . . *Of our elaborate plans, the end, of everything that stands, the end . . .*

⤜⤐

"I never heard you quote Morrison before," he said to her that night in bed. "What made you quote him?"

And she replied, her back to him, "I'm reading *Wonderland Avenue*. A memoir by Danny Sugerman. You should read it; it's the most fascinating book."

"I don't read about Morrison. I'm not a fan," Jared said. "He is too self-indulgent."

"Who? No."

"Oh, it's all so beautiful and lyrical," continued Jared. "He free verses, he rhymes, he combines death and thighs, Mexico and storms. What does it mean? Ultimately he's got no philosophy to hang your Mexican hat on. He's just a gifted stoner, being pretentiously superficial."

"He's not pretentious—what are you talking about?"

"Who's going to read Jim Morrison and say, ooh, man, that shit changed the course of my life? He doesn't make a lick of sense. He's about nothing. But unlike Seinfeld, he's not even remotely funny."

Larissa remained silent, her back to him.

"You know why?" Jared went on. "Because there's no there there. At its heart it's empty. It's shallow. Because in the end it's nothing more than drug-addled lunacy."

"Well, *I* like him," Larissa said. "Why does everything have to be profound? Why can't it just be?"

"Yes, but what does it *mean?*"

"Why does it have to mean anything?"

"If it doesn't mean anything, then why write it?"

"Why do anything?"

"Good question. Morrison himself said all he wanted to do was to fuck away death." Jared smirked. "How'd that turn out for him?"

Larissa had no response.

And on Monday Jared became mired in managed money and retirement accounts, and a pesky variable annuity that involved a

nearly insolvent commercial real estate account in Hoboken. There
was no time to think about the guilt of her madness.

It wasn't a question of him reading *Wonderland Avenue*. The only
thing Jared had been reading the last eight years of his life were the
Generally Accepted Accounting Principles, the annual reports of the
Fortune 500 companies, and the templates for auditing safeguards.
By keenly analyzing the relationship between regulation, quality
attributes, and diversification, Jared was sure he could keep at
bay that most undesirable of events, a tax audit—an unwelcome
intrusion by the public into your private business.

Chapter Four

1
Glad in the Guilt

Larissa was crushed against the hard white wall and her hands were up, perhaps around his neck, or flayed against the wall, like she was flayed, her gasping coming out in hot bursts of disbelief and ardor. One of his hands cupped her face as he kissed her, and the other . . . she was pawed, her dress, her arms, her hips; he raised her dress, put his hand under it, and if she breathed out, she wouldn't know because his lips were on her, and she lost her head, everything was lost but the hand under her dress, his full palm pressing against her. She wanted to put her own hands up but not in surrender, perhaps in a maybe; say wait, too fast, not fast enough, say, I have to go, though not yet, move away from his lips? though moving away from his lips was impossible, or moving away from his fingers and his spread out hand under her whimsical spring dress, so when she moaned, she moaned into his mouth, barely able to stand up, clutching him as he was panting. *Oh, Larissa*, he whispered, touching her; with his body he stopped her from falling, he just kept her pinned and confined, his tongue in her moaning mouth, his relentless fingers troubling her into a climax so unexpected and intense, she was condensed to sliding down onto the wooden floor while he kneeled down close by her, rubbing her thigh in earnest comfort, though there was no comfort for her.

"Oh my God, Larissa," he whispered. "Come on the bed."

Kai, I have to go, she mouthed back, her eyes shut in shame and desire. She couldn't believe what had just happened. *What time is it?*

"Please. Just for a sec."

Time was the damper—the worry that her belated appearance at her child's school might ring off a bell into the world, a warning signal she needed desperately to tamp down. Damper: a device to control vibration. His hands were trying to be dampers, pressing down on her legs. But her body was not cooperating. She was vibrating.

"You don't want to go, do you?" he whispered, on the floor next to her, his mouth in her neck, on her shoulder.

It's two o'clock.

He glanced at his watch. "Two fifteen."

"Kai!" Scrambling up, her knees liquid, her insides molten, she didn't look at him, couldn't look at him as she gathered herself together, straightened her dress, got her purse and keys that had fallen, her lipstick.

"I wish you didn't have to go," he said. It was Thursday.

"I know." She held onto his forearm, his bare arm that had just been unfathomably wrapped around her.

He drew her back inside, into his arms. "What are we going to do?" he groaned. "I can't . . . I need . . ."

"I know. But I have to go. Please . . ."

"Larissa . . ." Kai murmured in daylight, like a song, as he kissed her.

The aching nerves like twitching live wire, the aching insides full of fire and longing, the intemperate blinding desire to stay—nothing but the smallness of a waiting child could have made any woman take a step away from a man *that* inflamed, with lips that impassioned, his whole body begging her to stay.

"Tomorrow I'm supposed to work in Chatham till noon at the masonry yard, and then be at Jag by two."

"And I'm casting through lunch."

"I'll call in sick," he said, his hands squeezing tight her waist. "Come in the morning. Come," he whispered. "Promise?"

She was out the door and down the stairs. Down thirteen wooden steps, into her two-seater, reversing out of the drive, trying not to glance up at him standing at his open door.

2

A Dance to Lighten the Heart

In movies, Larissa knew, right after this moment—there was nothing. She walked down the stairs, drove off, and the film director cut to—

Cut to what? The next day, the next breath, the hands on her bare body, lying on his white bed, cut to the following afternoon. But this wasn't a movie. This was her life. There was nothing to cut to.

Gripping the wheel with both hands, afraid she would get into an accident, Larissa drove extra carefully five miles to her son's school, parking just as the first grade teachers were escorting their backpacked charges outside. She ruffled her son's hair, said hello to three other moms, including Donna, whom she forced herself to talk to for ten minutes even though her swollen mouth couldn't remember English and her ears certainly didn't understand a word of Donna's. But inside a forethought was forming: I may need her. I might be late one day, I may need her . . . And just as she was thinking this, and willing herself to smile, to nod, Michelangelo, standing somberly nearby, eating his fruit snack, pulled on her hand and said, "Mom, don't think I didn't notice you were almost late again today."

"Son, but I wasn't late. Almost late means not late."

"I know. But you *almost* were," said an unperturbed and

disapproving Michelangelo. "You've been coming almost late a lot lately."

Donna, pleasant and without makeup, smiled knowingly, lifted her eyebrows, and made some kind of joke—wittily, or so she thought—insinuating possible reasons for Larissa's tardiness, and Larissa right then and there knew she wouldn't be able to use Donna again to look after her way too precocious son. They didn't stay at the playground but came home instead, where they had an hour before Emily's bus. In that hour, Larissa put Michelangelo in front of her TV in the master bedroom and reluctantly took a shower. She didn't *want* to take a shower, she knew a shower would wash off the scent of her fevered trembling, and yet she *had* to take a shower.

When she came out, Michelangelo, splayed on her bed, paused Cartoon Network. "Mom," he said, "why did you just have a shower in the middle of the day?"

"Because I needed one." That was the truth.

"Why did you need one? What did you do?"

"Nothing. I was running around and got sweaty. What did *you* do?" She toweled off her hair.

"Weird, Mom. Freaky." He turned to the TV, pressing PLAY.

Larissa glanced at her watch: 3:15. What in the world was she going to do? How was the day ever going to pass? She couldn't imagine the next sixty seconds passing without collapsing, convulsing.

At 3:35 Emily arrived, inhaled a handful of grapes and a yogurt, ran upstairs, changed her clothes, ran downstairs, grabbed her cello and said let's go. Michelangelo reluctantly had to come with them. He was enjoying lying on his parents' bed. That was a treat he didn't usually get after school. After she dropped off Emily for her New Jersey State School Music Evaluation rehearsals, Larissa waited for Asher to come to the parking lot from track and tell her he was running ten miles in a row today and to pick him up not a second after 5:00 p.m.

She and Michelangelo came home, Maggie called. Larissa talked to her for five seconds. "What's the matter with you?" said Maggie. "Are you even listening to me?"

"Sorry, Michelangelo is pulling on me. I gotta go, Mags, gotta do homework."

After she hung up, she called into the den. "Hey, bud, let's go, let's do some spelling, turn off the TV."

At 4:30, they drove to pick up Emily, and then whiled time away in the car, listening to music, until Asher came out all wet and sweaty from the field behind the school promptly at five. "Mommy was sweaty today too, Ash," said Michelangelo after his brother got into the car. "She had to have a shower."

"Thanks, bud, for telling everyone about my day," said Larissa. She was sure Jared would hear about her impromptu shower.

By the time they got back home it was 5:20, and she started dinner: steak and French fries. At 6:20 p.m. Jared walked through the door. "You smell clean," he said after he kissed her.

"That's 'cause Mommy had a shower today." Michelangelo jumped into his father's arms.

"Did she?" Jared studied her bemusedly, moving his head away from his son's face.

"So I can be nice and clean for you, darling," said Larissa with a twinkle in her eye, prompting Jared to set down Michelangelo and usher him out of the kitchen.

"Come here, you naughty girl," he said, motioning to her.

But the steaks were grilling and had to be turned over, and the ill-timed fries were starting to burn, and the broccoli was soggy and unboiling. Impromptu sex after an impromptu shower was barely averted.

They ate, noisily, talked about track, cello, the spelling test, Spanish vocabulary, the meaning of alternating current, the plans for a new mall only twenty miles away in Orange County, the possibility of taking an adult theater class at Drew, and then Larissa looked at her watch, and it was 7:15 p.m. and there was still an evening and a night and a morning.

She offered to clean up without Jared. "Go, change your clothes, get yourself comfortable. You've had a long day. Go on."

He kissed her in gratitude and left her alone in the messy

kitchen. The kids played their instruments, did their homework, there was a fight over TV viewing privileges, and Stephen Marley on the kitchen stereo singing, *Hey Baby, hey, baby* . . . Bo called to invite them out to dinner Saturday night.

After Jared came downstairs he said they were going out Saturday night with visiting clients of his, here from California, and couldn't. "This is tax time, and we're having people from all over. Sorry. Reschedule with Bo, will you? Wait, let me call her. I have to make your birthday plans anyway. Is dinner in the city at the end of April okay? You know how crushed I am right now. It's tax time."

"Of course, darling. Whatever works best for you. We'll go out when you're less busy."

He left the kitchen to confirm birthday plans with Bo at the Union Square Café, and when he returned he said, looking puzzled at the counter, "Lar, did you . . . did you just wash all the dishes from dinner?"

Larissa hadn't realized she had. Instead of just rinsing them and putting them in the dishwasher, she had washed them by hand, polished and dried them.

"I'm feeling nostalgic for the old days," she explained with a light smile. "In Hoboken. When we didn't have a dishwasher. It's nice actually. Relaxing."

"Now suddenly it's nice and relaxing," said Jared. "Back then you called it hell."

"What did I know then of heaven and hell, Jared?" said Larissa, looking for something to dry her wet hands.

"I told you Mom was weird," said Michelangelo, hanging on to his dad. "Come, I want to show you my new karate chop." Jared said he couldn't wait and they left.

Larissa finished spraying the countertops, making a shopping list for tomorrow. After *all* the work was done, she looked at her watch: 8:01!

Another excruciating, slow-ticking hour inched by while she gave Michelangelo a purple-colored bath with bubbles. Somehow, by 9:30 the children were in their rooms, the little one asleep, the big ones reading. Larissa made herself a cup of tea, slowly walked from the kitchen to the den and perched down on the arm of the sofa. *When* would this day be over? *When* would the next day begin?

Jared came out of his office. "Sorry. I have so much work to do."

"It's okay, honey," she said. "I know it's tax season."

"Do you want to do something?"

They settled into the couch. The lights were dimmed through the house, the shades were drawn. Riot was chewing on what Larissa hoped was one of her toys and not Larissa's leather sandal. They watched *The Mexican*. Larissa didn't register a frame of it. Jared fell asleep twenty minutes in. She didn't wake him, but covered him, and as he slept, she sat next to him watching the TV screen, the eyes of her soul watching her being pinned over and over and over again against the wall, and then collapsing on the hardwood floor.

11:15.

11:32.

12:09.

Kai had forgotten his wallet. Larissa had to pay for the sushi, not that she minded. After they had finished eating he asked if she would mind giving him a lift to his place so he could get his wallet and his bike.

Oh, sure. No prob. No problem at all.

One turn off Main onto Cross, a left on Kings, a right on a road called Samson, and then into a rectangular loop residential road called Albright Circle, one of the oldest streets in the neighborhood, a block away from the train tracks that ran through Madison. He asked her to pull into a courtyard-sized driveway at the back of an old three-story clapboard house painted yellow. The driveway was a gravel parking lot, with enough room for a Mafia wedding. There was a detached garage, where she guessed he must keep his bike. She was right because he slid open the garage door and pulled the Ducati out. On the grass nearby Larissa spotted two cars on cinderblocks and a truck with its cab burned out. "I think the landlady's son does something with them," Kai told her, replacing the kickstand and grabbing his helmet. "He either fixes them up and sells them, or else he's the one doing the damaging. To this day I can't tell."

"Have you met him?"

"Oh, yeah." Kai grinned. "It can go either way." He started walking to the back of the yellow house to a long white wooden staircase that led to a white deck on stilts.

"It's nice here," Larissa said, walking across the gravel, following him. "Quiet." He was wearing light jeans, a black shirt and a dark gray sports jacket today. He had such a long-gaited, assured step, yet he bounced a little as he walked, like an adolescent.

"Yeah, quiet, except every twelve minutes the entire house rumbles as the New Jersey Transit train rolls past, blowing its horn. Every twelve minutes. It's enough to drive you mad." He threw his helmet in the air, caught it like a basketball. "Come up for a sec," he said. "I'm on the top floor. You want a glass of water?"

"Um, sure."

They walked up the steps. "I do like it here, though," Kai said. "The old lady doesn't bother me; her rooms are in the front. There was a tenant downstairs but he left; that could've been her son, so either he left, or . . ."—Kai raised his eyebrows as he turned around to glance at her—"he was taken."

"You should be a writer, Kai," she said. "Your imagination keeps running away with you."

"Don't it just?" They reached the deck. "Anyway, she lets me play my music, doesn't complain too much. It could be because she's deaf. Every time I speak to her, all she says in reply is, 'Yes, dearie.' I'll be a week late with my rent, Mrs. Sinesco. 'Yes, dearie.' I'm going to hold a Satanic Mass in your backyard, Mrs. Sinesco. 'Yes, dearie.'"

Larissa laughed.

He unlocked his door. "Come in," he said. "Hope it's clean." Tentatively she stepped in behind him.

"It's such a beautiful day," he said, taking his wallet from a small table in the front hall. "Hey, you want to go for a ride?" He smiled. "I'll take you to Glenside. Come on, what do you say? For, like, fifteen minutes. I'll find you another helmet. I've got a spare in my closet."

"For what, a spare head?" she muttered. "You know what I mean? If you lose the one helmet you've got, I'm thinking, chances are you're probably not going to be in any position to rummage around your closet for the spare."

He laughed, striding across the studio to the fridge. "So is that a yes or a no?"

She stood at the open door in a short entryway that led to a large light room on the top floor where he lived. It looked like an attic conversion, with vaulted ceilings and exposed whitewashed truss beams. With her hand still on the doorknob, she could see three walls of the studio, the fourth hidden from her view. He didn't have much furniture but his books were neatly stacked on the floor around his one overfilled bookcase. He had a soft-looking couch across from the TV and an efficiency kitchen with a small round table next to the window near the fridge. She imagined him eating his Corn Flakes in the morning, looking outside. He had two blue guitars perched near the couch, an acoustic and an electric. He had two ukuleles next to them, and two amps by the wall. She saw a stereo but no computer.

The bed had white sheets and a gray quilt and two pillows plus one large square one for leaning against the wall if he wanted to sit up since there was no headboard. He had one nightstand, on it four books and a lamp, and another ukulele propped up against the bed. His plankwood floors looked swept and clean with one small area rug under the coffee table. There were four tall windows, two flanking the bed and two near the kitchen area. The room was filled with sun. The white walls were bare except for two posters near the TV, both of Jim Morrison.

"So? About that ride . . ." He was in front of her, handing her a glass of water.

She had to will her hand to release the doorknob. Taking the drink from him, she pointed to her flouncy summer dress. "I really don't think a motorcycle ride would be appropriate today," she said.

He looked down at the hem of her dress, at her legs. Having handed her the water, he was still standing close. "Now why do you say that? A dress on a woman is perfect for a ride." Raising his eyes to her, he smiled.

"From a man's perspective, maybe."

"Well, exactly. Look, you just take the dress"—slowly he lowered his hand for a handful of it—"and then, hitch it up a little, and then . . . kind of tuck it . . ." His hand still down, holding a fistful of thin floral cotton, the knuckles of his fist grazed against her bare thighs. He lifted his dilated gaze from the dress to her eyes, to her mouth. "Tuck it . . . between your legs," he said very low. The water glass in her hand started to shake. He took it from her, set it down. They were still by the open door! Pulling her away, he pushed the door shut behind her, the hem of her spring frock still in his fervid clutches, and wrapped his free arm around her back.

"Oh my God," she breathed out right before he kissed her.

Oh my God, she groaned now, in bed, under covers, day done, everybody's but hers, Jared having awakened long enough to climb upstairs and throw himself into bed.

12:30.

She held the script for *Much Ado About Nothing* in her empty hands, pretending words could get in.

BEATRICE: I love you with so much of my heart that none is left to protest.

BENEDICK: Come: bid me do anything for thee.

12:49.

She tried to read. To concentrate. The house was quiet. Jared was snoring. Larissa even mouthed the words on the page to herself, to focus better.

How did it happen? One minute she was in her car, the next, she was parked in front of the stairs to the porch to his apartment, the next, pressed against the wall of his studio, her palms flat on the wall as if staying off execution. Blind me. Blind me. Turn me around.

Get behind me so I don't see. Press my face against the wall and hold my wrists before you kiss me before you kill me.

1:01.

What was she going to do?

How was she going to go to sleep, to make the night pass faster?

2:04.

The eyes were bleary. Twenty minutes earlier she had turned off the light, thinking she was sleepy, but lying awake in the dark was worse than sitting up pretending to read, and she jumped up and turned the lights back on. Her hands clenched around the book.

At 3:16 a.m. it occurred to Larissa as she was nearly unconscious and blessedly close to morning, that the whole afternoon, evening, sleepless night, the one thought that hadn't crossed her mind or clouded her judgment was: what am I going to do?

It was not even an unformed question. This was no epiphany, a standing on the ledge, looking downward, teetering, tottering, hoping something would save her. It was nothing but the gritted counting down of the merciless minutes until she could see him again. She wanted nothing to save her. This was not the stepback moment; it was too late for that. She couldn't be kissed like that, *touched* like that, and *then* apply cold reason to her burning heart. She was enflamed outside and in, and no bucket of icy logic was going to quench the arson inside her, was going to succeed against her in order not to save her, but to destroy her. She wanted only one thing, and every synapse of her body was crying out for only one thing. Not wrong, not right, just Kai, the means *and* the end, the beginning *and* the end, its own punishment, its own reward, its own reason and justification. Its own everything.

❧

At 6:13 she sprinted into the shower.

"It's too early," groaned Jared.

"No, it's time. We're always running late. I want to get on top of things." She brushed her teeth in a flurry, on speed-dial threw on her clothes, brushed her hair, made coffee, got the cereal bowls ready, took Riot out, got the backpacks by the door, got Jared's briefcase by the door, not a single thing to delay her, and at 7:00 woke the kids.

Jared was out the door by 7:30, thanking her for the coffee. "Oh, you're welcome, darling, any time," she said, as if behind a counter, flashing him her Starbucks smile, giving him small change. "Have a great day."

He stared at her, puzzled, with his travel mug in his hands. "Yes, you too. Enjoy the play."

"*Come, come, we are friends,*" she said to him across the island, quoting Benedick. "*Let's have a dance . . . to lighten our own hearts.*"

"A simple so long will do," said Jared as he left the kitchen. "But interesting that you omitted the words that end that line, about what else the husband should lighten by the marriage dance."

"*Fare thee well!*" She called after him. "*Let's have a dance to lighten our hearts and our wives' heels.*"

"That's better!" Jared called out as the back door slammed.

Asher was catching the bus, but Emily had to be driven to school for orchestra practice. Larissa packed up Michelangelo extra early, dropped off Emily, dropped off Michelangelo, ten minutes before the bell ("Mom, I've never seen the school this early! Well done"), and was back at the house by 8:10.

She debated with a pounding heart what to wear, what to do with her body, what perfume to put on, settling on the same white musk with a spritz of Escada's Moon Sparkle she had worn yesterday. She almost left the house with no underwear. Not forgetting. Deliberate. Almost. But it was too shameful. What if she got into a car accident? How would she explain to the doctors in ER, and to Jared who rushed to her side, why she had on no underwear to go to the supermarket?

He had told her to come in the morning. What was morning for him? 11:00? 11:30? 10:15?

She remembered, nearly belatedly, even though she sat at night and fake-studied Shakespeare, that she had auditions today. She cursed for ten minutes, squawking around her house, trying to find a way out. If she called and said she couldn't make it, Ezra would tell Maggie, who would bring it up over the weekend, in casual conversation, mention to Jared that dear old Larissa was too busy at ten in the morning to come in and stage a casting call for a hundred kids. She could say she'd gone shopping; the children needed clothing. Which was true: they needed shorts, sandals. But to say it would beg the question of why they continued to have no shorts, no sandals.

Out of options, Larissa drove to Pingry. She was on stage by 9:20 a.m., consoling herself that Kai was probably asleep and it was no good to wake a sleeping man. Was he a nocturnal? Or was he an early riser? Were stonemasons early risers? The delay was good; what was the point of him knowing that she wanted to rush to him like a wound-up schoolgirl at her first canteen dance.

Of course there was no one at 9:20 in the theater room. The casting call wouldn't begin properly until ten, when the kids would start their free periods.

She got the books out, the glasses of water, the little table and chair on the stage, checked the time: 9:26 (!!!) and then, to busy her frantic hands, she decided to begin painting the backdrop to Claudio and Hero's lovesick struggles.

She changed into the old painter's grays she found in the production room, opened and stirred the paint, got out the brushes. She was hoping as always to get lost in the colors, the right hemisphere of the brain coming to the rescue, useful like hypnosis. Not today. Today there was no relief in the 12x16 hunk of plywood that gradually became golden brown and red.

At 10:13, she changed back into her floral skirt, flimsy blouse, touched up her lipstick, easier said than done on her tremulous lips, and bounced back into the theater, where Leroy and Sheila were waiting, along with ten students ready to read.

With a stone face Larissa sat in the chair next to Leroy and every time he would ask, well, how is this one or that one? she would say, she's not bad, he's not bad, and she would pretend to make notes, which were nothing more than an endless repetition of the child's

name, Angela, Angela, Angela, Alison, Alison, Alison, What
time was it? Oh God, it was 11:02. Wendy, Ginger, Kate, Josh and
Michael. Josh Josh Michael Michael. What about now? 11:15. She
had to go. Right now. She sprung up.

"Where are you going?" said Leroy. "We're not done."

"I know. I've got some stuff that can't wait. Can you finish up,
please? You and Sheila."

"Be glad to," said Leroy. "But if you don't hear them, how are you
going to cast them?"

"Callbacks. Make notes, ask them to come back Monday." She
remembered Kai's day off was Monday. "Maybe Tuesday, okay?
Tuesday at ten for callbacks. That'll give us time to run through
everyone who wants to audition. We've got twenty parts to fill," she
said to Leroy, grabbing her purse, "so be watchful. Oh, and Sheila,
the last line in Act 5, Scene 1 reads, *'How her acquaintance grew
with this lewd fellow.'* In this context, lewd means worthless, not
what the kids will suggest to you it means. Don't let them snicker
and change the meaning, okay? You must be firm. Because they'll
run roughshod over you."

"I know."

"I know you say you know," said Larissa, "but not five minutes
ago, Michael put the wrong emphasis on it, and you didn't correct
him or ask him to read it properly. That's what I mean. You gotta
watch for that stuff."

Sheila turned red, became flustered. "I didn't realize . . ."

"I know. Please do. This is Shakespeare, not MTV. You, too,
Leroy. Help Sheila. Where is David? He can run lines to help us."

"He's sick today."

"Ah. Well, perhaps tomorrow. See ya, guys."

She was outside in the sunlight and eleven minutes later already
across the railroad tracks, Jag on the gravel, stairs traversed, her
clenching fist knocking on his white door. Before her knuckles
rapped the wood a second time, the door was opened, and he stood
in front of her smiling. He was extra casual, loose jeans without a
belt, a blue faded tank top. He was unbelievably thin, in that way

young bodies are when all they do is move. Only his lanky arms were flash. His hair was still wet, pulled back. He was so rad, so irresistible, so new.

"Where've you been?" he said, pulling her in by the wrist and shutting the door behind her.

"You said morning." She dropped her purse. "You didn't say a time. I didn't want to wake you." Wasn't she so composed!

"Not much chance of that," he said, grinning. "I've been waiting for you since 8:30."

"Since that early?"

"I called Lincoln Elementary and found out school started at 8:05. I made us coffee." He pointed to the stove. "Probably all burned by now."

She said nothing, standing awkwardly.

"Should I make a new pot?"

One of the windows by the bed was open a crack and the breeze was disturbing the curtains. How long could she stand like this, in silence, her hands twisted together in front of her, avoiding his eyes. "If you want," she said.

Reaching out, he took her hands into his. "You know what I want? You," he whispered, pulling her to him.

Not composed anymore, her legs weakened when he kissed her.

"You smell great," he whispered. "What is that? It's fucking amazing . . ."

She wanted to tell him, but she forgot. The name of the perfume had flown out of her head.

He was already panting, not composed himself, not still, not calm, breathing hard, fumbling with the buttons on her shirt, with the zipper on her skirt. She wanted to tell him not to bother with the zipper, just hitch the skirt up. She kicked off her shoes as they kissed standing up, their arms wrapped around each other; she was trying to absorb him through his jeans, through his blue tank, which he threw off, breathlessly acknowledging her opened blouse, her sheer white bra underneath, her hardening nipples.

"Oh God," he said, drawing her close, his hands pulling off her blouse, finding the clasps of the bra. "Larissa, what I want . . ." He stopped to collect himself. "What I want is to feel your bare nipples against my chest, but I can't. That's what I want, but I can't have it." He left her in her bra, her skirt unzipped but not pulled down. "I'm sorry," he said, pulling her to his bed. "I can't even open my eyes. I can't look at you naked, I can't even imagine you naked, all right?"

"All right," she moaned, watching him unbutton his Levi's. She sat down on the bed in front of him and was about to pull down his jeans and his boxer briefs when he took her hands away from him. "No, no," he said. "I'm not kidding. You can't touch me." With his body he pushed her down on the bed and climbed on top of her.

"I can't touch you, you can't touch me, you can't undress me." Her arms went on his bare back. "So what can we do?" His excitement was so conspicuous, so apparent, so blatant that Larissa moaned even as she uttered those normal words. To have him rub agonizingly against her in lust and shamelessness, to *want* to be pressed into the bed under him in lust and shamelessness . . . the panting evaporating memories and miseries and marriage, being drunk on untamed youth, not sinking but drowning, gulping for air.

He couldn't speak.

"Okay," she whispered, gently touching his arms, his back, opening her mouth under his searching frantic mouth. "It's okay."

"It's not okay," he said. He barely opened his jeans, finally did jack up her skirt without being asked; he didn't take off her underwear, just pulled it to one side and breathing shallow into her mouth, his eyes closed, he found her in an instant, thrust inside her, and before she could grasp his back and gasp . . . it was over.

"I told you," he murmured, after a few moments of panting silence. He gazed at her up close with a contrite but delighted smile. "I'm so happy you're here," he said, kissing her. "I was afraid you'd have horrible second thoughts, and then I'd be walking around with blue balls the rest of my life."

"That doesn't sound very likely," she said quietly.

"You not showing up? Or my blue balls?"

She laughed. It was bright in his apartment, even with the

shades drawn. There was nowhere to hide. The light kept coming through the cracks.

He was tanned the way people who have lived their lives in the sun are tanned—their skin changed color, was no longer white. He had little hair on his chest, almost like he was still growing it. She ran her elongated fingers with their polished nails from his chest down to his smooth table-top stomach.

Was there even a five-minute break? Ten? He had enough time to get her a drink of lukewarm water, throw some ice cubes in it. He undressed her, left her naked on his bed. "God, I knew you were going to be beautiful," he whispered. "I knew it from the moment I saw you."

"Did you?"

"Yes." He smiled, his fingertips running down her thighs. "Underneath that big parka, those loose sweats, hidden under that no-nonsense exterior you carry, like you can't be bothered with the world, I knew there was sweetness, there was hotness."

Straddling her, he sucked her nipples, kissed her, told her he was sorry he only had the one mouth and couldn't use it on her all at once, and she said she was also sorry for that because that sounded like something she might like.

And he laughed.

She tried to hide her star-struck wonder. Arching her back into the bed, she opened her legs. "Come here, Kai," she said, opening her arms, too. "Come to me."

He climbed on top of her, supporting himself with his wiry arms. "I don't know what to do first to please you, to make you happy," he murmured. "I'm ridiculous."

"No," she said. "You're not. You're fine. But there is just one thing I need, okay?" She took him into her hands, tried not to moan and failed, tried not to pant and failed, tried not to let him see her excitement at feeling him in her hands, and failed at that too, his face so close, his eyes roaming her face for meaning.

What? What? he kept saying. *You like touching me? Why? Tell me why.*

Now she was the one who couldn't speak. She wasn't ready for the blitz, for the groping hands and the seeking mouth seeking her mouth, licking her breasts, *wait, wait*, she kept saying, trying to hold on to him, to caress him, to keep him between her surprised and stroking palms for just a moment longer, *wait, wait*, and he kept saying, *wait for what?* Pushing inside, inside, inside.

Oh God, no honest, wait.

Wait for what, Larissa?

She wasn't ready for the klieg light of his unstoppable youth, ashamed of how uncontrollably she was moaning. Once she started to come, she panted for him to stop, but he wouldn't listen, and she kept coming and coming. *I can't take it anymore*, she kept saying.

Sure you can, he kept saying back.

I can't take it anymore, she kept whispering underneath him on his bed. *Honest, I can't*, on her back, on her stomach, on her hands and knees, spread out, stretched out, drawn, quartered, blankets thrown off, just the sheet on a mattress near the wall, her arms stretched above her head, searching. Not even a headboard for her desperate hands to grasp. She tried, she really did, to be circumspect in her vocal yearnings, the windows were ajar, but she wanted to scream, to cry out, I can't believe what's happening, I can't believe the fantastic of it, the joy of it.

No more, no more, she kept gently pleading. *Kai, stop, please, no more . . .*

More, more, she kept gently pleading. *Kai, don't stop, please, more . . .*

She was soaked, wet, and he was soaked, dripping sweat on her in the spectacle of his flagrant exertions.

Help me, please, oh God, help me. When will you come?

You want me to come?

If you don't soon, I won't be able to walk out of here.

Larissa, he whispered, and Larissa was coming even before he finished the question, *do you want to walk out of here?*

He was so beautiful to look at, but never more so than when he was naked. To see a twenty-year-old man nude, erect, that was a pleasure and a privilege Larissa didn't expect to get again. There wasn't a soft line to him, except for the pulpy excess of his mouth. He was reed lean, the arms that lifted stone like stone but on a sinewy body, not a gym rat's body. A body that worked for its living outdoors in the heat of dust, in the bowl of mortar. Not a scrap of extra on him anywhere, except in the extra there was too much and too young of. He really was the most beautiful man.

His youth became her. How else could it be for her when faced with the voluminous fire of a rapacious boy, who had it instant-on, like gas logs, press a button and *voilà!* at maximum volume in seconds? There was no start-up, it was just up. It had been a long time for Larissa, living inside such adolescent flame. Eighteen years married, and before that young and incautious, parading her new-found sexual freedom around the campus—that wasn't the same thing as being in love, was it?

It wasn't this.

Nothing was this.

She had been in love with Jared, though in the geographical landscape of her heart, that love now seemed as remote as New Hebrides was from Summit. New Hebrides? Exactly. An island in Micronesia.

"*Nothing* can be this fucking good."

Larissa couldn't believe it wasn't she who had uttered those words.

She was crying.

No, don't cry. Come. But don't cry.

Why can't I do both, Kai?

He tasted of mint gum, of black coffee, she thought faintly of cigarettes. What did she taste of? Was he the kind who would tell her? She couldn't ask any questions now; she was immersed at the moment in answers.

She feared that when it was over—and eventually, it *was* over— she would be deflated by her rememberance of things past, but that was not to be. She kept tracing the outline of his damp stomach with her fingers. He had a long scar on his left lower abdomen. *What's that from?*

Oh that? Well . . . I was on a demon ride, he said. *Fell off my bike.*

Demon ride?

Yeah. Riding the motorcycle in the dark with the lights off. Crashed into the side of a volcanic cliff.

Hurt?

Yeah. Pretty bad. He got quiet. *I had a girl with me. She got hurt, too.* He got quieter.

Is she okay?

Pause. *Depending on what your definition of OK is.*

Is she OK by any definition?

I guess the answer to that would be no. But she did make it out alive from the accident. So that's something, I suppose.

Larissa could tell he didn't want to talk about it. Leaning over, she put her lips on his stomach, on his scar.

After more than two hours of pageantry—two hours! How insignificant! How trivial! Time entering into eternals, how ludicrous, how degraded—she had to leave. Left his hands on her thighs, his soft lips on her bare stomach, left her own hands on his back, kneeling on the bed. *No, don't go*, Kai whispered, *I haven't . . .*

You mean there is something you still haven't done? Larissa almost didn't leave.

"I'm off Monday," he said as she was getting dressed. "I'll be here all day, waiting for you. Come when you can. Whenever. Just come, Larissa."

She buttoned her blouse, slipped on her sandals, smoothed out her hair, got her keys, her purse. Was she forgetting something? "This Monday?" What she wanted to say and couldn't was, *I can't wait until then to see you again. I'm not going to make it.*

His hands grasped her hips, his mouth was in the swell of her breasts. He cradled her to himself. "Every Monday."

3

All Else Shall Vanish

On Monday:

Shower	7 minutes
Drying	2 minutes plus air dry
Lotion	2 minutes
Hair	1 towel-dried minute, plus 1 minute for gel
Makeup	5 minutes for mascara
Dressing	5 minutes
Misc.	5 minutes
Total	**28 minutes**

Larissa was at Albright Circle by nine in the morning. His door opened as soon as her Jag pulled into the drive. He dragged her inside, shut the door, pressed her against it. "Good morning," he said, tilting his head, kissing her deeply, kissing her neck, staring besotted into her embarrassed eyes. "I bought croissants, bagels. I bought eggs. I didn't know what you'd like for breakfast."

Larissa didn't speak. She didn't trust her voice. Her eyes were closing at feeling him next to her again. But he was grinning so happily, still keeping her against the door, his hands over her body. "Did you miss me?" he said huskily. "Tell the truth, did you?"

"A little bit," she croaked.

"Did you think about me?"

"A little bit."

"What did you think about?" His hands were already under her skirt, between her thighs.

"Oh, you know, this and that."

"Well, what was it?" *This* . . .

Or that . . .

Still by the door! Against the door! Her keys falling to the floor, like she was about to fall to the floor.

"Would you like some croissants?" He unbuttoned her blouse, looked for the bra clasp.

"It's in the front."

"Ah, convenient." With one motion it was unhooked, her breasts spilled out, her nipples still raw from Friday, pleading for more. She pressed her fists against the door trying very hard not to moan.

He was panting, excited pupils black against the whites of his eyes, wet mouth on her. "Come with me," he said, fondling her, tugging on her nipples, making her shudder. "I see you came early today. Not like Friday." From ear to ear was his smile. "Why did you come so nice and early today, Larissa?"

Kai, come on, don't drive me crazy.

Why not? He picked her up, carried her to the bed, dropped her on it, fell on top of her. *You drive me crazy.*

They were instantly naked.

Kai, I want . . .

I know what you want. His hands were filled with her body. *I cannot believe how wet you are. I'm going to go insane. I can't believe it. But now that I know I can give it to you, I want other things first.*

She took him into her hands, moaning, bent down to put him into her mouth.

No, no. I mean, yes, yes. But later.

Now is when I want it.

I know. But now that I know I can give it to you, I want other things first.

He propped pillows underneath her, to arch her hips to him. He kneeled between her parted legs. He looked at her, gazed at her, lifted his gaze to look into her face, he panted, he shook his head in wonder. Larissa didn't think touching her at this point would be necessary. One hot breath from his mouth, and she would be finished.

Every girl is different. Will you tell me what you like?

Okay.

Will you tell me what you love?

Okay.

What I want, Larissa, he said, lowering his head to her, kissing her gently, touching her gently with his fingers, *is to make you come with my mouth. Can you tell me how to do that?*

If I remember how, she thought but didn't say. It had been a long time since she had come that way.

Turned out she remembered how.

And he turned out to be a quick learner. *Imagine what you might like me to do to you,* she whispered, clutching the sheet, his wild head, his hair. *Do it just like that, but much much gentler. No, gentler, Kai . . . please.*

Okay. Okay. Okay. What about my tongue?

Yes, also good. Very good.

What about my fingers?

Yes, also good.

Fingers everywhere?

Oh, God help me . . .

Is that a yes or a no, Larissa . . . ?

There was no more instruction after that, just current running through Larissa's third rail body until 2:15 p.m. when he was drenched like he'd run a marathon and she had to run.

◈

The other life melted away, like ice in heat. A frozen block started to drip, and before she knew it, it was a puddle on the ground, and the spring sun beat on. The ground became dry; soon there was no indication that once last winter in that place stood a house, a husband, children, day-to-day things, breakfasts, shopping, friends, theater! which had been the primary driving passion. Not even a damp stain remained where the old evaporated life had been.

And yet, there was Larissa. And she still had to get up, and get her children up and out, get their backpacks, first to school, and then their towels and bathing suits for their swim lessons; she had to make their lunches and wash their wet things, she still had to pick up Michelangelo from school. Every day. The balcony for the *Much Ado* production was built three inches too small for six-foot Trevor, who played Benedick and who kept hitting the upper beam with his forehead every time he stepped forward to sing, *The god of love that sits above, and knows me* . . . The balcony had to be scrapped and rebuilt from scratch; just another delay and headache for Larissa. There was still Maggie. Larissa still had to drive Emily to her friends' houses and to her music lessons, and she still had to go shopping, and think about dinner, and she had to come home and put the food away, and chop onions and marinate meat, and fix drinks, and help Asher with his Spanish words and Michelangelo with his addition. She had to unload the dishwasher, and clean Riot's paws and put gas in the Escalade and the Jaguar. She still had to smile for Jared when he came home, and sit at his table and listen to him talk about the impossible goals of lowering operating costs without laying people off while magically increasing revenue; she had to monitor the kids and clean up. She still had to undress and lie down next to Jared, and on the weekends she had to lie under him. On Saturdays, after running to Pingry to rehearse for three hours and paint the trap door for Hell and Ghosts in just the right shade of Sherwin-Williams cast-iron gray, she still had to spend the day with her family, and soon they would go to Lillypond up in Pennsylvania, hours away, and she simply didn't know how that would be possible. She walked, sleepwalked through her life with a vacuous but ever-present smile, and the fact that no one noticed told her that the vacuous, ever-present smile was not too far off from her previous smile, for it must have been the same face that the external Larissa had carried in the world for many years because now that her internal geography had altered utterly, no one noticed.

◦◦◦

Except for this. She moved faster. She sped down halls and staircases. She speed-dialed numbers, tapped her impatient pens and fingers, unloaded groceries at warp drive. Dinner was served and cleared before Jared had a chance to take off his tie. Kids were in bed on the dot of nine-thirty and out the door before eight. She took five-minute showers, she learned how to—she *had* to. No more anointing her head with two hours of lubricant. Her anointing was waiting for her at Albright Circle. She ran from the parking lot to the school and through the halls, and once Ezra caught her and yelled into her back, "Hey, no running in the halls! You wanna get written up?" And to Jared a few days later said, your wife was skipping through my school today. What do you make of that? Positively skipping.

"Skipping?" said Jared, like he'd never heard the word before. "You mean like with joy?"

"Well, I don't know. I'm just saying. It *was* odd."

"So what did you do?"

"Well, I told her to cut it out."

"Well played. And she?"

She, who was sitting right there at her own table, pouring Margaritas to everyone but herself (for she had reduced her social drinking—wanted to stay in control), said, "I haven't been written up since high school."

"Exactly. Bet you haven't skipped since high school either."

"What's with the skipping?" asked Maggie.

"Your husband is as always employing considerable literary license to state the plain truth. I was late to rehearsal, and was hurrying. But," Larissa added, "I *am* glad winter's over. It's good to be warm."

She wore her spring dresses, her denim skirts, her silken blouses, and then she lay down in the white bed with Kai while the gauzy curtains blew spring all over the room, wet and warm April, dry and singing May.

And Kai, in between the brief moments of waiting for ardor to return to his body, serenaded her with the ardor in his soul, by sitting next to her in bed and strumming the strings of his ukulele, singing to her a song she barely knew, hardly ever heard, yet he sang it like he wrote it and he wrote it for her.

> *Beautiful dreamer, wake unto me,*
> *Starlight and dewdrops are waiting for thee . . .*
> *Beautiful dreamer, queen of my song,*
> *List while I woo thee with soft melody . . .*

They lay on their backs, counting their fingers and toes, counting their minutes and their blessings. He kissed her between the shoulder blades and whispered murmurs of lust into her back, and she tried to listen, but the uncooperating body was keening, arching to find him, searching for him.

"Okay, tell me the first time you wanted to sleep with me," she said, turning over to lie on his chest, threading her fingers through his. Tick tock, the clock by his bedside went. Tick tock, tick tock.

"Hmm, lessee . . ." He pretended to think, looked at the ceiling. "If I had to guess, I'd say it was . . . that time in the supermarket parking lot."

She shook him, tickled him. "Come on. Be serious."

"What? It was."

"Kai, I don't have all day."

"No kidding. Okay. The first time, well, I guess if you're forcing me to tell you . . . it'd be that first day I saw you."

"What?"

"Of course."

"That can't be true."

"Why? Of course it is. Don't you know anything about men and women?" He tried to sound wise. "Sheesh. All guys, not just me, but all guys, and when I say all guys, I mean *all guys* as in every guy you've ever met, know within the first five minutes of meeting you if they want to sleep with you. To give you credit where credit is due, I probably knew with you after the first ten seconds."

"Come on!"

"It's true. But usually? Five minutes, tops. We don't need to figure it out. We have it all figured out. We don't need to look deep inside ourselves and say, she's a good friend, but do I like her in *that* way? We know immediately. Either we want to see you naked or we don't."

"Oh, so romantic."

"Romantic? You're the one who asked that prosaic question. When did you want to sleep with me?" He mock-huffed. "And *I'm* not a romantic."

"All right, all right."

"So . . . when did you first know you wanted to sleep with *me*?"

"I'm still deciding, lover-boy."

"Ahh. Of course you are. Well, you *are* a woman." His mouth bent deep into her breasts, to her swollen nipples. He cupped her, fondled her. "Is there anything I can do to help you make your decision quicker? Because I don't know if I can wait much longer."

She moaned.

"You know what I got? A flame Ducati, baby," Kai said, opening her softened body with his kisses, on his arms over her. "It can go one forty an hour, and it does, and it won't stop till it runs out of gas after it does things to you six of which I'm certain are illegal in the state of New Jersey. Decision: Yes?"

"God, oh yes. Please, oh *yes*."

4

Jared and Larissa's Dry Week

I'm not singing to an imaginary girl, Kai sang to her.

But I am, Larissa whispered. *I am imaginary. When I'm here, it is as I would like to be, wish I could be, wish I had been. But not as I am.*

That's not true. This is how you are.

No. No, this is how you *are. I'm only this because of you.*

But, Larissa, my delight is not imaginary. Remember acting out a motorcycle on stage, the pale rendition of what it is really like to be on a Ducati? Same here. My joy is real. And my joy is you.

I've never known anyone like you. No one who loves like you, who comes like you. No one who touches me like you. No one who wants to be touched by me like you. I simply don't understand how you exist. Is this what all women are like at forty?

No. Only me. Is this what all young men are like at twenty?

Yup, pretty much.

It's not that she didn't believe him. It's that to say those words, pressed against full soft breasts, a bare stomach, with white legs wrapped around you, with adoring eyes on you, with a mouth that's crying, chest against a heart that's weeping with ecstasy, all could be said at those moments. And all was.

It was a breath in her day. The other twenty-three hours Larissa spent doing nothing but ensuring that she could continue to take that one breath with which her lungs were filled, her soul was filled.

She made sure not only that she was punctual, but that she was a couple of minutes early everywhere. When Michelangelo was doing his homework at the island, she returned every phone call she missed during the day. She scheduled to be at play rehearsals on Saturdays, on Tuesday lunchtimes and Wednesday afternoons, and made sure she was always present. She drove to Pingry every morning at ten o'clock and helped with the sets, she oversaw construction and painting, she drove to Sherwin-Williams and bought the paints with her own two hands. She repainted the columns herself, she redesigned the discovery space underneath the balcony, and went to a curtain store to choose the curtains. Every dispute over teenage costumes she presided over, and she made sure that before she fled school, she sat down in Ezra's office with a coffee for him and went over the day and the play.

Preempting Tara's calls to go walking, Larissa called her herself. She called during times she expressly knew Tara wasn't going to be there. "Tara, darling, I've got to run to the school, but do you want to have a walk now?" she would leave as a message, and then Tara would call back and leave a message on Larissa's machine. Thanks so much for calling and inviting me for a walk. So sorry I missed your call. I was taking Jenny to playgroup. Maybe tomorrow?

And at home, Larissa became more of a mother. To make it easier on herself, she bought prepackaged brownie mixes, pre-made cookie dough, ready-made biscuits. But every day in the early evening, something sweet emanated from the hot oven, as Larissa poured a lemon marinade over her chicken, and helped Asher with his three-dimensional paintings and talked to Emily about the importance of dressing appropriately for formal occasions like the NJSSMA auditions. Larissa ran the rest of her life like clockwork, so that the one moment of undisturbed chaos would continue to be allotted to her. It was almost as if she were saying, look how good I am. I'm doing everything I'm supposed to, I'm excelling at my life. I'm juggling it all, keeping all the balls in the air, I'm not mixing my whites and colors, and I'm not pouring bleach over dry towels. I'm not forgetting ice cream in my trunk anymore, and I'm not learning words to the wrong play. I'm fresh-smelling and happy, my children are well-tended, their needs taken care of, and Jared is taken care of; I'm not forgetting him. I'm not forgetting my friendships. I remember to listen to my close friends about their problems. And for this, for being *so good*, I get one little tiny thing for myself. It affects nothing. Except the way I feel about my life. It's the thing that makes everything else so much more worthwhile. Nothing wrong with that, is there?

There was only one thing Larissa could not do, and the silence of that omission screamed louder than the noise of all her other actions.

Larissa could not write to Che.

༄

"Close your eyes."

"No, why?"

"No questions, just . . . close them." Kai met her outside his place on the gravel, down the steps and at her car before she barely turned off the ignition.

"I don't want to close them. I'm afraid."

"Oh, be afraid . . ." he lowered his voice to corn-husky. "Be very afraid. But close your eyes anyway."

"No."

He kissed her. In the driveway, in full view of the world, leaned in and kissed her against the car, smiling, happy, holding her hand. "I've got a present for you upstairs."

She looked up to his windows. "What is it?"

"It's a surprise. Why so much talking? Close your eyes, and in ten seconds you'll see."

"Is it a puppy?"

"No." He put his hand over her face. Closing her eyes finally, she allowed him to lead her across the courtyard to the steps.

"Is it a boat?"

"A boat? Careful, hold on to the railing here."

"Is it a . . . television?"

"You need a television, Larissa?"

"Is it a . . . pair of shoes?"

"Yes, because that's me. A shoe shopper."

"Is it . . . ?"

"Just go on up, two more steps. You'll see."

"Will it make me happy?"

"Well, I suppose you'll let me know in about five seconds. Keep 'em closed. We're almost inside. It's very important you keep them closed. Otherwise you'll ruin the surprise."

"Is the present in the surprise, or in the actual present itself?"

"I don't know how to answer that. In both?" Not trusting her, he put his hand over her face as he led her across the threshold, past the entryway, slowly across his wood floor.

"Will it make me cry?"

"You tell me." The backs of her knees hit the side of the bed. "Without opening your eyes, lie down."

"Lie down where?"

"On the bed."

She lay down.

"No, all the way, like you're on the bed. Feet, too."

She lay down on the bed, feet too. He climbed on top of her, nestling, grinding her, kissing her neck, her mouth. Her arms went around his neck.

"Now," he said quietly, "reach up with your arms over your head."

"Why? I can't touch you?"

"Just reach up, Larissa."

She reached up with her arms over her head and . . .

Brass rails!

She opened her eyes, tilted her head back. "You got me a headboard?" It was a high, curved, sleigh-bed-design brass headboard with nice thick strong brass rails.

He was beaming. "I got you a headboard. And a footboard. Just in case." He laughed, raising his eyebrows. "What do you think? You like?"

"Oh, Kai . . ."

"Does this make you happy? A big brass bed?"

"Oh . . ."

"Does this make you cry?"

"Oh . . ."

"Grab on, baby," he whispered. "And hold on tight."

⌒⌒⌒

What is it like to spend your hours in deceit? There is no gesture big or small, no word big or small, no thought, no breath that can be made with a clear, unmanipulated heart. The vigilance is 24/7. There is nothing that can, or must, escape your attention.

She was afraid of Kai's smell in her car. What if someone had seen her on the back of his bike like a skull and crossbones flag flying down to the Deserted Village, wind in her hair? What if she bought something in a place she wasn't supposed to be in? What if she bought something she shouldn't have bought, a see-through bra Jared had never seen, a black silk thong to drive a man to distraction? What if she was gaining weight from the sushi she kept having in Kai's bed, and the ice cream from his freezer, and the sugar in the two cups of coffee with cream she drank with him? What if she left a receipt for the sushi, a wrapper from a gum she didn't chew, a piece of candy she didn't eat on the floor of her car? What if a CD in the changer was one she never listened to?

What if—and this was a frightening what if—Jared opened the statement from her gynecologist and examined the details more thoroughly than usual and saw that in addition to an exam and a blood test and a cervical smear there was also a script for a six-month supply of birth control, matched by the billing statement for the prescription account they paid into? How could she explain to Jared that suddenly at forty she decided to go back on the pill as if she were a slutty college student without a boyfriend? What did married women who hadn't been on the pill in seventeen years need to be on the pill for? Last time she was on the pill was before

Emily was born. Now, she kept that pink wheel of 28 mother's little helpers hidden deep inside her cosmetic drawer, in a blue silk bag that contained the suede brush.

Can you hide? Isn't anyone watching? Thank God no one was watching, and you could maintain the shell of what was, though all the things that made you you had gone, replaced by another heart that beat and pumped blood for someone else.

On the theater stage, Larissa smiled and gave suggestions. "No, no Trevor," she said. "When you, as Benedick, have Don Pedro say to you, *Why, what's the matter, that you have such a February face, so full of frost and storm and cloudiness?* you cannot while you're hearing it, be chewing gum, grinning, and making eyes at Lynnette over in the corner. Try, Trevor, try as hard as you can, to have a February face. Otherwise you will not sell your character to the audience. Do you know how to have a face full of frostiness? Like this."

When Evelyn called, Larissa nodded into the phone and said, Lunch? Sure, when? Oh, no, not then. I'll call you. When Maggie called, she said, Mags, I'm running out, can I call you back? Che wrote: "*I know something is terribly wrong in your life because you haven't written me for so long and in your last letter you were so far away you might as well have been on the moon, and just as cold. Is it still about the car?*"

Emily learned to play cantabile on the cello and after dinner, she propped her instrument against her shoulder on the floor in the den and played for the family while Larissa stood and smiled and nodded, 4.2 miles and twelve minutes away.

∽⌒∾

The routine helped her, saved her like staging a play. During the week, Jared's work, the kids, the office, the TV, the clean-up, the day-to-day, meant that by midnight, there was no Jared left for anything more than a kiss and a snuggle, which Larissa was happy to give him, her eyes closed, his eyes closed. By Thursday he was stirring, his caresses becoming more arduous, but only slightly, and the kids being late, himself being late, rushing, running, putting on suits, getting his briefcase together, already thinking of the day ahead, meant that she didn't have to worry until the weekend and on the weekend, true, there had to be some highwire performance art from her, there had to be courtesy and warmth, some reciprocity of affection, there had to be lying in bed while being caressed by Jared, and all this Larissa dutifully performed because on the front burner of her mind was protecting the only thing that had meaning for her. Had she had qualms about Kai, had she had second thoughts, pangs of conscience perhaps, her Oscar-worthy effrontery would have been harder, but since she experienced none of the three, the same force of intense self-preservation she used to propel herself out of Kai's bed and into her car to pick up her small child was the force she used to lie in her own bed on the weekends and open her arms to her husband, as if to say, take this from me. I give it to you gladly, while I keep the most precious part of myself, the rest of myself, for someone else, not you.

5

Kai's Prayers

She got all dressed up on a Saturday at the end of April to go celebrate her belated birthday in the city, with her black peep-toe pumps, her dazzling sequined navy-blue dress. It came just above the knee and her legs, smooth, waxed, lean, were in black stockings. She had painted her nails red and wore red lipstick to match. She wore Jared's diamonds and rubies on her wrists and her throat, she wore black undergarments and her décolletage as an accessory. She sat in the darkened Jaguar with her arms wrapped around herself, as Jared chatted about work and how hard it was to reserve a table for ten at the Union Square Café, and how beautiful she looked for her celebratory evening, and was she feeling all right? Because she was quiet. But Larissa said, I'm not quiet, darling, I'm eagerly anticipating. The lights of the Manhattan skyline were green, sprinkled with night-time razzle-dazzle before they entered the Lincoln Tunnel, passing through Hoboken. She didn't pray, but now, the prayers she heard in her head were Kai's.

"Larissa, isn't there any way we could go out at night? Please?"

"No, Kai."

"Can I have you overnight? To sleep with you? To wake with you?"

"No, Kai."

"We'll go away for one night. I'll take you to a beautiful hotel. Anywhere you want."

"No, Kai."

"Larissa, can we go to Samurai Sushi, the new place that opened in Maplewood?"

"No, Kai."

"Can I meet your children?"

"No, Kai!"

"Can I have a day with you in the city? You and I, for one day, in the city of dreams, not Summit? We can ride the Circle Line."

"No, Kai."

"We'll go dancing."

"No, Kai."

"Oh, Larissa. Is there anything at all that you can do with me?" He opened her bare legs, now so elegantly closed.

"Yes, Kai."

"You won't see me outside of this apartment. You won't have lunch with me in Panera, ice cream with me at Ricky's, you won't have dinner with me, you won't sleep with me. Is there anything you *will* do with me, Larissa, or are you an imaginary girl?"

"Yes, Kai."

6

Surveillance, Electronic

Who designed the cell phone? Who thought *that* was a good idea? As an ideal, sure. But as a practical matter, a cell phone might as well have been Jared in Larissa's pocket. The phone would always ring. Larissa's hiding behind the "no signal" got her only so far. Jared said, "Where are you that you're in a no signal zone every time I call?" He called at lunch. He was busy in the morning and busy in the afternoon, but at lunch, between twelve and two was when he wanted to speak to her. Trouble was, at lunch between twelve and two was precisely when Larissa could not take Jared's call.

"I was at the mall," she said.

"Every day this week? What did you buy?"

"I bought nothing. Just window-shopping. Looking for spring styles."

But she had to make herself available. One way or another. She started calling Jared at 11:50, as she was racing from Pingry to Madison. Hi, honey. How are you? How was your morning? They had always talked during lunch. What good reason could Larissa give, did Larissa have, for not taking Jared's calls at lunchtime? What was she doing? Sure, sometimes she could have been having her own lunch, with Maggie, or Evelyn in Hoboken. But how often? And was she so involved with her friends that she couldn't pick up her husband's call? And since she actually *wasn't* going to lunches with Maggie, how long before this became apparent to both Maggie *and* Jared? Could she involve Maggie in her duplicity? Could she confide in her? No, not in any universe she lived in. Che maybe. Che hadn't played Scruples with the gang. Che's allegiance was only to Larissa. But Che was nowhere to be found in Jersey. With Bo, she had a proper and prim relationship. They met at the Met and talked about the externals of life, and there had been a need for that, though less these days. With Fran, they painted their nails. Her life was not to be doled out in twenty-minute pleas for fraud. Evelyn? Her little bookworm homeschooling Evelyn? Would she understand?

"Larissa, you want to have lunch?" Maggie called to ask.

"Oh, sure. When is good?"

"Any day this week. Monday?"

Monday was the worst. "This Monday is not great. How about Tuesday?"

"I'm working."

Larissa knew that. "Wednesday? Nah, Wednesday is no good for me. I'm supposed to go into the city, have lunch with Bo." This was true, strictly, the "supposed to" part. She wasn't actually *planning* on going. How about that, using one set of bogus plans to get out of another?

"Thursday?"

"Yes, sure. Thursday."

But by Thursday, Larissa called, not on her cell phone but from home, and said, "Sorry, Mags, have a blinding headache. Mind if we reschedule?"

Friday Larissa pretended to go with Fran to do her nails, like she used to. Except, Larissa now did her own nails, and since no one knew Fran, no one knew she wasn't meeting her manicure friend at Nail Art by Grace.

Mondays, Larissa spent not one hour but five in Kai's bed when the sun moved on the plank floor from one window to another

by the time she left. Mondays Larissa didn't need the cell phone.
Mondays she lay naked and was worshipped and serenaded for five
hours by a sun god.

But one Sunday Kai called her. "I miss you," he said. "Whatchya
up to?"

She had been gardening, her hands in gloves, the vibrating
cell phone in her shorts pocket. She was preparing the ground for
flowers, and being outside allowed her the privacy to dream of him,
while still being outwardly present in her life.

"Not up to much," she said quietly. "What are you up to?"

"Up to missing you, is what," he said.

"Kai . . ." she lowered her voice to a breathy whisper. "We have
all tomorrow."

"I can't wait. Can you get away for an hour?"

Can you get away for an hour was the sexiest thing anyone had
ever said to her. It meant his work would be quick, efficient. It
meant he couldn't do without her, would dispatch with her, then
release her. It meant he needed her for only one thing. She told him
no and hung up, but couldn't continue to sit, to garden, to hoe, to
weed. One couldn't garden and ache in the places she now ached.
Couldn't continue. Arms wrapped around herself, she stumbled
into the house to change clothes and said to Jared she wanted to
have a barbecue. She was going to run to the store to pick up some
ground beef and chicken wings.

"We got nothing in the house? Not even frozen? Oh, well. Okay.
I'll fire up the grill. Don't forget potatoes and corn. Oh, and you
might as well get some rib-eye. But on the bone, okay?"

She called Kai from the cell phone on the way to Route 124.

"I'm coming," she said.

"I'm waiting," he said. "Are you bare under your skirt?"

Yes, Kai . . .

"Totally bare, Larissa?"

Yes . . .

It was a miracle she didn't crash the car.

He was waiting for her at the open door at the top of the stairs.

She didn't know if they closed the door before he was inside her.

From zero to one hundred and forty, with hardly a breath in between, zooming all the time, in need, in want, in desire, on deserted roads, engine constantly revving, faster, faster.

Except . . . when he had complete control over himself and wanted to torment her, he would pin her legs, confine her and proceed to move slow and shallow. He would stand over her so he could watch himself and watch her and he would continue this past the point of all decency, past the point of all decorum, past the point of all sanity, until the only thing Larissa could do, since she couldn't get away and couldn't get free, was beg him, *beg* him to fuck her until she came, and then and only then would he free her.

That is what he did to her today. After forty-five minutes she crowbarred herself away from his naked arms and staggered down the stairs like a disaster.

She galloped through Stop&Shop, the chicken wings, the potatoes, the rib-eye, bone in. She forgot the cheese, the bacon. She forgot drinks, Coke, forgot brownies. She never looked at the list, which had fallen out on the hardwood floor at Kai's place.

"Cash back?"

"Oh, yes, please. A hundred."

"Max is fifty. Is that okay?"

"It'll have to be, won't it?"

Before she got home, he called her again.

"Kai, stop, we're going to get in trouble."

"I'm already in trouble, baby. This is me in most terrible distress."

"Kai."

"All right, I'll stop. I just wanted to say, I had flowers for you, I bought flowers."

She had glimpsed them, on the table, in a vase.

"I don't need them."

"You do need them. Fields of them. Monday?"

"Monday."

As soon as she hung up, she erased his messages from her phone.

As soon as she erased the messages from her phone, she realized that she could erase all she wanted, the messages, the little texts, "WOT R U DOING?" "WOT R U UP 2?" "MISS U." "CALL ME."

She could erase them to her little heart's content. She could spend all day erasing. Problem was, the itemized bill was available to Jared online, to Jared, who paid the bills, who paid the phone bill, who looked over the bills, because he was the accountant, not just of Prudential but of her life too. The list of phone calls was available to Jared instantly, at the moment of occurrence, like the saxophone booming buh-Buh-BUH, he could log on to their account, and as she was calling or being called, her husband could press Refresh in their home office, and there it would be. His wife out buying things for the family barbecue, and on her phone, a local number, one minute thirty-eight seconds in duration. The thump thump was not the sax anymore, it was the anxious drums of her heart. She would be found out, no question about it. She slowed down as she drove home, the chicken wings in her car. What to do? Nothing to do. She hoped Jared was too busy lawn bowling to go into his home office. She couldn't even text Kai to tell him not to text her anymore. Oh!

When she arrived home she found Jared playing softball with Michelangelo, with Asher standing grimly by, holding his own bat like he wanted to wallop somebody with it, probably his brother, for taking up too much of their dad's time. When Asher saw his mother walk into the backyard, he, who was not the storming kind, stormed into the house.

"He doesn't like to share his dad," said Jared, out of breath. "You were gone forever. Did you get everything?"

"Place is mobbed on Sunday afternoons. It was ridiculous. They were out of Diet Coke."

"Out of Diet Coke! And they call themselves a supermarket."

"I'm going to marinate the chicken."

"Yes, do. Can you get me a can of something cold?"

She brought him an RC Cola. He kissed her and said thank you.

To Kai on Monday, Larissa said, "You can't call me anymore. You can't call me on the cell phone."

When she explained, Kai looked skeptical. Skeptical but naked. "Does he really check such minutia?"

"He really does."

"Who's got the time?"

"He does. That's his job. This is what he does. He checks things."

Kai didn't roll his eyes, didn't even squint, just slightly narrowed his irises.

She got defensive, though he had said nothing. "Someone has to."

"I said nothing."

"Kai, whose job is it going to be? Mine?"

He shrugged in bed, shook her a little, to rumble her mood up. "I'm glad it's not me. Spending my day looking at little numbers on the screen, seeing if the dollar spent matched the thirty-second call."

"He didn't always do this," Larissa defended, defended her husband to her lover! While lying naked in bed, having barely finished arduous protracted congress, waiting any moment, any second to start again, windows open, cool breeze, leaves green, blooming spring. "Once we had no money."

"This is much better," Kai said. "Now he can count it."

"That's not all he does." Though actually that was all Jared did. That was his job. Counting money. $3.4 billion in net income a year. Somebody had to.

Kai didn't want to talk about Jared anymore. And neither did Larissa.

On Tuesday, she left rehearsal and stage production early and went to the mall, where in one of the kiosk stalls, she bought a hundred-dollar pre-paid phone, number untraceable. She paid for it in cash.

7

Surveillance, Human

Before, Larissa went months without seeing a familiar face; now she saw them everywhere. In Stop&Shop she ran into Rita, one of Michelangelo's friend's moms. "What are you doing all the way here?" asked a friendly Rita.

"I could ask the same of you," Larissa replied.

"I was in the neighborhood, thought I'd try it out. Looked big and new."

"Yeah, me, too."

"You want to grab a coffee? They've got a Starbucks right on the premises."

"Maybe another time? I'm in a bit of a rush."

And then by herself in Neiman's lingerie department. Suddenly: "Larissa!"

And it was her friend Diane, the wife of Frank, who happened to be Asher's guidance counselor, who once every couple of months played poker with Jared. She could see it now. Diane tells Frank that Larissa bought a $400 sheer lace black babydoll, and Frank asks Jared while he's laying down four queens if the black babydoll has paid dividends and Jared returns home inquiringly.

"Shopping for a friend's birthday," Larissa said. "As a gag. Trying to find something wholly inappropriate. Any suggestions?"

"Well, what you've got in your hands should do the trick."

"You think? Thanks."

Larissa, pulling out of Albright, waiting for the cars to pass before she could make a right, and an oncoming car, pulling up alongside her, window rolling down. "Larissa! What are you doing in this part of town?" It was one of Maggie's teacher friends, Amy.

"Having my car checked out," said Larissa. Such a trivial thing. Yet people clearly had little to talk about, little to do, little to think about. Because Amy told Maggie, and Maggie told Ezra, and Ezra the very next Saturday night said, "Everything okay with your Jag, Larissa?"

"Yes, of course, it's fine. Why?"

"Amy said she saw you were getting your car fixed."

"No, not fixed," Larissa said, trying to mask the exhaustion, the irritation, the fear out of her voice. "Not fixed. Oil needed to be changed."

Jared came back in the dining room with more drinks. "I thought we just changed the oil on it a few weeks ago?"

"Yes, but the engine was running rough on it. Rumbling. Sure enough, oil needed to be changed."

"Again?"

"Guess so."

Maggie chuckled. "How fast is Larissa riding that engine that her oil needs to be changed every two weeks?"

She and Maggie were ambling to Neiman's one Thursday and who should come walking toward them but Fran, her nail companion.

"Larissa, baby! Where've you been? I haven't seen you in monthloads."

"Hi, Finklestein. Maggie, Fran."

"Hi, Maggie." Fran, so smart in her skin-tight jeans, her loose striped sweater and spiky boots, turned to Larissa. "Have you found a better place?"

"No, but it hasn't been that long. In fact, I'm coming tomorrow."

"Ah, I can't tomorrow. Maybe next Friday?"

"Absolutely, Finklestein."

And as they walked away, Maggie said, "You haven't done your nails? But look at them. They're always freshly manicured."

"Mags, have you tried the Sally Hansen Diamond Strength Nail Hardener? The stuff keeps your nails forever. I just reapply every couple of days. You should try it."

Maggie showed Larissa her bitten-off nubs. "Not for me."

Larissa breathed out a small sigh of released tension.

Oh, but the joy ride on his bike. Straddling it, flying in the clover fields through the dandelions, their white florets raining down like daisies on postcards, like summer wishes. To think that Union County of the state of New Jersey could hold paradise.

8

Much Ado on the Stage

"I want to come to your play." It was set to open the first week in June, before the proms and after the interminable Memorial Day weekend spent without him.

"Are you crazy? No."

"Why can't I come? I'll sit in the back. I'll watch. After it's over I'll go."

"Kai, don't be silly."

"I'm not being silly."

"You're not serious."

"I am."

"You can't come."

"Why?"

"Kai. Do I really have to explain it?"

"It turns out that yes, you do."

"You can't come because if Jared catches one glimpse of you, he'll know. At the very least, you'll raise his suspicions. He'll start to snoop around. He'll become more watchful. He won't think it's a happy coincidence. He won't think it's normal. Why would you, of all people, come to my play?"

"I'll come on the day he's not there."

"I'm there every night, so he's coming every night."

"Even if he sees me, is he really going to think about it all that much?"

"Yes!"

"He won't see me."

"He will. By accident, he will. Michelangelo will run up your aisle and drop his Milky Way candy in front of your seat. Oh, hi, you'll say to my husband."

"I'll act like I've never met him."

"But you have! Kai, I'm serious. No."

"Really, no?"

"Really, no." And when she saw his wounded face, she said, "I'm begging you. Please."

"Am I even real?" asked Kai.

Funny, that. That's what Larissa kept asking herself. Was she even real?

Chapter Five

1

Split Rock

She told Jared she didn't want to go to Lillypond in the summer.

"But you love that house," Jared said. "What happened to, if we could, we'd live there year-round?"

"I'm not feeling the love this year, okay? Plus the children never get to hang out with their friends, they never get to do any of the fun summer stuff their friends do. They want to spend July at the Swim Club. Emily wants to go to music camp."

"No, I don't!" called out Emily from the computer in the den.

"Asher wants sports camp."

"No, I don't!" called out Asher from the TV in the living room.

"Michelangelo wants to go to day camp with his friend James."

"I do, I do, Daddy!"

Jared didn't understand. "Why even have the place if we're not going to use it in the summer?"

Larissa didn't say anything. "Well, maybe you're right, hon. Perhaps we should sell it. Is there an economic downturn? Is your job secure? Maybe this isn't a good time to be carrying two houses."

He looked at her funny. "Is my job secure? What are you talking about? You want to sell *Lillypond?*"

"I'm just saying. I don't want us to pay for that *plus* the kids' camps. It's too much. That's not being practical. We should be careful."

He watched *her* carefully.

"We'll do what you like, honey," Larissa said. What she was doing wasn't working. She had to try another tactic.

"I want to go to Lillypond. The kids love it there."

"It's hard for me, Jared," Larissa admitted. "You're not there for six weeks . . ."

"That's not true."

". . . I'm taking care of the house, the kids, the laundry, the cleaning, the cooking, the shopping, all by myself. It's hard. It's nice that you roll in on the weekends . . ."

"And a week in August."

". . . And everything is done for you. You play with the kids for a few hours and then go back to your grown-up world. But I'm with them twenty-four hours a day, I don't have any adults to talk to, and I just don't want to do it anymore, okay? It's too much for me."

Jared reached for her, but she was too far away. She moved herself too far away, imperceptibly, as she was speaking, and when he reached out, he couldn't touch her. "I didn't know you felt this way. Why didn't you tell me?"

"I'm telling you now. This is me telling you."

"The kids are getting older," Jared said in confusion. "It should be easier, not harder. It's not as hard as it was when they were babies, is it?"

"Maybe to you it seems this way," said Larissa. "But the cumulative effect of the years of taking care of the kids by myself must be having its toll. It's like the clouds. They don't seem like much, one by one, but get enough of them together, and there's a downpour. I feel a little bit like that."

Some of this was true. She did feel isolated. In the past she would go, hoping to read, relax, get away from the urban life, as she called the school year in languidly suburban Summit. But in the wilderness there was no Ernestina and no husband; Riot was always running in soaking wet and muddy, the kids always needed the rowboat pushed out, and everyone's clothes were in a perpetual state of filth even though they hardly wore anything but bathing suits. There was no time for reading. She never had a moment to herself. Michelangelo came everywhere with her. So did Emily. And Larissa was going to be three hours away from Madison! For six weeks. And then they were going to Miami. It just wasn't going to happen. She couldn't not see Kai for two months. Simply couldn't, that's all there was to it.

Jared and Larissa compromised. The children went to day camps for the month of July, and in August, Jared insisted on taking two weeks off to stay with her in Lillypond.

"I can manage two weeks on my own, Jared. Don't take off."

"No, I want to. I don't want a crisis on my hands, an unhappy wife."

"I'm not unhappy, darling. Not at all. *Believe* me."

"I believe you. I'm still coming. We'll spend the month together. Two weeks in Lillypond, then two weeks in Miami." He smiled broadly at her through his thick-rimmed glasses. "Happy?"

This is what happened when you made up bullshit reasons for your decisions to a good man who tried to help you. He helped you. She wanted adult company? He came and kept you company.

In July, Larissa lived like she suffered, she lived like she was blockaded and in famine. Kai worked from sunrise to sundown, from six in the morning till noon at Cortese Builders, seven days a week, and then at Jag from two until closing, every day except Monday. She carved out three hours every Monday when he was off in the afternoon and her kids weren't back from camp until 4:45. They spent those stifling summer hours in a tortured perspiring embrace, clammed up even as they were opened up.

"You're not going away forever," Kai kept saying to her. "It's just for a few weeks. I'll be here when you come back. Right here. I'm not going anywhere."

She couldn't speak, couldn't tell him that she couldn't do without him, couldn't be without him. She thought if he filled her up with himself those three hours, filled her up, like a tank of gas, all twenty-two gallons of him inside her, then she wouldn't run on empty when she was in Lillypond.

But when August came, and her family packed up the house and the kids and the two cars, and the dog, and drove out to their summer retreat in the woods on the lake, not a day went by when Larissa wasn't on empty, dragging her limbs, all of her listing down, down, down like a willow in the rain. After the first day, she couldn't imagine another hour without Kai, much less a whole month. The cell phone that was once her friend was now her enemy. There was no cell phone signal in Lillypond. In the previous years that was part of the delight, and now it was a blight on her soul like a plague of locusts. Not even a call to hear his voice!

After suffocating for two more days amid the pastoral sunny pleasures of the great outdoors, Larissa tore her bathing suit. Tore it with her hands, and told Jared she had walked into a tree branch, and look, she'd only brought the one.

"You only brought *one* bathing suit?" He was incredulous.

"I don't know *what's* wrong with me," she agreed. "I'll just run out and buy a new one. I'll be an hour or two. Will you be okay?"

"Will I be okay while you run out to buy a bathing suit? Yes, I think I'll manage. We'll go fishing. I'm going to teach Michelangelo how to row a boat. But where are you gonna get a bathing suit around here?"

"Oh, there must be a place somewhere."

"I mean, something you can actually wear."

"Well, you're right. That might require some searching."

She and Kai met at Lake Harmony, sixty miles away, about halfway between Lingertots and Madison, at the Resort at Split Rock, a sprawling vacation destination for families. There was no time to get a room, plus Larissa wasn't sure if the Great Pocono Lodge on Lake Harmony was the sort of three-star holiday establishment that rented rooms by the scorching afternoon. They met in the parking lot—they were used to that—and made feverish, clothed, cramped, desperate love in the passenger seat of her tiny Jaguar, parked in a remote corner at the edge of the forest. Lake Harmony was one of the Pocono lakes, the entire area given over to families coming with their children for fun and frolic in the fjords of Pennsylvania, where everywhere you looked were placid trees and lakes and gently rolling rising rocks and mountains, where oak and ash grew abundant over roads, and families came to play badminton and volleyball and rent boats for water adventures. In a secluded green corner of that unspoiled esthetic, Kai and Larissa succumbed to a corner of their own rising rocks and falling ash. He made her take off her clothes and sit naked on top of him for the second time around, with the windows open and the roof off, daring her to moan, to keep quiet, his palms on her wet back, his mouth at her throat.

They slumped afterward, their bodies glued together, until she told him she had to go, and he said of course you do, squeezing her hard nipples in his regretting fingers. After she went, she realized she hadn't gotten a bathing suit. The Resort Shop in the Galleria sold simple black one-pieces with the Split Rock logo stitched in. Larissa pulled out the threads that fastened the logo to the fabric with her teeth and brought the suit home without the bag that read, "THE POCONOS! ENJOY YOUR PLACE IN THE SUN AT LAKE HARMONY!"

Jared didn't think much of her choice. "This is all Wilkes-Barre had?" he said with a critical shrug. "You would've done better going back to Short Hills, to Neiman's."

"Oh, I'm sure you're right. But too far. I didn't want to leave for the whole day."

"Nonsense. You should," he said. "Me and the kids will be fine. It poured in the afternoon. We're going to go tomorrow to see if we can find any mushrooms."

"It rained?" Not sixty miles away it hadn't. "But Jared, you hate mushrooms."

He laughed. "I know. I'm thinking of the children."

"They hate mushrooms, too."

"It's time they learned to pick the things they hate," he said. "Go tomorrow, if you want. Leave early, though, so you have all day. Go shopping. Get yourself a facial. Pamper yourself. Go to a movie, buy some sandals, have lunch. Have fun." He brought her to him and kissed her, his amber eyes soft and affectionate. "I didn't realize how hard this is for you. I haven't been considerate. Go. I do this so rarely, it's a treat for me. I'll be mom for a day. I'll put on your apron, bake brownies."

"Jared," she said, still in his arms, "I don't own an apron."

"Maybe you should get one tomorrow."

With Jared's blessing, she went. Kai called in sick, to both jobs.

They rented a room at Split Rock, the "Woodland Retreat," on the ground floor, with a kitchen, a Jacuzzi, and a small patio overlooking the lake. Kai paid in cash. They bought baby oil at the hotel sundry shop, they ordered room service sandwiches, coffee, water, champagne. They put a "Do Not Disturb" sign out.

They had eight hours. It was like a waterfall.

2

Spilled Milk

"So how new is this life for you?" They were soaking in the Jacuzzi, sitting across from each other, their legs intertwined. She'd had too much champagne, was feeling woozy in the hot water.

"Which life?" Did he mean him?

"The house and all."

"Oh, the house is over seven years new. A little older than the baby boy." She probably should get out. They'd been in for a while. She was losing grip on her speech.

"The boy came with the house?" Kai chuckled, flicking water at her. "Why didn't you stay in Hoboken? Continue to teach theater."

"Why? This is a much better life."

He said nothing at first, his hands moving in clichés, in circles. "Is it?"

"For the children, absolutely."

He kept silent. "Did you do it for the money?"

"We did it for a better life, Kai. We were broke, fighting all the time, the kids were unhappy. And then our college friends Katie and Scott came over for dinner one night, and we found out that they paid their babysitter more per week than what Jared and I made. *Combined.* And we had all been English majors. English, theater. We had all been in the same boat at NYU, yet there they were and here we were. Chris had an MBA, and was the head accountant for

Shearson. And they didn't seem stressed and unhappy like us. They were happy. Like they didn't have a care in the world. So after they left we talked it over for weeks. We said we also have a choice. We can continue living Evelyn's life, and our life, and Ezra and Maggie's life, or we can try to build a different life. It was a joint decision. We both wanted it."

"Did you?"

"We did."

"No, that's not what I'm asking. I'm asking, did *you*?"

Larissa tilted her head back. And slowly blinking, closed her eyes. Definitely too much champagne.

She was speedwalking down Henry Street in Hoboken, nine months pregnant with Asher and huge like an elephant's ass, with Emily barely a year and in the stroller. She was carting a half-gallon of milk in a plastic bag hooked over the handle, because they had only one car and Jared took it into the city to look for work before he went to his night job, and the plastic bag broke, and the milk fell and crashed and spilled all over her shoes and coat and stroller—*milk!* All over everything, the small child in the stroller crying, hungry, and she cursed the milk and the stroller and the crying, and possibly even the small child, and resented Jared because he was out gallivanting in their only vehicle while she was rolling back the years, and stomped back to the store, wet with sticky milk, to get another gallon and this time she asked for a double bag, and it was a quarter-mile back home to the three-room apartment they were renting on the fifth floor, and when she got to the store, thinking it couldn't get any worse, her water broke.

Three years passed. The MBA nearly finished, one more year to go, and they struggled insurmountably to make ends meet. They couldn't afford to drop the milk because they wouldn't be able to buy another gallon, and she diluted the milk a little bit with water for the kids' cereal, hoping they wouldn't notice, waiting, waiting until the day the MBA would change their life and make it all go away.

"Yes, Kai," she said. "I really wanted it." She didn't sit up, didn't look at him.

He splashed her. She came out of it. "Are you happy?"

"Of course." She paused. "Though the Chinese food was better in Hoboken. But now I can afford it. And I can still get Chinese when I go visit Evelyn, but at least I get to come home to a house with a ping-pong table, a breakfast nook, a bills nook."

"You need that."

"Yes. Lots of bills to pay. Just like before. Difference is, now we can pay them."

He was pensive. "House *is* beautiful. The dog especially."

"Boy is beautiful, too."

"The boy that came with the house? Yeah. Must be nice to have kids."

She watched him carefully. Studied him. "It is."

"Do you have a chandelier? Mood lighting?"

"Yes."

"Fireplaces?"

"Three."

"I know you have a pool."

"With a diving board. And a movie theater room."

"With popcorn?"

"A popcorn *maker*."

"Drink holders?"

"And remote controls built into the arms of the reclining leather couches."

Kai whistled appreciatively.

"Three years it took us. Three years of grad school, of eating pasta, potatoes, counting every nickel we put into the jar. Paying for our weekly groceries with change the kids were saving to buy a new game system. No one handed it to us. We worked very hard to get here."

"It paid off. Look where you are."

Thing was, she was bare in his naked arms.

3

Simi and Eve

"You wanna go do something?"

"Like what?" They were in bed, and she was less woozy, but more raw. Cosily she was nestled against him, his body an ironing board, a stern taskmaster. He was the wire-mesh monkey mother, too hard for comfort, yet what comfort it was. The sheets were pulled over them, and he was tap-tap-tapping a fast beat on her back.

"Well, Larissa Stark," Kai said in his tour guide voice, "this is the Split Rock Lodge and Resort. We have many different activities for your entertainment."

"I think I may have already partaken too much of some of those."

"Well, yes, I see you have enjoyed our daytime portion of the program, a Hacky Sack game for adults, and I commend you on wanting to play it time and again, and improving your speed in reaching the finish line, but I wanted to draw your attention to other things we offer in this resort for you and your eager and able partner. Would you be interested in attending our Motivational Seminar called 'The Magic of Split Rock'?"

"Thank you, but I think I've already attended that. I'm sold."

Tap-tap on her back, kissing her on the head, kissing her mouth, contemplating her, Kai continued. "In the Galleria Main Lobby we have a Scrabble tournament this afternoon."

"I'm all scrabbled out."

"A little later we've got one-on-one basketball. Perhaps your lover can play you?"

"He's played me. One on one."

"We've got indoor tennis courts, a bowling alley, a fitness center, or boating if you're feeling outdoorsy and adventurous instead of sleepy and naked."

"But what if I'm feeling sleepy and naked?"

"Well, perhaps you'd be interested in our nighttime entertainment calendar. We've got jackpot bingo, and a family dance party with a live band. In our Benchwarmers Pub, we offer Big Willie Live . . ." Kai mock frowned. "I don't know if Live is his last name, or if Big Willie is being offered live."

"I hope he's being offered live," she murmured, her hand caressing him up and down.

"Will you consider coming to the Family Sing-Along?"

"Coming to? Or coming at?"

"No, no, we do not allow hotness. This is a family establishment. What about the Newlywed-Oldywed Game? How well do you truly know your young lover? This may be a good time to find out. That's at 10 p.m."

"Hmm." She was less sleepy, and he was less sleepy. She climbed on top of him, held him between her legs, kissed his face, his chest, kissed his eyes. His hands were holding her hips. "What about the Great Pocono Ping-Pong Challenge?" she asked. "The winner gets to have sex with the loser."

"Done deal," he replied, dancing rings underneath her. They kissed deeply. "But I want payment upfront."

"Done deal."

❧

They played Miss Mary Mack, all dressed in black, and were lying on top of the sheets in a quiet room with the curtains drawn, the windows shut, in welcome air-conditioning, the hum from the wall unit soothing out the silence.

"Kai, we have time," Larissa said. "We have a little time. Tell me things. Please."

"I was about to drift off, so happily, too. What things?"

"Tell me things about my young lover . . ." she whispered.

Kai sighed. He was on his back, but his arm around her became less embracing. "What's the point?" he said. "Is it going to make you want to come more?"

Was he being naughty? She peered into his face.

"Is it going to make you want me more?"

"I don't see how that's possible," she whispered. "I can't think of anything else but you."

"But what if it makes you want me less?" he said. "What if instead of pity and compassion, you'll be afraid, you'll stay away?"

"Kai," she said, "how in the world can I stay away from you? Please, yes, tell me *something* that will make me stay away."

"What will do it? What if I was in prison like my dad, for drug dealing?"

Larissa was quiet. Was he testing her or hypothesizing? She didn't think that would do it.

"I wasn't, by the by."

"Kai, you're so young."

"Only in body. I've been quite careless with things. You know how reckless you can be when you're young."

She knew.

"Look at the scar on my stomach. I went for a demon ride, but a girl was on my bike with me. I nearly lost my liver, but she broke both legs, a rib, and her front teeth. She could've been killed. But I wasn't thinking about that. She wanted to go so I took her. That's what I mean about careless. Slam! Right into the side of a mountain. At night. I was going way too fast and came to a hairpin turn and couldn't stop. With the lights off."

Larissa rubbed him to soothe him. "But the girl went of her own accord. You didn't force her to come with you."

"I should've known better. I knew the risks. She didn't."

"She went of her own free will. You didn't kidnap her."

Kai said nothing at first. "Sometimes you have to watch out for people you care about," he said at last. "Sometimes they make the wrong decisions. You have to try to help them."

"You think she made the wrong decision?"

"Surely she did."

Larissa cajoled him, but he remained reluctant to speak. Not angry, just withdrawing. She had not seen him angry.

"Is this not enough?" Kai asked, shying away from being tickled, probed. "We have it good. Why can't we just leave it like it is?"

"Is this good?"

"You don't think this is mad good?" His body was suddenly over her, his inquiring hand between her legs. "I don't mean *this*. I mean us. You and me."

"Will it be less mad good after you tell me?" Larissa moaned. Will *we* be less good? But she didn't ask that.

"I think it might be, yes." Kai pulled away, lay on his back again, his burst of energy spent. He did that thing she saw him do sometimes: when he was stressed, in traffic, or in a hurry, he would pull up, straighten his back, sit preternaturally still, frozen without motion, like a painting. He made himself a still life and dealt away with his anxiety. It was a Zen move and she loved it because it made her calmer too. She didn't want him to be tense. She thought of stroking him, but the result of him being stroked would not make him less stressed in the end, and he might welcome the diversion and a stop to the unwelcome conversation.

"Tell me anyway." Was she hoping somewhere in the recesses where a tiny breath of conscience entered that perhaps she might dim in her ardor? Wouldn't that be loverly, to dim in her ardor. "You're a kid. How much trouble could you have gotten into?"

"Plenty," Kai said. "And real trouble. The kind that's hard to walk away from."

Larissa hoped, almost prayed, the trouble she was in now wasn't that kind of trouble.

"I was a party boy. Lots of friends, lots of drink. Girls. My mom was working two jobs, and partying herself, my grandmother had raised me, but she was getting old, and my granddad had died. I was on my own, fending for myself since I was thirteen. Working, partying, whatever."

Funny how from a different provenance that had also been Larissa's life: her mother and father lovingly but deliberately hands off. "We want you to make your own mistakes," they told her. "That's the only way you will learn. We're not here to run your life." Larissa always suspected that after raising three boys strictly, they were done with serious child-rearing by the time they got to her and used the libertarian argument to justify their parental exhaustion. But the effect on her was the same: she had love but little guidance.

"One of the girls I met at a party," Kai continued, "was Simi. She was sixteen. Had a crush on me."

"Who wouldn't?"

Leaning over, he kissed her lingeringly, kept his lips on her as if he didn't want to continue. He sighed. "I hooked up with her one evening. With all that music blaring, I couldn't tell anything about her except she was cute. It was nothing serious, just one of those things."

"Have you ever had something serious?" Larissa asked tentatively.

"You decide," Kai said. "After I tell you. I kept seeing her. But I had a few other things going on . . ."

"Girls-wise?"

"Mmm. It didn't take me long to figure out that Simi was a junkie in the worst way. I mistook pinpoint pupils for doe eyes. She had been hoping I had the goods because she'd heard about my dad. She was thinking she'd sleep with me and I'd give her the H. I told her my dad didn't deal blow to his son, how sick is that? And he was in prison besides. Hard to sell dope from prison. I thought that'd be the last I'd see of her, but no. She kept coming back."

Larissa looked at his stomach, at his legs covered with a white sheet, at his lips. He had the goods. She tried not to quiver.

"Well, she continued with me like I was her methadone or something, but she was a real screwed-up girl, a nice girl, but so messed up, like . . . *messed* up." Kai lifted his arms as if in surrender, and broke off. "She was a cotton shooter. You know what that is?"

Larissa shook her nervous head.

"That's someone who's so bad addicted that when they're broke and can't get the man, they shoot up the residue from the cotton used to filter the H. Pretty bad." He clucked his tongue, but Larissa could tell from the way his bottomless eyes refused to look at her when he spoke, that this wasn't a gossip story to him, this was the source of much of his solitary inwardness.

"I didn't see her getting out of it," Kai went on. "You know how sometimes you can tell if people can get out of shit? Like you sense in them a way out? Maybe a bit of strength, or a bit of hope for themselves, maybe a little upbringing, a little ambition, God maybe? Something. It doesn't have to be much, but it has to be real. Well, Simi had none of that. Her home life was terrible. She was a high school drop-out, had no skills, lived with her stepmom, and stole serious dough from her to score."

"Where was her dad?"

"Out of Maui with another woman. Can you blame him?"

"I don't know," Larissa tersely replied. "I know nothing about him."

"I wanted to stop seeing Simi, but she was so tightly wound, I didn't think she'd take it well, and so we kept at it, me hoping she'd move on from me, find an actual balloon, um, a supplier," Kai explained. "But she wasn't moving on, floating, floating, promising me week after week when she was broke that she'd quit for good, and then we could have a normal relationship."

"Were you . . . on it?"

"What are you worried about?" He peered into Larissa's face, shaking his head. "Control over myself is my thing, my drug of choice. H wasn't my scene," Kai said. "You know what I believe, Larissa? Life is so fucking short, you never know when it's going to end, and I didn't want to spend a second of it in oblivion. Trouble was, Simi thought life was entirely *too* long and oblivion was exactly what she needed to make the hours run faster." Kai paused. Larissa was still lying down, but he was now sitting up bowling pin straight against the headboard. He looked down into his palms. "You want to know how the hours of her life crawled to a stop?"

"She OD'd?"

"She got pregnant."

Larissa put her face into her hands. Why were young women so wantonly reckless with their lives and bodies? "While on heroin?"

"Yeah, apparently those two things are *not* mutually exclusive. Turns out heroin is not synonymous with contraception. Who knew? It may stop you from coming, but not from conceiving. So how do you think a seventeen-year-old girl still living at home with no job, no education and a devastating King Kong–size monkey on her back would feel about this?"

"I can hardly guess," said Larissa.

"Simi got it into her head that the baby was going to be her ticket out. Suddenly she got religion! Here was this baby from God, and now everything was going to be okay with her and consequently with us."

Larissa sat up in a lotus position, her hands on his legs. "Were you okay with that?" She looked into his face searching for answers.

Kai shrugged inscrutably. "I wanted her to get better. She was a frail girl. And—you know, my mother had me at sixteen, had my sisters soon after. Many of my mother's neighbors had their kids young. I didn't have a problem with it."

"But a baby for you at eighteen!" Larissa said, wistfully anxious.

"My dad wasn't much of a dad. I wanted to do better. I thought I could do better."

Did Kai have a baby waiting for him in Hawaii? That was coldly inconceivable. Rather, Larissa didn't want it to be true.

"So I said to her that if she quit the H, I'd marry her."

"You'd *what?*"

"Yeah. It was the right thing to do. I said I'd marry her. I'd graduated high school, I was working, *lots* of business for a stonemason with the luxury hotels and the condos springing up everywhere. I was making money. I said, why not? We'll do it right, Simi."

"You're crazy."

"That may be so, but she got pretty excited."

"Kai, is Simi the girl who was in the motorcycle accident with you?"

He was utterly quiet for at least a minute. It seemed like he wasn't even breathing, his chest not rising nor falling.

"Yes," he finally said.

"Oh, Kai."

"The accident didn't happen when she was pregnant. It happened the first night I met her. That's how we found out she was a junkie. She went into mojo withdrawal at the hospital."

"So you hooked up, went for a demon ride, and both nearly died?"

"Yes."

Larissa herself fell silent. She became frightened—of him. Of the calm that hid life-threatening danger just below the surface.

"Anyway . . ." Kai made a rolling forward gesture with his hands, like he wanted to get on with it. His usual animation was nowhere to be seen. "You want to hear more?"

Larissa didn't. She imagined no good endings. She nodded.

"Simi decided she would cold turkey it and get off H, but the doctor at the free clinic said never. You should've quit before you got pregnant, that's how you do it. First quit, then get knocked up. Now it's too late, you're out of options. You quit now, the baby dies for certain. If you want this baby to have the remotest chance of living—and Simi desperately did—you have to continue the heroin, in the smallest dose you can manage without going through withdrawal, and we'll do what we can to keep the baby inside the womb as long as possible. Heroin babies are usually preemies. If we can get to thirty weeks, thirty-two, we stand a good chance. Then you and the infant can go on methadone."

Larissa was so silent, she could hear a boat rev its engine in the water, beyond the hum of the AC, through the closed windows. She could hear a woman calling down the hall, a siren wailing off in the distance. She could almost hear the hands of the clock. Thirty weeks of tick tock.

"Simi tried hard to eat, to sleep, to take her vitamins, to only shoot up when she absolutely needed the fix."

"Where was she living at this time?"

"With me. We rented a one-bedroom. We weren't strapped for cash. I kept bringing home the bacon and she kept buying heroin with it." Kai broke off; Larissa could see how unwillingly he continued.

"I'd be happy if I never had to talk of this," Kai said. "I don't want to get it off my chest. This is not something I need to work through. It's just the way it is. Nothing you can do. After she got hooked, nothing anyone could do." He breathed in, his back in a straight line, nothing on his body moving. "Well, she managed real well, longer than anyone'd expected. She carried that baby nearly to full-term. We all thought the worst was behind us. The baby was doing great. They were going to induce at week thirty-six, just to be on the safe side. But then, during a routine check-up at thirty-five weeks the doctor couldn't find the baby's heartbeat. They did an ultrasound, and . . ." Kai opened his hands to the heavens. "That little baby had died. Simi had to give birth to it dead." Kai did not look at Larissa. "I told you it was no good. Simi had to be sedated before she could be induced, she was pretty hysterical."

"Oh, Kai."

"We buried the baby right before Christmas, and broke up a few months later in the spring. She said to me, you can still marry me, Kai, you know. I just gave her my weekly pay. I said an addict can't live with a normal person, Simi, and she said, I can live with you, Kai, you're not normal because you make me better, you make me calm because you're calm yourself. You bring me peace. I said, yes, but you don't bring *me* peace. We can't be in the same room together while you shoot up, busted up with grief over our baby. She said she understood. What she didn't understand was that what happened wasn't just against her, it was against me, too. She thought she was the only one suffering. So . . ." Kai took another pained breath. "She moved back in with her stepmother. I continued to send her money. We stayed in touch. I wanted her to be okay."

"I'm so sorry." Poor Kai. Poor Simi. Much of Larissa's sorrow was for the heroin-addled heroic mother who carried a baby to term because she thought it was going to save her. There was something visceral and paralyzing in the knots twisting shut Larissa's own womb when she imagined addicted Simi from Hawaii, who loved Kai and wanted his baby even more than she wanted heroin. What Larissa felt for Kai at that moment was beyond primitive sadness. It was a burden of churning current, but heavy. Like sand and cement in her gut.

"Was it a boy?" Why didn't she want the answer to be yes?

"No, it was a girl. Simi named her Eve. Eve Passani." Kai clicked his tongue together, tightened his grave and unhappy mouth. He was still looking down. "And not long after that, my dad died, just to, you know, complete the vortex of parental malfunction swirling around Maui at that time. Simi continued to be so depressed, on all kinds of meds, totally unable to deal. She was taking anti-psychotics morning and night. The doctor would say, but Simi, if you keep taking Klonopin, you'll never deal with it, and then when you go off the meds, two years from now, three years from now, it'll be like it happened yesterday. And Simi said, who said I'm going off the meds? The doctor said, well, eventually you'll have to go off. And she said, who said? The doctor looks at *me*, helplessly! I said, what the fuck are you looking at me for, man? Give me some of that, too. Who wants to deal with it?

"But you know, after months of this, I'd had enough. Simi wasn't going to get better on my watch. I was fooling myself into thinking I could help her. When I got Dad's bike, I left for good. Came here. Escape, man. Anything but stay and watch her destroy herself."

"And Simi stayed with her stepmother?"

"Yes."

Larissa didn't speak.

Kai didn't speak.

Larissa didn't speak.

Kai didn't speak.

"Did Simi die in April?" she whispered.

"She did."

"Oh, Kai."

"She was doomed. Doomed before I met her. I just didn't know it. 'Cause sometimes you don't. You think you can play God, be the big man, help the poor, heal the afflicted. Like you're Jesus or something. Well, it's all bullshit. You can't help anybody. She had become personal assistant to a moderately unknown rock star in Hawaii," Kai said in a dull voice. "I think he supplied her with all kinds of shit. After a party one night she tried to drive home and crashed. And they tried to blame him! It's his fault, her stepmother cried. He never should have given her the shit. But was it his fault? Was it mine for knocking her up? For giving her the money for the heroin? Who has the responsibility for their own life? You? Or everyone around you? Makes you feel pretty hopeless, though." He paused. "We buried her next to the baby. Same gravestone and everything. Simi and Eve."

Larissa cried.

"No, no." Kai got off the bed. He couldn't even look at her. "I'm not the guy for that," he said. "Seriously. You wanted me to tell you and I told you. But I can't have this." He waved in the general direction of her face. "It's hard enough. I can't deal with it."

Larissa wiped her face. "I'm sorry."

"Yeah. Me too." He looked at his watch. "Have you seen the time?" It was nearly eight. "You better go, you have an hour's drive." He put on his clothes in six seconds.

It took her a little longer to wash off, to get dressed. She wanted to touch him but she could tell he didn't want to be even secretly glanced at.

At the car he kissed her. "Except for that last bit, this was a pretty good day, wasn't it?"

It was all she could do not to weep in front of him.

"So what do you think?" Kai asked forlornly. "You want to say goodbye? I'm tainted goods, Larissa."

"Not quite," she replied, pressing her body against him in a long embrace. "Not quite ready to part with you just yet."

"Funny, that's exactly what Simi said to me right before she died."

4

Family Fun in the Poconos

Where were the bags from this all-day shopping trip? Where were the sandals, the dresses, the bathing suits? Something for Jared, maybe some red, white and blue boxers, a sundress for Emily? Makeup from Bloomingdale's? Where were the things he sent her out for? If she sent Jared to get milk and he came back without milk, what would she think? What will he think? Larissa was so filled to bursting with Kai that she returned home at nearly nine in the evening with no bags.

"Mom's back!" Asher and Emily and Riot ran to her, the dog first. "What'd you get?" The house smelled of fish and of brownies.

"Nothing. Though not for lack of trying. How was your day?"

"Great! We went fishing," said Asher. "You should see the size of the fish I caught, Mom."

"It was a tadpole," said Emily, pushing him out of the way.

"It was a bass, Mom."

"Why don't you just tell her you caught a dolphin if you're going to make crap up?"

"Emily!"

"Sorry."

Larissa put down her purse, took off her sandals. "Where's your brother, your dad?"

"Brother is sleeping, finally, thank God," replied Emily, rolling her eyes.

"Hey, look who's finally home!" Jared came in from the den. In the background, she heard a ballgame. No wonder he didn't come out to greet her right away. Game must be close. "How was your day?" He kissed her. "What'd you get?"

"Well, look, I took half of your advice. I pampered myself. I didn't make it all the way back to Short Hills." She shrugged. "I had the greatest day, though. I wanted to try something else, find something around here that was kind of fun. I drove around everywhere. I explored."

"Oh yeah? Where'd you go?" He was absent-minded. Game must be tied.

"Guys, I have to take you to this place I found. I was on I-80, and I needed to use the bathroom, plus I was thirsty, so I stopped off at one of the Pocono resorts."

"Which one?" He looked back toward the den. Tied game must be in late innings.

"Split Rock. Do you know it?"

He crinkled his nose. "Isn't it cheesy?"

"No! The kids would love it. It's got an indoor waterpark, and boating . . ."

"Indoor boating?"

Larissa pinched him. "It's got bowling and Scrabble tournaments, and family sing-alongs. I brought home a brochure so you could see. It looked fun. It was filled with happy families. Maybe we can go for an afternoon?"

"Maybe," said Jared, skeptically and noncommittally.

Emily and Asher began fighting over the brochure. Jared shook his head. "Kids, stop it. Or I'll rip it in half. Go finish Scrabble. It's almost time for bed. Go! Let me talk to Mom." Still fighting over the brochure, they rollerballed into the den and Jared and Larissa were left alone. "You look tired. You okay?" He touched her face, her hair.

"I'm great. Yeah."

"So what did you do there at this Split Rock? Don't tell me you went to a family sing-along." He smiled.

"Well, of course not. I didn't have my family with me. But I walked around, window-shopped. They have some nice stores. A book store. I had a beautiful long lunch. And then I went to their spa. It was quite something. They had a few openings for a facial, for a massage. I only had to wait an hour or so. I sat in the sauna, I think I fell asleep there. I went in the Jacuzzi. I had a great ninety-minute massage."

"Mmm," he said, rubbing her neck as she stood close to him. "With a female, right?"

"Of course." Larissa smiled. "As always. Michelangelo sleeping? Did he go down okay without me?"

"Well, not okay. He went down. I read him four books. He didn't like any of my choices. I sang him 'Rocky Raccoon' five times. He told me you lie down with him for twenty-two hundred hours. I said that can't be right."

"No, that's about right." Wanly Larissa stared at Jared.

"But you still didn't get a bathing suit? What are you going to do?"

"I guess I'll wear the terrible one I bought yesterday. Besides," she added, walking into the kitchen, "I'm gaining weight. Everything I tried on looked terrible on me. Terrible. I became so depressed."

Emily and Asher were fighting over a word in the other room. Asher was accusing his sister of cheating; she was telling him to not be such a sore loser. The ballgame was on, the windows were open. Dusk was settling, and the sky was deep violet, like Lillypond.

"Michelangelo caught a big fish."

"Oh, yeah? What kind? And I thought you were going to go mushroom picking today."

"Dunno. Big kind. We ate him for dinner. Kids loved it. And we did pick mushrooms. We had a whole full day. We did both."

Larissa sank down.

"Are you hungry?" Jared asked. "I saved you some fish. You don't mind it cold, do you? It's cooked."

"No, I'd love some food. I'd eat the fish raw at this point. I'm starved."

Jared put a thick piece of fillet in front of her, some cold potatoes; she inhaled it, not looking up. He got her a drink of water, a glass of wine. She gulped gratefully.

"You're not gaining weight," he said, coming around the butcher block island to inspect her. "What are you talking about? Just last night I was noticing how slim you were." He put his hands on her hips. "I meant to tell you."

"I look like a fat hog in those fluorescent fitting-room mirrors," said Larissa.

"Can't believe you didn't buy anything."

"You mustn't be so surprised. I often go to the mall and don't buy anything. We'd go broke if I bought something every time I went shopping. You should feel blessed."

"I do feel blessed." He patted her behind, kissed the back of her head. "I'm going to check on the game. It's 4-4 in the eighth. Be right back."

He didn't come back. Larissa finished eating alone, staring at the wood-grain island top. Her soul, full just an hour ago, was already being drained of life. She couldn't stop thinking either of him, or of Simi and her dead baby. Simi's story felt like a separate sorrow that happened to a whole separate human being. But that was *his* baby that died! He hooked up with a troubled stranger and almost got a baby out of it. A child. He wouldn't be a kite on a bike now, he'd be a father of a little girl. Larissa mustn't think this way. Had Simi and Eve survived and got dry and clean, Kai wouldn't be in Summit on his Ducati. Simi had to be doomed so Larissa could fall. Incongruously this girl's fate, her baby's fate were tied up with Larissa's. Had Simi escaped injury on Kai's old motorcycle, maybe Kai would not have felt so responsible for her, so personally liable for her untenable recovery. He was going to marry her because it was the right thing to do. What a fat lot of conscience for a twenty-year-old.

Larissa trudged upstairs to her rustic boudoir and had a shower. When Jared came upstairs, she pretended she had fallen asleep on top of the still-made bed, and he covered her quietly and went back downstairs.

The week creaked by. Larissa busied herself with cooking, with cleaning, with doing the family's laundry. They swam, fished, rowed their little boat. They went for walks and blueberry picking, they played hide-and-seek in the abundant woods and built a water park for the twenty frogs the kids caught and named them all. She baked. For this she needed supplies. Cake flour, baking soda, cardamom, Arborio rice, raisins, brown sugar. This allowed her to drive to the country store in nearby Nanticoke across the Susquehanna River, and to call him from her cell phone. Unfortunately Emily wanted to come with her, and there was no good reason to say no. Larissa managed to get away for a minute, "to use the facilities," to call him.

"Hey. It's me."

"Hey, you."

Briefly, painfully they talked about the impossibility of taking another day like the one they had.

"Every day now feels like seven years," she said.

"I can come to Sugar Notch," he said. "Just thirty minutes away from you up river. I can come Monday afternoon."

But Monday afternoon Maggie, Ezra, and Dylan were going to be here, staying for the week.

"You can't get away? Not even for an hour?" For the first time he said to her, "I wish you could get on my bike right now."

"Me, too, Kai."

"I'm not being metaphorical, Larissa. I mean, really. Get on my bike, we speed away from here."

"Speed away from here to where?"

"I don't know. I don't know the way out. No one knows where they're going. As long as I'm with you, I wouldn't care."

Larissa lived on those words, flew on them, as her house filled with guests, and what should have been, and always had been a pleasure—them together, relaxing under the stars, under the sun— instead became torture, as she tried to make herself more present, yet failed at everything, even dinner conversation.

5

The Cagesweepers

"Man is not free. Freedom is an illusion. Who is free?" This is what happened when the evening ran long, when the children were happy and entertained in the other room watching a Jim Carrey comedy and Riot was asleep under their feet. This is what happened when Ezra had too much Domaine de la Romanée-Conti.

"You're being ridiculous," said Jared, loosened up on Romanée himself. "Right, Lar?"

"Right, darling." She was barely paying attention.

Ezra turned to Larissa. "Larissa, can you not pick up the kids from school? Can you not cook dinner? Well, maybe Maggie over here can *not* cook dinner, but all the other wives, like you, can *they*?"

"Ezra, you're being a pedant," said Jared. "I'm talking about big things, not stupid bullshit."

Ezra shook his head. "Picking up kids from school is not stupid bullshit, Jared." He shook his head, swirled the wine around in his mouth. "No one is free. Not you. Not Larissa. Not me."

Maggie was pensive. "Ezra, that's not what Jared means. He's saying at any time we can change our life, if we put our minds to it."

Ezra laughed. "You think so?"

"I *know* so," said Jared. "Larissa and I were trapped in a life that was wrong for us. It started out pretty good, and then soured real quick. So what did we do? We didn't sit and whine about it. We changed our life. So the answer to your question is yes. We really think so. Right, Lar?"

"Absolutely." She couldn't connect the threads of the words.

Ezra snorted. "That's not freedom," he said. "You've just switched cages."

Jared laughed, unbaited. "Well, give me the cage of Lillypond and Bellevue Avenue any day of the week."

"I'm not saying life is not good in the cage," said Ezra with an agreeable nod. "Life is very good. The cage is clean. The straw is fresh. You can even see the outside if you come real close to the bars. And every once in a while you can go out for a walk. Are you free to just keep on walking?"

Larissa was silent. *That* she heard.

"Exactly! Not in any meaningful way are you free to keep on walking. Loosening the bonds is not possible. This is your life. Accept it."

Jared and Larissa and Maggie exchanged an inebriated, exasperated glance.

"You can do many fun things in your cage," continued Ezra. "You can watch TV, you can paint, like Maggie here, you can read, keeping your mind fresh, thinking up ideas." He swallowed the rest of his wine. "Honestly, I think it's impossible to lead a life *too* examined. I don't think a spiritual death is leading an *un*examined life. I think a spiritual death, and many other kinds, is leading a *too* examined life. That's when people go nuts."

"And you're the proof, man," said Jared.

"Ezra, are you really saying there is no way out?" asked a skeptical Larissa.

"I am saying," Ezra replied, "that there is *no* way out. Pass the wine, Jared."

"It's all gone, dude. The good stuff is gone. Down your gullet. I have beer."

"Chasing down a two-hundred-dollar bottle of Romanée-Conti with Bud? There's poetry in that. I'll take a cold one." Ezra turned back to Larissa and Maggie. "In all ways, girls, in your small yet delightful ways, you are free to make your corner of the world liveable. That's about all you can do. Here's my final statement on the meaning of life: Drink with grace from the cup you've been given. Both of you, by the way, excel at that. We picked ourselves some fine women, Jared."

Jared came back with two Buds, two glasses, patting Larissa on the shoulder as he passed the beer to Ezra perching on the bench next to his wife.

"But, say, you don't have a family or kids like us," Larissa said pensively. "You're alone. You and your guitar. A hitch-hiker by the side of the open road." She managed a small smile. "Aren't you free then? Free to think only of yourself?"

"No!" Ezra was jolly like Roger. He took a swig of Bud. "You're much worse off."

"Get out. Worse off *without* the kids?"

"Of course. Then you're just a slave to *your* needs. You're a slave to your own petulant wants, different every day. Every day you'll want another thing. There'll be a new desire you must satisfy at all costs. Now that you're not swayed by the needs of people who depend on you, you'll be corrupted by your moral emptiness, because you'll be drowning in yourself with the full approval of your so-called conscience. Are drug addicts free? Are thieves, petty con artists free? Are prostitutes free? Alcoholics?"

"He's like this every day," said Maggie to Jared and Larissa. "It's stand-up every night at our house."

The uneroded Ezra continued. "This freedom business is the wrong approach to figuring stuff out. It's bound, by the limitations of its own argument, to lead us to destruction or manic depression. It's much better to focus on other things. Which are: how closely does the life I'm living resemble the life I've always wanted to live? Am I making the best of the hand that's been dealt me? Do some of the things I do every day bring me joy? Is there something more I would like to do, would like to be?" Ezra nodded. "*Those* are good questions. Unlike the false choice Scruples questions you keep tormenting us all with, Margaret."

Larissa knew how much Jared loved evenings like this, spent renegotiating the motivations of Othello's murder of Desdemona, debating free will and the fifth proof of the existence of God. Jared's mind was filled to the brim with the details of his work, weekend and weekday, and he loved it except for the gray erosion of the cliffs of soaring argument that had once allowed him to shine like the intoxicated Ezra, to talk with reasonable likable people about things that mattered most.

Larissa knew these evenings were Jared's way of drinking with grace from the cup he had chosen. Jared, in a crisp white tee and a gray sweatshirt, his gray-brown hair shaggy all month, the eyes inside his black frames so smart, so sparkling. She put her arm around her husband, smiled, and raised her own emptied glass to her lips for the last red swallow.

∽∾

Every time Larissa went to the store, Maggie said, I'll come with you. And of course, why shouldn't she? They went out to lunch. Once they went to the movies. They played gin rummy and Scrabble, watched the Yankees and *Die Hard*. They swam. They fished. Not a day of rain, except for the down-pour in Larissa's heart. The prepaid cell phone criminally without signal, except when she went to Naticoke, and there'd be ten text messages from him that she would read and one by one erase. And once she was in produce, getting peaches, thinking of him, of his back, of the small scars that adorned him, of the one long scar, her hands were on his stomach feeling it, moving lower, as she was in the store buying peaches! and the ding dong of the text message sounded, and Maggie, right by her side, said, "Look, you got a message."

Larissa didn't know what to do. Why hadn't she put the phone on silent! Well, she couldn't remember everything, could she? The web of Kai spun the sticky treacly poisonous thread of sham through every detail of her life, so that even something as simple as turning off the "You Got a Message" alert became a source of danger. Like hiding her pill wheel in Lillypond. What to do now?

"Aren't you going to see who it is? What if it's Jared and he wants more beer?"

She couldn't pull her prepaid phone out. Maggie knew Larissa's regular black phone, and this one was silver and red. She should've bought a phone that matched her regular phone. Damn. So many things she just couldn't think of.

"It's Evelyn," said Larissa, pulling out her regular phone, glancing at it quickly and then snapping it shut. "She says hi."

When Maggie turned to get a plastic bag, Larissa read the text on her prepaid. I CAN'T LIVE, the screen read.

Slightly trembling, she pressed several buttons in a row with her thumb, to delete all messages, even that one, the one she wanted to engrave and hang on a plaque nailed to her heart.

"Evelyn, huh?" said Maggie, squeezing the peach too hard, pulsing the juice out, and then gingerly putting it broken and oozing into a plastic bag so she could pay for it. "I thought you told me they went to Montana to visit her family?"

"They did. She texted me from Montana."

They moved on. "I didn't know you and Evelyn were on such intimate texting terms."

"Well, you don't know everything, do you?"

"Clearly."

6

Miami

After the DeSwanns left the following Saturday, the Starks packed up and left too. They said goodbye to the woods and the frogs and drove back, past Split Rock, past Lake Harmony. Jared drove the Escalade with Michelangelo and Emily, Larissa drove the Jaguar with Asher in the passenger seat.

"Mom, isn't that the place you were telling us about?" asked Asher, pointing to the billboard off the Interstate. "The place with the indoor waterpark and the sing-alongs?"

"Yeah, maybe. I think so, son." But Larissa got stuck on the billboard next to it, peeking out from behind, where a single question blared at her in bold black caps: **"WHERE ON EARTH ARE YOU GOING?"**

"It looked really fun in the brochure. Sad we didn't get to go. Maybe next summer?"

"Yeah, maybe." What was that even an advertisement for? *Where on earth are you going?* What a strange question.

"Or, you know, it's open year-round," Asher continued. "The indoor waterpark in January might be fun for a weekend. We never go anywhere in January. Maybe we can go in the wintertime."

"Yeah, maybe."

The following day, which happened to be a Monday, Larissa told Jared she had to go to the mall. They were scheduled to fly out to Miami and she had deliberately booked their flight for Tuesday morning, knowing that Mondays Kai was off. "I guess I have no choice but to go buy me some bathing suits," she said to Jared. "I can't be in Miami without appropriate attire."

"Absolutely. Don't come back without something extremely sexy. Maybe a two-piece?"

"You're crazy. I'm forty years old. I'm not buying a two-piece."

"Okay. Maybe we can find you a nice topless beach, then." Jared grabbed her to fondle her. "One of those European-style beaches, where you and your teenage boobs are lying out in the sun, burning up, browning."

Lightly she wrestled out of his arms. "Hardly teenage. And is that a topless beach *with* the children, Jared, or without? You're thinking of a different sort of vacation."

"Clearly, but suddenly I'm not thinking of vacation at all."

And after they had sex, in the middle of the afternoon with all the children awake, in the house, and downstairs, Jared announced he was going with her! He was going with her to the mall. He said, I might as well come. I have to buy some shorts.

"To the mall, Jared? I can buy those for you."

"I know, but I want to try them on, plus, we can have lunch at your little Neiman's Café." He nuzzled her. "It'll be my way of saying thank you for some rare love in the afternoon." He was humming happily. "Emily! Come here. She'll be thrilled to watch Michelangelo, won't she? Emily! Did you hear me? Get your butt over here!"

"Dad! No!"

What was Larissa going to do? What excuse could she make? Her husband, in a rare display of spousal affinity, was coming shopping with her! For bathing suits. Shopping. Normally you couldn't catch him *driving* past a mall. Wasn't there a game on or something? Apparently Monday was the Yankees' traveling day. Larissa was out of excuses. She couldn't even pick a fight. She couldn't even call Kai to tell him she wasn't coming.

And then Miami, a two-bedroom ocean front suite at the

Alexander Resort, the sun, the green warm ocean, the Spanish guitar playing nylon string melancholy all day and night, Black Orpheus day and night with seafood and salsa, and beautiful sun dresses and burns on their faces. The kids all went to tennis camp, though Larissa wished they hadn't. Kai had stopped texting her, never responded to her message apologizing for skipping out on him on Monday.

In a cover-up tied around her waist, Larissa took walks by herself around the hotel grounds in the simmering heat. Miami in August was not the smartest of vacations; it felt as if they were wading through the steam from a boiling pot of water underneath them while above them the ruthless sun beat down. Oh, but how brown she got, how perspiring and tan with white crisscross lines on the tops of her feet from the flip flops. She took a picture of herself and sent it to Kai when the signal was strong. What a dream. What a fantasy. How hot, how unbearable it was.

How unbearable.

While Jared golfed with his new buddy Mark, Larissa lay out by the pool, near the ocean, near the beach, big black sunglasses on, in a Christian Lacroix black bikini; she was slim and long legged, graceful and burned, and she dreamed of Kai, wished only for Kai to see her like this, tanned like in high school, or maybe like an Island girl in a peach tube top around her brown breasts, a floral bandana and pink flip flops. He could kneel between her legs, pull down the tube top and suck her nipples in full view of the admiring public by the shimmering blue pool, near the warm ocean. And then he would take her non-stop right on the chaise longue, under the blistering afternoon sun while the nearby flamenco singer strummed Albéniz's *Malagueña* to drown out her desperate moaning, her desperate coming, her legs splayed, quivering.

And then one afternoon, when they were both out by the pool, she in reverie, Larissa opened her eyes and saw Jared reaching into her purse to find some singles to tip the man who brought the Mojitos, because all Jared had were twenties. Larissa watched in horror as he opened her purse, rummaged around to find her wallet, underneath which, in full view, next to the pink gum, the Kleenex, the lipstick, and the Band-Aids was her silver and red prepaid cell phone.

"Here we are," he said, giving the patiently waiting boy four dollars.

"*Gracias, señor.*"

"*De nada.*" Jared turned to Larissa. "What's wrong with you? Why are you white?"

"I think too much time in the sun," she said in a weak voice, her heart down in her stomach. "Can I have my bag, please? Must put some more gloss on."

"Yes, we like you nice and glossy. Drink up. Nice and glossy, and tipsy." He leaned over, smiling. "And naked."

She gave him a pasty smile, clutching her bag to her knees. "I'm going to go use the restroom," she said, struggling up from the chaise, "but start thinking where you'd like to go for dinner. I heard that Creek 28 at the Indian Creek Hotel serves one of the best skirt steaks in Miami."

"Sounds good. Do they take children?"

"Yes. And credit cards." She smiled, standing in front of him appraising her in her bathing suit. "I'll be right back." And as soon as she walked inside the ladies room, with shaking hands she fished out the phone from her purse, turned it off and threw it in the garbage. How many narrow escapes like that would she have, how many freebies before the entire jig was up? How dumb of her. Did she *want* to get caught? Try explaining to a happy husband on vacation with his wife and family in Miami, why his perspiring and panting wife, while lying by the pool almost nude, keeps a prepaid phone turned on by her side, vibrating messages into her trembling legs as she tans with her eyes closed and her parched mouth slightly parted.

7

Dracula

They returned to Summit Labor Day weekend. The children were about to start another year of school, Michelangelo second grade, Asher eighth, and Emily ninth at the high school. Kai might have been off Mondays but Labor Day Monday, as always, the Starks had a big bash at their house. Fifty people came. Caterers. Booze. Clear and jazzy music, Dizzy Gillespie, Ella Fitzgerald, and Ben E. King crooning over the grass to Larissa, that he who had nothing loved and adored her and wanted her so.

The pool lights were on, guests in bathing suits, colored floods on the trees at night, intoxicated animated adults dancing, laughing, and Larissa getting compliments left and right.

"God, Larissa, look at you, you've never looked better."

"Jared, look at your wife! She is stunning."

"Lar, what have you done with yourself?"

"Lar, did you drink from the fountain of youth?"

Even Ezra noticed. "Larissa, they're right, you're glowing from within. You look twenty."

"Twenty years younger or twenty?" countered Larissa, and Maggie, standing close, pinched Larissa's slim brown tricep and cooed, "What's the difference?"

Monday, Monday, Monday. She hadn't spoken to him in over

two weeks, not since she blew him off and never called him. What must he think?

Soon this will be over, Larissa thought, smiling for her guests, carrying the drinks and the strawberries, dancing with Evelyn, with Jared. Tuesday will be here, the children will be on the bus, gone, Jared will be in the car, gone, and I, too, will be gone.

On Tuesday morning, after she got all the children successfully off to school and was getting herself ready, Ernestina came too early with her crew. Larissa's anticipated first morning alone in months turned into ducking four non-English-speaking girls. She closed her bedroom door to shine herself up like a slick apple in the produce aisle, and then had to walk past Ernestina with her vacuum cleaner.

"Oh, Miss Larissa, you look so beautiful. Where you going?"

"Nowhere, just shopping."

"Oh, no, you look too beautiful for shopping!" The girls giggled. "Maybe Miss Larissa has a hot date."

She stormed out of her house without looking back. She must do something about their banter.

She called Kai on his cell from a phone booth near the Summit train station, hoping no one who knew her would see her standing in the middle of town at a *phone booth*. What good reason did Larissa have to use a public telephone?

"Hey, it's me."

"Ah. It's *you*," he said. His voice was cold.

"Kai . . ." She was lost for words. "Did you get the picture I sent?"

"Picture? Of yourself having a blast in Miami? Yeah, I got that."

"Why didn't you text back?"

"Didn't see the point. Why didn't you text me back after I sent you twenty messages in Lillypond?"

He was upset.

"I'm sorry about Monday."

"Which Monday would this be?"

"Kai . . ."

"What happened to your phone?"

"I had to throw it out," she said. "Jared nearly found it in Miami. It was a miracle he didn't."

"Yes, uh-huh, a miracle."

"What could I do? Don't worry, I'll buy another one."

"Oh, I'm not worried. And what makes you think he won't find the next one?"

"I'm not going to be with him twenty-four hours a day, am I?"

"I don't know. Aren't you?"

"Kai . . . when are you getting off?"

"One, probably. I'm at a job now. I have Jag at two."

"I know."

"I was off yesterday," he said pointedly.

"I know. But we had a party."

"How nice for you."

"Listen . . ." she lowered her voice, so it wouldn't break, "I'll come and see you at one, okay?"

"I don't know, will you? You said you were going to come and see me two weeks ago, and yet I don't recall running into you. So I'm not optimistic."

Cold and damp inside, Larissa hung up and drove to Pingry for her eleven o'clock with Ezra and the Gang of Six Naysayers, the play committee. Denise, as it turned out, was not coming back. She was staying home with her baby. Larissa remained the director. The eight of them suffered over what play to put on for the fall.

"I suppose I can't talk you into *Godot*?" Leroy asked.

Larissa was hardly listening. To conduct her outer life when her inner life was screaming took all the resources she had; the power of speech fell by the wayside. She let them bicker and discuss for a while, but when she noticed Ezra's curious, slightly puzzled eyes on her, she blinked and came to it.

"Okay, this is how it is," Larissa said. "It's fall. We need a big production, lots of pizzazz. I'll give you a choice. You can have *Dracula*, or you can have *The Wizard of Oz*. What will it be?"

"Why does it have to be those two?" said Leroy.

"Yeah," said Fred. "Maybe it's a false choice."

Here it starts again. "No," Larissa said slowly. "It's not a false choice. You know how you know? Because it's the choice you've been given. I know you might like a different choice, but that's not one of the choices. Out of these two no good, awful choices, pick the one that's least objectionable."

"But *why* does it have to be one of these two?"

"Because I said so." They were like children.

This time it was Ezra who put his foot down. "Let's do *Dracula*," he said. "The kids will love it. It's a real crowd-pleaser."

The rest of the table grudgingly agreed.

"Great," Larissa said. "Leroy, immediately put out a casting call for twenty parts, fourteen girls, six guys. I want Lucy to be played by someone dark and small, mention that in the notice. Van Helsing by someone tall. The guy who played Benedick last year, Trevor, he was excellent. *Much Ado* was a big success because of him. I hope he auditions. Sheila, please order at least thirty-five copies of the script. Last time we ordered twenty-seven and it wasn't enough. Order them today, though. We need to get started. We're putting it on right before Thanksgiving—plenty of time to do it right. Fred, you're very good with words, would you like to write the casting call?"

Brimming with pride, Fred nodded.

"Excellent. Vincent, we'll need to start sketching Dracula's Castle for Act I as soon as possible. That has to be done just right. Ask Dara, who runs the art department, to come and see me at ten tomorrow. I want to use some of her students to help us. This is a big project. They should all be involved. Sheila, better order forty copies of the script. I have a feeling we're going to need them." Larissa stood up from the table. Everything had to look and function as normal, more than normal. It had to buzz with efficiency and sameness, temperature 72°F at all times, oven 350°F, burners on medium, nothing singed, burned, left unattended, nothing out of place, nothing, nothing, nothing.

8

Love

She was against the wall, suffocating under his hands, she was on the wood floor, suffocating under his body, she was being ravaged with his starving lips, his bare and starved body. "Larissa," he kept whispering. "Larissa . . ."

She was a song without words. He didn't even admire her outfit, her tanned legs, her tie-up wedge sandals. He admired nothing. She was certain he hadn't looked at her before he took her, groping for her in darkness, though the September day was hot, was blazing glory sunshine. And she was moaning and crying and crying and coming. Not long ago, I lay in a chair under the sky and imagined this. Why is reality so much more bitter? "I missed you," she whispered into his neck, her arms, her legs around him, his sweat dripping on her. *I love you.*

"Really?" He was panting, his eyes closed.

"I can't take it anymore . . . please."

"Please what?"

She didn't reply.

"Please what? Please more, or please stop?"

She was crying.

"You have never been fucked like this," he whispered. "And you never will be again."

Larissa didn't want it to be true. But she feared it was.

He didn't leave her. He remained in the space that contained them both, until he was ready for her again. Afterward she washed herself with cold water, no soap or shampoo, just water, to erase the smell of him, to soothe the swelling sting of her bare flesh, to calm herself.

She sat naked on the unmade bed. She was about to get dressed, leave, but she didn't want to. She *had* to. She had *no* choice. This was not a false choice. She had no say in the matter. Whatever *she* wanted to do, the New Jersey Central School District didn't care, it let the kids out every afternoon at 2:40 p.m. with absolutely no thought to what the mothers were doing, whether it be feeding the homeless or sitting here in a bright room, not feeding but falling.

Except . . . it was good. It was beautiful.

It was everything else that was the not-beautiful.

Kai sat up; Larissa quivered. To look at him, to see his hands stretching out for her, to swallow her. One day she was going to simply forget it was 2:40. Conveniently forget. She would live a life in which 2:40 no longer existed. It would be just like 1:40, or 5:45. Just another meaningless minute. The way Che lived, the way Bo lived. And in that minute, his hands would remain outstretched to her, and she would not get off his bed.

"Oh, Kai," she said, an elocution for the lost, a declamation for the longing.

"I can't live without you," he said, watching her.

"Please don't say that."

"It's true. I can't live without you," Kai repeated. "And yet I watch you after not being with you the whole summer walk out of my bathroom, washing my love off your body. Washing *me* off your body. You say you love me, yet this is what you do."

"Did I?" Larissa said, sinking down, defeated, hanging her head. "Did I say that?"

"Yes. In your most fragile moment, you did. You say you love me. Yet, this is what you do."

PART TWO
SCYLLA AND CHARYBDIS

I was not in safety, neither had I rest,
neither was I quiet; yet trouble came.

Book of Job 3:26

Chapter One

1

The Disappearance of Tenestra

"Did you hear that Abel's daughter Tenestra has disappeared?" Ezra lowered his voice. Abel was one of Ezra's Classical Lit professors.

"She ran *away* from home?" They were playing poker, but Larissa dropped her cards on the table.

"Well, sort of. She ran away from rehab."

"Rehab! Get out. Not Tenny. Impossible."

"Be that as it may."

"Rehab for what?"

"Crack."

"You are *so* full of it."

Ezra raised his glass. "All right. Whose turn is it to deal?"

"Mine," said Larissa. "Maggie, is it true?"

Maggie shrugged. "He tells me it's true. Is that the same thing?"

"No!"

"Why are you so surprised?" Ezra asked. "Because it's Tenny?"

"Yes, because it's Tenny." The girl was the valedictorian of her eighth grade class. Granted, that was three years ago, but still. Why did it make Larissa sad to hear it? She palmed her Margarita glass.

She didn't know what was more distressing, Tenestra on crack, or Emily coming home last week and dramatically flailing her arms, telling her that her friend Jemma, all fifteen years of her, was seeing a nineteen-year-old sophomore from Drew. Jemma, whom Larissa had known since Jemma was seven, seeing a boy *nineteen years old*. It was oppressive.

In the here and now she heard Ezra's voice. "What, you think valedictorians don't have serotonin?"

"What?" Larissa struggled to get back on track with crack.

"You think they don't have reuptake inhibitors? They don't feel euphoria? Haven't you heard? Crack is the greatest high you can have."

Larissa didn't believe it; she didn't believe crack was the greatest high you could have.

"But humans are so perversely made," Ezra continued, reaching for the cards. "That the greatest high is accompanied barely two hours later by the greatest low. All you want is to be up again, be that happy."

"Ez, I don't believe it. No one runs away from rehab at Christmas," Larissa said.

Ezra laughed. "There are so many logical fallacies there, I don't know where to begin. Is it that no one runs away at Christmas, or is it that no one is in rehab at Christmas? Which is the thing that galls you most?"

"I don't know where to begin," said Larissa carefully, watching Ezra shuffle. "So where is she?"

"If they knew where she was, we wouldn't have a missing person, would we?"

"What's her father doing?"

"Going nuts. What do you think he's doing?"

"Yeah, really, Lar," said Maggie. "Imagine it was one of your kids." She shuddered. "I can't even begin to think of Dylan getting involved in something like that. The thought alone is intolerable."

"No, no, Dylan is a very good boy, don't worry."

"Yes, tell that to *valedictorian* Tenestra!"

. From the corner of the dining table where she sat, Larissa glanced through the wide hall into the open space of the den where Emily and Asher were on the floor playing hide the ball from the dog, while Michelangelo sat on top of Asher's back and tickled him.

"Are they looking for her?"

"Of course! Larissa, what's wrong with you? Of course they're looking for her."

"Where?"

"Everywhere. There's an APB out on her. She's a runaway minor."

"Does she have money on her?"

"This worries Abel more than anything," said Ezra.

"The fact that she does?"

"No," Ezra said. "The fact that she doesn't."

2

Jonny and Stanley

Bo had been desperately calling Larissa all Monday morning and unable to get through. No one was picking up the phone. Bo was a clarion of frustration. She wanted, *needed* to see her friend immediately. And Larissa usually picked up the phone. She was known for it. What did Larissa do on Mondays? Was she having lunch with Maggie? Bo could never be sure on which alternating day Maggie worked and on which she hung out with Larissa. She didn't want to have lunch with the two of them. She needed Larissa all to herself today. Maggie was all judgment, and Bo needed counsel not judgment. She lived in a two-bedroom apartment in Chatham, which she shared with her boyfriend and her frightfully hypochondriacal mother, going downhill ever since the divorce eighteen years ago. Her mother's last wish, as she would (very often) state, was to see her daughter finally marry the boy she'd been with since college. Though it was theoretical. Mrs. Purch was in love with marriage, not Jonny. Jonny her mother couldn't stand. Bo and Jonny had quite a fire going when they were sophomores at Rutgers. But that was ten long years ago.

Bo had Larissa on speed redial and speakerphone as she continued to put on her makeup in front of her big oval mirror. Mondays the Met was closed, but sometimes Bo went in anyway (as a press writer for the Met art exhibits, her job never ended), though not today. That's it. If Larissa didn't pick up, Bo would drive to her house. Was that rude to just pop in? What if she was washing the floor? Or taking a shower? Or indisposed in some way? Bo herself would be mortified if someone popped in on her when the breakfast dishes from two days ago were still on the table. Or if her mother was still in her robe. Bo spent half her day—which meant half her life—being humiliated by her mother's lack of personal hygiene. How Jonny continued to live with her under these conditions she didn't know. Sometimes Bo brought up a "facility," and her mother glared at her as if Bo were a gargoyle. "What are you talking about, nursing home?" she'd say. "I'm in perfect health. I'm only sixty-nine."

Bo didn't want her mother's nursing home death on her conscience. She was waiting her mother out. A small apartment, a sick mother, two cats, one of whom peed all over the house, and the appetizing sight of sunny-side-up eggs half-eaten, dried on the plate, left on the round Formica table. Yes, if someone just popped in, Bo would be mortified. She'd have to stop being friends with them. She'd have no choice.

It was all about appearances with Bo. As long as no one saw her actual life, but saw *her*, neat, ironed, straight slick hair freshly brushed, a ready smile on her face, then all was okay. Bo was an attractive woman. She was tall and stately, and though she seesawed in weight, even the extra twenty pounds, which is what she was packing at the moment, distributed itself around her hips and breasts. Because she was five-ten, it was hardly even noticeable. She owned all her clothes in two sizes; she would wear the larger size and that would be that. Appearance was the thing.

Dressed as if for work, Bo made sure her mother had a cup of tea in her hand, the TV was on, a window was cracked open despite heavy protestations, and made for the front door.

"You're going to work so late!" said Mrs. Purch. If ever there was a reason to get married, it was so she wouldn't be Bo Purch anymore; what a name! But Jonny's was not much better. Jonny Zolle. Bo Zolle? No luck with the last names. She wished she could have

Larissa's. Stark. And even her maiden name had been elegantly nondescript. Connelly. Larissa had all the luck. "They're going to fire you," added Mrs. Purch.

"Just running a little late, Mother. It's fine," said Bo, wishing she could strap her mother to the couch. *Just to make sure she was safe.* Chatham was ten minutes away from Larissa's house. Seven if she made the lights near the intersection of the highways.

~∽⌐∾~

Larissa showed up at 3 p.m. with Michelangelo in tow.

Bo jumped out of her Saturn. "God, Larissa! I've been *desperately* trying to get in touch with you all day. Where've you been?"

"Food shopping." She popped open the trunk to get the grocery bags. "Whazzup? Michelangelo, be polite, say hello to Bo."

"Hello, Bo." He stood close to his mother with his navy school bag. Larissa handed him a bag of paper towels and tissue boxes.

"Hi, honey." He was so cute, that curly head of blond hair made you want to squeeze him, tousle his hair. So Bo did; she squeezed him, she tousled his hair. "How was your day? How was school?"

"Good. I had art today. We painted. Wanna see?"

"Sure, let's go in." And to Larissa, Bo said, "I really need to talk to you. I stayed home, hoping we could have lunch."

"Why didn't you call me?"

"I did call you!"

"On the cell?"

"Yes!"

"You know, the phone never rang. Don't know what's wrong." Larissa shook the phone, put it to her ear. "Here, call me right now, let's see if it works—oh, wait, no, let's do it later, I've got to get the food in or the ice cream will melt. Is everything okay?"

"No, everything is not okay."

"Sorry about that. Would you mind grabbing a couple of bags?"

Bo took two bags, looking baffled at Larissa. Why was she acting as if Bo weren't standing in her driveway in dire straits? She was acting like this was the most normal thing, Bo taking off, waiting in

Larissa's driveway, wanting to talk to her! As Larissa walked by her, coat open, Bo couldn't help but inhale Larissa's scent. She became even more puzzled. Because under the halfway normal Larissa smells of deodorant and faint perfume, Bo could swear, could almost swear in a court of law, that she could smell the sweat of sex. There was no other smell quite like it, fluids and perspiration from man and woman intermingled on the woman. That smell was like the smell of firewood. Unmistakable. But was Bo mistaken? Didn't Larissa say she was out food shopping? Maybe Larissa hadn't had a shower since this morning, Bo reasoned. Perhaps this is what she and Jared got up to before he left for work. No wonder they had a perfect marriage. If that was Jonny, maybe Bo wouldn't be coming to tell Larissa what she wanted to tell her.

"We can talk in front of the boy," Larissa said as they walked through the back door to her kitchen, "just euphemize, 'kay?"

Bo watched Larissa mill around the kitchen, unpacking the groceries. She was wearing light skinny jeans, a snug cashmere Henley with the seams exposed. Were the jeans *too* skinny? The four-inch-heel boots that went with them—chocolate suede, Gucci?—were definitely too high. Is this how Larissa went food shopping?

"How's everything with *you?*" Bo asked slowly.

"Good. You know, same old, same old. Nothing exciting ever happens here. Hey, want some ice cream?" Larissa asked cheerily. "Or a sandwich?"

"A sandwich might be nice. I'm hungry."

"I'll make you and Michelangelo tuna. Honey, want some tuna?"

"Yes, Mommy. On an English muffin. With pickles. But can I have a little tiny snack while I'm waiting?"

"You got it, bud. Take your folder out. We'll get started on the homework while I make your snack appetizer and snack main course." Larissa turned to Bo from the fridge. "What would you like to drink, Bo? I can make us coffee."

Larissa then proceeded to tell Bo about the six different varieties of coffee she had at her house, and how they each tasted, especially when run through the espresso maker. What was Bo in the mood for? "The French roast is bold but not too spicy, and the Colombian is very mild but good, then I've got some Italian espresso which is quite strong, and the best of all is the Jamaican blue, though it's deceptively mild. Which would you prefer?"

"I guess, um," Bo said dully, "the Jamaican blue."

"Good choice. Coming right up. Now do you like half and half, or milk in yours?"

"Larissa . . ."

"And sugar or Splenda?"

Bo turned to the island to glance at Michelangelo, who was cutting and pasting a dinosaur while munching a cup of dry Cheerios, a string cheese, a cookie, a glass of milk, and a fruit cup, while waiting for the tuna sandwich. "Lar," Bo said lamentably, "I met someone."

"Oh, yeah?" Larissa was grinding the coffee beans on a loud setting, while breaking up the tuna into little morsels in a steel mixing bowl with a metal fork and putting boxes of tea in the cabinet, which she then slammed shut. The English muffins were toasting. "Who'd you meet?"

"Larissa!"

Larissa turned around, still mixing the tuna.

"You're not listening! I *met* someone," Bo stage-whispered, raising her groomed and freshened eyebrows. Larissa should know all about stage whispers.

"You *what*?"

Finally something got through. Larissa went to sit at the island next to Michelangelo and across from Bo. But only for a second. A second later, she was up again because the English muffins had finished toasting. Bo let Larissa make the espresso and the tuna sandwiches, and *finally* they sat down, and Larissa nodded invitingly, ready to listen. Bo began to speak. She spoke for a long time. When she finished, there was a pause between the women. Fortunately in the middle of the monologue Michelangelo had sneaked off with his sandwich to watch TV in the den.

Larissa's pause lasted unusually long on her inscrutable face. Eventually she spoke. She said, "You're thinking of having an affair with someone named *Stanley?*"

Bo was taken aback. "That's *all* you have to say?"

"No . . . that's just the beginning. That's where I'm starting."

"What's wrong with Stanley?"

"Nothing . . . just doesn't seem like a name for an *affair.*" Larissa took a long sip of her coffee. "Coffee's good, isn't it?"

"It is, yes. There are names that are more suited for affairs?"

"Well, I'm just saying. Does Stanley have a good voice?"

"What does *that* mean? Is that also one of the criteria for an affair? A sexy name and a good voice?"

"It doesn't hurt. Is he attractive?"

"He's not, um, conventionally attractive."

"He's not *conventionally* attractive?" Larissa paused again. "Jonny is such a good-looking man," she said. "And he has a very good voice."

"I live with Jonny! I don't need to have an affair with him."

"You're right. Well, what's this Stanley like?"

"He's riveting, and interesting, and I love to listen to him, he is incredibly smart, and he's in a band. I'm completely taken with him, Lar. I'm not thinking of being with him because I want someone conventionally attractive. Jonny is plenty handsome."

"This is so true. Hey, would you like some cheese strudel? I bought some at your Chatham Bakery, and it's unbelievable. Come on, share a piece with me."

Bo began to suspect that Larissa was going to be surprisingly little help. "What do I do?" She fidgeted with the tips of her fingers.

"Well, *I* don't know!" Larissa stridently replied. "How should *I* know? What do you *want* to do?"

"I don't know. What do you think I *should* do?"

"What do I think you *should* do? Who am I, the Pope? How would I know, Bo? Why are you asking *me?*"

"Because you're my friend."

Larissa came around the island and put her arm around Bo. "I'm sorry. Of course. But, darling, it's not my life, it's your life. What do *you* want to do? And I thought Jonny got a job?"

"What does that have to do with *anything*?"

Larissa looked pensive. "I thought you *wanted* him to get a job."

"I did! But again, what does that have to do with anything?"

"Well, I don't know. I thought it made things better."

"I'm not unhappy with Jonny. I'm just not happy. We're in a rut, stuck in the same place for years, bored, spinning our wheels."

"Huh." Bo watched Larissa studying her, chewing her lip. Larissa with her light flawless makeup, so composed and polite, so exquisitely superficial, smiling, pleasant, groomed. Her hair shiny, straight, parted, down, perfect. Bo had never come to Larissa with anything personal before, and maybe this was why. They'd been friendly, but in that adult way—when you talk about everything but the state of your life. Perhaps she had been wrong to give Larissa her confidence. She tried one more time.

"I think I still have feelings for Jonny, Lar."

"Of course. That doesn't go away immediately. You've been together so long. You have a family, you built a life, you have children . . ."

Bo narrowed her eyes at Larissa. "What are you talking about, Larissa?" she asked. "You know we don't have any children. *Who* are you talking about?"

Larissa blinked. "Uh—you know what I mean." She emitted an embarrassed chuckle.

Bo studied Larissa carefully.

"You know what I think, Bo? I think we should get Maggie in on this."

"You don't think she's too judgmental?"

"No, no. She is very smart. And she is kind. She has excellent ideas. Let's all talk it over. Because you see, I have to run, unfortunately. I've got to pick up Emily from school. She is auditioning for the talent show, and it's almost 4:30. And Asher's got cross country till 5:00. I'm . . . this is a terrible time for me to give you my undivided attention. I feel a little distracted and that's not fair to you."

"I've been calling you all day," Bo said plaintively. "Where've you been? I even called Pingry, but Ezra said you're not always there on Mondays."

"This is true."

"I don't know what to do. I'm bored, I guess. I want to add a little spice to my life."

"You're *bored*? Bo, how can you be bored? You go into the city every day. You work at the Met, for goodness' sake. You work on fantastic exhibits, the best in the world, you meet powerful, fascinating people, you travel. You have a cute boyfriend who's smart, and who now has a job."

"I know all that. But we are getting stale. We're so familiar with each other . . ."

"So break up with him, Bo," Larissa said. "You're not married. It's easy. You're so *lucky*. You've got no kids, no commitment. Isn't this why you didn't want to get married? So you could leave your options nice and open?"

"No," Bo said defensively. "Larissa, you have it all wrong. I didn't want to get married because both Jonny and I don't believe in marriage."

"But that's great! That's so convenient! Now you don't want to be together anymore, so break up."

"Who said?"

"Well . . . didn't you just say . . . ?"

"I didn't say. I said I didn't know. I'm not even sleeping with Stanley yet."

"Oh. Yeah . . ." Larissa trailed off. "You're making it all needlessly complicated, I think. You know what I mean?"

"Larissa, me and my mother are living in an apartment that was left to Jonny by his mother when she died. I can't just pack up and move out. Besides, I don't even know if Stanley would want me to move in with him. We haven't even . . ."

"Oh. Right. Yeah, you might want to . . . first . . . and then afterward ask him if you can move in."

"I don't know if I want to break up with Jonny, Larissa. I love Jonny."

Larissa smiled. "*Now* we're getting somewhere."

Bo couldn't believe that she had just professed her love for Jonny.

"I gotta run, darling," Larissa said. "You're welcome to stay for dinner. But I have to go get my kids."

"No, no," said Bo, getting up off the bar stool. "I think I best be running along."

"Let's have lunch with Maggie. We'll come out to the city like we used to."

"You haven't done that in a long time," Bo said.

"Yeah. Been so busy. You know how it is."

"Do I?" said Bo, as Larissa ushered her to the back door. "Can you come to the city tomorrow?"

"Tomorrow? Let me call Maggie, see if she can do it. She's been feeling under the weather lately. Hasn't been up to doing much. I'll call you tonight?" Larissa kissed Bo on the cheek, opened the door, waved genially, and before Bo was at her car, the back door was slammed and Larissa had vanished.

3

Middle of the Night

The phone rang at a strange hour. It was 2:30 in the morning. Larissa was startled out of sleep. Her first reaction was not to answer it. She didn't have a plan, but who on earth and for what good reason would be calling this late at night? Sure it could be her mother with some scary health news, but with Larissa's bad luck, it could be bad luck calling. Her heart thumping a hundred times in the four rings before the answering machine picked it up, Larissa lived through Kai's voice, and Jared's voice, her life twisting yet again, metal breaking screeching—

It was Jared who harrumphed out of bed. "You don't hear that?"

"Hear what?" she said in the dark, with no lights. Her voice didn't sound like her own.

Jared answered it. "Hello?"

Larissa couldn't hear the rest, whether he listened or responded. She was panting, deaf to him. She felt him nudging her arm, passing her the phone. "God, it's for you . . ." He rolled away. She put the phone to her ear.

"Hello?"

"Larissa, baby!" The voice was dim, the satellite connection fragmented. It was Che.

"Che! Oh my God! Che!"

Jared groaned with judgment, pulling the covers over his head.

Jumping out of bed, Larissa, relieved beyond measure, her spirit revived, her heart resuscitated, left the bedroom and ran downstairs.

"Che, it's nearly three in the morning! Is everything all right?"

"Larissa Stark, you tell me. Why do you think I'm calling? What would make a penniless woman call her best friend in the middle of the freaking night?"

"I don't know." Larissa thought about it, rubbing her groggy eyes. "Wait . . . you're not . . . are you . . . you're *pregnant?*"

"Yes!"

"Ahhh!"

"Ahhh!"

"That's the greatest thing I ever heard!"

"Isn't it?"

"Oh my God!"

"I know! Oh my God! Isn't that the greatest?"

"The greatest."

"Finally."

"Finally."

"Oh, Che, I'm so happy for you. I'm so happy."

"You're the first person I called. I miss you so much."

"I miss *you* so much."

"Larissa, I can't believe it's *finally* happened."

"How many weeks are you?"

"Like two minutes. We had sex yesterday."

Larissa laughed. "How do you know you're pregnant?"

"The nuns told me."

"The *nuns* told you?"

"Yeah. They know this stuff. They're like soothsayers."

"Hmm, Che, maybe you should go to a doctor? You know, just to be on the safe side."

"Oh, I went, silly. He confirmed today what the nuns told me two weeks ago."

"He did a blood test?"

"Yada, yada. Yeah, he did a blood test. But the nuns, Lar, they *knew* because they felt her soul inside me."

"*Her* soul?"

"Oh, yes. Sister Agatha told me."

"She can tell this?"

"A girl soul? Of course. Oh, Larissa . . . you have to be here for the birth of my baby. I can't give birth without you."

"You conceived without me, didn't you?" They giggled.

"Ahhh!"

"Ahhh!"

"Is Lorenzo happy?"

"I don't know. He's gone fishing. He's trying to start his own business as a fisherman, like his parents."

"How's it going?"

"Slow. He says there are no fish. Between you and me, I don't think he's a very good fisherman."

"Oh, Che."

"Oh, Larissa."

"How much time do you have left on your calling card?"

"I don't know. We may be cut off at any time. Why the hell haven't you written to me in over six months?"

"I'm sorry."

"You should be sorry. Something is very wrong. I can tell."

Larissa started to cry.

"Lar, are you crying? Oh my God. It's Jared, isn't it? What has he done? I'll kill him. What has he done?"

"No, no, Che . . . it's nothing like that."

"So what's the matter, darling? Why on earth would you be crying? What could possibly be the matter?"

"Because I'm in desperate trouble, Che," whispered Larissa. "I'm in terrible trouble. I couldn't write you about anything because it's just too awful to put into a letter. But I really need your help." The words were coming out unintelligible. "I have no one in the world to turn to. You're so far away, and I need you so much. I can't tell you how much I need you." Larissa blew her nose, wiped her eyes. "Che? Are you there? Did you hear me? Che!"

They'd been cut off. Larissa couldn't go back to sleep, pacing around her dim silent house. The next morning, she went to the mall, bought fourteen maternity outfits, two for each day of the week, and sent Che a package, with a money order for a thousand dollars. She included a congratulations card but no letter. She had absolutely nothing to say.

4

Larissa the Epicurean

Ezra and Larissa were having their monthly lunch to go over department things.

"Why do you look so nice?" Ezra asked.

She was wearing a denim Escada jacket and black True Religion jeans. "Not that nice, Ez," said Larissa. "Jeans and a jean jacket."

He looked her over. "I don't know. Pretty put together for a Tuesday afternoon is all I'm saying."

"Well, thank you. And I like your green corduroy blazer. It goes with your purple tie." She smiled.

"Uh-huh. So listen," said Ezra, "Have you been thinking about the spring play?"

"No! It's January! We're still in rehearsals for *Godot*, with that insufferable Leroy."

"Here's the thing. We're reading Shaw's *Saint Joan* in AP English. It might be a nice parallel for the kids to perform it while they studied it."

Larissa considered it. "*Saint Joan*? Spending three months listening to Bernard Shaw apologizing for the English?"

Ezra smiled thinly. "*Saint Joan* is brilliantly written, and it's got like twenty parts in it. But who could play Joan? The whole play is in her casting."

Larissa sighed. "I don't know. Tiffany?"

"Give me a break," said Ezra with tired bemusement. "She was okay and camp in *Dracula*, but she's not serious enough. *Saint Joan* is about sacred things." They both petered off; Ezra looked down into his coffee, Larissa into hers.

"Can we make it into a musical, Ez? With interpretive dance numbers. Maybe when Joan is getting burned at the stake the dancers can sing, 'Dawning of the Age of Aquarius.'"

"Too avant-garde for me."

"What about a melancholy guitar that from stage left punctuates the action with song?" Larissa stirred her cold coffee. "Listen, it's not the worst idea you ever had. Let me find it at home, and I'll reread it. I'll let you know."

"No need to search," Ezra said, pulling out a copy from his worn briefcase.

"You're something else." She took it from him, noticing the gaunt red look around his eyes.

"You okay, Lar?"

"What do you mean?"

"I don't know. You seem . . ."

"I'm fine." Larissa frowned. "Why do you ask?"

"I dunno," he said. "You've been a little off lately."

"Off, like spoiled milk?"

He smiled. "Off, like something is not right."

"Funny, because I was going to say the same about you."

"I'm fine." Ezra paused. "Maggie hasn't talked to you?"

Larissa became alert instead of inert. "About what?"

He sighed. "She hasn't been feeling well."

"She's mentioned that, yeah."

"Well. She's got this . . ." He broke off.

"She told me a while back," Larissa continued for him, to help him, "that she keeps getting . . . what is it . . . oh, yes, urinary tract infections."

Ezra's lip twisted. "Actually . . . I'm surprised she hasn't told you, but she's been diagnosed with chronic kidney disease."

"What? No. Poor Mags."

"Yeah. Not quite a UTI, is it?"

"No. What causes that?"

"High blood pressure in her case."

"Maggie has high blood pressure? I didn't know that."

"She's been on blood pressure meds for years." Ezra frowned. "What do you mean, you didn't know that? She had hypertension with Dylan. Had to deliver him six weeks early. It's the reason she can't have more children."

"Yes, of course. Funny, I thought it was pregnancy-induced and temporary." Larissa hurried past Ezra's puzzled, scrutinizing eyes. "But now what?"

"Now she's sick all the time. The kidneys aren't filtering fluids like they're supposed to. They keep getting infected."

"What do they prescribe for that?"

"Believe me, she's taking one of everything. Twice a day. She's still miserable."

"Well, inflamed kidneys will do that."

"Yeah." Ezra was not looking at Larissa. "It's changed her life, our life. And not for the better."

"Oh, Ezra. Are you worried about her?"

He waved his hand. "A little bit. She'll be okay. It's just that . . . I don't know if she's spoken to you about this, but one of the effects on her is this thing sapped her of all energy and health. She's been constantly sick."

"This I've noticed."

"You girls haven't been out much, not shopping, or lunch."

"No, nothing."

"She's actually thinking of stopping teaching."

"No!"

"I know. Seems inconceivable. I told her, why? You're going to stay home and do what?"

"Exactly," Larissa agreed. "I should talk to her."

"Please. But I don't want her to think I'm complaining to you. She won't like that."

"You're not complaining. You're worried about her. That's different."

Ezra wasn't looking at Larissa again. "Except for one tiny thing . . ."

"A little complaint?"

"Tiny one." He cleared his throat. "This whole kidney business has really put a damper on our, um, love life."

"Really?"

"Yeah."

"Like how much of a damper?"

"Like . . . a dam sort of thing."

"Hmm. Dam: a little water released every once in a while?"

"No, uh-uh. More like totally dry beds."

"Dry? Really? For how long?"

Ezra was silent at first. "Since summer."

Larissa was shocked. "But, Ezra . . ."

"You're telling me."

"Oh, Ez. I had no idea."

"I thought she might've mentioned it."

"It *is* strange she hadn't."

"You know, Lar, Maggie says she's finding it harder than usual to talk to you these days."

A disconnected Larissa didn't ask for clarification.

"She says you're not listening."

"To what?"

"To anything."

"Well, that's silly. Of course I listen."

"You're very good at covering up. I'm just telling you what Maggie said."

"Maybe that's why she hasn't talked to me. Because she thinks I'm not listening."

"Perhaps."

"I'm going to try to do better," Larissa said. "Okay?"

Ezra nodded. "She could really use a friend right now."

"Exactly. And who can't?" She gazed at Ezra with sympathy. "I'll talk to her, I promise. I'll be very tactful."

He scoffed. "You can try. But a heads-up—you know how Maggie is. She's been trying to figure out why this illness has been given to her."

Larissa shrugged. "Oh, not that again. Why does there have to be a reason? Why can't it just be given?"

"Given by whom?"

"Isn't that the eternal question?" She laughed lightly, becoming more animated. "But why can't Pozzo in *Godot* be right? One day he woke up and he was blind as Fortune. Why can't we get sick because of dumb blind fortune?"

"You know that Maggie doesn't believe things just happen."

"Not even headaches?"

"This isn't a headache. It's total body misery. And it affects her life, her entire family. She feels responsible."

Larissa chewed her lip. "But look, she's asking too much of her body. She didn't get kidney disease on purpose."

"'Course not. But she's trying to figure out"—Ezra tightened his mouth as he continued—"if this is Thomas Aquinas's warning or an Epicurean struggle for her to work harder to achieve the absence of pain."

"Epicurus seems to be losing."

"No kidding."

"What did Aquinas write?"

"He wrote," said Ezra, "that pain *is* given to us by God so that we can protect our material body and stop doing whatever it is we are doing that's causing us pain, and thus, by protecting the material body, we protect our immortal, immaterial soul."

Larissa was thoughtful. "Immaterial, like not important?"

Ezra chuckled. "You *would* ask that. No. Immaterial like standing outside matter."

"But didn't your Epicurus say that nothing exists outside matter?"

"Yes, but Maggie is suffering. She needs to come to terms with this transformation of her body and consequently her entire life."

"But why can't it be nice and plain? Why *can't* blind Pozzo be right?"

"Because she's not getting better, Lar," said Ezra. "And this causes spiritual suffering for her. Maggie thinks that her pain means she's breaking some boundary, transgressing laws put into her mortal body by a life-creating force. Perhaps she's been careless or overindulgent. She's not a naturalist. She doesn't obey *random* laws of nature. She is an ethicist. She obeys the laws because she sees in them a divine source."

"Careless?" Larissa shook her head. "That's not Maggie."

"She likes her food, she likes salt, doesn't drink enough water, hates cranberry juice."

"Oh, Ezra. You don't get *punished* with kidney disease!"

"She thinks she did."

"She just got a lousy set of genes from her parents. What does that have to do with her?"

"Because it's her life that's being altered," Ezra replied. "And mine."

"Well, I don't know how blaming herself is going to help," said Larissa firmly. "I'm sure Epicurus agrees with me."

Ezra smiled. "Sure, to swirling atoms, all this blather about ethics is meaningless."

"There you go. Isn't that more comforting?"

"Maggie doesn't think so. But she *is* trying to work toward the Epicurean model."

"A fine goal to shoot for," Larissa agreed brightly. "What does Epicurus say about the soul?"

"Oh, brilliantly, he says we ain't got one."

No soul! Larissa widened her clear eyes. "No soul, really?" She mulled. "That means no God?"

"Right. In his day it was gods, but same difference, yeah."

No, God, no soul!

"Wouldn't that be easier for Maggie," Larissa asked, "to live in a soulless universe?"

"Would it?" Ezra shrugged. "Without a soul, the here and now would be all you'd have, all you would ever have."

"Exactly!" Larissa became lively, encouraged.

"But in the here and now, Maggie's body is sick," said Ezra. "If Epicurus is right, and the only thing she has is her body, her body is failing her. That doesn't provide as much comfort as you might think."

"I guess." Deflated, Larissa palmed her coffee cup. "But you know what? If there's no soul, there is no God, and if there's no God, there's no judgment. And if there's no judgment, with a little bit of hard work, there could be no conscience." No conscience! "No moral boundaries, no ethical laws, see? No consequences means no punishment. Tell Maggie that. Then you don't have to suffer. You just have to feel better."

"How?"

"I'll talk to her, Ez. I'll set her straight. I'll tell her that if God doesn't interfere with nature, he doesn't interfere with man's mortal body. If there's no God, it means you can reason yourself out of anything." Or into anything.

"Reason yourself out? But by what method, Larissa? The swirling atoms?"

"Right! Because atoms can't reason."

Ezra smiled. "Exactly. Matter must somehow learn to stop contemplating itself. That's a neat trick. Maggie hasn't mastered it yet. Have you?"

"Well, it's not easy," Larissa agreed.

"Yes, because first you have to explain by what method you manage to examine yourself in the first place. Molecules can't, can they? Atoms can't reason. They're neither naturalists nor ethicists."

"Right, they're nothing. Just nothing," she said. "Why isn't that comforting? *I* feel better already. Tell Maggie to drink some cranberry. It's miracle juice for the kidneys."

"She hates cranberry juice. Perhaps I forgot to mention it."

Larissa suddenly jumped up. She grabbed her lunch plate and cup like an efficient waitress.

"Where are you going? It's only noon."

"Gotta get stuff and do stuff. Who's going to go food shopping while we sit here and contemplate our molecules? I don't have cleaning people anymore."

"You don't? What happened to Ernestina?"

Larissa slid her hand across her throat. "I had to let her go."

"What? Why? When?"

I hear them walking, walking. I want them to stop, I have to get the phone in case it rings, but I can't open my door, and they're always knocking, every two seconds, asking me if I want coffee, clean sheets, if they can do my bed now, clean the bedroom, if I need anything at the store, where the paper towels are. I'm going crazy. They're outside in the hall bathroom, they're in the hallway, vacuuming, every time I turn around, they're right there. One, another, a third. I tried to switch them for a different day, not Mondays, but they have no openings. They come to my house at 8:30. The children have barely left for school, and they're already knocking.

"I'm getting ready, no, no, thank you. I don't need anything."

I hear them like mice, like squirrels outside my door.

"Look, how nice you look! Where you going, Miss Larissa?"

"To the school, Ernestina. I'm directing a play."

"Look so nice. So pretty. You dress up for the store like I dress up for my boyfriend."

Larissa shrugged. "I was tired of them being in my house, Ezra. Besides, I think one of the girls might have been stealing." This wasn't true. It was just to end the conversation.

"Really? So what are you doing now?"

"Cleaning my own house." When Ezra looked at her incredulously, Larissa said, "What, you don't think I can do it? Think I'm afraid to get my hands dirty?" She rushed out of the cafeteria.

"Larissa, wait!" Ezra caught up with her in the hall. "One more thing."

"Quick, Ezra. I gotta run."

"I don't want to do *Saint Joan* unless we agree on the lead. She has to be right."

"Okay. How about Megan?"

"Megan! You're joking. You're not paying attention to me."

"I am." She was nearly running.

"She is pampered and overweight. How is she going to be the dynamo that frees France and restores the King to his throne? She is *round*!"

"What, round people can't be martyrs?"

"Larissa, you're not taking this seriously. Megan is wrong for the part."

Larissa shook her head, speeding up. "How about Tiffany?"

"No Tiffany!" Ezra called to her departing back. "No running in the halls!"

She was *running* out.

"Megan will be fine, Ez," she called back to him, waving. "You'll see. We'll play her against type, she'll be fantastic. Soft and chubby on the outside, lethal on the inside."

～◌～

She was early, and he was late. She sat in her car, and waited, wondering if she should use her key and go in.

What's the key for? Jared had asked a few weeks ago and Larissa replied she didn't know. Huh, he said. Odd. A nervous Larissa was going to give it back to Kai, sensing trouble brewing, but he said, no, don't give it back. It's your key. I can't give you jewelry, cars, pretty things. I can't give you anything. But I give you the key, like a key to me. As long as you have it, you know that my door is always open. If she could've put the key around her neck on a gold chain, she would've. The best she could do is drive around clutching it between her fingers. She bought a gold-plated key ring for it, with red Swarovski crystals, and when Jared saw, he said, "Is that Swarovski?"

"No, darling. Costume jewelry at the trinket kiosk at the mall."

"Ah. Looks pretty authentic."

"Doesn't it, though."

But what if I used the key to come in when you're not home? she had asked Kai.

"And do what? Snoop?" He grinned naughtily. "That's *so* hot. What are you looking for? Naughty things?"

"Well, I don't know."

"What do you want to find? Old love letters?"

More like new love letters, she replied quietly.

His mouth was in her neck, his hands in her hair. "Well, tell me," he murmured, husk, husk. "Have you been writing me much?"

So now Larissa waited. It had been snowing and freezing for two months. Yesterday they had their ninth snowstorm. Today was fifteen below. After another minute, she heard his Ducati revving up on Samson. He pulled up next to her in the driveway and hopped off, helmet still on, a ski cap under it.

"Man, it's *freezing* out. Come on," he said, smiling. He kissed her through the open window. "You're like my good luck charm. I sold three Jags today, last one just five minutes ago. That's why I'm late. Couldn't leave. I have another appointment with the couple right after lunch." He worked full days at the dealer in the frigid winter, taking a break from masonry. From his small trunk he produced a large paper bag and a bouquet of supermarket-bought flowers. "For you," he said. "Also the sushi."

"I have things for you," she said.

She had a box for him, beautifully wrapped at Neiman's.

She had a cake for him, his favorite, a cheesecake. She wanted to make it, bake it with her own hands, but since that was out of the question, she went to the best bakery in Chatham, bought the cheesecake and left it in the back seat of her Jag. She brought candles, and matches to light them.

They didn't eat first. They never ate first. Afterward they ate, still in bed, naked, the sheets pulled up over her, pulled down on him.

She retrieved the matches from her purse to light the cake. "You're finally old enough to drink."

"Isn't that awesome," he said, popping open the champagne. Cristal and strawberry cheesecake for his birthday lunch. She bought him an Armani jacket, classy greige, size 42 long. She thought with jeans and a white shirt he would look splendid.

"Blow out the candles with me," he said when she asked him to make a wish. The cake was on the bed, between their legs. And after the blowout, with champagne on his lips, he asked her what she wished for.

"It's not *my* birthday." She was lying in his arms, rubbing his chest. Seventeen minutes left. "What did *you* wish for? To be able to shave?"

He pinched her. "I do shave, smarty-pants. If you ever saw me in the evening, you'd see my five o'clock stubble."

"No, wait, I know. You wished to be able to rent a car."

He pinched her again.

"My mistake. You have to wait four more years for that."

"Extra funny today, are we, Mrs. Stark." He tickled her, not allowing her body to tighten. "You want to know what I wished for? There's a town, in New Mexico, off Route 66. To call it a town is almost unfair, it's a street with no name, a gas station, a general store . . . I want you on my bike behind me, and I want us to see it. I want to stay in a tiny bed and breakfast, all dusty and strange, and wake up where the sun is out three hundred days a year."

"That's a fun wish."

"You on my bike, Larissa," he whispered, climbing on top of her, "holding on for dear life to my leather jacket."

"Okay." Spoken like an exhale.

Twelve minutes left.

"Or," he said, his body gently rubbing up and down against her, rubbing his naked chest against her breasts, "I want to show you Maui. The red flame trees that grow in the spring on the black volcanoes. We'll get up at dawn and take our bikes up the mountain, into the Maoloa."

"Will you take me for a demon ride too, Kai?" She moaned, the nerves in her body raw with him, from him, spine tingling, skin burning.

"If that's what you want. Would you like that?"

"So much." She closed her eyes, not to see the merciless clock. The blue birthday balloon burst over her head.

I wish we could go to the movies, she said to him. *I wish we could go to dinner at the swank Italian place down the street, and then bar hopping. I wish we could stay at the Madison Hotel, white like a wedding, like a dream. I wish . . .*

Don't be sad, Kai whispered to her. I told you, I'll take you any way you want to give yourself to me. And if this is how you give me you, then that's how I will take you. Is this ideal? Many things are not ideal. What *is* ideal, though, he said, is you. To have *you*, I will have this. If you said to me, it's either this way or nothing, I would choose this over nothing. It's not sex with you I want. Don't you understand? All I want is you.

All I want is you.

Eight minutes.

Six.

Three.

She got dressed as she was. She washed at home.

Kai put on his faded jeans, black boots, a white crisp shirt, the Armani jacket. He looked splendid.

Wetting his hands in the sink, he slicked back his growing-out kinky hair and smiled at her, ruefully.

"That is what I wished for, Larissa," he whispered to her back, as she was *running* out. "I wished for you."

∽◦∾

Emily had a cello lesson at four and voice at 4:30. Michelangelo trooped along for his karate at 5:00 in Chatham. Asher was playing with his buddies in a basement band until six. On the way home, the kids discussed a teacher who pushed a kid, and Emily had forgotten her lunch and was *starving* hungry, and Michelangelo forgot his karate robe and they had to go back. The kid on the morning bus was, apparently, "simply vile" and Emily didn't know how he was still living.

That night they had take-out Indian for dinner; Jared was happy to eat Tandoori and talk to her about Jan at work, who was just promoted to deputy company secretary, and Jared didn't know what *that* was about, declaring Jan not yet reliably off the sauce, but whatever. They talked about their plans for the weekend, which apparently included going to South Mountain Reservation with Doug and Barbara on Saturday ("For some reason, Doug's insisting we drive in *his* car. I think something may be up"), and on Sunday driving to Greenwich to have brunch with Jared's boss, Larry Fredoso and his new wife.

The kids were in bed by ten, and Jared had some work, thank God. Larissa sat in the den with her cup of tea, her hands shaking, and closed her eyes so she wouldn't have to see the fire Jared built, or her books, or the house. She sat on her couch, legs drawn up, head thrown back on the pillow, squeezing shut her eyes so tears wouldn't spill down her face like rain.

"Larissa?"

Opening her eyes, she found Jared standing, staring at her with concern. "You 'kay? What's the matter, tush?"

"Oh, nothing. Just tired." She tried to smile.

"What?" he perched next to her. "Did the kids do something?"

"Of course not."

"Did *I* do something?" he chuckled, with the giggle of a man who says the most ridiculous thing he can think of, because he knows he is beyond reproach.

Reaching to touch his face, Larissa shook her head. "Of course not, darling."

"I'll be just another couple of minutes; almost done paying the bills. Want to watch *Seinfeld* at eleven?"

"Very much."

And they did. She didn't laugh once. Upstairs, Larissa spent so long in the bathroom that Jared was asleep by the time she stepped into the bedroom. She lay down, careful that no part of her would touch any part of him, and stared at the ceiling to find some answers there.

She had no one to turn to. All her friends had drifted away one by one, departed from her, detached. With them she had the regular things. My kid is flunking math. Do you want to see a movie? Can I borrow an iron; mine broke. I'll tell you if your dress looks good, if you've got a tag sticking out, if you've got lipstick stuck to your teeth. This is what friends do. But when you come to me because you actually need my help, I stop hearing you. I become deaf. You're talking too low and asking too much of our friendship. I've got my own problems. You want to complain no one listens to you? Boo hoo. No one listens to me either. Join the fucking club.

That's what it was. No one listened to anyone. At the heart of our life, we all walked around with our head hung low, or our eyes raised high, begging for someone to hear our prayer, to hear us speak to the deepest sorrow in us, to our deepest longing.

⌒◡⌒

Dear Larissa, my friend,

I want to tell you about my life.

I'm sorry we got cut off the first time in years I got to hear your voice. The card ran out of money.

I was floating on happy clouds for three weeks. Nothing troubled me. Nothing could.

Lorenzo became the most protective of boyfriends.

He didn't want me to work with him anymore. He said it was too dangerous. So I asked Father Emilio if I could help him out at the orphanage for a few pesos, and he let me, but the kids were always getting sick with stuff, and soon I got sick. I caught some awful fever swamp thing and started to bleed, and couldn't work at all. I couldn't do anything but lie in bed, and Lorenzo said he would work for both of us, and did. He was gone from the house

*morning till night. He never slept anymore, and you remember how
much my Lorenzo loves his beauty rest. He distributed pamphlets,
sold trinkets, was a cycle messenger and then a rickshaw driver.
Lorenzo made us money, and Father Emilio came every day on his
walkabouts and brought me fruit.*

I was feeling better. And then the most awful thing happened.

*Lorenzo was hired to protest against the Manila/MILF
agreement. MILF is a faction group, a breakaway paramilitary
organization, the Moro Islamic Liberation Front. For years they've
been raising Cain in Mindanao, where Lorenzo is from, claiming
the island is theirs, wanting independence from the Philippines,
but, Lorenzo's parents live there, and millions of other native
Filipinos. After years of arson and assault and street attacks, the
Philippine government finally agreed to give part of Mindanao to
the Muslims. You'd think that would be the end, but no. MILF
kept asking for more. To get peace, the government has been
giving them more. And more. More land, more resources, more
autonomy—and still no peace. Over two hundred thousand lives
have been lost in the fighting. So Lorenzo goes to protest handing
over 712 more villages in Mindanao to the Muslims, and not two
days later, his mother's uncle comes down to Las Pinas, finds San
Agustin, finds us, and tells Lorenzo that both his parents, both his
parents!, died a month ago when their village was torched during
an occupation by the MILF rebels. They were killed at Sulu Sea on
their boat in the early morning, while rowing to shore.*

*The rebels surrendered to the Filipino commander, and there
were many other civilians killed but what good is that to Lorenzo?
He has lost his mind. He is completely inconsolable. And raging
at his poor Papi and Mama too, because he's been begging them
to leave Zamboanga for years, ever since the worst of the troubles
started, but they kept saying it was their home and they wouldn't go.*

*I don't know what to do. My poor Lorenzo. Just at the time
when we should be so happy. Instead, he is sick with grief. I draw
a little sad face on my letter. Hope you're doing better. Can't
imagine you could be doing much worse.*

I keep praying there won't be any more trouble, but when I look at Lorenzo's stricken face, I get so afraid, like all the trouble is still to come.

Thank you for your package, the clothes, the money. Money was most appreciated. The clothes, don't be mad, but I think you forgot how tiny I am, they were all too big for me. Plus, they were winter maternity. And it doesn't get cold here. I sold them, and made some money from your top-of-the-line American merchandise. I paid my rent for two months with those clothes. I love you.

5

Doug's Jaguar

"I want to show you something! Come look."

Jared was sitting at his desk at work, sorting through his bank and credit card statements. Something in them vaguely bothered him.

"Come downstairs for a sec."

"Doug, downstairs where? Like outside? We've got a board meeting in fifteen, and we still have to go over—"

"It'll just take a sec. Come on." Doug was like a kid.

Out in the parking lot covered with mounds of snow, Jared saw what Doug was so excited about. It was a gray Jaguar sedan.

"Oh, man, I can't believe you did it!" Jared walked around the car. "You took the plunge!"

"Yeah, baby! Will you just look at it! XJ8. Vapor Gray metallic. Are you seeing it with your eyes?"

"I'm seeing it. It's amazing."

"No fucking kidding. I got tired of you going on about Larissa's Jag, so over the weekend the wife and I went to check it out, see what all the fuss was about. Well, one minute, we're window-shopping, and the next I'm forking over the whole Christmas bonus for the down payment and signing on the dotted line. I don't even know how it happened!" He opened the doors, had Jared touch the soft black leather. "You wanna go for a ride?"

"Doug, what about the board meeting in ten minutes? How about we go at lunch? I'll let you take me out."

"Done. I can't believe you bought your wife a convertible Jag," Doug said, his hands on the hood. "I didn't know what that meant until we drove this one, which is already like a space ship and the salesman said, yeah, but the sports model has 420 horsepower. Did you buy Larissa the regular or the supercharged?"

"What do you think?"

"Oh, man, you're nucking futs!"

Jared shrugged. "It's what she wanted. Might as well have the best, if you're going to go all out. Otherwise what's the point?"

"Yeah, well," said Doug, "we didn't want to spend that kind of money and not let the kids inside it. I bet Larissa never lets hers in."

"You bet correctly."

Doug shook his head. "See, we didn't want that, Kate and I. Sedan seemed so much more practical."

Jared studied Doug. "Douglas, you're my friend, and we go back a long way, but what the hell are you talking about? It's a fucking Jaguar. Who wants to be practical? This is supposed to be a mad car."

"Not when you have kids. You have to be a little bit sensible. We're not teenagers anymore."

Jared just shook his head. "I guess. And like you could afford this when you were a teenager."

"Too true. But isn't it incredible?"

"Beyond belief. Congratulations."

"I know. I'm excited like I had another baby or something! Should I pass out some cigars?"

Jared laughed. "Absolutely. But what I don't understand is, did you buy the car for yourself or for Kate?"

"For Kate; why do you ask?"

"So then . . . what are you doing driving it?"

"Well, just look at it. Do you even need to ask?"

"So you bought her a car, and then took it for yourself?"

Doug demurred. "I just drove it today, to show you."

"Uh-huh."

"And besides, Kate works in the city and takes the train in. Be a shame for a beauty like this to sit in our garage all day, lonely, undriven, in that cold mean dark space. I can't believe you'd even suggest it."

"You're right, what was I thinking?"

"Do you know it's got an Adaptive Restraint Technology System?" Doug chuckled. "I don't even know what the hell that is. Plus, look, a DVD-based navigation system. That cost another three grand. You guys have one?"

Something about that itched Jared in the chest. It was those words. *Navigation system*. Not just by itself, but somehow related to the statements lying on his desk upstairs. What did the navigation system that Larissa bought nearly a year ago and the credit card statements from last month have to do with one another? Both gave him the same bad feeling. "Come on, Douglas. We gotta go."

Doug locked up and they started walking back.

"Did you go to the Madison Jag?" Jared asked.

"Yeah, of course. That's the one you recommended."

"Did I? I don't think I did. Maybe Larissa did. Who helped you?"

"Um, I can't remember his name. Weird name. He was a good kid, though."

"Kai?"

"Yeah! Your salesman, too?"

"Yeah. I wasn't impressed."

"Oh, no, the wife and I loved him. He knew *everything* about the car, was patient, let my wife drive for an hour, gave us the history of the vehicle. And he gave us a fantastic deal. I sent him a bottle of Cristal to thank him. And he must be doing something right, because he was wearing an Armani jacket, cut like you wouldn't believe. The commissions must be rolling in."

"He talked to you?"

"What do you mean, did he *talk* to me? He's a salesman!"

Jared shook his head. "Odd. Because I just hated him. He didn't say a word to me. If it weren't for Larissa, I never would've bought it from him. He was like a deaf mute."

Doug laughed. "You must have made him mad. He was nice as apple pie to me and Kate. What did you do to piss off your salesman?" He pressed the button for the fourteenth floor in the elevator.

"Nothing," said Jared, already mentally at the board meeting, where he had to present a new proposal for the Financial Services Division to outsource the work because the investment managers could not handle the case load, and to listen to an introduction of innovative methodology for the life assurance funds, and in the recesses of his mind, right before the summary of the new reporting requirements to benefit consumers, Jared realized what it was that was bothering him about the bank statements.

Larissa wasn't shopping.

~∽⌒∾~

"Larissa, you haven't been buying anything," Jared said to her that Saturday night after tenderloin and before ice cream.

"We haven't been to the mall in *ages*," Maggie said. "Since before Christmas."

"Before Christmas? That can't be." Larissa shook her head.

"Mags is right, Lar," said Jared. "You know how I know? I see the bills. And there aren't any. You're not buying anything except food at Stop&Shop and shampoo at the drugstore."

Larissa shrugged, a study in casual indifference. "I'm not buying anything because I have everything."

"Since when has that stopped you in the past?" said Ezra. "Maggie over here has more hair products than can fit in one medium-sized house. Does that stop her?"

Larissa smiled. "I don't have curly hair like Maggie. I don't need quite so much."

"But what about shoes, Lar? You don't need new suede boots?"

"Nope. Have a pair from last year. And the year before."

"A new sweater?"

"Have dozens I never wear."

"Makeup?"

"Too much of everything, Jared," said Larissa, smiling benevolently at him from across the table. "What's this? The husband is complaining that the wife doesn't shop *enough*?"

"Well, your not shopping *is* new. I'm bound to notice," he said. "And you go to the mall. You're always telling me you're at the mall."

"I like to window shop."

"There's a red Escada jacket in the windows of the Macy's in Newark," said Jared. "It would look smashing on you."

Larissa turned her elongated neck to Jared. "Hon, you want me to go all the way to Newark to buy a jacket?"

"I'm just saying."

She lives in secret, hides between words and minutes, while her soul remains in a 20 by 20 room between the hours of twelve and two.

While waiting at the red light, she thinks, I can't take much more of this.

That lasts eleven minutes, on the way to Lincoln from Albright. Then she picks up her boy and gets home, and then the school bus delivers more (of her) kids. There is subtraction, a Social Studies project on the Badlands, and a twenty-line free-verse poem on a bar of chocolate. There is a phone call from Jared asking what's for dinner, and Larissa saying, "What, if it's something you don't like, you won't be coming home?" and him laughing. "Just tell me what's for dinner and then I'll decide."

There is a basketball game on Friday, a dinner, a movie, a birthday party, and two more, lunch in Connecticut with friends, and then on Monday another week begins, and Larissa is grateful that things remain as they are, just a hazy Summit week, where the mother of three gets up on a Monday, kisses and dresses her children, packs them off to school, kisses her husband, tidies up the kitchen, showers, barely dresses, and then zooms down Main

Street in her supercharged Winter Gold rocket with a navigation system, nine minutes if she hurries and makes all the lights, turns into Albright, parks the Jag, sprints up the stairs. He is waiting, open arms, smile on his face, ardent lips, ardent everything. And she thinks: I will take as much of this as I need to.

They showered together, makeup running down her cheeks, they made love in the shower, bubbling up the lava place inside from where she craved him, with which she craved him. And then— having to go.

"I don't want to go," she said when two o'clock came, 2:15 came. It was 2:20 and she was still there.

"I don't want you to go," Kai said. They had bagels by the bed, coffee. The music had stopped. No sounds at all, except them, in bed, pressed together, laughing when they weren't coming.

At 2:25 she threw her clothes on, anointed with sex, sweat, moisture, anointed with Kai on her bones, in her pores, like sacramental sacrilegious perfume.

She gazed at him, longingly, regretfully, lying naked on top of the bed, stretched out, absent-mindedly caressing himself, looking at her. Her whole body ached as she put her shoes on. Nothing was right on Monday afternoons. It was like cramps, like labor. I must go. I haven't worked it out any other way. There *is* no other way. I must go.

"Larissa," he said, "imagine a world in which you wouldn't have to leave me. Can you imagine such a world?"

Too well, she wanted to say.

Not at all, she wanted to say.

She was late: 2:35 and she was twelve minutes away from the school. When she got there, with Michelangelo waiting with Mrs. Brown inside the doors because it was so cold, she smiled apologetically.

"It's fine, Mrs. Stark," Mrs. Brown said, "but I *have* been noticing that every Monday for the last several months now you've been coming late to pick him up. Could you leave ten minutes earlier?

Because I've got teacher assessments to do on Mondays and I'm always here waiting with your son."

That evening Michelangelo said over baked ziti, "Mommy was late picking me up again."

Jared looked up from his garlic bread. "*Again?*"

"She's late all the time, Dad."

"Michelangelo! I pick you up five days a week. I am not late all the time."

"The teacher yelled at her today."

"Really, yelled?" Jared glanced at her with amusement. "What was Mommy doing that she was late?"

"Getting stuck in traffic in Chatham, that's what," said Mommy. "There was an accident."

"Yes, but what about all the other times, oh late Mother?" said Michelangelo.

Larissa rolled her eyes. But after that, she tried very hard not to be late. The following Monday she was only five minutes late. Mrs. Brown raised her eyebrows.

In the evening Michelangelo said, "Mommy was late again."

Jared raised his eyebrows. "Accident in Chatham?"

"No, a horrible woman at Neiman's was paying in cash and they didn't have any change. Can you imagine, a cash register not having any change! The salesgirl had to go across the entire floor to get change."

"Ah. Nice to see you finally shopping," said Jared. "I hope whatever you got was worth it."

"Well, I didn't get it, did I? I couldn't wait anymore. I dropped everything and ran."

"What was it?"

"A trench coat."

Two days later Larissa came back with a Gucci trench coat to show Jared. And the following Monday she tried *very* hard not to be late.

Kai, lying on top of his sheets naked, perspired, icy wind through the curtains, frosty daylight outside, the wood floor shiny, the sheets white, the male bed full of Kai, his twinkling eyes, his bare chest, his long legs splayed out, his lovely wet mouth whispering, "Don't go, Larissa." Singing in a whisper, "Beautiful girl, stay with me . . ."

She couldn't imagine where this was headed, and she couldn't imagine where she was headed, except down Main Street to Albright Circle.

Chapter Two

1

Paolo and Francesca

Larissa and Maggie met at last at Summit station to take the train to New York to have lunch with Bo. Maggie wore loose, dark, non-descript clothes, while Larissa was decked out in a fitted short bloodred Escada jacket and boot-cut white jeans.

"It's winter white," she said to Maggie, who stared inquisitively.

"Ah." Her curls stifled in a severe bun, Maggie turned her head to the window. The train passed the monastery of the Dominican Nuns of Summit in the distance. "Do you know," Maggie said, "that I've taken to going there and sitting in the chapel? They make the most beautiful music during lauds."

"Lauds?" Larissa repeated as if she'd never heard the word before. "What time is that?"

"At 5:55," Maggie replied in a voice that sounded like it was still at the chapel. "On Sundays it starts ten minutes later, at 6:05."

"Ten whole minutes later? And how would you know?"

"Because," said Maggie, "I go there on Sundays, too."

Larissa studied her friend's hair, half turned gray. Maggie stopped coloring it long ago, and her pale face was devoid of makeup.

Something stirred inside Larissa, like something she was supposed to do, or talk to Maggie about, but for the life of her she couldn't remember what it was.

Larissa wanted to ask why Maggie started going to lauds at the monastery, but what she asked instead was, "I didn't know their chapel was open to the public."

"Of course," Maggie said, turning her face away from Larissa. "It's a church."

"No, I know, but isn't a monastery supposed to be a cloistered affair? Like aren't the nuns supposed to be hidden or something? Because they're Dominican, right? I read something about that. They, like, mainly pray for the salvation of souls but lead a hidden life."

"It's a church," Maggie repeated. "Their mission is one of intercession. How hidden could they be if their mission is intercession?"

"No. Right. But it's confusing, don't you think? The word cloister means something with walls around it, presumably to keep others out, unless of course, it's used primarily as a prison, to keep you in. But I don't think the nuns mean it in that sense, right? They can leave if they want to, no? I'm just saying. Cloister, and then intercession . . . you can see why a layperson like me might get confused. So!" Larissa continued, in a segue from the nuns to Bo, "Have you heard from her? I hope she's okay. I fear we may be too late. We were supposed to go talk her down before Christmas, and now it's January, and I haven't heard from her."

"I talked to her," said Maggie. "She can still use our help."

"Almost like *we're* interceding." Larissa chuckled.

"Interceding, really? She told me about your conversation." Maggie gave Larissa a peculiar cold look. "Maybe it's best you let me do the talking."

Larissa didn't think there was anything wrong with what she had said to Bo. Smiling genially, she made a mental note to study her words more carefully. Had she said something off kilter? She didn't want to probe too deeply.

"I haven't been feeling well," Maggie said suddenly.

"Have you been under the weather too? I'm so sorry. My God, I had Emily and Asher both home last week with sore throats." Larissa rolled her eyes, adjusting the collar on her jacket. "I thought I was going to go insane, them being home all day every day, and sick too. Michelangelo thankfully didn't catch it, good boy that he is."

Maggie turned to stare out the window. Larissa busied herself with the messages on her phone.

"How's your friend Che?" Maggie asked. "How many months pregnant is she?"

"Oh, she's good. I think a few. Three? Four?"

"She must be excited."

"She is, yeah, everything is going swell." Lorenzo's troubles would mean nothing to Maggie, so Larissa didn't share them.

Soon they were under the Hudson.

The Met had a café on the fourth floor. It was a Tuesday, yet the place was hopping. They met the impeccably coiffed Bo at the top of the wide staircase, and as they were about to walk into the packed lunch place, she nudged Larissa and motioned to her left. Larissa looked. Up the stairs and out of breath puffed a tall wide sloppy-looking man in an ill-fitting suit.

"That's Stanley," Bo whispered.

Larissa widened her eyes. He and Bo didn't acknowledge each other as he passed barely two feet from the three women. As Bo led the way into the café, Larissa tugged at Maggie and mouthed, "Oh my God." Stanley was astonishingly slovenly. By no measure that measured these things could he be described as attractive, his pants unable to contain his beer-gut stomach, his hair in need of a comb and a cut, and he certainly wasn't in the least as good-looking at Jonny, who spoke well, wore sharp suits, was smart, appreciated Jim Morrison's poetry, laughed, was an all-around great guy, albeit one who took a bit of his sweet damn time getting a job. What in the world could Bo possibly see in Stanley? Moreover, he didn't even glance Bo's way.

"We're keeping it cool," Bo explained. "Everybody at work knows I'm with Jonny."

It took the women a while to order their soup and sandwiches and find an empty table. "So? What did you think?" Bo asked them while they were standing waiting in line to pay.

Maggie spoke before Larissa could speak. "It's not up to us, honey."

"I know, but what did you *think?*"

"Well, he seemed like an interesting fella," said Maggie. "Right, Larissa?"

"Yes. So interesting. He seemed like he had a lot on his mind. Like he was very busy. Thinking interesting thoughts. Does he have an important job here? What does he do?"

"He is one of our art collectors. He buys the art. So yes, very important job."

"Exactly. I saw that," Larissa said, relieved they managed to get a table, and weren't going to have their lunch huddling in the corner with their trays in their hands. "He looked like he was thinking about important things."

At that point, Bo dropped the conversation, Maggie stirred her soup, and Larissa scraped the mayo off the bread. "Why do they always slap on the mayo?" she asked rhetorically. "Don't they know tuna salad already has mayo in it? Why overload?"

"We're *so* busy at work," Bo said to Maggie.

Maggie turned to face Bo. "Oh, yeah? Tell me about it."

"One of our special exhibits during this quarter is 'Art and Love in Renaissance Italy' and I have to write up yet another emergency press release for it before closing. I can only stay for a little while." They ate.

"Yeah, me too," said Larissa. "I've got to make sure I catch the train back in time for 2:40." She couldn't say that time out loud without wincing. It burned her tongue to say it. She was glad the girls weren't looking at her and didn't notice.

"Lar, did you hear about Dora?" Maggie said, putting on an effort to act normal, to sound normal. All Larissa saw was the effort. Why so much effort to say the simplest things? Maybe because it was awkward that they came to talk about Bo's beau, such as he was, and Bo wasn't talking.

"No, what's going on with her?" Dora had been one of Maggie's teaching assistants last year and she and her fiancé, Ray, really tried to become friends with the DeSwanns and the Starks. Larissa invited them over for dinner a few times. Bo met them. Dora did not fit well into their little group. She was so painfully shy that she had trouble looking even her friends in the eye.

"She's going to night school at Drew."

"Well, good for her," said Larissa. "Nothing wrong with trying to improve yourself."

"You know what she's going to night school for? Wait for it . . ." Maggie smiled. "Marriage counseling."

"She needs marriage counseling?" said Larissa. "I didn't think she and Ray were even married."

"Fool! She is going to *be* a marriage counselor!"

Larissa's eyes widened like she'd just envisioned their statuesque, pristine, calm-mannered Bo under the sprawling Stanley. "Get out!"

"I told you."

A silence washed over the table. Not even a fork clinked in the mouth.

"Well, that's great," said Larissa slowly. "How long's the course?"

"Two years."

Everybody's eyes turned inwards, on drinks and napkins and cheap metal spoons. What to say? Dora could not function when Ray was out of the house, constantly imagining him with other women. The fights they had over this issue was the sole reason Ray had not proposed even though they'd been together for fifteen years, having met in school. The worst thing that Dora could imagine in the whole world, in the universe, of all the bad and evil and awful and terrible things out there, was infidelity. She couldn't speak about it without hyperventilating, herself readily admitting that she *might* be a tiny bit overwrought, but it wasn't her fault that she perceived the entire perilous relationship as one big jealous paranoiac swampy outrage from which she could only be spared by death—and maybe not even then.

So when she heard that Dora was thinking of going into *marriage counseling*, Larissa's first thought was, it must be a form of mental illness. When you looked at things that were and saw them as completely different from how they really were. How *you* really were. It wasn't *wishing* them to be different, it was just delusional. It was like studying to become a surgeon when the sight of blood made you faint.

No one could be more ill-suited to advise couples on the state of their marriage than Dora. Counseling *implied* you were going to try to work things out. In Dora's mind, there was nothing to ever work out if the man ever so much as glanced at another woman. She'd be advising the girlfriend/wife to dump the cheater, grab her four small children ranging from three months to five years and run to a shelter for abused women.

But of course, as Larissa, Maggie and Bo sat at the table and digested this, having come together, after all, to talk about Bo's imminent infidelity, the first thing out of Larissa's mouth was, "Well, Mags, I'm sure she'll do great. It's really a shame you couldn't bring her with you today. We could've tested out her nascent skills on Bo here."

Humorlessly, Maggie and Bo stared at Larissa, who dug into her tuna sandwich, took a sip of her ice tea, regretting all the things she wasn't doing at the moment, the rooms she wasn't in, the body she wasn't touching, the voice she wasn't hearing. Here, away from the heart of her heart, she became upset at Bo for being silent and at Maggie for implying that had Larissa been more empathetic two months ago, they wouldn't be sitting here today.

"So tell me Bo, has there been any progress?" Larissa was done with dilly-dallying.

"Progress with what?"

"With the situation with Stanley."

Bo looked into her ice tea. "Well," she said. "I guess you can call it progress. Last week I finally slept with Stanley."

Maggie gasped. Way to go, Mags, way to be non-judgmental. I'll just leave it in your capable hands to deal with it. Larissa remained quiet. "What else? I sense a pause."

"Oh. Also, I told Jonny."

"You *what?*" exclaimed Maggie.

"I did. I know. It was eating me up. I just couldn't hide it any longer."

"But, Bo," Larissa said slowly, "how could you have consummated the act and become so ridden with guilt all in a span of seven days?"

"See, I don't think it was guilt. You know why I think I told him?" Bo sighed. "Because I wanted *him* to propel me toward the next thing. I couldn't do it myself. I was torn, unsure. I just didn't know what to do and couldn't make a decision. So I told him."

Larissa stopped eating, stopped drinking.

"What did you want the next thing to be?" she asked, leaning forward, wanting to hear, wanting to know, not wanting to know.

"Well, I wasn't quite sure myself. But I wanted us to have it out! We're so placid, honey this and honey that. Everything was so ordinary. I wanted drama."

Maggie sounded aghast when she said, "Oh, poor Jonny, what did he do when you told him?"

"Poor Jonny? Why are you siding with him?"

"No one is siding with anyone," Maggie said hastily. "But I imagine he must've been upset when you told him."

"He was. But what about me? You don't think this is hard for me, too?"

"Bo, it is hard," said Larissa. "Of course it is. The conflict is overwhelming."

"Yes!" Bo exclaimed. For some reason she sounded thrilled with the overwhelming nature of the conflict.

"So what did you want from him?"

"I wanted him to, I don't know, tell me to leave. Kick me out. Throw me out. Liquidate me. To tell me what he really thought of me." She paused. "And then after a huge screaming meltdown, I could go and tell Stanley that Jonny found out about us and threw me out."

"Good use of the passive voice, Bo," said Larissa. *"Found out about us.* Good. As if Jonny was doing all the investigating."

"Oh my, you already told Stanley, too?" Maggie paled in confusion.

"No, I haven't told him yet," Bo replied. "I'm going to tell him tonight. I'm going to go over his place after work and tell him."

"Does he know this yet?" Larissa asked.

Bo frowned. "Know what?"

"That you're going over there tonight?"

"No. But what difference does *that* make?"

"How many times have you slept with him, Bo?" asked Larissa. She resumed eating heartily. Maggie and Bo had stopped.

"Just once," Bo replied. "But how many times do you need before you know that it's right? When I told Jonny, in the back of my mind I think I was secretly hoping it might bring back the spark that used to be between us, bring back my other self."

But Larissa knew: nothing could bring back that other life.

Pat and insipid confessions couldn't do it. She was surprised at Bo. Confessions were so tawdry. How could you? I'm sorry. I didn't meant to. How could you? I'm sorry. I didn't mean to. How could you . . . I didn't mean to. *Ad nauseam.* She wanted to vomit imagining it.

"Jonny is just where you left him, Bo," said Larissa. "But nothing can mend what's not there anymore. The piece that's missing is you. Not him. No. He is right there on the couch. The house, the boyfriend, the toys on the floor, the books, the packages that arrive at the door. They are all where you left them. But not you."

Maggie and Bo raised their eyes to stare at Larissa. "Toys on the floor? What are you talking about?" said Maggie.

"What *are* you talking about?" said Bo. "I'm still here. I'm exactly the same as I always was. I just want a little excitement."

Larissa looked into her empty glass. There were things that were real, and there were things that weren't. There was imagined conflict, manufactured conflict, and there was real conflict. There was imagined love, manufactured love, and real love. There was imagined trouble, manufactured trouble, and then there was real trouble. Sometimes it was hard to know the difference, especially when you were talking about yourself. Ezra was right. Walker Percy was right. We spend all our days with ourselves, and yet we are the person we know and understand the least. We know all about the paths of the planets around the sun, but ask us where we're headed in the next five minutes and why, and we have no answers.

"Your problem, Bo," said Larissa, "is not going to be easily resolved by *deus ex machina* exits. No grand gestures of destiny will save you."

"Destiny, what destiny? I don't want destiny to save me," Bo said. "I want to be with Stanley. Do you think that's wrong?"

"Do *you*?" asked Larissa. "Do you really want to be with Stanley?"

"Yes! I'm completely enamored of him. I'm fascinated by him."

"But Jonny loves you so much," said Maggie.

"I think Stanley does, too," Bo countered.

"The issue isn't whether Jonny loves you," said Larissa. "The issue is how *you* feel about Jonny."

"Well, I love him, but I'm not *in* love with him. But my problem is . . ." and here Bo nearly banged the table in her frustration, her disbelief at the mystery of the workings of man, "is that Jonny didn't do any of the things I wanted him to do, or the things I thought he would do. I thought I knew him. I wanted him to go nuts so I could go and tell Stanley, hey, my boyfriend found out about us and flipped out . . ."

"Good plan," said Larissa.

". . . And threw me out, which would allow Stanley to react with a 'Thank God!' or a 'Now you're free!' or even a 'How do you feel?' Except Jonny didn't do any of these things. He didn't throw me out. He didn't tell me I was trash. He didn't even get mad," Bo said with incredulity. "Jonny sat on the couch and cried."

"Jonny cried?" said Maggie, incredulous and ready to cry herself.

"I *know*, Mags!" Bo made a gesture with her hands that made the wet straw from her Diet Coke glass fly out and hit a woman passing by. After apologizing she turned back to Maggie and Larissa.

"I didn't know what to do. I didn't expect him to . . . God!" She shuddered. "Anyway, I became ridiculously upset with him, and after half an hour, it was Jonny who was apologizing to *me* for his inappropriate reaction toward my appalling affair." Bo was breathing heavy. "I told him, I don't want to be in a relationship with you anymore. I want out."

"You said this to Jonny?"

"Sure did."

"Where was your mother during all this?"

"Making my life a living hell," Bo replied. "We put her in the bedroom, and she kept coming out every five minutes. Do you want tea? Do you need some water? Should I open the window? I'm like, Ma, *basta*! But she wouldn't. She said, I think I'm getting a migraine, Bo, can you get me my pills, I can't see so good. It could be the glaucoma. My blood pressure must be through the roof. My pills, Bo! Honest to God, I don't know if I dreamed it or lived it, it was so surreal. It was like a Dali infidelity scene. Nothing in it made any sense."

"And yet somehow remarkable sense. Bo," Larissa said calmly, "let me ask you a question. You know how you just said that Jonny didn't react or behave in the way you either wanted him to or expected him to . . ."

"Yeah?"

"Well, is it possible, just possible, that Stanley might also not react or behave in the way you want or expect when you tell him that you want to break up with your boyfriend and go out with him instead?"

"No." Bo frowned. "Stanley and I have talked and talked about it and about us. We have a very strong connection."

"I'm sure you do." Larissa stood up, and placed her plates and bowls on the tray. "Nothing you can do now. You've embarked on a course you've got to see through. Talk to Stanley. You've left yourself few other options. Now, Mags, are you coming? Because I've got to start back."

"I'm going to finish eating," Maggie said, looking into her uneaten soup. "You don't mind, do you?"

"Of course not." Larissa gladly left them, but instead of heading to the train, she went downstairs to the third floor and explored the "Art and Love in Renaissance Italy" exhibit, showing a passing interest in the Childbirth Bowls and Trays by Castel Durante and an intense fascination in Gustave Doré's black and white drawings of Paolo and Francesca, Dante's Fifth Circle desperate lovers, both married to other people, murdered by the cuckolded Giovanni before they were able to repent, clinging to each other for dear life while the hurricane of souls swirled around them.

Would Jared render her blameless, accept her Epicurean arguments? Could Larissa persuade him with her airtight logic? But Jared, she could say. I came home. I cooked you dinner. I spent the weekends with you. I still picked up your starched white shirts from the cleaners, on the way home from being soundly assaulted with love, someone else's, not yours.

She knew: in no way would anything be made easier for Larissa by having her free will compromised by acts of fate. There had only been one act of fate—her going to Stop&Shop because King's parking lot was full—and one act of free will: when she went back. After that, just like now, it all remained in Larissa's clenched and sperm-drenched hands.

After a trance that lasted many minutes, Larissa startled herself out of it, ran downstairs out of the marble lobby and hailed a cab. To avoid accidentally running into Maggie, she took the cab all the way home to Summit.

∽ɔʊɔ∾

At six o'clock the next morning, her phone rang. Why did the phone ringing frighten her so much? She couldn't help it, she thought it was going to be bad news.

It was Maggie.

"Maggie, do you have any idea what time it is?"

"Yes, it's lauds time. And I'm not going today. Oh my God, did she call you?"

"Call me? Who? What?"

"Bo!"

"No, she didn't call me. I thought she was with Stanley." It's Maggie, Larissa mouthed to Jared in the bed, and got up to take the phone into the bathroom.

"She was! Listen to this, but pretend you know nothing if she calls you, okay?"

"Okay."

"She went to Stanley, and she said to him, Jonny threw me out. And do you know what Stanley did?"

"No, what?"

"Stanley said, oh dear. Threw you out? What are you going to do now? Bo didn't know how to respond to that. She hemmed and hawed for thirty minutes. And then he said to her, get this, Bo, *I'm sorry, I didn't realize you were coming by tonight. I'm actually going out.*"

"He was going *out?*"

"Right! So Bo asked if she could come. And he said, not *that* kind of going out."

"Not *that* kind of going out," Larissa repeated. "So what did she do? Did she turn around and run for her life?"

"Would *you* do that?"

"Um, *yeah.* Faster than you can say, see ya."

"Yeah, me, too. But maybe once again, like you said, my Ezra is right. No one knows what anyone else is doing. We don't even know why *we* do half the things we do. Bo did not leave, did not run. Larissa, Bo stayed on Stanley's couch while Stanley went out."

"She *what?*"

"I don't think we gave her good advice, Lar."

"No kidding. Well, I tried. I tried to tell her that perhaps a week of sleeping with another man was not enough time to determine such a definitive course of action. But did she seem to you like she was listening? She just wanted what she wanted. She was paying us lip service."

So the evening ended with Bo sitting on Stanley's couch while he went out and left her alone, and Jonny sitting on his own couch, while Bo went out and left him alone. Larissa pressed her forehead against the cold tile. Remarkable.

"She sat and waited for Stanley to come back," Maggie continued. "He strolled in at two! Bo wanted them to redefine their relationship. He didn't even ask her what *she* wanted from the relationship. She had to tell him! Stanley, Bo said, I'm in love with you. I want to stay with you. I want to be with you."

"After sitting for three hours alone on his couch while he went out with God knows who, this is what she said to him?"

"Yes! And Stanley said nothing. It took him until four in the morning to cough up the ugly truth."

"There's a truth uglier than what you just told me?"

"He told her he wasn't in love with her!" Maggie hissed into the phone.

"I don't believe it," said Larissa. "That lardball told our lovely Bo that *he* was not in love with *her*?"

"That's like saying that the bell ringer of Notre Dame was not in love with Marilyn Monroe," said Maggie. "I'm sick for her. My God, I've forgotten my own troubles."

Larissa wished she could say the same.

"Stanley said he thought they were just having fun," Maggie went on slowly. "He was not interested in more. Not from her. I don't feel about you *that* way, Stanley said to our Bo."

"I cannot believe what you just told me," said Larissa. "That blubbery fool." And then she remembered Jonny.

"Bo left Stanley . . . and took a cab back home. Cost her a hundred and fifty bucks. And on the couch back home she found Jonny waiting for her, still awake, eyes red from tears."

"And she called you this morning?"

"I just got off the phone with her. She said she and Jonny were going to try to work it out."

"Really?" Larissa tried to imagine Bo's dull flat voice as she spoke those words to their friend Margaret. *We're going to try to work it out.* Whole insubstantial dream faded. All the drama bubbled and burst in the span of one week.

Lucky Bo? Poor Bo?

"Obviously Jonny thinks she's worth keeping."

"I'm shocked," said Larissa. "Worth keeping even though she regards him as second best? Possibly third?"

"Listen," said Maggie, "she asked me, begged me not to say anything to Ezra. Can you please not say anything to Jared? She doesn't want Jonny to be humiliated when we all get together. I know. The irony. But please. I know you don't keep any secrets from Jared, but can you try with this one?"

"Mags," said Larissa, "let me ask you a question. A tiny one. Did you already tell Ezra?"

"Oh, yeah. Everything."

Larissa laughed. "Well, I am going to try to keep it from Jared," she said. "It won't be easy. But I will try."

Jared came into the bathroom and turned on the shower. "Keep what from me?"

Larissa told him the whole tale before they were finished brushing their teeth. "And there I was, thinking Jonny had the upper hand in that relationship," she finished. "Who knew, right?"

Jared rinsed his razor under the warm water. "What a chump Jonny is."

"What?" Larissa smiled, glancing coquettishly at him. "You don't think you'd be on the couch waiting for *me* with red-rimmed eyes?"

"Oh, I'd be on the couch, all right. But instead of a box of tissues, I'd be holding a Howitzer."

Larissa wanted to study Jared extra carefully to see if he was joking, but wouldn't allow herself even a glance at his reflection in the fogged-up mirror.

2

Stories on the Ceiling

And Kai?

She watched him and her heart slammed against itself like a swallow not seeing glass and shattering. "Who do you need to talk to, baby?" he said. "I'm right here. Talk to me. I'm all you need."

"What's there to talk about, right?" she said, leaning over him to cradle his face in the crook of her arm. He allowed himself to be smothered, and then wrested free to continue playing his harmonica. The singing answer to everything was apparently in the jungles wet with rain.

She told Kai about Stanley and Jonny. He said nothing. He listened, but inscrutably, and after she was done, he clucked his lips, opened his hands with an *oh well, what are ya gonna do* gesture and shrugged. "What are you looking at me like that for?" he said. "It's not us."

"Well, yes. First of all, you're not three hundred pounds."

"Not yet. But—more important—*you're* not coming to tell me your husband threw you out, and you're here to stay." Steadily he gazed at her. "Exactly. So why have a hypothetical conversation about bullshit? Come closer instead. I want to play you a new song I learned."

"You had me at play you," said Larissa, crawling over, unable to gaze at him steadily or any other wayily.

He played the verses on the ukulele and the wordless chorus on the harmonica. It sounded in a washed-out way like an old standard, sadness about the pyramids along the Nile, and photographs and souvenirs, except nothing like it. Taking the harmonica away from his lips he sang the last of it to her a cappella. When you're home again, he lamented in a whisper croon, just remember who you belong to . . .

"Please," Larissa whispered. "Don't do that . . ."

"I'm just singing, babydoll," he said. "I'm not crying."

"Am I *Francesca*, Kai?" She struggled close, her face at his face. "Are you *Paolo*?"

"Ah," he said, one hand on her, the other on his ukulele, strumming it with one hand, strumming her with the other. "What's your question? In what way are we like Dante's lovers?"

She said nothing. He put his ukulele down. His arms went around her.

"We're clinging together like doves. We are surrounded by a storm of souls. We have not repented." He paused. "Is your husband Giovanni? My answer is, no one knows. Not even him. Most men aren't until the moment they are."

He was unchanging. He was like the moontides. Every day with a smile, a poem, a nod of the head, his naked body, he touched her, he kissed her, he brought her food in a paper bag and he opened champagne and poured it into plastic flutes, and played acoustic guitar and the electric ukulele, he wailed through the harmonica, soft and bluesy, perfect, perfect. All music, like life, was of two types: either moving toward God or away from God. Blues was moving away from God. Moving away from God, but toward Kai.

He didn't help her or not help her. He just was. She couldn't talk to him about this. About other things, but she couldn't sit and say, Kai, oh my God, what do I do? He didn't know the answer; it wasn't blowing outside in the snowy blizzard wind; it wasn't heard in the whisper of the willows. There was no answer.

He had told her. Larissa, all I want is you.

All I want is you.

All I want is you.

Was that helpful?

No.

But yet . . . all he wanted was her.

That *was* helpful.

Larissa lay on her back next to him. Thirty more minutes. They were on the bed, swamped with the toils of their labors, he was on his stomach, pretending to snooze, while she stared at the ceiling, imagining the paths open to her. She wasn't Bo, she didn't want a cataclysm, a shallow confession without remorse, she didn't want the hand of fate to intervene. Or did she? This was more real than her own two feet on which she traveled the earth, and yet she lived alone with it inside her heart, like a misty vapor, a muted haunting. The only true Larissa was nude on her back in an attic room in a yellow house in Madison.

Snatches of time, dammed, damned with the shackles of time. Was it easy to live this way? Was it easy for him not to see her at night, to be alone Friday nights, Saturdays, weekends? To wake up alone. To go to sleep alone. They couldn't have pancakes together out, couldn't go shopping at the mall, couldn't go for a ride on his bike except up and down Glenside in an infinite spin of a dead-end loop. Couldn't spend a night together at the Madison Hotel! Couldn't go on vacation, couldn't go swimming, couldn't fly.

They could go on like this, but Larissa felt that this was beginning to sully the very soul Epicurus swore she didn't possess. Is this how she wanted to live, is this how he wanted to live, like outlaws? She didn't dare ask him in the dread that he would say *no*.

She was sure Dominick the UPS man saw her car parked in driveways not her own, because every time he gave her a package and said, "Have a nice day," what she heard was, "You trollop. You lying slut. You heartbreaker."

She felt, one way or another, this couldn't continue. Jared would soon find a speck of a price tag off a silk Cotton Club camisole bought for six hundred dollars, gorgeous like black diamonds, draped around her afternoon body. She left it with Kai, in the drawer he emptied for her in the dresser of his life. She bought slinky things, brought them here, left them here. But every once in a while in her purse, she'd find a tag from another flimsy fandango chemise bought in haste, used in haste, repented not at all, dreamed of in leisure. One of these days even Jared would stumble upon it. Even a broken clock was right twice a day. Even a blind man would eventually trip upon the one obscure door in his life that opened into another world.

Larissa had.

And then what? There'd be railing and false apologies and even falser remorse, and she'd have to grit every nerve ending in her body, but the chasm between synapses would open too wide for speech, and to keep the outer shell of her existence, she would have to let Kai go, and repent repent repent. And go on.

Without him.

She would have to turn her back on the impossible vivid dream next to her naked heart and go back to what she left behind. The ceiling couldn't help her here: after it all crashed to a hideous end, the exposed rafters could not beam sugarplum visions of her looking out of her Georgian sash windows onto the golf course and the mall in the distance and the sunshine, planning another vacation and camp for the kids, and maybe some summer school for Asher since he was doing so bad in math. She'd figure out when best to exercise. Maybe in the mornings she could swim in her pool for weight loss. Surely she'd need to do something. In the afternoons she could cook. Bake from scratch maybe.

The girls could come over and she could show them how to make rubbed-down jerk chicken with cracked pepper sauce. On the weekends, they could ride in Doug's Jaguar to South Mountain.

There was no exit. There was no way out.

Oh my God, Kai, what do we do? she whispered helplessly.

"It's 2:30, Larissa. Your son is up on a hill at Woodland."

⌇

Dear Larissa,

We are in so much trouble, Lorenzo and I. All that protesting meant nothing until it meant something, and as soon as it meant something, everything else went ruined and run down.

When we did it for money, we protested anything. But as you know, you cannot serve two masters.

Our life has come down to one thing: Catholics against MILF. After what happened to his parents, it's the only thing Lorenzo cares about. He was going to protests and meetings, and then he needed to buy a typewriter, and even Father Emilio complained about how often he was using the rectory copy machine. He was out of the house all the time too, but the money stopped coming in. Like one minute there was money, and the next there wasn't. I don't know if you know what that's like, Larissa.

I asked him what he thought he was doing. He said he had never cared about nothing before, except drinking and having a good time. But MILF was taking over Mindanao. And we had to stop them. I wanted to ask who "we" was but was too afraid. Mindanao cannot be MILF island. This country is ninety-five percent Catholic. For forty years they lived side by side with us, but not peacefully. The government wanted to end once and for all the Christians being killed daily on Manila streets, and also to stimulate the tourist trade in Mindanao, which had vanished because of the unrelenting attacks and burnings and deaths. So the government agreed to something called the Memorandum of Agreement on Ancestral Domain, a long-standing MILF demand. Lorenzo said the government simply surrendered the island of Mindanao to the MILF in return for peace. "But they don't understand that they'll have neither," Lorenzo said. This meant war.

I said (I may have yelled), Lorenzo, what are you talking about? What war? We are going to have a baby.

He said our baby will not be safe. Like his parents, apolitical fishermen in tiny Zamboanga, were not safe. No one is safe anymore, he said.

Two weeks ago he joined the Peace Brigade, which is another name for street fighters, and he's taken to the streets in full riot gear—a flak jacket, a helmet and weapons! Of course, the MILF rebels are raising even more trouble than the Peace Brigade, to make the government ratify the agreement faster.

I don't know what to do. I have no one but Lorenzo, and he's gone mad. He won't even go to Father Emilio to be helped. All the work he does now he does pro bono for the Catholic League, and they feed him in return, and Father Emilio feeds me, but we live in a shack that costs three thousand pesos a month, and Lorenzo no longer makes any money. This is my pregnancy. He's insane with grief and rage, he talks like I've never heard him talk, of nationalism, of separatist insurgencies, of continued clashes and protests on Manila streets until the government stops negotiating with terrorists, of what's right, of revenge.

And the worst is, Father Emilio is not on my side! He thinks Lorenzo may have a point! He says, how can the rebels consider themselves autonomous when ninety-eight percent of their operating revenue comes from the Philippine government? After fifteen years of having an autonomous region, they haven't created any other significant source of sustainable income, and yet they want more autonomy? And they're killing Filipino civilians every day as if it's their right. "Lorenzo is fighting for justice," says Father Emilio.

Larissa, help me. I'm lost. What do I do?

3

Chris Chase

Attempting to carve out an occasional evening for her and Kai, Larissa found a new colorist in the city on 21st and Ninth. She scheduled an evening appointment and told Jared that was all they had. He looked miffed, and when she pressed him, he said, "Yeah, I'm ticked off because you color your hair once every six weeks, and I don't want to get into a crazy habit where you're going into the city every month at night when you can get color at Kim's until 2:30 every day."

"Paul at Chris Chase is the best."

"Where did you read that?"

"*Allure*."

"*Allure*. Swell. You've been going to Kim for seven years, and now suddenly you're going to the city for *hair color*? Honestly, Larissa. If you were meeting Bo for dinner, if you and Maggie were going to see a show, if you were doing something fun, I'd say, absolutely, by all means."

"Would you?" she said quietly. "What's the difference?"

"To go in at night to get your hair done? It's odd. It's not normal."

Gritting her teeth, turning away, Larissa said with her back to him, "I already made the appointment." It was obvious this was not going to be the success she'd hoped for. She was trying to work it out so that once a month she and Kai could have dinner together.

The colorist really *was* supposed to be great. She scheduled him for Wednesday, which was Kai's early day; he finished at six and agreed to meet her in the city by seven.

She was done with her hair a few minutes before seven and waited for him, ridiculously excited on the corner of 23rd and Ninth, decked out in a sea-green clingy cashmere tunic over black leggings and high patent leather boots. She wore her shearling coat open, her jewelry sparkling, her breasts rising and falling with anticipation. She stood on the sidewalk near a short fence, looking at her watch, flinging around her beautifully done head of hair, long, silk straight and smooth, with red lowlights and blonde highlights on a base of light brown; it looked fantastic; *Allure* was right, Paul *was* a magician. She licked her lip gloss, eagerly impatient in the cold, fluttering like she was seventeen going on her first date, and bitter-sweetly realizing that aside from sitting in the car or being in his apartment, this was indeed their first time out anywhere, and, even through her excitement, feeling a pang of sadness for Kai that he spent his weeks and days, his months and hours waiting for her to grace him with an hour of her presence. She was still standing, tapping her heels on the pavement when she heard a female voice say, "Larissa?"

Paling, Larissa stepped slightly away from the wrought-iron fence and turned in the direction of the voice.

It was Kate Grant, Doug's wife.

Doug, Jared's co-worker, accountant, office manager, second financial officer, friend, and there was his wife, on a New York City street, smiling at Larissa, just as it was falling dark and 7:10 and Kai would be upon them any minute.

"Hi, Kate, what a surprise! What are you doing here?" said Larissa shrilly, stepping forward to kiss her hello.

"My law firm is on 23rd and Tenth. I walk this way every night to catch the subway." Kate smiled. "The surprise is to see *you* here."

"Oh, I'm—I just got my hair done."

"I was going to say it looks smashing."

"Thanks. So how are the kids?" Larissa desperately tried not to fidget.

"Good, everybody is good." Kate looked Larissa over. "All of you is looking pretty smashing tonight," the woman said. "I'm impressed. You dress like this to get your hair done?"

Larissa laughed loudly. "You're funny. So how's Douglas?"

"He's great." Kate rolled her eyes.

"And the new car? You enjoying it?" Larissa willed herself not to turn to the busy street to scan the crowds of faces. Maybe he would be a few minutes delayed and Kate would leave soon. Maybe, maybe, maybe . . .

"The new car is all the rage. It was supposed to be for me, except I never see it. Doug takes it everywhere, like a purse."

Larissa fake laughed again. "You must put your foot down. I didn't even know you worked in the city, Kate."

"Of course you did. You just forgot. Legal secretary. Been with the same firm fifteen years. Any minute now I'm going to get a gold watch."

"Hey, better than a golden handshake. And who takes care of the kiddies while you're away?"

"Oh, we have a lady from Nepal. She's our third one. We like the Nepalese. The language skills aren't great, but they're wonderful with babies."

Larissa tried hard not to glance down the street, not to look for him, not to look like she was about to have a heart attack, fall down. She stepped closer to the fence, to grasp one of the wrought-iron poles in her cold white hand.

"Are you taking the train back?" asked Kate.

"I am, yes."

"Great. You want to walk to Penn? It's not too cold out. We can bundle up, burn off a little lunch, ride home together."

"Um, yes, that would be wonderful . . . I meant I'm taking the train later. I'd love to walk with you, but the thing is, I'm meeting a friend for dinner."

"Oh." Buttoning up her big down coat, Kate smiled at Larissa's black shiny boots. "Well, listen, the four of us must go out to dinner and spend all evening arguing about the various merits of our respective Jag models."

"Yes, let's," said Larissa. "There's supposed to be a great Italian place in Madison."

"Madison? A little far, but okay. Doug will be happy to drive, no doubt." They kissed, they hugged, and Kate was about to walk away from Larissa when she said, "Kai? Kai Passani?"

Oh my God. She knew him! Of course. He sold Doug and Kate their Jaguar. What a nightmare.

Larissa was forced on a darkened street to endure watching Kai shake Kate's hand, express surprise at seeing her, and answer her exclamations.

"Yes, nice to see you, too. Oh, you're welcome for the car. My pleasure. Thank you for the Cristal. Much appreciated. Yes, of course; I put it to very good use. What? Oh, just meeting up with a couple of friends. And how are you enjoying your new vehicle, Mrs. Grant?"

Kate spent three minutes telling Kai how much her husband was enjoying her new vehicle, and all the while Kai expressed vocal amusement while Larissa stood nearby and pretended she didn't know either of them, didn't speak English, was like the lady from Nepal, just standing on the corner, waiting for the truck to run her over or take her back to the old country.

"I'm sorry, how rude of me. Kai, do you remember Larissa Stark? You sold her a convertible!" Kate was ebullient. "She's the reason we came to see you. The way she *raves* about that vehicle."

"Well, she's right to. It is a fine car," Kai said, tilting his head to Larissa. "Nice to see you again, Mrs. Stark."

"Yes, you too," said Larissa, barely moving her numb lips.

The three of them stood for a long moment, and Kai said, "Well, ladies, have a wonderful evening. Enjoy your cars." He bowed his head to Kate and walked past Larissa, who clenched her mouth in mute acknowledgment of his passing her by, but didn't otherwise allow herself even a blink at his leather jacket, at his jeans, at the profound look of condemnation and distress in his eyes as he walked by her, not six inches away from her on a busy street, turned his body toward her instead of away from her to pass, and said, "Excuse me," in a bark too cold and clipped for a stranger, while Larissa stood motionless, speechless, but when she turned her head to wave goodbye to Kate, she caught the woman watching them, and there was an odd glint in Kate's frowning puzzled expression, imperceptible if only it weren't so tangible, like a darkening realization of something untoward and electric right in front of her tired eyes.

Larissa did the only thing left to her. She had to deny Kai. She had to deny him with all her heart.

"Kate, wait!" Hurrying, Larissa caught up with her. "Can you hang on a sec?"

"I'm going to miss my train," Kate said coolly.

"Yeah, just a sec. I don't know why, but my friend is not showing up. She's a half-hour late. And she's not answering her cell. I wonder if she got held up or something. Hang on, okay, I'm going to check my messages."

Silently, Kate waited. Larissa checked her fake messages on her real phone. "Can you believe it," she said, tutting. "I've been standing here like a fool for thirty minutes, and she'd called at six to say she couldn't make it. Damn. You mind if I walk with you? Maybe we can take that train back home together after all."

That seemed to deflate the balloon of suspicion inside Kate Grant, because she smiled and relaxed, looking noticeably relieved. They started walking toward Seventh Avenue without giving Kai another backward glance. And Larissa, falling inside, horrified for him, for herself, for her own fucked-up, slowly unraveling life, could only imagine what Kai must have been thinking as he stood on the street watching her walk away.

They caught the 8:02. It was thirty-three excruciating minutes to Maplewood, forty-five to Summit. They sat by the window across from each other and chatted, and when fifteen minutes had passed, Kate tittered nervously. "You want to know how silly I am? You know when we were standing there, and we ran into our car salesman . . ."

"Yeah?"

"I don't know, it's almost funny now, oh, it's so dumb, but for a second, as he walked past you, I saw him look at you like he knew you."

"Who?"

"The Jag salesman."

"Well, he *does* know me," said Larissa. "He sold me the car."

"No, I know. But there was something else in how close he walked by you. I mean he looked at you like he *knew* you."

"On a crowded rush-hour city street?"

"Exactly! But you didn't move away, you see. You didn't even step away." Kate giggled. "I think I've watched too many *Days of Our Lives* in my youth. For a minute there, I could've sworn you were meeting *him* for dinner, the way he walked by you, staring so intensely into your face. And you wouldn't even lift your eyes to him. Watching it from the outside, it was really quite a stunning moment. Glowing with possibilities."

Larissa giggled herself. "Kate, that's quite an imagination you've got there. You should be a writer."

"Really? Funny you should say that. I *have* been dabbling a bit . . ."

"*Have* you? Why don't you tell me about it."

Kate beamed, and was off non-stop for the next ten minutes until Maplewood when Larissa kissed her goodbye.

She couldn't get a signal on the train, but as soon as she was at her car in Summit, she called Kai. He didn't pick up. She left a message. "I'm so, *so* sorry," she said. "Please forgive me."

She texted him.

There was no answer.

She sat in her car with her head on the wheel. Two more trains came.

Then she drove home. Drove slow like the mob were waiting for her, having accused her of breaking the law of omerta, about to dip her feet in liquid cement and after it had hardened, throw her into the Passaic River.

~~~

"Emily! Have you practiced your cello?" she barked as soon as she came inside and found the children in the den playing video games and watching TV.

"Um, no."

Larissa slapped off the TV. "You know the rules. You don't sit down until the work is done. Go practice. I knew you were going to take advantage of your dad. Go!"

"I was watching Michelangelo for you!" Emily yelled. "I was *babysitting*! How am I supposed to practice when I'm playing trucks with him?"

"Always with your excuses!" Larissa yelled. "How do I manage to cook dinner and clean the kitchen, and help you with your homework and Asher with his while I'm playing trucks with Michelangelo? Go, I said. I don't want to hear anything but sounds of cello for the next thirty minutes!"

Emily stomped off. Asher sat at the computer desk quiet as a mouse. Michelangelo came and hugged Larissa around the leg. This was all before she took off her coat. Jared silently watched her from the entrance to the kitchen.

"Well, hello to you, too," he said.

"Hello. But you *know* she is supposed to practice her cello."

"I don't know what she did and didn't do before I got home."

"You have no right to be that oblivious. She's got her winter concert next week." She stormed past him.

"Well, maybe you shouldn't be gallivanting around New York when your children need you," Jared said, following her into the kitchen. "I don't know what's going on. I barely remembered to bring home pizza. Good thing Em called to remind me."

But Larissa had stopped listening. "Asher! How many times do I have to tell you—after you're done with your homework put your damn books away."

"I just got done."

"So put them away! Don't wait for me to yell at you. Just do it!"

"I put my books away, Mommy," said Michelangelo.

"Well, you're a good boy," she said. "But I did notice that you didn't put your trucks away after you were done playing with them. You know the rules. Done with something? Put it away." She grabbed on to the side of the counter to steady herself.

"I wasn't done playing with them," the boy said.

"Well, I suggest you get to it. It's bath in five minutes."

"I'll give him a bath," said Jared staring at her coldly. "You get yourself sorted out."

But there was no sorting herself out.

Kai told her. It's not that she didn't listen. It's that there was nothing she could do then, or now. In one minute, the life she was living, the entire house was going to come crashing down on her head if she didn't find a way to get herself together.

Funny thing about righteous anger, righteous frustration at the impossibility of the way things are, of wanting to change them and being unable to, of wanting to scream her love from the rooftops and being unable to, of wanting to be free, and being unable to be. Of wanting and wanting and wanting, and being constantly thwarted, of being desperately afraid, the vigilance of every day taking the toll on her nerve endings. She stood in her kitchen being blackened in ways she did not expect. She felt her vision go blank, her legs go slack. What's happening? Am I fainting?

And the next thing she knew she was down on the kitchen floor, opening her eyes and Jared kneeling over her.

He helped her up, got her to the bar stool, got her some water. "What's the matter? You're not well? I knew it as soon as you came in. You looked terrible. You must be getting sick."

"Looked terrible?" Larissa held her head, which was hurting, but not as much as her sore heart was hurting. "Do you not see me? Do you not see my hair, my boots, my sweater? Do you not see my hair? Looked terrible? What are you talking about?"

"Come on, you know what I mean. I can't see past you falling faint on the floor, okay? To me that's not a woman who's feeling well."

"I may not *feel* well," she said through gritted teeth. "But to you that's how I *look*, too?"

He began to speak to defend himself, but Larissa cut him off. Cut him off or tuned him out. She was so tired of living like this. She thought she could do it, juggle it all; after all, that's what mothers did. They multi-tasked to the max, no one could juggle life as well as a mother, and yet the balls seemed to be at her feet at the moment, except for the lead ones in her gutted stomach. She thought she could do the kids, and keep the house, and cook and shop, and prepare *Saint Joan*, and open *Godot*, and go out with reasonable people, get her nails done and her hair, buy clothes for her growing family, entertain in her beautiful home, schedule activities for the weekend, little trips out, big vacations, do all this but keep the core of her life, the love of her life, preserved on Albright Circle like a dragonfly in amber, pristine, unbroken, untouched by misfortune. Kai said he was okay with it, and she was relieved, because she wanted him to be okay with it. They had so few options. It was the status quo or it was nothing.

But something had broken inside her. To leave Kai in the middle of the street, having deliberately gotten him out there, having him pass three inches away from her breast, to set him up just to reject him, to *betray* him, it screamed injustice to her so loudly that she could not endure another second of Jared's solicitous face. *Now* he was solicitous! She had treated Kai poorly. And when you treat people you adore poorly what's left? What does your life mean when you can't even be good to the ones you can't live without?

What if he got fed up? What if he said, I've had enough.

Frankly, that's the only reaction Larissa expected from a young man left on a street corner by his dreadful married lover. He knew he would never come first. Not second. Not even a distant third. On street corners, he couldn't even place. He was not a qualifier.

How long could Kai put up with this? She didn't think much past tonight.

"Excuse me," she said faintly to Jared, moving past. "I'm not *feeling* well. Suddenly I feel as awful as I look." Larissa didn't know what to do. Not only had she no answers, she was out of questions. But this is what she knew. If tomorrow when she came to grovel to Kai, he said to her, I cannot do this anymore, she would be finished. There was no more life for her except with him. Whatever was going to happen, one thing that could *not* happen was she could not lose him. That she knew. That was the one true thing. Everything else was on the negotiating table.

She went upstairs, into Emily's room, sat down heavily on her bed, asked her about her day, her science quiz, her book project and listened to her play Dvorak's *Humoresque*. She went into Asher's room, told him to turn down the stereo and go have a shower before bed, walked past the bathroom where Jared was giving Michelangelo a bath, thought of coming in because she loved seeing her little boy all soapy wet and happily playing, but just then remembered that she left her purse downstairs, and in it the cell phone, and what if Jared looked through her purse concerned about his wife's peculiar behavior, and found the phone? As she trudged back downstairs, to throw out yet another pre-paid cell phone, she miserably thought I wouldn't care if he found it. I want him to find it, I want to have it out, I want something to change. I'm with Bo on this one. I can't do this anymore.

When she took out the cell phone, there was nothing from Kai.

She went outside, by the bushes in her back yard, and called him. He picked up this time.

"I'm so sorry," she said. She started to cry.

"Calm down," said Kai. His voice was cold. "Are you home?"

"Yes."

"Don't do this. Get yourself together. Don't . . . it's fine. I'm a big boy. I can take it. Just calm down."

"Oh, Kai."

"Hang up, go tend to your family."

"Kai . . ."

"Larissa, stop. Remember, no man knows what he is going to do until he is faced with it. Now I'm faced with it. But if you don't get yourself together, are you sure you're ready to find out tonight if Jared is merely a sitting and wailing Jonny or something else?"

Larissa fell mute. They hung up.

She dropped the phone deep inside the Hefty bag in the outside trash, cleaned up her face and went back inside. Jared was in the kitchen. "What were you doing out there?" he asked.

"Throwing crap out," snapped Larissa. "I'm not happy with you, Jared."

"What did I do? Did I not play my cello?"

"Go ahead, make fun of me raising my kids," said Larissa. "Jared, every single day you get to come home late if you need to, early if you want to, you get to go out with clients to dinner, you never have to worry about a thing. I ask for one evening every six weeks to go do my fucking hair in the city, and you give me shit about it."

"I didn't give you shit."

"Oh, no?" She mimicked him. "Why don't you just do it during the day, why don't you do it with Kim?"

"Well, why don't you?"

"Because I don't want to! Because I want one evening every month where I go to the city and have my hair done by a guy who got written up in *Allure*, and then have a little dinner, and maybe go to a movie, or go to Barnes and Noble. Why is that so hard to accept? Why do I always have to fit my life into a little snippet of time you allot me? Jared, I'm scheduled up the ass, I live and die by the clock."

"Welcome to the adult world."

"Yes, yes," she said with tired impatience. "But you can have a three-hour lunch if you want to. I can't. You can be out all day driving around, checking out real estate. I can't. You go to nice restaurants and hang out with adults. I don't. I'm scheduled to the clock of children. That's a huge difference."

"But you have time during the—"

"I have no time during the day! You know what I have during the day?" Larissa broke off under the weight of the deception that wasn't quite ready to fall off her shoulders, to slide trippingly off her tongue. Kai was cool on the phone, not livid, and this gave her strength and hope. She was going to try one more time to make this right. "You take me completely for granted. You have no idea what I do during the day and worse, you don't care. For your information, besides cleaning your house and cooking your food and taking care of your children, I'm recasting, painting, rehearsing."

"Whose fault is that?"

"Which part, Jared?" she asked quietly. "Which part is my fault?"

"I told you theater was going to be too much. You can't complain now."

"I *can* complain, and you know how you know? Because I'm complaining. But the only thing I'm really complaining about is your awful attitude." She ran her hand through her sleek hair. He hadn't even noticed. "You know what? I need to talk to someone. I need to talk to a professional."

"What?"

"Yes. I can't . . . I can't do this anymore. I'm going to have a fucking breakdown. We need to stop speaking, or I *really* won't make it."

"Why did you fire our cleaning lady if you needed help?"

"It's not about the cleaning lady!"

"*She* helped you."

"That's not the kind of help I need! I need talking help. I need to be by myself help. I need a night class in Drew help. I need . . ."

"So talk to me."

"I'm talking to you now and you're not listening! You're going on about Ernestina like she's the answer to all my troubles."

"I didn't know you had troubles," said Jared in grim puzzlement. "I thought we were living an enchanted life."

"*Your* life is fucking enchanted," she spat. "That's how oblivious you are to everything that's going on."

"What are you talking about? I—"

"I had my hair done today! Did you notice?"

"You came in, in the middle of a boxing match with yourself!" yelled Jared. "I'm hardly going to be commenting on your hair!"

"Yes, because otherwise you're very observant, Mr. Reconnaissance man!"

Jared rubbed his face. "Is that what I need to be in my own life, in my own house? Unless you tell me, how do I know you're not happy?"

"I'm very happy. I'm extremely happy," Larissa said, with a cruel face, wet eyes, mascara running. "But I'd like to talk to someone about all my happiness, all right? I have so much happiness I can't deal with it. I feel I'm going to explode from the joy."

"All right, enough."

"Enough is right. Because, word of fair warning, if your wife ends up in the loony bin, you'll be rushing home every night, not just once a month, and then we'll see how you like it when you have to figure out how to get Emily to her cello lessons twice a week while Michelangelo has karate and Asher has cross country, and orthodontics, all at the same time. Let's see how many late dinners in the city you can have then, Mr. Chief Financial Officer."

"Larissa, calm down."

"Why is everybody telling me to calm down?"

"Who is everybody?"

"I will not calm down," she said. "*You* calm down. You say things and act in ways that are mean and upsetting, and then you get all high and mighty like *I'm* the unreasonable one."

"I'm not acting like anything." He opened his hands. "I'm sorry, okay? How do I act like this? I'm trying to understand."

Larissa got Jared to apologize to *her*! "Well, understand this. Once a month, your wife needs an evening alone without you and without the kids."

"God, why do you have to make such a big deal about it? Why didn't you talk to me last week when it came up?"

"Because I wanted you to do the right thing on your own! I wanted you to be considerate, say, okay, Lar. The way you did last summer in Lillypond when you let me have a day on my own. That's what I wanted. But if you like, I'll hire a full-time babysitter so she can cart the kids around while you work."

"What are you talking about? Stop it."

She was panting. "I'll get myself a full-time job in the city, and then I'll also be away from the house from seven till seven, and maybe then I won't hear any more bullshit from you about me spending two hours every two months to color my fucking hair."

"Larissa! What's gotten into you? Calm down."

"Oh, I'm calm, Jared. I'm calm like the Pacific."

"Larissa . . ."

"I have to put the baby to bed. Are we done?"

"You tell me," barked Jared.

"Oh, we're done." She stormed off upstairs like she was Emily.

4

"Shall We Go?"

Godot was opening for three nights on the following evening, and there had been stage setup all that Thursday morning and a final rehearsal of the last act due in the afternoon. By the time Larissa got to Kai's, it was after 12:30. He was fully dressed and sitting at the round table by the window.

"Hey."

"Hey."

He sat like a sphinx, straight up against the chair. His eyes followed her from the door to his table. She sat down across from him. He seemed inaccessible and unmoving.

"Kai . . ."

He raised his hand to stop her. He didn't say anything. He just sat with his back up and stared at her, mouth unsmiling, eyes unsmiling. Larissa desperately tried not to break down.

"Don't be mad at me, please," she whispered. "I beg you. You know how hard this is for me. I was trying to do something for us, and look what a botch I made of things. I didn't want to upset you."

He sat.

A tear ran down her face.

"It's the middle of February," Kai finally said.

"I know."

"Your play is opening tonight. Valentine's Day is this weekend."

"I'm not going to dinner with him," Larissa said. "I have the play. And then it's our wrap party."

"No romantic dinner with him, or with me. Soon it'll be March. A year since we started this little fandango, as you call it, this happy dance between us."

"Kai . . ."

"Larissa, I take it all, you know I do. I do because I have a life which I live while I wait for you. I read, I play my instruments, I work. On Sundays I ride up to Rahway and visit Gil. He's going to be paroled early, we hope, for good behavior. Then I'll have my buddy back. But in the meantime, on Friday nights I go out with his roomies, Harry and Mark, and we go to Newark with our guitars to jam at the local bars, and I pass the darkened Prudential building, and I think of you being with your family."

She couldn't sit as straight as he. Her back was curving. His eyes were so neutral and his voice so flat.

"Let me explain, so you don't misunderstand," Kai said. "It's not about yesterday. Yeah, that was pretty abominable, but it was just one evening, and like I said, I can take it. It's not about that." He paused to draw in his breath. His curly hair was loose and wet, his eyes somber, his face clean-shaven. He was going to work soon, and he looked almost ready to bolt out the door. "You know what it's about?"

She shook her head.

"It's about my life. And it's about yours."

"Please don't be upset with me," she repeated in a whisper. "I'll make it up to you, I promise. I don't know how, but I will."

"Yesterday *was* you trying to make it up to me," he said. "Trying to make up to me for the twenty-three hours a day you deny me. But you understand it couldn't have gone any other way?"

"No, it will, it'll be better."

He shook his head. "It'll never be better. This is the way it is. That was the best it could be."

"No, there's something I can do—"

He emitted a short skeptical laugh. "Maybe you can leave him. Come here and live with your Stanley."

She didn't say anything, the shame and degradation of that impossibility denying her the voice and the resources to answer even in the negative.

"You must've thought about it. I know I have. We don't talk about it because there's no point. We don't talk about it because we both know it's impossible!" The exclamation at the end was the only time today Kai had raised the pitch of his voice. Larissa didn't know how he did that, talked so calmly about calamities. She would have preferred he yelled, howled, got up, threw things. At least that would have been understandable. And yet his composure, his placid, equable nature was the thing she kept returning to—the thing that bonded her to him so utterly: that he, of all the chaos out there, didn't make her life hell for the hallowed trap they found themselves in. When she was with him, it was always sunshine. Which is why she kept coming back. But today she needed the Kai that didn't exist, the Kai of resentful words, of shouting, because this guise of pretend preternatural cool frightened her.

She shook her head. "Talking isn't pointless," she said.

"You and I both know," said Kai, "you can not, *cannot*, move in here with me, and have your children come visit you here, sit in this small space, at this table and look across the room to the bed where a young kid, a few years older than your son, just fucked their mother!" He paused, staring at her breathless. "You and I both know it can't be done. This is exile. You will lose your children. You will humiliate them, and they won't be able to look you in the face, the older ones especially. They'll choose not to see you. You'll be able to get only supervised visits, with a court-appointed stranger present. You'll be condemned. You know how I know? Because my own father had to leave his family rather than introduce us to the nineteen-year-old mango seller he got all sweet on. Or was it he couldn't introduce *her* to us? He turned his back on his kids either way. And we condemned him. Anyway, without me telling you, you know this. Which is why you've never brought it up."

Tears trickled down Larissa's cheeks. She kept wiping them with her cotton sleeve. Reaching over, he ripped off a paper towel and handed it to her. Ezra was right. An examined life was no picnic.

"We had it pretty good for a while, Larissa," Kai said. "But I think you and I reached the end of the line."

"Kai, please! No. Let's wait. Just a little while . . . let's . . . please, I'll work it out. Give me a chance."

"A chance to what?"

"To fix this."

"You can fix this?"

"I can."

"I don't see how."

"I will. You'll see. What happened yesterday won't happen again."

"Of course it will."

Mutely Larissa shook her head. She was shivering. Opening her hands to him, she whispered, her voice quivering, "Kai, please . . . have mercy on me."

Sighing, blinking, finally rising out of the chair, Kai did.

In bed they lay naked facing each other. Her arms were wrapped around him. His were resting on her but distantly, like Pacific atolls.

"Kai, you know how I feel about you," Larissa said. "You *know*. I don't have to tell you."

"You don't have to tell me," he agreed. "I know. But, Larissa, I'm at the end of my rope with being your leather-jacketed toy. I never asked myself how long I'd be able to take it. Last night, I had my answer. Not much more. I'm just about done."

His face was between her palms as she kissed him, tasting her own salty tears.

"Don't give up on me just yet," she whispered. "I'm going to go talk to a psychiatrist. He'll help me figure things out."

"Will he?"

"Absolutely."

His hands drifted down between her legs. His mouth drifted down to her breasts. He kissed her nipples while he caressed her.

"If this can't help you figure things out, I don't know what the good doctor is going to do for you. Perhaps he has moves I don't have."

She moaned. He opened her up. She opened her mouth to taste him.

Eleven minutes.

"The play should be called *Waiting for Larissa*," he said, pushing inside her.

Clutching him around the neck, she moaned, lifting her arms to grasp the headboard. "You don't have to wait for me, my whole heart, my lover," she said, crying from love, from sadness, from fear. "I'm right here."

Four red walls of roses later, thirst amplified not slaked, he whispered, quoting Vladimir: "*Shall we go, Larissa?*"

"*Yes, let's go.*"

They do not move.

5

The Mungo Wilderness

Godot, much to Leroy's irritating self-satisfaction, was an unqualified success both with the parents and the children, despite a cast of four and a set of one barren tree in stage fright.

Maggie put her hand on Larissa, who was sitting in the dark, waiting for the curtain to rise with the script on her nervous lap. She hoped no one would forget his lines. There were so many lines, and on that bare stage there was no hiding.

"You can come with me," Maggie said solicitously.

"Come with you where?"

"To the monastery."

"Monastery! Why on earth would I do *that*?" She was trapped between Jared and Maggie.

Maggie lowered her voice. "Jared told us you're having a hard time."

"I'm not having a hard time." Larissa couldn't even move away, because it meant moving closer to Jared! "I'm fine."

"Jared said you needed someone to talk to."

"Not like that, Mags. Not a priest or anything. Somebody, you know, professional."

In the darkened theater with other people chatting about movies and TV shows and ice cream flavors, this is the conversation Larissa was having!

"The nuns sing beautiful psalms, so beautiful they pierce your soul. You really should come." Maggie closed her eyes. *"O my God, I cry in the daytime . . . deliver my soul from the sword,"* she softly murmured.

How's it been working out, the deliverance? Larissa wanted to ask. Taking a breath, she said instead, "Has it helped you?"

"Yes."

"Really?"

"Of course. I found peace. You think it's easy to come to peace with the fact that your body is giving out?"

"I should think not. But singing isn't quite what I'm looking for. Believe it or not, I'm all good with songs." Do the nuns play acoustic strings? Do they have deep baritones? Do they sing of soul kitchens and soft parades?

Maggie still hadn't taken her sympathetic hand away from Larissa's forearm. What was the etiquette for yanking it away?

"You can always talk to *me*, Lar. You know that. I understand things. I finally figured it out!—why I'm suffering. Why we all suffer—"

"Excuse me for a sec." Larissa patted Maggie on the arm and quickly stood up. "I need to make sure they remember to enter from stage left so they walk across the entire stage. I'll be right back."

For a moment, as she scanned the darkness of the school auditorium, her breath stopped because she thought she saw Kai up high, in the rafters. She wanted to call out to him, up in the tower. You know what my soft morning laud is? O grant me one more day, one more hour when I can still travel the street in the cold to sit in warmth for a blink in the afternoon before everything—beauty, sadness, doom in that blue attic room—comes crashing like skulls tumbling down stone mountains.

All the performances were sold out, even this Thursday one, but she didn't see him, not even when the lights came on at the end. She must have imagined his eyes on her.

The small cast got a long standing ovation and flowers. Larissa and Jared had made up, had come to a truce. She apologized, he bought her roses and chocolates. "Are we really not going out to dinner for Valentine's Day?" It was like he couldn't believe the confluence of events that would make the closing night of *Godot* fall on Valentine's Day.

"How can we, Jared? The play is at seven, and at ten, we have the wrap party." She told him they would go to dinner on Sunday; the celebration would be a day late. But on Sunday, they took the kids to Watchung Mountain and went sledding. They were gone all day, and in the evening as they were coming back, it was inconceivable that they should go back home, drop off the kids, and then go out to eat by themselves. It was already so late. They found a perfectly nice hibachi steakhouse in Mountainside and had a lovely family dinner with their chatty and tired children.

On Monday after Valentine's Day, Kai had one hundred and forty-four red roses for Larissa at his place, twelve for each month he had known her. They were scattered around the room in twelve glass vases, on the nightstand, on the coffee table, on the counters, and two vases on the floor by her side of the bed. She now had a side of the bed, like she belonged here on Sunday morning. It was near the open window from where the distant oceans waved their salty winds into her gasping mouth.

They had a belated Valentine's Day celebration of their own, with rainbow sushi, chocolate cherry-chunk ice cream, excellent espresso, another bottle of bubbly. They had love, not dry silent kisses, not sleep; they had wild fires and shining naked unmasked storms. They tasted from flame-trees while cast out of Eden, but yet, oh but yet, why did it feel like bright and bitter Eden?

"Larissa," Kai began, his excited eyes burning, his breath shallow. "On Route 66 there's a town." He rose on his elbow to look down into her face. The roses in vases framed his brown-blond head in red.

Why did she go numb in the fingers? She tried not to close her eyes, not to turn away.

"In Arizona, near Flagstaff, in between the mountains and the canyon, away from the desert and the forests, there is a little town." He paused. "Not too far from the Canyon. Wouldn't it be great to open a tour company? We'd make so much money. We'd buy a little bus, maybe a 1936 Yellowstone bus, with a tarp roof and a big old wheel in the back."

"Buy it with what?"

"What do you think I've been doing with my commissions? Everything is in the bank. Anyway," he went on, "we'd charge twenty bucks for a roll around the Grand Canyon. We'd go out three times a day, in the early morning, after lunch, and at sunset. Wouldn't that be something?"

She didn't say if it would be something. She said, "What happened to touring Jersey?" She wanted to mention the Second Watchung Mountain, and how the snow glinted, all packed down by sleds and snowboards, and how Michelangelo beat his older brother in a race and thought it was the greatest day of his life.

Falling back on the bed, Kai flung his arms behind his head. "Nah. I want to ride my bike on the great prairies, in the distances between the seas." He paused. "With you on my back."

"Like a little monkey," she said quietly.

His hands caressed her hips. Rolling over, he kissed her arm, the side of her breast. "Do you want to know the name of the town?"

"Is that the important thing?" She glanced at him. "The name of the town?"

"It's not un-important. Names of towns define the life within. Summit. Mountainside. Paradise Falls. The one in Arizona happens to be called Pine Springs." Kai smiled, his infectious toothy smile lighting up his face like Christmas windows. "Doesn't that sound great?"

She didn't know. She couldn't say. There were plenty of pines in Jersey. Millions of them. Pine Barrens. There was the Great Swamp. There were springs in Jersey. No canyons, but there were mountains.

Love, sushi, coffee, cold Cristal, bare beautiful Kai. He was sheepish, wrenchingly endearing. "Larissa, hear me out, okay? I don't want you to shake your head, or talk, or say anything."

Not to worry, she wanted to say. I won't shake my head or talk or say anything. Her voice was in her heart and her heart was in her stomach and couldn't be heard from the black deep.

"The dude with the wife who ran into us on the street? Doug Grant? He was going on and on to me about his trip to the Australian outback." Kai dreamed "Apparently, he went on a five-hour tour in saddle country near a place called Jindabyne, southwest past Canberra, near nowhere. He went in a modified Jeep." Kai's fingers were caressing her leg, down and up from the shank to the flank. "So it got me thinking. We could have a Jeep, a safari jungle Land Cruiser for cheap, and take tourists out to the bush and narrate about the snakes and the land, and rocks, and some such."

"What?" she breathed out.

He put a finger to her lips, jumping up into a lotus position, his face shining with excitement. "You said you wouldn't say anything till you thought about it."

"Thought about what? Australia? Are you kidding?"

"I'm not."

"We know nothing about Australia."

"We'd learn. And I know a little. What do you think I've been doing while waiting for you?"

"Obviously going insane."

"Yes," he said. "Insane for you. We'd go on a vagabond adventure. Canberra or Alice Springs, or a place in the outback, a wilderness called Mungo. Doesn't that sound exotic, fantastic?" Kai squeezed her hands, brought his face down to them, kissed them, put his head into her lap. He was so close.

"Kai—"

His mouth was at her mouth, stopping her. "Ah, ah. You said you'd think about it, not speak about it. Come on, the Kai & Larissa Tour Company." He laughed with joy. "Doesn't that sound awesome?" He kissed her face, her hands, her lips. "Yes, my love," he whispered. "Is that the grandest plan or what? I've saved a lot of money. You won't have to worry about a thing. I've been salesman of the month for nearly a year. One more month, maybe two, and I'll get my own Jag. I'm that good. Then we could sell it back, get another sixty, seventy grand. And you must have a little money, but even if you don't, it doesn't matter. I'll take care of us, and when our business starts making money—"

"Kai . . ."

"Yes?" The whites of his teeth, the whites of his eyes were inches from her stunned face. "Close your eyes and imagine it. Tell me you can't. Tell me you can't see it vividly?"

"Kai," she said in a faltering, frightening voice that didn't come from the voice box, but from somewhere deeper, from the small provenance of all life. "You own my heart, but . . ."

"There is no but after that," Kai said. "*But* is not allowed after those words. You may speak only of love. I can't believe I'm worthy enough to be loved by you, Larissa. I didn't think I was worthy of much, of anything. But to have *you*, how much the gods must think of me. So please. Don't say *but*."

She said nothing. It was time to go. Michelangelo wasn't going to pick himself up from school.

"What about my children, Kai?" she whispered, barely audible even to herself. The curtains were open, and through the open sunny windows she could hear King Street traffic near the railroad. It was cold. She was burning.

Lowering his gaze, he swallowed and raised his shoulders in a faint question. "Pine Springs then?" he said. "In Oregon, I have a buddy, Roland, who told me the Louis and Clark Trail winds through the forests to the ocean. We could do a sight-seeing tour. That would be something. In Colorado, we could do skiing tours through the Rockies. I can't ski to save my life, but so what? What about the Badlands? The Montana rivers? We could teach the tourists how to flyfish."

"But fish don't fly."

"Ha!" He clapped his hands at her. "We don't know how to do anything. Isn't it grand? I once didn't know how to sell cars or lay paving. But we'd learn. My friend Don lives in Missoula. He said he would help. Or, in Northern California we could do a Redwood forest tour and live on the Pacific bluffs."

"You have a friend there, too?"

He kissed her. "Who do you think comes to Maui? Tourists. I help them out, get them the best sushi, the best mangos, fragrant flowers for the missus, and as a result I got friends all over the world."

"Not in Australia."

"Yes, in Australia. My buddy Bart lives near Canberra. He owes me a solid for hooking him up with a chord progression that melted his girl Bianca's heart. Now they're married." He rattled her a little, ruffled her hair. "Doesn't it sound incredible?"

She said nothing.

Time to get dressed. Despite the terror in her heart, or perhaps because of it, she wanted him again, and as she was pulling on her Theory black slacks, a vile thought flickered by: if I went with him, I would have him again. Any time I wanted.

They kissed, bounded downstairs. He hopped on his bike, put his helmet on. "Larissa," he called to her.

She turned around.

"What I want is for you to get on my bike, and for us to roar down Main Street together, and not be afraid. You'll think about what I've asked you, won't you?"

"And of nothing else."

Larissa couldn't even see Main Street as she drove home. She blundered through two red lights and a stop sign, nearly crashing into a van that had the right of way. The screaming horns barely registered.

Chapter Three

1

Heart Strings and Alice Springs

Larissa found a doctor in Madison. He did not come with a recommendation. Because Larissa couldn't *ask* for a recommendation. He came from the Yellow Pages. She chose him because she liked the tag after his name. "Dr. Kavanagh: Specialising in depression and matrimonial difficulties." As if the two went hand in hand. Like lovers.

She turned out to be a tiny, superbly dressed, exquisitely wrinkled woman in her early sixties, clearly a smoker, whose eyes were too sharp for Larissa's liking. Larissa would've preferred her clinical help to be dull and opaque.

She didn't know how to feel about the issue of the doctor's sex. Would a woman be more or less sympathetic? She sat down on the leather couch, eyeing the doctor unsympathetically. Kavanagh sat in the task chair, twisted into a yoga pretzel, legs tucked under her. And is that what Larissa was hoping for? Sympathy?

She didn't know what she was hoping for. She was in a fog of blind confusion and she wanted a nanosecond of clarity—so she could see either what was around her or what was in front of her. She couldn't see anything besides him.

They spent twenty-five minutes on the vapid minutia of her life.

"Where were you raised?" the doctor asked.

"Here. Well, there. Piermont, on the Hudson, just under the Tappan Zee Bridge."

"I know where Piermont is, I used to have a practice in Nyack. Where are your parents?"

"Divorced. Dad moved away. He's dead now."

"When did they get divorced?"

"I was twenty."

"And did you say you were the youngest of four?"

"Yes."

"So, when they split up, your parents must have been . . . ?"

"In their late fifties, yes. Too old to get a divorce, I know."

"Hmm. You're never really too old for hate. Or love. Where did you go to school?"

"NYU. Theater."

You're married? How long? How many children? How old? What does your husband do? Where do you live now? Are you religious?

"Not really," Larissa said. "I'm ambidextrous. My parents taught us to study things carefully, have an open mind, examine everything, then make our decisions. They were highly educated and, I believe, agnostic. That's how they raised us."

"You *believe* they were agnostic?"

"They had a curiosity about metaphysical things, but were too skeptical and intellectual to lean one way or another. They believed in science, in culture."

"They *believed* in science?" The doctor paused, squinting. "What about now?"

"What, me or them?"

"You, Larissa."

Larissa thought about it. "It's just not part of my life." She remembered Ezra. "I have heated discussions with my friends about ethics and meaning and whatnot. But just devil's advocacy, you know?"

Dr. Kavanagh studied her, as if she didn't know. She remained inscrutably blank. "Tell me why you're here."

Finally, twenty-five minutes in, the question Larissa came to have answered, and now that she was asked, she had nothing to say. Her mouth went dense and dry. She didn't know how to begin. She grew uncomfortable, started to fidget, to chew her nails, the skin around her fingers.

"You seem agitated."

"I'm not agitated."

"No?"

"No. What I am is . . ." She trailed off. What was she? Larissa didn't know what to say. There was no beating around the bush. What could she say? Start at the beginning? It was too tawdry. What about now, it wasn't tawdry now? It was all decent?

Decent: moral, good, kind.

Tawdry: cheap, gaudy finery.

Yes, that's what it was. Glad rags dressed as ceremonial dress.

"I'm involved with a man who is not my husband," blurted Larissa. It was an emancipation to speak. She started to cry. Kavanagh was quiet. Nothing on her moved except a hand extending a box of tissues.

"How long?"

Not long enough. Unacceptably too long. "Months."

"Two months? Six?"

"A year."

Kavanagh whistled. "That's a long time for an affair."

"I didn't say it was an affair. I said . . ."

"Yes, yes, I know. Has the husband found out? Is that why you're here?"

"No. And no."

"No?" Kavanagh seemed surprised. Was she alluding to Jared's blindness? "How do you feel about it?"

Larissa blew her nose. "Feel about what?"

"Your relationship with this man. Your marriage. Yourself. How do you feel about what you've just told me?"

"Clearly I'm confused."

Kavanagh pursed her lips. "I don't know if that's clear."

"I'm here, aren't I?"

"And is confused what you feel?"

Larissa had no answer for that one.

"Do you want your husband to find out?"

"No," Larissa said quietly, almost whispering. "I don't know. I don't want to think about it."

"Well, what *do* you want to think about?"

"What to do, I guess."

"You want to *think* about what to do?" Kavanagh said dryly. "What to do about what?"

"I have no one to talk to."

"Yes, you said this." Kavanagh's voice softened slightly. "Do you want to get out of it?"

"Get out of what?"

Kavanagh was watchfully silent.

"It hasn't been easy, I see by your face," the doctor said from a throat that had had forty years of nicotine. She sounded like Joe Cocker. "Leading a double life is not easy. A year is a long time to live with deception. You feel like you might have to make a choice soon. Your family, your husband, or your lover."

"I suppose." Larissa noticed her hands were clenched on her lap, but she was powerless to unclench them.

"Is this why you're here? To figure out what to do and then do it?"

"*Is* it why I'm here?"

"Larissa, are you answering my questions with questions?" Kavanagh might have looked amused if she didn't look annoyed first.

"I'm here because I wanted to talk to someone. That's the honest truth. My husband and I have mutual friends. I don't want to humiliate him."

"Yes, words can be very humiliating," said Kavanagh, and Larissa couldn't help feeling that the doctor was mocking her. She remembered her own similar reaction to Bo's worry about Jonny. For some reason, Larissa liked that about Kavanagh, liked being judged. It got her blood up.

"A friend of mine recently had a situation," she said, "and we all knew, and now we're all looking at her boyfriend like he is a chump for staying with her."

"Is that what you would think of your husband? That he would be a chump for staying with you?"

"I don't know . . . I was just talking about my girlfriend. That it's better to keep that stuff hidden, because your friends never look at you the same way."

"Is that what's important to you?" Kavanagh asked. "Not if your husband will look at you the same way, but if your friends will?" and before Larissa had a second to get indignant, continued, "Let me ask you another question. If this could work out just the way you want, what would that be?"

Larissa opened her hands. "I don't know."

Kavanagh looked skeptical.

"I have no time to imagine the future," said Larissa. "I'm spending every minute just managing the seconds of today." That'll be one hundred and forty dollars for the lies today, thank you.

"But I have to know what you want, so we both have something to work toward."

"Okay, you want to know what I want to work toward? I want it to work out without everyone involved getting trounced."

"Who do you mean by everyone?"

"I mean . . . *everyone* involved."

"You?"

"Well, yes. Me, too, I guess."

"Your lover?"

"Yes."

"Your husband?"

"Yes."

"Your children?"

"Yes."

"Who the least? Who do you want to hurt the least?"

Larissa didn't want to answer the doctor's question. She didn't. Because the small answer was: herself. She didn't want herself to get trounced most of all. Because she had to remain with herself till the bitter end, and she didn't want to live with her failed and beaten self.

Kavanagh wrote something down in her little notebook. "Do you see it continuing?"

"See what continuing?"

"The extra-marital relationship, of course."

"As opposed to what?"

"As opposed to ending it and rejoining your family life."

What a terrible idea it was to come here!

"I cannot imagine it *not* continuing," Larissa said into her fists.

"When you first started, what did you think?"

"I didn't."

"You gave no thought to the future?"

"Not much," Larissa admitted. "I guess at first I thought it was going to be a short burst. Brief, extinguished. I didn't imagine . . ."

"Tell me how often you see him."

Larissa told her.

"Wow. It seems both insufficient and incredibly excessive. What does your lover want?"

"I don't know. I haven't asked."

"Is he married?"

Larissa couldn't tell even her psychologist! "No."

"Does he have children?"

"No." Kai's sorrow wasn't Larissa's to tell.

"You know," said Kavanagh, "it's not easy to maintain a relationship with a married woman with three children."

If the doctor only knew.

"How does he feel about your children?"

"He's never met them."

"He does know you have children?"

"Of course." Why did Larissa feel constantly indignant with this woman?

"And you've never talked about the future?"

Larissa desperately didn't want to say. So she didn't.

Kavanagh bent her head appreciatively. "And all this time your husband hasn't found out? He must be a very trusting man. This isn't easy to hide."

"I was a theater major in college."

"Ah. That helps. One more question before we go. Do you want to save your marriage? Is this why you're here?"

Larissa paused, like she forgot the words.

"Hmm," said Kavanagh. "Okay, then. See you next week."

∾⚬∽

On the way home, on impulse, disbelieving herself, out of bounds, knowing it and helpless, Larissa, without calling or thinking any further about it, drove to Albright Circle, parked the car, walked up the steps and knocked on Kai's door. She hadn't planned it; she just pulled into the driveway, walked—thunderously, she thought—up the wooden staircase and knocked. She heard the guitar and the sound of his singing voice. Outside was dark and cold. The roads were icy.

"Larissa!" He pulled her inside. "What are you doing here?"

The TV was on but without sound, song books, the guitars and ukuleles on his bed, cartons of half-eaten Chinese food, opened cans of Coke and Corona. Kai, wearing loose navy sweats and a gray tank, barefoot and scruffy, was thrilled to see her. She breathed a palpable sigh of relief.

"Oh, I was headed back home from my new shrink," she said. "Thought I'd say hi. Sorry I didn't call. My phone was out of power." Nice, Larissa. Lying to Kai now, too. *Nice!*

He pulled her onto the bed, swept the books off, moved the guitars to the side, laid her down, jumped on top of her, like a kid. "How long can you stay?"

Her heart aching, the talons of fear inside her still scraping away, she said, as he grinned, pinning her arms, kissing her neck, kissing her lips, "Fifteen minutes."

"That's fourteen more than I need."

Unpinning herself, wrapping her arms and her legs around him, she realized belatedly she would smell like him when she returned home. And she couldn't take a shower, come home after seeing Kavanagh being damp or smelling of soap. "What kind of shrink *is* this, Larissa?" Jared would rightly ask. But she also couldn't come home having red prickles of her lover's fresh stubble over her throat. Yet his lips were on her, and his face was rubbing against her neck, her clavicles, her chest. His wiry hair was in her hands, and he was kissing her and murmuring and smiling, something about how happy he was to see her at night, what a gift it was.

She stayed a while. It wasn't an embrace in the public square but it was kisses of youth, silver guitar strings, dirges with drum beats. She came upon him suddenly, and he was himself, at night as during the day, one hour then or now: just happy to be with her like he was a sailor and she was an angel.

February had twenty-nine days that year. One extra day.

⌒⌒⌒

To Kai's question Larissa had no answer. She was hoping it would vanish in the ether like dandelion fuzz, and it did, and, like a dandelion, planted root where it parachuted down, sprouting like weeds in the grass, forcing its way through the pavement by the side of the open road.

What will it be, Larissa? Yes or no. You've got a house you need to clean every day, and vacuuming hasn't been done since Tuesday week. You're down to your last roll of paper towels, and Michelangelo long ago ran out of white paint because you haven't bought him any. You never did go out for Valentine's Day dinner with Jared, but otherwise, every night you're making your family dinner, baking store-bought cupcakes, frozen pizzas, potatoes in a box, corn in a can. Yes or no.

Megan is abominably wrong for *Saint Joan*, but the die has been cast, and you've got to make the best of her. She cannot be strong, her voice is whiny, and every day you tell her, deeper Megan, you are Joan of Arc, the original and presumptuous! Joan is a warrior, built not for romance but for something greater. To make her a flirt would be like making Caesar a flirt; it's unseemly. And Megan, wilting by the backstage, would say, what does Caesar have to do with the Maid of Orléans? They were both warriors, Megan! Assert yourself, don't stand timidly at the curtains, remember Joan is the eighteen-year-old girl that led France to freedom. She doesn't whine, Megan. She roars.

Larissa could've been talking to the curtains. Megan didn't know how to roar. Megan thought the manatee, a sweet and gentle creature, was unfairly maligned with an insulting moniker: the sea cow.

This is tragedy, not melodrama, Megan! Do you know the difference? And the girl would shake her shy head.

Tragedy: where everything happens because of a flaw or an excess or a void in the main character. The hero directs the action of his own play—heroic struggle, followed by crushing downfall.

Melodrama: literally, drama punctuated by melody, orchestral music, little songs, sensationalized; external events, not tragic flaws, direct the traffic of your life. Do you see the difference?

And Megan would shake her woeful histrionic melodramatic head and chirp, *"One thousand like me can stop them! The shortest way to save your own skin is to run away!"*

Yes or no, Larissa.

ᘎᕠᕤ

The doctor was pensive. "Tell me, is being a wife and a mother important to you?"

"Of course." Larissa once thought it was her whole life. But independent of what she thought about it, it was what it was. Her whole life. Tears came to her throat again.

"What do you think your husband's reaction would be," Kavanagh asked, "if he were to find out?"

"I don't know." I don't want to think about it.

"You've never discussed this issue, even hypothetically?"

"We've discussed it." In Scruples with *other* couples. "But never with me as the guilty party."

"Why?"

"Because I'm not that person. I was happy in my marriage. Happy to be married. When I was a girl in a pink room, my life now—rather, a little before now—is what I dreamed of. This thing—it's not me."

"Oh, but clearly it is." Kavanagh studied Larissa, wearing a pencil skirt, high-heeled pumps, a cropped cream sweater. "You're an attractive woman," she said at last. "Men, I'm sure, must consider you sexy."

"My husband is a handsome man. We're evenly matched." Larissa gave off a whiff of harried irritation. "And . . . he is a good man."

"Okay, but not so good that you want to save your marriage."

"How can you save what can't be saved?" asked Larissa.

"*Nothing* is beyond saving."

Funny, that's what Maggie kept telling her. Maggie, with her swollen ankles and muscle cramps.

"Doctor, but what if you didn't want to be saved? Could you be saved then? Against your will sort of thing? Like divine intervention?" Like Che—once, not now.

Kavanagh sat in judgment of her from her pretzel-like presiding. "Is this supposed to be a joke?" She looked down into her lap—at her notes? "Okay let's get down to the brass tacks: if your husband gave you an ultimatum, said it was either him or your lover, what would your answer be?"

Larissa exhaled. Her guilty eyes drifted to the carpet, and when she looked up, Kavanagh was staring at her, scrunching up her small wrinkled hands with elegant fingers the way she scrunched up her small elegant brow.

"Honestly, I don't see any confusion in you, Larissa," Kavanagh said. "I see crystalline clarity. Tell your husband you don't want to be married anymore, move out, let him file for divorce, work out custody, and move in with your lover."

Larissa turned her head to the window. She couldn't believe it was windy March already. Time was marching on. The steady beat of it, drum drum, one more day at home, one more unfinished project, one more forgotten task. One more minute late to everywhere. One more phone thrown away, bought again, thrown away, bought again . . .

"Our time is up," said Larissa. If she hurried, she could spend an hour with Kai. She would've liked to fire Kavanagh, but because of the good doctor, she now saw Kai in the evenings.

Another week of sushi, sex, love, *Saint Joan*, deep in frustration and rehearsals, another financial quarter ending, late nights for Jared, sculpting for Michelangelo, his white dry clay like hardened cement all over the wood floor of her house, and Kai's question and Kavanagh's question hanging in the air like lilac helium balloons, drifting, floating, colorful neon numbness.

Soul, soul, be gone from me.

On the way back from Kavanagh every Tuesday, she made a handy right left right, ran up the wooden steps two at a time, and spent one glorious hour at *night* in his company. They made love, had hot snacks, watched snippets of sitcoms, innings of ballgames, talked about the aesthetics of retaining walls in masonry landscaping, she listened to the sound of his deep singing voice one week, the strums of his guitar the next, and then . . . .

~⌘~

"There has to be an end to this, Larissa."

"No."

"One way or another, something has to change."

"Why?"

"What do you mean, why? What do you see happening?"

Who said this to her? Could've been her doctor. Could've been him. She hoped it wasn't him.

"Even if your husband doesn't find out, eventually your

lover might get tired of sharing you with another man, no?" said Kavanagh. "Men can be funny about that."

So it was the doctor. Larissa felt a rising prickle of irritation.

"Have you asked yourself why your lover hasn't?" Kavanagh said calmly. "A man who loves a woman usually prefers not to have his woman share another man's bed. Why hasn't he?"

"I don't know why. He is calm. He doesn't poison me with petty jealousy. He knows how hard everything would be if he did."

"Or perhaps," said Kavanagh, "this is convenient for him too. Juggle you, and other things?"

"No. It's not like that."

"That calmness of his must come at a price. What is it? Are you just one hour in twenty-four for him also, Larissa?"

Flattened, Larissa drove home, as if she had been rolled over by a sand mixer. What was wrong with Kavanagh? This is what talking got you. No solutions, but instead a knifelike burrow inside her chest. She couldn't take a breath imagining Kai touching another woman. How did he live imagining her with Jared? Don't think about it, Larissa! Don't think about it . . .

$\sim\!\sim\!\sim$

"What are your plans?" asked Kavanagh.

A plan by definition involved the future. "Haven't got one."

"There's something you're not telling me. I feel it. I've seen this thing too many times before. What's the missing piece? Why won't you leave your husband?"

Larissa said nothing.

"Tell me more about your lover. What is it about him that drew you? Is he very different from Jared?"

Larissa described Kai.

"Car salesman? Stonemason? Drives a motorcycle? How old is he?"

Larissa said nothing.

Kavanagh opened her eyes, and pulled the legs out from under herself, leaning forward in the chair. "He is *young*?" she exclaimed, startled.

"Not very young," Larissa said, bristling. "He's a little younger than me."

"How much younger?"

"A few years."

"How many?"

"I don't know, Doctor. Maybe ten. Or so."

"Ten, *or so*? Larissa, to help you I need to know the truth."

"He's twenty-one, all right?"

Falling back in the chair, Kavanagh whistled softly. For a few minutes she said nothing. Then she spoke. "So where do you meet someone like that, a woman like you, a housewife, a mother?"

"Stop&Shop," Larissa replied.

"Ah, well," said Kavanagh. "That explains it. I don't usually shop there, which is probably why I've never run into someone like that. I go to Shoprite. It's cheaper."

"He goes to Stop&Shop for sushi."

"That may be another one of my problems," Kavanagh said. "I don't like sushi."

"Yes," said Larissa. "I didn't either."

"What does he want with you? He is a boy barely out of his teens and you're a married woman with children. What are *his* plans for the two of you?"

Larissa couldn't tell Kavanagh about the wheels of the Ducati landing on the pavement in Pine Spring, in Willowbend, in Invercargill. Lewis and Clark and the Redwoods, and the whole damn volcanic mist over the ocean, the beaches and the sailboats, and the Mungo outback dreams before her sunset eyes.

"You really should've told me about his age, Larissa." Kavanagh shook her head in disapproval. "I understand your predicament better now. And it *is* a predicament. All this time I've been saying to you, why don't you just do what other people do. Move out. Retain custody of the kids. How fraudulent of you to let me continue giving you advice based on your giant omissions."

"Is your advice different now?" How can there be visitation, right? How can a mother be a visitor to her own children, be a guest in their holiness? If Larissa clenched her fingers any tighter they would fracture.

But afterward, an hour with Kai. O pine smoke bliss.

Except . . . he also can't resist asking her things she can't answer.

He is looking at her puzzled and questioning. She wishes they all would stop asking her things. She's doing her best, can't they see that?

Once I was Larissa. Then I was Jared's wife. And then I was Emily and Asher and Michelangelo's mother. And then I was Kai's lover. But long after I will stop being someone's wife, or someone's lover, I will continue to be a mother. I cannot resolve the unresolvable. The paralytic with a broken neck cannot walk, no matter how much he wants to, no matter how often or how passionately he talks about it. I am a mother. I cannot walk.

But then another small voice clears its throat and croaks. Yes. But before you were a mother, you were Larissa. What will you be if you stop being a mother?

Every Tuesday at seven she drove to see Kavanagh to help her figure out the primordial mire of her life, and afterward Kai was waiting for her. That's how she made it all better. By finally figuring out how to see her Maui lover at night! And maybe soon there could be a jazzercise night, and maybe she could take a painting class at Drew, or sign up for pottery and French. *Oui, oui, madame. La passion est la maîtresse due.* With any luck, she wouldn't have to be home at all.

The Ides of March passed.

～⁕～

"I love him," she said to Kavanagh.

"You don't think you're bandying that word about too lightly?"

"I don't bandy."

"You love your children, don't you? You love your husband? Your parents? You yourself said you're living a dream life. Perhaps what you really mean is infatuated. Which is not permanent, you know. But the decisions you make based upon this infatuation *are* permanent."

That was almost advice! And the doctor looked spent after giving it.

"Everything you say is entirely correct, Dr. Kavanagh," said Larissa, trying hard not to fidget. "Except I don't think you understand. Am I having a hard time explaining it? It's not infatuation. It may not have stood the test of time like my eighteen-year-old marriage, but it doesn't make it any less real. I was one kind of person, one kind of woman before I met him, and I was plodding along, and I thought I was doing pretty good, but then what happened, you see, is that everything inside me got reordered."

"Somehow, I don't believe that's true," Kavanagh said quietly.

"I don't mean awakened," Larissa hastily went on. "I mean, broken down and remade. The outside may be the same woman, but the inside is not. I can no more deny what I feel for him than I can deny my own name. Now we may argue that it's wrong, we may argue that I need to feel other things too, like guilt, obligation, responsibility, we may argue that I need to put my feelings aside, which is a separate discussion, but let's not talk about how what I'm feeling isn't real. It's more real than anything else I know. If it isn't real, then nothing is real. Nothing."

"It's a bright flame," Kavanagh said. "It burns out."

"But after it burns out, isn't true love what's left?"

"What if nothing is left?" The doctor stared hard at Larissa. "You say you once loved your husband. Where did *that* go?"

Heavily, Larissa got up off the couch. She wanted to crawl away. "You really *don't* understand. Wow. I keep saying it over and over. It's like I'm talking to a wall. I can't end it with him. I can't. In the scale of my life, he outweighs everything else."

"*Everything* else?"

"Doctor, what are you talking about?" Larissa exclaimed. "There are sixteen schools of psychotherapeutic thought, but only one second law of thermodynamics. Take a good look at *me*, not into a book. I'm spinning into chaos right in front of your eyes. I'm paying you—my husband is paying you—a hundred and forty dollars an hour to notice. Don't you notice?"

Kavanagh was cold and calm. "Your lover or your children, Larissa."

She slammed the office door so hard on her way out, the glass jar on the glass coffee table rattled and fell over.

∽◡◠

Dear Larissa,

Why haven't you written to me? Why do you only send me money with a superficial note full of platitudes?

You cannot believe what's happening to me. I've wanted to be a mother for so long. At forty, I'm finally having the baby I've been praying for my whole life, with a man I love so much. I can't believe what's happening.

Lorenzo went out to protest with that cursed Peace Brigade, and he was given weapons to carry with him for the demonstration: three knives and a smoke bomb. The protest got out of hand, a fight between the mob and the police ensued, and Lorenzo got carried away and threw the bomb. He was told by Agas Ilocano, the council leader of the Brigade and his close friend for seven years, that it was a smoke bomb, just a little tear gas to let the cops taste some of their own medicine, but he was duped. It was a nail bomb. And it exploded into a hive of cops. It blinded two of them, and critically injured several more, including one who got a nail stuck in his temple. He was taken to the hospital, and died three days later.

Larissa! My Lorenzo has been charged with a cop's murder! Nineteen people saw him throw the bomb. He told his public defender that he absolutely didn't know it was a nail bomb, or he never would've thrown it. So the prosecutor asked Lorenzo to name names of the leaders of the Brigade, and Lorenzo refused.

Bail has been set for two and half million pesos! It might as well be two hundred and eleventy bazillion pesos. We don't have a hundred pesos for a bus to the free clinic. I, with my big belly, have been visiting the people Lorenzo worked with, trying to elicit sympathy, but no one is willing to risk even ten pesos on him because they all say he is a flight risk. They take one look at my belly and say he is a flight risk!

They're right. He is. If he got out, he wouldn't stay a second in Manila to await trial. He says the Brigade leaders tricked him, deceived him and abandoned him. They knew he never would've thrown a nail bomb. And so far they're in hiding, and none of them has come forward to say Lorenzo didn't know it was a real bomb. No one. But he's still not willing to rat them out, because he says he wouldn't survive five minutes on the street if he did. He thinks even as they're quiet, they're secretly raising money for his bail. He is so deluded! But I keep saying, Lorenzo, if you don't tell the truth, you're going to go down for murdering a cop!

I get money from Father Emilio to take the bus to come and see Lorenzo in the city jail. He says I'm the only person in the world who loves him. He says he is an orphan now and I'm all he's got.

Thank you for the money you sent me last month. You know I've stopped even pretending I don't need it. I live on that money you send me. I love you.

Remember I wrote to you about wars and rumors of wars? How it was just the beginnings of sorrows? All I keep praying for right now is, dear God, please please let this not be the beginnings of my sorrows. Do you know what I mean, Larissa?

It's starting to feel like I'm running flat out of options. Do you know how that can be sometimes? When you've just flat run out?

◦◦◦◦

"Larissa! I got my free Jag. It's April already. Have you thought anymore about Pine Spring?" Kai asked. It was a Friday.

"Of course I have."

"Well, you haven't said anything. Hard for me to know."

Fridays were difficult. A weekend without him was about to descend on her. Friday afternoons were heavy, this one made particularly wearing by the weight of his question and the promise of his offer, like an anchor into quicksand. Is he for real? she wondered. And how will I know? How can I know? Is this a pursuit thing? Is it a pride thing? Is it malice? Is it true?

What if Kavanagh is right and I'm blind to the truth; can that be? Of course it *can* be; but *is* it? Kavanagh certainly thinks so. But she's not in bed with him. Larissa is in his bed, and he is naked, so lean and young and beautiful. He's almost ready to go again, they have ninety minutes today, he makes sure of that, and he gives himself to her prolonged and twice, so that the aching until she sees him again is doubled, not halved. And today he's asking her questions to which he wants and expects an answer.

"What do you want me to say, Kai?" Why is it that the gift of her answers is divided not multiplied?

"Yes would be nice." Slowly he gathered her nipple into his fingers and pulled on her gently, as if buzzing for an answer. His hand remained cupped around her breast.

"Kai, you know it's not as easy as me saying yes. You know I want to say yes. But you also know I can't. I have to think long and hard about what to do. I'm trying to figure a lot of things out. A *lot* of things."

"What have you been doing all this time with me?"

"Drowning moans and flames."

He gathered the whole of her into his arms, lay flush with her on the bed, inhaling the smell of her hair. "Larissa," he whispered. "What we've been having is not enough for us. Not for you. Not for me. It's not *enough*. We need more. Can you just imagine us, Larissa?"

When she did allow herself a blink's worth of reversed imagery behind the eyes, the picture of the future was not like a sweet and sunny summer morning. It was more like photographic negatives of carnivals. Black was white, and white was black.

"You want more choices?"

She would. Choices not offered here.

"Alice Springs, Pine Spring, Missoula, Monte Carlo. It doesn't matter. Without knowing the way, we'll figure it out. We'll go where no one knows us. We'll go to lunch together, in a public place, not with paper bags in bed. We'll have our own little place where we'll go to sleep at night, naked in *our* bed, and we'll wake up in the morning, naked in our bed. Together. We will make eggs and coffee. And we'll work together. We'll travel everywhere. We'll build a new life, far away from bad things, from bad memories, mine and yours. We'll be unencumbered, like gypsies. We'll be free."

She wanted to say she had no bad memories, but she sure was making them as he spoke. What are you talking about? she wanted to say. Don't you know I'll never be unencumbered, never be free. Oh God! How easy it was to imagine the graffiti world he spray-painted with his words. "It will never be simple like that for me, Kai," she said in a gutted voice. "Going with you—you know what that means."

He bowed his head, fell back on the pillow. "I know. But children are resilient, Larissa. They adapt. They adjust. I know this for a fact. I adapted. My sisters too. Soon your children will leave home. The younger ones have short memories. They forget."

"I won't forget," mouthed Larissa, stifling a groan.

"I'm sorry. Only you can know whether it's possible or impossible."

Even talking it wasn't possible.

"No kidding," said Kai, and she realized she'd spoken out loud. She must be more careful. "Kai . . . we could try . . . I could tell Jared—"

"Your husband," he cut in abruptly, "will not let you go."

"Why do you say this?"

Kai was quiet. "Something tells me he will not be Jonny."

"*Why* do you say this?"

"Because," said Kai. "I have you in my bed. I know what he must feel when he has you in his."

She ran her hand across Kai's chest, down to his navel, she caressed him with tender fingertips, she ached for him again, and hurt from the navel all the way to her eyeballs. Her skull was cracking with sadness. "You're wrong about Jared, Kai. He doesn't feel about me like that," she said.

"You don't know or understand men," said Kai. "Trust me about Jared. But if you think you're right, then go ahead and tell him about us. He's a good manager and has sharp business acumen; he is mild-mannered and moderate. Why don't you ease him into it, by explaining about his dry bed, and my overflowing heart, and the glare of the supermarket, and how love just *is*, how it's not caught or found, it just is and becomes you, how it swallows you whole. Explain that to him, sitting down in your dining room over a cup of tea. Tell him you're going to leave him, leave your children, and go away to live with me. But please," he added, "say goodbye to me first. Because I'll never see you again."

❧

Dear Larissa,

Write to me! Tell me what you think of my unholy mess. Do you know what crazy Lorenzo has been saying during my visits? When the Peace Brigade makes bail for him, he says he and I are going to run into the mountains and stay with the Tasaday until everything blows over. The Tasaday! They're natives who live in the rainforests of Mindanao. That's six south islands away! The eye of all MILF trouble, and he wants us to escape there. We'd have to get there by outrigger canoe, by small merchant boats, by the kindness of strangers.

But Lorenzo says we'll be safe with the Tasaday for a while. He says they live without money, radios, watches, modern medicine. They live in the woods and eat frogs. Also weeds and grubs. Sometimes they come down into the lowlands and fish. They make baskets out of bamboo and give them away. They spin and loom their own clothes. They live in mud huts, which they build themselves. Because they're on high ground, they don't get much flooding, except during the monsoon season, during which they sleep in hammocks and then rebuild the huts from scratch. A completely natural existence free from all strife of modern life.

No protests, no demonstrations, no Moro warriors, no murder, no 400,000 displaced-by-violence people. But I tell him, Lorenzo, what you're proposing is that we are going to be displaced by violence. We are going to live in exile. He says we won't need any money. This is what he dreams of, sitting in jail. Going to live like the Tasaday!

I said to him, Lorenzo, what about our baby? He looked like he was surprised I brought it up. He looked almost like he was going to say, "What baby?"

"I'm about to have a baby, Lorenzo," I said.

"What, the Tasaday don't have children?"

"I don't know. Do they? I'm eight months pregnant. I can't fight my way through the jungle in my condition."

And do you know what he said to me? "Che," he said, "you can stay here. But I can't. I have to go. Don't you understand? I'm going to be put to death for murder. The president has not abolished the death penalty yet. So you pick. Either Mindanao, or death, or at best prison for the rest of my life."

I said to him, what bail? We don't have any money. I know he keeps hoping the Peace Brigade will come up with two and a half million pesos, but I find myself hoping we won't get it, and he won't get out. Is that terrible? It's excruciating.

"Don't you love me?" he says to me.

Would that it were that simple! Would that love were the answer to everything. I once thought it was. "Of course, I love you, Lorenzo," I say, praying he won't make bail. Why am I a bad person, Larissa? I've already been the girlfriend, the lover. I just want to be a mother.

2

Mothers

Larissa kept looking at her hands. She and Emily painted their own nails nowadays with Michelangelo's abstract art help, but all three of them weren't very good with the cuticles. She must go back to Grace's soon and get a proper manicure. In the meantime she and Kavanagh were having another unhelpful conversation about family. Why ask unanswerable questions, trying to get to the bottom of a bottomless morass, when all Larissa wanted was to be flying, up up up, not down down down like planes from skies? Talking about Jared, her home, her family was *so* depressing. Why do it?

"I don't want to talk about them," she said. "Can't we talk about something else?"

"Sure," said Kavanagh. "Let's talk about your mother."

Larissa groaned.

"You don't want to talk about her either?" The doctor sighed. "Would you like to talk about movies? I just saw *The Prince of Tides*," she said. "It was good."

"My mother is an attractive woman," Larissa said. "Okay? Pleasant. Nice."

"Do you see her?"

"Of course. She is the children's grandmother."

"I didn't ask if your children see her."

"When they see her, I see her."

"What about your father?"

"He's dead. So I don't see him as often as I'd like. Before that he was in Florida." They were divorced the year Kai was born. Larissa went pale, had to gather herself for a few moments by remaining silent and licking her dry lips at the sour-bitter taste in her mouth.

"Amicable?"

"Not particularly." Wasn't that the understatement of the day.

"When you were growing up, what kind of a relationship did you have with your mother?"

Larissa paused. "Why do we need to talk about this? I'm an adult. I don't live with my parents. What's happening to me now has nothing to do with my mother or father."

"Larissa. What's happening now is you are having an imbalance in your feelings for your actual life on one end and your lover on the other."

"He is also my life."

"Yes. But—"

"My relationship with my mother was strained when I was growing up," Larissa cut in. "My brothers were grown and out of the house. My parents had me late in life. I was their only daughter. My dad adored me."

"And you?"

"I adored him back."

"What about now?"

"Now he is dead."

"What about before he died?"

"I don't want to talk about it," said Larissa.

"How long were your parents married?"

"Thirty-three years."

"That's a long time." Kavanagh studied Larissa, who absolutely *hated* to be studied. "Did he leave your mother for another woman?"

Deeply reluctantly Larissa answered. "Guess so."

Kavanagh looked at her with understanding. "And you," she said, "who always sided with your dad against your mother, as an adult was faced with the fact that your father did an unforgivable thing. Suddenly your mother needed your sympathy. How did that go?"

"Distantly. I was in college. I had my own life."

Kavanagh was quiet. Larissa was quiet.

"Is your relationship with your mother strained now?"

"No, it's polite. Cordial."

"She's polite?"

"And I'm cordial."

"And underneath?"

"Don't think much about it. Don't need to."

"Would you describe your mother and you as close?"

Larissa chewed her lip.

"Warm? Comfortable with each other?"

Larissa didn't answer.

Kavanagh looked into her lap. "What about your own daughter?"

"What about her?"

"How is your relationship with her?"

"Very good. She is my *daughter*." For some reason, like a steel trap door coming down, Larissa didn't want to talk about Emily even more, if that were possible, than she didn't want to talk about her own mother. Wow.

"Are you and Emily close?"

"Doctor . . ."

"I can see this is making you *extremely* uncomfortable; why?"

"Because it's *so* unnecessary!"

"It's making you uncomfortable because it's unnecessary?"

"Not that."

"What then? Talking about your children?"

"We're not talking about my children, are we?" Larissa flared up.

"By all means, let's talk about them."

"No! Look," she said, trying to sound calm. She was trying to emulate Kai. "Emily is fifteen. That's not an easy age. She's a good girl, a devoted girl, but sometimes she says I try to make her into something she isn't. So I leave her alone, but then she accuses me of not caring about what she does."

"Does that mirror your relationship with your own mother?"

Larissa quickly went on without replying. "It's a fine histrionic line with her. With the boys everything is simpler. Moods are easy. Food, drink. Video games, trying to get away with stuff. Very normal. For some reason girls are harder for mothers."

"Were you hard on your mother?"

"My mother was hard on me."

"Was she? I thought you said she was hands off?"

"Our time is almost up," Larissa said. "But I'll tell you why I have minimum contact with my mother. Because when I was growing up, I hated myself and the person I was. Everything about me was awful to me, particularly when I was in my house. But when I was with my friend Che at her house, she and her mom were so close and human, and full of regular up and down human interaction: they fought and argued and laughed, and cooked together, that being there felt more comforting than being in my own home. So what I did when I left is I remade myself into a person I wanted to be. When I was with my mother, I didn't like myself. And that's probably why our contact is minimal. Because when I'm around her, I still don't like myself."

"Where is Che and her mother?"

"In the Philippines. Her mother died." Larissa didn't want to say it felt like losing her own imagined perfect mother, the mother she wished were hers and wasn't.

"You do realize, Larissa, that you haven't remade yourself at all, you just hid the parts you didn't like?"

"Keeping the parts of yourself you hate under control is a tremendous feat, Dr. Kavanagh," said Larissa. "It requires will and a strong spirit."

"I couldn't agree more."

"But I can't keep myself under control when my mother is around. So what I do is limit my exposure to the person who brings out the worst in me."

Kavanagh was looking at her from the chair, wrinkled, frowning, wise. "And how would you describe what that is?"

Larissa stood up and grabbed her bag. "Always looking for a way out," she coldly replied. "See you next Tuesday."

∽ひ๑〜

Dear Larissa,

Lorenzo finally realized I've been dragging my feet on the bail. He accused me of wanting him to rot in jail. He told me if I really loved him, I would ask you for the money. I said, Lorenzo, are you out of your mind? Your bail is set at two and half million pesos because they're afraid you're going to run. Which is exactly what you're going to do as soon as you walk out the jail doors. You do understand how bail works, don't you? If you run, Larissa doesn't get her money back. You're asking me to ask her and her husband for over $50,000 that she will not see again. What world do you live in?

And he said to me, "Che, what world do you live in?"

I started to cry. I said, I just want to have my baby. That's all I want. I want to have my baby.

And he said, what about me, Claire? Do you want to abandon me? He called me Claire. I don't think he's ever called me that before. I didn't know if he was intensely imploring or detaching himself from me.

I said, it will work out, Lorenzo. It always does.

He said, "Work out, will it? How long do you think it will be before the scum I worked with will get caught, the scum that have been hiding all these months, even though they know I'm in jail and you're about to have a kid? This band of thieves to save their own skins, you don't think they'll point you out to the police as my accomplice, so they can get a lighter sentence?"

They won't point me out, I mouthed to him in terror.

"No? Didn't you hear? They caught my friend Agas Ilocano! They found him finally, hiding out in the swamps of Batangas! I

worked with Agas for over seven years. Seven years, and I thought we were tight. But after five minutes of interrogation he swore under oath that he never gave me the nail bomb. It's now my word against his, the cops told me. They're putting pressure on him to expose the others. How long do you think it'll be before they reel in the whole nefarious gaggle of them? And to save their own craven asses, they will tell the cops I didn't work alone, that I worked with you. And then what do you think is going to happen to you, Che?"

All I could whisper was, "Lorenzo, I'm having a baby." I could barely get the words out.

Help me, Larissa!

∽◡∾

As usual, they celebrated Larissa's birthday belatedly. Jared was swamped with the end-of-the-quarter tax reports, and couldn't take the time to plan a get-together. They had cake with the kids on April 4, but didn't invite their friends until almost May. Jared wanted to go out, like always, to reserve a room at one of the great city restaurants, perhaps Tabla, but Larissa, after feebly suggesting Nobu—which in itself was strange since it was a famous *sushi* place—said she would prefer to stay home. She found a new recipe in one of her cookbooks and wanted to try it out. They hadn't had a dinner party in so long, she said. She'd like to keep it casual, and have the kids with her. The kids had been sick, Larissa said, and she didn't want to leave Michelangelo when he was just getting over a cold.

Jared invited Maggie, Ezra, Bo, Jonny, Doug, Kate, Evelyn, Malcolm, and even Dora and Ray. On the day of the party Dora called and inexplicably cancelled, saying only that something came up. Jared found that perplexing, even more so than her clipped and awkward manner, especially considering her unrestrained enthusiasm the week before when she had thanked him profusely for inviting her. Doug and Kate were away and couldn't come.

At the house, Evelyn mentioned that she hadn't seen Larissa in a long time. Evelyn's reaction at seeing Larissa unsettled Jared.

"God, Larissa, have you not been outside?" she exclaimed. "You look frighteningly pale." Jared studied his wife. *Did* she look pale? "Oh my God, Jared, her skin is like porcelain, and I don't mean that in a good way, Lar. It looks translucent."

"What, like you can see right through me?" Larissa went back to stirring something on the stove.

"Yes, like that."

"Plus," said Maggie, "she's wearing black. Why would you wear black in April, on your birthday, Lar?"

"Didn't you hear, Mags?" said Larissa, not turning around. "Black is the new black. How are you feeling?"

"Today, a little better, thanks for asking. I'm getting used to living with my new warped and tired body. That's all I can ask."

Larissa didn't turn around. "You definitely look better."

Jared didn't see what Evelyn saw; he thought his wife looked pretty good, no matter how black-clad and pale she seemed to others. The jersey dress draped over her slim figure, she wore high-heeled black pumps, her hair was down.

That was at the beginning of the evening. Larissa stayed in the kitchen until dinner was served, and during dinner she must have gotten up three dozen times, without exaggeration, to help the nine kids with their food. Larissa got up to bring them butter, to cut their bread, to pour more drink, to scoop the peas from the bottom of the pot, to get a new spoon for Michelangelo and a straw for one of Evelyn's children. She spent the entire dinner bent over their table, cutting up food, buttering, spreading, pouring, salting, fixing napkins and mouths. "Larissa! Sit down. The kids will be fine," Jared kept repeating. This wasn't just a different-looking Larissa. This was a different Larissa.

"Yeah, really, Lar, they can fend for themselves," said Evelyn.

"They're only children," Larissa said. "They need our help."

"Oh, it's time they learned," said Malcolm. "They'll be out on their own soon. Right, kids?"

Usually there'd be a witty riposte from Larissa. Not tonight. She was back at the kids' table, hovering over Michelangelo. Her own food got cold. "I don't mind," she said when she came back to Jared's side. "I always eat it lukewarm anyway." She had made beef bourguignon and potato skins with bacon and cheese. She didn't touch her tepid food.

"Why aren't you eating?" Bo asked.

"I can't tell you how much I had while I was cooking." Larissa chuckled mildly. "I didn't realize how stuffed I am."

"Lar, you want more wine?"

"No, I'm good, thanks."

She was good if by good she meant her wine glass was still full, the red bobbing in the hollow bottom. Oh, she swilled it, she just didn't swill it down. Carefully Jared laid his hand on her hand. Carefully she smiled, turning to him halfway like an animatronic Disney figurine, and then bobbled slowly away, on a little spring that wouldn't let her turn all the way to face him.

Much of the dinner conversation was taken up by the travails of *Saint Joan*. Larissa barely contributed. The troubling Megan was Larissa's responsibility, and Jared thought she didn't want to be blamed again for Megan's obdurate softness. Why did Joan *have* to wear boy clothes, Megan wanted to know. Did she really hear saints' voices? Could Joan be made into a secular Joan? She had done the impossible *with* God; could she have done it without Him?

Larissa might have participated in her own defense had she not been up at Michelangelo's elbow, wiping up the melted cheese he dripped over his brand-new sailor suit.

Jared and Jonny had a long discussion about which era was best for rock music. Malcolm and Ezra and Evelyn got into a heated debate about who was the greater military leader, Saint Joan or Napoleon. Maggie and Bo chatted about the Met's newest exhibition of "Truth and Illusion in Contemporary Photography." Jared caught the tail end of that when he stopped talking about who had the greater influence on modern music: The Who or The Stones, and heard Bo say, "Sugimoto was stunned by the fact that no matter how fake the subject, when photographed it became completely real."

Jared realized Larissa was not back at the table. Excusing himself, he got up and went to the kitchen. She was cleaning up. "What are you doing?" he said quietly.

"We're going to have cake soon. I want to get the table ready."

"It's your birthday, I don't want you to clean up after cooking all day. Come on, sit down. You're making everybody feel bad."

"Who's everybody?" said Larissa, wiping down the granite. And it was true, the noises from the dining room were of happy people drinking and talking.

"Do you want me to help?"

"No. You go sit. Otherwise that would be plain rude, the host and hostess both missing."

So Jared went back, and she cleaned up, and then served her own cake. They put candles on, a number 4 and a number 1, and after they sang "Happy Birthday," she blew out the candles before they had finished the last note.

"Whoa, Larissa," said Maggie. "You blew them out so fast, I don't think you had time to make a wish."

"Well, I already made a wish on my actual birthday," said Larissa. "No sense irritating the gods with repeat wishes."

Maggie nodded with friendly approval. "Did you hear that, Ezra? Our Larissa doesn't want to irritate the gods."

"It's so considerate of Larissa to even think of them," remarked Ezra.

Silently Larissa moved her own slice of cake around on her plate for a while and finally got up, disappearing again.

Half an hour had passed and she wasn't back. When Jared went to look for her, she wasn't in any of the bathrooms, nor in the bedroom upstairs. Puzzled he came into the den to ask the kids if they'd seen their mom, and found her on the couch, watching a Nickelodeon show, with Asher on the floor by her feet, Emily leaning against her right shoulder, and Michelangelo on her lap, pressed against her as she embraced him with both arms. He watched her from the back for a few seconds; she hadn't stirred. He tapped Emily on the shoulder and mouthed, "Is Mom awake?"

By way of answer Emily pointed to her mother's face. Jared walked around the couch and witnessed a glassy Larissa sitting blank-eyed, unreacting and unemoting. "Larissa?" he said, expecting her to snap out of it, the way people did when they've spaced out for a moment. But she didn't snap out of it. Slowly she blinked, and then raised her eyes to him, as if she had not been entranced at all, but fully aware. "What are you doing?" he asked. "Come to the table."

"I will, hon, in just a sec. I cooked and cleaned all day. I'm a little tired."

Lowering his voice, he said, "That was your choice. No one made you do it."

"I'm not complaining." But she had already turned her attention back to the TV. "I just want to sit with my kids a minute."

"Yeah, Dad," said Michelangelo, nesting against her. "Leave Mom alone. Can't you see she's busy?"

Slowly Jared returned to the table.

She didn't come back to the dining room. Half an hour later Jared found her upstairs giving Michelangelo a bath.

"Larissa!" he hissed in the steamy bathroom. "What the hell are you doing? We have guests downstairs! Evelyn and Malcolm are about to leave."

"Jared, the boy is not feeling well and needed a bath. I'll be down in a minute." She was kneeling against the tub. She didn't turn around.

"I like it when Mommy gives me a bath," said Michelangelo, splashing his mother, still wearing her black dress, "because she puts bubbles and colors in, and you don't, Dad."

Downstairs only Maggie and Ezra remained.

"What's wrong with Larissa?" asked Maggie.

"I honestly don't know," Jared replied.

"She's so out of it," Maggie said. "The shrink doesn't seem to be helping her."

"No kidding. I think she's worse. Ever since starting counseling she's been having awful mood swings, unlike ever before. She's either like this, or she's maniacally frustrated with the kids' shoes, notebooks, baseball gloves . . ."

"Maybe she's got a bipolar disorder?"

"What, she suddenly developed one after finding a psychiatrist?"

Ezra waved his hand at both Maggie and Jared, downing his remaining wine. "Don't be so overwrought, both of you," he said. "I talk to her at school. She is fine. Why is it unreasonable to assume that when she is in her own house, she might feel exhausted from being so front and center all the time? That exhaustion can show itself either in silence, like tonight, or in impatience. She's not a performing monkey. She is a human being. And sometimes, human beings get tired. You know?" He stared pointedly at Maggie.

Maggie lowered her gaze.

Ezra casually continued, "She is okay during the week. There's a lot of stress with *Saint Joan*. I feel partly responsible. I roped her into it, and I think she regrets it now. Blame me, but don't be so hard on her."

The three of them quickly changed the subject to Dylan's gifts in sports and arts, and how unfair it was that he had to choose one or the other before he entered college. Soon it was time to go. Larissa came downstairs to say goodbye. Upset with her, despite Ezra's mollification, Jared went to yell at her for spoiling her own damn party that he wished to God he'd never arranged now, and found her on the floor in Emily's room, playing Scrabble with Emily and Asher, and he wanted to say, oh, to talk to adults, you're all out, but to play Scrabble, *that* you've got a brain for, but the three of them looked so cute on the floor.

"You wanna play, Dad?" asked Emily. "We just started. We'll go easy on you. We'll give you a thirty-point handicap. Right, Mom?"

"Thirty? Let's give him at least fifty."

"No, you guys go ahead," said Jared. "I'll go check on the ballgame."

He didn't mean to, but he was also tired, and he fell asleep on the couch around midnight. When he woke up it was six in the morning and his back was sore and cramped from sleeping in a sitting position. He couldn't believe she hadn't come to wake him. She herself wasn't even in their bed! Larissa was with Michelangelo, sleeping on top of his covers, her arm around him. Jared thought about waking her, but reconsidered, leaving her where she was, where she wanted to be.

3

Scylla and Charybdis

"Larissa." Kai closed the door, but made no motion to touch her. She couldn't even smell him. Usually, he had his happy-go-lucky, come-hither-and-take-what-I'm-offering smile, but not today.

"What's the matter?"

"You know what the matter is."

"Kai . . ." Her arms went around herself.

"I'm waiting."

"You're not giving me time to think."

"It's been twelve weeks!" He made a helpless gesture with his hands. "Oh my God, no, it's been seventy weeks."

"It's not enough time."

"Not enough time for what? What are you waiting for?"

"I don't know." Oh, the hated phrase!

"Do you want me to call him? Go to his work? Come to your house?"

"No!" Larissa, still standing, backed away toward the door. "What are you saying . . . ? No. Never."

"Then what do you want?"

"Kai, what's wrong with you. You're never like this . . ."

"I'm like this now."

"But you've been . . ."

"Been so what? Patient? Nice? Tolerant? Adaptable? Easy-going?

Doesn't my cup ever get full, too? Doesn't it spill over?" When she didn't answer him, he said, "What do you go to your doctor for, if not to work this shit out?"

"I go so I can see you at night."

"Okay, but even *en passant*, without meaning to, don't you manage to resolve anything, since you do actually speak to her once a week?"

"Clearly, we haven't resolved this."

"Clearly."

She stood. He stood.

Minutes passed. "I can't do this anymore, Larissa," Kai said. "I can't do this for another day. I can't have you go to him, sleep with him, live with him. It would be one thing if you never touched him, but . . ." He trailed off. "I had been hoping that my love for you would make you see the light."

"I see light." I see lots of things. Darkness, too.

"Apparently not. Look, that's it. Do you love me? So stay with me. Do you love me, but can't? Then walk the fuck out that door."

"Kai . . ."

He raised his palm to stop her. "No more. Tell me we had a lot, and it was good, but what I ask of you, you can't do, you can't go with me." His young face was dry, grim.

"Not many could do it," she whispered.

"You're right. Many could not lie like you, deceive like you, pretend like you, live a double life like you, stay married to one man while saying you love another quite so well as you. Many women are not you, Larissa. But then I'm not with them. You can't do it? So tell me you can't do it."

Larissa didn't speak. Kavanagh had been right. Nothing could stay. This especially.

"Kai, I'm still trying to work out a way we can remain here," she said in a halting voice. "I leave him, and come to live with you, and then I can still see—"

"Larissa, don't fucking lie to me. You have *not* been working it out! You have been coasting and floating. You haven't been working out a single damn thing. Don't bullshit me. You've been taking Ambien at night so you never have to think about it, and you've been filling your days with all kinds of bullshit filler so you never have to deal with it. You're all about rehearsals and book projects for the kids, and driving around with the music on a hundred decibels! I know how loud you have it when you turn on your car to leave me every afternoon. To obliterate all thought, right? And every time in the last three months that I've tried to talk to you about this, you've refused! Plain refused. You've changed the subject, you've diverted me—oh, you're very good at that. You've asked me to play more music, play your guitar, Kai, play the uke, Kai, sing to me, Kai. More noise so you don't have to think for a single second about anything."

"I *have* been thinking about it, I have . . ."

"Look, there are two choices here. Either we go and live with what's left for you and me, or you go back to your old life."

She couldn't tell him the woman who had lived that life was gone. "I don't understand what the hurry is. Why do we have to go at all? We don't have to stay in Madison. We can move to—"

"I'm leaving," Kai interrupted. "I can't stay because I've been here about fifteen months too long. I came to spend a month with Gil, have some fun. And look what happened. My time here is finished. I'm not staying."

"Kai—"

"Larissa." He was immovable. He would not be cajoled.

"If I tell you I cannot do what you ask of me," she said in a breaking whisper, "you wouldn't stay then? You'd let me go?" She said it like she couldn't believe it.

"No! If *you* cannot do what I ask of you," Kai replied in his own breaking voice, "you will let *me* go." He stood against the wall, silent for a few moments. "In the beginning, I was out of my depth. I was an outsider. I'd never felt about anyone the way I feel about you. I knew it wasn't going to be easy." He took a breath. "But the longer we stayed together, the easier the dream became. Maybe for you it became harder, but for me, everything was so clear! It was as if there was suddenly daylight! *I* could see; how could you not?"

"I have more at stake than you."

"Oh, you think so? Hitching my star to a married woman twice my age, with three kids to boot, you think I've got nothing at stake?"

"Kai, come on, you're not being fair. I said not as much as me."

"What is this, a competition for who's got the greater price to pay?"

"Do you *have* a price to pay?" she snapped. Why was she being cruel to him whom she loved?

"I pay it every day, Larissa," he retorted, growing ever colder, "when I allow you to come here for one hour, feeling about you as I do, and then let you go, knowing you're going to sleep with another man. I know you think I'm okay with it, but for the record, I'm not okay with it, and I'm never going to be okay with it. But is this what we're all about? Pride?"

"There's nothing to be proud of here," Larissa said.

"Oh, wonderful!" he yelled. "You think this is degrading? You think it's cheap? You're ashamed of me? But it's *my* whole life! Just think about that for a second; for a second *think* about somebody else's pain but your own. Your abasement is my entire existence!"

"I'm sorry, Kai . . . I didn't mean it . . ."

"I'm tired of feeling like an outsider in my own life, which is how you make me feel when you tell me every single fucking day that you have something in your life more important than me. One of us is living a sham, and one a delusion. You don't see a problem with that? The most meaningful part of my life is the least meaningful of yours?" He ran his hands through his hair, trying to understand, find a way out for himself. "Oh, my God," he said. "Which one of us is really the fool here?" He laughed. "Sometimes when we're together I think we're the center of the universe, and I believe for a few stolen minutes that I'm the center of yours. And then you look at your watch, and it's like a balloon of joy bursting. I've been watching you do this and slowly realizing how much I fucking hate it, because it's not joy that's whistling out of those pop-up balloons in spasms, it's poison! Every time I see you glance at the time—like you're doing *now*!—you tell me I'm least important to you. *I'm* the outsider."

"You're not the outsider! Don't you know how I love you . . . ?"

"I don't care! I don't care what you feel anymore. I only care what you *do*." Kai stepped away from his wall and took a stride across the entryway. "I don't want you to go back to him, Larissa," he said.

"Please don't ask me to choose . . ." She started to cry. "You know it's not between him and you, you know that."

"I have to be worth something, too."

"You are."

"Then why are you still toying with me after all this time?" he said. "I want you to imagine what Jared might say if you told him this is what you've been doing with your afternoons. How would he react? Well, *I* know what you've been doing with your afternoons. And with your nights. I know everything. I'm always behind the door. You want to imagine how Jared *might* feel? Imagine how I *do* feel! Imagine how anyone might feel except yourself. Anyone else, Larissa!"

And Larissa saw by the menace in his body, by the panting mouth, by the fire in his eyes that Kavanagh was right. She heard her gravelly voice in her head. *I don't know what took him so long, Larissa*, Kavanagh kept saying. *No one else would have waited this long.*

But he's not like everyone else. He is like no one else. He gazes on blue and walks in waltz-time. He listens for Tai Chi, and stays warm. He brings nothing but calm and music to my life. Still his stance, his expression scared her. For a second, it felt like Tijuana at night, like the next thing could be blood in the streets. He could suffocate her. He could beat her. He could kill her. He could throw her down the stairs. He could drown her in the river. He could keep her and not let her go. As he was dying, she was living, and without her, he too had nothing. What if it was Kai, not Jared, who could not bear to part with her? Did he have a Howitzer to balance these scales?

She opened her shaking frightened hands to him. "Please let's not fight." Her voice trembled like her body. "We have behaved badly. This hasn't been beautiful, this has been brutally wrong."

"I'm glad you think so," Kai said through clenched teeth. "Because it's been the only thing in my life. Happy to know it was all in grave error."

"I'm not the ditzy receptionist who answers your calls, Kai! I'm somebody else's wife!"

"Oh, do I not know this! Will there ever be a minute that goes by that you don't inform me of this one way or another?" Kai took another stride to her. He was so upset. "But guess what? I don't want you to be someone else's wife." He grabbed her with angry hands. "I don't want anyone else sharing you with me anymore. Can't you understand that? I can't believe I even have to say it! How come I'm a generation younger, yet so much smarter? How come I see this, and you don't? How dense you are, how hopeless, how full of only yourself!"

She wanted to pull away, but couldn't. She wanted to leave, but couldn't. She wanted not to moan, not to cry out for him, not to cry for him, but couldn't. And he so shamelessly abused his ruthless power over her, he discarded her clothes and took her body for himself, he took off her watch! And turned all the clocks with their faces to the wall, he turned her face down on the bed, and he whispered hot things in her ear, while she was splayed, body and soul in the glare of her abandon for him. *Just so you understand, Larissa,* Kai whispered as he took the thing from her he could take, the thing that looked like love and was love, and yet wasn't; was more like a sonnet to a whore. *I am leaving next weekend. I've paid up my rent till the end of May, I've given my notice at work, and now I'm giving you notice. I think I may have misunderstood you. What you really have been hoping for, praying for in your own little secular prayerful way, was not that Jared would kick you out, but that I would. You've come to resent me because I'm not doing the thing the biker stud is supposed to do. I'm not becoming imaginary soon enough. It took me a while to figure this out. I've been an idiot. You've been waiting for a* deus ex machina *exit from me! Well, in exactly one week, you're going to get it.*

It was high tide. It was deluge. And afterward, as Larissa rummaged on the floor to find her clothes, pick up the buttons torn off her shirt, find the belt that had fallen, the watch he'd flung across the room (it was 2:50!), she said to him, "But Michelangelo is not Jared. He is not me. He is not you. When you make me this late, he suffers."

"When you leave me, you make *me* suffer," Kai said. "And I want to make *you* suffer."

"You think I don't suffer?"

"I don't think you suffer enough." His back was to her. He didn't turn to watch her go.

❧

Dear Larissa,

Lorenzo has cooked up a plan. He says I need to leave our house and go find sanctuary with Father Emilio and have my baby at the orphanage, and when we get Lorenzo sprung, we'll run, and leave the baby with Father Emilio until we get ourselves sorted, and then we'll return to get it. He said the nuns would take care of it while we hid out in Mindanao.

I said, Lorenzo, where are we going to get the money for bail?

He asked me to talk to Father Emilio. So I put away my shame, thrust my belly forward, and talked to Father Emilio. He stared at me silently a long time before he answered. He said, Do you want me to trade my good name and the name of this church to vouch for a man who plans to flee as soon as he is out and you, knowing that, are asking me to do this?

I cried. I said I didn't know what else to do.

He told me he would take care of me, the mission would take care of me and the baby, but his conscience would not allow him to lie for Lorenzo, and his parish did not have two and a half million pesos to lose to post bail for a man who would flee. He said the church would defrock him. He couldn't do it. His word in the neighborhood was law. Do you want me to ruin my reputation and the reputation of San Agustin so that the man who will not marry you can persuade you to abandon your desperately wanted child and run into the mountains with him?

I could barely get myself to my feet to walk out of the rectory.

Do you know, Larissa, sometimes, to my great shame—God will never forgive me, though I pray He is merciful and does— but sometimes I wish Lorenzo had died in that clash with the cops. Because then I could grieve, and it would be horrible but it wouldn't be intolerable, like now. I wouldn't have to make an impossible choice between my baby and my Lorenzo! Because I don't want to abandon my baby to run to Mindanao. I'm terrified we won't be able to find our way back.

On your end of the world, do you even hear me?

This isn't the beginning of sorrow—this is simply the worst thing that's ever happened to me. I cannot bear to make this choice.

<hr />

Painting her nails with Fran Finklestein on Friday morning, the shattered edges of Larissa's glassy numbness couldn't help but skid over into the classical hums of a peaceful manicure.

"You're *so* agitated," Fran said, her long-fingered hands stretched out for Sherry. "I haven't seen you in months. Why are you like this?"

"I *am* agitated," concurred Larissa, her long-fingered hands stretched out for Jessica. She clenched to get herself together. "I've been going to this psychologist and—"

Fran chuckled. "What do *you* have to go to a shrink for? You don't have any problems."

"No? Jessica, no, I *do* want the cuticles done today. Look at them. Thanks." Larissa turned to Fran. "Oh, I got some stuff. Nothing is perfect, Finklestein."

"So what's he doing for you?"

"*She*. Making me agitated, that's what. I'd fire her, but then I'd have no one to talk to." And other things, too, she wouldn't be able to do at night with guitars on beds and short tumblers of raw poetry. Memorial Day was next weekend. One week. Seven days.

"Talk to *me*," Fran grinned. She was bubbly and gum-chewy. She was twenty-four. She could afford to be bubbly and gum-chewy. Larissa too had been bubbly and gum-chewy at twenty-four. "I know stuff," Fran said. "I'm people-smart. And I won't charge you a penny."

Larissa steadied her gaze on the beautifully unclumpy black lashes framing Fran's dancing brown eyes. She was delightful. Why hadn't Larissa spent more time with her? They could've been friends. They could have gone shopping, had lunch. Fran had been unconnected to any other part of her life. It had never occurred to Larissa that she could've talked to Fran. Once, Fran had seemed too young to be friends with!

The wood life was chipping, and Larissa was sliding in prickles of pain in the splinters of it. How could Fran have noticed her suffering before Jared?

Yet . . . the girl seemed so happening and with it. She hadn't been around the world three times, like Kavanagh's weathered face suggested she had been. Fran liked Larissa. Maybe . . .

"Wanna go have lunch after?" Fran asked.

"I'd love to, doll. But I can't. I've got . . ."

"Things?"

"Yeah." I've got Albright Circles and ukuleles and promises of scars and fresh wounds.

"Okay," said Fran. "How about a hypothetical right now?"

"Well, the point of *talking*, Finklestein," said Larissa, "isn't a question and answer session. We're not engaging in the Socratic method."

"The what?"

"The point is to converse freely about topics of great interest."

"Check! I'm greatly interested. Oh, yes, Sherry, please, this Ballerina Pink for the nails." Fran winked at Larissa. "They'll go with my black boots and gray striped leggings."

Fran looked great. She always looked good. She put herself together just for the manicure. She seemed so accessible. Larissa chewed her lip. "Okay," she began. "A hypothetical."

Jessica and Sherry leaned forward. Larissa found this fascinating, considering their English was usually impaired by near-total lack of comprehension. Yet here they were: Larissa said *hypothetical*, and the foreign non-English speaking girls leaned forward!

Their curiosity duly noted, her own hands still outstretched, Larissa clammed up, and the girls started talking in Korean, and then she unclammed, but still, was having difficulty getting even the hypothetical words out.

"Finklestein," she said, "do you know the story of Scylla and Charybdis?"

"What did you just say?"

The Korean girls continued talking, while buffing the bare nails before applying the polish. Larissa had five minutes tops, and then some time under the drier.

"Scylla," said Larissa, "was a six-headed dog with twelve pairs of feet who lived under a rock and ate men who sailed by her through the Strait of Messina. Guarding the other side of the narrow strait was Charybdis, a sea monster with a gaping mouth into which it sucked huge amounts of water and created whirlpools that sank men's ships."

"This is your hypothetical? A dog and a sea monster?"

"Yes."

Fran laughed.

"Finklestein . . ."

Jessica applied the last coat of red on Larissa's nails. Sherry was quicker. Fran was already done.

"Is that your choice, Larissa? Between a six-headed mutt and a sea monster?"

"I'm saying, you're passing through the strait. You can keep to one side or the other. Staying in the middle, impaled on the stake of your own indecision, is no longer an option. Your choice either way is unacceptable." Intolerable.

"I would turn around and go back," Fran declared, her wet pink nails moving sideways under the fan of the drier. "Can you go back?"

"No," Larissa said. "There is no going back. It's either Scylla or Charybdis, Finklestein. Which one shall it be?"

Fran got up, all long skinny legs in high-heeled patent-leather boots, her lips shining, her eyes blazing, her hip flirtatiously bowed out, dancing hip-hop, fashion-plate, young, careless, free, and said, "I would go back if I could. But if I can't, you know what they say." She blew and burst a large pink bubble.

"No, Fran. What do they say?" Larissa was so tired. Of her wet nails, of gray horses galloping, of chariot races in the watery abyss.

"Don't sound like much of a choice if you ask me. But, if I had to pick, I'd say that if you ride the tiger, you gotta reap the whirlwind, baby," Fran said, blowing her a kiss and twirling out. "Reap that whirlwind."

∾ᑖᗢ

Larissa received another letter from Che barely three days after the last, the frequency of her friend's letters underscoring Larissa's own increasing despair.

> *Dear Larissa,*
>   *I'm out of options. I'm so sorry, I can't believe I'm asking you for this. Please. Please, I beg you. Could you*

Larissa stopped reading and put the letter back in the envelope. She was sorry, she really was, but she could not read another syllable of Che's frantic missives. She simply couldn't read about someone else's troubles, her dirty plate overstuffed with her sordid own. Odysseus chose Scylla, because he said he would rather lose a few of his men to a beast than the entire ship to a whirlwind. I'm sorry, Che, she thought, pushing the letter away into the depths of her dresser along with the others. But the love of Larissa has waxed cold.

4
Fever Swamps

She came to see Kavanagh on their usual Tuesday evening and sat down on the leather sofa with her hands in her lap. Watchfully she sat. Silently. It had been getting darker later and later, and tonight at seven, the last light of the sun streaked auburn through the windows, almost as if it were autumn, not the end of spring. There were no lamps on in the office. The paneled walls, the books, the wood desk behind the doctor, the notepad in the hands in which Kavanagh never seemed to write down anything, yet always remembered things Larissa had told her, Kavanagh and Larissa both steeped in lengthening shadows like curling smoke through a burning house. Tonight Larissa didn't fidget, didn't fret, or fuss with her purse. Her jeans, her spring-green blazer, her cream tank top were pristine. Her light makeup hadn't run from morning. She made figures out of clay with Michelangelo after school, fed her family burritos and fajitas, and home-made flan for dessert that took all day to make, and cups of fresh fruit. She had driven steadily with both hands on the wheel and now sat with both hands in her lap. She didn't speak. And the doctor didn't speak, waiting for Larissa to begin.

Larissa said nothing.

"Do you have plans for Memorial Day weekend?" the doctor asked.

"Not really," Larissa replied.

In this manner they sat for forty-five of their fifty minutes together.

"I should be getting back," Larissa finally said, getting up. "My daughter has a concert on Thursday night and I promised I would listen to her practice before she went to bed."

"Of course," said Kavanagh, also getting up. "Are you . . . all right?"

"I'm fine." Larissa smiled and then extended her hand. "Thank you."

Dr. Kavanagh shook it in confusion. "I'll see you next Tuesday?"

Larissa rolled her eyes. "Actually, my son managed to get into the Junior League baseball playoffs and they have a five o'clock game next Tuesday. I don't know when it will end. Can we reschedule?"

"Of course. Do you want to come next Thursday instead?"

"Let me call you, okay? Because it's sudden death at the Junior League, and if they go through, I don't know when the next game will be."

"So we'll reschedule?"

"I think that would be best," said Larissa.

✿

She knew the person she needed to talk to was Ezra.

"Lunch?" He glanced at the clock above her head. It read 10:45. "Um . . . ?"

"I know but . . . I've got things later."

She began casually, talking about the pesky epilogue problem for *Saint Joan*. The play was opening next weekend, at the beginning of June, and they still couldn't decide whether to have the epilogue or to scrap it. There seemed to be as many opinions as there were people. They rehearsed it both ways, and were still agonizing. Poor Megan remained terrible and miscast. Larissa had made a reckless choice and was now paying for it every day.

"Larissa, has anyone told you you've lost weight?"

She shook her head. "Not really."

"What, you think I can't tell?"

"It's an illusion. You know what Sugimoto says. The fake subject in front of you looks real when transposed onto a photograph."

"Oh, so you *were* paying attention to Bo and Maggie on your birthday? You and your unplumbed depths."

Oh, they've been plumbed, Ezra. Plumbed down to the bottomless maw.

"But which is it?" he asked. "Are you fake, or is your weight loss fake? Or is the weight loss the very thing that's making you a fake subject against a real backdrop?"

"You're making a big deal out of nothing. I'm five pounds up or down." Larissa was thirty pounds lighter. Everything hung on her like she was a cancer patient. She despised herself for her lying metaphors.

"Do you think I'm self-actualized?" she asked Ezra.

"Not if you don't think you've lost at least half a Larissa."

"I'm talking in a metaphysical sense. Look beyond the physical, Ez."

"The physical is a manifestation of our inner sanctum. That's why the soul is so hard to hide."

Is it? Anyone who ever loved could look at her and know . . . and yet . . . they all did love, and yet looked at her, and saw nothing.

"What's your question?" Ezra smiled. "No, I don't think you are self-actualized." He leaned forward. "But you know what you are?"

She leaned away from him. "No, what?"

"Half a Larissa."

"Now listen." She leaned forward again. "Ezra, what do you do when you have to advise your kids on big problems, like when you found our runaway Tenestra trying to give herself an abortion in the school bathroom?"

"Fortunately, in her crack withdrawal distress, she had gone into the men's bathroom," said Ezra. "I never would've found her otherwise."

"My question is," Larissa continued slowly, "what do you draw on to help her? Your education? Your intelligence?"

He shook his head. "Nothing in my education or intelligence can help me deal with a kid who's scared shitless."

"So how does *she* decide to go into the men's bathroom?"

"She puts away everything else and follows her fear. What is she afraid of most? Clearly, it was giving birth to a baby."

"Is that how we make all our decisions? Out of fear?"

"Tenny did. I don't know how *we* do." He studied her. "What are *you* afraid of?"

"Oh, no, not me." She smiled so lightly, so brightly, all her teeth sparkling at him. She took a sip of her coffee. Her hands didn't shake. Though she had to stifle the gag reflex from tasting anything that resembled nourishment.

"I see my kids, fifteen, sixteen years old," Ezra continued, "and they're confused, not ready to face life, and yet they have to choose a college, a boyfriend, whether or not to lie to their parents, have unprotected sex, drive when drunk. It doesn't end."

Larissa nodded. "Sometimes when the kids come to me to ask for advice, I don't know what to tell them."

"Sometimes I don't either."

"But what *do* you tell them?"

"What do you tell *your* kids?"

"You mean my real kids?"

"Yes, as opposed to the fake ones in the photographs. No, not your *children*. I mean the kids you teach."

"Well, this is where the trouble starts," said Larissa. "My heart is conflicted. I see two different paths for them. I can imagine an urban college or a rural one. I can imagine playing baseball, as in the case of your Dylan, but also guitar. I don't know how you can advise even your own son."

Ezra looked amused. "Those things are easy, Larissa. That's not a do I have a baby or not. Do I have unprotected sex or not. Do I sleep with my best friend's boyfriend, do I take my parents' car when they've expressly told me I can't."

"But what if you don't know how to make the . . . *right* decision?" asked Larissa.

"What I do then," said Ezra, "is ask: what is the overriding passion of your life? What is the *one* thing you can't imagine living without? If God came to you in a dream and told you He would take away from you everything but the one thing you couldn't part with, what would that *one* thing you were left with be?"

Crowded bazaars, caravans, freak shows, high wire dancing monkeys, and fire hoops. I dream to be dreamless. I want it to be like before, not after. I want it to be not now when hollow heaven is awash in charcoal. "What if there are *two* things?" she asked, almost in a whisper.

"Rare. You'd be surprised how decisive the students become when the choice is presented to them this starkly. What if everything else was taken away? What do you want to be left with? They all know. If it's piano, or baseball, or their singing voice. For some it's their long legs, or their best friend, or their blonde hair. Some say their little brother. Some say their dog."

"Does anybody say their . . . parents?" She could barely get the words out.

Ezra laughed. "Not a single one, *ever*. What does that tell you?"

Larissa tried to will herself not to look like she was going blind, torn, drained, like she was in a death struggle. "But what about the other stuff? Right and wrong stuff? Like taking the car when you're not supposed to?"

"That's harder," Ezra admitted. "But I say to them, do you know how you know what you *should* do? The thing that you don't want to do. That's how you know."

"Oh, I bet they love that."

"Oh, they do." He grinned. "They fling Epicurus to defy me, like monkeys throwing poop. They all suddenly become Lucretians, start quoting from *On the Nature of Things*." He tutted mildly. "I can't get them to remember one quote from Kant or Kierkegaard, but Lucretius they have memorized. The atoms, ho, ho, ho, Professor DeSwann, they move in an infinite void, and all we are is atoms.

The reality of atoms is unflinching, they inform me. Suddenly all the young ones are Epicureans." Ezra laughed. "I tell them it's not a philosophy that has stood the test of time. They vociferously disagree. When I mention that Epicurean philosophy condemned lusts of all kinds, condemned passions, immoderation, they don't want to hear it. They hear only 'reality of atoms.'"

Larissa was thoughtful. "Well, aren't your students correct, Professor DeSwann? We *are* made up wholly of atoms."

"You can't have it both ways to Sunday. Even atoms are not random. They move about in orderly, predictable ways, in ways that are designed and flawless. Even atoms are charged positively and negatively just enough and no more, the electrons do not fly away on whim and adhere to another matter just because they feel like it. The atoms behave along the lines of the natural order of the universe. Which is to say, not like human beings at all, who behave in all manner of appalling and unpredictable ways."

"You must be so popular at this point."

"Oh, I am. But then a boy takes the girl's pencil, the girl says it's not fair, someone gets a B instead of a B+ and complains heartily . . . In five minutes we move on from Epicurus because he can't help us even in the classroom."

Larissa drank her coffee. She tried not to look at Ezra, her friend since freshman year in college, her friend even before Jared. She wished she were wearing sunglasses. Her eyes felt swollen, she could barely make out Ezra's amused expression, his smart eyes, his tapping fingers. She didn't know much. But she knew this. He picked her up on his chrome Ducati. His name she knew, like it was tattooed in blue on her electric soul.

"So how do we live, Ezra, knowing we're a walking contradiction? Made up of orderly things on the outside, yet inside us chaos reigns supreme. We are the most erratic, inconsistent, uncertain movement in the universe."

"Yes, Larissa. Because gods cannot walk the earth," said Ezra, "without taking the form of beasts. Ask yourself: of all the things you endure, and wish for, and define yourself as, and long for, what is it that makes you break out of your false choices and become that impossible thing: an unbroken undamaged self?"

"Nothing." And this she did whisper.

"Ask yourself what you want to be left with."

"What if there is no answer?"

"How can there be no answer to *that*?"

"What if there is no *right* answer?"

"Really? Just atoms in a void? Well, then, that's your answer."

"I don't understand about your Maggie," exclaimed Larissa a little too stridently. "Her body is giving out, is getting completely out of whack, and she keeps going to Our Lady of the Rosary. How in the world does God help Maggie?"

"Maggie?" Ezra said surprised. "I thought this was about your students?"

"Oh, it is, it is."

Ezra stopped speaking, almost as if he wanted to say something and didn't.

"What if you can't be like her?" Larissa asked. "What if you don't believe?"

"You have to believe in something."

"What if you believe in . . . nothing?"

"In nothing? Who believes in this?"

"Well, some of my students."

"Odd. They usually have very strong beliefs, even if dunderheaded." Ezra smiled. "Delightfully dunderheaded."

"What does Jesus do for Maggie?"

"I think you may have the relationship reversed," said Ezra. "Jesus doesn't come and go as *you* please. He doesn't serve at *your* pleasure. He is an implacable source of all things, but He is not there for your convenience. That you must accept or you will quickly find yourself at a loss."

"*That* helps her?" It sounded most unhelpful.

"It does."

"Can someone be, say, a materialist and still believe in God?"

Ezra stared at Larissa with incredulity. "No, Larissa."

"Why?"

"What do you need God for, if physical matter is your only reality?"

"Why can't someone believe in God sometimes?" She pressed on. "Like when He is needed?"

"But He is not summoned. You don't wear Christ like a coat. Take off, put on when it suits. He is not dispensable."

"No kidding." Larissa shrugged. Or shuddered? "It doesn't seem like He makes life questions easier."

"He doesn't," Ezra agreed. "He makes them harder. He is an insuperable master."

"Why would anyone want that?"

"They don't. Which is why so many people turn away from Him."

"What's in it for Maggie?"

"Definite meaning and infinite comfort," said Ezra. "Because more so than with anything else, the universe for people with Christ in it is fundamentally different than for those for without. You can instantly tell the two apart. The struggle for their humanity, for significance, for the burden of obligations to others as well as for the destination of Self is markedly different for those for whom Christ does not enter into the equation of decision-making."

"And this *helps* Maggie?" Larissa asked skeptically.

"Sure. Her suffering is no longer meaningless. She is profoundly comforted. Like our Saint Joan, without these things Maggie cannot live." Ezra paused, and then spoke almost reluctantly. "You know, you never did talk to her, though, like you promised."

"About what?"

For a moment, Ezra and Larissa stared at each other. Soft rebuke was in his eyes; guilty puzzlement in hers, like she knew he was right, but couldn't even recall the conversation in which she had promised to do the thing for which Ezra was now chiding her.

"Sorry, Ez," she said. "I'll talk to her this weekend. I think we're going beverage shopping on Saturday for Monday's party. We'll have time alone then." Her coffee long finished, she stood up. "Still,"

Larissa said, "I don't understand why you can't put on Christ. Put Him on, take Him off. Johnny Cash did. Your own personal Jesus."

~ ~ ~

"Jared," Larissa said Wednesday evening after coffee. "What would you think of me going to visit Che?"

He had been reading the sports page and looked up half-heartedly, as if this was a conversation too big—or too trivial—to compete with the box scores from last night's games.

"Visit her where?" He looked back down. The catcher had hit three doubles. Was that a record for the catcher?

"In Manila."

Yes, yes, look! They said it. He broke his own record. Four hits and three doubles in one game. Wow. Would he be playing again tonight? "Manila?"

"Yes. I thought I'd go for two weeks maybe. Ten days? You know how long she's been trying to get pregnant . . ."

"If she's trying to get pregnant, maybe you're the last thing she needs." Who was pitching tonight? God, no, not him. They have not won once since he's been on the mound. Jared's whole outlook soured when he realized who was going to be taking the ball for the Yankees this evening. When was the game starting?

"Jared, Che *is* pregnant. Remember? She is about to have her baby."

"Oh, yeah. Maybe. It's not a bad idea." He glanced at his watch.

"*Really?* I can go?"

It was 7:30 already! He missed the first pitch. Swallowing the last of his coffee, Jared snapped shut the paper and got up from the table. "Sure, why not? Where did you say?"

"Manila, Jared," Larissa said, exhaustion in her voice.

He was halfway to the television in the den. "Manila?" He took a step back to her. "Manila, as in the *Philippines?*"

"That is where Che lives."

Jared rubbed his eyes. "Is that what you've been talking about? Going to Manila?"

"You just said it was fine."

"Lar, I wasn't paying attention! Are you out of your mind? When were you thinking of doing this?"

"Now, Jared. She is about to have her baby."

"Good for her. But you've got three babies of your own. Look, it's not that I don't want you to go visit your friend. But she's your *friend*. You've got a family here. How in the world do you think we're going to manage for two weeks? Even if I bring home take-out every night. How is Emily going to get to her lessons, and Michelangelo to his karate and Little League, and Asher to his playoffs? And aren't you putting on a play that opens next Thursday? I'm serious, Larissa. I don't think you've thought this through."

"I have." Her palms were on the table. She didn't look at him.

"No, I don't think you have. If you did, you wouldn't be asking. I mean, just think about it logically, and the answer will be so clear." He glanced at his watch again: 7:40. Damn. He probably missed the entire first inning.

"It's just for a couple of weeks, Jared," said Larissa. "It's not forever."

"Lar, they can't do without you for five minutes!"

"Maybe we can hire someone to come in after school."

"What, for two weeks hire someone? Where do you get someone to just come in for two weeks to live your life?"

"Aren't there some temporary childcare agencies? There is one that's called Parenting Plus. I heard it's very good. Empty Nest is another. Sort of an ironic name, but it comes highly recommended."

"Highly recommended by who?" Without waiting for her answer, shaking his head, Jared took one slow step toward Larissa, one eager step toward the den. "Please. It's the end of the school year. Emily has two recitals, Michelangelo has a concert. Asher is going with Dylan to New York for the Summer League pitcher tryouts. Emily wants a party. We're having two hundred people here for the Fourth of July. Oh, and by the way, lest you forgot, sixty people here in four days on Memorial Monday. Asher wants ten of his friends to sleep over this Saturday night. This is the *worst* time to go." That's it. Punt it. Like football. "Tell you what. Let's talk about it again in the fall."

"But Jared, in the fall there are birthdays and Halloween and the holidays, Thanksgiving, Christmas." Larissa lowered her head.

"That's true." Punt missed. Shame.

"There's never a good time to go."

He said nothing, widening his eyes, conveying to her that perhaps she had answered her own question. But she wasn't looking at him.

"I really would *like* to go," she said quietly.

"I know, Lar. And I really want to go hiking in Alaska. After college and before we got married I was an English-speaking tour guide in the Himalayas. I'd like to do that again. I'd like to live in Rome," Jared called out, leaving the dining room, his back to the questions, to the conversation, eye on the remotes, speeding up. "There will be time enough for all that again, when the kids are in college. We'll both go then. I promise. Now . . ."

5

Before You Go

The world was here in which the heart was lost, given away, surrendered to another human being. Was that not the world in which she wanted to live? Was this not the essence of her whole brief minute on earth? Find love, hold on to it with both hands. Love is all you need.

Love is the answer.

Well, okay then. Love was the answer.

Follow your heart, your heart's desire.

Going is easier when you're prepared. Research your options. Remove your contact lenses in case suntan lotion gets in your eyes. Bring your glasses.

Dress for comfort. Clothes you can slip on and off easily are a must. Loose, dark-colored clothing that won't show stains is best. Natural fibers are preferable. Cotton. Linen. Silk.

Eat, but not too much. You don't want to be famished, but you don't want to be bloated either. Fresh fruit. Perhaps a cup of coffee. Some cheese.

Travel lightly, and carry a small bag. Bringing less is best.

And the most important thing . . .

Leave all your valuables behind.

PART THREE
"EVERYTHING MUST GO"

To abandon: To give up absolutely; to forsake entirely; to renounce utterly; to relinquish all connection with or concern for a person or persons to whom one owes allegiance or fidelity; to quit; to surrender; to desert.

Chapter One

1

And Now for Something Completely Different

Monty Python's *And Now for Something Completely Different* played on cable. *"This is a frightened city. Over these streets, over these houses hangs a pall of fear."* Jared turned the movie to a more manageable mute while he sat on the couch, flipping the phone from hand to hand and watching the gangs of old ladies mug forty-eight-year-old men. He had put Michelangelo to bed, holding it together long enough to say good night to his children. "Where is Mommy?" said Michelangelo on this unprecedented Friday night. Jared had no answers.

He didn't know what to think. Had her cars not been in the driveway and garage, he would have thought car accident. But the vehicles stood glumly motionless, their engines cold. Had there been a note left to the effect of, I went to visit my mother, or I went to spend the weekend at Lillypond, he would have—well, he would have known. Could she have gone to stay with Che?

For a moment, he got excited. That was it! She went to visit Che! But no.

Her passport was in the house, in the red manila folder where they kept all their important documents. Their marriage certificate. The children's birth records. Social Security cards. Passports. Hers was there, next to his, acquired when they planned to fly to Paris for their fifteenth wedding anniversary but cancelled at the last minute because Asher got viral pneumonia. In two weeks, on June 15, it was going to be their nineteenth.

At eleven at night Jared called Ezra and Maggie.

"Mags," he said. "Sorry to call you so late. But . . ."

They came over. In the quiet house the three of them sat in the kitchen while Ezra made gin and tonics and Maggie made tea. "Margaret! No one is going to drink tea with gin and tonics."

They sat around the granite island and stared at each other.

"What could've happened?" said Maggie. "Maybe she got into an accident?"

"Something must have happened," said a stumbling Jared.

"Where's her purse?"

"By the front door. And no, nothing's missing, as far as I can tell. Her wallet, her car keys, her credit cards. Her makeup. Her script of *Saint Joan*. Headphones."

"Driver's license?" Maggie asked.

"Yes."

Ezra leafed through *Saint Joan* to see if there was anything out of the ordinary highlighted, marked. Jared made an irritated gesture with his hands, a defensive wrestling stance with palms flat, sweeping away pointless details off the table. "Ezra, please. But maybe she left a note and we missed it?"

They looked. They searched downstairs.

"Maybe she was run over. Maybe she went for a walk and was knocked down near Summit," Jared said.

All three went pale as they studied each other. "Knocked *down*?" mouthed Maggie.

"Well, what else could it be?" Jared didn't want to tell them he'd already called Overlook Hospital, a half-mile away, and was told that no white female without ID had been admitted to the ER on Friday. So if she *was* knocked down, it wasn't close to home.

"I think we have no choice," Ezra said finally. "We have to call the police. I mean, we can't ignore the obvious: it's nearly midnight, and she's not home."

"And hasn't been home all day."

"Well, we don't know. Who picked up Michelangelo from school?"

"He had a playdate with Tara's kids. She picked him up."

Ezra and Maggie exchanged a glance. "So she didn't show up for rehearsal," said Ezra, "*and* arranged for Michelangelo to be picked up from school?"

"How are those two things related?" said Jared.

"Call the police," said Maggie.

Jared dialed 911 but turned his back to his friends in case he lost his composure. He was perilously close to losing it anyway. To sit, to talk, to *chat* about this had a surreal quality, numbing like a Lidocaine needle piercing through his muscular lack of understanding.

"Sir," the female operator voice said, "state your emergency."

Briefly flummoxed, Jared recovered to say, "My wife is missing. Has gone missing."

"How long has your wife been missing, sir?"

"Uh"—he couldn't do the math. Did he talk to her today? No. They hadn't spoken. What time was it now? Midnight?—"Fourteen hours? Fifteen?"

"We do not file a missing persons report until forty-eight hours have passed. If your wife has not returned, please call back then."

"Forty-eight hours?" Jared was horrified. Forty-eight! What if she was hit by a car? No, no. "I can't wait that long. The children . . ."

"Are the children missing also?"

"No, but . . . can you send a squad car to my house? Detectives, maybe? I really need to . . ."

"Your address, please."

In less than ten minutes, two plainclothes officers were at his front door, flashing badges. Detectives Finney and Cobb. They were in suits, both middle-aged. Cobb was younger and stockier, his dull eyes apathetic. Finney, broad and soft around the middle, looked like he drank. It was a Friday night, and they acted as if they'd been expecting the worst, had seen the worst. What *was* the worst? Jared wondered as he led them down the back hallway past the washer and dryer into his kitchen.

He offered them a drink they declined, and then the five of them stood in the dimly lit kitchen with cream glazed wooden cabinets and soft yellow lights, with glass doors, carafés and tumblers, with under-the-counter lighting and black granite counter tops, everything organized and gleaming. Jared told the cops what he knew, which was little, and they said little as they listened. The first thing Cobb asked was: "When did you last see your wife?"

"This morning."

"The children saw her, too?"

"Yes. Like every morning. We got ready for our day."

"Who takes the children to school?"

"She does."

"And there was nothing strange?"

Jared frowned. "Like what?"

"I don't know. That's why I'm asking."

"No, there was nothing. She kissed me. Told me she was going to pick up my shirts. Hurried the kids along."

Cobb asked if Jared had called the local hospital. Yes. Had he called the area hospital? No. Cobb called Morristown Memorial himself, to learn that no unidentified women had been brought in the last twenty-four hours.

"What about identified women?" asked Ezra. Has anyone been brought in with injuries that might have limited the patient's ability to call home? Severed arms perhaps? Amnesia?

Jared perked up. Perhaps that was it. Perhaps his wife had been flattened by a small vehicle, unhurt, except for amnesia, a total loss of memory that prevented her from calling home. She came to in a fog. She didn't even know it was a Friday. She didn't know who she was, didn't know her own name. Didn't know who her husband was. Or her children.

Cobb's response deflated his musings. No unidentified females meant *no* females, not some females who had amnesia.

"But maybe she hadn't been brought in?" Jared said, hopefully. (With hope?) Was he hoping she had been knocked down, and not brought in? Just an amnesiac wandering the streets of Short Hills?

"It's unlikely, sir," said Cobb.

"My wife not being home the entire Friday, not calling, and leaving her purse, her wallet, her car keys is also unlikely," Jared said. "What else could have happened to her?"

Cobb said she could've been kidnapped. Was there any sign of struggle in the house?

"Kidnapped! Struggle!" Jared's raised voice was a small outward indication of the broiling turmoil inside him. "No, there was no struggle." He hadn't even considered it. Perhaps it was possible. She had let in—who? Who could Larissa have let into the house? "Who could have taken her? And for what?"

"People get kidnapped every day for all kinds of reasons. Ransom perhaps? Where do you work?"

"Prudential," replied an exasperated Jared. "But if someone had taken her and kept her for ransom, wouldn't they have called in the last fourteen hours? What kind of bogus ransom kidnapping is it if I don't even know about it?"

Cobb and Finney agreed it was odd. Still, they weren't dismissing the possibility, nor others by the looks of their discomfited expressions. They stood in the middle of the kitchen refusing a drink and glancing warily at each other. Jared couldn't figure out why they were studying *him*.

"So what do I do now?" he asked. "Usually I know where she is at all times. She has *never* not been home on a Friday night. I don't mean sometimes, or occasionally, or seldom. I mean, *never* not been home. Something terrible must have happened."

The rotund Finney nodded. The apathetic Cobb didn't. "Do you?" he asked Jared pointedly.

"Do I what?"

"*Do* you know where your wife is at all times?"

It took will for Jared not to raise his voice, not to take a linebacker step forward, not to lose his temper. "What does that mean? What are you asking?"

"Don't get upset, sir. I'm asking a simple question. You're at work all day, while she is here."

"She is *not* here," Jared said. "If she was here, I wouldn't be calling you."

Finally they began to jot down information about her in their notebooks. How old she was, how tall she was. Distinguishing marks? Color hair? Attractive? Yes, said Ezra, Maggie, Jared. Attractive. What she was wearing? Jared didn't know. It all depended on where she was going. Going without a purse or a wallet, he wanted to add. How would she dress if she'd gone out for a stroll, or a run? He kept coming back to that for some reason, that she'd gone out for a walk and was knocked down by a car. But . . . a woman didn't get knocked down willy-nilly in the middle of suburban neighborhoods without someone noticing.

Maybe she went out for a jog and—and what? How to complete that sentence?

—and had a heart attack and fell and died? And had a stroke and fell and died? Had a ruptured aneurysm, a cerebral hemorrhage. When morning came, if she was still not back, Jared would go look for her in the woods near the golf course.

And then Cobb spoke, to break Jared's reverie about Larissa falling down dead. "She could've been picked up by someone," he said. "Was driven out of the local area. Driven out of Jersey. To New York? To Pennsylvania? She could've gotten into an accident somewhere else. Or not." Cobb slapped closed his book. "She could be anywhere."

Jared got stuck on the first part of Cobb's words. All his earlier efforts had been jutting up against a blank wall of her vanishing. Now Cobb brought up something Jared had not considered. "Picked up by *who*?"

"I don't know, Mr. Stark," said Cobb. "I don't know your wife."

Finney coughed. "Was there any trouble in your marriage?"

"Any *what*? No! What are you guys talking about? Trouble in my marriage? What kind of trouble would make a wife vanish like this?" Jared turned to Maggie. "Maggie, is what I'm saying true?"

Maggie shook her head. "She never said a word." She paused. "About anything." Slightly she shifted in her chair. Jared noticed. Finney noticed. Ezra, who was looking down into his tense hands, noticed. "Recently," Maggie said, "she seemed more distracted than usual. It wasn't normal."

"Define recently," Finney said.

"Six months," Maggie said. She looked away. "Maybe longer."

"Distracted?" Jared said incredulously. "Six months? Maggie, what are you talking about? What does it have to do with today, with tonight?"

"I don't know, Jared," said Maggie. "Nothing? Everything? I'm just saying. She's been out of the ordinary for a while. That's what the officer asked."

"Her being distracted during your lunches when you haven't felt well for over a year doesn't translate into her being kidnapped out of her own home. Or falling down from a cerebral accident."

"What cerebral accident?" asked Cobb, and it was then that Jared realized: wait, they think *I* may have had something to do with it. They *must* think this. That's why they're looking at me like that. Like I did something to her.

Jared retreated. Literally took a step back and lowered his shoulders. His spine sloped, his mouth fell mute. There was nothing more to say. Desperate, he called the cops for help and instead of helping, they eyed him with suspicion. The raw injustice of it burned his eyes.

"My wife is missing," he said quietly, to no one in particular, wishing they would all leave his house. "You're here because *I* called you. I didn't know what to do. I still don't. Can you help me or not?"

Apparently they couldn't help him yet. But they did give him their card and told him to call and file a formal report on Sunday morning if she hadn't returned by then.

For the rest of the night, Jared sat on the sofa in the den, unable to go upstairs to their bedroom. He must have fallen asleep before dawn, though it felt as if he slept mere minutes before Michelangelo tumbled downstairs and, patting Riot, sleeping by Jared's feet, said, "Dad, where is Mommy?"

It was seven. Jared spooned some cereal into his son's bowl, poured the milk, patted his head. After putting the boy in front of Saturday morning TV, still in yesterday's clothes he walked down the driveway to Bellevue, made a shoehorn left along the golf course and slowly walked up the street, between the houses and the dewy glinting green golf course, looking for something, *anything*, that might clue him into the cluelessness. It was a crisp May morning. It smelled of the upcoming summer. The oaks had bloomed, the red impatiens were fluttering; it was beautiful, the silence of the street, the distant view of the mountains. What was he looking for? He walked the half-mile circle up to the main road, looked left, looked right, turned around and walked back down Bellevue. He found nothing. He walked again, slower. He walked the third time. When he got to Summit Avenue, he didn't know which way to go. The town of Summit was to the right, but what good did the town do him? She took no money with her! She wouldn't have walked to Summit; what would the point be? She had play rehearsal in the opposite direction. She had to get in her Jaguar and drive to where people were waiting for her. She didn't do this. Why? Jared turned around and started his fourth walk back home. It was after eight, he'd been out an hour. Tara was walking down her driveway in her robe, to pick up the paper. They lived in the large black and white Tudor two doors from the Starks. She waved.

"Good morning, Jared. Isn't it a nice morning?"

"Tara," he said, coming up to her, "have you seen Larissa?"

"What do you mean? Today?"

"Yesterday."

"I talked to her," Tara said cheerily. "She called to confirm the play date and asked if I would mind picking Michelangelo up from school along with Jen. I said of course I didn't mind."

"What time was this? The phone call?"

"Early. Nine? Maybe ten."

"Usually, would she pick him up?"

"Yes, usually. But that's okay. She said she had scheduled some errands that might run late."

"What kind of errands?"

"She didn't say. Why? Is everything okay?"

"I don't know," Jared said. "So you didn't see her all day yesterday?"

"No. Wait, I did see her, briefly."

He stopped breathing, holding Tara's words, trying to listen.

"I was running out to the car with Jess," said Tara, "and she was walking up Bellevue. I waved to her."

"Walking up Bellevue?"

"Yes, right here. In front of my house." Tara pointed behind Jared, to the street lining the golf course. "Like she does many times. She looked like she was going out for a brisk walk. But without Riot."

"Were her hands free? Was she carrying her purse?"

"Gee, I don't remember. Why? Come to think of it, I think she was carrying something, like a dark bag, maybe a duffel. Which is why it didn't quite seem like she was exercising, more like going somewhere."

"What was she wearing?"

"Oh, I don't know, Jared. I'm sorry. Jeans, maybe?"

Jared stared at Tara interminably. Tara became uncomfortable. "What's wrong? Is something wrong?"

"Larissa didn't come home last night," he said in a hollow voice. "She's still not back. I'm afraid something terrible's happened."

Flustered, Tara said nervously, "No, no, everything seemed

normal. When she called she sounded friendly, very much herself. Oh, my goodness. You think she got into some kind of accident?"

"Possibly. What time was this, when you saw her walking?"

"Not long after our phone call. Maybe 10:30? Quarter to eleven? Yes, it was probably closer to quarter to eleven, because Jess and I were going to the doctor at eleven, and I was putting her in the car. I drove past Larissa, opened the passenger window and waved to her. She waved back. I asked if she needed a ride. She said with a smile that no, she was fine. That was all. Everything seemed—"

Staggering backward, Jared had nothing more to say, nothing else to say.

At home Emily was awake, Asher still sleeping. "Em, hold the fort, okay?" Jared said. "I'll be right back."

"Where are you going? You've just come back! I have volleyball practice at eleven."

"I'll be back before then."

"Asher has his playoff game at 11:30."

"Way before then, Em."

"Michelangelo goes to art class with Mom at ten."

"Probably today," Jared said, "we will have to cancel art. We'll try again next week."

He drove slowly up Bellevue, made a right on Summit, and headed toward town. He drove up and down the local streets, drove past the hospital, drove past the library and the train station, past the diners and Maggie's Dominican Monastery. Could she be in there? Around and around he spun his wheels, circling the square of town, trying to traverse the bewilderment of the distance between himself and Larissa. What did St. Augustine say? Jared took a course on him in college; could he remember a blessed thing? *Don't you believe that there is in man a deep so profound as to be hidden even to him in whom it is?*

The streets are spotless, broom-swept clean. Not a thing out of place. Trash cans every fifty feet as required by ordinance. Flags on the lampposts. Nothing rusted or unpainted. Windex shine on all the glass in the stores, impeccable displays, cobblestones, pristine sidewalks, landscaped parks, sun shining. Everything like a picture. Like their house with the Christmas lights on and snow on the evergreens.

He didn't get back in his futility until noon, having lost all track of the hours. Emily was beyond herself. Asher, less enraged and more productive, had called up one of his friends and found a ride to his playoff game. Feeling himself a failure on all fronts, Jared scooped up a shoddily dressed Michelangelo and went to the baseball grounds downtown, where he stood blankly by the chain-link fence and when the other parents clapped or booed, he clapped and booed, while Michelangelo played on the playground, and Jack and Frank and Ted kept talking to Jared about Asher's incredible pitching arm, and the Yankees' terrible pitching. He heard none of it and all of it. He didn't know how he continued to stand. Sitting in the field bleachers, in the fifth inning, with his son's game tied and the entire season on the line, Jared called Larissa's mother.

"No, I haven't heard from her," Barbara said. "But why is that unusual? I never hear from her. Is everything okay?"

"Oh, yeah. Absolutely. Great."

"She did invite me for the barbecue on Monday. Do you want me to bring anything?"

"What barbecue?"

"What barbecue? The party you're having on Memorial Day. Jared! What's wrong with you today?"

Oh shit, the barbecue. "That's right. Thanks so much, wonderful, can you bring some of your potato salad?"

"I always do. Tell the children I have something special for them."

"They'll like that. Thanks, Barbara."

"See you Monday. Three?"

"Three is great."

When he hung up, the other team had scored four runs off Asher. Jared clapped. "Yeah! Go, Wildcats!" Except he was standing in a sea of dismal parents, who were booing and not clapping. His own son glared at him from the pitcher's mound as if to say, what's *wrong* with you, Dad?

What was wrong with him indeed. What time was it?

One.

O God.

And at home, Ezra's Subaru was in the drive, and Emily was storming out the side door, fuming, ready to castigate him, and before she opened her mouth, Jared took her by the shoulders and said through his teeth because he didn't want to upset Michelangelo, who was still in the car, "Emily, you need to look around you and see what's happening. Your mother is missing! Have you noticed this? I don't want to hear another word from you unless it's to help me. I don't want to hear about your missed games, or your cello, or your volleyball, or anything. Your. Mother. Is. Missing." He never talked to Emily like this. He left the discipline to Larissa.

"I know," she said sullenly but not particularly sympathetically. "But she's going to come back, right?" Clearly she thought whatever was happening would iron itself out like most adult things, but that her volleyball practice might have to go on without her was an irrecoverable travesty. Jared held the car door open for Michelangelo, nearly closing it on his son's hand.

Ezra and Maggie were in his kitchen.

Vacantly he told them what Tara had told him. He didn't tell them that he stood in the middle of Summit, in the middle of the street and listened to the dried-up screams in his throat. Where was she? What had happened? He was afraid they would think he was losing his mind.

When was the forty-eight hours going to be up? When could he file a report on a missing Larissa, and why would he want to engage Cobb and Finney again with their cold stares and presumptions of Jared didn't even know what. And yet, what else could he do?

Maggie and Ezra brought Dylan, who babysat Michelangelo along with Emily, while Maggie called their friends, asking them to daisy-chain the news that due to a short-lived emergency, the Memorial Day bash was being cancelled this year. She even called Larissa's mother.

"You're telling me *not* to come? But I just spoke to Jared, who told me to bring potato salad!"

"Yeah, so sorry, Mrs. Connelly. Everyone just like that fell under the weather. Larissa will be in touch soon."

Detective Cobb called at three. Had she returned? Because no one at the surrounding hospitals and precincts had any information. Cobb said once they filed the missing persons report there was a chance the FBI, suspecting cross-state foul play, might get involved.

Cross-state? Foul play? Jared hung up, his arms, his head, his eyes sore and hurting. Ezra fixed him a drink. Maggie fixed him some food. He didn't eat, he didn't drink. "I don't understand what could have happened," he kept repeating. "I simply don't understand. Is there an explanation?" He raised his eyes, his palms.

Ezra shook his head, his own palms opening, shoulders rising in rank bewilderment.

"*What* makes sense?"

"Nothing." He and Maggie exchanged a glance.

"What? What, you fear something? You suspect something?"

"I suspect nothing." Ezra took a deep breath. "But on Wednesday when we had lunch, Larissa was unusually distraught, not at all herself. She wouldn't touch her food. I didn't think much of it at the time, but I'm thinking of it now. She was asking me weird questions."

"What kind of questions?"

"Hypotheticals, she said, to help her deal with students."

"Like what?"

"Like . . . *is* there a right and wrong? How do you choose? How do you stop yourself from doing wrong? Are there absolutes in this, or is it a matter of perspective? She wanted to know about Jesus. And Epicurus."

"What's so weird about that?"

"How do you know what to do, she kept asking, if you don't believe in God? What do you draw on? What else have you got? Aside from experience, aside from common sense?"

Jared wanted to swipe all the glasses off the island. It was only through a crushing burden of his will that he didn't, remembering his small son in the den, not wanting to scare him with noise. "What the fuck are you telling me?" he asked. "Ezra, what are you talking about? What does *that* have to do with this?"

"I don't know, pal," Ezra replied. "But she was asking me for help in making tough life decisions, and now she is not here. I don't know. Perhaps it's a coincidence."

"You're damn right it's a coincidence. Ezra, you and she have been shooting the shit for twenty years. Religion, Epicureanism, principles of elocution, all you do is talk this crap. It's like verbal handshakes with you two. What you're saying is she woke up in the morning and brushed her teeth and now she's gone, so maybe it has something to do with her brand of toothpaste!"

Maggie tried to quell him. Ezra looked both deeply estranged and sympathetic. "There was a desperate quality to her questions." He looked down into his hands, balled them into fists, pressed them to his eyes.

"You only see it now!"

"She lost so much weight, man."

"She really had, Jared," said Maggie, her hand on Jared's back, patting him. He wanted to thrust himself away from her. Being touched was suddenly painful to him, unholy.

"A minute ago, you couldn't imagine what could've happened. Now suddenly she's losing weight and asking questions? And why are you talking about her in the past tense?"

Before Ezra could reply, Michelangelo walked into the kitchen. He was hungry. Maggie made him a sandwich, made everyone sandwiches. The kids sat in the dining room and ate. Asher didn't speak. Was he upset about losing his playoff game? Jared didn't know. He didn't speak himself. Jared didn't know what to say to his children. What *could* he say? All of Ezra's degrees, all of Maggie's years in public education, all of Jared's aptitude for investments had not prepared them for this, a missing mother in the middle of one's sacred life.

Somehow three o'clock became four, and four became five, and then, because they forgot to call and cancel, there was a knock on the door, and Bo and Jonny strolled in, with a bottle of wine and a dozen cannoli for their Saturday night dinner. They came in the kitchen, all smiles—evaporated just like *this* when they saw Jared's face, and Maggie's and Ezra's. Made Jared wonder who else they forgot to cancel, who else would show up Monday expecting a raucous bash in the backyard.

Maggie took Bo to a corner and (thought she) whispered, "Larissa's missing."

"Missing?" Bo said (loudly). "What do you mean?"

"What can one mean by this?" Jared said. "She is missing. We don't know how else to explain it."

There was a moment of silence. "Why didn't you call us?"

"I did," said Jared. "Remember, I called you yesterday and you said you hadn't seen her."

Ah, Bo mouthed, her brown eyes moistening. She surveyed the room in a way Jared found irksome; she remained so composed! How could one remain calm? If this wasn't the time for shouting, for flailing one's hands, when was? Wasn't there anything that wasn't sanitized, climate-controlled? All of them living in 72°F houses, no breeze, no bugs, always comfortable. The fridge at 45°F, the freezer at 37°, everything crisp and clean and glam. Ah, he wanted to groan. A guttural sound signifying uncontrolled despair. Ah.

The hands opened, someone touched his back, someone got him a beer, someone else patted him. Someone let Riot out and someone ordered Chinese because the children and the soldiers of the vanished had to eat. Lo mein came, shrimp with lobster sauce, fried dumplings. Jared, who hadn't eaten all day, took one look at the food, one whiff of the sweet soy sauce odor, and left the kitchen to void the void in his stomach. Afterward he didn't feel any better. Bile kept bubbling up to his throat.

"I can't think," he said when dinner was done and the children dispersed to be entertained by Dylan. "I can't figure it out. Like I'm missing something." Besides my wife. "Like there is a piece of the puzzle I'm not seeing." That infernal puzzle again! The missing piece was now a missing wife.

He searched the faces of his intensely worried friends, for comfort, for answers. In Ezra's eyes he saw another Epicurean attack, and snapped. "Ezra, this is not a theoretical coffee-hour discussion about materialism."

"I don't think it's theoretical, man," Ezra said grimly.

"I don't care that she was pale and without appetite. Tell me what you think. Could she have died?"

It was possible, Ezra agreed, distressed.

"Was she kidnapped?"

No one thought she was.

Perfect. Finding out what happened to Larissa by committee.

"Someone say something. What else?"

Dylan put Michelangelo to bed, and Jared put the older kids in front of a movie before someone answered his question. The person who answered him was Ezra.

"Dude," he said heavily, "is it possible she could've left you?"

"Left and gone where?"

"I don't mean that—" Ezra broke off, glancing at Maggie, as if for strength, staring at Jared for silent understanding. "I mean, *left* you."

Jared sat back in his chair. "Like up and left?"

Ezra nodded.

Now it was Jared's turn to search Maggie's face, Bo's face, Jonny's face.

"You tell me," he said at last. "Is that possible?"

After an agonizing pause, they agreed it wasn't possible.

"It's not likely," he led them. "Right? Not likely?"

After a terrible pause they agreed it wasn't likely. And yet . . . not a trace of her anywhere.

"Left me why?" Jared said.

They said nothing.

"Do you mean left me?" Jared said. "Or . . . left me for someone else?" He almost laughed when he said it. If she hadn't vanished, he would've laughed when he said it.

"It happens, man," said Ezra.

"Yes, to other people," said Jared. Bo and Jonny looked into their drinks, into their hands.

"No, I agree with Jared," Maggie said staunchly. "Not our Larissa. It's unthinkable."

"She is not here," Ezra said. "That's also unthinkable."

"Besides, I would've known," continued Maggie. "She couldn't have kept it from me. Or from Bo. Right, Bo?"

Bo nodded with uncertainty. She wanted to say something but, glancing at Jonny, reconsidered.

"Call Evelyn," said Maggie. "Call Tara. Dora. Call any one of her friends. They'll all tell you the same thing. It's not possible."

"And yet . . ." said Ezra.

"Stop it!" Maggie cried, expressing what Jared wanted to express. "Stop, Ezra! Until we know, let's not speculate. It'll just show how ludicrous you are when you're proven false." She turned to Jared. "Are you sure she hadn't told you she was going away?"

"How could I forget something like that? She runs this house. How could I forget she wouldn't be here for Memorial Day weekend, for the kids?" The kids! Jared allowed himself a small smile. "Ezra, look, even if what you're saying could be true, even if she could leave *me*, she couldn't leave her kids, could she? It's Larissa we're talking about."

"You're right about that, man," said Ezra, finishing his beer, reaching for another, reconsidering, pulling on Maggie to get up. "It's Larissa we're talking about."

They stayed with him as long as they could. But short of

staying overnight, eventually they had to go. Soon forty-eight inconceivable hours would pass without a word from her.

"She must've left a note somewhere," Jared said. "It must've blown away, or fallen on the floor, or was swept into the garbage."

"A note saying what?" asked Ezra.

"Maybe she needed to go away and think."

"About what?"

"Well, I don't know, do I?" Jared paused. Maggie left the kitchen. He heard her crying in the den, then calling for Dylan. "You really think she could've left me, Ez? This isn't how people go. They say something. They pack. They take their children. This isn't what they do."

"You're right, I'm an idiot. I'm sure there's a very good explanation."

"Ezra . . ." Jared was standing but felt like he was falling. "Left me for . . . someone else?"

"I don't know, man. I'm so sorry."

"But wouldn't I have known? That doesn't happen in a vacuum, there's no way to hide something like that. I would have known!" Jared exclaimed. "There'd be a thousand signs."

Ezra said nothing.

"What? Did you and Maggie talk about it last night?"

"About nothing else. We didn't sleep till sunrise."

"Well?"

"Well, what? Were there signs? She has been *very* distracted for months. But I do know that to do rehearsals, you've got to be completely into it to put on even a mediocre play."

"But could she have been hiding in plain sight? Behind plays, rehearsals?"

"Possibly. Maggie says for some time Larissa hasn't been engaged in her life."

"She's only saying this now!"

"No, dude. Maggie kept saying it and saying it. Something is not right, she kept saying: I'm so sick, I feel so bad, and she can't remember from one day to the next what's wrong with me."

Maggie came into the kitchen with Dylan, her eyes red, wet.

"Did you say this, Mags?"

"I did, Jared."

"But you didn't say it to me!"

"We didn't want to pry. Especially since winter, when she looked like she was having some trouble coping. We were sure you were working it out whatever it was."

They talked about this standing up, near the door, their car keys in their hands. Eventually they had to leave him, and he was again alone. Jared didn't know how he would get through another night. He heard a noise at the front door, he ran to it. It was just wind. He heard a noise at the back door, he ran to it. It was just Riot. The children were asleep, the house silent. He thought of taking Larissa's Ambien. She said it helped her sleep; it might help him. But he was afraid. What if the phone rang and he was out of it? What if the cops came, and he was unable to talk to them? What if the kids needed him and he was strung out on drugs? He couldn't do it.

Why did Larissa need to take Ambien? She said she was having trouble getting to sleep, and he didn't want her to have any trouble. When she started sleeping better, she was happier, and therefore he was happier. But why couldn't she sleep?

With the house unbearably silent, Jared sat on the couch in the den. He put on the ballgame he had TiVoed earlier, muting the sound, then turning it up to nearly full volume. He held a beer in his hands. All the lights were off except the dim ones in the kitchen, except the cold blue flicker from the TV. Riot was by his feet.

What in the name of God was happening?

She did sometimes seem a little distracted, but gently distracted, as if she were thinking about plays and lines and scenes. She would always get like that when she was hip-deep in staging, rehearsing. It wasn't unusual.

She *had* lost weight lately; it was hard not to notice. She said she was too busy to eat, always running around. In front of him a few weeks ago she ate a slice of cheesecake and a lemon meringue. They laughed about it, her becoming fluffy round like a lemon meringue herself.

She stopped shopping, stopped buying things. Was that proof of her restless heart?

Did they make love less? Jared didn't think so. Maybe a little less, he had to admit. But they were busy. Life intervened. She never asked for it, but she never refused him either. If he got busy and tired, and was sometimes too quick, too functional, that wasn't her fault, it was a product of their full life. On vacations, during anniversary weekends, in the summer in Lillypond, they more than made up for the utilitarian approach to their physical intimacy. For the last sixteen years this was how they lived, ever since the kids came. Sometimes when he looked down at her, her eyes were closed. But so? His were closed too. She was so sexy, to control himself, sometimes he didn't want to open his eyes and gaze at her. She kissed him, she did the things that good wives do. And also, she made his lunch and picked up his shirts, she made him dinner, dressed his children and bathed them, she was the perfect hostess on Saturday nights and let him watch baseball without complaining (too much). This is how she had been and that is how she was. Nothing in her recent demeanor suggested she was living a double life.

Except . . .

And it was only because he started to think about it, painstakingly raking over the grains of the days, the chaff of memory. Sometimes she really did seem more than just a little distracted. But he was a fine one to talk, stressed out about crises at work, about diminishing returns, unpaid dividends, capitalization, amortization, that he himself could barely see what was on TV unless it was a ballgame. When they sat and watched a movie, her eyes were open, she was looking at the screen, sitting close, eating popcorn, but once, a few months ago, she told Ezra she'd never seen *Zoolander*, when they had all watched it together a few Saturday nights earlier and laughed their asses off, even her.

But this was Jared projecting! Grasping at straws. Doug told him

Kate always fell asleep during movies. Was that a sign of treason? A wife who didn't open her eyes at the TV? A wife who didn't laugh at *Seinfeld*?

The money remained in their account. All her clothes were in her closet. Though how could he tell? She could have taken two pairs of jeans, a skirt, five shirts, ten, five bras, ten. He wouldn't know. It was almost summer, the winter stuff had been packed away. Her spring jackets hung in the hall closet. The suitcases were down in the basement. Her makeup and perfume were on her dressing table. Her reading glasses! She didn't go anywhere overnight without her Versace reading glasses, and they were still by the bedside. He checked.

Tara said Larissa had been carrying some kind of bag. But that could've been anything. Tara said she had been walking as if *to* something. She waved with the hand that wasn't holding the bag. Waved like how, Jared had asked. Waved like she was saying goodbye?

"Yes," said Tara. "But, Jared, she actually was waving goodbye. And I waved goodbye to her."

When was the last time Jared saw her? Friday morning. He was running late, they'd gone to bed late, woke up late; there was a direct relationship. As a result, he was barely able to kiss the kids, kiss her, grab the mug of coffee she made him, say, "G'day, fellas. Be good for your mom," and speed out the door. She waved (goodbye?) to him, too. She said, "Have a nice day, honey. Drive safe." Perhaps she didn't always say *drive safe*. Perhaps she never said it. But he was in a hurry. And she was engaged in the world around her. She wasn't distracted. She was getting milk for Michelangelo, and she smiled at Jared from behind the island. Her smile had been . . .

Again, it was only now. At the time, he thought nothing of it. Now he was animating her smile, personifying it with attributes it hadn't had. Now it seemed to him that she glistened as she smiled, that her eyes were wet, that she gazed at him longer than usual, smiled at him and studied him, as if what? As if she knew she wasn't going to see him again?

This was absurd! He had asked Michelangelo earlier. He was such a sensitive boy. Did Mommy seem different Friday morning?

"Different how?"

"I dunno. You tell me. Did she seem in any way different?"

"Nah," he said. "She seemed exactly the same. She hugged me for five minutes."

"She did?"

"Uh-huh. I was like, Mom, let go, I have to go learn something."

"What did she say?"

"Nothing. Said she loved me."

"Was that unusual?"

"No, Dad," Michelangelo said slowly. "Mom says she loves me all the time."

"Of course she does, son. And do you know why she says it?"

"Because she loves me?" he said happily, skipping away.

She hugged Michelangelo for five minutes. Her eyes looked wet when she waved goodbye to Jared, and smiled. She didn't remember *Zoolander*. She lost weight. She stopped shopping. The evidence was in, ladies and gentlemen! Clearly this woman was contemplating the unthinkable! The unimaginable.

◈

Did he even sleep? Jared didn't know. It was the second night he hadn't gone upstairs to his bedroom. He showered in the kid's bathroom and put on Asher's deodorant. He hadn't shaved since Friday morning and sported a formidable gray stubble that made him look "old and tired," as reported by Michelangelo, who was the first one up, climbing onto Jared's chest, turning on the TV, rubbing Jared's rough cheeks and saying, "Dad, did you fall asleep in front of the TV again?"

"Can you believe it?"

Michelangelo kissed him, patted his chest, climbed off, nuzzled close. "I can believe it because you're a weirdo."

Jared slept the broken shallow sleep of the anguished as his seven-year-old boy watched four repeats of *Full House*.

At ten on Sunday morning he called the detectives. After they came by, Jared spent an hour with them going over every detail he could think of for their missing persons report. They pretended not to study him as they took down the information. Except they couldn't help it; they both stared when Cobb asked him, "You sure there was no trouble in your marriage?"

"No," said Jared, in a defeated voice—because she wasn't home. "Nothing beyond the usual."

"What's usual?"

"I don't know. Occasional short tempers. Bad moods. Nothing serious. No yelling." Except for that one strange night in February when for an evening he thought Larissa was losing her grip on reality, on sanity. But that passed. It was an aberration. And it was nearly four months ago! She didn't go back to the city for the hair color, even when he tried to insist; she dismissed it, was no longer interested. Jared stopped speaking, worn out.

The cops continued to stare at him.

The husband is always the suspect, Cobb told him. That's who we look to first.

"How can I be the suspect? I was the one who reported her missing."

Husband always reports her missing. He is always distraught. He always goes on the evening news and pleads for his wife's safe return. He is always the one searching, calling us incessantly, boisterously lamenting her absence.

"Is that what I am? Boisterous? Calling you incessantly?"

You are searching.

"Are they usually found?"

Yes. The detectives said nothing after that, as if the silence was the meaningful part.

"Alive?"

No.

"Ah." Jared waited, thought it out. "Is the husband usually the culprit?"

Nearly always, Mr. Stark.

After that Jared fell silent. To find her, that would be good. Alive, even better. To prove them wrong, a corollary benefit. But that wasn't the question swirling around in his head. It was more vague, laced with torture and ambiguity and terror for his days ahead, like night covering the rest of his life.

"What if . . . what if . . ." How to say it? How to ask.

What if she is not found? Finney asked for him.

"Thank you. Yes."

What's your question, Mr. Stark?

"What happens then? In the past, what happens if months go by and the wife is still not found? Has that ever happened?"

They thought about it. Twice, Finney said.

"And?"

The husband called off the search.

"The *husband* called off the search?"

That's right.

Funny, that. Because Jared couldn't imagine doing that. And now he couldn't even if he wanted to. How could he? That's what the husband *always* did.

"Were those two women eventually found?"

Yes. Again with the laden silence.

"Alive?"

No.

Jared tried hard not to take a deep breath before he asked. "Culprit?"

"Who do you think, Mr. Stark?"

He heard that last part loud and clear. It was he who was responsible for Larissa's disappearance.

෴

At eleven in the morning, Emily came downstairs, still in her nightgown. "Is Mom back yet?"

"No." Jared didn't know what else to say. "Mommy might have gone to visit her friend Che," he added, struggling to say something that might sound like the truth. "She may have gone to the Philippines. But Che has no phone, so we're waiting to hear."

"Mom left for the Philippines without saying goodbye?" The child cut right through to the truth of things. The incredulous tone reflected the absurdity of that, the incongruity of it. "Dad, that's ridiculous."

"I know."

"So why are the police here again?"

"They came to check on things. See how we're making out. Tell me, on Friday morning when you saw Mom, did she seem out of sorts with you?"

"Not at all. We were running late. She shoved us out the door at 8:10. She yelled something that sounded suspiciously like I love you. We couldn't believe it."

"Didn't answer her?"

"No." Emily paused. "She hugged me before she shoved me out the door. *Actually* hugged me. Arms and everything. Kissed me on the cheek. I said, Mom, don't be so strange. What the hell is wrong with you?"

"She tried to kiss me, too," said Asher, strolling into the kitchen. "But I wouldn't let her. It's just not done, Mom, I told her. Mothers don't kiss their fourteen-year-old sons. Don't you know anything?"

"Then we ran off," said Emily.

"Yes," confirmed Asher. "We were late."

They glanced at him, three little pauses by the island. They looked hungry but didn't want to ask about the Sunday brunch Larissa always made. Jared poured cereal out of the box. Under duress, he agreed to toast a bagel for Emily, who was sick of cereal. As it turned out, they didn't have any bagels. Jared drove to get bagels at Bagels4U. Everything about Summit felt wrong to him this morning, as if . . . as if every road and every store hid the clue of what had happened to Larissa, except he didn't know which road, which store, and was forced instead to wander the streets like a bum until he somehow fell into it, lucked into it.

While he was waiting for the bagels, he remembered the psychiatrist! Larissa had been going to the woman since February. Surely, she would know! She'd know something. Reanimated, vivified, Jared flew home to call her, dropping the bag of warm bagels on the island, except the children wouldn't let him drop bread on the island as if they were ducklings by the pond. He had to toast the bagels, peanut butter them, jelly them, and only then could he pick up the phone—and only then did he realize he had no idea what the doctor's name was. Oh, Larissa had told him, but it was in one ear, out the other. But there were insurance and co-payment bills. Her name must be somewhere.

With black coffee in hand, the first bit of sustenance he had had since yesterday, Jared painstakingly went through Larissa's medical records back to January. There were two bills from visits to Larissa's ob-gyn, one for pupil dilation from the optometrist, and a stack of bills from the psychiatrist. Joan Kavanagh. He didn't care that it was Sunday. He dialed her number—and got her answering service.

"Is this an emergency?"

"Yes," said Jared. "Yes, it most certainly is." He left his own number, and then sat by the phone for fifteen minutes, for thirty, waiting for the callback. After 41 minutes, he called back.

"I passed on the message," the operator said.

"Did you say it was an emergency?"

"Yes, sir."

"I guess a psychiatric emergency works on a different schedule than a medical one, huh?" Jared said. "Because forty-one minutes—"

"I'll pass on your second message, sir," said the operator.

So he sat.

He had to come out of his office to look in on the kids. It was a Memorial weekend Sunday, warm and sunny. Asher, who hadn't even asked for the sleepover he had been planning for weeks, had gone for a bike ride to his friend's house. Emily was playing ball with Riot and Michelangelo. Jared went back to his office. Maggie called, Ezra called, Bo called, Jonny called, Larissa's mother called,

Evelyn called. The worst conversation was the accidental one with Larissa's mother.

"Is she feeling all right?" asked Barbara.

Jared didn't want to lie, but he also didn't want to talk about it. Why did he pick up the damn phone? "Barbara," he said, "I'm sorry, but the other line is calling, very important phone call."

"On Sunday, a very important phone call?"

"Yes, I'll—don't worry, we'll—I'll—"

The doctor still hadn't called. Forty more minutes. He went to the kitchen, looked inside the fridge. Kavanagh was a doctor; perhaps she was at her country estate. No one worked on Memorial Day. She was away. She could be out of the country. Jared went through Larissa's purse while he waited. He went through her wallet, pulled out all the recent receipts, looked through them. No supermarket receipts, no drug store receipts. On Thursday there was a receipt for filling up the gas tank. Fifteen gallons of juice. No reason to fill up the car if you were leaving it in the drive the next morning and footpedaling down the highway. He found a receipt for sushi at Stop&Shop. *Sushi?* Yet this is what the receipt said. Stop&Shop in Madison. Sushi.

Larissa hated sushi. Never ate it. Now she was buying sushi at a supermarket in Madison, not even in Summit?

Zoolander, sushi, kissing the kids on Friday, "*drive safe.*" What did it amount to? A hill of beans?

But she wasn't here! She wasn't here . . .

Jared held her suede patchwork purse in his lap, sitting behind his desk. It was remarkable how little there was inside it in terms of purchases. Rather, in terms of receipts. The purse was clean, the wallet clean. But Jared was an investment banker. He had been watching receipts for bigger fish than Larissa. He knew that one way or another, following the trail of money would lead him somewhere.

He went online to check the purchases on their American Express account. Other than gas, there was little else. He clicked to see which gas station she used, what time she gassed up. It was at the

Exxon station on River Road, once a week, around 8:50 a.m. Like clockwork. He went back seven months. Once a week, at the same gas station. Which wasn't the station closest to home, the one they always used, where she filled up her Escalade on the weekends. He checked the day of the week. It was Mondays. He went on Google Maps to see the station's location. It was on the way to Madison. He checked the location of Stop&Shop. Madison. And the shrink was also in Madison.

He sat, he waited. He thought. He threw on his jacket, took Larissa's Jag, drove to Exxon. The man who came up to his window was smiling at him with a friendly familiarity that vanished when he saw it was not a woman driving the Jag. "Can I help you?" he said.

"This car belongs to my wife," said Jared, taking out her photo. "You know her?"

The man didn't have to glance at the picture. "I know her well. She comes here all the time. You need gas?"

"Not today, I'm all set," said Jared. "Does she come in this car, or the other one?"

"I've only seen this one."

"So how long has she been coming here?"

"Oh, a long time. I don't know."

"How long would you guess?"

"I don't know, I told you. Maybe a year. Maybe more. Sorry, another customer behind you. Do you mind?"

Jared didn't mind. Slowly he pulled into a parking spot and sat rubbing his stubble.

What was it? His heart, his fear was getting in the way of his reason. Was there a connection between the missing wife and the unheard-of sushi from a supermarket, the fuel from a gas station they never used?

He sat for ten minutes, his hands on the wheel. Then he drove to Madison, to Dr. Kavanagh's office.

She wasn't there on a Sunday, of course. Much of what he was doing felt like an exercise in futility. But what other option did he have? Cobb said the FBI might have to get involved. He said it as if Jared should be afraid of it, but all Jared could think of was, when? Why not get involved now, immediately? Immediately was Sunday afternoon on a sunny day in May. His kids alone in the house while he stood outside an empty doctor's parking lot ringing the bell. That was immediately.

As he drove back, he tried to visualize Larissa. Was she hurt? Damaged? Was she gone, as in gone, gone? Did it feel to him like she'd had a stroke and fell where she was walking and never got up? No. It didn't feel like that. What it felt like was more incomprehensible than a freak aneurysm, but also more frightening. Because what it felt like was not chance, but design.

❧❧

What was Che's address? Jared wished he knew it by heart. But he didn't know much by heart, except the details of his investment funds, mortgage rates, differential dividends. All the information he carried in his head was on a strictly need-to-know basis. In any case, Larissa's passport was in the drawer! Che lived in the Philippines. And why would Larissa fly to the Philippines and not tell him, not even leave him a note? Hi, hon, I won't be long. I'll be back for Asher's graduation from middle school.

He had to put Che out of his mind. Larissa couldn't fly to the Philippines without her passport. That's all there was to it.

Then where was she?

What day was it when he got back from Kavanagh's parking lot? Oh God. It was still only Sunday.

He called Cobb. "We have no new information," the officer said. "It's only been two hours since we saw you."

"Since we filed the report, maybe," said Jared. "But she's been gone since Friday morning. Have we checked the hospitals again? The police blotters? Any reports of a woman who's hit her head?"

"I haven't checked all the police blotters myself personally," said Cobb. "But we checked the bulletins from the precincts in the Tri-State area. This includes Connecticut."

"Nothing in the bulletins?"

"Hundreds of things. Just no information about a fortysomething brown-haired woman."

"With blonde highlights." Jared hung up despondently.

Why was being at home waiting like this so unbearable? Why couldn't he do something with the kids? Maybe throw a baseball to Asher. But Asher just pitched a loss in his playoff game. Last thing he wanted was to see a baseball. Maybe go to the park? To Canoe Lake? Maybe pack up, take everyone to Lillypond? No, that was impossible. What if she came back? What if there was some news?

Came back from where?

What kind of news?

He called Kavanagh a third time. "I will pass on your message, sir. She will call you back at her earliest convenience."

"This is an emergency," Jared said, his hands unsteady, his voice cracking. "A real emergency. Please."

Another hour passed in despair.

Emily went over Alyssa's house. Asher went over James's house, taking his guitar. Michelangelo sat with Jared at the island, pretending to look at the news in the paper. "Daddy, so what do you want to do?"

"I don't know, bud. What do *you* want to do?"

"We can go play catch. Or you can take me on the swings. Or we can play go fish. I love that game. Wanna play? Or I have some awesome black Model Magic clay. It really is like magic. And it's black." Michelangelo grinned. "We can sculpt a vampire for Halloween."

After a full minute of thinking, Jared said, "Halloween is five months away."

"Never too early to get started on the decorations," said Michelangelo. "That's what you always say, Dad."

"I'm not always right, bud."

Jared watched his son mold the soft and pliable black clay into something resembling a head, with arms growing out of it. To do a cape, or white fangs, or blood rolling down the chin, that wasn't possible. The vampire looked like a bird. A nightingale.

The phone rang. Jared dived for it. It was Ezra. "We're coming. We're bringing dinner."

"No. Yes. I don't know."

"It's not a question. We'll be there in a half-hour."

"What time is it?"

"Three."

"Three!" What was happening? Why did time stop moving? Why was it that usually he couldn't get time to stand still, couldn't slow it down a millisecond, to sit at night, to dine with friends, to prolong his climax, to read the paper, one extra day on Miami beach, and now it stopped moving? Not just slowed down. Stopped. "It can't be three," Jared said numbly. It had been three all day.

Bo and Jonny came over too, brought snacks, drinks, paper towels, paper plates. They brought milk, bread, cereal. Maggie took Michelangelo into town for ice cream, and to Bryant Park. Asher came in, then back out to play miniature golf. Emily came home and baked some store-bought brownies she found in the cabinet.

The phone rang. It was Cobb. "Just wanted to confirm—you said you didn't find anything missing? Credit cards? License? Other ID? Money?"

"She never carried any money," said Jared, his temples throbbing. Maybe sleep is what he needed.

"Sorry, I know it's rough. It's Memorial Day weekend, everyone's away."

Yes, Jared thought, pressing OFF on the phone. *Everyone* is away.

∽৽⌒৽

Jared didn't know how he got through Memorial Monday. Because Ezra and Maggie and Bo and Jonny didn't leave him alone for a moment, that's how. They brought food, games for the kids, bats, gloves, Frisbees, balloons, tried to make it as normal as possible, put music on to drown out the noise in Jared's head, took care of everything. Ezra barbecued, though Ezra didn't know how to barbecue. They fed Jared, though he didn't eat, and they fed his kids, who were all, except for Michelangelo, walking around as if they were shell-shocked. Asher had withdrawn nearly completely. Even Riot was sleeping on the deck by Jared's feet instead of playing with the kids.

"You're going to have to talk to them, Jared," Ezra said. "You're going to have to say something." They were sitting outside on the patio while the kids were in the hammock deep in the backyard.

"Say what? What can I possibly say? I don't know anything!" He stood up, his legs unsteady.

That Monday night he went into Emily's room. He couldn't have a conversation with his sons, but Emily was a girl; he was hoping she'd go easy on him.

"Em, things have been upside down around here," he began, perching on her bed.

"You don't say." She half-turned from him; then, thinking better of it, sat up, hugging her knees. She wouldn't look at him.

"Look, I wish I could tell you what's happening. I'm sorry I'm so clueless."

"Don't be sorry, Dad. Your cluelessness is one of the things we love about you."

"The police are looking for your mom."

"But we don't want them to find her, right?" She looked at him hopefully. "Because that would mean that something really bad happened to her."

"You're right, Em," said Jared. "We don't want the police to find her. I'm hoping that Mom just went away to be by herself for a while."

"But why?"

"I don't know."

It was Emily who reached out and patted him on the shoulder. "It'll be okay, Dad," she said. "Everything will be fine."

Jared swallowed. Cleared his throat. Wished for a glass of water.

Wished for a lot of things. They sat for a few minutes in heavy silence. "In the meantime, we've got to hunker down."

"No kidding. But, Dad, what are we going to do? I don't mean . . . mean, *actually* what are we going to do? We've got stuff every day till the end of school. Who's going to drive us?"

"I'm taking a few days off work while I figure it out. I'll drive you. Maggie said she will come and help us. I'm sure your mom will come back any minute. But you're going to have to help me, Em. I haven't done this. I don't know when or how or where. And please—don't expect me to remember. Because I won't. Just write it down on a piece of paper. Stick it into my hand. Tape it to my car keys. Do whatever it takes."

"When are you going to go back to work?"

"I don't know. We'll see."

"But, Dad . . . don't you need to get paid?"

He almost smiled. "Maybe they'll pay me anyway. I've been working so hard."

"Don't use up all your vacation time," Emily said wisely, like a miniature Larissa. "We want to go to Lillypond."

It's remarkable what happens when your heart is no longer attached to anything else in your body. Things you never thought you could say, you say. Things you never thought you could hear, you hear. Things you never thought you could do, you do. As if you're walking through a darkened museum of a silent demonstration of someone else's ancient life, and in the back of your mind, you're thinking, in one minute, I'll be outside in the sun, and out of this black morass, and I can't wait for that. Thank God this isn't my life. That's how Jared felt as he got up and kissed Emily good night and shut her door.

He called in sick on Tuesday, saying he had to deal with a personal matter. Just today? the CEO, Larry Fredoso, asked him.

Jared wanted to say till September. But he didn't. "Let me have this week, Larry," he asked. "Okay? A very serious personal matter. Then we'll talk again."

How *could* he go into work? He couldn't even face the mirror to shave. In any case, Michelangelo needed to get to school by 8:10. Jared didn't even know where the school was. He had to look up the address on Mapquest.

"Mom doesn't drop me off here, Dad," said Michelangelo, peering out the Lexus window. "She parks the car on the road up here, then walks me down."

"She doesn't just let you out of the car?"

"No, Dad." The boy sighed.

So Jared parked the car up on the hill and walked Michelangelo down to the school. "Not these doors, Dad."

"But all the kids are going through those doors."

"Those are the kindergarteners. Sheesh. What grade am I in?"

And Jared didn't know. "First?"

"Dad! Second."

"Of course. I knew that. Sorry, bud. You're my little buddy. I can't believe you're in second grade already."

"Only for one more month, and then I'm in third."

"Wow." He brought him to the correct doors. Michelangelo waited. Jared looked at his son. "What?"

"Mom always kisses me."

"Oh." Jared bent down and kissed his son's curly head. "Bye. Have a good day."

"You, too." Michelangelo waved without turning around. "Don't forget to come get me at 2:40 sharp."

"I won't."

"Don't be late."

"I won't."

And afterward? He couldn't go back to his empty home.

He drove to Kavanagh's office in Madison. He passed by the Stop&Shop, remembered the sushi, became physically distressed, drove trembling through the little town, past the college on the left, forked to the right onto Park Avenue and once again pulled into the empty parking lot of a small white house before St. Elizabeth College. The doctor wasn't in. Jared opened his windows, and sat waiting.

From the parking lot he could see the road and the passing cars; they hypnotized him, the cars one after another, motorcycles, buses, zooming past, thirty, twenty, forty-five miles an hour, it was a Tuesday morning, windy, rustling green, almost June, and the road was provincial, yet busy, and so he sat and thought about nothing, and everything. The Ferris wheel at the local fair, where he let Larissa and Michelangelo ride by themselves while he stood at the bottom and waved each time they swerved past, and the flan Ernestina brought to his house that Larissa left for him because she knew how much he liked flan, and the color of the Jaguar in his garage, like the color of her hair, subdued and elegant, flashy in an understated way. Like her. Busboys clanging their dishes at the Summit Diner, dropping his grilled cheese sandwich last time he needed to have the inspection on his truck and he went and waited, thinking ahead to the evening, to dinner. It had been warm, and the summer was coming, and the birds were loud. Almost like now.

Were straitjackets always white? Did they pin your arms behind your back so you didn't hurt yourself—and them? Did you spend 28 days in the sterile bin, or did you stay there until someone else other than you decided you could leave? And who decided? And who decided if you should be committed in the first place?

When he first met her, she was the hippest chick on campus. She wore her hair long and brown, she wore no makeup but very short dresses and her legs stretched abundantly like flamingo pins, she was natural, yet complex, the sight of her made him want to quote Byron in the middle of a Wednesday afternoon. *She walks in beauty, like the night, of cloudless climes and starry skies.*

She draped over student union sofas drinking ceaseless cups of black coffee as she presided over the Footlight Players. Her face gleaming, she was tyranny with a smile. She told them what to do, how to play it, what to say, and they did it, they said it. They followed her blindly, listened to her agape. Whenever she was indoors she was always barefoot, she said she liked to feel the ground under her feet, and he wondered how she kept her soles clean, but when they started dating and he asked her about it, she stared at him squarely and said, "I wash them. How do you keep *your* soles clean?"

"I wear socks," he said.

He pulls into a gas station, and pulls out a gun. With heavy gasps he robs the till and runs and then is chased the rest of his days by the toothless man who exacts revenge in the form of paranoid, drug-fueled terror.

Was that a movie? A nightmare? Was that his life?

Was this his life?

Now he counted cars that flew by, none of them stopping here. Was Larissa in one of those cars? Not in her own, but in another car?

Another's car?

Everyone is the star of his own life. But she was the star of everyone's life.

She was easy on the heart, easy on the eyes. She was the hitchhiker with the contagious laugh. She got into the car of his life and rode with him, and just as suddenly got out, flashing her breasts and her whites and was gone.

Was she the sideshow?

Was he the sideshow?

Memories like acid.

Ten o'clock, eleven.

At noon, a large gray Mercedes pulled in and a wizened bird of a woman got out. By the time Jared slowly scrambled out of his truck, he felt he was not the same person who had opened the windows three hours earlier.

Warily she looked at him heading over to her in the parking lot. "Can I help you?"

"I don't know," Jared said. "I've been calling you non-stop since Saturday. I said it was an emergency."

"I'm terribly sorry, I was away for a few days. Is everything all right?" She frowned at him. "Who are you?"

"I'm Larissa's husband," Jared said, watching her face intensely. It was almost poker-like. Except for the three quick blinks, a zeroing in on him, a honing in, a sharpening of the wrinkled features, a breath before she spoke.

"What's happened?"

"She's vanished," said Jared. "She didn't pick up our youngest child from school on Friday. She wasn't there in the afternoon. She hasn't been home since."

Kavanagh was still clutching her purse. She slammed her car door. "Did she leave a note?"

"What kind of note?" said Jared. "She could be lying dead in a ditch after a brain hemorrhage. What kind of note do you leave for that?"

Jared hoped that she took pity, because after a brief *pitying* glance at his wretched face, she said, "Come with me. Come inside."

"Do you know where she is?" Jared said in the parking lot. "I don't want to come inside, because I'm afraid you're taking me inside to tell me to sit down, and I don't want to sit down."

"You're very perceptive as to my motives," said Kavanagh. Was it Jared's twisted imagination or did she place just a little too much unnecessary emphasis on the *my* in that sentence? "My next patient is not till one. I thought we could talk for a few minutes."

"Why can't you just tell me where she is?"

"I don't know where she is, Mr. Stark."

"Then why would I want to come inside?"

"You wouldn't," she said, nodding slightly. "But it's hot, and I'm not as young as I used to be. I'm sixty-seven, and not much of a fan for standing in the heat. I get easily winded, easily exhausted, and I have a full day today. I want to be fresh. By all means, don't come in. I hope the rest of your day will be better. I'm sorry about Larissa."

She started to walk toward the door of her office building. Jared followed her. "You don't think she is dead? Why don't you think so?"

"Mr. Stark," said a no-nonsense Kavanagh, her gravel voice hardening, "either come inside with me so we can talk, or have a good day. But don't engage me when I've asked you not to engage me."

Reluctantly he followed her inside, and she walked straight, without turning around, almost as if she knew he would.

The office hadn't been aired in days. It was stuffy, musty. The central air had been turned down to a minimum. Already shallowly breathing, Jared felt like he was suffocating. *Actually* suffocating. His chest was tight. He asked Kavanagh to open the windows. She started to protest about the AC, but then saw him gasping and relented. He stuck his head outside, to gulp the air.

"What's happened?" he asked dully, straightening up.

She put down her purse, took off her light gray jacket, cleaned her gray-rimmed glasses, tiny like the rest of her, and sat down, scrunching up into a small hard pretzel. She said nothing.

"What, you can't talk to me?"

"No, I can."

"Is this about some doctor-client privilege?"

Kavanagh smirked. "A little knowledge can be a dangerous thing, Mr. Stark," she said. "No, this isn't about some doctor-client privilege. First of all, this isn't a court of law and you are not the Feds. I assume and presume a crime has not been committed, but even if it was and you were and a crime had been, there is no doctor-client privilege in the United States. Marital privacy, yes. But no doctor-client privilege exists for my legal protection, or for Larissa's."

"So why are you reluctant to speak to me then?"

"I'm not reluctant," she said. And nothing else!

"Do you think she is dead?"

"Anything is possible," said Kavanagh. "But I don't think she is, no."

"So where is she?"

"I don't know."

"Is there *anything* you can tell me? Besides I don't know?"

"Is there anything you can tell *me*?"

"I don't know anything! I came home Friday, and she was gone!"

"What did she take with her?"

"Nothing. Not a thing. Not even her car, not her purse. Nothing."

"Money?"

"No, no money. She didn't carry cash on her, and no unusual amounts of cash left our account in the last few days, few weeks." Jared held on to the narrow windowsill, shallow of breath. "You're asking about the money because you think she was planning to go?" he asked weakly. "But she took nothing with her!" He didn't—or couldn't—ask the follow-up question. *Why would she go? Why would she want to?*

Why did Jared, with his limited perception, his bewildered mind and exhausted body still feel that this expressionless woman knew things she didn't want to tell him?

"She's been coming to you for months. She never told me why she needed to come. She just said she needed to talk to someone, and I accepted it without argument, without too much worry. She said she wanted her head clear. There was a day in February when she seemed to have trouble coping with things. She said she felt anxiety, sometimes got depressed. It seemed normal."

"*Did* she seem normal, Mr. Stark?"

Jared intertwined his fingers in a knotted twist. "Doctor, I beg you, don't analyze me in hindsight. Don't get me to discover what I clearly have not discovered. Just tell me what I need to know. I can't play these games. Can't and don't want to. I just want to know what's happened in my life. Friday at four o'clock it was one way, and one hour later it was another. What's happened?"

"Only in your perception, Mr. Stark," said Kavanagh, "has the change been that sudden. I assure you, your wife's miseries have been continuing for some time."

"What miseries?" he cried.

Kavanagh said nothing.

"You don't want to tell me?"

"I don't," she admitted.

"But she's vanished!"

"I can see," Kavanagh said, fighting for her words, "that this is deeply upsetting to you and—"

"Please—don't euphemize what I'm feeling," Jared said. "Don't cover up my agony with your psychospeak. Just tell me. What? Was she suicidal? Was she having an affair?"

"Yes," said Kavanagh. Like a slap.

It was almost as if he had been expecting it. When the blood rushes away from the heart and the lungs, it's easy to remain sanguine, because you've got no life to react with.

"She was?"

"She was."

"Is that what this is all about?"

"I suspect that since she's not in your home, it might be."

"So she, without saying anything to me or to the children, just up and left without so much as taking her purse?"

"That gives me hope that perhaps she hasn't gone far," said Kavanagh.

"Who was it?"

"I don't know."

"What, she spoke to you about it, but never gave you any details?"

"It was some man she had met."

"Met where?"

"Perhaps on her daily errands?"

"What man, what errands?" Jared was still by the window, grasping the sill with his bloodless hands. "This isn't what happens," he whispered. "This is *not* what happens. There's a confession. A revelation. The spouse begs forgiveness. The husband is loathe to give it. There may be a separation, followed by counseling. There are reparations, a period of mutual gloom, a blackness in the house. Everything seems pointless. They decide whether it's worth staying together. Many times they decide it is. They try to work it out. What has happened here that is so far from that truth?"

Kavanagh mulled her words. "Sometimes a confession is so

threatening," she said, "that most people would rather go on being deceived."

"Not me."

"No?"

"No!" Jared glared at her. "No," he repeated emphatically.

The doctor shrugged in acquiescence. "Perhaps had there been a discovery by you, that's what would have happened. Or perhaps something else would've happened, and she was afraid of it." She paused. "My guess is that's what will still happen. This could be her way of confession, and revelation. When she returns it will be followed by the other things you mentioned."

"She seemed exactly the same!" Jared exclaimed. "She did everything like always. She was beyond suspicion." His voice got lower and lower. "She was a good wife. This makes no sense. It can't be. I don't believe it's true." His voice got louder and louder. "What you're telling me is not possible. That is not my wife."

Kavanagh said nothing.

"Was she unhappy?" asked Jared. "Did you ask why she didn't talk to me?"

"She wasn't unhappy," the doctor replied. "She said she got herself in too deep."

Got herself in too deep. What did that mean? "Did she . . ." An incredulous Jared couldn't get the words out, ". . . *love* him?"

Kavanagh looked into her own twisted hands. "Yes. She said she did."

Jared's legs weakened. The draining of blood, the evisceration going on inside him made it difficult for him to stand. He took a few shaky steps and sank into the hard chair by the window.

For a few minutes neither of them spoke. "I'm very sorry," Kavanagh said. "I tried for months to get her to talk to you, to look at her life in a different way. Your wife loved you and the children very much."

"How could you tell? Do her actions speak louder than her words?"

"She got in over her head. She thought she'd be able to continue living a double life."

"How long had she," Jared asked in a dying voice, "been living a double life?"

"When she came to me," said Kavanagh, "she said she'd already been involved with him for a year."

Jared drooped flaccid against the back of the chair. *How long?* he mouthed inaudibly. Kavanagh didn't respond.

They just kept on coming. One after another. Gasping to stave off shock, he hyperventilated into his hands; he covered his face. "Are you telling me she was having an affair for eighteen months and I didn't know it?"

Kavanagh said nothing.

"Who was it?"

"She never said."

"Was it one of our friends? Was it Ezra?"

"Ezra?" Kavanagh frowned. "*Your* best friend?"

"No, *her* best friend."

"No."

"What, you think *that* would be beneath her?"

"I don't know. I know it wasn't him. In any case, is Ezra still present in your life?"

"Yes, of course."

"Well, then, she is not with him."

"No, but . . ." He raised his head. "Maybe she was so distraught over what was happening that she killed herself?"

"I don't think that's likely," said Kavanagh. "Have the police looked into it?"

Jared started to shake, from his effort to think, to get his heart to pump again. His lips trembled. "She could've drowned. We may be looking for her in the wrong place. What if she couldn't deal with it anymore, and left us, and him, and ended her own life? Somewhere we haven't been looking." He said this with the fiery excitement of a man on electro-shock therapy, all twitchy and disconnected. "I mean, that's *possible*, right?"

Kavanagh conceded it was possible.

"There! At least . . ." He broke off. "We'll need to broaden our search, widen our efforts." He had to look away from the doctor's slowly blinking raisin eyes. "Did she tell you his name?" He jumped up.

"I don't remember."

He was pacing frantically. "You didn't write it down in your little notebook?" He stopped in front of her.

"Do you see a notebook? And no, I didn't write it down. She did tell it to me once."

"So? What was it?" He clapped his hands together, half a dozen times, like applause during an intermission. "Come on, come on, come on. You must remember."

"I mustn't," she said. "Sit down, Mr. Stark."

He went back to pacing. "I can't. What was his name?"

"It was a weird name, not usual. Not a name I heard before."

"Unusual, like . . . Ezra?"

"Not Ezra."

"Jonny?"

"No."

"Fred? Richard? Tim? Jeff? Bob?"

"Bob is unusual?" Kavanagh thought about it. "But short like that. Like a clap. One syllable. Bob. Bob. Bob." Thoughtfully she clapped her hands together, trying to remember and then glanced at Jared. "Why do you want to know who it is? Is that going to help you?"

"If she's not with him, that's helpful, no? Then we know my theory is correct, something terrible's happened to her. Can't you remember?"

"No."

"What about now?"

"Don't badger me, Mr. Stark." She kept clapping her hands.

"Kai," she finally said. "It was Kai."

Oh my God. The car dealership! That salesman he hated from the first time he saw him. Oh my God. But he . . .

"No, that can't be. That's wrong," said Jared, shaking. "That kid was barely out of high school."

Kavanagh said nothing.

It was like Jared was hit by a fastball in the temple. She flamed up, burned through, settled down into her betrayal, over the course of sixteen, eighteen months, seventy, eighty weeks, six hundred days, mornings, nights, and all the while he lived his life, worked, slept, made love to her, as if things were normal. He felt sick. He started to retch. He was sick in the wastepaper basket.

"How old was he?"

"Twenty-one."

As he staggered out of the office and drove blindly down the street, Jared knew this wasn't Kavanagh's fault, but he wanted to blame her. Eighteen months! He couldn't imagine what he would say, but it didn't matter. Creativity in action always followed rage.

It was Tuesday nearly 1 p.m. when he stormed into the Jaguar dealership. The receptionist, a vacant-looking chick with braces said, "Can I help you?"

Wild-eyed he searched the floor. "I don't know if you can help me," he said. "Is Kai here?"

"Who? Oh, Kai. Um, no. Unfortunately he, uh, he doesn't work here anymore."

"What? Where's the manager?"

"Jim?"

"Yeah, whatever. No, Chad. He around?"

"I think so. Let me page—"

But Jared was already walking to the business office in the back, where four men stood behind the counter, having sandwiches for lunch.

"Hey," said Chad who had recognized him. "How you doin', man? Everything cool with the car?"

"What car? Oh. Yeah, absolutely."

"So how can we help?"

"Is your salesman here? Kai?"

"No, sorry. He quit. But Gary can help you. He's excellent."

"Quit? Do you know where he went?"

"I don't. He just said he had to be movin' on. Salesmen come and go in this business. He was a young kid. He stayed a lot longer than we thought he would. What a tremendous salesman. Actually won a Jag for himself. We haven't had that happen in seven years. Traded it in, got some dough, then quit."

"I knew we should've never traded it in for him. He'd still be here."

"Well, how could we not trade it in? That's ridiculous."

"Yeah, but now what are we going to do? Our sales will be in the toilet."

"We're temporarily screwed. We gotta get someone else as good."

"No one's like him. And I'm a salesman twenty years. Takes a lot for me to admit that."

Chad and Jim suddenly turned their attention back to a waiting Jared, head lowered, fingers gnawing the counter, his own palms. "Um, everything all right? Can we help you with something else?"

"Yeah. Does he live around here?"

Chad became less friendly. "What's this about anyway?"

"Not much. Just have to ask him a quick question. I gave him a copy of my tax records. Turns out I misplaced the original. Wanted to see if he could make a copy for me."

"Your tax return from *last* year?"

"Yeah. Don't have it." It's a good thing they'd forgotten he was the CFO of an investment bank.

"Well, he didn't leave anything in his desk, if that's what you mean."

"You don't happen to have his cell, do you?"

"We do, but he turned off his service. We tried to call him ourselves this morning."

Jared took a step back, turned around, walked away. The receptionist became friendlier when he stopped at her station and pretended to chat with her. He was inventing small talk on the fly; it was like learning English.

"So he left, huh? Bet you miss him around here. He was good, right?"

"He was the best," she said wistfully smiling, all metal braces, name-tagged Crystal. "He really was. He was so fun, and great with the customers. We went out a couple of times. I was sorry to see him go. We all were."

"He didn't say where he was going?"

"Nah. He didn't talk much about his business. He just said it was time to start movin' along."

"Strange, right? He was so successful," prodded Jared.

"Oh, he was," said Crystal, lowering her high-pitched voice to a dog whistle whisper that grated on Jared like a tree saw on metal. "We all think something major was up. He didn't get another job, he just left." She raised her painted eyebrows. "In a hurry."

"He probably got a job at the BMW dealer down the street."

"Nah. We know those guys. He's not there. Kai would've told me."

"Well, he has to pay his rent somehow. Doesn't he live around here?"

"Yeah, right on Albright Circle, a block or two away."

"Albright what?"

"Here, let me check for you . . . I have his records in the computer . . . here it is. Albright 12. I just sent his last paycheck there on Friday."

"He didn't come in for his paycheck?"

"No. Thursday was his last . . ."

Jared was already out the door.

Twelve Albright was a large old yellow house. He couldn't imagine a young kid living there unless it was with his mother. He parked in the front, knocked on the front door, knocked again loudly, waited.

She came to the door, an old woman in a housecoat, awake but barely dressed, her hair gray and mussed.

"I'm looking for Kai," Jared said.

"Who?"

"Young kid who lives here? Kai."

She shook here head. "Not here no more."

"What do you mean?"

"I mean not here no more. Paid me till the end of May, then split last week. Just like that. One day here, moved out the next."

"When was this?"

"Right before the long weekend. Paid me and split."

Jared couldn't stifle a tortured groan. The landlady looked at him funny.

"Do you know where he went?" he managed to ask.

She shook her head. "I don't ask. He pays me my money, I don't ask nothing."

Unsteadily Jared took out a picture of his wife. "Have you seen this woman around here?"

She squinted. "I don't have my glasses," she said. "There *was* one woman who used to come by here. Drove a sports car."

"What color?"

"What color woman?"

He grabbed hold of the railing. "What color sports car?"

"Oh, I don't know. Some funky thing. Non-descript. Like the color of water."

"I see. Thank you."

"Do you want to see the place?" she said. "Maybe rent it?"

"I don't—" But how do you pass that up? "Yes. If you don't mind."

"I don't mind," she said. "I'm Mrs. Sinesco. Who are you?"

"Jared."

Slowly she came down her stairs and they walked around back to the gravel lot. "What did he drive?" Jared asked.

"He had a motorbike," she said. "Very flash. Hid it in the garage. Loved it like a child. Bathed it every Sunday." Slowly she made it up the stairs. "I used to tell him, Kai, you gotta love somethin' else in your life like you love that bike, and he would say, why do I gotta? Gotta paint these again," she muttered, going slow, lifting her legs, clutching the chipping wooden railing. "Paint's peeling bad. Sorry about that. If you move in here, I'll paint for you. I'll give you a discount on the rent if you help. What did you say? Speak up, because I can't hear too good."

Jared was lifting his own legs slowly, clutching the railing. "I didn't say anything," he said. He crawled up the stairs like old deaf Mrs. Sinesco.

She opened the door and he walked in to the sunlit room, large and wood-floored. The place was furnished, and the brass bed stood at the wall between two windows where the white curtains fluttered. The bed was freshly made. All the personal things were gone. The bookshelves were empty, the open fridge turned off. He stumbled around, even peeked in the bathroom. All was gone. Not even a smell of her remained.

"I cleaned it real good," Mrs. Sinesco said. "Lots of bleach. To get it ready for the next tenant. It's a nice open room, don't you think? A good bachelor pad for someone."

"Yes." He grabbed on to the door.

"You okay? You want to rent it? A thousand a month."

"I'll think about it."

And he did think about it.

∽∾

But he couldn't think about it too long, because he had to race from Albright Circle to make it to Michelangelo's school by 2:40. He was a few minutes late. Both the teacher and Michelangelo glared at him. "We've never met," said the teacher. "I'm Mrs. Brown."

They shook hands. He took his son's hand.

"So will you be picking him up from school from now on?" the teacher asked.

Jared tried not to stutter. "I don't know," he said. "Maybe."

"Because pick-up is promptly at 2:40," she said.

"Yeah, Dad," stage-whispered Michelangelo.

When they came home, Jared immediately went into his office. He slumped into his chair and . . .

"Dad? What are you doing?" Michelangelo was standing in front of his big polished cherry wood desk.

"I don't know, bud. What are *you* doing?"

"Well . . . I'm standing here. I need a snack. Then another. And a drink. I need my show put on. Then we do homework. What day is today?"

"Tuesday."

"On Tuesday Emily has to be picked up with her cello from school and driven over to her lesson."

"Where's her lesson?"

"I don't know. But I have karate at 4:30."

"Where's that?"

"I don't know."

"Where's Ash?"

"Well, he *was* playing baseball, but I guess now he isn't anymore. So he'll be walking home."

"Okay." Jared dragged himself up. "What do I do first?"

"Feed your son, Dad."

∽◦∾

The next morning after dropping off the boy, he went back to Kavanagh's.

"You really should make an appointment," she said when she opened the door to her waiting room. "I have patients all day."

He waited three forty-minute sessions for someone to cancel. And then sat in the room on the couch for ten minutes before he was able to speak. "Is this where she sat?" he asked.

Kavanagh pointed to the other end of the couch. Jared remained where he was. "The guy left, too," he finally said. "Quit his job, moved out. They're not here anymore." Which seemed almost right, because he didn't feel her here. From the beginning, Jared felt her resolutely absent from the geographical sphere that had made up his past life.

Kavanagh said nothing.

"I think something terrible may have happened," he said.

Kavanagh said nothing, but raised her brows in a faint question, as in, *something worse than this?*

"Yes. I don't think she went with him. She left her ID behind. If someone is leaving for good, wouldn't they take that?"

Interrogatively the doctor shrugged.

He put his face in his hands. "She could've drowned herself in the Passaic," he said, his voice muffled.

Kavanagh said nothing.

He lifted his gaze to her. "She could have."

"She could have," agreed the doctor. "Is that what you want?"

"You know what I want? My wife back. My life back." Jared squeezed his hands together. "Why didn't you say something to her? Why didn't you say to her, you can't do it. Why did you tell her what she was doing was okay?"

"Just the opposite. I never said it was okay. She hated me because of it."

"Why didn't she tell me? Like other people."

Kavanagh mulled his question. "And what would you have done, Mr. Stark, had you known?"

"I don't understand! Who does this? Who leaves without a word or a note or an explanation? I don't know a *man* who does this!"

Kavanagh nodded. "It *is* awful. But these things burn out. Give her a week or two. I think she'll come back. This is why she left without taking anything. It's a temporary thing. She'll come back."

"Who'd take her back!"

Kavanagh stared at him and he looked away.

"How funny it is," Jared said at last. "When you imagine it sometimes, on the drives home, you think you'll never forgive it, never be able to live with it. But now I'm not so sure. I can't face my kids, I can't go back to work, I can't talk to my friends. I've lost my life. If she came back, I don't think I would even question it."

"I know," Kavanagh said, her voice full of heavy-hearted sympathy.

"How can you be so sure she didn't kill herself?"

"She didn't seem the suicidal type."

"There's a type?"

Kavanagh gently stared. "Of course." Shrugging, she made a motion with her hands as if she were bringing a cigarette to her mouth. "He's a young kid. She is a woman with children. They'll wake up soon enough, come out of their dream. It won't last."

"Nothing lasts," Jared said. He had to stop speaking.

"Yes. Not even the way you feel right now. Not even that." But Kavanagh was wrong. The way Jared felt lasted.

∽⌁∾

Was he responsible for this, by wanting to get her a car?

"Jared, don't be ludicrous," said Ezra, after the fiftieth fruitless conversation about the hows and the whys. "How could you be responsible for that?"

But again Jared got the feeling that there was something, some accusation that Ezra was not voicing. Ezra could've been distracted by the crisis going on in his theater department, since the director of the play opening tomorrow was absent for dress rehearsal, final stage prep, the dress rehearsal dinner, absent without explanation, to the great detriment of the cast and crew, who were in panic mode, especially Megan, who, without Larissa's stern voice and firm direction could not raise authority for her pliant Joan. Ezra told him that he said Larissa had had to leave on emergency family business and wouldn't be back for a while, but Jared, staring at Ezra glassy-eyed, said, "Ez, I don't give a shit about the play. Can you understand?" So Ezra stopped talking about it, but this might explain the hostility in Ezra's voice when discussing Larissa's disappearance. Perhaps he was angry at Larissa for ducking out on the last theater event of the school year and making him look bad. It was so inconsiderate.

"Are you listening to me, Ezra?"

"I'm listening, Jared." It was late Wednesday. Ezra came over after the dress rehearsal that he said went terribly. Ezra himself was pale and gaunt-eyed.

"I mean," Jared asked, "was she perfectly content, and then one day met him? Is that what contented people do? Implode at the slightest provocation?" He told Ezra everything about Kai except the salient thing, the appalling thing—his mortifying age.

But there *was* something else, Jared thought, as he got Ezra a Corona and some chips and salsa left over from Memorial Day. Jared wasn't remembering it accurately. He had to think back, but finally it came to him. The conversation at the dinner table.

He didn't mention Jag to Larissa. He wasn't even thinking Jag. He was thinking of something half the price. She was the one who said, "Jag?" Which meant she must have already known that kid, known that he worked there.

But still—she didn't bring it up. *He* brought it up. She never hinted, she never said, oh, wouldn't it be nice to get a Jag, she didn't in any way plant the idea inside Jared's head. That was all his doing. He was driving to work one morning, thinking of what special thing to get her for her fortieth birthday and he was smoked by a red Firebird, so close it almost hit his Lexus truck, and first he swore under his breath and then a light went on, and he said to himself, wait a minute! That's it! I'll get her a sports car! A car for youth, for beauty, because she is beautiful and deserves it. She's always driving the kids around, and the Escalade is filled with candy wrappers and old homeworks and melted crayons. I'll get her a car in which no kids will be allowed, a car that only she or I can drive, and we'll feel like we never felt when we were twenty, because then we had nothing. But look at what we have now.

"Forget the Jag," said Ezra. "If you didn't get her a car, she would've gone there pretending to shop for one. Once the possibility was open to her, she would've figured out a way. The thing of it, man," he continued (another day? Another conversation? Or the same endless one that followed the same endless day?), "you're looking at it wrong. It's not: how could it have happened when things were going well, it's: it could never have happened when things were going badly. It's all about the struggle. Without it, the organism falls into disrepair. It's all over the animal kingdom. And in the human kingdom, the organism falls not just into disrepair but despair. And the worst is when it 'lives' and doesn't even *know* it's in despair. When it doesn't even know to look out the window, or to question its own self, or read for discovery or take up art. Striving is the condition required for all life."

Jared heard and didn't hear, listened and yet not, understood, and yet didn't.

"We didn't stop striving," he eventually said. "Our life was busy. We had a thousand things to do every day."

"For seven years that's what she did. That's a lot of days staring out onto the golf course while picking up the kids' toys."

"I don't know what you're saying. Peace is good. Struggling is bad. Worry, anxiety, they're bad things."

"Clearly the organism doesn't think so," Ezra said gently.

"Ezra, you're full of shit. Read any self-help book. They all say the opposite. Peace of mind is all they talk about, serenity."

"Has it helped? How are all those books working out for us? Are we helped? Are we at peace, serene? Have we learned to let go of our fears? Not to worry so much? Where have all those books gotten us?"

"Where have your books gotten you?"

"Nowhere," admitted Ezra.

"So what's the answer?" Jared whispered.

"The answer," said Ezra, "is perhaps in that question alone. With or without books, with or without faith, how do you become a worthy keeper of your immortal soul?"

"Ezra, do you have any answers at all?"

"None," the red-tied man replied. "I don't even know if I'm asking the right questions."

"You're asking the wrong fucking questions," said Jared. "As always, you're making this an intellectual exercise, hiding behind your books, when something real is going on that you can't deal with, can't help, can't solve."

"It's true," said Ezra, lowering his head. "I can't deal with it. I can't believe she would do this. This is how I hide. Maggie hides in other ways. What do you do?"

"I don't have the luxury of hiding," snapped Jared. "Michelangelo has karate in twenty minutes, and Emily finishes volleyball at five. I have to go."

"Will you come to the play?"

Jared glared at Ezra as if his friend had twelve Medusa heads.

Maggie asked Jared to come to the monastery with her on Sunday morning.

"You know, Maggie," Jared said bitterly, by way of raw refusal, "in the very beginning I was afraid she was dead. The fear was like a sickness inside. You know all about that. So I prayed. Dear God, anything. Just don't let her be damaged, suffering, kidnapped, dead. Please. *Anything.* That's what I prayed for. That's right, Mags, *don't* look at me. And isn't it nice to know that even without going to Sunday lauds, there is an interventionist God who answered my fucking prayers?"

∽◡Ꮕ

Barbara had called him on Monday, Tuesday, Wednesday. Finally on Thursday, after he brought the kids home with McDonald's for dinner, Jared, afraid she would drop in unannounced if he didn't pick up the phone, picked up the phone.

"Jared!"

"Everything is fine, Barb. How are you?"

"What are you doing home so early?"

"I took a day off today. So what's going on? I was just running out . . ."

"Can I talk to Larissa? Isn't her play on this weekend? I wanted to drive in and see it. Can she leave a ticket for me?"

"What play?" said Jared.

"*Saint Joan!*"

"Barbara . . . she won't . . . I'm sorry . . . she won't be at the play, she's had to drop out . . . what? She didn't tell you? Yeah . . . sorry about that. You can still come, but we won't be there . . . oh, she's not here at the moment, she just stepped out . . . may I take a message?"

"What are you, a hotel operator? Dropped out of the play? For heaven's sake, why?"

"She'll call soon, explain it all, I'm sure."

"I'm not going to hold my breath. Don't forget to give her the message."

"Course not."

That was Thursday, seven days *after*.

∾⌿∽

But on Saturday, what Jared feared happened. There was a brusque knock on the door around lunchtime, and Barbara, impeccably dressed as usual, strolled in. Michelangelo ran to her. Emily and Asher waved hello from the den. Emily had a recital for WWII vets at Calvary Episcopal in a few minutes. Asher had band practice. Jared was about to drive the older kids and then take Michelangelo to Old Navy to buy him some summer shorts. Everyone was in flux, and Barbara had the knack, not just today, but always, of intruding at the least opportune time. There was a period in their early marriage, before Hoboken, but after the arrival of Emily, when Jared and Larissa were so broke and jobless that they had to live with Barbara in Piermont. Jared loved the proximity of the grand Hudson River, loved the small town life, loved Orange County, but both he and Larissa agreed that no visual esthetics could ever again outweigh the stress of living with your mother-in-law, even temporarily. "Not just any mother-in-law," Larissa had said, "but *my* mother."

"Hello, children," Barbara said, hugging the smaller boy.

"Hello, Grandma. We were just leaving."

"Where are you going? And where is your mother?"

Emily glanced desperately at Jared, who shook his head, and said, "She's not here."

It was Michelangelo at Barbara's hip, who gave away the farm. "She hasn't been here since like last year," he said, time sands shifting. Is that what it felt like to him, Jared thought, stepping forward and pulling the boy away from the imperious gray-haired woman who had straightened up and leveled a cool look at her son-in-law. Jared had always suspected he didn't measure up. But then Larissa all her life suspected much the same: that she didn't measure up. Which was odd; who did measure up then?

"What do you mean, she hasn't been here?"

"Mommy's gone," Michelangelo said. "The police are looking for her. Dad too."

There was a slow-motion moment of silence. No one moved, no one blinked, no one spoke. Jared felt that it wasn't because they didn't want to, but simply because the digital camera of life went click, and was still processing the image and they were stuck in it, frozen, while the little round clock timer whirred and whirred.

Ah, there it was. The moment before—and the moment after.

"Jared . . . ?"

"Barbara, everything's fine," he said. He didn't want to panic the kids. "Come in the kitchen. You want some coffee? Em, take Michelangelo upstairs and dress him. We're going out."

"Dad, we have to go in fifteen."

"I'll be ready," he said to her. "Will you be ready?"

With a roll of her eyes, Emily rolled away.

Asher, without a word, walked upstairs to his room.

In the kitchen, Barbara turned to Jared. "I don't want any coffee."

"That's fine," he said quietly. "Because I wasn't going to make any."

"What's going on? You said everything was fine."

"Everything is fine." Jared didn't look at her. "No one knows what to think. She's not here. Sort of mysterious, I admit." He shrugged, tried to appear casual, failed, he could see, by the panicked look on his mother-in-law's suddenly old-looking face. Well, she *is* old, Jared thought. Nearly eighty. But, boy, is she feisty. Drives herself everywhere. Dresses well. Perhaps this is what Larissa would have looked like in old age.

"Jared!"

"I'm sorry. What?"

"What are you talking about?" Barbara put her palm on her heart. "What's happened?"

"I don't know. No one knows. No one has seen her since Friday."

"Oh my goodness! She must have been in a car accident!"

"That's what we thought. But . . . her cars are here."

"In someone else's car!"

"Hmm. The police are looking into that."

"Since *last* Friday?" She held on to the island. "Over a week?" When Jared didn't answer, she pressed for more. But he didn't have more. Certainly nothing he would tell her. "If they haven't found her yet, they're not doing a very good job looking," she finally declared.

"I agree." Jared told Barbara all he knew, that Larissa's purse was still at the house, giving the *impression* of an unexpected departure, or perhaps of an imminent return. She didn't mean to go, he wanted to say.

She just did.

How he wished he hadn't gone to see Kavanagh. Hadn't gone to the Jaguar dealer. Hadn't gone to Albright Circle. How he wished he was still in the dark and blind. If horses were wishes.

Barbara sat for five minutes slumped on the bar stool. Emily came down, Asher.

He had to drive his kids, Jared told her; did she want to wait? He didn't want her to. His relationship with her had been cordially strained. He never spent more than five minutes with her without Larissa present.

That was a good way to describe most of his adult life. Not five minutes of it had been spent without Larissa by his side.

Leaving Barbara in the kitchen, he drove Emily to the church, and she said, "Dad, why can't you stay? This is a public performance." But she had so many of them, and there was only one of him. They should have thought it through, got Barbara to come and listen, but they didn't. Silent conflict played on Jared's face, and Asher got out of the truck with his guitar, and said, "I'll stay, Dad. Don't worry. I'll stay, and then I'll just walk to James's house. It's five minutes from here. I'll be fine. Let's go, Em."

Clearly, Michelangelo would have no summer clothes, ever. Jared parked the truck on the street, and they all went in and sat in the pews, while the string quartet and the Summit high school choir played melancholy for an hour. Afterward, Asher walked to James's house, while Emily went over Jemma's. Jared took the cello and Michelangelo back home.

By the time they returned, Barbara had already cleaned the kitchen, the living room, the den. She cleaned like Larissa. Methodically. Or was it right to say Larissa cleaned like her mother?

After putting last year's swim trunks on Michelangelo, Jared threw him in the pool, and made iced tea for Barbara. They sat outside and watched the boy and Riot swim. It was warm, sunny, nearly 90°F. Jared himself didn't have any tea. The normal things had gone from Jared's life.

But as he sat across from Barbara, surreptitiously glancing at her, trying to study her without her noticing, he wondered: what is it about this woman that had made Larissa turn into the woman she became? Barbara and Larissa had always seemed polar opposites. Larissa was warm, funny, quick with the joke, unmeasured, natural, nice. Barbara was proper, respectful, no-nonsense, dry, serious. They both had a calmness, but Barbara's brusqueness was replaced in Larissa by a smiling affability. Barbara kept everyone but the children at arm's length, while Larissa kept no one at a distance. The thought of that pricked him, pierced him in the place from which he felt and breathed, like air was being let out of his lungs. That's right. His crunching jaw set against his teeth. She kept *no one* at a distance. And with his firm face, he examined his mother-in-law for clues.

What was he looking for?

Finally Barbara could no longer ignore it. "What are you looking at me like that for, Jared?" She frowned haughtily.

He leaned forward in his chair, his hands clasped. "I'm trying to understand what's happening."

"You're trying to figure out how I'm responsible?"

Jared said nothing.

"You silly boy," she said. "I've got three sons all older than you—I can call you this. You silly boy. Haven't you figured out yet that her whole life Larissa has been grappling with the same question. How to blame me."

"Blame you for what?" Jared asked. "She was wonderful." He clenched his fists. "And she had a good life. Why would she blame you for anything?"

"Why are you referring to her in the past tense?"

Jared wasn't about to answer.

And she didn't answer him. "Blame you for what?" he repeated, but his lungs had deflated. He couldn't speak anymore, his anger deflated also.

After five minutes of stunted silence, Barbara spoke. "What can I do? How can I help?"

"Do you have any idea where she could be?"

"Of course not. Why would I?" She put down her empty glass. "You know she didn't confide in me. Even if something was terribly wrong, Larissa always pretended that everything was fine. Her whole life she did this. Inside turmoil, but on the outside, all smiles and neat clothes! That's why I didn't know she was failing science, and Spanish, didn't know she was involved with a bad crowd in high school, until one of them got arrested for shoplifting in a supermarket and another attacked by security dogs while trying to steal drugs from a walk-in clinic. What, you didn't know this? You know what else I didn't know? That she loved theater. No interest in it in high school, and suddenly she's majoring in it in college. I should've known she was all about the drama and secrets. About pretending to live outside society's rules while doing the traditional thing. How she adored that false Romantic dichotomy."

"What are you talking about?"

"You two eloped! Wanted to do things your own way. You weren't going to be dictated to. But you eloped to get *married*—can't get more conventional than that. Traditional rebels you were—and thinking only of yourselves. You didn't even give me an opportunity to participate in a proper wedding of my only daughter."

"You misunderstand," stammered Jared. "We were broke, and we didn't want you to spend the money." He said it guiltily. He had never been okay with it.

"You let her rope you into that?" Barbara said. "Selfish! Selfish. To deny me the pleasure of seeing my only girl be married. To deny your own parents seeing their son get married. *I* didn't misunderstand. *You* misunderstood your role in your own life and in the life of your family. And you wonder why I've always been terse with the two of you. You let her connive you, convince you into running away."

"Stop it." Jared wanted to get up, run away himself. "Stop it! What does that have to do with this, with anything?"

"Well, according to you, nothing. Because you're still not making the connections. That's fine. One day, perhaps you will. You will see that it has everything to do with your current predicament." Barbara stood up. "Stop looking at me like that. I have no answers. I don't know where she is. I don't even know who she is." Lightly she touched his shoulder, and he didn't recoil. "The woman you think you know could not have done this. Yet she's not here. *That's* the trouble, my boy. *You* don't know who Larissa is either."

2

All Things Under Heaven

It took Jared two weeks to locate Ernestina's number. Two June weeks during which he went back to work and pretended everything was hunky and dory, and coordinated with Maggie about Michelangelo and Asher's band and Emily's all-State concert at the high school at which she was first cello. Maggie couldn't pick up Michelangelo every day because she had to be at the hospital for tests, and Jared spent his evenings calling Tara or some of the other class parents, asking them if they could keep his son for a few hours until six o'clock when he got home, and to everyone he said, "Larissa had to leave on some family business. Really hate to impose." He would've put the boy into afterschool Milk and Cookies program for working parents, but with the year ending in a few weeks, the option was closed to newcomers. "Perhaps in September, Mr. Stark?" said Joan, the program coordinator.

"Oh, I'm sure I won't need it then," he said. "But thank you."

Dinner was the hardest thing. When you don't cook for twenty years, merely pretend you cook because you fire up the grill and put the burgers on, which someone else seasoned and shaped into patties, it's a rude awakening to have to every single relentless day think about what to make for dinner for five finicky people. Take-out is what you make. Chinese, Indian, Thai, Mickey D's, diner food, Chinese again.

Jared didn't know Ernestina's last name, and she wasn't in the Rolodex; Larissa must have thrown out her card when she let her go. Jared found it in a box of Christmas cards from four years ago. And only because Ernestina's card said, "Merry Christmas from the Lopez Family." But because she ran a company called Lopez Professional Clean in Millburn, Jared was able to find her in the Yellow Pages.

"Mister Jared, I no know where she is," said Ernestina when she called back. "I so sad she fire me. I no hear from her a long time."

It took Jared ten minutes to explain what he needed. Mrs. Jared had gone missing. Did Ernestina remember anything strange about her last few months? Did she see anything, hear anything, out of the ordinary?

"No, everything was okay, Mister Jared, nothing was wrong. That's why I so surprised she fire me."

He spent another five minutes of trying to make the highly nuanced clear: not something wrong with you, but something wrong with *her*. Was she amiss? Did she do strange things?

"She did no strange things, Mister Jared. She good to me, she good lady. She never treat me bad till the day she fire me."

Five more minutes.

"Sometimes," said Ernestina, "she would take long time to get ready."

That was Larissa.

"And I would say, you sure look nice Miss Larissa to go to supermarket, and she would say, well, you never know who you gonna run into, Ernestina. But she always look real nice. That's all."

Ernestina didn't remember any phone calls, anyone coming to the house.

"The only other thing I notice," she said, "is that Miss Larissa stopped talking to me about cleaning this or cleaning that. One time I broke a Christmas figure and she didn't care. One time I forgot to clean shower curtains, she didn't care. She stopped asking me to do extra stuff. She always pay and say thank you, house looks beautiful, even when my girls did something wrong. Not like before."

When Jared hung up, he wondered what to make of that. Larissa was absent-minded about cleaning? It was hard to fault her on this; Jared didn't even know how much they paid Ernestina.

A few days later Ernestina called back. "Mister Jared, I remember something I want to tell you."

"Yes?" He jumped off the bar stool in the kitchen, his hand held on to the corner of the island. It was eight in the morning—Michelangelo was pulling on him to go. He gestured sharply to his son to stop and turned his back, to hear Ernestina better.

"Right before we got fired, one of my girls, she clumsy a little and she knock over a wooden box on top of Miss Larissa's dresser. She was dusting and she—"

"Yes, yes?"

"Well, a lot of cash fall out on the floor."

"What fell out to the floor?"

"Cash."

"Like *money*?"

"Yes, Mister Jared. *Lot* of money."

"How much is a lot?"

"A *lot*. I didn't count, I start helping Cindy pick it up, and Miss Larissa come in, and she upset with us, like, what are we doing? Maybe she thought we was stealing or something, but I been with her for six years, I don't take a penny that don't belong to me."

"She knew that, Ernestina."

"Yes, but it was very next week after that she fire me."

Jared remembered Larissa had said to him she thought the girls were stealing. But he recalled her saying "jewelry." Not cash. She wasn't a cash kind of girl.

"What kind of money?"

"Fifties, hundreds. I never seen so much cash in one place. She told me it was her Christmas tip fund."

Jared had hung up. He was racing upstairs.

"Dad!"

"One minute, son!"

"We're going to be late!"

"Yes, we're going to be late." He slammed the bedroom door behind him.

The large wooden box stood on Larissa's dresser, given to her years ago as a birthday present by Maggie. It was light wood, painted ornamentally with pastel flowers. Maggie painted it herself when she was in her stenciling phase. Jared held his breath, set his teeth, and opened the box.

It was empty. There was not a penny in it, not even on the bottom, under a business card for a hair place, a business card for a podiatrist in Sparta, a $20 receipt for a water gun from three years ago, and a ticket stub from a movie they had gone to see before Michelangelo was born and they were still going out to the movies. There was no money in it.

Michelangelo. The boy was waiting downstairs, his backpack on, his shoes and jacket on.

They were forty-five minutes late to school that morning. Michelangelo was so mad he wouldn't even let Jared kiss his head before he stormed tardily down the hall.

After Jared came home, he searched every drawer in her dresser, every nook in her closet, every pocket of her jeans, every book on her shelf. There was no money squirreled away anywhere. The phone kept ringing, but he ignored it. It was work. He'd forgotten to call in. The excuse he mouthed to Jordan the receptionist when he finally did call was pathetic. He emailed Larry so he wouldn't have to hear it in person. Sorry. Family emergency. I hope to be in tomorrow.

He went online, opened their bank account, checking and savings, and pored, poured himself into every transaction in the last twelve months, every single day. He found nothing that said unusual. She had taken out money to pay the cleaning people. A hundred here, a hundred there.

There was nothing in the account that said the wife was taking *other* money, ulterior money, money she could not explain withdrawing. Yet the wife was earning money. For a year she got paid a few hundred dollars a week from Pingry. The direct deposits went straight into their joint account. Every paycheck was accounted for. There were no justified parallel withdrawals of cash, in crisp clean fifties.

He drove to Bank of America in Summit.

Diane came out from her desk to greet him. "Jared! Long time no see." She smiled, smartly dressed, friendly, attractive. She'd been a young mom; now had a daughter in college. Jared had helped her with financing advice a while back, and after that she went out of her way to help him with a deposit, a withdrawal, increasing the overdraft, anything he needed. Personal service every Saturday morning.

Well, he needed something today.

Diane, he asked her, do you recall my wife coming in, a month ago, maybe two, and taking out a large amount in cash? Did she have a separate account that maybe I don't know about? That made him run cold, made him sit down. What could he do? He had to ask. He had to know.

No, Diane said, a worried look on her face. As far as I know, there was nothing. But let me check, okay?

She got him a drink of water while she went into her computer. No, look, just the one account you've had since you moved it over from our Hoboken branch. Checking and savings all tied up.

Nothing else?

No.

She didn't come in here and withdraw large sums of cash?

No, said Diane. Except for the international money orders we wrote for her every few months, for five hundred, a thousand dollars to her friend in the Philippines, Claire Cherenge.

Yes, that I know. Anything else?

Like what?

Well, I don't know.

Hang on, Diane said, reacting to his visible distress. Let me go ask the girls.

She came back five minutes later with Beatrice by her side.

Beatrice says, said Diane, that she remembered Mrs. Stark coming here a little while ago and changing a lot of small bills for some large ones. Changing twenties and tens for fifties and hundreds.

Beatrice called over the other teller, Missy. He'd never met either of them before. They looked young and new.

Missy confirmed she had also changed small bills for large bills for Mrs. Stark.

When, a month ago? asked a pale Jared. Two months?

A few times, said Missy, said Beatrice, a dull din in his ear. Beatrice said she saw Larissa after tax day on April 15, because she remembered teasing her about it. "I asked her if this was her tax refund, and she laughed and said it was her Christmas tip money."

Missy said the last time she changed money for Larissa was a week before Memorial Day. "She said you two were going to Atlantic City for the long weekend. She said she was feeling lucky."

"Do you have a record of these transactions? How much did you change for her?" Jared managed to ask. "Over the course of last year?"

Beatrice had to go check her records on the account. When she came back, Jared could tell she didn't want to tell him. He didn't want to ask.

They both said nothing.

She hemmed and hawed. The three women stood over him, like hushing hens, their skirts trying to protect him. From what?

Finally, after clearing her throat for the fortieth time, Beatrice said, "Altogether, thirty-seven thousand dollars, Mr. Stark."

How much? he mouthed numbly, shocked into muteness. The hole of her disappearance almost diminished because the hole of the quantity of that figure swallowed it this morning at the bank. He had to hear Beatrice repeat it. He didn't trust himself. He thought he had misheard.

She repeated it.

He had not misheard.

"But that was all together," Beatrice said hastily. "That wasn't all at once. She came in at least three times. Maybe more. Three were in the last four months." She stared into her piece of paper. "One right before Memorial Day. One right after Tax Day. And one back in February."

"Are you telling me that my wife came in here to exchange thirty-seven thousand dollars in singles and it didn't set off any bells in anyone's head?"

"It was in tens and twenties, Mr. Stark," said an anxious Diane. "I'm sorry. We didn't think much of it. We are a bank. This is what we do."

"She didn't withdraw any money?"

"No. Except for the money orders to the Philippines, no withdrawals."

Jared wanted to get up, but he didn't trust his legs. He felt ridiculous sitting in front of three conciliating women. He didn't know how long he was in a trance, but when he blinked reality back into his eyes, three bank tellers were standing looking at him with great financial pity. Poor man, the dollar signs in their eyes read. His wife took tens of thousands of dollars out of their joint account and he didn't even know it. Something else, too. If someone took fifty bucks out of my account I'd know it, their expressions read. Imagine living a life where forty grand can go missing and you don't even know it. He wanted to say to them: imagine living a life where a whole wife can go missing and you don't even know it.

He pulled himself up to turn away from the last thing in their gleeful uncomprehending glances: I wish I had that kind of life. No misfortune wouldn't be worth that.

He needed a cane to walk out of the bank. He didn't have a cane. He hobbled like a man crippled.

When he got home, he went into his office until 2:40. For four hours he pored over every withdrawal that dripped out of their account in the last fourteen months. He paid the bills, her Visa bills, the American Express, the Mastercards. He paid it all. On the charge cards, there was not a single cash advance, not one.

In their debit account, there were no unusual cash withdrawals, but there were "point of sale" purchases almost every day. Point of sale was the supermarket and the drugstore. Point of sale meant that as Larissa paid for the soap and the shampoo and the quart of milk with her debit card, she asked for *cash back*. Every day. For up to fifty dollars a pop. On some days there were two point of sale purchases.

$57.14.

$394.07.

$98.53. What mattered is that they were *all* over fifty dollars, which meant that conceivably Larissa could have easily taken $37,000 out of their account, and perhaps more. Took fifty to a hundred dollars a day, and he didn't even know it.

He became stuck on this. And then unglued by it. He felt perilously close to losing the center of his very being.

This wasn't an impulse buy, an impetuous running away. This was a premeditated attack on his life by his wife. For over a year, Larissa planned her escape. She got a job, got paid, but without drawing attention to herself she siphoned money out of their account, hid it, exchanged it, prepared. She planned all along to take those fifties and leave. For a year!

That was the look on Finney and Cobb's middle-aged veteran faces. They'd seen it all before—death, kidnapping, murder. They'd seen this, too. Which is why they hadn't pursued him as a suspect. He kept calling her a missing person, while they stared at him skeptically. Now he knew. Their expressions read: you *sure* your wife is missing? Maybe to you she's missing. But to her, maybe she's exactly where she wants to be.

He wasn't a suspect. He was just poor schmuck Jared.

Ever think of that, Mister Jared, as you sit and count other people's money for money.

He told the police none of his findings. Not about the Jaguar boy, the bank, the cash. He told them nothing. He wanted them to find her.

He wanted them to find her so he could kill her.

$\sim$

A manic, maniacal Jared, looking for he didn't know what, turned Larissa's wardrobe upside down, threw onto the floor every scrap of stupid crap she hoarded in her dresser drawers and went through it meticulously like he was looking for a way for Prudential to save three million dollars a quarter in operating costs. That's when he found Che's letters from the last two years and while waiting for 2:40 to come, he read them all one by one, ending with the last cry for help from a desperate and pregnant Che.

Dear Larissa,

I'm out of options. I'm so sorry. I can't believe I'm asking you for this. Please. Please, I beg you. Could you ask Jared to lend Lorenzo and me the money for his bail? We will spend our whole lives paying you back, but please, could you ask your Jared to send me the money so I could free my Lorenzo?

Ask him to help us. Beg him to help my unborn child.

The Tasaday, Larissa! Mindanao! Leaving my baby, running away, getting Father Emilio to vouch to the government for Lorenzo when I know I'm asking him to vouch for a man who plans to run out on that fifty grand and never be seen again. What's going to happen to me?

Larissa, I was wondering if I can come stay with you? Maybe you could send us a plane ticket and me and the baby can come and stay with you for a little while? Can you do that? I'll be safe with you and I'm not safe here.

I'm so scared. All these years I thought I was wild and free, and it turns out I'm neither.

I can't imagine running out on Lorenzo. It's like leaving him to be torn apart by wolves. To stand trial for something he did

*not do on purpose, to go to prison! How can I abandon him? He
needs me.*

*I won't be able to leave my baby. But I can't leave Lorenzo
either.*

Oh my God, Larissa. What do I do?

*Please write me. I need you, I haven't heard from you in ages.
I'd call you, but I have no money. I was kicked out of my house.
We hadn't paid the rent in six months. My baby is a week overdue.
Even she doesn't want to be born into this loony bin world. Father
Emilio feeds me these days. I eat with the nuns. I live with the
nuns. Where would I be without the intercession of His daughters?*

For a second after reading it, Jared was filled with a crazy hope that
Larissa took the money to pay for Che's boyfriend's bail. How absurd
that was. The cash back program began long before Che needed a
large sum of money.

Before he could clean up, it was 2:40. And at 3:30 Emily called
from the high school asking to be picked up with a bathing suit
and towel in hand and be driven to the Swim Club in Chatham.
Michelangelo wanted to go, too. Jared sat mutely by the side of the
pool while Michelangelo doggy-paddled in the deep end, every five
seconds yelling, *daddy look, daddy look.* Asher called when Jared was
still poolside and asked to be picked up with his amp and guitar.

He took the wet kids and the dry kids to an air-conditioned
diner, while at home, the things on the floor remained. Jared didn't
know what to do with the bits of paper, old receipts, with Che's
letters. Where is the place of organization in your house where you
might file for future use letters from the best friend of your wife who
has evaporated like morning fog? No good place in anyone's house
for something like that. Filed under: things that must not ever be
thought of again.

∼⌒∽

Also these: like satanic daily rites of ceremonial disembowelments,
Jared on a daily basis was assaulted with the hari-kari reminders of

his current condition. This is the passageway to hell, and it doesn't end, despite what Dr. Kavanagh professes. She is wrong; this is the dank narrow hallway of your present life.

Rite 1: he went in to Dr. Young's in town to fix his glasses that got loose, and Young's wife, also a doctor, said to him, "How does Larissa like her new glasses?"

"What new glasses?" asked Jared. He thought everyone in town had heard the news about him. Clearly not everyone. Didn't anyone maliciously gossip anymore, so he wouldn't have Larissa's name pulled out of a small-talk hat like that?

"Oh, her new Prada reading glasses. She said one pair was not enough, she was always leaving them by the bedside. So she got herself another pair to carry in her purse."

"She did. Of course. I must've forgotten. Refresh my memory. When was this?"

The female Dr. Young checked her records. "In April. They were deep gold. Very attractive. Come on. You must've seen them on her face?"

"I have. They're quite nice." His hands grabbed the glass counter. "Are we done with the repair?"

"Yes, almost."

This was never going to end. Dr. Young chuckled. "Larissa told me you'd never notice. She said she could have a diamond encrusted tiara on her head and you'd say, did you do something different to your hair?"

"That's me," mouthed Jared. "Not very observant." He extended his trembling hand. "Can I have my glasses now? I'm in a hurry."

Rite 2: after the optometrist, he called the gynecologist. He was going through all the medical professionals. Why stop at just the shrink and the eye doctor? There was a script on the insurance bill for something he didn't recognize, he told the receptionist. What was that? Larissa asked him to call in the prescription for her and he couldn't tell what Norethindrone was.

"Norethindrone? You mean the birth control pill?"

He slumped over the phone, over his desk. "Of course," he said in a muffled voice. "The birth control pill." It all makes perfect sense. "She says she lost the prescription. Our local drugstore doesn't have it. How long was it for?"

"The last prescription?"

The *last* prescription? Implying there were others before it.

"We gave it to her for twelve months. Does she want the doctor to call it in *again*? Because she lost it once already. We had to call it in a second time to a CVS in Madison. She told us she changed drugstores. Maybe it's still there?"

"Yes, let me check with . . . I'll call you right back."

"What? I can't hear you."

But he'd already hung up, and remained flattened at his desk until Doug came in and said, "What are you doing? We're late for the three o'clock on insurance derivatives. You okay?"

"I'm fine," Jared said, fork-lifting himself into a standing position. "I have to leave early. Emily has another recital at five."

"Larissa can't drive her?"

"Not today." He tossed his laptop into his briefcase, the newspaper into the trash.

Rite 3: Jared called Finney again, called to find out if there was any news. No, Finney said. I'd call you right away if we found something. Trust me. You'd be the first one we'd call.

"Nothing on her license? She hasn't surrendered it? Hasn't been stopped for a moving violation on it?"

"No," Finney said. "Nothing like that. She did report her license missing and was issued a new one, but it happened well before her disappearance—"

"Wait, wait," said Jared, rubbing his eyes, standing at the kitchen door, looking out on the yard where his two older children sat chatting on the red swings. "What do you mean, issued a *new* one. Why?"

"I don't know *why*. She reported it missing is all I know."

"Who told you this?"

"Um, the New Jersey Department of Motor Vehicles."

"When was this?" He couldn't look at his kids anymore. He closed his eyes.

"Late April."

"She reported it missing in late April?"

"April 28, to be exact."

April 28. A full month before she left.

"And then?"

"And then? She said it was lost," explained Finney. "And they issued her a new one."

"Why would she do that? Report it lost?"

"Maybe because she lost it?"

"Detective, you know she hasn't lost it. I told you it was in her purse."

"You sure?"

"Am I *sure*? Yes! Right in her purse, in her wallet, where it always is. Next to her insurance card, her credit cards."

"Huh."

"I showed it to you."

"Sorry about that. I misremembered. I thought we couldn't find it. So many details. So why would she report it lost, then?"

"You're asking *me*?" Jared shook his head. "Did you check the new license? Check if there's anything on it?"

"We checked. There's nothing. She hasn't been stopped, hasn't surrendered it."

"Well . . . I guess you might as well check her passport," Jared said lifelessly. "Perhaps she reported that lost also." His forehead was against the screen door. "And was issued a new one."

Evisceration Rite 4: She did.

April 20.

And she was.

❧

He laid out the daggers of Larissa's vanishing on Kavanagh's table, like a prayer feast for the faithless departed.

"Is this what you call her coming back any time soon? Forty thousand dollars taken from our account? A new license. A new passport. He is gone, she is gone. I'm asking you—does this seem to you like a person who planned to be back in a flash? Someone who's thinking it over? Someone who's left the back door ajar so she can slip in, unnoticed, like nothing was ever amiss? Why aren't you saying anything? Why?"

But the reason Kavanagh wasn't saying anything was because he wasn't in front of her. He didn't go and see her. He couldn't. All the answers were on his desk at work, where he went to hide when there was nowhere else. He didn't want to have the conversation with Kavanagh, he didn't want to see her pitying gaze, he could barely stomach Ezra's, to whom he told nothing beyond the bare bones of a hidden affair and a running-off like a dry-bank stream.

"She'll be back," said Ezra, said Maggie, said Bo and Jonny, and Tara, and Evelyn by phone from afar, all the way from Hoboken. Evelyn, sick at home with home-schooled kids, knew Larissa would be coming back. Perhaps if Evelyn had all the information: that Larissa, unlike Hansel and Gretel, left behind nothing that could be traced back to her, she would've come to a different conclusion. No one had that information but Jared. And he was growing skeletal with it.

3

Lillypond

Eventually the children began to notice their mother remained conspicuously not home. The less said of it, the better, Jared felt, and clearly his children felt the same way, for they said less and less of it. They all withdrew from one another, grew silent, grew mute with grief.

Michelangelo asked at first.

One night Jared overheard Emily in his bedroom saying to him, "Don't keep bringing up Mommy all the time."

"I don't bring her up all the time. I bring her up a little bit."

"Well, don't. Dad is waiting for her to come back and he gets upset."

"Why?"

Emily was stumped for a second. Jared stood in the hall. "Why? Because he wants her to come back, and she's not back yet and this upsets him."

"I want her to come back, too."

"We all do."

"I miss her."

"Yeah."

"Is Asher going to have a graduation party?"

"I don't think so. Don't bring it up."

"But he wants a party."

"No, he doesn't. Ash is so sad. We have to try to cheer him up."

"Like with a party?"

"Stop that. This isn't a good time for parties."

"Are we still gonna go to Lillypond when school ends?"

"I think so. Dad said."

"Yeah."

And that was the end of that.

⌒⌒

School ended.

When school ended, Jared had no plan for Michelangelo, and he behaved like a man whose life didn't stop on a Friday in late May, a man who was without a babysitter, a man who didn't have cleaning help. He behaved like a man whose wife was still home. Like a man who still had Maggie come in the afternoons, though Maggie hadn't been able to help him much in the last few weeks, and he wished he could remember why, but he was so absorbed in the labor of his own suffering that when she began saying she couldn't come, he stopped listening. He suspected it had something to do with the exacerbation of her renal condition. Over a week ago someone had mentioned "transplant." But again, when Jared heard it, in front of "transplant" he put the word *heart* not the word *kidney*. He wasn't thinking of Maggie.

So on the first Monday of summer vacation, he showered and shaved and dressed and came downstairs to find Emily watching TV with Michelangelo. "I'll see you later, guys," he called out to them, taking his briefcase. "Be good. Call if you need anything."

"Dad!" Emily shot up from the couch, still in her pajamas. "Where are you going?"

"Where am I *going*? To work, Em."

"Why are you going to work?"

"Because if I don't go to work, we can't pay our rent, or buy food, and the TV will get turned off and you won't be able to watch *Sponge Bob*."

"But who's going to take care of us?"

"Em, you're fifteen. You're not a kid anymore. You can take care of yourself."

"But Michelangelo is not fifteen! He can't take care of himself."

"He's got his sister and brother with him."

"Dad! That's not fair! Asher and I are going to the Swim Club."

"No, I'm going to band practice," said Asher, who'd just woken up and come downstairs. "Can someone drive me? I can't carry my amp on the back of the bike."

Jared stood in the hall, having almost been out the door, and looked at his three children, the sleepy head of a neutral, everything-inside Asher, the wild-eyed expression of everything-outside Emily, and Michelangelo, in *Sponge Bob* oblivion. Jared had been walking out of his house his entire adult life, every morning, Monday through Friday, in Hoboken when he was a teacher, and here in Summit when he was a chief financial officer. For twenty years, he walked out his door, got into his car, and drove to work, and never once had it occurred to him to think of how the children were going to be taken care of.

Because they always were.

"Emily," he said quietly.

"Don't say my name in that way!" she cried. "Don't make me feel like I'm being unreasonable!"

"Em," he said, gripping his briefcase tighter, the knot in his tie constricting his throat, keeping him from breathing. "You have to help me out. I know it's tough . . ." he paused. Paused or stopped? Loosening his tie, he thought only of himself, of the emptiness, of the wish for hunger. Everything was once so good. The kids were growing up beautifully. Things were becoming easier. They lived well. Saved money. Spent money. After the kids headed to college, Jared and Larissa planned to travel. She had already started saving the brochures for their unrealized dreams. They read books, newspapers, talked about life present and past. Everything was as it should be. "I'll pay you for babysitting," Jared said to Emily, "until I figure something else out. Just . . . look, take the boy with you. Take him to the Swim Club."

"I'm not taking him to the Swim Club!"

Jared turned to Asher.

"I'm not taking him to band practice!"

"Why don't you take him to work, Dad? Take him with *you*."

The straps of the briefcase in the hand felt as if they swelled in his hinged and frantic fingers.

"I will figure something out," he repeated slowly. "But for now, the two of you, help out your dad, will you?"

Emily and Asher grimly relented and Jared left for work. But he had not thought things through.

The thing he was in the middle of, the current nightmare, it wasn't even his nightmare. It was real in someone else's life. It wasn't real. Wasn't real.

He called Larissa's mother. "Barbara, I'm sorry, but I need your help," he said, defeated.

"Thank God," she said immediately. "You want me to come and stay with the kids?"

"God, yes, please. I'll hire someone. I'm just . . ." Not ready. He didn't want to tell her this.

"I'll come. I'll finish up here and jump in the car."

"Oh, and . . ." He didn't quite know how to say it. "Barbara, can you bring some clothes with you? I'd hate for you to drive back and forth to Piermont. We have a guest room. Stay with us for a few days."

There was silence on the phone. "Truly, the world is being turned upside down," said Barbara.

Jared called Ernestina and rehired her.

Afterward Jared sat in a corporate meeting about the new challenge of acquiring clients in an Internet world, and didn't hear a word, thankful only that he wasn't chairing it.

Barbara brought a suitcase. The children, who never had their grandmother stay with them at the house, were overjoyed. And she seemed strangely pleased also, almost as if she had planned it. Only Jared stood incongruously near the back door, feeling simultaneously grateful and revolted.

The days lumbered by, but then a week later he forgot to make the call at the end of trading to reinvest in a multi-billion-dollar account for a multi-billion-dollar subsidiary fund. By the time he remembered, it was too late, the Dow had closed and the price rose over what he was allowed to pay. The weekend came and went, and on Monday, Larry Fredoso met with him darkly in the large conference room and asked him to explain, and Jared had no answers. He was counting on Larry's goodwill, wondering, but only superficially, how long the goodwill would last. If he lost his job because of incompetence, what would they all do then?

Out of options, Jared told Larry the truth. Jared didn't tell him the whole truth, nasty, devastating, cruel—the kid was twenty! And she planned to run with him for a year. But he told him almost everything else. Things he couldn't tell Ezra and Finney, he told his boss. Fredoso listened and said only, "Holy fuck," and nothing else for a few minutes, and then added, "Holy fuck," another three or four dozen times and then fell quiet. After five minutes, Jared got up and left.

An hour later Fredoso came into Jared's office and closed the door. "I am useless in personal situations," he said, "my third wife has been calling me an asshole for seven years. What I meant to say before but clearly didn't was, whatever you need, you do. I'll help you. We can help. What can we do? Do you want to move closer to work? We'll find you a house in Newark, a nice one."

"I would, Larry, but no. I can't move. The kids will . . ." The kids. Yes, *them*.

"You need help. Who's taking care of them when you're here?"

"That's one of my problems. Right now my mother-in-law. But as you can imagine, that's temporary. She is seventy-eight besides."

"Ah. You should hire a professional. Hire the best. Get a live-in."

Jared said nothing. Like a live-in wife? he wanted to ask.

"What do you want? You're not saying anything. Do you want to take a leave of absence?"

"Yes," Jared said instantly.

Fredoso was taken aback. "Really?"

"I do, Larry. I know it's crazy. But I gotta figure out my kids. It's summertime. They're freaking out. I have to keep my family sane somehow. I—" And myself, too. I have to keep it together somehow, for my kids.

"Okay. Absolutely. Whatever you need. What, like family leave?"

"Family leave, bereavement leave. Whatever. I've got time built up. I can take some time paid. Then unpaid."

"No, we'll work it out."

"I can work from home. I've got an office. Send me the administration and the asset management reports every week. I just . . . I can't leave them with a babysitter yet. I know I might have to. I'm just not ready. And besides . . ." Though he didn't want to say what besides. He was hoping she would return soon. Which is something he didn't want to say to his boss, but Fredoso, for all his cluelessness, clearly knew what Jared was thinking.

Nodding full-heartedly, he said, "Yes. Leave of absence. Your kids need you." And then quickly turned and walked out.

So Jared stopped working. Barbara regretfully went back to Piermont, and with Emily's help, and Maggie's help, and Ernestina's help, he packed up what he could and in the middle of July took his family and his dog to Lillypond.

~⁓~

In Lillypond, the phone never stopped ringing. A distraught Doug apologizing so hard, as if Larissa had run off with him. I'm sorry, man. How could it have happened? Do you know who it was? Maybe something happened to her? Maybe . . . I'm sorry, man. I don't know what to say. Kate is devastated.

Evelyn; Bo; Maggie, subdued; Ezra, even more subdued.

Emily started making lists and Jared went shopping while she played mom and made them eggs and even tried Aunt Jemima buttermilk pancake mix and put blueberries in it just like Larissa used to. She made English muffin pizzas for lunch, and even tuna the way Michelangelo liked it. At night Jared barbecued. They had chicken, burgers, steak. Afterward Emily served ice cream sundaes with homemade brownies. Cleaning the place was harder. No one wanted to do it. Michelangelo used Windex on all the glass surfaces. Also all the wood surfaces. All surfaces. He used one bottle per cleaning. Emily swept the plank floor. Asher did nothing, but under duress, once he vacuumed. Jared taught Emily and Asher how to do their own laundry, but it was Michelangelo who was the only willing and eager student, dragging the pillowcase full of his clothes to the washing machine, and asking, "Dad, is it detergent first or laundry first?"

They went swimming and boating, Jared worked for a few hours, answered calls, looked over banking and trust services reports that were sent to him. One blind eye to the work, one blind eye to the life. He felt himself withdrawing, trying to remember the exact words of the note he left for Larissa back at the house. "We're at Lillypond. Kids really need to see you. J." Just like that. And while he was nested at the feet of the Appalachians, every day verdant and fragrant, he wondered if there could be anything more pitiable than to come back home and find the note just where he left it. He wanted to count how many days it had been, but he was afraid to. Would he soon have to measure the time in months, not days? And then? He watched Michelangelo collecting every twig he could find to build a house for a bear. Jared hoped it wasn't a real bear, but judging by the size of the twig pile, it was a false hope.

Like so many things these days.

At the end of July, Doug and Kate came to visit for a couple of days with their girls. Doug reported on things at work, while Kate judiciously avoided crossing even a passing glance with Jared. He found her to be tongue-tied to the point of being mute. It was just as well. Jared could barely look at Doug's Jaguar parked in his drive.

It was just as well they were only staying for a few days, because on their last evening, Jared and Doug were on the porch and Doug, after clearing his throat for five minutes, asked Jared if he knew who the guy was.

"I don't want to talk about it, Doug."

Hastily Doug apologized and moved on, but not far enough. "You'll have to forgive my Kate. Sometimes she gets these ridiculous notions and I keep telling her to dispel them, but she just hangs on and won't let go. It's the writer in her."

"What notions? She's barely said a word to me."

"Yeah, she's upset." Doug laughed nervously. "You want to hear why?"

"Not really."

"A few months ago," Doug continued, "in the wintertime, remember Kate ran into Larissa in the city? Well, Larissa had been waiting for a girlfriend to show up for dinner, and suddenly bam, who shows up but the salesman from Jaguar."

Jared paled in the night. Kate had never mentioned that part, though he had heard the rest of the story several times.

"He just passed them on the street and Larissa, of course, came home with Kate, so clearly Kate was imagining all the wrong things, and she thought no more about it, until your—thing that's—happened, and then she started thinking again."

"Thinking about what?"

"Well, let me tell you how crazy she is. She went in for service recently on the Jag and asked to see our salesman, and they told her he no longer worked there! He split. So of course—"

"Doug, I'm getting tired, sorry, man."

"Is that crazy, or what?"

"It's crazy."

"She can't get it out of her head, but I keep telling her he was just a kid . . ."

"Not quite a kid. Twenty-one." Jared, defending his indefensible age! His life was becoming a Monty Python sketch.

"I'm just saying, that maybe—"

"Kate's got an overactive imagination. You better watch out, Douglas. Good night." Was he going to have to get himself a new job? Was he going to have to move, sell the house, take his kids, leave everything behind? Maybe they could move to the Black Hills of South Dakota, to a small silver mining town in the woods, in the mountains. How could he continue to face his friends and their most trivial of questions?

And then not a week later, in the beginning of August, Maggie sat at his Lillypond Saturday night table, with the kids happily playing with Dylan in the next room, and said, "Jared, you won't believe what I'm about to tell you."

"Not only won't I believe it, I don't want to hear it."

"Do you remember Larissa's birthday celebration?" she went on. "How Dora said she was going to come and then suddenly cancelled? Well, I just saw her for lunch last week, for the first time in months, and I told her about Larissa . . ."

"Why did you do that?"

"She asked me how Larissa was. I told her. What was I going to do? Lie?"

Jared said nothing.

"Do you want to know what she told me or not?"

"I don't."

"She saw them."

"Saw who?" Jared said tiredly.

"*Them!* She says that one night in April she got out of her class at Drew around ten; she had parked the car by the train station and was about to drive away when they walked out of the Madison movie theater."

Jared said nothing. Was this ever going to come to a screeching end? *Ever.* He didn't look at Maggie, he stared blankly at the woodgrain in his pine table.

"Dora said they ran to her Jag, and he opened the door for her, and they kissed right at the door on the street . . ."

"Maggie!"

That was both Ezra and Jared.

Jared lifted his palms up. "I. *get* it. She saw them. I don't give a shit. It's too late now, isn't it? What's the point of telling me? Why didn't Dora come to me then? Why didn't she say something to me back in April when she called to cancel? She could've told me why she didn't want to come to our house. Why didn't Kate tell me earlier the snake oil salesman was also on that city street with her and Larissa? Back when it might've done some good. Or not. Why tell me this now?"

"Because I only know now."

"So what? Why are you telling *me* this now?"

"I thought you might want to know."

"Maggie . . ." said Ezra. "Why would you think that? Honestly."

"I thought this is what we were all about," Maggie said. "Honesty. Witnesses to truth." Her curly hair was nearly completely gray now, no red to speak of, and she had it cut to a bob. She looked a decade older than Ezra.

"So Dora and Kate were witnesses to truth and then carried it hidden for months?"

"But *I* didn't carry it hidden."

"Ah, see, but I wish *you* would have."

"All right," said Ezra, trying to mollify them. "All right. There's no point . . ."

"Well, there's some point in knowing the truth, no?" Maggie said.

"I used to think so," said Jared. "But what good is the truth to me now? So Dora saw her at the movies. Maggie, they were fucking for eighteen months! And she left me. She left her kids!" Jared doubled over. "I don't give a shit about Dora's confessions. Can you really be so thick and not see that?"

"Oh, yes, because *you* see so many things now," retorted Maggie.

"Yes!" exclaimed Jared. "In hindsight, it's true: I see plenty. Isn't it glorious to have perfect vision?"

"Guys, guys, okay," said Ezra, raising his palms. "Too much wine . . ."

Maggie scratched the table with her nails. "I think back about how closed up she'd become." Her voice sounded like nails on a table. "We stopped shopping. Our lunches became so short. And rare. And when we did meet, all we talked about was school or movies, just the lamest stuff, and she refused to talk to me about my illness. I didn't think it was normal even then, but now I know—it's because her life was being rearranged, and she was using up all her powers to hide it. She had nothing left for other people. How could we not have noticed?" Maggie started to cry.

Ezra sat looking at Jared, glancing at Maggie. "That's true," he said quietly. "Mags's got a point. How *could* something like this go unnoticed?"

"I don't know," Jared said. "But I *love* these pointless fucking disquisitions."

"It's not pointless," returned Ezra. "How else can we make sense of it?"

"We can't, that's how. She left her children. Make sense of that."

"When I saw her last," Ezra said, "she was trying to show herself to me. Here I am, what should I do? I don't know what to do. And I didn't see it."

"That's right," Jared said scathingly. "She asked you for help. And you didn't see it. And look! She's gone. What did you say to her, Ezra, that made her cut and run?"

"No, no, stop it." That was Maggie, wiping her face, standing up, going over to Ezra, stretching out her arms to Jared. But Jared didn't stop it. And now neither did Ezra.

"But *we* didn't live with her!" Ezra exclaimed. "We didn't eat dinner with her every day, lie down with her, get up with her. I wasn't her husband, was I?"

Jared jumped up, and Maggie got between them, shaking, pulling Ezra down, pushing Jared away, crying, please, please, stop it, she'll come back, don't do this, it's not your fault, it's not anybody's fault, sometimes these things just happen, they just . . .

"And no one knows? No one sees? How can that be? How is that possible?"

"Who cares? She's gone now! That's the only thing that matters. She's gone . . ."

Who said that with such naked anguish?

The next day Maggie and Ezra left.

Another day. Another day. Another day. Jared watched the ballgames just to get lost in something, in numbers, statistics, rules, strategies, to not think, to have the TV on, or music, anything to not be in grief or rage.

One night Michelangelo sidled up and sat by him on the couch, holding his yellow blanket and his favorite torn blue bunny.

"What's up, bud?" said Jared, taking his vacant eyes off the TV and focusing on his son. "You want to go to bed? Why aren't you watching *Hercules* with Asher? It's your favorite."

"I know. But I've seen it a bazillion times. What inning is this?"

"What *inning* is this?" Jared peered into the face of his seven-year-old son. "It's the fourth quarter. It's third period. Since when do you care what inning it is?"

Michelangelo pretended to thoughtfully analyze the TV screen. "Dad, watch the TV, not me," he said. "Look, the enemy almost scored a run."

"Yeah," said Jared. "Lucky for us they didn't. Because then we'd be getting trashed 14–3 instead of 13–3."

"Oh. That's not good, huh, Dad?"

"Not good, bud."

Michelangelo started watching baseball with Jared, sitting quietly with his bunny, staring at the TV, falling asleep, and when Jared would try to lift him to carry him to bed, he'd open his eyes, clutch the blanket, shake his head, and say, "No, no, I'm good. I'm awake. I want to watch with you."

Jared couldn't tell Maggie and Ezra about the money Larissa had taken, drop by drop, week by week, taken and taken and taken, slowly, methodically, out of their joint account, gradually so he wouldn't notice, but now all those sharp-edged twenties were falling like glass pain upon his heart as if Aeschylus had been writing about Jared's own despair. Taken it so stealthily and in such small sums that, against his will, wisdom was coming to Jared by the awful grace of God: Larissa had taken it as if she never intended to come back.

O God! Mad fevered girl galloping toward destruction while the earth bloomed with moss and frogs and blue battered bunnies. Jared didn't know how he woke up every morning, brushed his teeth, put pants on, put his feet forward, breathed. He didn't know how the green air got into his collapsed lungs.

Ezra had tried to comfort Jared by saying this was nothing but a random act of God. "Don't spend the rest of your life figuring out why you. Best to get on with it."

"I never say why me," Jared said, palming the last of the Mondavi Cabernet. "You know what I say? Why *not* me? What the hell makes me so special? That's not what I'm trying to figure out. But this wasn't a random act of God, Ezra. She didn't get kidney disease that she didn't ask for and didn't want. She wasn't hit by lightning, she wasn't mowed down by a drunk driver. She was a rational, conscious, sentient being, with a choice, a free will, and a conscience. With a heart that carried love in it. With a womb that carried life in it. And this is the choice that person made, the heart of my wife, the mother of all those kids in my house. That's what I think about when I wake up ice cold. Not why a random act of God. Rather, why a deliberate act of Larissa?"

Chapter Two

1

Parenting Plus

At the end of August, having been off work for seven weeks, Jared brought his kids back home. The note he had left for Larissa he threw in the trash.

He thought of calling Finney and Cobb; he hadn't heard from them since July; he wanted to ask if her passport had been stamped with an exit visa, but then he picked up a summer's worth of mail from the post office and opened half a dozen desperate letters from Che, and he knew he didn't have to call Finney because Larissa wasn't in Manila. He couldn't get through all of Che's letters, about Lorenzo and kidney sales and jail, but he got through the gist of them. Larissa hadn't been in touch. Her silence was breaking Che's heart.

❧

Jared attended to two pressing things when he returned.

The second thing was looking into hiring permanent help. How did one go about doing something like that?

Hadn't Larissa said something to him? Right before Memorial Day, when they were discussing her visiting Che, she said he could call . . . who? You can call so and so, they'll come and help you, she said. And he said, what, call someone for two weeks to come and help? Yes, she said. To come and help. You can call . . .

He sifted and sifted, battled against the encroaching amnesiac denials. Finally it came to him on a rush-hour drive home. Parenting Plus! Larissa, while readying the wrecking balls was also laying out new bricks to rebuild, stone by stone.

The woman on the phone was young and friendly. Her name was Lauri. She'd been running Parenting Plus for fifteen years, said she was sure she could find him someone very good.

"Quickly?"

She demurred. Someone good would require time. Quickly was a different story.

Jared couldn't tell if she was kidding. He'd lost his humor sensor.

She took down some information, and then asked, "A live-in, or live-out?"

He didn't know the answer.

"Nationality important?"

He didn't know the answer.

Young or old?

He didn't know.

How many hours a week did he need?

He didn't know that either.

Lauri fell silent.

"I'm conflicted, Lauri," Jared admitted. "But I really do need someone."

"You have to figure out *what* you need before I can send you someone."

"What if I don't know? I've never had to hire a babysitter before."

"Can your wife help?"

"Less than I'd like," said Jared. "Let me call you back."

But Lauri didn't wait. She had several good candidates. Would he like to set up some interviews?

"The first one I'm going to send you is foreign, but her English is very good."

"Where's she from?"

"Slovakia? Does that sound right?" Lauri chuckled. "It sounds made-up. Like Transylvania. But she says she's from there."

"I'll tell the kids she's from Transylvania," said Jared. "They'll be thrilled."

"Transylvania, is that like a real place?" asked Lauri.

"Yeah, sure. Why not?"

Maria Toledo came at three in the afternoon on Saturday when all the kids were home. When he talked to her on the phone to set up the time, from her voice he imagined her to be benevolently heavy, but she turned out to be tiny and slender. She wore a maroon peacoat and brown lace-up Timberlands, and her brown hair was pulled back in a French twist. She had good teeth. She smiled a lot. Her English was pretty good. She said she had been working as live-out for a family in Mountainside, but the husband recently lost his job so they didn't need her anymore.

"Do you need a live-in or live-out?" she asked.

"I don't know," he admitted.

"Because I can't do live-in. I'm married."

"Oh."

"And I'm looking for full time. As many hours as possible."

"That I've got."

She lowered her voice. "The children have no mother?"

"Well, they didn't spring from a rock," said Jared. "So clearly they have a mother. She's just not here."

"Oh. Is she coming back soon?"

"Not sure," Jared replied. "But in the meantime, the three children need supervision, the house needs upkeep, errands have to be run."

"I understand."

He told her what the job entailed, she listened. He liked her. He was a little worried about her request for vacation. Not just to be paid when he and the kids were away, but four weeks in addition to that, at the time of her choosing so she could go back to Slovakia to visit her family. He didn't know what to say to that. Was that normal, that much vacation? *He* didn't get that much vacation. For the lack of anything to say, he asked her where in Slovakia she was from.

"Oh, you know Slovakia?" She giggled. "Just a small little village outside Skýcov. Do you know where that is? Is that helpful?"

"You're funny," said Jared.

She laughed. "So? What do you think?"

"What do I think?" He guessed she meant about her. "Very good."

"Do you want to see my references?"

"Sure. But I have to interview some other girls, too."

She became noticeably deflated. "I've never been out of work before," she said. "I worked since I left school, twelve years ago. Never not worked. I'm worried."

"Give me a couple of days. I'll be in touch this week. Now, those references?"

The references were very good. But she was the first girl he met with. He had to see what else was out there.

Courtney smelled like smoke and had an artist air about her that Michelangelo loved, but which concerned Jared. She didn't seem the type that would stay.

Erin was young and attractive, perhaps *too* attractive for his fourteen-year-old son to have in the house; plus she had zero experience; he'd have to hire her solely for her looks.

Jaime had lots of experience, didn't want any extra vacation time off, was willing to start right away and do whatever he needed to, but she had bad teeth and her hair lay in an unbrushed clump at the back of her head.

Fern, at first glance, was ideal. She was fifty-one, energetic, good-looking, was a personal trainer for twenty years and had the body to show for it, and was funny when introduced to the kids.

Then she opened her mouth. For the next fifty-five minutes, Jared couldn't open his to even let her know what would be required of her. She told him about how unfairly the-soon-to-be-former boss was treating her, how she wasn't being compensated enough, paid enough, rewarded enough, and she went into some length about her empty-nest syndrome and how after her twenty-one-year-old son moved out, she wanted to die, and even for good measure about her hysterectomy and its attendant complications of bleeding and infection.

It was after Fern that Jared called back Maria Toledo and offered her the job, and she said, oh, I'm so sorry, Mr. Stark, I really liked you and your family, but I didn't think you liked me, you said you would call me in a few days and I didn't hear from you.

"Maria, you were the first girl I talked to. I wanted to interview other candidates before I concluded how perfect you were."

She giggled. "I know, and you were perfect too, but I already accepted another position."

He couldn't believe it.

"I know, I'm sorry."

"I called you within seven days of our interview."

"I know, but I was very worried about being out of work. Listen, I will keep your number. I mean, I've never had a job not work out, but if this one doesn't work out, I'll call you, okay?"

"Okay, Maria," said a very disappointed Jared.

Well, that was that. Once again he called his mother-in-law.

Barbara returned, ecstatically. There was no other way to describe the emotion on her face when she was still in the driveway with her suitcase. The children, even Asher, who never ran out to anybody, ran out to her. Larissa! Jared wanted to say to his wife— who would've thought a life was possible in which your mother was coming to live with me and I would be grateful?

But the first thing Jared did, even before looking for help, or calling Barbara, or organizing any Labor Day get-togethers, was sell Larissa's Jaguar. He had been doubling up on the monthly payments, and had paid it off four months earlier. He got half what he paid for it, which was no justice at all.

What in the name of God was he going to do with that money?

 ᴑᴠᴌᴑ

On Saturday following Labor Day (no party, but Ezra and Maggie came, not in a party mood) when he came home from food shopping in the late afternoon, Emily ran out to the driveway and hissed, "Dad, where've you been? Somebody's here waiting for you!"

"Who?" he motioned her to step away and slammed the car door.

"I don't know. Somebody from your work. She brought her two kids!"

"*She?*" Twirling his keys, Jared walked into his house.

Jan Skeels from work was sitting at his kitchen table with a big pot of food in front of her in a casserole container. She was casually but neatly dressed, and she sprung from the bar stool so fast, she knocked it over, which made her even more on edge.

"I thought I'd come by," she stammered. "I only just heard . . . I'm sorry. I can't believe I just heard. I'm so out of the loop on stuff . . ."

"How are you, Jan?" said Jared, putting his keys on the ring, walking over to the island. "Emily said your kids are here?"

"Yes, they're playing with two of yours somewhere. Maybe outside? I didn't know you'd be out. I just stopped by in the afternoon. I wanted to bring a little pot of food, thought it might be hard for a man on the weekends."

"Nah," he said, smiling slightly, "on the weekends, it's easy. We just go out. Or get take-out. Do you want a drink? We have Coke," he quickly added, belatedly remembering her ardent alcoholic troubles. "Or iced tea."

"No, I'm fine. Your daughter gave me a glass of water." Jan nervously tittered. "So what do you do during the week for dinner?"

"We just go out. Or get take-out."

And she laughed, less nervously. "I brought my little specialty dish I was making for me and the kids, and thought, why not? It's baked ziti. Kids like it."

"Yeah, mine too."

"There you go. I wanted to be a good neighbor, that's all."

"Thank you. Thank you very much." Neighbor? "You live around here?"

"Yeah, not too far," she demurred. "A couple of miles. Boys!" she yelled. "Come on, let's go!"

"Um, do you want to stay for dinner?" asked Jared.

"No, no, we have plans. I really just brought it over to acknowledge my knowledge—" Jan broke off awkwardly again. "My sympathy, I mean."

"Thank you."

"When my husband left, it was very tough. Without my neighbors feeding me, I don't know how I would've managed."

"Would that my neighbors fed me," said Jared. "They've all been too mortified."

"Yeah, people don't know what to say."

"No kidding," said Jared. "You sure you can't stay? You made plenty of food. And I have some Italian bread, some salad fixings. We might as well make a full dinner out of it. My mother-in-law is going to join us. You don't mind, do you?"

"No, of course, not. Well, I'll have to . . . let me . . . I'll just make a phone call."

"Sounds good. I'll have the kids set the table. Kids! Come!" He turned to Jan. He forced a smile.

∾⟡∽

Jan Skeels wasn't the only one. The bank ladies on Saturday morning *all* came out to greet him, nattily dressed, friendly, arrayed as if in a line-up, offering him coffee while he waited, a donut, making small talk, chit-chatting, commenting on the gray goatee he had grown, how much they liked it, how it made him look more distinguished.

And the women at work were undeniably more friendly—and

better attired. As if his daily life had become a fashion show parade. Mr. Stark! Please. Your eyes on the runway. And the next one is only twenty-seven! But after several bad relationships and issues with her mother that are being worked out in twice-weekly therapy sessions, she is ready to present herself to the world. Here she is, wearing an elegant Diane Von Furstenberg cotton tank dress with a sweetheart neckline and a lace-up front, size 6, color bloom. On her feet, she is wearing delightful multi-colored Dolce and Gabbana buckled slingbacks, and she is carrying a Bottega Veneta hobo bag with a suede inner lining. Makeup by Nars, hair by Frederic Fekkai. What do you think, Mr. Stark? This is the director of human resources at your firm. Not for you, you say? Next! Mr. Stark, please pay attention. Because they're coming to your office door two at a time now, and you have only a few seconds to assess. Focus!

It's like they all knew. The wildfire spread through the bank, the office, even Michelangelo's school. Once everyone knew, no one talked to him about Larissa anymore, blessedly, but the ladies smiled wider and dressed better.

There were things he had to make himself do, to begin to function again, to cease to end to function. He asked Ezra for help in finding a house painter. Ezra was happy to locate one, a father of one of his students. The man came one evening to assess the job and give Jared an estimate. Before he and his crew painted, Jared had the Salvation Army remove every single item from the bedroom. They took Larissa's clothes and her books; they took their old TV, and their two dressers. They removed their bed and the nightstands, and her makeup table with the cosmetics still in it. They took it all. And then the painters came and in two days his bedroom went from taupe or whatever to Sherwin-Williams Rainwashed, with Honied White trim and Nuthatch chocolate bedding and curtains. Maggie helped him pick those out. She and Ezra took Jared to Pottery Barn at the mall and selected a new bed with him, a dark stain four-poster king with a short headboard. White pillows, a Nuthatch cocoa quilt, a new dresser (just one), a leather chair, and a 50-inch LCD TV so he could watch his Yankees in High-Def style. He placed the bed against a different wall than before, made a seating area with new black bookshelves for his baseball and finance books. He even went on art.com and bought a Joan Miro painting, black framed and triple-matted to go over the bed, because the old things that hung there, the two pictures of Jared and Larissa in their simple eloping wedding clothes standing in front of the justice of the peace, had been taken down, as all pictures of her had been taken down and placed in a large plastic container that held her photos, their wedding albums, her plays from Pingry, and all the trinkets he hadn't donated to St. Paul's. This was a big project; it took all of September. But he could sleep in his bedroom again; that was something.

Also in September Jared got busy with school supplies, backpacks, pens, folders, three-ring binders, lunch tickets. Things he never had to do. He thought he had had it tough, dealing with a multi-billion-dollar business, stress, politics, personalities at work, office shit, rushing home. He didn't know how easy he had it.

It was warm for part of September, and then got cold fast. The fall jackets came out of the attic. The Halloween decorations went up. Jared hung the goblin lights, put the ghosts out, the coffin, the skeleton that talked. At the store they bought orange flowers. One Saturday in October he took the kids and Barbara to a farm in the country. They went on a hayride and through a corn maze and picked out five pumpkins, but Michelangelo picked one more and said, "This is for Mommy." No one else said anything. It was a cool beautiful afternoon. Afterward they went out to a steak place for dinner, and Jared sat with his kids, and cut up Michelangelo's steak, and they talked about Thanksgiving and Christmas presents in the most oblique way; sort of, we can't wait for Christmas, and should we buy some more tree decorations, and when can we start our wishlist? The gaping hole in the middle of Christmas they all left unsaid.

Thanksgiving came. And went.

At the beginning of December Jared got a call at work from a

Maria Toledo. He had to work to place her in his memory. It was the first girl he had interviewed, the girl with the Transylvanian accent.

"I'm sorry to bother you," she said. She sounded cracked, breaking up, struggling for words. "But back in September you said I could call you if my job didn't work out."

Now he remembered.

"I don't know if you hired someone already . . ."

"Well, my mother-in-law is helping us," said Jared.

"Oh. I see."

"Why? Did the other job not work out?"

"Well, this is the thing . . . I don't know if you would be interested in maybe having a live-in, but you know, I have been in child care my whole adult life, and in Slovakia, I lived with a family of eight children . . . that's a lot, right? And I did everything for the mother, I helped her, and I cooked, and cleaned, and took care of the kids, and then I lived in London for three years as an au pair for a woman with three children. You could call her for a reference, and then here in America, I worked for four years for two different families, and they'll tell you, I did everything for them, so I'm saying, I could help you, and you wouldn't have to worry about anything, your kids would be taken care of, and I'd do homework with them, and I love sports and playing outside. I'd take them to their after-school programs, and I know you said your youngest boy liked arts and crafts, well, I love arts and crafts, and I could do lots of stuff with them, and also I could walk your dog, because I bet she is lonely being by herself during the day; your mother-in-law, she probably doesn't walk her, does she?"

"No," Jared said slowly, "no, she doesn't. She's got arthritis. Makes it hard to hold the leash."

"Well, that's what I'm saying. Do you still have the reference letters I gave you last time? Because I can stop by tonight to drop another copy off if you don't have them."

"No, I probably still have them somewhere."

"I could start anytime for you. I don't have to wait until next Monday. I know it's Tuesday right now, but if you want, I can start tomorrow. And because I'd be a live-in, I won't need as much money. Oh, and I know you were worried before about me taking time off . . ."

"I wasn't worried."

"No, I could tell. You were. You thought it was too much time. And you were absolutely right. I won't take any time except when you go away. I'll just work around your vacation time. Because it must be hard for you . . . Your wife, she's not back yet?"

"She's not back yet."

"That's what I'm saying. It's not a bad deal. It would cost you less than a live-out."

Jared was quiet.

"Are you okay, Maria?"

"Oh, I'm fine," she assured him. "I just wanted you to know I was still available if you needed someone."

"To live in? But what about your husband? I don't think husbands like that very much, their wives living somewhere else."

She started to cry.

Jared turned his face away from the door in case someone came in, and pressed the phone tighter to his ear, as if Maria was crying right in his office and he didn't want his staff to hear.

"Well, this is the thing," she said. "The husband went on a fishing trip to Florida before Thanksgiving, and said he'd be back in two weeks, but two weeks passed and he wasn't back, and wasn't picking up his phone, and then finally over the weekend he called me and said he wasn't coming back at all, and he was going to send a friend of his to get all his stuff from our apartment. So I locked his friend out, and he called the police, and told them it was his apartment, which it technically is—his name is on the lease, but we're married—but the police are like, lady you have to move, so I don't know what to do, and the landlord, I found out, hasn't been paid since September! So now they're telling me I owe four months rent on an apartment they're kicking me out of! I mean, is that crazy, or what?"

"That's crazy."

"So I have a double problem. I need a place to live, and I have to earn enough to pay the landlord so he doesn't sue me."

"Plus the husband is in Florida."

She cried.

Jared hired Maria and paid her back rent. They bought her a bed and she slept in Michelangelo's room like Mary Poppins in the nursery.

∽⌁∿

After the tree went up, and the season to be jolly sped by, Jared and Emily together wrapped Michelangelo's presents on Christmas Eve. The radio was playing Christmas carols, Jared poured his daughter a little punchless eggnog, while he punched his up with a dose of brandy—and rum and whiskey besides. They were casually chatting, about how happy the little boy was going to be with his Hot Wheels set and his Batcave and his Star Wars Lego ship, and Emily said, "Dad, what do you think happened to Mom?"

Jared blanked, stood with the wrapping paper in his hands.

"I don't know, honey," he said at last. His mouth twisted, he was looking deep inside for a diplomatic thing to say, for the elegant thing.

"You don't think she's with Che, do you?"

"No," said Jared, knowing more than he wanted to about Che and Lorenzo. "I don't think your mom is with her. Detective Finney told me she hasn't used her passport to leave the country."

"What do the police think happened?"

"Finney doesn't know." Jared was making a mess of the wrapping. The scissors didn't function in his hand. The Scotch tape didn't tape. "He thinks she may have . . ."

He stopped, looked at his daughter. With her clear brown eyes, her open face, her ready smile, her straight brown hair, her light and steady posture, she looked so much like Larissa. So much like her and yet nothing like her. For Larissa had something else. The commonplace, yet unique. The eye-fooling thing. The heart-fooling thing. The mirage that told him she was all there.

The truth was in their bed, when she appeared wholly to be his—but wasn't . . . and soon, disappeared entirely, like a magic trick, like Houdini in the wilds, a vanishing act: drinking dirty martinis by the jamb of the door, smiling, wiling away the hours, candles burning on windowsills and mantels, while planning the impossible, hiding the impossible, hiding the missing fundamental part of yourself.

The part that would stop you.

What would Emily like to hear? What would a child prefer?

"What, Dad?" Emily stopped wrapping. "What? Does Detective Finney think Mom had some kind of accident?"

"He doesn't tell me."

Emily resumed wrapping. "No." She forced her voice to become steady and firm. Just like her mother used to. "No. She's just traveling. You'll see. She'll be back."

"Em . . ."

"She will, Dad. I know Mom. She'll be back."

"But what if she . . ."

"No. She is alive. I know it. I feel it."

"Do you?"

"Yes."

"You'd prefer that?"

"As opposed to what?" Emily put the garlands down.

Jared put his whole soul down. He couldn't face her, couldn't reply to her.

"So what do we do? We wait?"

"We wait," said Emily. "What choice do we have? But we live our life, too."

"Well, we can hardly help that part." But how did Jared do that? Live his?

"That's right. It'll be all right, Dad. Don't worry." She patted him on the back.

He waited for more wisdom from his teenager. All she ever learned, she learned in kindergarten. It will be all right if you put a Band-Aid on it. And then pat the wounded on the back with a brief word of comfort. "And if it doesn't?"

"I don't have *all* the answers, Dad. I'm only fifteen. Ask me again in a few years." Emily smiled. "But in the meantime, it's not too early to start thinking about my sweet sixteenth. I want to have it at the Swim Club. I want to invite a hundred people . . ."

❦

In the new year Jared went to see Dr. Kavanagh. She seemed stunned by his reappearance—if he was here, that meant that Larissa wasn't here. Or perhaps it was his *appearance*. Jared was pretty sure he didn't look like the same man. His hair had gone gray. He'd lost a remarkable amount of weight. The saddle of what had happened sloped his shoulders downward, the weight of it had shortened him. He felt half-man standing before her.

Kavanagh herself didn't look good. She looked collapsed. She was thinner, though that seemed impossible; she had started out so small. The bags around her eyes, the sallowness of her skin; Jared hoped it was the light, the lack of it. She really didn't look well. But then neither did he. And so they stood at the open door and eyed each other warily until she spoke. "Do you want to come in?" And he said, "No. But I will."

In her office he paced once or twice from the window to the couch, and finally sat. When he looked at her again, she seemed so tired. She wasn't curled up in the chair, she was just sitting, her hands falling onto her knees.

"Are you all right?" he asked.

"I'm a little under the weather. I'll be fine." She coughed. "Are *you* all right?"

"Oh, sure. Doing swell. Work is good."

"Kids?"

"Kids are good."

"They've adjusted?"

"As much as you can adjust to this sort of thing."

"Kids are resilient."

"Yes."

"Are you seeing anyone?"

"Seeing? You mean . . . ? Um, no. Not like that. There's a woman I work with who comes over on Saturdays, brings her two boys. We have dinner, the kids play."

"Is she nice?"

"She's nice." Jared was uncommitted. "A bit of a whiner. I'm not much for that. You know, everything's going to hell in a handbasket type of whining. I don't know what she expects me to do about it. I'm like, welcome to the club, sister."

"That seems insensitive. She must know about your situation."

"She does. But you know how quickly people forget."

"Yes."

"She says to me, I've been so unlucky in love. This is what she said to *me*! I mean, come on, that takes balls, don't you think?"

"Yes." Kavanagh shook her critical head.

"I said to her, What do you think love is, anyway? You think it's all dinners and walks on the beach? That's not love. Love is seeing the laundry, the unclean kitchen, the tired husband who still wants sex, love is the everydayness of it, and you know what? It's not sexy. It's not romantic. It just is. Like the kids. There will be one or two moments of pure joy, that oh my God feeling, like, I can't believe they're my kids, but most of the time, it's just doing doing doing. It doesn't stop. And even when you don't feel like it, don't feel like checking their homework or worrying about dinner or listening, or bathing them, or watching TV with them, you still do it. That's love. And you know, this woman looked at me like she had no damn idea what the hell I was talking about."

Kavanagh laughed. "Who takes care of the children for you?"

"Things are actually okay on that front," said Jared. "Larissa's mother was helping for a while, but she had a minor stroke and couldn't drive the car. She's better. Still lives with us."

"Larissa's mother is living with you?" Kavanagh seemed sharply surprised by that, as if she knew things. "That's good, Jared," she said, calling him by his given name for the first time. "That's very good."

"Is it?" He shrugged. But he knew Kavanagh was right. It *was* good. "But this girl I interviewed back in September came to live with us. Maria from Slovakia." Jared paused. "I hired her before Christmas. We're a little cramped at the moment. I never thought my big house wouldn't have enough room. But my mother-in-law is in the guest room, and Maria sleeps with Michelangelo."

"Is she working out?"

"Yeah, she's great. She does everything. I come home, the kids are clean, the clothes are folded. Her husband ran off to Florida, so she's not exactly a ball of sunshine. Except . . . she cooks this . . . Slovakian food that the kids and I are not used to." Jared smirked. "The kids are like, Dad, what's sauerkraut, what's kielbasa, what's barley?" He shook his head. "So Maria tries goulash, almost edible. Or these cookies made with sour cream. Listen, I'm not complaining. She works hard. I'm thinking of getting her a Betty Crocker cookbook."

"For when, Valentine's Day?" Kavanagh kept a straight face.

"What? No. Just because. Not as a gift. As a hint."

"Ah."

They sat for a few minutes in silence. He was hunched over, his elbows on his knees, looking at the carpet and his black shoes. She was squired into a tight twist roll, looking into her lap, breathing noisily.

"I'm not all right," Jared said.

A wilted mouth told Jared of Kavanagh's disappointment. As if she had a personal stake in this. "You seem better than before."

"Well, yes. Before, I was the walking dead. Now I'm waking up to things. It's the end of January. There hasn't been a single word. She hasn't even sent one word to the kids. I mean, how can that *be?*" He clenched his uncomprehending fists.

Kavanagh stayed silent.

"Doctor . . . ?" A faint interrogative. He took a breath. "You said she'd be back."

"I've been wrong about many things in my life. I'm hoping this won't be the last." She broke into a nasty coughing fit.

"Do you think she'll get in touch eventually?"

She didn't look at him. "Do you?"

"I don't think so," he said. The look in Ezra's eyes from the summer continued to prickle Jared, to burn him. That might be a conversation for another day: how to resume his intimate friendships with people he couldn't face. Maybe Kavanagh would tell him he needed new friends. "If she wanted me to find out about her and him, I would've found out. It wouldn't have taken much."

"More than it took."

"Yes. But she wasn't just careful. She wasn't just meticulous. She was preternaturally scrupulous. I mean, she took thousands of dollars from our account in practically singles! She knew I examined the account, so she did it in tiny increments, making sure I wouldn't notice. She left behind her license, but got herself a new one, as if she wanted to give herself a head start to wherever she was going. She left her passport behind, but got herself a new one. Why would she need a passport? She's never been out of the country, not even to Mexico. Last time I checked, Hawaii was still a state in the union. She doesn't need a passport to go to Hawaii, does she? She didn't take any of her clothes, as if she wanted me to believe she just stepped out."

"What's your point?"

"It was a commando operation from the start. It was a tactical nuke. I was ambushed. I know you keep wondering how I could've been so blind. What I'm saying is, I don't think she was hoping I would find out. Just the opposite. She was hoping I would *never* find out."

Kavanagh sat. Her hands squeezed together.

He sat defeated. To a medical professional, as if to a secular priest, Jared couldn't for certain, for one hundred percent, for absolutely, deny whole-heartedly that he wouldn't have killed her if he found out. His face felt too hot, even now. His heart, too.

"Don't be fooled by the premeditation," said Kavanagh. "For her it was nothing short of agony." She paused. "And I use that word deliberately. *Agony*, the suffering preceding death. The anguish of her choice—to stay, or to go. To lose her life, to regain it. I'm sure what she is going through right now is nothing short of the same."

Jared stood to go. There was nothing left to say. "What do you think this is for the rest of us?"

Slowly she nodded, breaking into a hoarse cough. "If you'll excuse me, I must go into the next room where my oxygen tank is waiting for me," she said, struggling up. "I have small cell lung cancer." He stood mute and sore with pity, with awkward empathy. "I know what it is for all of us," rasped Joan Kavanagh. "You know what another word for it is? This suffering preceding death?" She wheezed. "Life."

⚮

What was Jared going to do? Mark the day of her disappearance? Commemorate it with a party, a wake? Put a marker out in the field or a cemetery, bring his kids—her kids—to it? Could the flood of friends and food help him? Oh, he loved how they took care of him. Let's go to Vegas, forget your troubles. Do you want me to cook? Come to my house. Bring the kids. Leave the kids. Come on vacation with us. They didn't want him to be alone. He understood. Trouble was, inside he was in solitary confinement, weighted down, unable to move past. And move past what? If she was coming back, then he would grit his teeth and wait. But if she wasn't coming back, then what?

His kids were waiting, even as they turned eight, and fifteen, and sixteen. He was waiting, even as he turned forty-five. He repainted the back door. He bought a slide for the pool. He bought a kitten to keep Riot and Maria company. Larissa was not a cat person; that'd show her.

He bought new dishes, a new stove. He fixed the steps to the

deck and locks on the back gate. He patched up the fence that had
fallen during a storm, and even got a landscaper to plant a line of
four birch trees down the side yard by the driveway. Eventually, the
purgatory would end, no? He couldn't remain right here for the rest
of his life. He couldn't tell—was he in the middle of his life, or right
at the very fucking end?

And yet each day he got up at six and showered and got all
the kids up and fed and out. Every day, he didn't care what early
meetings he had, he drove Michelangelo to school. Every day at
four o'clock he stopped everything he was doing and called Emily,
to find out if she was home, if all was well. Maria couldn't help
Asher with geometry; Jared did that. And Emily needed help
with Roman columns made of Model Magic. But Maria bought
the Model Magic. Michelangelo needed to find a hundred pieces
of something to celebrate the hundredth day of school. Instead of
counting out a hundred Cheerios or a hundred pasta elbows like the
other kids, Michelangelo made a hundred hearts by hand without
a mold out of Model Magic, painted them red, and said, they're for
Mommy, and then he cracked half of them, and said fifty of them
are broken.

Every day there was something. Every night there was something.
Jared's head stopped being filled with financial numbers from the
latest quarterly meetings and started being filled with white paint
for the winter snow scene and the broken magic markers and the
dried-up glue.

Many things were rude awakenings.

Was his body gradually waking up from the shock of her
abandonment? One night Jared had a dream about Maria. He had
come home and there was no one else there but her. He asked where
the children were; she said they were at the Swim Club and Barbara
was out shopping. Maria was stirring something at the stove, but
when she turned around to face him, she was naked. The next thing
he knew, she was underneath him in the family room. He was still
in his suit. And then she was on top of him, between his legs, still

holding the wooden cooking spoon in one hand and whispering, "We have to hurry, or the *bryndzové halušky* will burn."

"We wouldn't want that," Jared said in his dream, and woke up flushed and too embarrassed to look at Maria for a couple of days, especially considering that whenever he came home she was always in the kitchen doing *something*. The ironic thing about it: he didn't even know what *bryndzové halušky* was. Did he make those words up? He'd never heard the term before, yet it was so clear in his head—as were the vivid other things.

"Maria," Jared said to her at dinner a few weeks later, in front of the children, as casually as he could, "in your country, is there such as dish as . . . *bryndzové halušky?*"

"Of course," she replied happily. "It's one of our national foods. Potatoes, flour, cheese, maybe a little bacon." She smiled. "Some people think it tastes like glue, but that's not true."

"No, no, of course not," he said, looking into his plate, cutting up the sausage. "And how would you even know something like that?"

"Exactly!" she said. "Would you like me to make it tomorrow?"

"No, that won't be necessary."

Can there be forgiveness?

Jared didn't think so.

Then why did his body so emphatically think so?

Oh, the treachery of also yourself, Jared thought, taking a sleeping pill every night so he wouldn't be forced to lie in bed awake and alone. How can you trust another human being when you can't even trust yourself? I'm outraged by Larissa, I can't think of her, speak of her, yet every night every physical thing in me seeps for her. Weeps for her.

∽ও৲

He had to do something. But what? Make a decision one way or another. Say to himself, admit to himself, she was gone, wasn't coming back. But every time he started to think this way, even for five minutes, another lunatic part of him began a maddening argument. People make mistakes. They learn the error of their ways. Like everyone, she'll learn it, too, and come back. How can she *not*? Every morning when he woke his kids and got them off to school, he thought, how can she not? Look at them. Of course she will come back. Her children are here.

But when the months flew on, and there was still no word from her, Jared concluded he might need to try another tack, another path.

2

Private Investigations

His name was Glenn Kelly. He looked like a front-loaded dweeb, not at all like Jared had been picturing him as he drove to Morristown. Kelly was running his office, "Discreet Investigations" out of a tiny light-blue cape, sandwiched between other similar-size homes on a quiet residential street. The blue house had a porch with a rusty screen door out of which the screen and the glass had long fallen out.

Inside was clean. Kelly's office was the living room. First thing Jared saw when he walked in was the enormous desk, an Oval Office–size desk. After shaking his hand, Kelly went behind it to sit down. He looked like a dwarf behind it, a dwarf with a large ungainly stomach. He wore an old blue Big and Tall suit (to match the house?) that had been tailored to fit his short, wide frame, he had on crooked glasses, and he chewed his pencils and his nails, and the corners of his fingers; he tapped incessantly on the desk with either the gnawed fingernails or the gnawed pencils, all giving the impression of a man not calm, not listening, but restless and barely contained.

"How can I be of service, Mr. Jared?" he said, slightly panting, his round face looking down into a piece of paper where he had scribbled down Jared's name. Kelly didn't come highly recommended; he didn't come recommended at all. How could Jared ask anyone for this sort of reference? He found Kelly in the Yellow Pages.

"Would you be requiring a drink, Mr. Jared?" Kelly asked.

"No, thank you. And it's Mr. Stark. Or you can call me Jared."

Kelly lost his nose in the piece of paper, examining it as if it were an FBI fingerprint sheet. "Yes, yes. Please excuse me. I must've written it down wrongly. Nonetheless. Will Jared be acceptable?"

"Please." Jared took a breath.

"What can I do for you?" asked Kelly. "How can my services be of . . . service?"

"Mr. Kelly, I want to hire you to find my wife."

"Ah. Yes. Of course. And how long, could I inquire, has your wife been . . . not in your possession?"

After a pause Jared said, "Since May of last year."

"May!" On his fingers, Kelly counted out the months until he ran out of fingers. Perhaps he could use his toes. Every folded digit was a nail hammered twelve times into Jared's palms and feet and heart. "Hmm." He glanced up, looked away. "That's quite some time to have had her missing, Mr. J—Stark," he said.

"Well, this isn't an active thing on my part," Jared said, "having her missing. I would prefer she weren't."

"Of course."

"I've been waiting for her to come back."

"No harm in that. A passive game, waiting. Not much is required. Do you have, um, any indication that she might be coming back?"

"No."

"And you don't know where she is?"

"If I knew where she was, why would I be here?"

Kelly laughed. "You're so right. Because you know"—he tapped his pencil three times—"she's definitely not *here*." He waved his fingers before Jared had a chance to glare. "Just lightening up the atmosphere, with a small, humorful remark. Now please. Tell me what you do know."

Jared didn't speak.

"Listen, Mr. Jared," Kelly said, indifferent to being correct or corrected. "Let me tell you something. It's your money. I charge two fifty a day for my time, except for this free consultation, which is free only if you employ my expertise, otherwise it's two hundred and sixty-nine dollars plus tax for the consult. So. Two fifty a day, plus expenses, hotels, food, travel, documents, etcetera. Whether I find her or don't, you still pay. So if you keep stuff from me that makes it hard for me to find her, well, whatever. It's your dime. Perhaps you don't like your money. You want to give it away? Fine with me. None of my beeswax. I'm just telling you, I'm not your parent. I'm not here to judge you or discipline you. Tell me or don't tell me, but I want my money up front."

Looking at the modest, to say the least, surroundings, Jared suspected that the $250 a day work wasn't coming as fast as it should, and perhaps that was the reason for the urgency of the tap-tap-tapping. At the same time, the irascible Kelly wasn't the first private eye Jared had gone to. The other four were even more wrong than Kelly, not to mention more expensive. Jared hadn't liked their digs: either in glass offices or in neighborhoods more seedy than this one. So he stayed put, though silent, though hesitant.

Finally he spoke. "I will pay you your rate," Jared said. "No matter what. But there's a ten-thousand-dollar bonus if you actually find her."

"Ten thousand?" Kelly whistled. "Okey-doke. All the more reason to be straight with me, Mr. Stark. All the more reason to tell me what you know."

Jared spoke for ten minutes. His whole marriage, seven thousand three hundred days in ten minutes.

When he was done, Kelly was quiet, rapping his moist ragged pencil on the desk, drumming, tutting, thinking.

"Well, well, well," he said at last. "You got yourself quite a situation here, Mr. Stark. You want me to find her? Really? You sure? There's no denying I could use that bonus. But . . ." Kelly looked up, poker-faced, panting, yet pitying. "What do you want to go digging in these black holes for?"

When Jared didn't reply, Kelly drummed some more. "I been in this business a long time. I was a night-shift beat cop for ten years, a detective for seven, then I got shot, now I do this. Been doing it for fifteen. I'm fifty-three. Got a couple of years on you. Been around the block, married four times, so clearly I'm not one to advise you in *that* particular department. But I will tell you that what you want me to do, no good can come of it."

"That's not true."

"Wait, let me finish. Most of the people who come to me are women, mothers, looking for their husbands, the fathers of their kids, who ran out and left them without child support. Seventy percent of my marital cases are like that. Ten percent are women wanting photographic evidence of their husband's misbehaviors to slam them in divorce court. Five percent are men looking for their wives who took the kids. They want their kids back. Ten percent are men wanting to know if their wives have been faithful."

"How does that work out?"

"Usually, by the time the man gets wind of it, it's very much blindingly obvious to everyone else. Easy money for me, so I don't complain. Men, I'd say, are pretty clueless in this regard." He coughed. "I speak from personal experience, so I don't mean no disrespect there, Mr. Stark."

"None taken," said Jared. He *had* been clueless. "That may be over a hundred percent there."

Kelly counted on his fingers. "I think we're right up to a hundred, give or take ten or fifteen. What I'm saying, is, sometimes the woman goes but takes the kids with her. In an abusive relationship that often happens. But to leave like your wife? I've had two cases before you of the wife skipping out without the kids, and both of them turned up floaters. One in the Passaic, one a little further out in the Ohio." Kelly smacked his lips and shook his head. "That was a beautiful river, though, by Westport, Kentucky. If it weren't for the body three months dead being dredged up, the sunset over the river was a sight to behold."

Jared fiercely rubbed the space between his brows.

"Did you say the detectives ruled out a kidnapping?"

Jared nodded. "They and I both. Besides, I already told you she was involved with someone. You mean she might've been kidnapped unrelated to the affair she was having? As a coincidence?" He tried not to scoff.

"No, that's not what I mean. But maybe she didn't want to go, and the lover forced her hand. Maybe he threatened her life, or her kids, or you, maybe he told her he would tell you unless she went with him? He could've blackmailed her into going."

"Is that likely?"

"Why not? You say she was taking money out of your account? Maybe she was giving it to him."

"He was Jag salesman of the month for a year straight. He got a whole Jag out of it. Sold it without driving it once, and pocketed seventy grand. He didn't need her money."

"Okay." Kelly shrugged. "All's I'm saying is, we don't know what happened."

"She could've gone with him out of her own free will," Jared said quietly. "She could've *wanted* to go. She could've gone with relief, with joy."

The investigator looked skeptical, as if he didn't believe that could ever happen. Only coercion and violence made any sense to him. "She would've written, in that case," said Kelly. "She would've come back, called, petitioned you for a divorce. Her silence is abnormal."

"What do *you* think happened?"

"She's likely dead," Kelly stated without preamble. "She'd be back otherwise. Perhaps he was murderously jealous."

"For over a year she got together with him and then came home to me. Does that seem like an act of Othello to you?"

"Who? Oh, yeah. Uh, guess not. But I don't rule anything out in a strange case like this. Its very oddity is the reason of a good chance for all kinds of shenanigans. Maybe she wanted to come back to you and he got so furious, he killed her. And then killed himself. You're waiting on your wife when you should be mourning her and moving on. You're a good-looking guy in the prime of his life, making money, suddenly unattached. I may be spitting in the wind here, but I bet there are one or two women out there who might, just might, find that combination appealing."

"You think?" Jared said evenly.

"Something tells me."

"Hmm. Well, I'll be on the lookout for that, but in the meantime . . ."

"You see?" Kelly exclaimed. "Her being dead is really the best thing that could happen to you! Then you can tell your kids that Mommy wanted to come back, but has bought the farm and can't."

Jared agreed closure of some kind would be nice, even though he didn't share Kelly's enthusiasm for it.

"Exactly. I definitely see it from your point of view," said Kelly. "But because you want to pay me good money, I also have to see it from a point of view that's not yours." Now it was Kelly's turn to hesitate. "There's also an admittedly small but real possibility that I might find her. And if I find her, there's a real possibility that she ain't coming back, and I don't know how to say this tactfully . . ."

"Not coming back because she doesn't want to?" finished Jared.

"Precisely!"

"Okay. But don't you think I need to know that?"

"I don't know," Kelly said, reaching across the desk and extending his hand. "Do you? Think about it and give me a call."

They shook hands. "I'm ready right now," Jared said.

"Think about it and give me a call, Mr. Stark. You'll thank me later."

❧

It was just bravado. Kelly was right. Jared didn't want to know. He couldn't live his life not knowing, but he didn't want to know. Perhaps in his body language, the private investigator, who, after all, got paid to see things about people, divined Jared's paralysis.

After days of thinking about it, or rather, thinking about everything else but that, Jared called Kelly back. "I want to do this," he said.

"Mr. Stark. I don't think you do. Ask yourself the most important question about this, as about everything: what do you hope to achieve? If she's happy as a clam, will that be good? What will you tell your children? And what will *you* do? See, I don't want to get involved in anything that might later on make me an accessory to a felony, Mr. Stark. I don't want no Armani legal suit proving in the court of law that I had had every indication that you would go and off her, and yet I still went and found her for you. I get twenty-five years for conspiracy to commit murder."

"You're shaking me down for more money," said Jared. "Fine. Twenty thousand if you find her. And I'll visit you in Sing-Sing once a month."

"That twenty grand ain't going to do me much good there," said Kelly.

They met, exchanged information, and money.

Jared gave him Finney's number, pictures of Larissa, the missing persons police report, her driver license number, her social security number, her passport number.

"Good-looking broad," Kelly said. "Looks happy in the pictures."

"Yes, well. Perhaps we'd do better to look at the things which are not seen."

And then Jared sat and waited.

And waited.

And waited.

~∽∽~

Two weeks went by. He couldn't wait anymore. After placing a call to Kelly, Jared had to wait another thirty-six hours before the call was returned.

"I'm working on it," Kelly said. "I was away on business."

Jared couldn't tell from the sound of Kelly's voice whether he conveyed optimism, pessimism. Whether there was hope, whether he was grim. Through the receiver, Kelly sounded as if he'd never actually talked to Jared before.

"Do you have anything to report?"

"Couple of things. I'd rather not say yet. Not sure they're helpful."

"Anything is helpful. Anything you got."

"Okay then. Personally, I don't think she's in this country."

"What?"

"Yeah. Either that or she's dead."

Now Kelly sounded chipper!

"What makes you think," Jared asked slowly, "she's not in this country?"

"Social's not been touched. Driver's license neither."

"Finney said she could've gotten herself a new driver's license."

"Yes. But unlike your little friend Finney, who didn't do his job, I called the DMV in every state. She hasn't."

"In *every* state?" Jared was impressed.

"Even Alaska and Hawaii. And if she was working somewhere, her social security taxes would be taken out. And they haven't been. So how is she making money?"

"Maybe she's waitressing."

"You been at Prudential too long, Mister Financial Officer. Waitresses also pay into their social security. They get two bucks an hour, and six cents on the dollar goes to the social. There hasn't been even twelve cents added to your wife's retirement account. Believe me. She's not working. How long can she live on the money she took? By now surely it's all gone."

"She could've changed her name." Jared was thoughtful. "You should look into Hawaii."

"Why? Because he was from Hawaii? But Finney already checked it out a year ago. He found nothing there. I'll check again if you want."

"Yes, check again." But there were other things that were bothering Jared. "Can you keep in touch with me? I need a weekly report on what's happening. Even if it's nothing, I need it. Five-minute phone call is all I ask. Agree to call me every Thursday evening, or afternoon."

"Weekly? I'm not in my office weekly. I'm heading to San Francisco tomorrow."

"For me or for . . ."

"Partly for you, yes."

"You think she's in San Francisco?"

"I didn't say that. I said I was headin' there. I gotta check some stuff out. Hang tight. I'll call you. This is the thing, Mr. Stark. You waited too long to call me. Her trail has run cold. People don't remember who they saw or spoke to a year ago. I'm havin' a hard time jogging people's memories."

"I understand. We have to work with what we've got."

"No kidding."

"Do you remember I told you he had a Ducati bike? That's not something you forget. Apparently he loved that bike. He wouldn't have sold it. He'd have kept it."

"True."

"I'm saying people might remember the bike even if they won't remember much else."

"What people?"

"I don't know." Jared stammered. "Whoever you're talking to."

"Right now I'm talkin' to you, and you know nothing. You know he drove a Ducati. Does *that* bring you any closer to where she is? Do you know how many Ducati Sportclassics were sold in this country last year alone? Forty-seven thousand. Twenty-one thousand in his color."

"Oh."

"Exactly. Like I was saying. Hang tight. I'll call you Thursday."

❧

"They got on a ship!" Kelly said when he called the following Thursday. "I got a sailor to remember and another midshipman to corroborate. They purchased a trans-Pacific fare from San Francisco to Wailea."

"They went to Hawaii?"

"Looks like it."

"Why wouldn't they fly?"

"A thousand reasons. Easier to get aboard a ship with no questions

asked. Only the driver is asked for a license and sometimes not even
the driver. In his case, he wasn't asked, because there's no record of
him getting on the ship. No record of her at all. But two people who
are still manning the ticket office to the cruise lines remembered
the bike, and vaguely remembered the guy on it. They remembered
him, they said, because he looked so damn young. They asked for
his license to check his age."

"When was this?"

"Last summer sometime."

"Huh. So now what?"

"Now? Well, clearly and unbelievably I'm going to have to go
to Maui." Kelly chuckled into the phone. "I'm a little excited. I've
never been to Hawaii."

"It's not a vacation, Kelly."

"I know. Still, you can't help but notice the scenery even when
you're working."

Jared wouldn't know about that. He hadn't noticed the scenery
since last May.

3

The Runaway Child

There was silence from the fiftieth state. The Thursday phone calls never happened. Jared kept calling Kelly's office, but since Kelly didn't have an assistant, it was difficult to get much information. He left one message, two, a dozen. After a month he stopped calling. Michelangelo had joined Little League, Asher was pitching with the big boys, Emily was practicing cello three hours a day for the state solo auditions, and playing all out for another volleyball state championship. Jared found it difficult to work past 3:30. Which was inconvenient to the CEO of an investment conglomerate, since the stock market didn't close till four. To compensate Jared came in earlier. He got Maria to agree to take Michelangelo to school, just so he could go to the Little League practices during the week and drive Emily to her games on Friday night, and be there for them even in his diminished capacity after school. Every day was filled to the brim with life while he waited and waited.

The trees morphed from fluttering green to deep yellow by the time he heard from Glenn Kelly. There was Lillypond and a two-week trip to Florida to visit his ailing parents, and a week's adventure drive to the Keys. Maria went back to Slovakia for the summer. School began again. Fourteen weeks had gone by since Jared had heard a word.

At 4 p.m. on a Thursday, in October during Halloween season, Jared's phone rang. It was Kelly.

"Oh my God."

"Sorry, mate, I know it's been a long time. I told you to hang tight. Did you listen?"

"Where *are* you? The connection is terrible." Jared could barely hear him.

"Yeah, sorry 'bout that."

"Where are you?"

"Australia."

"Australia! In the name of God, why?"

"Why? Why? Because I got credible information that's where they went."

"To *Australia?*" Jared was incredulous. "What for?"

"That part I don't know."

"Where are they now?"

"I don't know that either. But I had tracked down one of his sisters finally, now living not in Wailea, where he's from, but Honolulu, and she told me that she remembered them talking about sailing to Australia. Can you imagine that?"

If Jared didn't know any better, he could've sworn Kelly sounded impressed by their chutzpah. A sailing voyage!

"Kelly, I can barely understand a word you're saying. What's the matter with you?"

"Nothin', mate. Absolutely nothin'. But look, problem is, Australia's a big country, with twenty million people sparsely spread around. It's taking me a while to locate just two. I'm not optimistic. I've been—"

"Gone over three months and you haven't found them!"

"All righty, no need to shout."

"You're not on my retainer for three months of vacationing in Hawaii and Australia, Kelly."

"I never said I was. Will a month be fair? You already gave me two weeks up front. Another two weeks and we'll call it even?"

"Call it even on what? What did you find out?"

"The sister thought they wanted to start their own business. Some kind of bushwalking tour. So I've been keepin' away from big cities. That narrows it down a bit, but the red center is one big hunk of space."

"You haven't found them . . ." Jared became utterly disheartened.

"I haven't given up, despite the challenges. I've been up and down the eastern seaboard, I've been in the bush, and way up near Cairns in the bamboo forest. What a country, by the way. You wouldn't believe it. *What* a country! Makes me not want to go back."

"Makes you not want to go back where? To work?"

"Yeah. Who wants to work when there are things that take your breath away."

"Well, I'm sure. And I do appreciate the tourist report. When are you actually coming back?"

There was a five-second silence. Jared thought Kelly hadn't heard him, the connection was that bad.

"Look, mate," said Kelly. "I gotta level with you. I'm not coming back."

"Please don't say that."

"I'm going to rummage around the country, see if I can find them along my own travels. There are many places I haven't seen. Do you know that I'd never been out of the country before this?"

"That's swell, Kelly. But what's your plan? To be on my permanent retainer?"

"No. Just Western Union me the money you owe me until today. Forget the bonus."

"You think? Forget the bonus for finding her? Only if you think that's reasonable."

"Don't be sore with me, mate. I told you from the outset, this wasn't foolproof. You signed a piece of paper. I thought you understood. I never guaranteed my work."

"Are you really not coming back?"

"What for? I can work here. Off the books. I don't get much, but then I don't need much. I work as a security guard, a bartender. I have other skills. I go to where the tourists are, work for a few weeks, move on."

"Congratulations. I'm pleased you've got your life figured out."

"Don't be sore. If I find them, I'll get in touch. It'll be on my dime. You won't have to pay. If I find her, I'll call you."

"That sounds great, Kelly."

Jared couldn't believe Kelly wasn't coming back. He thought it was a ruse, that the detective didn't want to admit failure.

First chance he could, Jared drove to Morristown to Kelly's house. There was a "For Rent" sign on the lawn and the windows were boarded up. Old chairs and other tatty furniture were piled up on the porch with a sign: "TAKE. FREE CRAP."

So not only did his wife leave him, but the private investigator he hired to find her left him, too. Jared now needed a private investigator to find the private investigator.

Australia!

∾⟩⟨∽

Jared lost track of how many months had passed before he came home one evening to find the manila envelope mixed in with the catalogs. It looked foreign, exotic.

Jared's name and address were scrawled by a quick and careless male hand, and the return address was a post office box in Tailem Bend, Australia. He wanted to rip it open right away, go into his office, close the door and be with it, be done with it. But it was dinner time, and Maria was cooking. Tonight she had made a Slovakian version of shepherd's pie, and when he asked what that was, smiling she said, Polish sausage, tasso ham, and Italian sausage mixed with potatoes and onions. No cheese, but some breadcrumbs on top. Asher needed to eat fast and be driven to a youth leadership meeting in Millburn, and Michelangelo had to prepare an autobiography project for school—which they kept putting off for obvious reasons—but now it was a week late, and had to be in by tomorrow. Emily learned how to make pound cake with seven eggs and was waiting for Maria's pie to come out of the oven to start on her creation, the third try this week.

Jared opened the envelope in the car, after he drove Asher to Millburn. He sat in the parking lot in the dark, idling the engine; for ten minutes he sat before he could unwind the string of the manila.

Inside was a letter from Glenn Kelly and another white envelope with photos in it. He read the letter first, like opening the card before the gift, except this was a black mass gift, a black mass card. Jared's hands were clenched around the paper.

Dear Mr. Stark,

I know it's been a long time since you heard from me. I don't remember when we last spoke, could it be over a year already? I can't tell you what a royal pain in the ass it was to find her. But she is alive and well, living in a ski town called Jindabyne. He and she operate a little tour company in the summertime. I don't know what they do during ski season. It sounded to me from snippets of their conversation like not much. I went on the two-day tour with them, that's when I snapped the photos. I am sending you two, but like I said, you paid me way back, and I know we had an agreement for more, but being that I quit the gig I don't think it's fair to pay me the bonus, since I wasn't actively in your employ all this time. If you don't want to see, I think you shouldn't see. They run a pretty neat tour. The Americans were quite impressed, including me. Everyone raved about it. Don't look at the pictures if you don't want to. Just go on with your life, Mr. Stark. You still have so much of it left.

I don't know how long I'm gonna stay on the Murray River. I may be moving on soon, want to hike out to the Western Territories. Two local dudes say they make the two-thousand-mile trek once a year—on camels! Can you imagine?

If you want to get in touch, I'm here for a few more weeks.

Jared didn't know what to expect when he slid the two eight-by-ten glossies out of the white envelope. He squinted to see better under the interior console lights. There was his Larissa. She was sitting in some kind of a troop-carrying vehicle, tan-color, all-terrain, like a Hummer but bigger. She was shot with a long lens from the back of the truck; there were blurred heads in front of her; the image was grainy, fuzzy. There was unmistakable truth in the photo. Before she saw Sugimoto make the fake look real, she used to say that a picture didn't lie. It caught a snapshot of what was already there.

Here was the truth that Kelly's camera caught. Larissa, her hair straight, bleached light, left long, unstyled, sitting hippie-like, her lean legs casual and bare, in khaki shorts and a sleeveless safari jacket, smiling like a teenager, with open happy eyes—no, not smiling, laughing! She was responding to something that was good. She looked twenty contented years younger than the last time he saw her, gaunt and entrenched. She was tanned; she wore no makeup.

She looked so happy.

It was the worst photo Jared had ever seen until he saw the second photo.

The second photo was a wider shot of her and the driver in front of a truckload of tourists. The driver was him. He was sitting down, his hands draping over the enormous wheel. Beyond the front windshield were leafy eucalyptus trees, sagebrush, unpaved and dusty distances. He sat with his head turned to her in profile. He also wore shorts and a sleeveless safari jacket. He looked like a stalk with nearly black bare arms. His long hair was pulled back into a ponytail. He looked as if he was speaking, saying something to her, his eyes shiny, full of delight and good humor. But it was her face that was wrenching! Her unabashed adoring face as she gazed at *him*, laughing at something he said, her white teeth, her wide smile.

Jared didn't know what he had expected. Not this. Blankly, he willed his eyes away and stared into the parking lot, into the fluorescent streetlamps outside the youth center, at other cars. Look, he wanted to yell, at the people who weren't there, yell at Ezra, her friend, at Emily, her child. Look—is *this* a face that's coming back any minute?

Is this a face of someone who is ever coming back?

For the first time Jared thought, oh my God. I will never see Larissa again. I will never see her again.

He might have cried.

So years later, he finds her on the shores of some man-made lake, certain that she has man-made problems, and instead, she sits in a truck smiling, laughing, all tanned and twinkling. She looks twenty years old. She is carefree. She is in love. A hammer chiseled away at the hard ball of pain in the middle of Jared's black heart.

Kavanagh was right, Ezra was right. They said, you're never going to get away from the bitterness unless you let it go.

He screeched out of the parking lot and raced across two towns to Kavanagh's office. Perhaps she had evening hours on Thursdays. He needed to see her, needed to tell her about the worst of himself after discovering the best in his once wife.

The lights were on and the door was open, but Kavanagh's waiting area had changed. The furniture was different, the curtains had gone, the TV was a plasma, the magazines were *Architectural Digest*, and the person who opened the door was not Kavanagh but a tall man.

"I must be in the wrong place," Jared muttered. "Sorry about that. I was looking for—"

"Joan Kavanagh?"

"Yes."

"I'm sorry. She died. The cards had gone out; you didn't get yours? Seven hundred people came to her memorial. She was very close to many of her patients. They were distraught to lose her. You never know how people feel about you until you're dead, isn't that sad?" He shrugged. "I'm Dr. Messina. Can *I* help you in any way?"

"I'm sorry," said Jared, stumbling back. "She was a good woman."

"Yes. A good woman who smoked too damn much." Turning from Jared, Messina motioned to his next patient.

In the parking lot, Jared slumped against his car, the manila envelope in his hands. Last time he saw Kavanagh, after he helped her into the tiny adjacent cubicle room where she kept her oxygen tank, after he helped her into a chair and affixed the clear breathing mask to her mouth and nose, Jared stood, discomfited, upset, watching her hollowed out by sickness, thinking he was just like her—ravaged by real pain.

Kavanagh said to him, "You want to know why your wife left? Look at me. In me you have your answer. Because duty is an ugly word. Obligation, responsibility. It implies your requirements to someone else. And we have all been taught—some of us too well—that our responsibility is to ourselves first. Well, I smoked my whole adult life, despite what my two daughters wanted, what my husband wanted. Smoked two packs, one pack, twenty, thirty, forty cigarettes, pretending to everyone it was only six, or eight, or that some days I even skipped entirely. I didn't need to smoke, I lied. But I wasn't fooling my body. It knew. And knowing I was weak and frail, knowing that I'd been getting respiratory infections the last twenty winters, knowing I was on constant antibiotics, that I had the beginnings of emphysema, knowing my daughter was finally pregnant with a boy after having two girls, ask me if I stopped smoking. It's a rhetorical question. You know the answer already. Knowing it could kill me, I didn't stop." The mask went back over her lower face. "Jared," Kavanagh called out to him, whistling cancer out of her trachea, "try to judge her less harshly. Remember: Larissa cannot give you what she doesn't have."

Jared sat in the car with the manila envelope in his hands.

He would rather have her dead than happy. That's what love looked like inside Jared's heart. Like hatred. He was angry with Kavanagh. I thought you promised me she was suffering, he wanted to yell. Isn't that what you said? But he was covering for his own shame, trying to erase from his mind the words of his daughter. "Dad, I'd rather Mom left us than died. If she's alive somewhere, there's always hope she might come back."

He sat alone in Kavanagh's parking lot, with his life in his hands. Not a thing was taken, not a thing was stolen. One day she was, and the next day she simply wasn't. She went out to get a gallon of milk, some paper towels, she went out to paint the set for *Our Town*, stage the puppet scene for *The Sound of Music*, and on the way to lunch in Hoboken, one moment she was driving, paying, getting her cash, and the next—

She just wasn't.

Everything else remained intact. The children, their hectic schedules, their classes, their music, their sports and friends and movies, and rooms with the bedspreads she bought and patched with her own hands. She taught them all, even the baby boy, to make their bed in the morning. She left them that. Jared had to teach them nothing. They got up, they brushed their hair, their teeth, they made their bed. They had breakfast, grabbed their backpacks, waved, shoved their way onto a yellow bus, were gone for seven hours, then came back.

She didn't come back. She made the life, then left it.

But she left it good. She didn't leave it in shambles. Only her absence was shambles.

Dare he say it?

It was as if she *had* died. And seven hundred people might've come to *her* funeral because she was once the moon that reflected in every pool.

In the state of New Jersey, when the spouse has been missing for more than two years, and all relief efforts of the police to locate her have failed, she was presumed dead. The marriage was dissolved. The husband was free to marry, to love again.

Jared stared into his hands while he suffocated.

With his whole heart he saw Larissa as he had known her, the person she once was. Nothing in over twenty years he had spent with her was helping him at this moment.

That's what he had been searching for in the rubble of ashes and burned paper and metal and shards of grieving steel, this very thing: a bone, a sliver of calcium that would tell him, yes! Yes, this is your loved one. But she is dead. Now you can put her in an open casket, bury her and finally get on with your life.

He started up his truck and gunned it to Millburn to get Asher from youth club.

The picture of Larissa in Jindabyne was the open casket.

When he saw it, he knew the truth. He knew she was never coming back.

∽∿∽

"When we were twenty and before she met you," Ezra was telling Jared, late one night, the two of them in Joe's Tavern in Summit, kids home, Maggie in the hospital waiting for a new kidney, "I remember waiting in the last row of the dark theater for her as she practiced the lines for a play she was rehearsing. She was so good, so bohemian with her big black skirts." Ezra was intoxicated, nostalgic.

"She was." She had been gone over three years.

"She was a moveable painting. Something out of Caravaggio, yet she walked, breathed, spoke in loud tones of plague and misfortune. I listened to her on that gray stage. She was reading both sets of lines, but when she caught a glimpse of me waiting for her, she changed tone suddenly, decided to have fun with me, and started reciting lines she had memorized from Anne Sexton. No college gal can go four years without memorizing Anne Sexton."

"Unthinkable."

"The lines had stuck in my head. She could've read anything, recited anything. She could've been funny or tragic, she could've been eloquent or profound. Instead, do you want to know what she read?"

"I'm not sure I do."

Ezra took a breath.

> *"I live in a doll's house*
> *with four chairs,*
> *a counterfeit table, a flat roof,*
> *and a big front door.*
> *Many have come to such a small crossroad.*
> *There is an iron bed,*

(life enlarges, life takes aim)
a cardboard floor,
windows that flash open on someone's city
and little more."

Jared drank his beer. Ezra fell silent. "Later I asked why she chose that poem," he said. "Was it to torment me or to showcase her talents? She replied that it was neither. 'It's simply the saddest thing I could imagine,' she said, 'living a cardboard life. I wanted to know if I could carry it off, not knowing what it means to actually live it.' It was just an exercise in evocation of imagined emotion, nothing more." Ezra swallowed. "I told her she had carried it off beautifully."

"Carried it off pretty far, Ez," said Jared. "All the way to Jindabyne."

They ordered another round. They chased it down with tequila. Ezra wondered how they were going to get back home, without Maggie to drive them. Jared said that Maria would come pick them up.

"We're about to get embarrassingly plastered," Ezra said.

"About to?"

Another round, more tequila, more lime, Jared's head willfully foggy, everything gaseous, floating, until nothing hurt. Ezra became morose. She'll be all right, Ez. She'll be fine. Maggie will get a new kidney, she'll be as good as new. Lucky for her, her brother was a match, and was willing to give it, Ezra said.

"Do you know something?" Jared said. "Father Emilio came to the Philippines originally because he was a doctor. It's fascinating. Apparently there's a huge market in kidneys in the Philippines. It's a booming business. The British doctors go there and marry the Filipino kidneys to desperate Westerners who can't find a match in their own countries. That's why Father Emilio went to Manila. He had been a surgeon and wanted to help."

"Jared," said Ezra, "are you hallucinating? Who is Father Emilio?"

"Che's priest. I read about him in her letters to Larissa."

"Che's priest was a renal specialist? Were you going to recommend him if Maggie's brother didn't work out?"

"Nah. I think the San Agustin parish is his only work nowadays."

"I'm not saying that's not helpful. But why are you telling me about him now?"

"I find it interesting that he began life as one thing and ended up as another. Don't you? I mean, to go to university, to medical school, through residency. That's no small thing. He went to Manila to be one man, and became another. I wonder what made him do it."

"Hmm. What about if we poured the tequila straight into the beer? Would *that* be interesting?"

"Fascinating," said Jared.

And they did. And it was.

Ezra kept trying to open his mouth and tell Jared something. He was having trouble getting the words out.

"You don't have to tell me anything, Ezra," said Jared. "Nothing I don't already know."

"I miss her," Ezra said. "Like a limb."

"I know. Me too."

"I once loved her," Ezra said.

"I know." Jared raised his glass. "Me too."

"Wait—you knew?"

"Of course. The husband always knows," Jared said with a black ironic tilt of the head.

"Since when?"

"Since college."

Ezra stammered. "But you said nothing!"

"What was there to say?"

This stumped Ezra.

"What was, was. It was before she and I got together. It was over and done with. It was fine."

"But how could you never have said anything?"

"It amused me. Had I felt threatened, I would've said something. But I thought I knew her. I felt safe with her. And we were all friends. I didn't want to make you feel awkward."

"I asked Larissa if she ever told you and she said no."

Jared nodded. "That was true. She never told me. Now that I think about it, I find that peculiar, don't you? Like another sign I missed. She knew how to keep secrets. But I knew anyway, Ezra. When you looked at her, it was so obvious. You used to look at her with a longing that I used to look at her with. Not easy to hide."

"Wow, dude."

"It's okay. It's all good."

"We were such good friends."

"Yes. The four of us were always close."

"I didn't know, Jared. Believe me. If I knew I would've said something." Ezra looked downtrodden.

Now it was Jared's turn to pause. "Would you?" he said. "Like what? And to who? To me? To her?"

"She was always happy with you. You were the one she was meant to be with." Ezra swilled his beer. "For a while this bummed me out, years ago. That you were the one she was meant to be with, not me."

"Believe me when I say this, Ezra, but how I wish to God I weren't the one she was meant to be with."

They both sort of laughed, except Ezra less, and this amused Jared. Was Ezra thinking that perhaps Larissa might have stayed had she chosen differently back in college? "Funny how our preconceptions become misconceptions," Jared said. "Had you seen that I *wasn't* the one she was meant to be with, you might've seen the other thing in her."

"The thing we all missed?"

"Yes." Jared looked away to the blue light shining down on the bright glass bottles of top-shelf liquor. Her mother hadn't missed it. Which is why Larissa wanted nothing to do with her. "You missed it because you looked at an illusion. You saw the crystal glass from the outside. How were you to know that the flute was empty?"

They both agreed there was no way to know.

Ezra sounded like he was crying, dry-heaving, but it was hard to tell for sure because Jared couldn't look at him. "Hey, did you catch the Queen retrospective on MTV last weekend? It was quite good, but the whole two hours was worth a split second of Freddie Mercury's face toward the end. He was singing in his last ever video performance, and the song was 'These Are the Days of Our Lives.' And in this video, Mercury is like Skeletor. He can barely move, and when he does, it's in slow motion. He is heavily made up to disguise the unmistakable fact that he is *this close* to Death—and knows it. Gaunt, eaten away by illness, he stands, barely moving, and sings, *'You can't turn back the tide,'* and then he stares into the camera and whispers, *'Ain't that a shame.'* And in his eyes you see his life, and his regret, and his imminent death, and how much he wishes he had lived differently then so he could live a little longer now. If you blink, the moment is gone—like many things—but that blink is how I feel. I wish I could go back to the days before, when I thought I was happy. Just one more week in that walk-up in Hoboken, us broke, diluting milk, and yet happy."

"Dude, it wasn't one thing," said Ezra. "There's no one moment you can go back to and say, if only I did this differently. Besides, you're looking at it wrong." Ezra turned to Jared on the bar stool, his liquid eyes animated. "It wasn't up to you! Her leaving was not your choice. But how you now look at your life *is* your choice. You can look at all that's been taken away from you. Or you can look at all you still have."

"Ezra," said Jared. "Haven't you noticed? I vacillate wildly between both."

"I know, man," Ezra said, subsiding, throwing his arm around Jared's shoulder. "Me, too."

Another hour went by. Or two. Was it closing time? What if Maria was asleep? They'd never been out this late.

"I picked her, Ez," Jared said. "I was in love with another girl before her, a real wild child, but I never slept at night. Yvonne was not the girl to give anyone peace."

"What about when she wasn't with you?"

"Especially," Jared replied, "when she wasn't with me."

"Ah."

"Larissa, on the other hand, had everything except the thing that made me nuts inside, and I mean that in a good way. She was goofy, she was funny, she had interests, she was smart. She was beautiful."

"Yes," said Ezra, and the way he said it, Jared didn't know if he was saying yes to the last thing or to everything.

"But the main thing was, I looked at her and saw a life with her. I thought that together we could build something that would stand."

"And you did."

Jared contemplated.

"You wish you'd stuck it out with wild Yvonne?" said Ezra. "I knew Yvonne. She walked around campus with no underwear, and when she thought someone behind her might not know it, she would pitch forward to pick up something off the sidewalk. So that they would know it."

Jared elbowed Ezra. "This is spoken from experience?"

"The bitterest kind."

Jared laughed drunkenly. "Wasn't she swell? In hindsight, she seems so charming and innocent."

Ezra laughed. "Does it make you feel better to think about her?"

"I dunno. I wonder what she's doing now."

"She's a flight attendant."

Jared stared at Ezra in surprise. "You speak from experience?"

Ezra nodded solemnly. "The bitterest kind."

Now Jared gaped. "Don't tell me she's kept her wanton ways."

"Okay, I won't tell you."

"God, Ezra! That could've been my wife! And Larissa could've been yours."

"I'm not sure," confessed a tearful Ezra, "that I would say no to that, even now."

I once hoped it was me that you saw when you were alone in the daylight, Jared wanted to say to Larissa, but it was much too late.

He wasn't her song in the daylight. The rest was moot.

∽◡◠

It all went up like a dream, and suddenly living became like sleeping. Your heart is raw, and somewhere inside it still hurts but all the details have gone, all the memories have been banished in the plural from the singular of your soul, and sometimes you still reach, reach for her heart, your fingers stretch to remember what you dreamed about, the thing that's forever gone. But you can't. After grasping at the nebulous half-images, you rise, and you dress, and you go about your day.

At the moment life no longer feels like ether. And it doesn't feel like a dream either. Jared's feet are firmly planted on the ground. His eyes are open. He is realistic, pragmatic, practical. He knows he is blessed with much. And if a part of him remains closed, well, that's the price he pays for drinking from his half-empty cup with grace.

Sometimes he wishes he could remember her better. That he hadn't thrown out most of her photos in an act of Neanderthal fury. That he had saved at least their wedding photo. She was a different person then. He was a different person then.

He has mellowed. Nothing fazes Jared nowadays. Nothing can. Sometimes he wishes he could feel that clarifying hate again—for anything.

Kavanagh's words often return to him. At least something returns to him. *She cannot give you what she doesn't have.*

That is almost comforting. Almost as if the carefully wrought destruction was out of Larissa's hands, almost as if it was nothing more than just a casual demolition of his life, an earthquake, a blizzard, a fire.

Except . . .

When Jared went through Larissa's things to throw them away, he found a poem she'd written, buried thoughtfully underneath the sheath of careless papers, a poem undated and untyped, written in her long and flowing, precise and elegant hand. It was titled "Runaway Child."

I'm a runaway child.
Full moon. Hopscotch. Summertime.
Nothing lasts.
When we eloped
You sang Marry Me by Train
And toasted me with cha-cha-cha champagne
But that was then.
Haven't you had long enough with me
Long enough with my tirades and sympathy.
The shooting stars have popped
our red balloon,
I floated down,
I wore my best perfume.
Because it was Friday
and on Fridays I loved you
Today and every day
I ironed your shirts and folded your troubadour ties,
Left hot cocoa for you on the stove,
Babies and house my disguise
Earthbound I stepped out
Poems put away
Every every Everything
Neatly put away.
Maybe someday, one day
Down the road one Sunday
The weight will lift
And you'll forget
I done you wrong
Put me away
And think of me
As just another thing in life
That's come and gone.
Memories like flowers.
Love like lime blossoms.

∞ე⌐

One Friday night, almost like any other, when Jared came home from work and was upstairs getting changed before dinner, Michelangelo yelled for him.

"Dad, phone!" his son called from the bottom of the stairs.

"Take a message."

"Can't. Dude says he's from the Philippines. He says his name is Father Emilio."

Jared was downstairs before Michelangelo had finished speaking. "I'll take it in the office, bud," Jared said. He closed the door behind him. He sat down at his desk. He took a deep breath. He closed his eyes, as if in silent prayer. Then he picked up the receiver.

"Hello, Father Emilio," Jared said. "Is everything all right? Is it about Larissa?"

"Hello, Jared," Father Emilio said. "Yes. It is about Larissa."

PART FOUR
MISS SILVER CITY

What fresh hell is this?

Dorothy Parker

Chapter One

1

The Walker

Larissa dreamed she was dreaming, lying on her back staring at the ceiling and sash windows with white transparent curtains, hearing the subzero freezer humming downstairs, the pattering noise of the shower through the partly open door, and when she opened her eyes, she found herself under the cream yellow quilt with golden petunias, goose down and starched white sheets and four pillows under her head. She felt her well-washed silken sheets under her palms and jumped out of bed, seeing the bookshelves, not yet emptied of stories, and her dresser by the window that had a view of green sloping golfing hills and downstairs a boy's voice instigating an eager dog to bark. "Speak, Riot, speak!" And she did. Larissa, still in her silk nightgown, ran downstairs, and found the three children around the granite island with Emily serving cold cereal in plastic bowls. "Plastic bowls for easy clean-up, Mommy," she said, smiling a bright new morning. "So you won't have as much to do when we leave for school."

Larissa felt profound relief, like a torrent pouring down from her heart to her numb arms hanging by her sides. Thank you, God, she mouthed, standing barefoot in her kitchen, her stomach falling as though she'd been thrown from a plane, falling and falling, staring at them, extending her fingers to reach for Michelangelo's curly head. Thank you.

∾⌒∽

She lay in a small hard bed, with gray sheets so stiff they abraded her back and bare thighs. The crooked blinds were partly open. The room was dark because the windows faced west and it was morning, and wintertime. No, that was wrong, it was summertime, it was July.

Everything was askew. Was it even morning? Or was it evening? Was the third day the seventh? Because wasn't she supposed to rest on the seventh day, which was now a Tuesday? Was black white and white black? Were tears joy and joy tears? Was lack of money really wealth, was a surfeit of love really a dearth of it? Or was there a dearth of love?

She didn't know. And before she got up, she studied the ceiling, granite gray and cracking, like the walls, like the curtains, like the sheets. Who thought it was a good idea to paint everything gray?

Larissa. She was the one who had painted it. Kai wanted a manly color that wasn't blue. So she picked gray. Was the whole cottage like this? What a travesty. Crawling out of bed, she walked naked past the window, indifferently glancing outside to the blue lake, spilled out in an expansive ink stain, and beyond it the foggy Alpine hills and rolling plains asymmetrically arranged for maximum beauty. Except it was July, which was January. Nothing was beautiful in January. It was just waiting for beautiful to begin. It was cold in the house—to save money they turned off the heat at night. As she walked to the radiator to twist the hissing knob open, she recalled herself on Burns Street in Hoboken, bending the same way, but eighteen years younger and two cold, squalling children fuller. Michelangelo wasn't even a curly thought back then. They didn't know how they would pay next month's rent. Later they had joked that if they had had him, they might have sold him.

When Kai and Larissa first got to Jindabyne, they felt lucky because they found this place right away, on the peak of a hill overlooking the silver lake, in a cul-de-sac in solitude, three hundred feet above sea level, at the very tip of a dead-end street named Rainbow Drive. Even the name of the street was optimistic. Behind the ash-colored greening eucalyptus stood a little old bungalow. The weatherboard romance of it attracted them. So secluded! Up on a hill! Private. Tiny. Removed. Distant. Far away. The view was a plus, a bird's-eye glance at the ever-changing lake, the clear of Jindabyne, bluer than blue, and when they stood on their tiptoes at the edge of their property and tilted their heads, they could see the church steeple down left in town center, four miles away by the banks of the lake. It was splendid.

Well, yes, in the beginning it was splendid. But splendid couldn't walk 7.2 kilometers down Jindabyne Road to town, to get work, to eat, to find a job, to keep one, to shop, to socialize. The Ducati did that, and when Kai was on it, he was in town. They had their tour bus, but Kai took the battery out in the wintertime to preserve it, so Larissa couldn't drive the bus if she wanted to—even if she could drive it.

In the winters she had no way of getting anywhere except on her own two feet. Which was okay with her. For the first three years it was okay with her. The four miles down the hill had been doable, manageable. But if she bought anything, carried anything, the four miles back up was a real drag, and in the fourth year, it began to get old. She started accepting rides from strangers just to get around. When Kai found out, he became upset. She promised she wouldn't do it anymore; she knew it was dangerous.

"You have to be safe," he said. "We'll get you a car."

"I'd settle for a Vespa," she said.

After a good chuckle of fond remembrance of Jaguars past, they scraped up a hundred Australian bucks for a bicycle for her. It was old, the rims weren't balanced, and the seat was made of stone, but Larissa didn't complain until she was hit by a car while on it, and then she said, you know what, hitchhiking was safer. Jindabyne Road was narrow, and the lady who hit her was trying and failing to make a U-turn. She was so intent on avoiding other cars, she didn't see Larissa pedaling uphill. So the woman hit her. Larissa swore under her breath, dusted herself off, and lightly cursing the whole way, limped home leaving the mangled bike by the side of the road. Kai saw the bike as he was returning. His panic when he ran into the house was a sight to behold; Larissa forgot all about her broken rib and broken toe. She told him she got away lucky. Heartily agreeing, he made her sympathetic tea every night for six weeks, but because she couldn't work, he had to work double, and did, and was never home. Her rib healed over a year ago, but Kai was still never home.

This morning he'd gone out to find work at the ski shops. He was happy to do this, wake up each morning not knowing how he was going to make money. They had been saving decent money through the summers, knowing from experience the winter months were meager, but last summer was particularly hard. They hadn't made any profit; everything went on operating expenses and living costs. There was too much competition. What Kai and Larissa offered was a quality overnight tour, which attracted a hefty price tag and a particular clientele, while the competition took the daily tourists out for a quick fix down Alpine Way to Khancoban, maybe stopped for lunch at Crackenback, perhaps drove past the Strzelecki monument and was back in three hours to pick up another tour. That wasn't Kai and Larissa's tour.

Sure, during winter season all the tourists and students came for the toboggans at Perisher Blue and the snowboarding at Thredbo, and the place was hopping, but also the itinerants flocked to find temporary work in Jindabyne. They worked for less money than Kai could accept. There were more people than jobs. Kai became like a migrant worker himself, renting skis, sleds, clothing equipment, selling coffee and cigarettes, pumping gas, and then scuffling for more work after he was let go for a man willing to work for half of Kai's pay. This winter was more meager than usual. Perhaps there was an economic downturn somewhere. It was like that late-night joke: he couldn't get a job at a ski resort in the winter.

When Kai was leaving that morning she asked him, what am I going to do today, and he said, do anything you want. Read. Paint.

I don't paint, she said. So read. I don't read anymore, she wanted to say. The mind wouldn't let her, wouldn't keep still on the words on the page. So cook something. But the stove was electric and erratic. Nothing she baked ever came out right, though everyone claimed Jindabyne was best for baking because of the high-altitude mountain air. Cakes were lighter, pastries were crisper! As far as Larissa was concerned, it was good for nosebleeds and little else. She either burned the roast or it came out wet. Mejida, their landlady, said she would replace the stove for a fifty-dollar-a-month increase in rent, which was six hundred dollars a year. Every year. They thought about it and decided to buy their own oven. And here it was, the replacement oven. Yet Mejida, a friendly Indian woman, newly married, who lived next door, would bring rice pudding with cardamom, sweet samosas, naan, and everything she made tasted delicious. Larissa wanted to blame the oven. I used to bake so much better, she wanted to explain. I used to make brownies, pound cake.

She thought about cleaning the house after she showered and dressed. Except there was nothing to clean. And nothing to clean with. She'd used the last of the Windex last week. She had no new vacuum cleaner bags, and the one that was in the Hoover was so full that every time Larissa turned on the vac, the dust blew wildly out the exhaust vent and made the house smell like old people's closets.

They had stayed out too late yesterday and her head felt it today, all parched and sore, like there wasn't even sugar in it, just hops and rye, and maybe cranberry. Perhaps there'd been some mixing of the alcoholic liquids; she couldn't remember. KISS and AC/DC had been on too loud, two bands she never particularly cared for, but at Balcony Bar, girls didn't choose the music. To fit in with the younger crowd, Larissa dressed in Billabong jeans, tight sweaters and high-heeled cowboy boots she got on sale for thirty dollars, which crushed her feet as though she were a Chinese female, yes, feet bound, but overall feeling pretty lucky not to have been drowned in the river at birth.

It was still early. Larissa didn't want to look at the clock. She didn't want to face the actual time, because then she would have to face down all the hours alone until he came home. A gutter child with ceaseless feet, she decided to walk to Caldwell's. She had to go early, otherwise all the fresh meat would be gone. One way or another she was determined to make Kai dinner this evening. They'd been eating out every night, burgers here, sandwiches there, sometimes nothing but bar food, or the hot snacks their friends Bart and Bianca put out. Bart and Bianca always seemed to have more money than Kai and Larissa, though Larissa couldn't understand why or how.

She didn't think she was eating enough, judging from the sheer woman in the mirror, unrecognizable even to herself. She had never been able to regain the pounds since the last months in Summit.

The passing days spun into forever, but the things she carried inside were eternal, operated by their own clock, their own intervals. Which is why it was so hard sometimes to tell how much time had elapsed since this event or that, a birthday, a concert, a phone call, a car accident—everything was *crash* and over. But the thinking about it afterward lasted a lifetime. It was one endless cross-country trek separated by the bridgeless divide between the lifetime before and the lifetime after.

One more morning. Snow. Sunny. The mute mountains white with foam stand wrapped in pine-clad crystal trees, in disconsolate willows. In the mirror is Larissa's pallid face. Everything is as it's always been. In the afternoon after school Michelangelo will be running around the den with Riot in smaller and smaller circles, trying to get himself so dizzy he'll fall down—on top of the dog. Emily will be at cello and then volleyball. She will need to be picked up at five. Asher will be at track or band practice. Jared is at work. Larissa stands in front of the mirror in one hallway, in another, her heart grown hollow with gladness, with sorrow, and wonders what it's like to be dead.

Once you got dressed up, shopped for food, enjoyed pleasures big and small.

And then you were dead.

The other things receded with almost no regret. Just the distant clicking of the hoofs of constant horses that carried off the years and the memories in their empty saddles. Carried off things that no longer mattered. Now other things mattered.

What were they?

This was the thing: Larissa knew a little bit about many things, but not a hoot about anything. She wasn't like Jared, who knew everything about investments and accounting practices and the profit-loss margins of multiconglomerates, and about runs batted in with two outs in late innings with a runner on third and the home team trailing by a run. She wasn't like Ezra who read prodigiously on varied topics and was thus able to fake deep and expert knowledge even on concrete pavers. No, Larissa knew a little bit about fashion and hair, more about books, still more about theater, modicum about rock music, less about jazz, tiny bit about history, and knew least of all what moved and spurred on human hearts, especially hers.

She thought if only she could understand her father, then other things might become clear. But she never understood him, and so much else in her life remained nothing but a hard floating January cloud. No promise of anything in the air. It wasn't spring, it wasn't even the amber heaviness of decomposing fall, it wasn't the green heat and salt water of summer. It was a bitter clear void of January. Everything felt like neither before nor after. Seasons came and went under the Southern Cross. When was Christmas? The joys of the season had gone for Larissa, the weight of all the resolutions she couldn't keep was upon her shoulders, no Valentine's day, no winter break, no planning of a week's escape somewhere, the Easter Fair, the Food Fair in Dalgety. It was day in and day out of the blue and red Summit swings not moving in the subzero cold.

Except it was *July*!

She stood for a long time naked in front of the mirror in the subdued and dusky house, all alone, before she finally went and turned on the shower. Afterward she got dressed in old sweats and a hoodie, layered herself up with T-shirts and a Henley, put on a ski hat, a scarf, some gloves (they might have been Kai's), put on walking shoes, and left the house. She had brushed her hair, but that was all. Her mascara was running out and she didn't want to spend another six dollars on a new one, not until they knew for sure if Kai could get some steady work. The six dollars she had in her pocket was for dinner tonight if she planned carefully. She would do without thicker blacker lashes as she walked down the mountainside, the frosted dry grass crunching under her feet.

It was colder than she wished, but not as cold as Summit had been, with its icy blizzards. In July, though, Summit was not cold. In July Summit sparkled with green sunlight, and Italian ices were sold at every corner, and she and the kids spent June at the Swim Club looking for lizards in the bushes, and then six weeks in Lillypond, where the mosquito nets were up, and the lake was warm. They were water rats, jumping off the wooden float, chasing dragonflies through the murmur of the swaying reeds, the moonlit fields.

This blue lake was not for swimming in July. The dry crispness in the air hurt her nose, it started to run, felt like it was bleeding. She wiped it with her glove. It *was* bleeding. She continued down the slope. She really should get it cauterized; in the wintertime, the nose gushed blood twice a day like a clockwork geyser.

Briskly she walked to Caldwell's with her hands in her pockets and her hat pulled down over her ears, the way Asher had worn it until his thirteenth winter, when he suddenly decided he was rejecting all winter attire for one whole season, for no other reason than he was protesting winter. The advantage was: it made Emily dress warmer in protest to his protest. Michelangelo didn't have a choice: his mother dressed him, and besides the little boy didn't like to be cold.

Larissa's head was cracking open. She should've taken an aspirin. If she had one, she would've. They could afford aspirin in balmy December when they worked non-stop from dawn to dusk. The irony was, she was too busy to get headaches in December. It was the rum! she realized. The fermented sugar cane did something funky to her brain, it always had. Usually she stayed away from it, but yesterday it must have been free, for how else to explain the raging head? No liquor affected Kai, except to make him dance and sing. He drank a lot to dance and be happy, but the next day always got up and went to work. He wasn't like Che's Lorenzo.

Larissa hadn't heard from Che for so long. Whatever happened to her old friend? She lost count of the summers that were winters and the winters that were summers. Did she have to count them twice? Because that would make Larissa over fifty. She stopped celebrating her birthday on April 4. Her birthday was in spring, not fall. She was born when everything in the world was beginning, not ending; she wasn't born when the leaves fell off the poplar trees, when it rained and the air got cold. She was born when the days were resurrected by forsythia and daffodils and yellow tulips. She wasn't born in rain and wind. There were so many degrees of wrong with that (180 to be exact), that the first year they were in Jindabyne and April washed over May, Kai said to her, suddenly remembering, did you have a birthday last month and I missed it? Larissa shrugged and said *meh*, and he consoled her with, you're forever young to me. That was sweet. She went with that. Ran with it. He didn't mention it again, and neither did she. His birthday was in January and he loved celebrating it when it was hot and the Alpine daisies were out, and they had resumed their tours and were making money again. They cleaned their Land Cruiser troop carrier, bought new hiking boots, invested in new tents, new fishing lines, summer jackets, flasks, Thermoses. And every twenty-third day of January they went out and got extra-expensive tequila at Balcony Bar and partied till closing time and then came home and partied some more, just the two of them. He was *so* good. Didn't agave used for tequila have sugar in it? Weren't the flowers edible, and had sugar, like rum? So maybe it was the cheap tequila that was cracking her head open this morning.

She clutched her stomach through her jacket pockets as she walked.

She wished she knew how to ski. How did learning that skill

pass *her* by? No surprise that it passed him by, Kai of the Hawaiian volcano beaches, but how did it pass her by, from the New Jersey mountains, where there was a ski lift on every hill? When she was a child she didn't ski. They lived near the Hudson River and when the town pond froze in Piermont, they ice skated, but there wasn't much call for ice skating in Jindabyne. After she got married and had kids, skiing was too expensive. By the time the children were older and there was money, there was no time for skiing. No time for skiing, or theater, or a job. No time for much of anything, yet every day was filled to bursting. Here in these summers/winters she had nothing but time.

But not for long. She decided she was going to get a job at Caldwell's. It wasn't too far; she could walk it every day. She could make some extra, sorely needed money to put toward the business. They could buy new tents and tune up their safari troopie, repaint the signs, upgrade the microphones and the radio, invest in new disposable cameras for the customers, make sure they had enough money left over for worms, lunch pails, trout lines, drinks, sun hats, for advertising online. They ran a beautiful tour. They designed it themselves, researched it, wrote it. Larissa performed it while Kai drove. Her theater training came in handy. Three times a week she put on a twenty-eight-hour-long performance. They took eight people a hundred and twenty miles into the wilderness, down the Thredbo, through the mountains and the Great Gorge and the Great Dividing Range of the Snowy River, to Tumbarumba. They sat on granite boulders and fished for trout in the Thredbo and the Murray, and for salmon in the streams. They cleaned and cooked their own fish while the wallabies grazed nearby and the wombats hid in the grasses. They bushwalked and talked about the high country wildflowers and poisonous snakes and the music of the Grateful Dead and the Animals; they drank beer, sang "The House of the Rising Sun" by the campfire, accompanied by Kai's spectacular ukulele, sang "Like a Rolling Stone," and "Angie," and slept under the everlasting stars in the Australian Alps.

Right after Halloween, Larissa would tell her favorite ghost story

by the flickering flame, the story of the Snowy Mountain River
Dam project. To dam the river to divert the water into the driest
part of New South Wales, to grow the businesses and the farms and
the vineyards, the government created the artificial Lake Jindabyne
in the flat valley between the hills, and all would have been fine
except the old town of Jindabyne was laid out in the flat of that
valley. Can't dam a river without burying a town or two, and so
Jindabyne was buried in a watery grave, and in the heat of the
summertime, when the tide is low and the water level drops, you
can still see the church steeple rising out of the lake like a phoenix,
like something that will out, no matter how well it's buried. The
myth says there were people in that town, and now they're in their
watery grave, too, and every Halloween their souls rise up from the
lake and wander the new city. They buried a real town to make a
fake lake, Larissa would say. Does that make you shiver?

And one time, a heavyset, out-of-breath American man said to
Larissa, "I have stories of destruction perpetrated against human
beings by other human beings that would make you shiver. What I
have seen with my own eyes is true terror. Wanna hear?" He stared
at Larissa too pointedly, too intensely. Now *that* made her shiver, to
the chill of her heart.

And funny enough, that dark night, no one wanted to hear.

The next morning they drove on to the sprawling grape-
growing country near Tumbarumba and partook in a tasting tour
of the region's best cool-climate sparkling wine made from Pinot
Noir and Chardonnay grapes. They took unmarked trails out, and
on the way back to Jindabyne drove down the almost inaccessibly
narrow Alpine Way past Mount Kosciusko, through the snow gum
and Alpine ash woodlands. All the new bushies were exhausted and
exhilarated. Many said it was the best tour they'd ever been on.

Larissa knew what they meant. The first time she and Kai marked
the tour on the dirt roads that ran parallel to the paved highways,
she never thought her lungs could breathe so deep, her heart could
beat so profoundly, that she could feel so happy. She was giddy with
the altitude, with rapture, chanting the name of her grandest lover

under the stars, his mighty limbs the length of grace. Kai . . . Kai . . . There had never been anyone like him in the open country.

After two years, when the birth control pill ran out, she didn't go to the clinic to get more. Let's see what happens, they said with an excited shrug. If it's meant to be, it will be. She wanted to say to him, you know, children are a big responsibility, but didn't. He had lost one of his. She had lost three of hers. No use dredging up the bottom-dwelling grief.

There was no baby.

They shrugged. Obviously it wasn't meant to be.

And things had changed in the five seasons they'd been here. Without getting a second vehicle and hiring more people, they reached a ceiling to the money they could make off eight people for a twenty-eight-hour tour. They were busy, but they weren't growing their profit. Last summer all the money they made went right back into renewing the supplies and repainting the desert-tan Land Cruiser a jungle camo color. It felt like business was drying up, like there was no way out.

Caldwell's market was before town, on the downhill road overlooking the lake. They knew her there; Caldwell, the man who owned the store, kept trying to sell her kangaroo tail. "Jimmy, I just want ground beef," she would say to him. "Got any of that?" Not giving up, Jimmy kept trying to convince her kangaroo soup and stew were just the ticket on a cold winter's night, and she couldn't explain that it was July and wasn't supposed to need winter stew. She kept buying ground beef because she wanted to make a summer barbecue. "Do you have some chicken wings, Jim? I want to marinate them," she said to him this morning, rubbing her hands together to get warm. Caldwell didn't have chicken, but he ground up some chuck for her.

"Jim," she asked tentatively, her palms on his glass counter, "is there any work around here?"

"What kind of work are you lookin' for, darling?" he said. He was a short man, perpetually in overalls and a plaid shirt. He had told her he was from Scotland, but his wife was Polish, and she made stuffed cabbage sometimes and pierogi that Larissa loved, having never had them before. Such foreign tastes, but good. Every once in a while Anna asked her if she needed a cleaning woman, and Larissa was surprised by that, as in: the Caldwells own a store that's open seven days a week and is the only provider of fresh produce and packaged foods for miles around. And yet Anna asks if she can clean Larissa's house, as if Anna is the one who needs the money and not the other way around.

"Oh, no. There's no work here," Jimmy Caldwell said. "Our son wants to go to England to college next year. We don't know what to do. How to explain to your only son that you can't afford to send him?"

"Is he smart?" said Larissa. "Does he have sports or musical ability? Maybe he can get a scholarship?"

"I don't think so," Caldwell replied. "He rides horses. He fishes. Do they even give out scholarships for that?"

Larissa was about to offer Jared's sage advice. Mortgage your store, she wanted to tell Jimmy. Take out a large loan with your business as collateral. That's what Kai and I would do, if we had a child. Sending one son to college in another country was a big expense. Now imagine if you had two children, barely eighteen months apart, and they were both in college at the same time. Imagine they went to private universities that cost tens of thousands of dollars a year. Those parents would have to mortgage their business, their house, their cars, their jewelry, everything, wouldn't they, to send two grown children through four years of higher education. Larissa suddenly felt sick. The feeling came again, falling straight down, all oxygen sucked out of her lungs, unable to catch even a shallow breath, the steepest rollercoaster drop but without the childhood and the joy, and the rollercoaster. First it assaulted her only during dreams, the awful rushing plunge, but now it started to come during the waking hours too, hatefully increasing in frequency.

"I'm sorry, darl," Caldwell said. "Don't look so sad. I want to help you. I would, if I could."

"No, that's fine." But he looked worried; she must have lost the

blood in her face. Long ago she lost the color in her hair. She started
bleaching it herself, dousing it with peroxide and lemon, to remove
all color. She removed it, all right. She wasn't so much Winter Gold
now, as winter ash. Kai said he liked it; called it lemon blonde.

Caldwell gave her a pound of ground beef and two baked
potatoes on credit until Wednesday. He gave her coffee for free. She
drank it black, without sugar, the way she hated it, and then slowly
walked back uphill to Rainbow Drive, carrying the little plastic bag
of food for Kai.

A woman was taking out her garbage. "Good morning!" the
woman said. "Isn't it lovely out? Did you see the lake today? It's
absolutely gorgeous."

"Good morning," said Larissa, speeding up. She didn't glimpse
at the lake.

What was it that haunted her? She had been doing well for so
long.

Was that true? Had she been?

After she got home, she scoured the kitchen for something to
eat. The bread was stale (though she didn't throw it out, just in
case; after all, what was a little mold when you were hungry), and
the milk was sour. She thought of taking the six dollars and walking
downtown to Gloria's Jeans, where she could get a coffee and a
delectable pear and raspberry bread and sit and read the newspaper.
Often there was news from back home. America this, America that.
Even New Jersey was in the news once, something about a governor
resigning amid charges of flagrant impropriety. "This is my truth,"
he had said. Larissa liked that formulation so much. My truth. She
had some truths of her own. Inarguable really.

Maybe instead of reading the paper, she could ask Serge at
Gloria's if there was any work. She could serve coffee to the
migrants.

She didn't want to walk so far again, but she liked the idea of
being there, the smell of the coffee, the sitting down in a warm
place full of food and people. Hearing other voices. No wonder she
couldn't put on any weight, all that walking. Larissa didn't think

Kai liked her this thin. She didn't know for sure, he never said, he wasn't mean, but . . . when they were in bed and he fitted in behind her, he didn't say, you feel so good, as he ran his hands over her. He didn't compliment her in clothes or out. Well, what was there to compliment? Her clothes were his clothes. Jeans, Henleys, boots, Akubra hats, his a Cattleman, hers a Stylemaster. Her body was his body. If it weren't for the breasts, she'd be narrow-hipped, long-legged and tall like him. Her hair was straight, his was kinky, but when they put it in ponytails, put on their safari jackets and hiking boots, from the back who could tell they were man and woman?

From the front who could tell they were lovers?

Once you could tell.

Yet at Balcony Bar on Wednesday nights after he got paid, they drank and danced, and she put on a little lipstick, and let her hair down. She still looked pretty, she thought; did she still look young? Ish?

The bungalow they rented came sparsely furnished. In the years they lived in it, they bought a new mattress for the bed because they broke the old one; all the coils burst out of it one night, a slasher movie about the evils of too much sex.

The TV flickered, and there was no radio, except for the clock by the bed that hissed the AM stations and was full of static on the FM as if the DJs walked on carpet as they spun the records. In the kitchen, there was a small table for *almost* four, in the living room a brown couch and an armchair by the window. The curtains remained drawn. They had no pictures on their walls. No framed and well-placed photos of their families, of her children in the pool, of each other. She had started to acquire some second-hand books, to rebuild her collection, but when the brakes went out on the troopie, they pawned the books and what remained of her jewelry to get them fixed, and then let the deadline pass for getting her things back. At night, they rode the Ducati to town to drink. Sometimes, when they were *really* broke, they stayed home. They weren't much for TV, but they read a little bit—when they had books. They played cards, pretending they were in Vegas or Reno. They had a pretty good time, sipping whiskey mixed with heavy cream to make it taste like Bailey's. But whiskey was expensive, and heavy cream went off. It cost three dollars, and sometimes they didn't have it. So they played cards without whiskey and cream. Sometimes, she lay down in bed and pretended to sleep. Like now.

❧

At first, things had been too exhilarating to be frightening. Though they were a little frightening.

Larissa left at 11 a.m. that Friday, with a small bag newly bought, clothes, passport, license, and crisp cash. She didn't turn back to look at her house one last time, she didn't turn her head to glance at the golf course. She just kept her eyes to the ground and her feet steady. It seemed like forever to walk that one mile to the train station. But it only seemed that way. Because she powerwalked, was almost running. She left the house at eleven, and by 11:16 she was already on the train, at the window, her face pressed to the glass as the train glided away, gaining speed, its urgency calming her, comforting her, as she daydreamed of the life she was about to live the only way she wanted to—together with him, somewhere where it never got cold. She was a gothic traveler, her pounding heart full of lush imagery of the future, heading not east to New York City, but west to Hackettstown, the last stop on the Jersey Transit Rail, where he was already on his Ducati, waiting for her and her little bag. "You okay?" he said. "I'm great," she replied. That was one of the few times they had discussed IT, the thing that would not be discussed, the unnamed disarticulation. Why talk when they had wilderness to explore? She hopped on, and they sped away with the wind in their hair; she clutched to him with both hands like she did during love, and pressed her cheek to his leather-jacketed back. They had jumped on his bike like baby joeys. He had sold his gift Jag; they had money. Larissa wished she could have sold *her* gift Jag for being a good wife seventeen years out of eighteen. She was filled with equal amounts of terror and elation. She had never felt more alive.

For four glorious hours through the Alleghenies, in full late spring, the wind in her face, she gulped for breath, holding on to him. The open road, the greening sloping fields, the up and down of the rolling hills, the breathtaking beauty of western Pennsylvania. They stopped for food and gas in the field country store in flat Ohio. They stopped for good when it got dark near Indianapolis, found a cheesy motel off the Interstate and made abandoned love on the white sheets until four in the morning, and then slept till noon.

They didn't want to leave; they hadn't ever had this, a night together, waking up together, mornings, a full day stretching out ahead.

"How can I be so lucky?" whispered Kai, caressing her bare stomach with the tips of his fingers.

You are my salvation and my refuge, she wanted to say to him. It sounded like a psalm Maggie might sing. She closed her eyes, losing herself in her own romantic posturings. This was all just prelude to the boundless adventure about to begin. Nothing was known, not a single day. There was no certainty, no plan. Every minute was strange and new. By the time they finished pancakes and French toast at Waffle House, it was nearly three, and they giggled like schoolgirls, like Che and Larissa at the playground, about the indolent decadence of not having to get up for work, for school, for *anything*.

They rode through Illinois, spent another purgative night at a roadside motel in Des Moines, Iowa, and it was there, at a deli on Capitol Avenue with a full view of the gilded capitol dome, that they had their first disagreement. She wanted to ride all the way to the west, across the country she'd never seen. "I want to be the bike girl from Chico," she said, reaching for his hands. The girl from Chico rides the back of a man's bike, and never thinks of tomorrow. Where did this dream of herself come from, this hazy yet clear definition of herself?

But he, pulling his hands away, wasn't interested in the Chico girl. He wanted to get to San Francisco ASAP because a ship was leaving for Maui and he wanted to be on it.

"We're going to Hawaii?" That was news to her. She told him she'd never seen the Great Divide, or the salt flats of Utah, the endless expanse of the Western sky in Nevada. The Pony Express, Kai, she pleaded into his indifferent face. She wanted to see these things all the more, partake in the exploration of the wilderness because she would see them from the back of his Ducati, pressed against his back, the back she grasped at night. What about this was so hard to understand? I want to get lost with you, she said to him.

"They'll kill us in the west for my bike," he said. "We'll be good and lost then, won't we? I can't leave it anywhere. What about *that* is so hard to understand?"

She sulked. She said let's get a gun to protect ourselves. Larissa said this. "*Get a gun.*" She, who'd lived in Rockland county, in a little suburban house, who'd gone to college in New York City, who lived in Hoboken, and then tranquil Summit, who'd never even *seen* a gun up close, was now advising her twentysomething lover to get a gun to protect them against the forces of evil in the lawless west. Afterward she was sore and raw from love, the excitement of her life pouring into night, the excitement of the night spilling over into life. It was all one, and the gun was part of it.

Kai refused to get a gun, citing registrations and records and waiting periods, reminding her they were on the run, on the lam. Did they want to be found? Is that what *she* wanted?

No, she admitted. That was the *last* thing she wanted. To be found. That was the truth of it. Lost is where she wanted to be.

Kai told her they would come again to these parts, would see the things she hadn't seen, there was so much time, not now, not today, but in the boundless future. He was ardent and persuasive and she believed him. I don't care where I am, she whispered to him in anonymous motels, as long as I'm with you. They took a train from Omaha to Union Station in San Francisco, and alighted a ship headed for Wailea, Ducati in cargo. It took three days to cross the Pacific, and Larissa spent most of the daylight hours on deck, standing at the rails, looking out onto the vastness of the slate ocean, just sea and horizon in every direction, humming to herself a vague, half-forgotten Marianne Faithfull tune that she stopped humming immediately upon realizing what it was: "Falling from Grace." She deemed it inappropriate. Of all the things to hum!

Kai was less impressed with the sea. "I liked the train," he told her. "I like looking at people's lives outside the train stations, imagining if I could live there, too. Here, there's nothing to imagine."

"Yes," she said with a falling face. "But lots to think about." She had had no way of telling Jared that Michelangelo couldn't go anywhere without his blue bunny, no way to remind him to take the bunny when they went to Lillypond or to Boston to visit her brothers, or to Piermont for dinner with her mother. There was no good way to nudge him about something like that. But that wasn't even the truth. *She* had forgotten all about it. Had she remembered, she would've figured out a way to slip in a sentence about the importance of the blue bunny to the blond boy, but she was preoccupied and didn't. And now Jared had no idea. They were so absent-minded, both father and son, they'd be halfway round the world before they remembered that the little boy couldn't sleep without his bunny. What could Larissa do about it now?

"Thinking? Not a good thing," Kai said, smiling, prying her clenched fingers away from the railing. He was besotted with the idea of love on the open sea. He said it felt like Bacchanalian debauchery. He couldn't get enough of her.

Kai and his joyful welcoming smile, like he hadn't a care in the world, just a guy rolling through life. He was a magnet, an instant polarizing elixir against the plagues of the heart. Smile, Kai, pull me away from the bottomless ocean. When I see you, there is nothing else but you. The ornery stubble, the soft mouth, the frizzy hair wet from shower, the restraining hands, the unforgiving bounty. For Larissa, her journey had already begun and this was part of it: learning how to take responsibility for her life unstoppably intertwined with his. It was on the ship through the Pacific that she flung herself in the waters, cleaving herself into the Larissa before and the Larissa after. It wasn't her sins she wanted the water to wash away, because that would imply there had been wrongdoing, and there wasn't, there *wasn't*. There was choice and freedom, and owning her actions, all virtues, admirable, dignified, every one. The two of them were full of goodness—look how profoundly still the ocean and the skies were around them. Kai and Larissa were one with nature. They were in sync with the earth. Long after she ceased to be, nothing would change in the great Pacific. That was reassuring, for she felt herself to be part of a larger creation, a freeform tone poem in the center of the classical symphony that was the ordered universe. What the vastness of the ocean succeeded in doing was to wash away her past life so that the mind didn't fly to it, didn't wallow in it, didn't stub the toe on it; it was put in a compartment inside, locked, excised and heaved into the salty straits, so that by the time they alighted in Hawaii, Larissa was reborn and new. Such a clean break, not even the nerve endings twitched. The limb of Past was severed and healed during the passage over the sea.

They were barefoot wanderers, plunging into the waters, foregoing the expensive wine. They didn't need it. Kai was like air. Without him Larissa could not live.

∽৩౿৫

Jindabyne was cold. Larissa hadn't expected it. This was incongruous to her about Australia. It was like Africa being cold. How could there be snow on the ground, sharp air filled with woodsmoke, ice around the edges of the recessed span of the lake, blue cold winter light reflecting off the distant hills? It was *August* when they got there! It was supposed to be only gold hues, orange, red, yellows and greens in Australia. Where did this violet cast come from, this aberrant chill? Larissa shivered as she asked these questions of Kai, who was cheerful and unbothered.

"It's winter. Of course it's cold."

"But I thought we were going to live somewhere warm." Like Hawaii. Why couldn't they have stayed on Maui a little longer? He didn't want to; Larissa could tell. Hawaii was like the 7-Eleven in the strip mall off a suburban tract highway for him. He didn't see anything in it. His associations with it were not a balm for the soul, the way beauty is supposed to be. Not the warm water, nor the fire flowers, or the mangoes.

"It'll get warm soon. You'll see."

But it was still wrong. It made no sense. At the Lake Jindabyne Motel they stayed at, the cast-iron radiator was on, pumping out heat! What was this, winter in Jersey?

Larissa had no warm clothes. No sweaters, no parkas. Wistfully she thought of all the winter jackets she had left, the downs, the Thinsulate, the thermals, the furs hanging in her closet, the cashmere scarves and gloves, the woolen hats, the ear muffs. Maybe she could write away for them. *Dear Jared, sorry I'm gone, but be a dear, forward my favorite sheepskin, it's freezing here in the Red Center.*

It's not the Red Center, said Kai. It's the Snowy Mountains. These are Australia's Alps and skiing villages. This is where the Australians come to enjoy the winter sports. Thredbo and Perisher Blue is where they ski. Let me take you there, so you can see. It was icy atop his bike, with the wind chill frosting up the windows of her eyes. Pressing her face against his leather jacket didn't shield her from the bitterness. Were they really planning to *stay* here?

He took her to a waterfront cottage on the shores of Lake Crackenback where they remained two weeks, sleeping, making love, pretending to figure things out, and every morning the frosty mist rose from the lake like a shapeless Loch Ness, and the lake underneath the rising haze looked like a winter glade, crystal bright and sparkling clear.

"What are we going to do? Do you know someone here?"

"I told you. My friend Bart and his wife, Bianca. They love it here. You'll see. It'll be stupendous."

"So we're definitely staying?"

"At least through the summer."

She listened to Kai's bold plan: a tour through the rivers and the mountains, legends of times long past, fishing, fires, songs and stories. It did sound remarkable, every syllable.

"But what about the wintertime?"

"We'll make so much money in the summers, we won't care.

We'll hibernate and recreate. Come here. I'll show you what we'll do."

She came, but she wasn't convinced. Still, she didn't want to be a spoilsport. It just wasn't what she imagined. It wasn't quite what she had signed up for.

～～

Larissa made dinner for him, but he didn't come home at six or seven or eight or nine. She didn't know what was going on. It was Tuesday, and he wasn't getting paid till tomorrow, and yesterday they'd already gone out. After they came home, he felt so dirty and broke, he said he wasn't going out again for a week. And here it was the next day and he was out—without her. He didn't even call. Perhaps the phone had been turned off; Larissa picked it up. No, the damn dial tone. She didn't have enough money for a cab, and she wasn't about to walk to town, seven kilometers without a shoulder or a sidewalk in the dark. After she angrily ate her hamburger, she thought of throwing his out, but hunger and frugality stopped her. She sat and waited in the silent house, without even the TV on to break the silence.

At ten, she went next door to Mejida's house. Mejida and her husband owned a car service business; sometimes Mejida helped her out and rolled the car fare into the rent.

"Sorry to bother you again," Larissa said. "But I think something is wrong with Kai's bike, and I can't get in touch with him. I'm afraid he might be stuck in town. Would you mind terribly . . . ?"

"I don't mind driving you," Mejida said. "But it's three weeks into July and you haven't paid the rent."

Larissa was shocked and embarrassed. Kai usually paid Mejida; Larissa thought it had been all taken care of.

"Not only *not* taken care of," said Mejida, "but Kai paid me only half of June. I won't even mention the hundred dollars in cabs you took between then and now."

"Oh," said Larissa, stepping off the porch. "Thank you for not mentioning it. I'll be ready in five."

She sat like a stoic in the passenger seat, not even enough guilty courtesy for a grateful conversation, too mortified that a month and a half's rent was due, and she knew, *knew*, they didn't have even a hundred bucks put away toward August. Mejida was an attractive, heavy Indian woman who always smelled of curry spices. Cumin, coriander, and cardamon like a savory rice pudding. Tonight, the sickly sweet spices were making Larissa subtly nauseated.

"So is it true what Bart tells me?"

"I don't know, Mejida. I didn't even know you talked to Bart."

"Of course I do." Bart and Bianca rented out skis and toboggans to the tourists whom Mejida and Umar then drove to Thredbo. How could Larissa forget. "What does he tell you?"

"Well . . ." Her soft Indian voice belied the bluntness of her words, "Bart said you had a husband and children in the United States you left to be with Kai."

"Bart told you this?"

"Actually, Bianca."

Larissa stayed composed. "Why would Bianca talk to you about me, Mejida? That's weird."

"No, not weird. I complimented you and Kai on your commitment to each other despite your age difference, and Bianca told me that you sacrificed quite a lot to be with him."

Larissa said nothing, digging her nails into the palms of her hands to force herself to keep steady and silent. She didn't remember ever telling Bianca anything. She didn't talk about personal things to their new friends. Perhaps Kai did? Except Kai was even more closed-mouthed than she. He talked only about the weather; he sang songs; he told jokes.

"Well, I think it's incredible," continued Mejida. "Not everybody can do it, view the rules of society as nothing more than a contrivance. Kudos to you. The individual triumphed over social constraints. Have you kept in touch with them?"

"Have I kept in touch with them?" What a strange question! The rules of society? What was she talking about? It had nothing to do with that. It had to do only with love. When were they going to be there? Didn't Mejida see the arms twisted around Larissa's stomach to stop her from hearing anymore blather?

Mejida clearly didn't see, busy driving down dark winding roads, because she continued evenly. "It's odd to imagine you as a married woman with children." She chuckled. "It doesn't seem like you at all. You fit so perfectly with Kai. You both give off a slightly dislocated vibe. Like two journeymen. A mother, a wife doesn't jibe with that."

"Doesn't it?"

"I can't imagine you as a mother at all," Mejida declared as she drove. "Motherhood is a word that has too many geographic limitations. I don't feel that with you, either the sacrifice or the convention." She smiled pleasantly in profile.

"You don't have any children, Mejida?"

"No, we just got married."

"Three years just."

"We hope to have children soon, when the business is more established. We want to be a little more secure."

"Yes, it's always good to be certain of the future," Larissa said through her teeth. She and Jared waited to have Michelangelo until they were more secure.

"Well, you probably don't think so. You've proved that. But it's important to us."

Larissa said nothing, wanting this conversation to end, this ride to be over.

"How come they haven't visited you?" Mejida asked. "They'd like it here; all children do. They could learn to ride horses, ski."

"We have horses in America," Larissa managed to get out.

"Yes. But I'm sure they'd like to visit you."

"I suppose," Larissa said.

"Oh, my goodness," exclaimed a startled Mejida, turning her face to Larissa. "I just understood. You haven't been in touch with them at all, have you?" She sounded shocked. She stammered a little. The two women fell silent.

Staring straight ahead, Larissa spoke scornfully. "Mejida, obviously I can't explain it to you. You don't have children."

"Ah," said Mejida, calm again, mild. "Do you think, Larissa, that if *I* had had children, it would make it easier for you to explain to me how you could have left yours?"

"This'll be good," Larissa blurted. "Drop me off here. It's fine."

Mejida pulled into a little parking lot near a closed trinkets shop. They were still half a mile away from Balcony Bar. "Thanks so much for the ride." Larissa slammed the door so hard, the empty beer can standing upright nearby fell over and rolled down the roughly paved lot.

∽༩∽

She was glad for the walk in the dark, to will herself to calm down. She had never liked Mejida. She felt judged by her, critically appraised and dissected. She couldn't believe Bianca talked about her to that woman, of all people! Oh, the spirit of idle talk, the malicious banter. What did Mejida care what Larissa did with her life, anyway? Since when did she become Larissa's confessor? Larissa couldn't believe they owed that woman and her lewd husband rent money. But perhaps that's why Mejida talked to Larissa like that—because she knew she could. The conformity of it, the illusion of control, the threat of eviction, of blackmail. Larissa wished she had longer to walk to get to Balcony Bar.

The place wasn't busy since it was Tuesday and none of the locals or the migrants got paid till Wednesday. There were a few people at the bar, a few at the tables, the music was subdued, which meant Creedence instead of Van Halen. She spotted Kai right away, standing in a social circle—Bart and Bianca (damn her) and laughing people Larissa had not seen before—holding a tall glass of frosty beer in his hand and telling a joke. His ukulele lay behind him on the barstool. He looked like he hadn't a care in the world. What was she going to say to him? Didn't he know that she'd been alone all day? And was that his responsibility?

When he saw her he waved and, pushing through the group, walked jauntily toward her. He was wearing ragged jeans, black boots, a jean jacket over a gray hoodie. His hair was tied back away from his stubbled face; he left in the morning without shaving. "Hey," he said, "aren't you a sight for sore eyes. Whatcha up to?" He kissed her without hesitation. And why not? Did she expect hesitation? Was she looking for it?

"Why are your eyes sore?" she said, standing close to him. "I was waiting for you. I made you dinner."

"I'm sorry." He put his arm around her. "I didn't know you were cooking. I thought we had no money."

"Yesterday you said you were tired of going out all the time."

He laughed. "I was supposed to get *dinner* from that?"

"But you went out—without me."

"Just a quick drink after work."

"Kai, it's ten in the evening. Everything closes at six. What 'after work' are you talking about?"

The bloom washed off his face, a frozen smile drifted across it. "No fighting," he said. "I'm sorry I didn't know you were making dinner. How was I supposed to know? What'd you buy it with?"

"What are you buying drinks with?"

"Billy-O bought the rounds tonight. I told him I'd take care of him tomorrow when I got paid from Snowfield."

"Who is Billy-O? And tomorrow we're going out again?"

"Well, it *is* pay day." He grinned. "Come, I'll introduce you. Billy O'Neal. He's one of the drifters looking for work."

"Oh, so more competition."

"No, he's a brumbie hunter. Different business from me. Come."

"You just met him and he's buying you drinks?" Larissa glanced in the direction of the group by the bar, watching them, waiting for Kai.

"I didn't say I just met him." His arm was still around her. His face was close. He kissed her again, sweeter. "Come on. Have a drink. They're nice. Bart. Patrick. Billy's hysterical."

"They're *all* nice?"

"They're all nice." His free arm went around her waist, to pull her to him. "No one's as nice as you."

But when Kai introduced her to his new friends, Larissa was suddenly not so sure that no one was as nice as her. Billy-O's squeeze in particular . . . perhaps the girl was tipsy, or perhaps this was the way all Billy-O's broads giggled at Kai's jokes, but this one seemed especially pleased to be having a drink in his company. Who was she again? Billy-O was a ranger, a sloppy-looking tiny, tiny dude out of the bush, worn, faded from the sun. He was wiry like a jockey, his face looking like it spent twenty hours of every day outdoors. Larissa assumed he was in his twenties, but the weathered lines in his hands and cheeks made him look fortysomething. The girl's age? Younger. She was smooth-skinned and pale; she wore a wide-brim hat to shield herself from the Australian winter sun.

With Creedence desperately wanting to know if she'd *ever* seen the rain coming *down*, Larissa couldn't catch the girl's name, her rank, her connection to the proceedings, her connection to Billy-O. She couldn't even catch Billy-O's connection to Billy-O. Who was he again? *Horses?* Well, then, how did Kai know him?

"Billy-O came here to find work a few months ago," Kai told Larissa, "and stayed. He doesn't ski, just like us, but he found work in the local stables taking care of the horses for the winter. He wants to go round up some brumbies for his own business."

"Billy-O has a business?"

"Yeah, he runs a stable out west. He's got an amazing life. He goes out into the grasslands, finds wild horses, brings them back, tames them, and then sells them. But now he's looking to keep a few of his own; he wants to start a horseback riding business in the National Park. They need to be really docile, though, to withstand tourists on their backs. Most of the horses he owns are barely tamed."

Larissa stared at Kai through the puzzled pinpoints of her troubled eyes. "You sure know a lot about him."

Kai shrugged. "We got to talking, became friendly."

"But where would you meet someone like that?"

Kai shrugged. "I went to look for work at the stables in Thredbo Valley."

"You? The stables?"

"I know a little bit about horses. I used to clean them on Maui before I got into masonry. I can handle a horse. Anyway, it's work, what do I care?"

"Did you get, um, work?"

"Not yet. Listen, you want a drink or what?"

Or what, Kai. Or what. Out of their remaining few dollars, he bought her a Jäger. They lived without cell phone service, without a bicycle, without a car for her, and the rent was two months late. But he *had* to spend three bucks to buy her a Jäger. If only they had something to drink at home, maybe they could go home to drink it. Maybe if they had something . . . but what was it? What did she want from her cottage on Rainbow Drive? Perhaps a little bit of Bellevue Avenue? But which part? The domestic part? The cleaning and cooking part? The laundry part? The unread books? The soft down bed in which she spent her winter mornings? Or something else? It was something else, something larger, yet smaller, something indefinable. The glass of Red Bull and Jägermeister liqueur in her hand started to shake, duly noted by Kai because he turned his shoulder to her and started talking to Billy-O and his girl.

As he was talking, Larissa, with incomprehension, watched Kai pour off a little of his beer into Billy-O's girl's glass. She hadn't even asked! As he was chatting away, he just held the girl's glass steady and poured. Maybe Larissa's narrowed eyes were failing her. It was dark in the bar, and Creedence was now demanding to know *who* was going to stop that damn *rain*, and then Steppenwolf informed her they were on a *magic* carpet ride, and all this questioning noise and darkness made it hard to think in a place where the jukebox was loud and other people joyous, standing too close to hear each other; other people, not Larissa. She was squinting, constricted, tired, feeling unbeautiful, standing wondering who it was that had the emptying glass into which her lover poured a bit of his cold beer. When were they going to leave? When would this end?

The girl's name was Cleo Carew. Larissa found her name pretentious and pornographic. It sounded made up, created specifically for stripper work: first name from the name of her horse, second name from the street where she lived as a child, e.g., Bunny

Highland or Josie Mary. As if her real name had been Martha and she changed it to appear more slutty. As if she needed help in *that* department, with her jeans three sizes too small and her pink sweater too thin, too small *and* too low. She wore a horror-show amount of makeup, laughed obnoxiously loud, flung her slick blonde hair around and thought herself disproportionately attractive. Yet Kai poured his beer into her glass. What was up with that?

Larissa couldn't wait for the opportunity to ask him.

"Ready to go?" she said after another half-hour had passed.

"One more drink and we'll go." It wasn't a question.

She wanted to shake her head, say, look, no more drinks. After all, I'm on the back of your bike. The uphill road is dark and twisting. But he obviously didn't want to go home. And something inside Larissa rebelled against making him. If he couldn't see straight to the time of day, she wasn't going to be the one to point out to him it was quittin' time. Not here, anyway. She shook her head to another drink, and tried in vain to participate in a conversation she neither heard nor cared to hear. Cleo was giggling non-stop.

She watched Kai drag out finishing his drink, like he was chewing gum long after the flavor had gone out. She watched him as he talked, his animated face, his straight-up spine. And when she glanced away for a moment, in the dark, she noticed that Cleo was watching him also, his animated face, his straight-up spine.

"Well, it's time I go," he said to Cleo. Not time *we* go, but time *I* go.

"So soon?" whined Cleo. "Come on, have another drink. My round."

"Thanks, but no." He smiled. "I won't be able to ride my bike."

"I'll drive you. I got a car."

"I think the designated driver might need a driver," muttered Larissa, and Cleo laughed, and Kai too, and Cleo said, your girlfriend may be right about that, and Larissa cringed after being so superficially acknowledged by this female stranger.

Cleo stuck out her hand to Larissa. "It was nice to meet you," she said. "You have a cool accent."

"I don't have an accent," said Larissa, reluctantly shaking hands. "You're the one with the accent."

Cleo laughed like it was the funniest thing she'd heard all night—and that was saying a lot. "You're in our country, now," she trilled. "Do as the Romans do."

Larissa didn't know what that meant. Was an accent something the Romans turned on and off at will?

"Does she even know who the Romans are?" she said to Kai as they walked out.

"Oh, come on," he said, taking her hand. "Sure she does. She's a good kid. Nothing wrong with her."

"Who is she?"

"Not quite sure. Friend of Billy-O's, I think."

"What's she doing in town?"

"Looking for work. Like everybody."

"Gee, there must be something a girl like her could do around here," remarked Larissa.

"Hey," he said. "What's with the tone?"

"What tone? No tone. You had too much to drink."

"Be that as it may, there was still a tone."

Thing about a bike, it wasn't like a car. You couldn't fight on it on your way home, so that by the time you reached your house, you were halfway done arguing, and all that was left was the makeup sex. On the bike, Larissa had to hold on to him, sit behind him, and he had to concentrate on the road so he wouldn't crash. They didn't speak. When they got home, they hadn't even begun.

❧

His tactic when they walked inside the house surprised her. He took her in his arms. "I'm sorry," he said, bending to nuzzle her neck. "I'm sorry I didn't come home and eat dinner. I know you're upset, but I don't want to fight with you. Honest." He smelled like strong beer, like smoke; he held her tightly.

"Kai . . ." she wriggled away so she could look at him, "why would you go out knowing I'm home and we have no money and I have no car, and I'm waiting for you?"

"I'm sorry, Larissa," he said. "It was thoughtless. I wasn't thinking. I lost the job at the Ski Village. They didn't have any more work for me. I was upset, and I needed to think."

"To think or to drink?"

"To think."

"You went to a bar to think? You lost your gig, the money that comes with it, and then you went to a noisy smoky bar and spent money we don't have so you could clear your head?"

Now it was his turn to let go of her and step away.

"I thought I asked you not to fight?"

"Well, you did ask me," she said slowly. "But when there's stuff unresolved, it's hard to keep silent."

"What stuff?"

"Look, I don't want to fight either. But I think I'm going to have to get a job."

"Why are you saying it like that?" The front door wasn't closed all the way. The Ducati keys were still in his hands. He dropped them on the coffee table, went to close the door.

"Like what?"

"In that accusing tone. Are you getting a job to *punish* me?" He scoffed. The door slammed. "That's *weird*, Larissa. Get a job because we desperately need the money. Don't get a job to get back at me."

"Is there something I have to get back at you for, Kai?" asked Larissa.

"Don't be silly." He fell down on the couch, spread his legs, threw his head back. "I'm so fucking tired."

"You're drunk, not tired," she said. "Kai, why didn't you tell me that you didn't pay June's rent? Or July's?"

He didn't even lift his head. "I didn't want to worry you."

She sat down next to him. Outside was black night and the only light in the house was fluorescently flickering from the undercabinet in the kitchen. She could barely make out his features.

"Where did the money go?"

"What money? Larissa, there *is* no money."

"But you've been working . . ."

"Yeah, paying for gas, for our food . . ."

"For drinks at Balcony Bar?"

"That's not much. We go there twice a week maybe."

"We? I didn't see a *we* there tonight, Kai."

He squinted at her. "Oh, you weren't there tonight?"

"No thanks to you."

"We can't afford drinks for *me*, and *you* want to come to spend money we don't have?"

"*You* do!"

"Please don't shout. I got friends who buy me drinks."

"Mooching off your friends?" said Larissa. "Nice. Yeah, I have friends, too, who can buy me drinks."

"I'm sure you do," Kai said, letting acid creep into his voice. "Like Coty the bartender?"

"Who?"

"Don't pretend. I know he gives you drinks for free. It's pretty galling, don't you think, for me to go up there to *buy* drinks for you, considering that with a little flash of your smile or perhaps your boobs, you can get all the free Jägers you want."

"What are you talking about?" said a flustered Larissa, jumping up. "You buy me drinks because it's the chivalrous thing to do."

"Oh, yes," returned Kai, still splayed on the sofa. "Knights in shining armor, that's us."

"Besides, he doesn't give *me* drinks," Larissa continued. "Every once in a while he says one of our drinks is on the house."

"This isn't worth our time. I'm wiped out. Let's regroup tomorrow. I'll go out, find work. The ski lodge in Perisher or Charlotte may be looking for loaders to help with the ski lifts. I'll check there tomorrow."

"Yes, but while you're checking, how am I going to check if the ski shop on Wagner is hiring? I heard they might be."

He paused. "I can take you there. But, Larissa, if you get a job in town how are you going to get there day in and day out? We saw what happened when you rode a pushbike."

"It's too cold for a pushbike anyway." They didn't mention the irony of it—not being too cold for his Sportclassic motorcycle that rode a lot faster than a pushbike. "Maybe we can get me a cheap used car?"

"With what? We'd have to sell our tour bus to do it."

"No, no, we can't sell that."

"That's right, we can't even pawn it," said Kai. "Because we don't have the money to get it out of hock."

"Did I say anything about hocking it?"

"You talked about selling it! Sell it and do what? It's our only means of making money."

"Well, where is this money?" she shouted. "We're supposed to save during the summer so that when winter comes we have enough to live on. What's happened to our money?"

"What's happened to our money? Larissa, where do you live? Who do you think you are? You're not some housewife anymore where the rich husband takes care of all the expenses while all you do is go food-shopping and fuck him!"

"And not just him!"

"No, that's right," Kai said. "Are you still keeping up that little charade?"

She would have slapped him if she were closer. But she wasn't so she didn't. All she did was exhale and fall mute, twisting her fingers into knots.

"Look, you know where the money is. We spent it," Kai said, much quieter. "We lived on it. We didn't make any extra and couldn't save any. You used to work some winters, but last winter you didn't. Or this one."

"You're gone from the house from seven to seven! How am I supposed to get anywhere? I've looked for work. No one will hire me."

"I'm not complaining. I understand. But why are you giving *me* shit? I'm not accusing *you*, am I? I'm not demanding to know from you where the money is!"

Her hands went up. His anger was distressing. It made her weak and uncomfortable. Kai didn't raise his voice. He didn't fight. He was the peacemaker, the tranquil diplomat, who made things better by quiet, not worse by shouting.

"I'm sorry," she said. "But what are we going to do? Are we going to continue to live like this?"

A heavy breathing pause from Kai. "As opposed to what?" he said, his voice measured and slow. This is what he did during their infrequent arguments: to infuriate her he became deliberate, soft-spoken, and the more agitated she became, the calmer he became. He would tell her afterward that it was his way of dealing with conflict, which he hated, but she took it personally.

"Kai, stop speaking to me like this," she said, the fight getting hot, inflaming the back of her neck.

"Like what?" he said in a conversational voice while she panted. "It's a serious question. What do you propose we do?"

Why did his question frighten her? She backed away. He saw it, even in the dark. Especially in the dark. And she knew he saw it, that she had no power, no leverage, and no solutions.

"This is stupid," she said.

"That's what I've been saying."

"You're in no mood to fight."

"I'm never in a mood to fight, Larissa, you know that."

"Right. So let's not."

"Absolutely. Let's not."

They were naked and entwined in seconds on the couch, and then falling off, on the floor, in twisted knots like her hands, broken needy coupling, fractured crying from her, no sound from him but panting, eyes closed, mouth parted, single-mindedly focused on the eternal thrust. Was it real, or was it a showy burlesque? His hands gripping her head, her legs, her hips, it was a carnival of souls, on the floor sandwiched between the coffee table and the sofa, boundless groaning wretched lovers.

After they were in bed, he lay down behind her. She waited for his hands. For a few minutes there weren't any, as if perhaps he'd fallen asleep. But then, here they were, on her hips, on her ribs, on her back, between her thighs. She felt his lips on the back of her neck. "Come on, *Larissa* . . ." Kai whispered, once again, using the three syllables of her identity as a mating call. Using herself against herself. She moaned lightly; he turned her to him.

"I don't want to fight," he whispered. "I never want to."

"I know," she whispered back.

He caressed her face. "It's going to be okay. You'll see. I'll get work. I'll work the stables. Billy-O says he might be able to help me. We'll muddle through. And for next Christmas we'll advertise in the *Sydney Morning Herald*. We'll get the Americans to come here."

"Americans like us?"

"No one is like us," he said, his hands freely roaming, softening her, appeasing. But she was afraid of just the opposite. She was afraid they were like everyone else.

She lay in his arms while he stroked her back in sleepy caresses; she thought he was drifting off, but his fingers were strangely insistent on her spine, between her shoulder blades.

"Are you hungry?" she asked him. "I can warm up the burgers I made for you."

"I'm not hungry for burger," he said. "I'm a little hungry again for you." He continued to stroke her. "I'm needy tonight. Don't know why." There was a protracted pause. "I think Cleo found you attractive."

"What?"

"Hmm."

"What are you talking about?" Larissa was befuddled. "What does she have to do with me? It's not *me* she found attractive."

"It is."

"How do you know?"

"She told me. She said, your goil is hawt."

"She said this to you? Seems rather forward. And what did you say?"

"I said, I know." He fondled Larissa's breasts, pressed his stubble against them.

"Oh, is *that* what you said. You and Cleo, Billy-O's girl, talked about me being hot. Where is Billy-O during this conversation?"

"In the loo."

"Where am I?"

"In the loo."

"I really don't know why you would tell me this," Larissa said. "Who is she? I don't know why you would talk to her about me."

"I thought it would please you."

"Discussing my physical appeal with a twelve-year-old with tits you just met in a bar—you think that would please me?"

His body was over her, his legs pinning her, his arms holding her, his mouth deep at her throat, on her lips. He was breathing heavily, hotly, the alcohol continued to fan his desire. "Come on, admit it, you found her a little bit attractive . . ."

"No! Did you?"

"It's not about me."

"Isn't it?"

"Not at all. I just wondered if *you* thought she was sexy."

"Kai, tonight these thoughts did not enter my head. You know what I was busy thinking about? What are we going to do when the money runs out?"

"*Runs* out? We're out, baby." His hand was between her legs. "So what about her?"

Larissa didn't push him away. Opening her legs for him, arching her back, she let him caress her, her moans, his whispers, the tap dripping. Drip, drip. "Come on, what do you think? Do you ever think about it, even for a second? In the abstract. Like you did back in college?"

"Think about what? You? Yes." Her moaning got louder as his fingers became more insistent.

His put his lips on her nipples, still whispering. "You're so fucking sexy. You got twenty-year-old breasts, an amazing body. Come on, you want to get it on with a girl?"

If Larissa hadn't been so indisposed at that moment to think clearly, she might have opened her eyes, might have heard him better. But she was pulsing and panting to the tune of a different master. She thought they were fantasizing, speaking in arousing hypotheticals, as they occasionally did, using erotic language as an aphrodisiac. "Sometimes," she replied. "I told you. Out of curiosity. But the time for all that came and went when I was in the first bloom of youth."

"Ah, except I'm still in bloom, baby," he whispered. "And I think Cleo might be amenable to being asked, if you're interested."

That's when Larissa opened her eyes. "Asked what?" She moved away from him on the bed.

He didn't reply, just gazed at her from his pillow with his seductive look of lusty existentialism, as in: I know I'm going to catch shit for it, but I don't care while I pretend I don't know what all the fuss is about.

"Are you *kidding* me?"

He reached for her. "A little spice. Just for fun. Nothing serious."

"Well, that's good to know. As opposed to what?"

"We don't have to if you don't want to."

"I don't want to."

"Okay." But he said okay in that way people do when not only is it *not* okay, but in one minute they're going to pick a fight over it. This was definitely not a fight Larissa wanted to have.

"Kai, why would you think for a *second* I'd want to?" She wanted to pull the blankets over her naked body, but they were too far down on the bed.

"It's a turn-on, not a life-change."

Larissa could tell he wanted to say something else about it, but either wouldn't, or was saving it. The other thing, the love thing, remained in the bed unfulfilled.

"I can't believe you would ask me."

"I can't believe you're making such a fuss about it."

"Am I? Am I really?"

"I think so."

"Well, how about if I asked you if you wanted to invite Bart into this bed, how would you feel about that?" Bart was a good-looking, built-up guy who, though he was married to Bianca, flirted shamelessly with Larissa all in the name of harmless fun.

"Bart?" Kai snorted. Shrugging, he lay on his back. "If you want to, I'd be okay with it."

"I don't believe you."

"I would, Larissa. It's all good." Climbing on top of her, he pressed his damp body against her, into her. "You know why I'm not worried?"

She moaned, shook her head, upset at herself, incensed by her desire for him, by her inability to push him away even at times like these. "It's all good," he continued, while she groaned and clutched him, trying to listen, but hopelessly, "because I know"—he broke off while waiting, almost calmly, for her to begin gliding against him in her imminent flaming panic—"that you have never been fucked like this . . ."

Larissa vehemently shook her head, crying and coming, and whispering, no, stop, don't say this.

". . . and you never will be again."

He said this to her once before. Except then, an elephant's lifetime ago, it meant one thing and now, in an unprotected universe where families and children and laws and husbands, and petitions for clemency and forgiveness faded, it meant another, a shuddering awful injustice she could not and would not face. Don't say that, she whispered again, trying hard not to shiver, not to cry. It's not nice.

"It is nice. Oh, it's so nice . . ." His hands were squeezing her thighs open. "A little excitement, nothing more. Nothing wrong with that. It's not like you're going to go off with Bart, is it?"

"He's with Bianca."

"So what?" Kai shrugged, rolling off her. "Let's just say Bianca doesn't care who comes over to swim in her pool."

"What?"

"You didn't know? Yeah. She's quite a libertine, that Bianca." Kai faced her, saying these outrageous things in the tone he might say, yeah, whatever you cook, chicken or fish, will be fine with me.

"What do you think? You want to?" He scooted closer, embracing her, rubbing his rough chin between her shoulder blades. "Because if we ask Bart, I'm thinking we can then ask Cleo."

"Kai!" Shoving him away, she sat up. "Is that what we want? To ask Bart?" She paused, fell mute, couldn't find the words. "Or do we want to ask . . . *Cleo?*"

He said nothing.

"Would Cleo make you happy?"

His answer didn't come fast enough for Larissa. What answer could? With a suggestive smile playing at his lips, he said, "Just to see the two of you together. It's a male fantasy. It's so hot. That's all."

"Kai, I'm not interested in Bart," Larissa said, disbelieving this conversation. "I'm not interested in Cleo." They were out of money, they had no car, she couldn't get a job because they lived so far from town, he was about to go thirty miles into the mountains to look for work at the horse stables, and they were talking about a threesome with Cleo, a foursome with Bart. Or was it a fivesome with that witch Bianca?

It wasn't dark enough. That damn silver lake. When would the day come when she would never see it again. It was freezing Kai from the inside out.

"Let's just forget it," said Kai. "Clearly you have *no* interest in this."

"You *think?*"

"Let's just slog along, like we've been doing. That's what we should do, living in paradise, great food, great bars, nice people, lots to do, yet we have no money, we can't ski, we can't work, we can't pay our rent, we can't grow our business, and when summer starts we're going to have to spend three thousand dollars on new supplies and mechanical work on the cruiser and we have no money." He paused. "We have nothing."

"We don't have money for August rent, which is due in ten days, plus we're two months late, and you want to bring Cleo into our bed?"

"Not Cleo. Bart, too."

"Oh, Kai," Larissa whispered, "what's happening?"

"Nothing. That's the problem."

Somehow, she didn't know how, he fell asleep, just like that, on his side, still uncovered. She covered him and remained sleepless and heavy and hollow—bodied and hearted—staring up numbly at the ceiling, hoping once again to find the answers there, because she didn't want to seek the answers in their narrow double bed.

The next morning he went out early. She was still asleep. She slept until two in the afternoon. Maybe 2:40. What else was there to do?

He came back that evening—with dinner! He brought takeout from Milly's on Lakeside, linguine with white clam sauce, Larissa's favorite, a bottle of red, chocolate fudge cake and flowers.

"Wine and linguine?"

"That's right, baby!" He was in an excellent mood. The pensive despondency from yesterday had vanished. Happier herself and hopeful, Larissa lit two candles.

"I found work," he said when they sat down at the kitchen table. "Now, I want you to keep an open mind, okay? It's not ideal, or permanent, but . . ."

"Well, we don't want permanent," she said. "Just something to tide us over till summer."

"Exactly right. We need a break now, and I think I may have found it."

He opened the wine as she watched him, gazed at him. His faded Levi's and gray T-shirt looked so good on him. His face was animated, optimistic. She took a glass from his hands. They clinked. Raising himself up and leaning over the table, he kissed her deeply. "I love you," he said. "Listen to my idea. You know Billy-O, right? The wrangler from Mungo?"

"Well, I've heard quite a lot about Billy-O," Larissa said. "I don't *know* Billy-O."

"Right. Well. He needs someone to build a bigger stable and paddock with him. He asked me to help."

"Help what?"

"Build the stable. He and this other guy go out on brumbie runs, but he needs stable help, and then help selling the horses. He needs a second-hand man for that stuff."

"He has money to pay you?"

"Yup." Kai grinned and drank. "He got a small business loan."

Her smile faded. If they had been in the country legally, if they had been Australians, perhaps they could've also gotten a loan, bought a second troopie. That was one of the problems with the work she and Kai could get. It was always off the books, and the opportunities were both competitive and limited. She forced herself to smile through her stab of jealousy.

"What do you think?" Kai sounded elated. He held her hand while they ate.

"Where is this Mungo?"

"Well, actually, the stable's on the edge of Mungo National Park, outside a little river port town called Pooncarie."

"Never heard of it."

"Yeah, tiny."

"How close to here?"

"Not that close. But you know what?" He pulled out a wad of cash out of his pocket. "He gave me money upfront—"

"You already accepted?" she said, frowning.

"Larissa, what was I going to do?"

She tried to unstress herself by taking another gulp of wine. Then another. "I don't know," she finally said. "Perhaps talk to me first."

"I wasn't near a phone, and I didn't have any other offers. We had to eat tonight. And we need a plan, Larissa. For the future. Don't you feel like we're slowly running out of options?"

She didn't want to nod in assent. "Maybe we should go," she suggested carefully.

"To Pooncarie?"

"No . . . just . . . go." She raised her eyes to him. "You and me. Away from here. I think you're right. Perhaps our time here is drawing to an end." She didn't want to tell him about how sad that made her, or about her appalling conversation with Mejida. She wanted to concentrate on the great unknown. "Kai, we've never seen Perth. Cairns. Ayers Rock, Adelaide. A baby dingo. Let's blow this shanty life, and travel on down the road."

"Larissa . . ." Now it was Kai's turn to frown. "Are you already disillusioned in the hopes and dreams you had just yesterday?"

"Of course not," she quickly said, feeling the crestfallen mountains oppressively black and close.

"You want to be traveling on? Resume searching for the thing that's perpetually out of reach?"

She reached for him, stammering through her stunted replies. What do you mean, she thought she said. It's not out of reach. You're right here.

"You may be right," Kai said. "Perhaps it *is* time. But two things . . . I *love* our summers here. Lazy, relaxed, quiet . . . dried-out orange groves, dips in the lake, kangaroos everywhere. I'm not tired of anything yet. I like having my own thing. I like what we do. I want this to work."

"I know. But it's not working."

"And second," Kai continued, "we don't have any money. Did you forget that part? Where can we go? Into the Red Center? You want to go up to Cairns? To Darwin? Maybe I could be a busker on the streets of Perth out west, I can play my uke and the Aborigines can put quarters into my Akubra?"

"I can wait tables," she tried. "If we didn't live so far from town, I could do it here. Maybe we should move from Rainbow Drive then." She feared that part was inevitable; something felt ended, wasted.

"Look at our little bungalow." He said that so sadly. "*The stuff that dreams are made on* . . . Look at our view."

"The shades are always drawn, Kai," said Larissa. "I'd rather save what we can than have the entire dream vanish into thin air."

"Well, that's what I'm trying to do, Larissa," Kai said, "with this stable thing."

She had lost her appetite and sat at the table looking at him in the dim light from the flickering candles.

"Where did you say Pooncarie is?" she asked with a resigned sigh.

"Well, here's the thing . . ." He cleared his throat. She listened intently. Why was there always a thing? "It's a little way away."

"How little?"

"I dunno. I'm not too sure."

"How long did it take Billy-O to get here?"

"He wasn't sure."

"Kai! You're being evasive. Is it forty miles? A hundred miles? What?"

"No, I think . . ."

"It's *more* than a hundred miles?"

"You know, I'm not sure."

Taking matters into her own hands, Larissa went to get the local map out of the kitchen drawer. Pooncarie wasn't on the local map. Taking out a map of Australia, she spread it on the floor, searched for Pooncarie, couldn't find it, searched for Mungo National Park, found that, looked up the legend, measured the distance in the inches on the floor. Finally she looked up. "Kai," she said in a stunned, empty voice, "it's over twelve hundred kilometers away!"

"No. That much?"

"Yes! That's over seven hundred miles."

He kind of slumped at the table, chewing his lip and rubbing the wine glass.

"Kai, did you really tell Billy you were going to do it?"

"Well, look, I knew it wasn't close, like commuting distance. I know . . ."

"So what are you proposing?"

"I'm proposing," he said, smiling anew, trying to sell it to her like a good smooth-talking salesman, like the young guy in a white shirt and black jacket and ironed jeans, selling her a Jag with quad tailpipes to drive from the gas station to the supermarket, to drive from the cleaners to the elementary school to pick up her smallest son, who fit so nicely inside her tiny two-seater, "I'm proposing that

I go live with Billy for a couple of months, through the winter, work with him, help him build the stable, help him sell the horses, make some dough, and then come back in the summer with money and resume our tour."

"What about me?"

Kai cleared his throat almost without pause. "Here's the thing. Billy-O said his place is too small for the two of us. I can crash on his couch, but we both can't. We can't put him out of his own bed, can we?"

"So you propose I stay here and pay rent on this place?" Stay here, next to Mejida, without a car, without a job and without Kai? Larissa looked up at him from the floor, her eyes shocked and wide.

"No. We can't pay rent here and try to save money for the summer. We've got to be smart about this."

"Smart, yes."

"So here's what I was thinking." There was a small pause there— for thought, for a breath, for tactics? "What about you going to visit your friend Che?"

"Che?" Larissa said dully, something inside her melting into numbness.

"Not a bad idea, right?"

"You know Che lives in Manila, right?"

"I know. Remember how often you told me how much you wanted to go? Back in Jersey you kept talking and talking about it. This is a great time to do it."

"I'd have to get to Sydney, and then fly to Manila."

"I know. There's a bus twice a day that goes to Sydney."

"But, Kai, we don't have money for rent or food! Where are we going to get a thousand bucks for a flight to Manila? Plus I'll need money when I'm there. I can't just show up and expect Che to feed me."

"Why not? All that money you had been sending her, you don't think it's worth a little reciprocation? A little quid pro quo?"

"She was broke last time I spoke to her. She doesn't bail me out. I bail her out."

Kai said nothing.

"Also, I haven't heard from her or been in contact with her since I left. What if she's not there anymore?"

"She's lived in the same place for years. Why would she not be there?"

"I don't know. But I'm not in Summit anymore, am I? She was having so much trouble when she last wrote . . ." Larissa could not remember what that trouble was. Something about her boyfriend . . . ?

"I could get a job, too," she offered shrilly. "In Pooncarie. At a local bar."

"We got nowhere to live," Kai repeated, "except with Billy, and he doesn't have room."

"So we'll rent a room."

"And pay rent again. Pooncarie is a small town, perhaps only a one-bar town. What if you come and there's no work? What are we going to do then? We won't be able to save a penny."

She waited. "Why don't we cross that bridge when we get to it? I'll find work. Why can't I help you and Billy-O at the stables?"

"Help us do what? Build a barn? Tame horses?"

"Either. Both."

"Larissa, be serious. We have nowhere to live!"

"So that's your grand plan? To ship me off to Manila and move to Pooncarie?"

"Not ship you off. Let you go do the thing you've always wanted to do. And not move but migrate. Go where the work is."

"What about this house?"

"I'm too sad to speak about it," Kai said, not looking at her, "but we will have to let this one go. Nothing we can do. We can't pay for it. Next summer we'll find ourselves a new place. Closer to town, though, so we won't have this problem again."

"What about our Land Cruiser? What about your bike?" She was still on her haunches, on the floor, her hands on her lap, looking up at him in the chair. She was trying to find her way clear but coming into dark alleys. They spent over sixty thousand dollars on that eleven-seat safari vehicle five years ago. What was it worth now?

"The bike stays with me," he said. "But we'll pawn the cruiser."

"We're going to pawn the cruiser?" She gasped.

"Just for three months. That way we'll have plenty of money to get you to Manila, and I'll earn enough to get it out of hock come October. What? Don't look so glum. It's just temporary."

"Everything's temporary," whispered Larissa.

"No, not everything."

And later, in their bed, Kai said to her, "I have to solve this, can't you see? Right now there's no work for me here. We're hurting. And it's hurting us."

He was right. They were hurting. The open catgut feeling inside her now lasted twisted protracted periods throughout the day, constantly making her feel like she was falling, even while walking, *especially* while walking, always with the breathless sensation of the never-ending plunge.

"We need to get through the lean months." Kai was soothing her with his voice, with his long and gentle caressing fingers. "We'll make it. We're strong; this is what strong people do—what they have to. We're regrouping, that's all." Leaning over her, he kissed her easily. "Remember when we wondered: what are we going to do when the money runs out? Well, now we know."

Larissa thought she was all closed up, shut in, boarded up, condemned, a Chico girl without a ride, but Kai made love to her that night as if she were the hospitality committee at the welcome inn. Everyone was invited, the doors were flung open, and the rooms were free.

2

A Motherless Child

And just like that, days later, she was on a bus alone to Sydney and then on a plane to Manila.

Don't worry, Larissa, an unwashed and unkempt Billy-O assured her, I'll take good care of Kai for you. Right. Because *that* made her feel relaxed inside. She brought with her a suitcase; she brought with her everything she owned—which wasn't much and fit in a suitcase. It was remarkable how little she had accumulated in the bungalow they'd fled.

They never paid Mejida. When Larissa confronted Bianca before she left, asking why in the world she would talk to Mejida about her past, about her life, Bianca looked horrified and bewildered.

"I never talked to her about you, Larissa," she said. "Not a word." She paused. "But Mejida's husband, Umar, did tell Bart that a little while ago someone had been snooping around looking for you, asking all kinds of questions. A big guy with a gut. An American." The blood turned to ice in Larissa's veins. That was part of the reason why she let it all go so quickly, why she barely protested Kai's tangle with Billy-O. They owed over a thousand dollars to a woman who knew something about Larissa. Some American man came snooping.

Even in this seemingly simple life, something was happening she couldn't control. Something was amiss in the blue universe, in the frosty glades.

In Manila it was hot and sticky. To explain this was impossible. How could a country just a few hundred miles north of where she lived have a completely different climate? It's not in the same hemisphere, the Manila cab driver who picked her up said to her. There it's winter. Here it's summer. "But why would you come here in July, miss? We're on the equator. It's the absolute worst month to come."

"Really?" She settled in the back of his old beat-up cab. "You think something could be worse than July being winter?" She glanced outside at the morning rush hour crowds in the damp heat. "Looks okay to me."

"Does it? It's monsoon season. A typhoon a day. And in Parañaque, where you're headed, everything floods. It's a swamp down there. Good luck to you."

She stared outside at the mess of traffic, the palm trees, the loopy jaywalking mothers with strollers, the racing bike messengers, the jitneys. "When do the rains go?"

"Late October."

She'd be gone by then. Her return date was late October.

They only had a few miles to travel from the airport to Che's address, but it took them over an hour; the highway wasn't moving.

"Must be flooding somewhere in Las Piñas," the cabbie said. "It always happens. This whole southern strip from Manila to San Pedro is two inches above sea level. One high tide and we flood. Bays on both sides. It just pours in. Roads are made impassable by waters."

"Hmm," said Larissa, her face pressed to the dirty window. "Must be good for the crops." In Jindabyne the orange groves dried out in the summer heat.

"Maybe good for crops," said the cabbie. "Not so good for people." Whistling, he smiled at her in the rear-view mirror. "But we don't mind. We take it all as it comes. It's all good, miss. *Bahala na*. It's all how it should be."

Is it? Was it? When the driver finally got off the parking lot that was the highway, and Larissa started looking at the signs, she became perplexed by the street names. Turkey. Texas. Libya. Syria. *Hawaii.* That one pinched her heart. And then after the crop fields and the public park, Benevolence. Kindness. Goodness. The poorer the neighborhood, the more virtuous the street names. Gentleness and Humility were framed by Meekness Extension.

Che lived in a gaggle of shacks spliced together between San Pablo and Humility. Larissa asked the driver to wait, but he got another fare and wouldn't. She was left standing with her bags in the middle of a shanty town. She wasn't used to the humidity, her clothes stuck oppressively to her body, her lashes stuck together every time she blinked, her mascara ran and she wasn't even crying, but it did feel like the next time she blinked, she might not be able to open her eyes again. Pulling her suitcase, she struggled down the dirt road. Was there even a chance Che's place would be air conditioned? Maybe they could scrape up some cash and buy a used AC unit, because Larissa could not live like this for three months. Could not. Che described her house as number 37 from the top of San Pablo, or number 12 from the bottom of Humility. But you really have to count carefully, Larissa, Che had written jokingly. They're not marked and it's easy to mistake two little houses for one spacious abode.

Larissa counted. Just to make sure, she traipsed back to San Pablo and counted again. Did Che really live in a tiny shack made of straw and bamboo, patched together with scraps of plywood and stitched-together cardboard, a handmade doll's house with no windows, just openings for air that flashed open on someone else's city? There was no one to ask, and Larissa stood in the middle of the road with her suitcase, her purse, her black carry-on, the same one in which she had carried away her other life, too, carried away her other self. When she knocked on the counterfeit door it nearly came off its one hinge. It was morning. Was it ten? Perhaps Che was sleeping. Or at work. Did she really live here?

A small man came out, still in his pajamas, barely awake. Smiling he asked her, a stranger, if she wanted to come in. No, thank you, Larissa said. I'm looking for my friend, Che—Claire Cherenge. Is she here?

"I'm very sorry, miss. No one by that name lives here," the man replied.

"You sure?"

"Am I sure? Look at the size of my house. You think I wouldn't know if a woman named Che lived here?"

"How long have you been here?"

"Three years. And before me and my family, an old woman lived here alone but she died. That's how we got the house. But no one young like you describe. Maybe you have the wrong address." They both looked at the scribblings in her tiny handwritten address book. But no. This was it. This was house number 12 from the bottom of Humility.

"She doesn't live here, I'm sorry. You sure you don't want to come in?" the man said regretfully, before closing his paper door.

Larissa stood in the middle of the street. What in the world was she going to do now? Behind the row of huts were wet fields, and down the street on Goodness, a morning market. Was this where Che had sold fruit for Father Emilio? The ground was sopping; all the dust was mud, but mud with a rising vapor because it was hot and getting hotter. Kai had given her two hundred dollars from pawning the cruiser, and she'd already spent twenty of it; was a hundred and eighty bucks enough to live on for three months, even in Parañaque? Where was Che? Not here for at least three years. Larissa glanced at the house before she walked away. How could her friend have lived here? She never described it like this in her letters. She talked about Lorenzo, their simple life, the church, the priest, wanting a baby, selling fruit, demonstrating for hire. She never wrote to Larissa about *this*. Once, a long time ago, when they were adolescent small-town girls on swings in shorts and ponytails, didn't they have the same dreams?

I want to have a little girl, said Che happily, so I could torture her like my mother tortures me.

I want to travel the world, said Larissa. She grinned. On a white horse. They were sitting astride a seesaw in a dusty playground in Piermont. School had ended. They spent the afternoon chalking the lines and playing hopscotch. At four the ice cream truck came and they scraped together enough nickels for one, a cherry bomb banana float, and with it sat on the swings rocking back and forth taking turns with the ice cream.

Che told her favorite joke. Two muffins are in the oven, Che said, and one muffin says to the other muffin, "Oh no! I think we're going to get baked," and the second muffin says, "Oh no! A talking muffin!"

Perhaps no, not even then. They didn't have the same dreams.

∾ⱱ↶ↄ

The cobblestones hurt Larissa's feet, and the sun blinded her eyes. She stumbled down Humility and Goodness and Gentleness, all narrow and winding, with their pungent smells of rotting fruit, unwashed humans, and seaweed all marinated in stifling wetness, the overhanging delapidation, the sad-sack windows, the chipped frames, and yet above it all, palms, and below it, red flowers, and drenching humidity like the ocean. She walked, dragging her heavy suitcase behind her, carrying her duffel on her sore shoulder; it felt like drowning, the air was so dense with moisture. Hobbling away from the thing she had come to find, Larissa almost couldn't breathe. Except it was a sunny morning and sauna hot, and the birds were chirping. Parañaque, a haven for farmers and fishermen, was close to the sea, sandwiched between Manila and Laguna bays, and it smelled like the sea—salt and fish—all through the thick air. The chaotic outdoor market was filled with haphazard tables displayed slippers, weaved baskets, bags of rice, bananas, mangoes, and yellow pears. Larissa would've bought a pear from a beseeching woman in flagrant red garb with a little baby on her lap, except for the falling sensation in her gut. Looking away from the mother and child, she could barely wheel her suitcase over the rough ground.

Where was she going? What was her plan? Should she find a bed and breakfast until tomorrow, then fly back, somehow make her way to Pooncarie, back to Kai? They'd have to make it work somehow, they would just have to. For God's sake, she couldn't stay in *Manila* all by herself! But changing the ticket would cost her money in penalties, and she didn't have it. Maybe Kai could wire her the money. What was she going to do? She'd have to call him at Billy-O's, tell him she got in okay, but Che was nowhere to be f—

Through her trance, she heard a gravelly voice. She raised her eyes, blinking, focusing, and glimpsed a tall salt-and-pepper-haired man in a black frock with a pronounced withered face. "*Is it nothing to you*," the man said in a British accent, his hands pressed together, "*all that pass by here?*"

That made Larissa stop walking cast down.

"*Look and see*," the man continued, opening wide his large lined-by-life hands and beckoning her to him, "*if there's any pain like your pain.*"

He was standing on the steps of a small adobe white church, sandwiched between a green garden and three wooden houses. He had a composed manner about him, penetrating contemplative dark eyes that seemed all the more striking against the gray hair, and an air of juggling too large a number of thinking balls. His mind seemed busy with inner things.

"Excuse me, what church is this?" said Larissa.

"San Agustin of Parañaque."

San Agustin! It was like a miracle.

Larissa stepped closer, still in the street, and walked a few feet toward him. "I can't believe it. Is there only one San Agustin?"

"In Parañaque, yes."

"By any chance do you know a priest named Father Emilio?"

"I am Reverend Father Emilio," said the man in black cloth.

"Oh, I can't believe it! Thank God." Larissa put her hand on her heart and started to cry. Stepping forward, Father Emilio placed his hand on her back, gently patting her. His expression changed, as if he put down some of those bright juggling balls and focused solely on her.

"Yes, you're right," he said. "We should thank God for all mercies, great and small. Would you like to come inside?"

"Inside where? Father Emilio . . ." Larissa wiped her face. "My name is Larissa Connelly. I'm looking for my friend Che. She used to—"

"I know Che very well," said Father Emilio, staring at Larissa, studying her.

"Has she ever mentioned me?"

"Yes, she talked about you, Larissa. I feel I know you already." His blinkless gaze, inquisitive, sober, remained on her. "I thought you were Larissa Stark?"

Larissa stammered. As with Mejida, she found it distressing and mortifying that strangers thousands of miles away from her physically and metaphysically would know anything about her. "She—um—used to, I'm pretty sure, live near San Pablo," Larissa went on haltingly, "but . . ."

"She hasn't lived here a long time," said Father Emilio. "She left perhaps five years ago."

"Left and went where? When she was writing me, she said her—" Larissa broke off. She didn't want to say. She couldn't remember.

". . . Boyfriend was in jail awaiting trial for murder?"

"Something like that."

"They made bail. And they ran. Took everything and vanished to Mindanao."

"And she hasn't been back since?"

He shook his head. "They joined the Peace Brigade there."

"Peace Brigade? She told me they were going to live with some tribe in the mountains."

"Yes, the Peace Brigade soldiers," said Father Emilio. "I heard that during one of their daily skirmishes with the police and MILF, Lorenzo was killed and Che was arrested. This is just a rumor, mind you. No one is sure of anything, and it's so hard to keep track of people, especially down on the islands. Our parishes can only help so much. Sometimes they lose the string of information. But then a year later I heard that Che might have gone to prison for aiding and abetting a cop killer and a fugitive from justice."

"Prison! Father Emilio . . ." Larissa's hand was on her heart. "Please . . . what are you telling me?"

"Only the truth, Larissa. Would you like to come in?"

"I don't think I would, no. But . . ."

Except where did she have to be? Where could she go? If not for this man standing on the steps of his adobe house, where did she intend her feet to carry her?

"I have some real problems, Father Emilio," said Larissa. "I may be in serious trouble."

He opened the side door to his church and stood waiting for her to pass by him.

~∾~

He took her into his rectory, a large comfortable room with tall windows overlooking the street. Larissa wheeled in her suitcase, dropped her duffel and purse and, with relief to finally sit down, sank into an old leather chair. Father Emilio sat in the red leather chair across from her. The windows were open, and the sun was out. There was a fan in the room, swirling the mugginess around, but it was better than being outside. There was a faint smell of incense and mosquito repellent.

She sat like this for many minutes. She didn't really want to talk, just enough to get her bearings and perhaps ask him to help her. But help her what? Did she want him to give her money? She couldn't look at him, at his silence, at his calm brown eyes.

"Is it true," she said when she finally spoke, "that you used to be a renal surgeon?"

"Hmm. Random," he replied. "But, yes. It's true."

"You became a doctor here?"

"No, in London. I came here on a grant with Our Lady of Peace Hospital."

"To do kidney transplants?"

"That's right."

She paused. "So how did you get from there to"—she circled the air with her hand—"here?"

Nodding, he smiled slightly. "Now I see. That *is* a good question. I decided I could be more useful here."

"You think so?" she said. "Rather than help people get new kidneys?" She tilted her head. "My friend had kidney disease. She kept going to church, but what she really needed was a transplant."

"I think that's a false choice," said Father Emilio. "After all, why can't you do both?"

Did this man just say "false choice"? Her old friend Ezra used to say that all the time. Larissa studied the priest more carefully.

"*You* didn't," she pointed out, finally.

"That's true. But now I'm not limited by a scalpel or by my area of expertise. I cast my net a little wider. As I said, more useful."

"I guess." Larissa shrugged. "Poor Che. So you don't know what happened to her?"

"I don't."

"From what I remember, wasn't she due to give birth?"

"Yes." He didn't say anymore, waiting for her, while she waited for him and sat in the quiet. There was something undeniably comforting about his composed, non-judgmental silence. It was in this silence that Larissa began to speak, almost like thinking.

"I might have screwed up my life pretty bad," she said to him because he had kind eyes. "You won't believe what I've done."

"You've messed up your life. I understand."

"You don't understand."

"Then tell me."

"I've been wicked."

"Okay," he said. "You've been wicked."

"I can't change anything. I can't make it better. What's worse is I'm afraid I may have made a fatal error in judgment. I may have subordinated reason to my . . ." Love? Carnal desire? Was there a difference? She thought there was. Her life with Kai was carnal, but sterile.

"That's very possible."

"Do you know about me?"

"I know about you a little bit, Larissa Stark, née Connelly," said Father Emilio sounding as if he knew everything. "But tell me some things I don't know."

She told him in staccato words. He sat and listened.

"I can never make it up to my children," she finished. "I will never make it up to my husband."

"Do you want to?"

"I don't know. Look at me. I don't know what to do. I came to Manila because my only remaining friend in the world lived here. I have less than two hundred bucks on me, my . . . boyfriend is sleeping on someone else's couch for three months. I've got no job, no money—" Larissa kept crying, weeping, into her hands, her eyes swollen, the raw anguish of her cries echoing through the empty halls. I don't know what to do. I don't know how to do anything. I don't know how to live.

He stared at her calmly, while she carried on. "Stay with us," he finally said. "See if you can work it out."

She stopped crying. "*Stay* with you? What are you saying?"

"You can stay with us as a guest of the monastery."

"I thought this was a church, not a monastery?"

"I can give you a tour of our grounds if you like, before you decide," Father Emilio said dryly. "We have the church for the laity, for the parishioners of Moonwalk, which is a district in Parañaque, that is correct. But we also have a small, all-female Augustinian monastery, twenty-two nuns in all, and attached to that, an orphanage with sixty beds. At the moment they're all full. Well . . ." Father Emilio cleared his throat. "Fifty-nine of them are full. We had an eighteen-month-old severely handicapped boy, left on our doorstep at birth, who died three days ago. We're burying him today." He paused. "So fifty-nine beds full."

"Is that what you want me to do? You want me to stay with the nuns? Or the orphans?"

"Your choice," Father Emilio replied. "But who do you think takes care of the orphans?"

"You're saying either way I'm with the children?"

"For as long or as little as you need."

"You're telling me to stay—" She broke off. "But I'm afraid I'm losing *him*, Kai, losing my life, and he is my whole life, don't you understand?"

"You're sitting in front of me, aren't you?" said the priest.

"What does that have to do with anything?"

"This is also your life."

"This isn't my life." She shook her head. "This is a break from my actual life."

"This seems like a break to you? You're destitute, your closest friend is in prison, or dead, and the young man you left your husband and children for has sent you away to another country."

"He didn't send me away!" Larissa exclaimed, horrified. "He . . . we were . . . we had no money, he had to work. No, no, no. You're mistaken about that. Completely mistaken. We did what we had to do to save ourselves."

"Yes," said Father Emilio, his steady eyes on her. "Sometimes to save ourselves we must do outrageous things."

"Look," Larissa said. Was there any way *now* of asking him for money to return to Australia earlier? Damn! "I'm in no condition to help with the children. Honest. I'm . . . I'd like to stay for a few days, just to, you know, but . . . I'm in really bad shape. I . . . this isn't what I envisioned." She was supposed to come visit Che! What in the world was this?

Father Emilio sat motionlessly, fingers pressed together and coolly stared at Larissa without speaking. After a few minutes she glanced at him, inquiring mutely about his silence. He opened his hands. "This is God's house," he said. "The doors are always open. In and out." He pointed outside. "They're open right now." He rose out of his chair and extended his hand to her. "It was very nice to meet you, Larissa. If Che ever comes back, I'll be sure to tell her you stopped by. Now if you'll excuse me, I must go conduct the noon service and then I have a funeral to prepare for."

"No, Father Emilio," Larissa said, standing up. "I didn't mean I wanted to go. I'd like to stay, like I said. I was merely saying that I'm not used to—and I'm so upset over things, and Che not being here . . . this wasn't what I had planned, that's all."

"All right," said Father Emilio. "This isn't what you planned. Probably life doesn't look pretty to you at the moment. But come with me. I want to show you something."

Larissa followed him, but she was sure she didn't want to see. "Father, I don't want to see the dead child," she whispered.

"Don't worry," he said, squeezing her hand. "You can't save *him*. But I *would* like to show you a live one."

After walking down a long corridor that led from the rectory to the back of the church, they swung open two glass French doors and entered an almost empty enclosed courtyard, a stone square enclosure with ferns in pots and the subdued moist sun shining. Through an archway across the yard, Larissa glimpsed a green lawn and trees, but here on a wood bench in the corner, Father Emilio pointed to a wan girl playing with horses made of sticks. A tiny dark girl, with short, pin-straight black hair and deep-set eyes. She was wearing a gray smock, a pinafore too big for her, and her feet were bare. She looked up at the two adults, her eyes smiling familiarly at Father Emilio and then drifting to stare warily at Larissa.

A gasping Larissa put her palm on her heart.

"This is Nalini," said Father Emilio. "Che's daughter. She has been with us since birth. Che left her with me and the nuns when she and Lorenzo ran to Mindanao. She said she would be back for her." He lowered his head. "But that was five years ago."

"Oh, don't worry, Papa Emilio," said Nalini in a high clear voice. "Mama will be back."

Larissa kneeled in front of the girl, kneeled on the stones in front of the bench where the girl who looked like her friend Che, except for the Lorenzo eyes, sat with her sticks. Larissa took several deep breaths before she trusted her voice to speak, to sound bright. "Hi, Nalini." Barely audibly. Not good. Have to try harder, Larissa. "Whatcha doin'?"

"Playing." She stared at Father Emilio. "Is it time for lunch?"

"Yes, child," he replied. "But don't be impolite to our guest. This is Larissa. Talk to her. You'll like her. She knew your mother."

Nalini jumped off the bench, the horses dangling in her hands. "Really? You knew my mama?"

"I knew her very well. She was my best friend when we were your age, when we both lived in America."

"My mama lived in *America?*" Nalini was wide-eyed. She looked up at Father Emilio. "Papa, where is America?"

"Very far away. Now come. You can show Larissa the kitchen, and then you must run to the chapel with the others. Larissa, you must be hungry, too, no?"

The three of them walked at a child's pace out of the courtyard, which is to say they couldn't keep up with her skipping through a stone corridor that led to the orphanage dining hall with long tables and a galley kitchen at the sunny end.

"What do *you* like to eat, Nalini?" Larissa asked.

"Nalini, stay with us!" Father Emilio called. "Don't rush so far ahead. Larissa is tired; she can't run as fast as you."

The girl skipped back. "I *love* Nutella—" she broke off, glancing sheepishly at the priest. "I *like* Nutella, very very much *like*. But we don't have it here anymore. Do you know what it is?"

"I do. It was your mother's favorite thing to eat. I used to send it to her."

Nodding, Father Emilio smiled. "Occasionally Che would donate one or two of your jars to the nuns. They treated it like a holy relic. It would take them a year to eat one jar."

It made Larissa wish she could buy a boxful right now. There had been rows and rows of it at King's, ye olde market.

The kitchen was splendid and empty except for the two silent nuns in the corner preparing something sour-smelling in a big pot on the stove. The rectangular bright room had three floor-to-ceiling windows that had southwestern exposure and faced the green park-like grounds at the back of the church. Larissa wanted to sleep in this kitchen, wake in the mornings on the long wooden table in front of the sunny windows.

"They have Nutella in America?"

"Oh, yes," Larissa replied. "They're swimming in Nutella."

Giggling, repeating, "They're *swimming* in Nutella!" Nalini peeked at Father Emilio for tacit approval and then took Larissa's hand, pulling her to the large stainless steel refrigerator. "Sometimes we have cut up mangoes with our lunch, little pieces," Nalini said, taking two large mangoes out of the fridge. "Little pieces because there are so many children here."

"I'll cut them up for you. Here, let me," said Larissa, taking the mangoes out of the girl's hands.

"Just disinfect the skin first with vinegar, Larissa," said Nalini. "Before you peel."

Shaking her head in confusion, Larissa carefully put down the mangoes. "Many children are nice," she said. "But noisy." She turned to Father Emilio. "Do you have room for me, Father? Sixty children, twenty nuns . . ."

"There's always room. After service and lunch, Nalini will show you to your quarters on the second floor."

"Come, Larissa," Nalini said, pulling her by the hand. "First I show you the chapel. We're going to be late if we don't hurry." She nodded. "Children are *so* noisy. The little ones won't keep quiet during service." She smiled up at Larissa. "Are you a mama, too?"

Glancing back at Father Emilio, Larissa took deep breaths, of Australia, and America, and Micronesia, of the Atlantic and the Pacific, of Jindabyne and Madison and now Moonwalk in Parañaque. "I used to be a mother," she said in a voice not hers, yet only hers. "But not anymore."

3

The Play

The imposition of someone else's routine, while stifling, was also soothing. Every morning Larissa simply got up and did as she was told. The daily rituals of the nuns and the orphans comforted her by taking the responsibility of decision-making away from her. She got up at six, sat half asleep through lauds; oh, if Maggie could see her now. Helping Sister Mary and Sister Miranda, she cooked oatmeal or shaped together brown rice cakes for the children, and afterward she washed the floors of the kitchen and the dormitory; on her hands and knees she scrubbed them, and remembered other distant floors, and sneakers, and rubber balls, pencils and gum wrappers, empty cups, newspapers, and drink holders, and straws, and a napkin of doodles from the blond-curl artist, a drawing of a woman holding a child's hand, and two arrows. One arrow: "Me." The other arrow: "Mom."

From the get-go, Nalini was a big help. "No, Larissa," she would say, "you're putting too much brown sugar in the rice cakes, and the coconut shavings don't go inside, they're sprinkled on after the rice cakes cool."

"No, Larissa, you can't just freeze the water, you have to boil it first. Freezing won't take the bad stuff out of it."

"No, we don't eat raw fish here at San Agustin, we have to cook it, or marinate it in vinegar for like two days. Let me show you where the vinegar is. You can make *sinigang* for lunch if you want. Boiled sour soup with vegetables."

"How come you don't cross yourself at Mass, Larissa? Is it because you don't know how?"

But Larissa had things of her own to show Nalini when she wasn't pickling the fish in vats of vinegar. "Do you know how to play hopscotch?" she said to her one early afternoon when they were ambling around the courtyard. Nalini was never much for the imposed siesta.

"No," Nalini said, jumping up and down. "But it has the word hop in it, so I already like it."

"Very good. Also scotch, which means a scratched line. Now where's my chalk?" Pulling it out of her jeans pocket, she drew the hopscotch court with just six squares, to teach Nalini. They found a centavo, threw it on square 2, and Larissa hopped on the rest of the squares. At first Nalini kept hopping on *all* the squares, but very soon got the hang of it, so soon that Larissa had to draw another two squares and then two more. They spent the afternoon hopping the course until the flood from the sky came and washed the white chalk away. The next day at sunrise, the first thing Nalini said to Larissa was, "Can we play hopscotch?"

"We can, but first you have to show me how to make *halo-halo*." *Halo-halo* was a Filipino fruit salad. "You're not really supposed to put vegetables in fruit salad, are you?"

"We don't have anymore *pandesal* bread, Larissa," Nalini told her. "It's all been eaten. We should make that first. Then we'll play hopscotch."

Father Emilio always made a point of coming into the kitchen in the morning to say hello to Larissa and to have a cup of coffee in her presence, and after the noon service, he ate lunch with her and the children in the orphanage dining room. During the siesta, he took a few minutes away from his work to walk with Larissa and Nalini. Sometimes he would sit on the bench and watch them play hopscotch.

If she could've, Larissa would've lived in that kitchen. The room she had been given to sleep in was spartan, and the only reading material in it was the Bible, and of course she had brought no other books with her. So she spent her days in the large kitchen, marinating the chicken for the adobo stew, cutting *pandesal* for bread pudding, constantly boiling and cooling water. She volunteered to go to the market in the mornings while the children had their lessons, to buy the fresh guava and mangoes and bananas from the local vendor. It made her feel closer to Che, remembering her friend's attachment to the market. She wished she could buy Nalini a floral sundress, something delightful. It was sad to see the child in the gray frock day in and out.

Two days after she had arrived, Larissa asked Father Emilio if she could use the phone. Apparently the only phone was in the rectory. While the priest stood outside the open door to give her an illusion of privacy, Larissa dialed the number Kai had given her for Billy-O. It rang and rang. No one picked up. What time was it there? Plus two and a half hours? Or minus two and a half? It was either early morning or the middle of the day. They were probably working. She'd try again. In the meantime, she asked and was given some stationery and envelopes and wrote Kai a letter. And another. And another. Father Emilio gave her stamps, the postman came, took her mail. After a week had passed, she started asking the postman if anything came for her, care of the parish church. She had not been able to reach anyone at Billy's house. And of course Billy had no answering machine, as though he lived in medieval times. Every night, since there was nothing to do in her room after compline, Larissa wrote Kai long expansive letters about their years together, about Che being gone, about wanting to return earlier; how did Kai feel about that? Was there perhaps more room in Billy's house than was originally indicated?

Soon her letters became plaintive. Kai, I haven't heard from you. And I can't reach you by phone. Please write me. Every morning she waited for the postman outside the narrow side door leading to the street. Anything today, Macario? Not today, Miss Larissa. Who is this child by your side? Oh, that's Nalini, Che's daughter. Nalini stood in the mornings with Larissa, holding the stick horses, also waiting for a letter. Anything today? No, Miss Larissa. What about me? Nalini asked brightly. Anything for me today? What are you waiting for? the postman asked. A letter from my mommy, she replied. Not today, Miss Nalini. And Nalini smiled, like a big girl, and the next day stood at the door, looking down the street waiting for the postman.

Che was missing, Lorenzo was dead. Kai was not answering the phone, not replying to her increasingly desperate missives. Only the girl remained. And Nalini followed Larissa around like a puppy. She washed the floor with her and prepared lunch with her; she shadowed her, barely speaking; she crossed herself and showed Larissa how. It's easy she said, to make the sign of the cross, it's like this. Nalini looked inside her own drink before taking a sip as if searching for her own answers there. She stood on the church steps in front of Larissa and was now the first one to say, "Anything today, Macario?"

"She's becoming very attached to you, Larissa," said Father Emilio, holding Nalini's hand as they walked down the corridor out of the chapel.

"She is a good sweet girl," replied Larissa, touching the back of Nalini's silky black hair. "Where do you take her in the late afternoons? I notice you're both gone for a few hours each day."

"For our neighborhood walkabout," said Father Emilio. "There are some people who want to but cannot come to church—too sick, or too old—so Nalini and I go to sit with them for a few minutes. We visit different homes each day. We alternate. Right, Nalini?"

"Right, Papa. I like the beautiful blind lady."

He smiled. "Yes. Dimagiba just turned ninety-seven and is bedridden, and she can't see through the cataracts, but every time Nalini comes, the old woman somehow sees her." He ruffled the girl's hair. "You just like her because she gives you chocolate." He continued to Larissa. "We go, we read Scripture to them for a few minutes. I give them the Host. Nalini helps me; she's my little helper, right, Nalini?"

"I hold your Bible for you, Papa," she said, making galloping motions with her two stick horses. "Soon I will be able to read with you."

"Well, you already know so much by heart."

"Yes! *Are the consolations of God small with thee? No, very great!*"

"She is quoting from Job," Father Emilio said, placing a pleased hand on Nalini's shoulder.

It was true. Larissa noticed that the child was able to mouth the recitations of a number of very long passages during the daily services. Well, sure, from hearing them five times a day. Larissa, when she rehearsed *The Tempest*, also knew it nearly by heart.

"Why do you take her?" Larissa asked, making a subtle face of distaste. "I mean, for a small child, to see all that unpleasantness, sickness, and such . . . she has it hard enough, don't you think?"

Father Emilio lightly shook Nalini's shoulder. "How do we answer that question, Nalini?" he asked. "We say, of course, it's not as beautiful as a garden of flowers or a park with birds, but . . ."

"It might not be as beautiful," Nalini said. "But it's more holy."

∽ↄ

The children have never performed on the stage, Father Emilio told Larissa. Are you staying through Christmas? Maybe we can do something? Che had mentioned you loved theater. Perhaps a small play?

Like *Twelfth Night*?

Father Emilio studied her with gentle curiosity.

The Tempest perhaps? *Now my charms are all overthrown, and what strength I have's mine own. Which is most faint.* Larissa wondered if he was appraising her, wondering how good her kidneys were, whether she should be asked to volunteer to donate one, or three. Maybe old habits died hard with him. *Now 'tis true, I must be here confined by you.* Too much time on her hands, despite the near constant obediences. The stillness, the quiet, the lyric chants of the nuns, the repetition of the psalms, the boiling of the water, the disinfecting of fresh fruit, the pervasive vinegar smell mixed in with tamarind leaves, flowers, and the heavy sweet smell of brown sugar and coconut, the scouring of the soup pots, and the incense permeating all the solitude hours spent not in prayer but in remembrance, as

Larissa checked the window screens at the orphanage for holes the awful dengue mosquitoes could get through, all the while composing letters to Kai in her head.

"Well," Father Emilio, after minutes of contemplation, finally replied, "*Tempest* is good. But I was thinking more along the lines of a Nativity play."

And release me from my bands, with the help of your good hands . . .

"Maybe you could write it for us, and we could rehearse it to get ready for Christmas?"

"I'm not staying through Christmas, Father," Larissa hastily reminded him. "I'm going back in October. Plus I've never staged a Nativity play." She shrugged nonchalantly.

"Children don't perform Christmas pageants in America?"

Not her children. She went cold. "I don't know." *Now I want spirits to enforce, art to enchant.* "I'm not familiar with that. When I was a child, my mother believed I should judge for myself, decide for myself—but only when I got older. It's just not in my background."

"Did you?" he asked. "Judge for yourself when you got older?"

"No." And her kids hadn't either. She passed that on to her children, the nothingness. *And my ending is despair unless I be relieved by prayer . . . which pierces so that it assaults mercy itself and frees all faults.* Mouthing Shakespeare by rote, not feel.

Larissa wanted to defend her mother on this rainy afternoon inside her favorite place—the kitchen overlooking the lawn. There were *plenty* of other things she taught me. She taught me to be polite—to strangers *and* my family. Not to be too demonstrative. To have good manners. I have very good manners. I learned to stay calm through crisis because of my mother. I am not a histrionic like Che. I can handle anything. Skinned knees, broken bones, bee stings, dog bites.

Obviously there is something she had not given me. But my mother was always a libertarian and proud of it. Live and let live was her motto. All my friends envied me for her *laissez-faire* parenting, for all the books I was allowed to read, for the no-limits approach to any adult material. Find your own way. Teach yourself. Play music, or not. Read, or not. Believe, or not. Whatever I wanted was fine with her.

But there was *one* thing. At the very end, when Dad was leaving, it was the only time she saw a chink in what she now knew was her mother's armor. Larissa heard her all the way from upstairs, screaming at him, and she had *never* heard her mother scream before; it was so guttural and jarring. She heard it only for a moment before she slammed the pillows against her ears. *I lived my whole life only for you!* And other things. It went on and on and on. It was unbearable. It was as if Dad had taken a crowbar to her.

The bitterness that flowed from the black end to their thirty-five-year union never dried no, which is another reason Larissa couldn't visit her mother too often, because it hurt to look at her. Dad died soon after and they never got an answer to their question that, like rhetorical cyanide, remained in her mother's heart and in hers: what was so completely missing in him that he couldn't see, what blinded him to the scales on which all of them were outweighed by one pretty stranger twenty years younger?

She thought that a scruffy boy from the wrong side of Maui who extended his hand to her made her blind. But what if she had always been blind just like her father, and just didn't know it?

Larissa blinked, came out of it, smiled blankly at Father Emilio. "Come on," he said. "You do theater, we do Jesus. Let's muddle through the Nativity play together. It'll be like the blind leading the blind."

Larissa looked away, trying to shake off her reverie. "Does Shakespeare do nativity?"

The priest chuckled. "You tell me, Larissa. *You're* the drama expert."

"May I use your phone, Father? I'm going to try . . . try to call Kai one more time today." Morning, evening—why didn't he *ever* answer the phone? Though in Kai's defense, the rectory was closed after compline at 8:30, which was 11:00 p.m. in Pooncarie, so perhaps they were out drinking. She didn't know. The phone just rang and rang.

Nalini wanted to be one of the Wise Men. But you're not a boy, Nalini. I can be anything I want, said Nalini. Why can't I be a Wise Man? I want to bring myrrh.

"How about if before you bring myrrh, you and I go to the market and get us some fabric so we can make costumes? We need cloaks for the Shepherds, and robes for the Wise Men, and a dress for Mary. We need ornamental rope to use for belts, and silk or satin scarves to tie on heads. Plus we'll need some thick paper and paints, because we've got to make crowns."

"For Jesus?" Nalini squealed, jumping up and down.

"No, not for Jesus. For the Wise Men. Jesus is not a king."

"Of course He is," said Nalini, puzzled. "He's the King of kings."

"I meant," Larissa corrected herself, "he's just a baby inside the manger."

"Yes! We should get Him a halo. And Mary too. And Joseph."

"Joseph needs a halo?" Larissa didn't know if she was going to be up to this.

Nalini laughed. "You're so funny. You're joking, right?"

"Yeah. Sure I am. Well, if we get gold foil, we can make some halos."

They made sheep and goats out of cardboard. The orphans painted them in rainbow colors. They shaped an angel out of white clay. Father Emilio suggested they build a cave. They got wood, and nails and hammered boards together. They ripped grass out and when it dried, they had hay. They got Christmas lights and hung them around the wooden structure so it lit up like a Christmas tree. The afternoon rehearsals morphed into morning rehearsals, and evening rehearsals. All the children who could walk and talk wanted to participate, all thirty of them. Larissa made it happen. The Narrator, Joseph, Mary, King Herod, three Wise Men, three Shepherds, and twenty angels dressed in white sheets with silver halos, Jesus was played by Benji, a severely cleft-palated three-month-old, born without any left limbs, who lay in the manger during rehearsals.

Larissa stood by the door to the common room watching them. So simple to teach them, yet so hard for them to learn. First, to teach them to be someone else, to be other people.

Perhaps if she had been other people, she could've remained more of herself. Perhaps had she been given alternate lives to play on the stage, she could've come home and lived in a place with the tall oaks and the view and the cold windows. Perhaps she could've continued to touch with her hands the faces she loved while during the day walking out into the cold and ascending three steps, four, to the wooden platform in a darkened theater, standing on it, and lifting her gaze to the rafters, the way Nalini, standing in daylight, lifted her gaze to Father Emilio as she learned the words that were hard to remember, memorized the cues that were hard to keep.

Nalini is quite something. She wants everyone's lines, not just her own. She wants to live many lives, not just her own, not even her one part as Magi Number Three. *"Myrrh is mine: its bitter perfume, breathes a life of gathering gloom—sorrowing, sighing, bleeding, dying, sealed in the stone-cold tomb."*

The little girl loves to sing that and bellows with all her might, but then her little hands go up, and her black eyes sparkle as she mouths, then whispers along to the words of the Narrator too! *Glorious now behold Him arise!*

Nalini, pipe down, beckons Larissa, standing across the room from Father Emilio, while Sister Martina, excellent on the piano, plays "We Three Kings," and the children sing, and uncontained Nalini jumps up and down. "How am I doing, Larissa? How am I doing?" Though she is not the Prophet, she speaks with the prophets, as Larissa rolls her eyes, yet with pride, with desperate tenderness at the child's vulnerability. She wants to promise her, swear to her that she will never leave her, that she will never again be the one to break that bond.

Except Larissa is not who Nalini longs for. All the vows in the world can't bring Che back to look after the child that stands in the light of the ancient adobe room and announces with the Prophets, *"Look! The redeemed of the Lord shall return, and sorrow and sighing shall flee away. Come, everyone who thirsts, come to the waters; and he who has no money, come, buy and eat!* How am I doing, Larissa?"

4

Happiness

"I watch you," Father Emilio said to her in September. "You've been with us over two months, and I still don't know how I can help you."

"What do you mean? I'm fine." Larissa was in the kitchen, in the afternoon. She had just finished kneading the dough for *pandesal* and was taking a tea break. The tea was good in the Philippines. She hadn't been much of a tea drinker before. But here they got their tea from somewhere aromatic. China Oolong? Green? It was soothing and fine.

"You're not fine. You're a gloomy Gus. Look at you."

Well, who wouldn't be gloomy? In two months she had received one letter from Kai. One! You want to talk about memorize? She memorized that letter. It wasn't hard to do, the letter being so short and all. Sixteen lines. Including the Dear Larissa.

Dear Larissa,

    I miss you too. I'm not a great letter writer, and I'm sorry about that, but I think about you all the time, think about the good times we had. Billy and I are working from sunrise to sundown. The stables are coming along nice. Almost done, remarkably. You'd like them very much, and the horses are doing well. Billy is an awesome wrangler and all-around great guy. We have big plans, Billy and I. I want to tell you about them when I see you. When

*will that be? Not soon enough. When are you coming back? I wish
you could call me sometime. I love your letters, it's like you're right
here with me. Though not quite. ☺ Please keep writing. I really
look forward to receiving them. Nalini sounds like a great kid. Your
friend Che would be happy to know you're keeping an eye on her.
I'm going to go now, but I'll write again soon, and I think about
you every day.*

    Love,

    Kai

"There's nothing you can do," Larissa said to Father Emilio.
"You can't fix this. You can't fix anything." *Love, Kai?* That's what
she got? She had written him thirty, forty letters, and this is what
came from him? She sat and stared out the window. It was pouring
rain, water like a tidal wave was washing away the hopscotch
course, the chalk outlines of momentary joy. The grass was sodden
with standing pools. After the children would wake up from their
afternoon nap, the greatest fun of their day would be to run around
barefoot in those shallow ponds full of lilies.

"Larissa, look around you," Father said. "Sixty girls and boys
in our Christ the Redeemer orphanage are growing up without
mothers and fathers. Some of them are disabled, some of them are
blind, can't walk, have heart valve problems, cleft palates. One
died last week from dengue fever. I know she was already sick and
small, but still. Despite this, they manage. Nalini, too. They skip
rope, play cards, invent games out of rocks, they hide and go seek.
They've been transformed by your play rehearsals. You should hear
them in their beds, in the morning, in the yard. It's all they talk
about. Every day they do this: find cheer despite the seeming misery
of it. Why do you sit there and cry over your own sorrows? Even
while you bake bread, cook sweet rice pudding, cut up fruit for *halo-
halo*, make costumes for Mary and the Wise Men, I see you lead a
joyless existence; why?"

"I don't know how *they* do what they do," Larissa replied. "I don't
understand them at all."

"You should feel a sense of sacred awe toward all mystifying things you don't understand," said Father Emilio. "The mystery of life is legion, that's why we continually pray for guidance and comfort." He nodded coolly. "You would do better not to view them with the scorn I hear in your voice."

"There's no scorn, Father. But they're children! I'm hardly going to take an example from them. They don't have to live with what I have to live with. No pain, no regret, nothing."

"No pain, no regret, really?" Father Emilio said so quietly. He folded his hands in front of him.

"I mean, they're not waking up every day saying they would do anything, *anything*, to live their life over."

Father Emilio watched her. "No, they probably don't do that, though I can assure you they wake up in the dead of night from all manner of other unimaginable things. But is that what *you* do?" he asked. "You wake up every day and say to yourself that you would do anything to live your life over?"

"Yes," Larissa said to him—and meant it. All she wanted was to live *it* over. To get up every morning with joy, see, once there was joy! and run toward her day, toward that one hour when she was in bliss on Albright Circle. One hour a day to feel young, to have love. Father Emilio wanted her to find it? She *had* found it. And now look.

"Larissa, please. Don't be keeled over like this, choking on your guilt and despair. Learn to live with the choices you made. Would you like Sister Margarita to teach you how to make *macapuno*?" It was a thick coconut dessert delicacy.

"Not today. Look what's happening to me," she said. "Love is vanishing. Yet it's the only thing left."

He stood up. "I must go attend to my other duties," he said coldly. "But, Larissa, love is not vanishing. It's everywhere you look, every single place on this earth. You can't get away from it. And everywhere love is, God is. And God is not where love is not. Open your eyes, and cast your glance on something other than yourself. And if you can't do that yet, then look inside your heart. When were you happiest? When did you feel most fulfilled? What place do your memories take you to? Go there, and see if you can find a way to keep yourself."

◦◦◦

After college and before she hooked up permanently with Jared, who was off looking for himself while being a tour guide in the Himalayas, Larissa spent the summer as one of the performers in Great Swamp Revue, a traveling band of improv actors, who rode in one bus from town to town in New Jersey and lower upstate New York, performing in local theaters, up north to Woodstock and west to Allentown. Ron Palais, their road manager, booked thirteen Saturday night gigs and seven Sunday matinées. There were eight in their theater group. Evelyn was one of them. So was Ezra.

It was the happiest summer of her life.

They lived in cheap motels and slept on the bus on the way to the next gig, they showered sporadically, read constantly, talked and smoked incessantly, recited tragedy and comedy under the pulsing beat of the Clash and the Ramones. They did not want to be sedated, they felt and saw and heard everything like they were on ecstasy. After each performance they went out drinking, continuing to rehearse, to riff off each other, to sing. *Did you stand by me? No, not at all.* They danced and paired up with unlikely partners. Larissa stopped wearing makeup and a bra. Evelyn performed Job on stage, the whole thing by herself in a soliloquy. Larissa had been blown away, but their manager told Evelyn not to do it anymore. "People aren't going to get it, Ev," Ron told the disappointed and incredulous woman. "The whole suffering thing. Nobody wants to suffer." Ezra said he agreed: suffering was for chumps. "No point in suffering for its own sake. It's self-pitying, self-indulgent, and stupid." He smoked three cigarettes in the time it took him to utter those few sentences. "Do you know why we suffer? So that the works of God can be made manifest in us. That's Job. Ev, can you convey that in a five-minute speech to families on a Sunday afternoon after church?"

Ezra was teasing her, but Evelyn didn't give up; she persisted despite Ron's orders, despite Ezra, who must have been a little bit in love with her also. Who wouldn't be? Larissa herself was a little bit in love with Evelyn, and while Ezra and Larissa were in bed, their eyes became moistened with the image of Evelyn's lovely mouth incanting, *I was not in safety, neither had I rest, neither was I quiet; yet trouble came.*

During this Renaissance Fair summer of her life, when Larissa's hair was cropped like a boy's and her face plain of makeup, she had joy every day and knew it, was cramped and didn't care, had few comforts, no money, was always broke, and didn't care. She lived not understanding why she was living and even less why eventually she had to die, and didn't care. Every night she got up on stage trying to imitate the inimitable Evelyn reciting long-suffering Job, with her own fruitful efforts from *Romeo and Juliet*, and Prospero's speeches. *We are such stuff as dreams are made on . . .*

Larissa knew it was fleeting even then, but fully believed it would come again, in another form, to be happy like that, so *alive!* packed up on a bus, all her life's belongings in a duffel bag under her feet, hung over from the night before, rootlessly drifting from town to town, singing karaoke in the smoke-filled bars. *Did you stand by me? No, not at all.*

And almost everything but the happy did come again.

❧

"I don't know what you think of me, Father. You must judge me. How can you not?" During a lull in the afternoon, after lunch, before vespers, when the children were having a short siesta, she and Father Emilio, with the tiny shadow that was Nalini, were taking a short walk in the monastery gardens before it downpoured again.

"I have nothing but profound sympathy for you," Father Emilio said. "Do you judge yourself?"

"Oddly, only since I've been here."

"That seems odd to you?"

"A little bit. After all," said Larissa, "this place is completely removed from anything I've ever known. I can't figure out what's stirring my conscience. Nothing in it is familiar, nothing rouses the senses or the memories."

"Nothing?"

Larissa chuckled. "No, and I must admit I'm not a fan of the vinegar and the pickled fish. Though I enjoy the coconut."

"But the thick liver sauce poured over the crispy suckling pig, that doesn't move your conscience?" Father Emilio smiled a little.

"No." Larissa chewed her lip. "You know . . . I really didn't mean for it to happen. This thing with Kai."

"Didn't you?"

"My pockets weren't empty and the devil wasn't dancing in them. I had a good life."

"Yes. Che was quite envious of you. I kept telling her to struggle is okay, too."

Larissa shook her head. "I've had both. Believe me, a comfortable life is better."

"That's what Che told me, and she hadn't had both."

"She was right."

"Was she? Your life got easy—and empty—and your soul started looking for a way out. The question you have to ask yourself is why? Larissa, you had love in every room in your house. Why wasn't that love enough?"

Larissa didn't like the formulation, the premise, the implied conclusion. "That's not true," she said. "It was enough. It had nothing to do with that."

"What then?"

"I told you, I wasn't vigilant."

"True, vigilance is essential in virtue."

"It's not about virtue." Larissa frowned. "It's about what feels right in your heart. But in the beginning, I wasn't guarded enough. I should've been more careful. I should've never pretended to myself even for a moment it was nothing."

Father Emilio nodded. "That's how it always happens. I told Che to be careful with Lorenzo, to guard herself against his destructive passions. All she wanted was not to struggle. I said to her, but Che, when you're struggling, conflicted, in a panic, you're always calling on God, praying to him, begging him for help, and few things please our Lord more than to give solace to the souls that cry for him."

"Hmm."

"Do you find yourself closer to God when things aren't going well?" Father Emilio asked carefully.

"Hmm," Larissa replied in a ponder. "Not particularly. I feel angrier, I think. When life's in the crapper, I feel like I can't believe this has happened to me. Like it's proof of the random, unfair nature of it all."

Father Emilio stared somberly ahead, his head shaking slightly.

"I really don't think God has any time for me, Father," said Larissa.

"Never, or not now?"

"Not now especially. But I guess never."

"You think He has no time for you," asked Father Emilio, "or . . . do you perhaps have no time for Him?"

She smiled restlessly. "You're right. It's probably mutual."

Father Emilio shook his head. "No," he said. "It isn't."

Larissa waved her hand. "He's got no sympathy for the likes of me. Not when compared to Benji and Bayani." Bayani caught hemorrhagic fever and had to be quarantined. Benji was the malformed infant playing baby Jesus, missing, among other things, the part of his jaw that allowed him to drink from a bottle. Milk had to be dripped into the open cavity that was his mouth.

"You're right, Benji and Bayani receive extra grace from our Lord. But let me ask you, have you been reading the Bible? At night after evening prayer, do you open it?"

Larissa didn't want to admit to him that she didn't, that instead she feverishly wrote and wrote and wrote her own testament to the rover on the Ducati, the wrangler of horses, the builder of barns, the taker of hearts.

"I didn't think so," said Father Emilio. "Because if you did, you would notice something very striking in all the stories of the Bible, Larissa, in the Old Covenant and certainly in the Book of Books, and that is: there is *no one*, no matter how small, how seemingly insignificant, how sinful, who is not fixed and fortified with everlasting and personal compassion from God. Not the woman at the well, not the blind leper, not the tax collector or the Pharisee, not Nicodemus or Job, or Joshua or Jonah, or the girl who died. No one is cast away from God's grace. No one. That's what should jump out at you. How full of intimate profound mercy God is to all souls. So yes to Benji and Bayani, but also to Nalini, and to you too, Larissa. Whatever joy or sorrow touches you, it touches God, too."

They made circles through the grounds, walking slowly. Larissa didn't want the rains to come. She liked talking to this man. She held on to Nalini's hand.

"In a regular day filled with small moments of outward insignificance," she told him as if reciting from her own new covenant, "one nothing led to another, and suddenly he was in my car, and suddenly he was in my heart."

"And nothing became everything."

"Yes. But he loved me, Father! And I loved him. I know I once loved my husband—"

"*Just* your husband?"

"No—you're right." Letting go of Nalini's hand, Larissa wrapped her arms around her sinking stomach. "But suddenly my whole self belonged to another person."

"No, Larissa," Father Emilio said. "Then, as now, your whole self belonged only to you."

She didn't know what he meant. But he was a priest. He didn't know what it was like to love. She didn't want to say this out loud. In the beginning, Kai and I had breathtaking fire, she wanted to say to him. We were all ablaze, and I was eighteen with him, an eighteen I'd never been. He was a joy above all joys.

"The question is," said Father Emilio, "what remains after that inauspicious beginning? What's left?"

Was he being ironic with her? *Inauspicious? Ominous?*

Foreboding? Sometimes she couldn't tell. "Love is left," said Larissa. "That love you keep talking about. That's how I know it was real."

"Does he still love you?"

"I hope so." Larissa bent downcast, undeniably upset and disordered by the absence of letters, by her inability to speak to Kai by phone. "We're fully committed to one another," she said. "We have one life."

"Have you noticed how often people make promises they can't keep? Look," said Father Emilio, "can I ask you a hypothetical question? If you had known then that you would never see your children again—never!—would you *still* have done it?"

Larissa didn't look at him. She didn't even nod or shrug. It had started to rain, blessedly, and they went inside.

What if the answer was *yes*?

∽∾

In this manner Larissa moved toward another winter, counting out the days until October 20, toward another falling of the leaves, other daffodils in other deserted towns on other continents. Or was it toward summer, the greening of the trees, the blooming of the flowers, the glow that sprung from renewal?

She dreamed she lost them and she kept opening and closing her cupboards, opening and closing her drawers, walking into people's houses, then walking out, looking in cars, in bars, in woods and bushes. She just kept wandering, her hands opening, closing things. What are you looking for, Father Emilio once asked. My children, she replied. I seem to have misplaced them. I put them somewhere and can't remember where.

5

Jared Stark

"What is she doing?" Larissa asked Father Emilio one afternoon. "Why is she always sitting apart? Here, or outside on the steps. Why doesn't she go play with other kids?"

"She does. She plays all the time."

"She always comes back here."

"Yes. During her moments of solitude, she does. She is waiting."

"Solitude? She is *five*. Waiting for what?"

"We all need to sit and think in the silence. The child sits and waits for her mother to come back."

"Oh my God!" Larissa stared at Nalini on the bench playing with sticks. "Is *that* what she's doing?"

"Of course. What did you think she was doing?"

The rains didn't come every day now. It was still warm and humid but without the torrents.

"I don't know. Just sitting?" Lowering her voice to almost a whisper, Larissa said, "Do you think it's feasible? I mean, you don't think it would be better for Nalini to know the truth?"

"I tried telling her the truth." Father Emilio smiled ruefully. "But Nalini sees it differently. She tells me her mother often comes to her in dreams, and vows to return to her as soon as she is able."

"Oh, Father," Larissa said, "why do you let her believe that? I don't think it's kind. You should disabuse her of the notion."

"Why would I? I don't know for sure Che won't come back. She might."

"Come on now. If she's not back already . . ."

"She could be in prison."

"She would've written," said Larissa. "Che was the best letter writer." Unlike the horse rider from Pooncarie. "And you know how she felt about having a child. If she were in prison, or alive, she would've written her daughter."

"You'd think that, wouldn't you?"

"So you agree with me, Father. Talk to her. Honestly, it's not good for her to do this. It's not healthy."

"Well," Father Emilio drew out, "you may be right."

"You know I'm right."

"Except for one example that makes me want to give the benefit of the doubt to Nalini." He tapped Larissa's arm. "*You.*"

"Me? What do *I* have to do with Nalini?"

"You're not dead," said Father Emilio. "You're not even in prison. And yet *you* have not written to your children."

There was that sensation again, of precipitous calamitous falling, the stomach dropping out. "That's different. I'm different. I don't know what to say to them . . . you're comparing two totally separate situations, there's no comparison, two totally . . . I don't even know—"

"I agree with you," he interrupted her stammerings. "I would prefer if Nalini had someone to take care of her. But I can't get an adoption placement for her without the mother's death certificate, which I don't have. She certainly does need someone, though." They both gazed at the little girl. "She is such a vulnerable child. Then, of course," he added, "are all children."

"I still don't understand where Che could've gotten the bail money," said Larissa. "She was always penniless and frantic. I mean, it's inconceivable that Lorenzo could've made bail. Did he sell his kidney or something?"

Father Emilio said nothing, but his gaze lifted from Nalini across the yard to Larissa next to him. "Do you really want to know how Lorenzo made bail?"

"Of course. Why wouldn't I?"

He stood up. "Come with me. Nalini, we'll be right back," he called out to the girl. "Stay where you are."

"Okay, Papa." She got up from her bench and followed them inside.

He sighed. "Sit outside, okay? I have to talk to Larissa in private."

"Okay, Papa." She slid down onto the floor, the two sticks in her hands prancing, all saddled up, as if in dressage.

In the rectory, with the door closed, Father Emilio turned to Larissa. "Your husband was the one who sent Che the money for Lorenzo's bail."

"*What?*"

"Yes. He sent the money, care of this church, for Lorenzo's bail."

"That's impossible!" Her hand flew up to steady her thumping heart. "He didn't know anything—he knew nothing about Che's—when did he do this?"

"Five years ago."

A stunned Larissa collapsed against the chair. She found this inconceivable and wrong, the connection between that world and this one, like a séance gone awry. She thought she was a ghost, and suddenly Jared's material presence made itself known, and with his presence the presence of the other thing, the thing that constantly made her feel like she was plunging from the skies.

"You want to see what else he sent?"

"Father!" she cried, putting out her hand to stop him. She was terrified he was about to fling at her the painted hands of her children, their painted feet, with helpless words scrawled in their unformed handwriting. *Mommy, where are you? I miss you.* There were some things Larissa could not endure. This was one of them. "Please . . . have mercy . . . no." She could take anything but a physical reminder of them.

From a safe behind his wood desk, Father Emilio pulled out a white business envelope and handed it to Larissa.

"I will not look at photographs," she said, her voice hoarse and low.

"Don't worry, no photographs. Look inside."

In the envelope was a stack of crisp one-hundred-dollar bills. "Money?"

"There's four thousand dollars in there," Father Emilio said, "marked for Che and the child, with your Summit, New Jersey address and phone number. Che had asked for a plane ticket to come stay with you. Jared sent her a note explaining your silence and your absence, but he did send her the money for the tickets." The priest pointed to the envelope in Larissa's hands. "The note is in there if you want to read it."

I'm not sure I do, Larissa mouthed inaudibly. I'm not sure I can. I'm pretty sure I can't. I'm certain I don't.

After sitting in the chair a while, almost hoping to be stung by a mosquito and get dengue fever—bonecrushing pain, fever, rash, seeping hemorrhage—for she imagined it to be better than this, Larissa opened the folded piece of paper. In Jared crisp firm block letter handwriting, the note read,

Che, Larissa is gone. Without a note or a goodbye she's left us; left me for someone else, and I fear she's left us for good. The money I'm sending you is from the sale of her car, which she clearly no longer needs. I'm sure she'd want you to have it. Please don't sell your kidney, Che, even though I know a wonderful woman who could really use it. You need both your kidneys. After all, you now have a baby to take care of. You're welcome to come and stay with us any time you want. You're always welcome, and I sincerely mean that. I enclose cash for you and the baby for two first-class tickets.

Jared

PS. If by chance you see her, tell her that no matter what, she is still the mother of my children, and always will be.

Her throat constricting, her fingers trembling, Larissa carefully put the note back in the envelope. Breakbone fever would've been preferable.

"The money is still here," she said dully. Four thousand dollars—in cash.

"Of course it's here. Che hasn't come back."

Larissa looked out the screened window into the front yard. Three small boys were playing soccer in the street. It was busy in late afternoon, teeming, women carrying shopping, men coming back from work, children returning from school or sports. Yet inside was sanctuary. Four hundred thousand people in Parañaque, eleven million in Metro Manila, yet inside San Agustin was like being inside the secluded abbey in Mount Athos in Greece, exquisitely isolated.

"Nalini dreams of going to America," Father Emilio said. "She is convinced when her mother returns, they will go and live in the place the ever-loving nuns keep telling her about. The place with snow."

"Does she know what snow is?"

"No. I tell her it's white and cold, but she doesn't understand. She doesn't know what cold is. It doesn't get below seventy on the equator."

Larissa held on to the money in the envelope. "But you and I know Che is not coming back. She could've died long ago in Mindanao forests. We will never know." She paused. "Please don't look at me like that, Father. We talked about this. Che is not me."

"You are alive. You remain."

"Yes."

"Larissa," Father Emilio said, stretching out his hand to her. "There's money in your hands for two tickets back to the United States."

"Yes."

"Go back home."

She jumped up.

He jumped up, too, grabbing hold of her arms. "Go back home," he repeated imploringly. "And take the little girl with you."

"Let go of me—please . . ."

"Your husband owes nothing to Che or her daughter, yet he sent them money, to change their life, to help them. That's the kind of man he is. He owed them nothing, yet he helped them. Don't you think he would do even more for you?"

"No! He will kill me."

Father Emilio shook his head. "A man who sends fifty thousand dollars in bail money to the Philippines to help the rebel boyfriend of his wife's childhood friend is not the man who will do that. He will help you."

"Please," Larissa whispered. "Let go of my hands . . ."

Father Emilio let go.

"There's no bringing it back. There is no reliving it." She covered her face. "Who would take me back now?"

"Your husband would. Nalini adores you, Larissa. And she desperately needs you. She shouldn't live in an orphanage."

"They love her here."

"She needs a proper home, you know that."

"Father . . . Che could come back any minute. And Nalini won't leave without her mother."

"You just said you were certain Che wasn't alive. Nalini will leave with you. To America? In a second."

Larissa shook her head.

"Don't you see how much she wants to be with you?" Father Emilio continued intensely. "She follows you around because she is afraid you will leave her, too."

Larissa shook her head. "I beg you, don't say that. *Please.*"

"And if Che comes back," Father Emilio went on in rapid-fire fashion, "I will make sure she gets to you and Nalini, wherever you are."

"There won't be any money left."

"You have my word," said Father Emilio, "Che will get to America." He beseeched her with his steady gaze, blinking compassion at her, kindness.

"Jared will never forgive me," Larissa said, casting her eyes away.

"He will. He already has. Didn't you read his letter?"

"Father, I've done an unforgivable thing . . ."

"There is no such thing."

"What are you talking about? Of course there is."

"There is *no* such thing," Father Emilio said firmly. "You think you're above God's forgiveness? That's what Judas thought. No one is above it."

"I'm above Jared's."

He raised his questioning shoulders. "I'm not saying your marriage is intact. I'm not even saying that your husband is in the same place. You wouldn't want him to be grieving for you all these years, would you? You wouldn't want your family to suffer? You'd prefer they moved on, found relief, am I right?"

"Of course."

"In the context of that new life, the man who sent fifty thousand dollars to a stranger will not turn away the mother of his children. Married people are bound by Divine law forever."

Haltingly Larissa breathed. "How can I be forgiven?" She whispered.

"You have to want it, you have to ask for it, repentance is first. But how can you continue to live unforgiven? If Jared forgives only what is forgivable, what kind of forgiveness is that? That's not forgiveness, that's justice. And you will not be judged until the end of your days. So you have some time. Forgiveness means forgiving the unforgivable."

Larissa shook her head. She wanted to put her hands up, to cover her ears from the terror. Her gaze remained down.

"I know you're disheartened. I see you every day. I've spent much time with you, watching the tides of your sorrow," said Father Emilio, his hands on Larissa's shoulders. "But, Larissa, catch sight of yourself, catch sight of your brave and strong soul, of your need for regeneration. You're not doomed, you're blessed! God takes hold of your heart and He gives you a new heart. Open your eyes—there's grace everywhere, inside you and outside you. It's solace you seek, and comfort. Remember what Nalini said. *Are the consolations of God small with thee? No, very great.* You are a child of God, too. You have a soul, that holy of holies, which is your true value. You are to live forever."

"You're frightening me much more than you intend, Father," said Larissa, clenching her hands against her chest, her blood pounding in her face.

"You are the essential missing piece in the swirling center of your own life, you are the integral element," Father Emilio exclaimed. "It won't come to you. *You* must enter into your own salvation. But grace *always* flows into the emptied soul that's crying out to be delivered. Grace is waiting for you. I know it. I feel it. All you have to do is say yes."

Barely able to move her lips, Larissa whispered, "Can I think about saying yes?"

"Promise me you will?"

"I promise you I will."

"Listen to me," said the priest, "I know that your time here is running out. But now your husband has offered you another way out rather than back to Australia, where things may be at a dead end. But even if you don't take his offering, you have another way. You're loved here. The nuns, the children deeply care for you, your bread pudding and your plays and your hopscotch. You have become a vital indispensable part of our small community. You bring a smile to everyone," Father Emilio said, "even when you are moping." He smiled lightly. "I won't even talk about what you mean to Nalini. Because you know. You've made our lives better by your presence here with us, Larissa. As I suspect you had in your American life."

She bowed her head. "Perhaps. You've given me so much to think about, Father. I promise I will think about everything. I'll figure it out."

"I hope so," said Father Emilio.

❧

A week went by.

"Father," said Larissa, coming into the rectory. She used her dramatic training to still her hands so they wouldn't fidget on her lap. "I've thought very carefully about what you said. You're completely right. I will go back to New Jersey. It's a good idea. And Nalini, I know, will be happy to visit with me, even if we don't stay for long, because truthfully, I really like it here in Moonwalk with you and the children and the nuns. I feel comfortable here, Father. So. I want to take her with me, and would like to take her, and will, as you suggest."

Father Emilio sat. He didn't speak.

"But here's the thing." Larissa cleared her throat, smiled her big smile, her blinking eyes on his motionless face. "Kai will be waiting for me in Sydney tomorrow. He is picking me up. I know things have been odd with us, stressful, and he hasn't written often, and we haven't spoken, but that's because he's been working so hard, earning money for us, and with the time difference, and my work here, it's been hard to communicate. But frankly I just don't feel it's right to leave him standing in the airport, after he's traveled two thousand kilometers to meet me in Sydney. It's just not right. I can't be correcting one wrong by making another." She shook her head. She banged her chest. "In here, it just *feels* wrong. So what I'd like to do, with your approval, is fly to Sydney, meet up with him, and have a conversation, and make sure, *sure*, we're on the same page and want the same things, but you are absolutely correct, I can't continue with him unless I know that we're both square with each other and are traveling together. In any case, if it ends, I want to end it with him properly, decently. I don't want one more thing on my conscience. I want us to meet, to talk, to finish, if that's what we must do, with dignity. I owe him at least that, don't you think? He deserves that simple human decency, don't you agree? And then I will come back, and Nalini and I will fly back to the States. I'll bring her some beautiful summer dresses from Australia. Sydney has lovely shops for children."

Father Emilio sat. He said nothing.

"It's wrong to just skip out, leave someone standing in the middle of the airport, in the lurch like that, waiting. You know, Father?" Swallowing, Larissa continued quickly. "Here's another thing, though . . . I've been with you for three months, working, completely voluntarily, of course, but as you know, I'm a little bit broke, and so I was wondering, about Jared's money . . . you know, Nalini and I don't need to fly first class, and Jared left enough money for first-class, which we really don't need, we'll be fine flying coach, Qantas gives you lots of leg room now and DVDs with your flight, and good meals, we'll be fine in coach, so I was wondering if I could take a little bit of my husband's cash, because Kai and I have some debts on the other side that haven't been paid, some back rent, equipment costs, etc., and I just want to make sure I have all my pegs in a row, and nothing outstanding. I don't want to be indebted to anyone. Because that would be wrong. So . . . do you think I could take, um, a few hundred dollars?"

In the only gesture he made, Father Emilio pointed to the safe, ajar behind him. She hurried, gingerly pulling out the envelope, looking inside, handling the crisp unused hundreds. He didn't turn around in his chair to watch her. He continued to sit, his fingers pressed together in prayer, facing the windows to the street.

"Thank you so much," she said, putting the envelope back in the safe. "Thank you for your understanding, Father. I'm just going to take . . . if you don't mind, I'll take two thousand, and what I won't need, I'll bring back, and this way, two thousand is left, which is plenty for two tickets, more than enough. Thank you so much." Rolling up the money, she stuffed it into the leg pocket of her khakis. "Well, if there's nothing else, I appreciate your understanding, and I must run, because it's nearly lunchtime and the fish adobo needs to be warmed up, and the bread put in the oven." She headed out of his office.

Go back. The return. Reversal. You left, jumped ship, and are now floating back to the Jersey port, to the town of Summit. You look around and suddenly the place you left has dignity, simplicity, grace! It's all the things you need, you want. Return of the native. Return of the prodigal son. You kiss the furniture, lie down on the wooden floor, beg for that elusive forgiveness, you scrub your life with your own two hands, saying, this is all I want, this is all I want, this is all I want, you chant home home home from the roof of the homestead.

And then . . .

You're not home home home thirty minutes before you drive to the local Dairy Barn for milk and a sentence of conversation with the insipid cashier makes you realize that you need to *run* not walk back into the well of the Summit train station, and not even ask where the next train takes you, just wait for the doors to open, jump inside, press yourself to the window, and thank all the Southern Cross stars that you barely escaped the plodding slog of your inevitable asphyxiating life.

"One more thing." Larissa turned to Father Emilio when she was at the open door. "Nalini is so close to me, and I can't find the words to explain to a five-year-old what I need to do as a grown-up. She won't understand, and I fear she's going to break down if I tell her I'm leaving, even for a couple of days. I desperately don't want her to get upset. Could you . . . do me a favor, Father, and please . . ."

"Don't worry," said Father Emilio. "I'll take care of Nalini."

Abandoned love. Eros. The hurricane of two souls.

Kai and Larissa forever.

There was no more anything.

There was Kai and Larissa, until the end.

We go through life praying it will never happen to us.

We go through life praying that it will.

6

Land of the Dry Lakes

He wasn't even there! He wasn't at the airport, he wasn't waiting for her. Obsessively Larissa called the only number she had for him, called it over and over. She had arrived in Sydney in mid-afternoon, and it wasn't until five in the evening that the phone was finally picked up.

"Kai's not here," said Billy-O. "Who is this?"

"Billy-O, it's Larissa!"

"Oh. Larissa. Hi." He said her name like he had no idea who she was.

"What happened to him? He was supposed to be at the airport."

"Airport. Oh, I'm sure he knows, yeah . . ."

She felt a smattering of relief. "When did he leave?"

"Uh—days ago, maybe four, five."

Relief shattered. "Oh my God," she gasped, "something must've happened to him."

"No, no," Billy-O said quickly. "Don't worry. He was making a detour in Jindabyne. Hang tight. I'm sure he'll be there soon. He probably underestimated how long it was going to take to get to Sydney. He does that a lot. Underestimates things."

Did Kai do that a lot? This wasn't a little underestimation, like, say, twenty minutes, a half-hour. Her plane landed over three hours ago.

"Do you know if he found a new place for us to live?"

"I don't know, darlin', I couldn't tell you."

Most unhelpful. And perplexing.

Larissa got herself some airport fries, a lukewarm panini, a Diet Coke, and sat lumpbacked with her luggage in the Qantas arrivals terminal. She calculated that from Jindabyne to Sydney airport was a five-hour drive, so even if he left late morning he should've been here already. This was inexcusable. She called Bart and Bianca.

Bart was friendly, but in a detached way; there was none of that, Larissa, baby, I haven't heard from you for three months, how-you-been talk. It was just, Hey. Yes, Kai came a few days ago, yes, stayed with us while he took care of things.

"Do you know if he found us a place to live?" she asked.

"I don't know that he was looking," Bart replied. "But he should be there soon. He'll tell you all about it. He left after lunch."

After *lunch*! When he knew her plane was landing at two?

She sighed. "How've you and Bianca been, Bart?"

"Oh, good, good, fine, yeah, everything's great. Listen, we were just running out to meet some friends, so if there's nothing else . . ."

"No, Bart, there is nothing else." Larissa hung up.

She heard Kai's voice calling for her across the crowded echo of the terminal. "Larissa!" He was strutting to her, his hands open, smiling. He had cut off his hair! It was all gone, just a thick light brown fuzz remained. He had a big smile on his face and didn't look remotely sheepish.

"Kai!"

"Oh, I know." He ran his hand through his crew-cut head as he came up to her and opened his arms. "You don't like it? It was too bloody hot. Come here."

They hugged, she frowning, puzzled. "Did you lose more weight?" he asked, his hands moving up and down her back.

"No, I think I gained a bit. I did nothing but eat sweet rice pudding morning noon and night." She stepped away from him, to look at him. They kissed. She was still frowning, yet was *so* happy to see him. "Kai, you're nearly five hours late. My plane landed this afternoon."

"No!"

"Yes. I told you. Before I left, I wrote it down in your little book so you wouldn't forget."

"Lar, oh my God. I'm sorry. I thought you were flying in *tonight*."

"I wrote it down for you!"

"I know, but I accidentally left my notepad in Pooncarie. I was sure it was tonight. I thought I was early."

"You *thought* you remembered? Why didn't you call Billy?"

"I thought I remembered correctly," he repeated doggedly, the conciliatory smile fading.

"Did you throw my letters out? Because I wrote in my last letter what time I was arriving."

"Ah," he said, pointing like a teacher with his index finger. "When did you send it? Because I didn't get it. The mail takes four months to get to Pooncarie. It's like the Pony Express. You'd write me in August, and I'd get the letters in late September."

She stood, staring at him, saying nothing.

"So actually," he said cheerfully, "I did pretty good, all things considering. Hey, it could've been worse, I could've mixed up the days."

"I think that would've been difficult, seeing that I wrote the date of my arrival at the top of every letter I sent you. It would mean you didn't read a single one."

"And that wouldn't be true." He hugged her again in *re*conciliation. "I'm sorry," he said into her neck.

"Oh, Kai. I've missed you so much."

Nuzzling, he didn't answer her. She backed away to appraise him. He was wearing distressed rolled-up jeans, a wide belt, old work boots, a black T-shirt, a jean jacket. He didn't look like himself without the kinky hair falling to his shoulders, but he was still the most fly guy around.

"Kai . . ." Larissa wasn't angry anymore. She was tired, and so happy to see him. They stood holding hands in the middle of the airport. Tiptoeing up, she kissed him. "Forget it. Just a mistake. Don't worry . . ." She was ready to cry. "I can't believe we haven't spoken in three months. I wish you could understand how much—"

"I know. It's been such a long time." His hands squeezed her hands.

"I called you every day. Every single day. You never answered the phone." She couldn't believe she was lucky enough to have him for her own, to feel him. She had put on jeans, a raw silk ivory blouse. On the plane she applied some makeup for him, brushed out her hair extra sleek and shiny. She spritzed on his favorite perfume, Moon Sparkle, donned his favorite G-string, a lacy see-through gold La Perla. Everything was for him. All the scattered ruins of all the other hearts were at his feet.

"It's true, we were never home," he said. "We've been crazy busy. And of course Billy doesn't have an answering machine."

"Why would he? But why didn't *you* spend twenty dollars and get one?"

"It's not my house," Kai said evenly. "I don't tell Billy-O what to do. Besides, they don't sell electronics in Pooncarie. I'd have to go down south to Adelaide for that."

"Oh, Kai." She leaned against him and closed her eyes.

"Let's go. No use standing in the middle of the airport. You must be hungry. I'm starved."

"What are we going to do? It's nearly eight," he said.

"Yeah, it's too late to drive back," she said. "Let's get a room."

"It took most of my dough to get our cruiser out of hock. We need the money. I don't want to spend it on a room."

Smiling, she showed him the hundreds in her purse. "We got us a little bit of money."

"Nice! Where's you get that? Nuns hold a fundraiser in your honor?" He grinned.

"Actually, funny story there, about the money. Wait till you hear. But let's stay somewhere nice. I've been sleeping practically on a rack for three months, with itchy blankets, oppressive humidity, no AC." She caressed his face. "And I'm sure Billy's couch was not exactly a luxury suite."

"So true."

"So let's splurge. What do you say?"

Reluctantly he agreed.

"What's the matter? You're worried about the money? It's found money, Kai."

"I know. But . . . I too vividly remember not having any money at all. Kind of hard to spend hundreds on a hotel room."

"You've been working too hard. I can tell by your face. You're so tanned, though. Must've been outside a lot. Come on, don't worry. Our tour season is starting in two weeks. We'll be fine. Let's go have a nice dinner."

"I brought nothing to wear."

She lowered her voice. "We'll get room service."

"Ah."

"We'll have sushi for room service," she cooed, gazing up into his face, kissing his chin, stroking his hedgehog head. "How did you get here? On the bike?"

"How do you propose we put your suitcase on my bike? No, on our safari jungle boy." He kissed her and picked up the handle of her suitcase. "Ready?"

"Where's the bike?"

He paused. "It's in hock."

She stopped walking. "You pawned your Ducati?" she said incredulously.

"Billy-O wanted to buy two beautiful horses from the local wrangler." Kai said. "They were stunning. He promised to pay me back ASAP."

"I don't understand why Billy-O would need to borrow money from you," Larissa asked slowly. "Isn't he paying *you*? And didn't he get a business loan?"

"Yeah, for the stable, not to buy expensive horses, Larissa. We've never seen mares like these. They're pale white. Come on, let's go."

They walked out of the terminal and crossed the street to the parking lot.

"Billy said you've been in Jindabyne a few days," Larissa said. "Did you get a chance to look for a new place?"

"No," Kai said. "But we can have our old place back if we want. I paid Mejida."

"You did? Why?" she exclaimed. "She was such a witch."

"Be that as it may, it wasn't her fault that we owed a witch money. I don't like to leave debts unpaid. What if I do business with her again? Bart and Bianca depend on her, and she was harassing them, threatening to stop driving Bart's customers. Too much bad blood all around."

Larissa shrugged, speeding up when she spotted their tour vehicle, happy to see it. "I guess. But I could think of many uses for the thousand bucks we owed her."

"Thirteen hundred."

"Look how nice it looks! You washed it? Did you get it tuned? Because it needed it."

"I did it all, Larissa."

In the troopie, Kai drove them into Sydney, to the Intercontinental Hotel on Macquarrie Street. Larissa was about to run to reception to see if a king deluxe room was available with a Harbor Bridge view, on a high floor, but she was stopped by the valet manager who said there was no how, no way that the hotel could park a vehicle *that* size in their garage. It simply wouldn't fit, he said. It's was a tank. A wartime troop transporter. There's not enough headroom, no clearance for this vehicle. Sorry, can't do it. He and Larissa argued, while Kai stood nearby, saying nothing.

Larissa was so disappointed. "Kai, how come you're not more upset? We could have had us a soft downy bed and a hot shower." She pouted.

He was philosophical about it. "Nothing we can do," he said. "I don't like to rail against things when there's nothing I can do. I would like to, however, do something about my hunger."

They got take-out from the snazzy Café Opera at the

Intercontinental; Larissa ordered black bean squid and soft shell crabs, and tuna, and in a little white shopping bag, she carried it out to the cruiser, and they drove off, parking in a metered spot on a side street near the Opera House, and sat on the bench side by side looking out onto the Sydney Harbor, eating their sushi on their laps just like they once used to. Was it her imagination or was he reticent? But the harbor looked so pretty as they sat. A little bit like the Tappan Zee Bridge looked over the Hudson River when she and Che were kids and would sit like this on the banks of a park in Piermont and watch the white sailboats in the fading light.

"Everything's fine. I'm just hungry, Lar," Kai said. "When my mouth is full, it's kinda hard to speak."

"Do you want me to tell you about Parañaque?"

"You mean something you forgot to put in your letters?"

She chuckled. "Were they effusive?"

"You could say that."

"Yeah, unlike yours." She poked him. "What was that one letter you wrote me? It wasn't a letter, it was a telegram. Dear Lar. Stop. Things are good. Stop. Miss you. Stop. Have nice day. Stop."

Kai smiled into his squid, licking the black bean chili sauce off his fingers. "You don't know how hard Billy and I worked. I couldn't lift a fork to my mouth at night. Every time I'd try to write, I'd fall asleep."

"But every time I called, you were never there. Where were you sleeping?"

"First off, Billy doesn't have caller ID so we had no idea you called. And second, we're men, we don't cook. After work, we'd run back, shower quick and then head out for a bite to eat. We had some other guys working with us, so we all hung out and what not." He fell quiet while he finished his food. It was nearing ten, and the last light had left the sky. The harbor went from violet to twinkling navy. Larissa had a sense of the unreal, a material awareness of herself being central to the elusive meaning of her own life. Just to think—she, a girl from a little town near Nyack who'd never been out of the United States, would be sitting in the middle of her life with her extraordinary Hawaiian boy, looking out on the harbor in Sydney, *Australia*, a hemisphere, four oceans, six continents away from home.

"What a fascinating place, the Philippines," she said finally. "I wish you could've seen it."

"Really? All that vinegar and boiled water? No, thanks. I'll take my Pooncarie any day."

"So you liked it there? It wasn't horrible?"

"Liked it?" He shook his head. "Larissa, it's like nothing else in the universe. Honest. It's transcendental there."

"Hmm." Pensively, she stared at him. "But we're going back to Jindabyne, right? You didn't leave anything behind in Pooncarie, did you?"

"No," he said without emotion. Why did Larissa get the impression he was struggling not to sigh? Instead he pointed quizzically to the sushi she was dismantling by separating the tuna from the rice. "Whatcha doin'?"

"Not eating the rice is what. I should've ordered sashimi." She spread the wasabi on the last piece of her raw tuna. "I've had enough of rice, thank you very much, to last me the rest of my days. If I never have it again as long as I live, that'll be just fine with me." She watched him get up, collect his garbage. "So tell me more about Pooncarie. Did you make good money with Billy-O?"

"Yeah, he took care of me. It's not about the money, though. Listen, you want to head out? We'll drive out of the city, find a campsite."

"Okay," she said. "I'm kind of ready for that campsite right now." She pressed herself against him.

"Yum," he said. "We're in a public place."

"So?"

"Aren't you frisky."

"I've lived with nuns for three months," said Larissa. "Frisky? I'm positively feline. You're lucky I don't ravish you on the bench in front of the Opera House."

"Lucky? I dunno. It'd be one hell of a story to tell the kids."

And just like that, the conversation guillotined by cliché. Mutely she threw out her garbage and got into the troopie. Usually Kai prided himself on being scrupulously careful, avoiding verbal gaffes like invoking the word "kids" in jest. But perhaps after three months he was out of practice.

He drove them to Bondi Beach, where they parked up in the deserted secluded hills, and lay down on a blanket in the dune grasses under the stars. The rhythmic ocean crashings served as background love music. She gave him all the love she got.

Don't cry, he kept whispering, through his own rhythmic crashings, *don't cry*.

Kai, do you have any idea how much I've missed you . . . ?

I have some idea. Please don't cry.

There was something fragile in their lovemaking, tentative, as if the magic rite was faltering, as if they both had to be extra careful lest the parchment leaves in their ancient books would crack and fall like cigarette ash. Larissa couldn't quite put her finger on what was wrong. Was the rhythm off? Was there less panting? Was there one less *Oh my God* than there should've been after three months apart, after three months of silence?

Afterward she lay on her back, stretched out, arms flung out in a perpetual eternal cross, questioning, asking, receiving few answers tonight. He was tired, he said. He had worked and driven and had to haggle down the price of the cruiser buyout. He was exhausted. He needed to sleep. So that's what he did. He fell asleep and she lay under the sky. Bondi was dark and warm but dry; it wasn't sticky or muggy like Manila.

Something was flowing out without blessing, Larissa thought. I don't know what it is. There was a detail in him that was assembled incorrectly. There was no assurance, no gold underwriting in the man sleeping next to her. Imperceptibly he was simply saying the wrong things. But what? He was looking at her the wrong way. But how? She couldn't put her finger on it. She put her finger on his heart. *I'm flying flying flying*. The wooshing breaking ocean soothed the raw ends, filled in the hollow, ill-defined fear. Everything was going to be fine. They'd drive back to Jindabyne. Larissa looked forward to seeing the lake again. Summer was coming, the best time for them, the happiest time. They'd go to dinner with Bart and Bianca, go out drinking with Patrick. They'd find another place to live. She was done living on top of hills. She wanted to try the banks this time, in the aromatic eucalyptus-forested shores on the way to Thredbo. Not too far from town. And maybe this time they could look for an unfurnished place so she could nest and buy homey things for it: pillows, cotton throws, vases to put fresh flowers in. Everything would be all right. They had a fundamental union with each other. Things are never perfect, Father Emilio had told her. We are human and we are not perfect, he had said.

It's better than it was before I left, Larissa decided, when we didn't know what was going to happen from one minute to the next. The future's more certain now, *that* part is assured. We'll get back on track.

Still though . . . something was bothering her, was not letting her sleep.

Throwing on a T-shirt, she got up and in the dark climbed inside their vehicle, dug out a flashlight from the storage compartment, and unzipped Kai's travel duffel behind the driver's side. His jeans were in there, T-shirts, socks, a toothbrush, a few dollars, a little notepad where he wrote down things he didn't want to forget, like her arrival date except that page had been ripped out, and sandwiched in the notepad, an unsealed envelope addressed to his sister Muriel.

Larissa put the envelope back, and was about to zip up the bag and go back to him on the blanket, but a small tingle of curiosity prodded her, only because she herself had received but one letter from him and here was his sister Muriel with whom he had barely communicated in the last how many years, getting what felt like three folded pieces of handwritten paper right around the same time Kai told Larissa he was too tired to write.

She took it out.

Dear Muriel,

I wish I could make you understand the inexpressible longing I feel when I am here, on one of our horses, clomping through the uncharted desert over the rocks. I've lived in only a few places in my short life, and I know there will be many more, but honestly I can't imagine ever feeling as completely part of a larger universe than I do when I'm in the Aboriginal wilderness. And when I say wilderness, Muriel, I mean, visibility unlimited, horizon infinite, nothing but the earth and sky as far as the eye can see, and I'm sitting atop a saddled mustang, and my lungs can't take a deep enough breath to inhale all the things I feel, to speak all the things I want to say.

For some reason when I am here in the saltbush sands, I feel like I have found meaning behind human life. I used to think I had to invent meaning, manufacture it, even when it wasn't there, imbue things with significance that I myself made up. But here, I understood something—meaning is something that is revealed to me, if I so choose to open my heart and see it. Which is why before it was all about momentary satisfactions. Here it is about a permanent state of grace. My woes have vanished, my sufferings gone away. The cypress pines were here long before I came, the bluebush will be here long after I'm gone. And in the meantime, I have a happiness I haven't felt for a while and confidence that I can build a meaningful life. Maybe after I make things right and we're settled, you can come to visit us here, the land of the red sand and the pink cockatoo, and see for yourself the astonishing dry earth, the vastness of the wide open rangelands, and the profound seclusion. The world and all its cares are a million miles away. There is mystery in everything.

Your brother, Kai

How long did it take Larissa to fall sleep after reading that? She couldn't stop thinking about the letter he wrote to *her*, penned as if he had just weeks earlier learned how to write. Okay, she had thought; she'd never seen his writing voice before, and not everyone could be Nabokov, not everyone could dream up, *light of my light, fire of my loins*. She had accepted that Kai was a man of many gifts, but writing was not one of them. And yet . . . in the little missive he carried with him, he somehow managed—to his sister of all people!—to express the physical and the lyrical, to find poetry in a dried-out landscape, to feel things and to reflect on them with significance on paper, to spin together earth science and myth and legend and a numinous metaphysical confession. While in his letter to Larissa, he couldn't be bothered to make an adjective into a proper adverb. *The stables are coming along nice.*

What to make of this? And why did it hurt so much?

And more important—or was it less important?—what to make of the content of the letter, if she could will herself to forget the form of it?

What did Pooncarie have to do with their current life?

And how to mention this to the sleeping naked man?

Larissa was missing something, some essential component, a key piece of the puzzle and she didn't know what it was.

❧

They set out quietly the next morning. She wished they were a little louder, because it was something else to open your eyes and gaze upon the Southern Ocean sparkling crystal green in its morning glory, to want to walk the hills, to swim, to sit with the beautiful people and drink coffee . . . Larissa wished for a carefree morning in Bondi instead of the one offered to her today. After buying coffee and an egg sandwich, Kai looked over a map and got on the road. Five hours passed slowly and not slowly enough. Time flew and crawled. Larissa said once it was hot.

"Yeah, we're having a heat spell here the last week or so. But whatever temperature it is in Sydney or Jindabyne, it's twenty degrees hotter in Pooncarie."

"What does that have to do with us?" Larissa said. "We're not going to Pooncarie, are we?" Challenging him to speak up.

"Guess not," he said to the road. "Though I would've liked for you to see it."

"Would you."

And then nothing for another hundred miles.

"You would've liked the horses," he said. "You've been on a horse, right?"

"Yes, Kai, we went together on Maui. Up to the volcanos, remember? Horses scare me, though. They're unpredictable."

"Yeah, they're large powerful animals. But they're incredibly resilient. They do well in the desert."

"Like camels. But Jindabyne is not the desert, Kai," she said.

Another hundred miles.

"Was Nalini okay when you left? She wasn't upset?"

"Upset? Nah," said Larissa. "She was fine."

"Really? You wrote she brushed your hair, braided it. She tried to get you to pray. You two sounded cute together."

"She's a sweet kid," said Larissa. "But it's not me she wants." Her arms crunched around her stomach, to keep the falling from the pit of herself.

"Funny," Kai said. "From your letters, she sounded like she might've given you a harder time about leaving."

"No, she was quite nonchalant about it." Larissa couldn't tell even him the truth. Well, why not? Was he telling her the truth?

Another hundred miles.

They got to Jindabyne after lunch. Kai suggested crashing at Bart and Bianca's which Larissa thought was a dumb suggestion, but what she craftily said was, "We haven't seen each other for three months. Privacy might be good, don't you think?"

He agreed, but not before saying, "I haven't seen Bart and Bianca either."

"You're not having sex with Bart and Bianca," returned Larissa.

"Okay," Kai said. "But after twenty minutes, then what?"

When she stared him down, he said, rolling his eyes, "Just kidding. Sheesh."

They rented a room at the Crackenback Inn, the place they had stayed at when they first came to Jindabyne, by the alpine lake in the glaze of a valley, surrounded by the Australian Alps. For a few extra dollars they got a white chalet on the water, with a balcony and a fireplace. Larissa was trying to re-create the sense of awe they both had back then, to be here, to have each other, to be alone. But awe is a funny thing. Awe: reverential respect mixed with fear and wonder. Only one of those words could still be applied to Larissa's current state of being—one more accurately described as dread.

In the morning she said to Kai, let's take a ride, talk to Darien, our old buddy at Snowy River Real Estate. He'll find us something to rent. She got all dressed up and smiley, but after an hour Kai was still in bed. "You go," he said. "I'm not feeling well. I think I'm coming down with something. Been working too hard. You go, and then if you see something you like, come get me and I'll go take a look."

"Are you serious? You want me to go by *myself*?" He seemed serious, because he was still in bed, face in the pillow.

".I do." His voice was muffled. "Or let's wait till tomorrow. I'm sure I'll feel better then."

Had she not read his letter to Muriel, Larissa wouldn't have known what to make of him. But she had read it. And still she didn't know what to make of him. She had zero interest in bringing the letter up. She called Darien and went out without Kai, filled with that "dread" part of awe, hoping that if she found them a lovely place, it would make everything better.

She found four lovely places, one better than the next. Two had spectacular access to the lake, and the one on the Banjo Patterson Crescent was brand spanking new, with wood floors and a fireplace, a terrace and bay windows. It was unfurnished and the price was right. She couldn't believe it hadn't been rented.

"Just came on the market yesterday," Darien said. "It won't be around past the weekend, I guarantee it."

She dragged Kai to Banjo House that afternoon. Kai, still mopey and not feeling well, didn't like it. "It's too bright, too much sun, everything we have will fade."

"What will fade?" said Larissa. "We have nothing."

Slowly blinking into the distance, Kai shook his head. "It's too new. It feels like a hospital, all white and prim. Don't like it. Got anything else?"

"Not at the moment," said Darien, eyeing Kai with spectacular disdain.

Larissa asked Darien for a few minutes alone with Kai.

"No matter how many minutes alone we have," Kai said to her, "I'm not going to like it any better."

"Kai, look at this place! It's cleaner, larger, nicer than the Rainbow Drive bungalow, which you said was the best place you ever lived."

"Clearly I was mistaken."

"Is this an excuse?" she demanded to know. "Is there some other reason you don't like them?"

"Why are you always looking for an ulterior motive? I just don't like them. Why can't we leave it at that?" He looked pale and tired. His mouth was tight. The shorn head made him look gaunt, haunted.

"We have to find a place to live soon. We can't stay at the waterfront chalet forever."

He wasn't convinced. As in, why can't we? Or worse. I know we can't, his stiff and apathetic body language seemed to be saying, but I don't have another solution.

She told Darien they were going to think about it, but the next afternoon when she called, the realtor told her the place had already been rented. Larissa was intensely disappointed.

"It wasn't meant for us," Kai said, strumming his ukulele, sitting on the balcony. "If it was meant for us, we would have it."

"We don't have it because you said no to it!"

He kept looking out onto the water and the mountains. He said nothing. Strum, strum, something lonely in a minor key, with lows and lows and hollows in the notes.

She tried to humor him. Would you like to go for a bicycle ride in the mountains? Would you like to go swimming? The pool is heated. Would you like to go bowling?

"Larissa, which part of I'm not feeling up to it don't you understand?"

"The part where I don't understand what's on your mind," she said to him after another *two days* of sitting and staring at the lake had passed. What's the matter with you, she wanted to ask. Why are you acting like this?

He repeated that he was coming down with a bug, though he had no fever and no outward symptoms of debilitation. How Larissa wished she hadn't snooped on the letter to Muriel. She didn't want Kai to say he didn't want to stay here. After Parañaque, Jindabyne had suddenly acquired a mystical appeal. The lake was beautiful. The weather was beautiful. The snow-capped mountains surrounding Crackenback and Jindabyne were beautiful. The trees, the hills, the friendly people, *everything* was beautiful. Hoping for a crack in the bad mood, she kept asking Kai every night if he wanted to go to dinner with Bart and Bianca, and he kept saying no. Do you want to go for a drink with Patrick? No. You don't want to go to Balcony Bar and hang out?

No.

And worse than that: the refusals kept coming even when she asked him to go shopping with her for their business.

"Kai," she said, "we need two new tents; the old ones ripped. We need eight fishing lines. We need two more blankets, four flasks, a new cooler, disposable cameras, a cell phone."

"We have a cell phone." He waved it at her. "I reactivated our service in Pooncarie, knowing we'd be needing it." Because no one went upstream without having even a weak signal in case of dire emergency.

"You reactivated our service in Pooncarie?" Larissa asked quietly, her brows knitting together.

"What's the big deal?"

"And didn't write to let me know so I could call you?"

"I just had it done! I didn't do it two months ago but last week because I knew we'd be needing it in Jindabyne. Geez, Larissa. What is this?"

"Okay, scratch cell phone," she said after a few moments of digesting his words. "But our first-aid kit is down. It needs restocking. And the season starts in a week."

"I know." He sighed.

"Do you want me to go get these items myself?"

"No. Yes. I don't know."

"We have to do something," she beseeched him. "We already have the first tour set up." They got the reservations and the deposits through the Thredbo Valley Tourism and Visitors Association website. They had always used the site to advertise their guided bushwalk and got quite a lot of international business that way. "What do you want to do, cancel it? We'd have to return all the deposits."

"No, we shouldn't cancel it." He just sat strumming the strings, seven minor sevens in a row, like a broken blues scale.

She perched close to him on the balcony, leaning against the little tea table for support. "Is everything okay, Kai?"

"Of course. It's fine."

"Well, we need the tents. Otherwise four of our clients are going to be sleeping on the rocks by the Murray with salmon under their heads."

"You're right," he finally said, not looking at her, staring out onto the lake. "We'll go get the stuff we need. Do you want to shower first?"

Larissa went first. At least something was happening.

When she came out, still wet, Kai was frantically pacing around the living room. It wasn't the same Kai who had just twenty minutes earlier been sitting on the balcony like a slumping lump, like inert matter. "Plans have changed slightly," he said, twitching. "I just got a call from Billy-O."

"Oh." Larissa towel-dried her hair. "I didn't hear the phone ring."

"You were in the shower," he said. "It's a little trill. How could you have heard?"

"That's true." She didn't want a fight. "What did he want?"

"Actually, he needs a huge favor from me." Kai continued his caged walk across the hotel room. "He's out on a brumbie run—you know he's a rover, he goes out into the bush to look for the feral horses, brings them back, sells them, or keeps them, but he's starting his new trail ride business in a week and he just realized he hasn't planned his course, and he has to submit the guided tour route to the Broken Hill Tourism Board and Review so they can approve it and post it on their website, but he's away and can't do it. He begged me to come and mark the trails for him. Otherwise the deadline will pass and he won't be able to do the trail rides until next year, and he's counting on the income as a major part of his new business model." Kai was panting in his agitation.

"I thought it was the *only* part of his new business model," said Larissa.

"I told him about what we did here," Kai went on without breaking stride, "and he's really keen to try it but with horses."

"I know about his interest in the trail tour." Larissa stopped towel-drying her hair. "When does he want you to do this?"

"Right now."

"As in . . ."

"Look, here's what we'll do. *I'll* go, mark the trail tomorrow, and come straight back on Thursday. You and I will go shopping on Friday, in plenty of time before the start of the season." He smiled at her, a beaming smile, the first one of the week. "Sounds like a plan?"

"A lame one," she said. "But I don't understand your agitation. Explain why you've been dragging your feet the last few days? You didn't know Billy-O was going to call you for an emergency equine favor, did you?"

"I haven't been dragging my feet. Honest." But Kai didn't say anything else.

"Plus, Kai," she added, "what do you mean, *you* go? What, *alone* into the desert to mark a trail ride for Billy-O? You know the first rule of ranging—you *never* go out alone. I don't know what you're talking about." She patted herself dry, threw off the towel and stood naked in front of him. "I'll go with you, of course. We'll mark the ride together. You can show me your great amazing Pooncarie." She smiled.

He stared at her like she had gone mad. Perhaps the world had gone mad.

"You want to come *with* me?" He sounded high-pitched. He was sweating. "But *why*? I'll only be gone a day."

"Why would I stay here by myself?" said Larissa. "At Crackenback no less, with no car, even farther from anywhere than Rainbow Drive had been."

"Why would you want to leave?" asked Kai. "Look how beautiful it is here. The stilts of our chalet are in the lake. It's incredible. And I'll only be gone a couple of days."

"I don't know what you're saying." Her face was one big confused frown. "You need someone with you. You know you can't go out alone. You *know* this. And I don't want to stay here alone. It's a win-win for both of us." Questioningly she smiled at him. "What's the problem?"

"There's no problem."

"Okay, then. Don't you *want* to show me Pooncarie?"

"I do . . . but Billy-O has no room for two extra people."

"Perfect," said Larissa. "Because he's not going to be there."

"It's really a pigsty," Kai said. "It's going to make you feel bad."

"You know what's making me feel bad?" Larissa said. "You acting like you don't want me to come. There's not a single reason why I shouldn't come. For your safety I'm actually necessary. Tell me what this is really about." Was Larissa wrong? Was this *not* about the graceful sentiments expressed to Muriel?

"Why wouldn't I want you to come?" Kai asked, wiping his forehead. "Of course I do. You're being silly. I just thought it'd be quicker if I went by myself. It's a long trip, thirteen hours."

"That's okay. I don't mind a drive. Now, would you like to order in or drive to the Thredbo winery for lunch?"

"Lunch?" Kai shook his head. A look of heavy-jawed resignation fell over his face. "No, if we're going to go, we might as well go now." He bent to grab his ukulele off the table. "If we hurry, we can get there just after nightfall. Because to go out on the horses, we'll need to leave tomorrow morning at six or seven the latest. By the afternoon it gets too hot in Mungo."

"So let's hurry," said Larissa. "We don't want it to get too hot."

∽⌣∾

In the Land Cruiser, with their stuff piled inside, Kai remained animated, nervously energized. Pooncarie had obviously got inside him, Larissa realized, and he didn't know how to tell her. So he told her piecemeal about the things that he kept hidden.

Was there fly fishing? Was there canoeing? Larissa asked, wanting to engage him, to keep him talking about happy things.

"Not in the summer months," Kai told her, "because the rivers and streams are dry. But wait till you see the colors of the sediment, the deep red core of the dunes. Oh yes, Larissa, there are dunes in the desert." He shook his head in wonder. "They're called the Great Wall of China. Once there'd been a lake there, and though it evaporated, the dune residuals remain on the lake beds. The Aborigines used to fish there, ten, twenty thousand years ago, but it's saltbush now, eroded by wind and water, all layers of desert of sand and clay." He breathed unevenly, remembering. "If we're lucky, maybe we'll see a giant wombat."

"See, I keep thinking if we're not lucky, we'll see one."

He laughed and went on about the addictive nature of the 360° horizon as they left the Jindabyne Alpines and the snow peaks, the extensive pine forest flora of the wild outdoors by the mountain valleys. Larissa had to admit she couldn't imagine the place Kai was describing. Everything around Jindabyne was hilly and densely packed around the flowing rivers. Mungo sounded like an arid dustbowl to her, but what did she know? She hoped she was wrong. By his attraction to the area, she clearly was.

The drive on the two-lane narrow Snowy Mountain Highway was a slog. The foliage got sparse and burnt, the land leveled out, and then grew green again and sloping, but the mountains had gone;

it looked like the American prairie. Until it didn't anymore, and was replaced by languid hills and patchy pine and eucalypt forest. They got stuck behind a car traveling leisurely and remained stuck for a hundred miles on the open road. Their cruiser was a sturdy vehicle and could withstand all kinds of terrain, but it couldn't overtake another car: it had no pick-up.

After a hundred and forty miles, they turned onto Sturt Highway. Around Gum Creek Larissa said, "Kai, there's nothing here." And there wasn't. No trees, no birds, no rivers. Nothing. Just a narrow road, and pebbly sand as far as the eye could see. Oddly it was overcast.

"Imagine what this would look like when the sun is out," Kai said.

"I don't need to imagine. Much like this. Nothing. With the sun beating down on it." It was eerie, ghostly, and otherworldly. It was peculiar and strange. There was no talking herself out of it: the barren bushland gave Larissa a stone-cold feeling, piled high on top of the other boulders that pressed down into the pit of her empty gut. It's not going to be like this in Pooncarie, is it? she wanted to ask Kai, but didn't. She couldn't imagine it would be. After all, ten miles can separate flatlands from forested alpine mountains and wine valleys from eucalypt jungles. Anything could change in ten miles.

But Sturt Highway proved to be an entirely different kind of travel. The only thing that changed on it after ten miles—and then two hundred miles—was that the barrenness that came before was nothing, *nothing*, compared to the utter desolation that came after. The land became flatter, emptier, the sense of being absolutely nowhere grew staggering and suffocating. And the road just went on and on and on, through the uninhabited vastness.

"How long are we on this road for?" Larissa asked in a constricted voice. As if that were the important thing. It wasn't the road. It was where the road was taking them.

"Five hundred more miles."

Five hundred miles! "How does anyone live here?"

"No one lives here, as you see."

"But what if you break down?"

"Best not to."

"No kidding. Does your cell phone have a signal?"

He looked. "No."

Of course not. Why would it?

"The land is a blank slate," Kai said. "You need to imagine the things you want it to have, the things that were on it a thousand years ago."

"You mean before the sun burned them away?"

"Yeah. Imagine the water flowing into Lake Eyre, miles from here, the largest inland lake and the lowest point in Australia. Once all the rivers flowing from it were full, meandering through the abundant life."

"Is Lake Eyre full now?"

"The lake has only filled up a few times in the last two hundred years," Kai replied, whistling "Zip-a-Dee-Doo-Dah." *Zip-a-Dee*-Ay.

"All right, Kai," Larissa said, closing her eyes to stop seeing the bleakness. "I'll imagine the boat cruise on the wetlands, the flightless birds, the giant marsupials." Bushriding through the scrub. How much longer? Maude . . . Yanga . . .

Yanga was slightly more vegetated, and she grew optimistic, but ten miles later by Benanee, it was back to the nothingness. Larissa glanced at Kai, to see if he could see what she could see. But he was tapping on the steering wheel, humming "Give a Little Whistle," eyes single-mindedly focused on the road. He didn't see.

In Monak, the earth acquired a red hue; "That's the red sand," Kai exclaimed. "Ain't it something?"

"Sure. Is there anywhere to stop?"

When they alighted for gas and an early dinner, he continued to regale her about the sunsets. The more cruel the heat, the more spectacular the sunsets, he said. Always something given, something lost. Larissa was so hot, too, on top of everything. There was no respite. Was something being lost now? In that case, what was being given? Oh, she thought, please let it not be wisdom—by the awful grace of God.

"You don't think it will be cooler in Pooncarie?" She wiped her soaked face. She didn't eat; she had no appetite.

"Twenty degrees hotter, I told you. It's in the basin."

Ah, basin. As opposed to this, an elevated butte perhaps, or a vista-like winding passage through the Alleghenys. She already missed the Alpine afternoon breeze of Jindabyne. She missed summer leaves that weren't brown. She missed noise and good music from young men and singing from the country girls, fueled by fermenting hops and darkness. She missed the things that were rampantly missing here. She was afraid of Pooncarie and couldn't say why. She hadn't been afraid of Parañaque.

Was this common to all human beings? No matter what you had, you always wished for what you didn't have? Every landscape, every season, the leaves, the views, the white mouldings, the cold windows. The ice, the snow, the ocean. Saltbush, desert, bluebush, devegetated dunes. She felt a little bit like the last.

Larissa suspected it didn't *always* turn to nothing, though it was difficult to believe that now, driving through the nothingness. Vaguely she recalled Father Emilio and the dusky subdued room where Larissa sat with him every afternoon, listening in comfort to his voice telling her that she was a witness to her own life, that God would bless her emptied-out soul if it needed Him, that He would not send the women to the tomb but that He Himself would come to the poor devegetated creature sitting in front of Him in sorrow, if only she would seek the comfort. Every minute of Father Emilio's day was given over to make heavy hearts a little lighter. She saw that on the faces of the orphans whose heads he patted as he strolled by. Well, that's why he is a priest, and I'm not, Larissa thought. He is a saint. And she'd said to him then that she didn't need comfort, not really. What she needed was answers. Specifically the answer to: *How is it best for me to live?*

And now she had neither answers nor comfort.

How much longer to drive? she asked Kai. It was going to get dark soon.

But Kai was telling her things and didn't reply. "I told Billy-O he should offer different types of tours," Kai was saying. "Half a day, a whole day, even a week-long tour all the way to Cairns or Uluru. Wouldn't that be something?"

"To Uluru on a horse?"

"No. In a cruiser. Like this one."

"Yeah, but," Larissa said pointedly, "where's Billy-O going to get a cruiser like this one?"

Kai didn't take the bait. "I told him he could ride out from Lake Munga all the way to Lake Eyre in a ten-man jungle vehicle. Sure, it's better if there's water there. Fly-fishing, kayaking. But still. Even without the water, tourists love an adventure. He could do what we do, make it a camping trip, with tents. A nice campfire, a potluck dinner. We'd sing songs, tell ghost stories of Australian outback horror. Ritual burials, wombats eating dingoes, that sort of thing." He laughed happily.

"We, Kai?"

"What?"

"You were talking about Billy-O, but you said *we*."

"I meant him. I misspoke." But after that he stopped smiling and stopped speaking.

Larissa grew irritated in the heat. "You're telling me Munga Lake is a salt flat, all fly-fishing joy evaporated by the red blaze, no rain, no rainbow trout, and you think the hapless tourists are going to fall for that? Sounds like a whole bunch of disappointment." She smirked mirthlessly. "They should call it Lake Disappointment."

"Nah. There's already a Lake Disappointment way out west."

"I might like to see that," she said.

"If you wish, Larissa," Kai said. "Though do we really need to travel that far?" He was biting in his dry reticence, like arid beds, like the river that was a dirt road for seven months of summer. And now *she* didn't take the bait, falling quiet instead.

In Trentham Cliffs, the woods grew in patches in the sand, but by this time, Larissa felt so disconnected from civilization and all life that the trees did not impress her. She knew they were just cover to hide the emptiness. Under the trees was still desert. The road was called the Silver City Highway, which sounded romantic, almost inspirational! Silver, image of something sparkly, shiny, accessible, yet enigmatic. And city, of course, could be the shining city on a hill. Yet . . . after Wentworth, the Silver City Highway became unnamed. It wasn't even the plodding Sturt Highway. Where they were going, the roads were unnamed. Good luck finding your way out. Was it any wonder that doom seeped inside her pores and settled in her aching bones?

Larissa withdrew from the conversation, detached herself from reality, which was not difficult, for reality had no landscape, *imagined herself in the kitchen in San Agustin, making pandesal bread, evaporated milk, egg, sugar, salt, butter, yeast, breadcrumbs, and then sitting by the tall windows waiting for the bread to rise, watching the deluvial monsoon fill up the green yard, the monastery an ark in the floodwaters.*

Imagined herself after the afternoon rains at Blizzard Beach water park in central Florida, having the park all to themselves and running up the stairs over and over to go on the family tube ride, racing wet in their bathing suits a hundred and fifty steps, to slide down in a huge round tube that bounced off the walls as it careened downward, all five of them, Larissa, Jared, Emily, Asher and Michelangelo, screeching and squealing, and finally the fifth time around, Michelangelo, who was about three, saying to her, "Go ahead, Mommy, hurry, go without me, save yourself. Because I have no feet left." And Larissa picking him up and carrying him up a hundred and fifty steps.

It was dark when Kai said quietly, out of the blue, "We're going nowhere."

Larissa opened her eyes. Closed them. "But we're going there together."

7

Pooncarie

They ran out of gas a mile away from Tarcoola Street at midnight. Kai thought they would have enough. Of course, his cell phone had no signal. And who would he call anyway? Billy-O was in the bush.

"Well, how did *he* call you earlier then?" Larissa said, sitting in the cruiser, belatedly realizing a logical fallacy inherent in modern technology.

"Who?"

"Billy-O."

"What do you mean? He called on his cell."

"Yes, I know. But he's out in the red desert, where there isn't a single signal tower. We know. We haven't had signal for seven hundred miles. How in the world did he get a signal to call you?"

"I don't know Larissa. Do I run Telstra?" He locked the cruiser. "Come on. Take your purse. We'll come back for everything else in the morning."

"I thought we were going into the National Park in the morning?"

"We are. Clearly I'll have to do it before we go."

"Gas stations open that early around here?" she asked. "Much demand for gas at six in the morning, you think?"

He stared at her coldly from the road. "Are you coming?"

They walked one mile in silence. In the night the mile seemed like twenty. How long was it between her Bellevue house and the Summit train station? Was that also only one mile? She shuddered.

Billy-O's house, right off the main drag on Tarcoola Street, was locked from the front. "Don't worry," said Kai. "He usually leaves the back door open." But that was locked also.

"Now what?" said Larissa. "We have to be up in five hours. Can you call him? Maybe we'll get lucky and he has signal again in the bush."

"He's probably sleeping."

"We're doing *him* a favor," said Larissa sharply. "Can you please call him?" She couldn't tell what Pooncarie looked like because at the moment it was darker than ink. Kai called Billy-O with no luck.

Two blocks away on Tarcoola Street there was a gas station, which was also a hotel *and* a beer garden. The gas station part was closed for the night, and the hotel was full. Full! As in "no vacancy." Why did Larissa find that not credible? But the beer garden was open till two, and Poon Pub was hopping, crowded like a Greenwich Village dance club on a Saturday night.

Kai didn't want to go in, claiming sudden exhaustion, but she was thirsty and asked for a cold beer. They walked inside.

And because nothing was ever so bad that it couldn't get *instantly* worse, the first person Larissa spotted sitting at one of the tables talking to a group of other poorly dressed young girls, was Cleo Carew, the blonde-haired chick from Balcony Bar.

The opening chasm in the stomach came first, followed by recognition.

Sinking down at a small sticky table, Larissa stared at the back of Kai's head at the bar for the few minutes it took him to fist-pound the bartender and to buy two beers. Slack-jawed, she watched Cleo's face a few tables away, talking to her friends, yet raising her eyes as he turned around with the beer in his hands and acknowledging him with a nod and a smile. Kai acknowledged her with barely a blink.

Larissa didn't know what to think. They had just driven over twelve hours across thirteen hundred bone-crunching kilometers to a hole-in-the-earth town with a hundred and fifty residents in the middle of a salty playa, a silver mining town, where they went ostensibly to do an emergency solid for Billy-O, and here at a nameless bar—in Pooncarie!—was the girl that would not be named, nodding to Kai, as if to say, glad to see *you* finally arrived. Not, what are *you* doing here? Not, what a surprise. Not, I vaguely remember you from somewhere. But, *finally*. You're here. The girl hadn't in any way acknowledged or greeted Larissa.

But what Kai didn't do was what people normally do when they see a vaguely familiar face. *Oh, hi, it's you . . . how you doing, what's happening?* What they don't do is pretend they barely know the person whose empty glass they refilled in another bar in another town.

Returning to her side, Kai passed Larissa a cold beer, which she suddenly didn't want, and he asked her about food, which she didn't want either, though not five minutes earlier she had complained bitterly of hunger, but now there were so many other things to complain bitterly about. The girl, surrounded by natives, looked ludicrously young, barely out of high school, though looked stupid enough perhaps never to have gone to high school. She had a vapid drop-out look about her, and too loud a laugh in a public place, a self-conscious, stare-at-me laugh. Her clothes were slightly baggier than at Balcony Bar, the relaxed-fit jeans, the empire waist top falling loose from the over-exposed ludicrous breasts.

Turning her frozen gaze away from Cleo, Larissa leveled the stare into Kai's expressionless face. He drank, sat calmly, smiled at her politely.

Larissa downed her beer in five gulps. "Let's go."

"Go where?"

"Kai, what do you propose? That we sit in the bar all night until we have to go out in the morning? Let's go climb through the window or something. Or try Billy-O again. Maybe he'll pick up."

Kai was inscrutable. "I'll try him again. I'll go outside so I can hear. But I'm starved," he added. "I'm gonna get myself a sandwich. Sure you don't want anything?"

"No, Kai. But thank you." Always so polite. Larissa couldn't sit anymore so she stood up and leaned against the wall, waiting for him, watching his back, the shape of his head, the crew cut of the kinky hair that had been too hot to keep long, and now he looked like a soldier with his tall reedy build, his buzzed dome. He looked like a different man. Certainly he behaved like one.

Cleo got up! She got up and toddled over to the bar, twenty feet long, ten of it unoccupied, but of course she had to stand right next to Kai, motioning to the bartender. Their heads didn't bob or lean into each other as Larissa watched them from behind. It was noisy in the pub, sweaty and loud, and there was no tilting from them, no shoulder swaying, no recognition from their bodies. Kai was draped over the counter, beer in his hands, waiting for his sandwich, and she was standing sprightly, ordering another drink. If Larissa hadn't been struck by her presence in the town where there were barely any people, she would've sworn under oath the girl and Kai were strangers, who happened to be standing at the bar at the same time ordering food and drinks from the same waiter.

And yet.

Unmistakably, the silent language of their bodies looked familiar, not foreign. They didn't stand together like strangers. They stood together as though they were speaking without moving their heads.

Kai got his sandwich, paid, and returned to Larissa, food in hand. Their table had been taken so they stood by the wall. He offered her a bite, which she refused with arms crossed, and after he was finished, they left. In utter silence, they walked back to Billy's place, where the doors were still locked and the lights were out.

They sat on the porch steps, waiting in darkness. But for what?

Kai called Billy again. This time the phone was picked up! The two men spoke briefly in man code. What up, dude. I'm sitting in front of your house, and I can't get inside. He hung up the phone. "He'll be here in a sec."

"All the way from the outback, he'll be here in a sec?"

"He came back with three horses. But he's going back out again tomorrow morning."

"So tell me," Larissa said suddenly, "is that why you came here? For her?"

"What are you talking about?"

"Are you playing dumb with me or games with me? I can't figure out which."

"I don't know what you're talking about."

"Kai!"

"Larissa!"

The raised voices on someone else's porch, in someone else's yard. Larissa sat on the busted-up concrete steps, elbows on her knees. She didn't look at Kai, she looked at herself, seeing the flash of dust that she was, the speck of person, a thousand miles from the nearest ocean in the Southern hemisphere under the bright and clear sky on a desert island, a thousand miles away from other continents, other countries, ten thousand miles away from the highway that led to a street named Bellevue, *a beautiful view*, a road shaped like a horseshoe for luck, staring inside her brittle emptiness.

"Why can't you be honest with me?" she asked quietly, not shouting, her voice not her own. "Why do you act like I'm an idiot and I'll believe anything you say? I know I want to. I don't want to think you're lying to me, deceiving me. But we drive this far, and you tell me that you don't know what I'm talking about when we run into the one person we're not supposed to ever see again?"

"Why is she the one person we're not supposed to see again?"

"Kai, how dumb do you think I am?"

"I don't know the answer to that question," he returned. "But how dumb do you think *I* am? You think I'd bring *you* here if I was coming for her?"

"I don't know. Would you?"

"What do you think?"

"Why do you keep answering every question with a question?"

"Why do you keep asking so many fucking questions?"

"Why is she here?"

"I don't know! Am I her keeper?"

"I don't know. Are you?"

"Oh, fuck!"

And then suddenly out of a neighboring house, a window flying open and a man's grating voice: "Keep it down! It's two fucking o'clock in the morning! Bloody fucking hell! People work during the day!"

They kept it down. Real down, like mute.

"She lives here, okay? She lives in this town," Kai said quietly, looking at the ground. "You knew she lived here. What does that have to do with me?"

"Yeah, okay. Was tonight the first time you saw her since Jindabyne?"

"No. There's only one bar in town. Clearly I've seen her, I come with Billy, she comes with her friends."

"Then why didn't you say hello to her? Why didn't you smile and say, Hi, Cleo."

"I. Don't. Know. What. You're. Talking. About." Kai rubbed his face. "Why would I say anything to her? I didn't say anything to the thirty other people in the bar either."

"Yeah, okay, Kai." Was that a lie? Was that the truth? Was it a lie that sounded like the truth? Was it the truth that sounded like a lie?

Not five minutes later, Billy-O's busted pick-up truck pulled up. "Oh God," he said, jumping out—or falling out?—springing over the short rusty fence, jingling his keys. "You been waiting long? Sorry." He shook Kai's hand, nodded to Larissa. He was obviously intoxicated.

"Why'd you lock all the fucking doors, man?" Kai said. "You always leave the back open for me."

"I didn't know you were—I forgot. Sorry, dude."

They stepped inside the tiny bungalow with torn musty furniture. Larissa didn't know why Billy would be locking anything. There was nothing to steal. Kai had been right: there was no place for Larissa here. There was barely room for Billy-O, with all the clothes on the floor and over chairs, the open containers of old food, the bags of chips, the cans of beer. "Sorry for the slight *dis*-array," Billy-O said. "I'm saving up to buy a new couch." As if those two sentences were in any way related. "Don't worry, Larissa"—he burped—"I got a bed for you two. I'll be fine right here." He plopped down on the couch and started to roll a joint. "So what are you two up to? She gonna come with you? You gonna go out into the Mungo, Larissa? Ever been in the bush, darling?" He clucked his tongue as he lit up. "It gets hellishly hot out there. I know. I nearly died today. Don't forget to bring a hat. You have a hat, don't you? Kai, I still don't know how you think an unsuspecting tourist is going to spend six hours out there in the saddle. I think the business is going to go belly up in two days." Billy tutted. "Well, Larissa can be our guinea pig. If she can do it, I say fine. Otherwise, I think you should limit the trail rides to an hour or two. The city folks ain't gonna last. They're not you and me, bro."

"It'll be fine," said Kai, shaking his head at the proffered joint. Since there was no place for Larissa to sit, she didn't, meandering awkwardly through the mess trying to find a place to perch. As she walked by the phone, a red number was blinking. She looked closer. The number said 7. As in *7 messages*. She picked up the cordless receiver and studied the buttons. CID, one of them said. She pressed it. Sure enough, the caller ID numbers popped up, one by one. Carefully replacing the phone on the cradle, she straightened up to hear Kai and a slurring Billy-O arguing whether it was possible to get all the way from the stables to the holy grail of the National Park, the Great Wall of China lunette dunes, on horses. Billy-O was skeptical. He was also drunk, so he couldn't win.

"You think the pampered crowds will remain on the horse in the godless heat? I don't know what you're thinking, dude," Billy-O said. "I'm telling you, we should just do the safari ride and forget about the horses. The birds are still here," Billy mused as he smoked the whole joint alone. "The cockatoos, the finches, also the kangaroos and jackrabbits. The ladies can take pictures, snap, snap. Them Americans *love* the kangaroos. The culling season hasn't started yet, so not too much blood in the sand." He chuckled.

"The horses is what's going to draw the Internet tourist in, Bill," Kai said. "Trust me. Because you've got too much competition in the vehicle tour area. Here, you're offering something new."

Larissa stepped away into the alcove kitchen. Kai kept telling her it was Billy-O's idea to do the trail rides. Sure didn't sound like it from *that* little snippet of dialogue. Looking for water, she opened the fridge. There was something awful and spoiled in it. It smelled like a dead snake. All she wanted was a cold drink. Billy-O called to her to drink from the warm tap. "Tomorrow we'll get you some bottled H_2O for the ride. Make sure you two bring enough of it," he said.

Larissa walked back to the living room, and studied the two men sitting side by side, Billy-O, small, unassuming, tired, drunk and slightly drugged, saying, "Why are you in such a hurry to go tomorrow? I'm committed to Kelvin for the mustering run. I already got paid for it, so I can't say no. If you wait a day, we'll go together the day after tomorrow." And sober Kai, laser-eyed on Billy-O, replying, "You have to submit the proposed courses to the tourism board tomorrow so they can post them online, remember?" And Larissa, perspiring, thirsty, exhausted inside and out, the prickles, the needles of jaundiced malign piercing her through a million pores in her skin, listening to Kai now and hearing him loud and clear *then*, his steady excited voice in her memory. It wasn't even the past, it was the just-lived-through present! This morning he told her that Billy-O had called him from the bush and asked him for this favor. Yet Billy-O sat in his own house smoking and talking about the trails as if he'd forgotten the hastily arranged details—like asking for the favor in the first place.

Billy slapped Kai on the shoulder, glassy eyed, fuzzy-balled, unsteady even while sitting. Larissa continued to stand in the alcove between the kitchen and the living room.

"Bill, what time does the gas station open?" Kai asked.

"Eight."

"Eight? You sure?"

"This is something I know very well. I run out of juice a *lot*."

"Anywhere to get some gas now?"

"It's two in the morning," Billy said. "Who the hell is going to be up at this hour?"

"All right." Kai stood up. "Come on. Give me a ride to the troopie. I need to get our shit out of there."

"I'm in no condition to drive, dude," said Billy-O falling back on the couch. "I'm in no condition to go anywhere . . ." His eyes were already rolling back.

"A great brumble culling you're gonna have tomorrow." Kai sighed. "Just give me the keys." He turned to Larissa. "I'll be back in a half-hour, okay?"

She waited for him until four in the morning. Billy was passed out in a sitting position on the couch. The place was revolting. She couldn't go and lie down in someone else's bed. She perched in the corner of the sofa away from his stoned frame, and mindlessly stared into the dark.

"Billy," she kept whispering, "Tell me what's going on. Tell me, what's happening. Billy, can you hear me . . . ?"

At one point she thought she heard Billy-O whisper back, *Go, Larissa, leave tonight, don't stay . . .* But when she sat up to look at him, his eyes were closed.

She woke up to Kai shaking her shoulder. "Get up. We have to go."

As Larissa suspected, Billy-O did not want to go. Bleary-eyed herself, she stretched out her sore body and stared up at Kai, still in yesterday's clothes. "What time is it?"

"Time to go. Seven in the morning."

"You said you'd be back in a half-hour." She struggled up. Billy was slumped on the other end of the couch.

"I was back. You were asleep. I tried to wake you, but you wouldn't wake for nothing." Kai made a disgusted face. "Plus Bill hadn't changed his sheets, and I didn't know where the clean ones were. I didn't want you to sleep on that."

"So you left me sitting up on the couch?"

"Better that than those sheets."

But for some reason he didn't look like he'd slept on those sheets either. She wanted to ask him if he got their things, if she should shower, if they would eat somewhere, get coffee. But she didn't have the energy to ask. She didn't have the energy to ask him anything.

8

Demon Ride

They didn't leave the stables until nine in the morning. Billy-O was convinced it was going to get too hot for them, that it was too late, that they should stay an extra day and go out tomorrow. Kai said no. The route plan had to be in by the deadline, otherwise he wouldn't be able to submit it for approval until the next tourist season. Larissa agreed. To stay one more day in Pooncarie was unthinkable.

What surprised her was Billy's stable. To think that a man kept his own accommodation like a trash dump, yet the housing for his horses like the Ritz-Carlton, was paradoxical. Yet his stables were spotless, and his horses were clean. There was hay in bins, and fresh water sparkling in metal buckets. It all looked painted and repaired and very well tended. Billy loved his horses and it showed.

"So where are these famous white mares?" asked Larissa, walking through the stalls.

Billy-O showed her. "What do you think?" he asked. "You think two horses are worth a whole Ducati?"

Larissa didn't know the answer to that question, though the large pale animals were very beautiful. But then so was the flame-orange bike. Kai hurried them from the stalls.

"When you return, just leave the horses in the paddock, they'll be fine," Billy-O said to Kai. "Don't forget to feed them tonight when you come back. One bucket each, chaff and grain. You can give them carrots. And don't forget to refill the water. It evaporates in the heat."

"Don't worry, man. I know what to do. I've been doing it for three months. I'll take care of it."

Leaning to Larissa, Billy said in a quiet voice, "Oh, he loves to go out on the horses, but taking care of the horses, not so much." He saddled and bridled two tamed Walers, one gray and light for Larissa, a brick-brown medium for Kai.

"No white horses for us?" she said with a smile.

"No," Billy-O said. "Kai says they're for tourists only—"

"We gotta go, Billy. Hurry up," Kai cut in.

"These are better," Billy told her. "They're both mixed breeds. Since they bred in the wild, I have no idea of the pedigree. I call yours light, Larissa, because it's quick on its feet, not too heavy, but you see, it's still a big animal." Affectionately he patted Larissa's horse's nose as he adjusted the bit and the bridle. "They're both excellent trail horses. Yours is especially docile. She is a seven-year-old mare. I can put six-year-olds on her. Right, Shiloh? Right, baby?" He kissed the horse, and then helped Larissa into the saddle. "You okay? Now, think about what you want to bring with you, what you want to leave behind. Because that jacket you're wearing, you'll get too hot in it after thirty minutes."

"I get hot, I'll take it off."

Billy shook his head. "Whatever you wear out there is what you keep on, because you can't take your hands off the reins—not for a second. You let go of the reins, you lose control of your horse."

Larissa thought that was sound advice. She took off her jean jacket, and was left in a sheer white blouse.

"How's Kai going to write things down about the trail if he can't let go of the reins?"

"Don't worry about me, Larissa," Kai said. "I hold the reins with one hand, I write with the other. But let's wrap this up. We gotta get moving." He sounded impatient from atop his chestnut Waler named Hal.

"She can't go yet, man, she doesn't know how to handle her

horse. Sheesh." Billy-O looked up at Larissa. "You hold the reins in your left hand, you hold on to the horn with your right."

"Why can't I hold the reins in each hand?"

"You can try. But what are you going to use to steady yourself? Now listen. When you want to go left you pull the reins left and kick her with your right foot, when you want to go right, you pull right and kick left. When you want to stop, you pull up on the reins and yell 'Whoa.' When you're in trouble, you yell 'Yihah.' Got it?"

"Got it. Doesn't sound too bad."

"It's not too bad. You're sitting on a nine-hundred-pound animal, though. Respect that."

She smiled at him. "Thanks, Billy-O."

"No prob. Kai, man, don't forget to put the maps back when you return."

"Will do. Ready?"

"You got everything? Hold on to the saddle, Larissa."

"We got everything."

Billy was still patting the skirt on Larissa's horse. "Water?"

"Yes."

"For you and the horse?"

"Yes."

"Pen and notepad to mark the trail?"

"Yes," Kai called out.

"First-aid kit?"

"No."

"Oh, dude." Billy-O shook his head in reproach. "That's just wrong."

"Ours is not filled up."

"Well, you're not supposed to take yours. You're supposed to take the one that comes with the horse." Disappearing into the stable for a moment, Billy came back with a leather medical pouch. "Trust me when I tell you, it's your insurance. The one time in my life I went out without it, my horse spooked, I fell off and got caught in the stirrup. The horse dragged my sorry ass upside down half a mile across the central Australian plain." Taking off his hat, he showed Larissa a six-inch horseshoe scar on top of his head.

Larissa paled. "For heaven's sake. How did the medical kit help you with *that*?"

"It didn't." Billy-O laughed. "But the fall only happened because I didn't have the kit. Every other mishap I've had since has been mild by comparison. Because now I always bring it."

"All right, Mr. Superstitious," said Kai, tying the small kit to the rigging ring in front of him. "Does it actually have anything in it, or is it just a talisman placebo?"

"It's got some shit. A Band-Aid. Some aspirin, Super-glue for the big stuff, like my head, and an anti-venom syringe for the really nasty motherfuckers out there." He grinned. "Pardon my French."

"Right. Now, can we go?"

"Kai, do you have your phone?" Larissa asked.

"I do, but it's out of power," he replied. "I forgot to put it on the charger yesterday."

"Don't worry, Larissa," Billy said cheerfully, "there's no signal where you're going even with a full charge." He patted the neck of Larissa's pale horse. "All right, you. Be good for the missus. Kai remember, however long you spend heading out, it'll take you that plus another half-hour to get back."

"Billy! I know." Kai sounded exasperated. "I've been out fifty times. I know the drill. We just need to time the ride for breaks, for mileage, and for scenic view points. I'm on it."

"I'm just saying. Come back before the heat in mid-afternoon. You have a compass?"

"Don't need one. I know where I'm going. Come on, Larissa."

Billy's hand reluctantly left the horse's neck. "Larissa, be careful," he said. "I told Kai he *had* to bring back the horses, but I said nothing about the riders." He grinned. "Seriously, though, always hold the reins, okay, when you drive the horse."

"Don't worry, Billy." Squeezing the reins with one hand, Larissa leaned down and patted the little man on his plaid-shirted shoulder. She was changing her mind about Billy-O. He was a decent dude.

"Don't forget to gently cue her," he went on. "Not rough, okay? Shiloh needs the mildest instruction. Do you know how to use the anti-venom syringe?"

"Bill, for fuck's sake!" exclaimed Kai. "We're not getting off the horses. There and back in four hours, stop clucking like a mother hen!"

"Billy," Larissa smiled, "forget about your mustering run. Just saddle up and come with us. Will that make you feel better?"

"Love to, but can't. Kelvin is about to kill me for being three hours late. Don't take your hats off, you'll get heat stroke." He tipped his own hat to Larissa. Kai was already clopping ahead. Billy gave Shiloh a nudge in the quarters, and Larissa's horse rocked from side to side as it lurched forward.

～～

Being on a horse when you're tired is terrible. The legs have to work so hard to control the horse, to carry you slightly upward to protect you from the horse's constant rocking bounce. Larissa's right palm that gripped the horn was sore, the left arm, slightly outstretched holding the reins was sore. After an hour of driving the horse through the dusty plain, Larissa was *done*. Kai was in front of her, marking the trail. All she saw was his back in a Jim Morrison "Riders on the Storm" T-shirt, almost as though they were on his Ducati, except they were on horses, separated by ten feet of desert. He kept stopping, writing things down in the trail journal, moving on. He rarely glanced back to check on her. The cypress and the mallee were sparse and far away. The blue-bush grasses were near, boulders, pebbles, uneven terrain, sand, stone, clay, blistering sun, not a cloud in the sky.

"I thought you told me Pooncarie was a river port town?" said Larissa.

"I did," he said. "It was."

"*Was?* Like, what? Forty thousand years ago when the Aborigines ruled the wetlands? And you know, in Jersey, the dinosaurs once roamed the earth. I don't say, yeah, Summit is a prehistoric Jurassic town."

"You could say it. I wouldn't care."

"It's misleading is all." Because this is what Larissa was going to waste her precious breath on. Kai's ability for dissembling.

Every once in a while when she reached down to grab the water flask, the leaning over made her feel as if she were losing her balance, so she put up with unquenched thirst to continue sitting steady and straight in the saddle. Shiloh scared her. Sure the animal walked meekly now, but Larissa suspected that had nothing to do with her, and if suddenly the Waler decided to bolt, to career from side to side, or to kick back on its hind hocks with a loud neigh, there would be nothing she could do. Pulling her wide-brim Stylemaster over her face and wrapping the reins around her wrist, Larissa held on to the horn as tightly as she could. She wasn't driving the horse. The horse was driving her. Kai and Larissa were riders on two of the four horses in the Book of Revelation. What did the colors of the Apocalypse mean? She had studied the lines for a Great Swamp Revue soliloquy at the same time Evelyn had been studying Job. How handy. Kai's red horse was what? War? *And there went out another horse that was red, and power was given to him . . . to take peace from the earth, and that they should kill one another: and there was given unto him a great sword.* And what of her own pale horse? Larissa didn't want to think about it for a second further. Was that the *Hippos Thanatos?* . . . *And I beheld, and lo, a pale horse . . . and Hades followed with him.*

Ridiculous. Look at Kai, take an example from him, how relaxed he was. Clearly three months in the bush made him comfortable in the saddle. He wore his riding boots, his big Akubra to keep out the sunshine. And there was some fierce sunshine.

But it felt as though she were three years on the horse. Her legs were so sore.

"What time is it?" she called to him.

"Eleven."

Only eleven! "You want to stop soon?"

"Not yet. Stop drinking so much. Then you won't need to stop. And hold on to your horse." Kai glanced back. "Don't tie up your wrist in the reins," he said. "If something happens . . ."

"What can happen?"

"A million things, Larissa. The horse can see a snake. They get startled by snakes and make sudden jostled moves. You heard Billy-O. If you fall off the horse and your wrists are tangled in the leather, Shiloh will drag you for a mile before she stops galloping. So do yourself a favor, okay, and don't wrap the reins around your wrists."

The side-to-side motion of the horse's hind quarters worried Larissa. She felt like an uncooked egg on top of a car that was about to race down an unpaved road. "What kind of snakes are around here?"

"King Brown everywhere in Australia, including here," Kai replied. "But it just so happens that in this part of Mungo, there is a small narrow habitat for the very uncommon inland taipan. The only location for it for hundreds of miles, by the way. Isn't that amazing?"

When they first got to Australia, both she and Kai had been fascinated by the plethora of dangerous, poisonous, extreme wildlife abundant in the country. That passed. But Larissa remembered well the inland taipan, cousin to the western taipan, the most venomous snake in the world.

"We're not getting off the horses, so quit worrying."

But this was the thing. Larissa *was* worried. She *needed* to get off the horse to rest her limbs. She was getting hotter and increasingly achy. Her legs in the constantly extended position kept hurting without relief. Much like her heart was hurting, and it wasn't even in the saddle. She hated it here, hated everything about this place. She would rather live a thousand lives in Che's broken-down shanty than spend another day in this burnt-out wilderness.

She kicked her horse awkwardly to speed up a little to sidle up next to Kai so they could ride neck in neck. They did. Silently.

After a while he said, "We'll turn around soon. I really want to get to the Great Wall of China dunes. What a treat that would be for the tourists."

"It wouldn't be a treat," she said. "It'd be torture. Like it is for me."

"That much's obvious," he retorted.

"I hate it here. I want to leave as soon as we get back."

"You can leave any time you want," Kai said. "You could always leave any time you wanted. I don't know why you didn't."

"I like your friend Billy very much," Larissa said, ignoring him, not responding to him. "I was wrong about him. He's a good guy."

Kai didn't say anything for a few minutes. They stretched out the mute moments in a timespace continuum around them. Clomp, clop, heat, silence. They were both looking ahead at the desert, not at each other.

"Larissa," Kai said. "I'm not going back to Jindabyne."

"What?"

"I'm not. I don't want to. I want to make a new life here."

"Here where?" she gasped. "In *Billy's* house?"

"No . . . in my own house. There's a little place I found, near the stables. I want to stay. Run the trail ride business."

"You want to run the trail ride business, do you?" Larissa squeezed the reins into her fist. Had the horn not been made of durable leather, it would've burst under the stress of her clenched hand. "Tell me, was this trail ride business really Billy's idea—or was it yours?"

"It was mine," he admitted.

She glared at him, judging him for his lies. "And hocking your bike for Billy-O, was that a lie, too?"

He paused. "I didn't pawn it. I sold my bike. Sold it to pay for two unbelievable mares."

Larissa was speechless.

"I cannot be*lieve* you sold your bike," she said at last.

"I love the horses, what can I say?"

"Like you liked New Jersey, liked your Ducati, liked Jindabyne? Not too long ago, you were telling me how much you loved it all."

"I did like all those things," he said with a nod. "But I hadn't seen this."

"This is hideous!"

"To you it's hideous. To me it's transcendental."

"Oh my God." Letting go of the horn, Larissa wiped her face, perspiring in running-down beads. "Is that why you were dragging your feet, torturing me in Crackenback?"

"Yes. I was done with Jindabyne and didn't know how to tell you." Kai had put the paper and pen away, and was holding the reins, not looking at her.

"And when you see the next thing, what happens? Whaling perhaps? Farming? Coral-gathering? Crocodile-hunting? What are we going to do then?"

"When I can't stay here anymore, I will go," Kai said. "Larissa, I'm looking for new frontiers, for remote settings, can't you see? I am seeking refuge in nature in my quest for beauty. I don't need money. I never needed it. I'm longing for unattainable fulfillment."

"Unattainable is right," she blurted out. "But what about me? I hate it here. Does that mean anything to you? That I'm going to be miserable?" And then things sprung into her head she didn't want to think about. The answering machine he said wasn't there. The caller ID. The cell phone service he told her didn't exist. The letters to her he never wrote. The sending her away to the Philippines. Oh no. Did he . . . ?

"We were on a wonderful adventure," Kai said quietly. "We had a grand life. But I believe it's time for the next chapter."

"What are you saying?" She could barely speak. Her mouth went dry. The hand that held the reins was shaking, and the horse started behaving erratically. It didn't know what Larissa wanted it to do. It would slow down, then go faster, turn its head, move its quarters in an odd way. Larissa's hands were not cooperating. She couldn't hold the horse steady.

"I need to move on," Kai said. "That's the truth."

"Move on from what?" Her voice fell into a hoarse whisper. "As in . . . move on from *me*?" She said that disbelieving, as if she made up the craziest thing she could think of, knowing it would be instantly rejected.

But he didn't reply, pulling up his horse to walk at her pace, shifting Hal from foot to foot, clomp to clop in the pebbled dirt, staring at the ground. He didn't want to look at her, didn't want to look into her face.

"What?" she whispered. "Was nothing real?"

"Why are you deliberately misunderstanding?" Now Kai stopped his horse. She belatedly realized it was because Shiloh had stopped, because Larissa had accidentally pulled up the reins in her distress. Kai turned Hal around and moved to stand close to Shiloh, muzzle to tail, tail to muzzle. He faced Larissa. Holding the reins, Kai put his fist to his heart. He and Larissa stared at each other. "What we had was real, was beautiful," he said intensely. "We had a profound everything. I loved you with all my heart, Larissa," Kai said. "But it's over. Tell me you don't feel it, too? Come on!" he exclaimed. "We don't have anything near what we once had, and we haven't had it for a good few years. We've been running down down down, and now"—he clucked his tongue with a *c'est la vie*—"we're at the end of the road. Before you left for Manila we'd become *so* mundane. What do you want for breakfast, pass the paper, what do you want to do in the afternoon. Yadi-ya-da. We'd been domesticated, like Hal, like Shiloh. Think of the feral animals we used to be." He shook his head, raising his brim. "Don't you want that back? With someone else? Because it isn't me, baking in the kitchen, unloading groceries. I don't want a routine with you. I walked about with you. I toured with you. I sailed the high seas with you and rode my bike with you, I shared my bed with you and loved you in more ways than I thought possible. We've done everything. There's nothing left for us to do but move on."

Larissa couldn't speak, couldn't get her words out. Dropping the reins she put her face in her hands and started to cry. Her good horse, despite the slack reins did not pull away, but continued to stand calmly next to her red partner.

"Larissa, what are you doing?" They were close enough that

Kai, reaching over, tried to pull her hands away from her face. She yanked her arms from him, nearly losing her balance. Panting, crying, she grabbed on to the horn.

"I don't know if this is acting," he said. "Are you putting me on? Why are you crying? Don't tell me you didn't see this."

"I knew we had problems, but everyone has problems. We were together, we were committed. I thought we were in love! I thought the whole point wasn't to bail, but to live together . . ."

"Problems!" He laughed lightly. "We didn't have problems . . ."

"Why did you bring me all the way out here!" she cried. "Why didn't you tell me this back in Jindabyne?"

"I tried to tell you! I told you in every single way but with my words."

"You *tried* to tell me?" She was gasping. "How did you *try* to tell me? Why didn't you just *tell* me?"

"I didn't want to hurt you. I wanted you to see the truth of what I'm saying to you now, to come to the blatantly obvious conclusion, to save some self-respect. What's the point of getting all histrionic about it? I hate scenes."

"Is that why you sent me to the Philippines?"

"I sent you to the Philippines to give us a much-needed break, to clear our heads, to clear our hearts. I honestly thought that you would see by my lack of engagement where the wind was blowing." Kai tilted his head in frustration. "I thought you would see the writing on the wall and not come back."

"You thought I wouldn't come back?"

"I was hoping," he admitted sincerely. "It would've been so much easier than this."

"Writing on the wall?" Larissa shouted. The rudderless horse trembled. "Why didn't you just write me yourself? Clearly I wasn't getting your obvious truths—why didn't you write me and tell me not to come back?"

"I should've. I made a mistake. But Bart, Bianca, Billy, they all told me for sure you'd never come back . . ."

"They *all* knew?" Larissa couldn't breathe. She bent over the horn and the saddle, she dropped her head into the horse's mane. She couldn't sit up, felt like she was falling down. "Is that why you didn't come to pick me up at the airport? You thought I wouldn't show up?"

With an apologetic shrug, Kai nodded. "When Billy-O called to tell me you were waiting for me at the airport, I admit I was pretty shocked." He half smiled. "Made pretty good time to Sydney, all things considered."

Larissa was going to keel over and faint. Kai's casual expression in the face of her uncontrolled grief was too much for her.

"Why didn't you tell me?" she groaned. "I know it would've been hard, but your deception, your lies, my paranoia, my desire to trust you, this is what people do, they trust each other. You saw I wasn't getting it; all right, I was dense, dumb, I was an idiot, I thought we would work it out, considering how much we gave up to be together." Wildly she pressed her fingers into her eyes, wishing for blindness. "I didn't think it was going to be over because you didn't want to be *domesticated*."

"Don't demean me. It's not *just* about that."

"Me demean *you*? Why didn't you tell me?"

"I thought it would be hard for you."

"Nothing could be harder than this," she whispered.

"I know that now." Kai opened his hands with a sheepish shrug. "I'm just a kid. I'm still learning."

"But what about what's left, Kai?" she whispered, choking on the tears in her throat.

"*What's* left?"

"What about love?" Her voice was gone again. "What about the thing that's left?"

He was silent before he said, "I'm sorry. There's not much left, Larissa. Not like we once had."

"Is any of it left?"

He shook his lowered head.

"You don't love me anymore?" she said. She couldn't believe it.

"I'm sorry." And Kai looked sorry. But not too sorry. "I don't love you anymore."

Shiloh chewed on some dried-up scrubgrass. The sun was like fire. For a few moments Larissa didn't speak.

"It's her, isn't it?" she said. "You pretend it's all about your noble search for answers, but in truth, it's all about that dumb bitch Cleo."

His face hardened. "Stop. Don't talk about her like that."

"Don't talk about her like what? It's always been about her. You met her in Jindabyne, asked me to have a threesome with her, because that's the kind of girl *she* is, and then sent me away like a coward, so you could come here and be with her. Tell me that's not true."

He twisted his mouth from side to awkward side, while his hands rubbed the saddle. He didn't look at her.

"What the fuck is wrong with you?" Larissa yelled. "Why did you bring me all the way to this fucking hole where she lives to tell me? Why didn't you tell me in Crackenback?"

"I tried to come here without you, but do you remember how insistent you were? I'll come with you, why can't I come, I want to come. Well, here you are."

"Come here without me? I didn't want you to come here without me, you craven bastard! I wanted you to tell me."

"I didn't want to have a hysterical scene like this one."

"So your grand plan was to run to Pooncarie like a little girl while I stayed in our hotel room and then just not come back?"

Kai didn't say anything. "I didn't know what to do. I was desperate. This is very hard for me, too, Larissa."

"Is it? Is it hard for you? I can't believe what you're doing," she said, bending in desperation over the horn, trembling on the horse. "I can't believe this is what you have been reduced to, have reduced me to."

"It's been a long time coming. You were blind. You didn't want to see it. It was right in front of your eyes."

"I don't mean that. I mean *her* . . . that fucking ugly slut—oh God!"

"Don't talk about her like that! You're being cruel."

"*I'm* being cruel?"

"To her, yes. You're being very mean. She is not ugly," he said by way of non-sequitur defense. "For your information, she won a beauty contest in Broken Hill last year. She was crowned Miss Silver City." He said it so proudly.

"Oh, she is Miss Silver City!" Larissa laughed while crying. "The competition must've been pretty dire if a dumb double-bagger slut like her could win."

"Larissa! I won't listen to this anymore, stop."

"Kai . . ." She kept wiping her face, struggling to stop sobbing. "But you and I . . . we gave up so much . . . don't you owe *me* anything?"

"I don't know, Larissa," he said hotly, taking off his hat, rubbing the sweat away from his head, his face. "*Do* I owe you something? You mean like you owed your husband and children something?"

It was like he had slapped her, hit her across the face.

"And actually," he said, "I'm treating you better than you treated them. At least I'm finally telling you what's going on."

"How can you say this to me?" Larissa became nauseated. Her face, despite the heat, was clammy and cold. "How can you be so heartless."

"Look, you'll be fine." Kai sounded almost chipper. Even now he was still selling her a car. "Just go back home."

"God forgive you, you don't know what you're saying," she mouthed numbly. "Who'd take me?"

"Oh, come now. Why not? Look at what you said about Nalini. She's still waiting for her mother. Well, your children are still waiting for you. It's never too late. Go home. Tell them you've made a terrible mistake. Tell them you're sorry."

"Tell them I'm *sorry*?"

He shrugged. "Tell them something. You can take the bus back tomorrow."

"Take the bus back tomorrow," she repeated. "And you?"

"I'm staying put, like I told you." Lightly he smiled. "Did you notice last night at the bar? Cleo's loose clothes?" He nodded excitedly. "Larissa, she is pregnant!"

Larissa stopped breathing. She put her hand on her throat.

He went on speaking in a ghastly cheerful voice. "I mean, I know this is hard, you . . . and me and *everything*, but from my point of view, isn't it something? I mean, come on, can't you be a little bit happy for me? You know about me, how hard it's been, you know what I've had to live with. After Simi and Eve, I haven't been the same. This is my second chance, to have a kid, to finally be a father. You know what this means to me; I don't have to tell you. I'm so happy. I rented a house for us and the baby. Before Cleo gets too big, we're thinking we're probably gonna get married—"

Maybe it was the awfulness of his face, so casual while speaking truth to power, so humiliating. He could've been talking to her about atoms, or baking, or snorkeling practices off the coast of Wailea. So mild, not like mercy. Larissa didn't know if it was the face or the brutal words or the vicious indifference in his eyes to the years they had spent together. Or if it was the yawning chasm between his contentment and her despair. All these things, none of them. Maybe it wasn't the years. Maybe it was the children. Remark about her family followed by his merry birth announcement. Whatever it was, Larissa had spent the last few months before Manila living in such lonely misery, fighting with him, extracting from him make-up love and false promises. She stepped to the brink, to the brink of the end of herself. This cannot continue. I cannot continue. She started to scream. She didn't know how she pushed him. But she did. She lunged for him, making an animal guttural sound of fury and hatred and heartbreak, a sound she knew you make only as you rage at those you love who have blackly betrayed you.

With the full force of her body and fists, she shoved him, shoved him so violently in his face and chest and throat that Kai fell sideways off his horse, shoved him so hard she lost balance and fell off her own horse. There was that sensation—the falling out of the sky, plunging down. Not out of the sky, but off a horse, onto her knees on the hard desert boulders.

She must have passed out from the pain because when she came to, she was on the ground, holding her knee and screaming, groaning from the raw agony of an open wound in her body, and yet it still didn't hurt like when he had savaged her.

Their two excellent, adaptable horses, tough and stocky, supposedly bomb-proof, yet terrified by the sudden protracted incomprehensible human suffering, bolted and loped away, far away so they wouldn't hear her scream. She slumped in the dirt. She may have fainted again.

When she opened her eyes, pain swallowed her. She groaned, trying to focus, to lift up her body, to find Kai. She saw him in the sand near low-lying bushes. He was convulsing.

She couldn't figure out why he was so stiffly unnatural, lying on his side, his body gyrating, his legs and arms flopping. He must have hit his head, broken something. This is what happens: you fall off the horse, you hit your head, and the horse is supposed to stay put, reins down, nose down, looking for some grass to chew in the outback. Larissa groaned again, but Kai didn't make a sound. His eyes were bulging. He was breathing, rasping. Blood trickled from his white-foaming mouth. She wanted to be less angry, but the pain in her knee terrified her. She wished she could gallop away like Shiloh. She was afraid she'd been badly injured.

Kai was only a few feet away from her, the width of two horses or perhaps the width of a bed they once shared. She feared that he broke his neck in the fall. She shoved him, he fell and she fell, but she was sitting up holding her knee, while he was down on his side and couldn't move. His eyes were moving, though, his mouth. He was whispering something to her. She couldn't hear him through her panting, and was afraid to come near him. Not just afraid. Couldn't.

Look at me. I'm sitting on the ground, covering up my knee

because I'm afraid to look. So I look at Kai instead, and he looks afraid, too. So afraid. He is mouthing to me, *Get help, get help*. It sounds like he's saying, *Remember me*. No. He's saying *I've been bit*.

"What?" Her voice trembles. It isn't fair! One second, one moment, you're overwrought like you've never been overwrought, and the next you're both on the ground. You can't move your leg, and he is whispering mute things to you that sound like *I've been bit*.

But he just told you he didn't love you anymore! He just said you should take a bus back home, mosey on home, to your *family*! He took you, took your heart, took from you everything. You're still panting from his unfathomable betrayal. It hurt so much you wanted to die. You wanted him to be dead. You shoved him off a horse wishing his soul harm, and suddenly he is begging you for help. He is begging *you* for help!

A few minutes ago, you were begging him for help. Where did that get you?

Yet . . . the thing you felt for him is still there. The thing that made you want him dead in the first place. The thing that is now making you struggle to crawl to him.

"What's happened?" she says.

I been bit, he mouths again. *Please. Help me.*

When you take your hand away from your knee, you see the source of your own physical troubles. You may not see the source of his because it's back under black soil in the arid Ayers land, in the shrubs of that transcendental mystical wilderness he so loves, but you finally see the source of yours. You see what ails you. Your knee is ripped open to the white kneecap, oozing plasma and blood. Gloopy white bits fall out in chunks.

Larissa starts to hyperventilate. Her knee is open! And they're miles from anywhere. What is she going to do?

She weeps.

Kai doesn't. He is paralyzed, she sees that. He can't move. He lies in his awkward bones like they have crumbled in a heap on top of his live body. The convulsions in his legs and arms become more pronounced. It's terrifying to look at him, and yet even more terrifying to look at herself. All she can do is hold her knee together with both hands, surprised it isn't bleeding more profusely from a gash that open, that deep. If only the horses would come back. His horse has clopped away what seems like a short distance, looking for food or water. Her horse is near, just not near enough to grab on to, and in her shocked confusion, Larissa has forgotten its name.

"Maybe somebody will come soon," she says, enervated by fear, drooping down, her head low. She is still panting but shallow now, stealing glances at Kai's desperate and pleading eyes. Behold your lover.

"Larissa," he whispers. "Get the anti-venom. It's on the horse."

"What anti-venom?" The sun is merciless. Many things are merciless. Then she understands. *I've been bit.* "By a snake?" Now she definitely doesn't want to crawl to him. Has it gone? Has it slithered away? What if it's still there, close somewhere?

"Which horse?" she says. She means to say, which snake? That little leather pouch on the side of the saddle. Billy-O sure knew what he was talking about when he told them to carry a syringe in case of animal bites, particularly the reptilian chordate kind.

Was it the inland taipan? One bite can kill a hundred adult humans. She remembers that from their days of faded fascination with the Australian world entire.

Tick, tick, tick. Panting breath, no other sound, except the slow clomping of a confused and riderless horse. Taipan, paralyzing venom. Nerve damage. Muscle damage. Kidney failure. Larissa's hands are twisted over her open knee. She tries and can't get up. She can't move her leg at all. Kidney damage. Maybe this is what happened to her friend Maggie. She was bitten by a taipan and didn't know it. What did Maggie once tell her? *So long as they believe there is a God, men will go on praying to God long after they've ceased to pray for the changing of the wind.* A smart man had written that. Who was it?

Is it too late for Larissa to pray for the changing of the wind?

Kai's horse, whose name is Hal, is a scrubland away with the anti-venom. A train station away. A city street. Perhaps as far as the golf course had been from her red front door. Perhaps as far as his Ducati had been from her Escalade that first winter day. Just keep walking, Larissa. It's so cold, and you've got a little boy to pick up from school, and a track meet to attend, and a cello recital, and Bo is looking for a new lover, and Maggie wants to teach you how to paint, and Ezra wants to tell you about Epicurus, and Jared is about to buy you a shiny metal spectacle on wheels that roars down Glenside through the Great Swamp, through the Deserted Village, to Albright Circle and Lillypond where you left your heart. The red horse with the anti-venom is *that* far away.

"I can't get up," she says to him, to the skies. "I hurt my leg. I don't know . . . something is wrong."

"Larissa!" Only his bleeding mouth, only his eyes move, dart this way, that. His stiff body is shaking. She sees that his fingers have started to swell, his neck too. His lips protrude; he becomes harder to understand.

But the horse! The horse is already in the past, on the river of memory, inexorably moving toward the sea into which all rivers flow. You can't touch the same water twice, you had one chance, that was it. The horse has gone.

O Lord, help me . . . Why have you forsaken me? Bring back the horse!

She sees Kai trying to get up, to sit up. Is this real? She blinks. No, he is still down, not moving, just looking at her. But there he goes again! As clear as love, Larissa sees Kai sitting up, turning around, staring at her with profound, imploring eyes. Is that his soul sitting up? She blinks. He is back down.

Limply she remains on the ground in insurmountable motionless sorrow.

It takes an eternity for him to die.

9

Seven Ages of Larissa

What do you think of when you're alone in the desert? Well, it depends. For the first four parsecs of time? Or the last three? In the beating downward drive of the sun, or when the blackness around you is so great that you actually begin to pray. Pray! You're begging God you have never called on for help. Oh, the trench-warfare hypocrisy of it. Dear God, dear God. Remember me. Help me. Don't forsake me.

Her father, whom she loved more than anyone before he betrayed the family, used to say to her, "Larissa, living a life is not like crossing a field."

She never knew what that meant, but, boy, did he love to say it.

But now she knows. She wants her horse. Shiloh, Shiloh, Shiloh of Cyrene . . . so it can help her cross the field.

This is a National Park. Like Yellowstone, like the Grand Canyon, like the Great Swamp in New Jersey near her house . . . where are other people, one person, one other human being . . . ?

There are fossils of humans here, as old and far back as 40,000 years. Kai called it time before history. Bushwalk through the sparse and shrubby mallee, through the cypress pines, hoping for a glimpse of the red kangaroo, of the wedge-tail eagle. That's what Kai told her, and perhaps he was right, but all Larissa sees in the gibber, in the desert pavement are rock fragments, pebble size, cobble size. She doesn't see the goosefoot wildflowers in the scrubland, or colorful leafy chenopods. She doesn't see Kai moving anymore, sitting up, not even when she blinks.

What's happening? The heroes in their own stories can't die. She was a theater and an English major. She knows this. You can't afflict them with death.

Except this isn't Kai's story. This is Larissa's. And she is no hero. Aside from the three children she heroically gave life to—and look where *that* got her. Children, behold your mother.

She turns her body away from Kai's body because seeing him dead while she remains so precariously alive is unbearable.

Precariously alive is a good way to describe everyone. One moment on a horse, the next . . . If she could walk, she would. But her tendon must have been severed in the fall. She can't walk *at all*. She cannot in any way stand up, put weight on the leg, move forward. She needs the horse, but the horse is not Riot. It will not come when called. It won't come even at random, just because. Just saunter over to find some dry scrub near her. No.

Did the horses run away from her desperate cries, or did they gallop away from the snake? And does it matter?

Larissa sits on the ground, and when she can't sit any longer, she lowers herself into the sand and drags her body sideways, away from Kai's, drags it slowly like a foot soldier, until she is fifty feet away, a hundred. Until he is a speck, an illusion in sunlight. A mirage. She is so thirsty.

She has to get herself to the horse. Then . . . she will mount it, she doesn't have to walk to do it, she just has to pull herself up to do it.

The severed tendon is like paralysis of the limb. The leg that once was is now no more. Did she sever her patellar tendon? And is this something that needs to be repaired surgically? To even think of those two words, repair and surgical, in the context that Larissa today finds herself in, is comical. On a flat unpaved terrain, as far as the eye can see dirt, bush, scraggly eucalypts. Nothing else. No phone. No hospital. No other people. Snakes, though. Heat. It isn't that the horses had gone. It's that there is no way to get to the horse. Damn animal!

After college, Jared, while playing weekend league football, tore his Achilles tendon. It was awful for him. He had to have surgery and couldn't move for weeks. Larissa was on the field when he injured himself, and as she ran up, she could see he was in terrible distress. Can you stand, the trainer had asked him. He tried. His leg hung under him as two grown men lifted him by his underarms and put him on a stretcher. Can someone lift her, put her on a stretcher?

Come here, Shiloh, come here, Hal! The water flask is strapped to the Waler's side. Near the anti-venom syringe. Larissa cringes. Leaving herself in just a bra, she takes off her blouse, tears it into strips, and ties the knee up as best she can. It has swollen under her hands and has become so painful to touch that she lets out curdles of screams before she can tie the shirt around the knee. She had thought the bandage might make it easier for the leg to function, but that's just a maladaptive thought disorder on her part, a delusion. Bandage or no, the leg is useless. A severed tendon is worse than a broken bone. You can still stand on a broken bone right after the injury. Having broken her ankle in the unfortunate hairdresser incident, Larissa was still able to get up off the dirty rug in the hallway outside the salon, to gimp to the car, even to drive. It wasn't until four hours later that Jared took her to the emergency room.

Here, she had a non-working limb even before the shock of the gaping wound wore off. To be replaced with other shocks: the wandering horses, the fear of snakes, the anguish of the calamity of broken love, the sight of the broken man she hitched her wagon to, and then, the blaze of the sun and his foaming paralysis, both of them falling in slow motion, from excessive force, from irrational violence. Under her hands Larissa still feels his chest and shoulder, his unshaven stunned face, both fists shoving him, her throat emitting that agonizing groan, him trying to grab on to her, failing, falling. The horses startling and pitching forward, causing the loss of balance in the riders. Yes, but what about the loss of his life? Did they cause that, too?

What hubris it was to think it would last! That it would last because of the magnitude of her sacrifice, the exorbitant price she had to pay to be with him. Or that when the flame went out, something deeper would be left, like Love, like with Jared. But here, after the curettage, nothing was left in the scraped-out, abandoned cavity of the suffering mutually theirs.

The horse, his? Hers? It might as well be three miles away. She can't get to it. She tries. She crawls. She is so thirsty.

How long has she been crawling? Is it almost evening? Can't be, the sun is still so high. She can't tell by the color of her skin, but she thinks she might be burned pretty bad. Some of the skin on top of her wrists has begun to bubble up. The Akubra Stylemaster is loose on her head, but the body can't be covered with its wide brim. The knee throbs every time her heart takes a beat. She counts. Sixty, fifty, forty stabs a minute of severed wickedness.

Out here in the open, truth and consequences plays in her heart when there's nowhere to hide from them, when there's nothing else to think about, and the pain is great every time she breathes, every time her heart beats.

It becomes hard to believe she is not being flayed for her sins.

She has to get to the horse before the sun goes down. That is a must, there is no choice. She cannot, will not, spend darkness in the desert.

Jared, I'm sorry.

I'm sorry, children, your mother is sorry. But even as Larissa said it, she felt worm-like in her eleventh-hour contrition. When she ran from them, she didn't allow herself to think of them. She rode on the back of his bike with the wind in her hair, she gulped mountain air, she was hot, she was salty, she was Love, she was alive! She convinced herself that her family would be fine.

But were they fine.

It was hard to tell from her vantage point of being in prehistoric Australia, in a nest of human-eating taipans, indifferent Walers, treacherous men. How do you replace love with knowledge? How do you repeal your self-obsessed agenda? How do you change what could not be changed? No, that part was finished.

If only she could get to that horse. Is she moving closer to it, crawling on the ground, or is it just a mirage? Is it moving closer to her perhaps? Larissa blinks. Shiloh momentarily vanishes and is replaced by a sepulcher of tall branchy trees, and a gate, with a man slowly riding a horse through the sloping golf course. The Short Hills Country Club would do that in the wintertime, arrange for a rider on a white horse to celebrate the winter solstice. Larissa tried never to miss it. Except for the last two years when she didn't even know it was happening.

How do other people summon horses? What would Billy-O do?

Here, horsie, she calls out, thinks she calls out.

Here, here, horsie.

Is she calling a horse or a cat? Neither would come. Riot would come. She was a good dog. She would come. But she can't ride Riot out of the apocalypse, can she? She can't mount her Labrador retriever.

What did Billy-O tell her? She can't remember. He told her . . . he told her . . . don't tell the horse to "whoa" unless you want her to stop. If you want her to slow down, say, "slow." Don't say "whoa."

Larissa calls out. She summons her powers, her lungs, takes a deep breath and yells, "Whoa!" She yells it again and again. Trouble is, she can't tell if the horse is moving, stalling, slowing, stopping. Is the horse still? The sun makes everything shiver. The air is trembling, and the horse, too. Larissa crawls on the dusty ground, dragging her leg. Her elbows are hurting, are scraped raw, her forearm is bleeding for some reason, bleeding right into the dust. "Whoa, Shiloh. Whoa."

She is a field away from the horse. Living a life is not like crossing a field.

What if the horse isn't there? What if it is also a mirage?

All of it a mirage. Even her. To be this hot, this arid, to hurt so much, to have so much pain, inside and out.

Una palabra. What is the *one word* I'm looking for that I can't find, one word that will bring me comfort, or stop my horse, or save me? Why don't I know that *una palabra?*

Where has the time gone?

Fickle friends. Now she knew why Bart was so apathetic to her. They knew. They all knew Kai loved someone else, that he was done with her. And they were lying for him. The only one who didn't know was her.

O God! Why are you forsaking me now? Help me . . . I just want to go to Manila and see my friend. That's all I want. I want to see Father Emilio and say to his kind face, you were right, and I was so stupid. To see Nalini.

Larissa cries into the dirt, and breathes in too much of it, chokes, spits it out, sputtering, hacking, panting. She is so thirsty. She thinks she might feel better if only she weren't so thirsty. The sun torments her from above. She needs water. Feebly she cries out. Help, help. Yihah . . . yihah . . .

All stories end with death.

Yes, just not mine.

His.

Not mine. Eve's. Simi's. Kai's. Not mine. I'm the narrator in my own story. I have to get myself back on the horse, and then I'll be all right. I'll find my way. I'll go see Nalini. Together she and I will figure out what to do. I can still do stuff. I'll drive a bus. I'll fish. I'll sell Father Emilio's fruits.

There must be other things I can do after I get to the horse. I'm so close. It's not far, it's right within reach. Whoa, she keeps whispering. Whoa.

She hears the Dylanesque sound of his harmonica, blowing plaintive notes of a barely familiar tune . . . He plays, and then he stops and sings. They're in her car, and it's lunchtime. It's before much, but after much also. There's nothing yet to return from, and because of that it seems so simple, so happy, and it hurts the heart. He blows, and then he sings.

"*Beautiful dreamer . . . wake unto me . . . starlight and dewbright are waiting for thee . . . beautiful dreamer . . . queen of my song . . .*"

He is laughing and she is laughing too and he is looking at her kind of endearing and kind of funny, and nothing is what it is now, it just is.

How could he do this to me? He loved me so much, how could he do this.

What did Dante say was the worst sin? Not that Dante was such an authority on sin. Larissa doesn't know Dante's personal history, but she's staged enough Shakespeare and read enough of the Greeks, and most important, she's seen *The Godfather*, and taken a Corleone course in college, to know that all the poets and all the writers, pulp and classical, the United States government and Jesus himself were pretty specific and consistent on what constituted the gravest of all sins. It wasn't a toss-up between murder and aggravated assault with a deadly weapon. It wasn't between gluttony or perjury. It wasn't fortune-telling or indolence.

It was betrayal.

Oh, Kai.

That was the one. The U.S. Constitution was plain. "*The President of the United States shall be removed from office for Treason.*" And just so you knew where you stood, the Founding Fathers capitalized Treason for you, in case you had any doubts.

Mark Antony's eulogy of Caesar was no less indicting. "*Brutus, as you know, was Caesar's angel. Judge, o ye gods, how dearly Caesar loved him . . . then I and you and all of us fell down, whilst bloody treason flourished over us.*"

Father Emilio: *Man is not punished for his sin. He is punished with his sin.*

Larissa's skin is bubbling up under the sun.

My question to Father Emilio, when I see him next, is this: why is the gravest of sins the hardest of all the commandments to keep? Why is it the easiest to break? If it's so terrible, why do we all do it?

Why are so many of us faithless?

Betrayal: *be*: to completely; *tray*: to hand over. Betrayed: *utterly handed over*.

Larissa can almost hear the voice of the man of the cloth replying: first answer about yourself, Larissa Stark. Not why are others faithless. Why were *you* faithless?

I wasn't faithless! she cries. Perhaps she needs more time to think about that one a little later. Her priority now is to get to the horse. She is almost there! The horse is still and Larissa is moving. Her left side from her shoulder to her ankle scrapes the dusty ground.

I wasn't faithless! I loved them. I loved them still. I don't let myself think of Emily's nails she keeps breaking when she plays volleyball but keeps wanting to grow because she wants them long like mine. I don't let myself think of Asher sitting on my bed playing me a song on his guitar he learned just yesterday, or of Michelangelo running through the porch door in Lillypond saying, Mom, come, I caught a whole family of frogs, I put them in our boat, come.

It wasn't because I didn't love them. I just wanted what I wanted. The allegiance was to me first. I hoped Jared would get on with it. I hoped the children would get over it. What's the big deal anyway? People do it all the time.

That last one is true. People do it all the time, betray the ones they love.

That Ninth Circle must be filling up by now, spilling over the Hades banks. No more room in Lucifer's mouth. The icy rooms are full.

But why am I singled out? Larissa cries, crawling on one side, on one arm, when other people do it too? We talk about how betrayal is really an act of rebellion against possession. Obligation is all about what you owe someone else. It's about commitment, vows, the promises you made. Well, we rebel. We don't like to be told what to do. It's not so much betrayal as assertion. We proclaim who we are to the universe. This is what I am! I don't want to be pigeon-holed. I don't want to be narrowed. Obligations are anchors around your neck, and you want to be free like a bird.

It isn't about other people. It isn't about husbands. Or even about children. It is about Larissa.

Larissa wanted Kai. Larissa wanted adventure. She wanted passion. She wanted, period. In the end, that trumped everything.

A small thought bubble takes the breeze out of her self-righteous sails for a moment. Then why is Kai's betrayal so devastating to her? He also wanted what he wanted. Why is she steeped in justification when thinking about herself, but deems it unforgivable when thinking about him? Look how upset she was: she lost her mind, she shoved him. They fell. Now he is dead.

Why did he have to die for no longer wanting to carry his obligation to her?

She didn't mean to hurt him. *Certainly* she didn't mean to hurt herself. She lost her mind. Now it's back. She was so angry. She didn't mean to hurt him. Still, though. What he did was unforgivable.

She can't get to the truth of it, like a needle in the heart. Why is the consequence of *her* action nothing but a beautiful execution of her noblest instinct, and yet the worst thing *he* could ever do?

Ah! She is getting closer to the truth here in the blinding white wilderness. It is only betrayal when your lover turns his back on you. When you walk away from your family, it is principled self-determination, independence, personhood. It is freedom. It is love. All falling under the category of positive qualities. Almost like virtue.

It occurs to Larissa that this is the first time she even voices her abandonment in these terms. She has been calling it all sorts of things, starchy, self-justified. She has never called it betrayal.

Betrayal is what someone else does to you.

We expect so much of other people, thinks Larissa. So much of them, and yet so little of ourselves. Is that unfair? Oh, well. What's done is done. And it is done. You know what's unfair? That she can't move her leg! That she can't find the horse.

"All I do is pick up after the children. That's what I do. I went to school, grew up, went to college, worked hard, studied hard, dreamed BIG, got a job, briefly, thought much of myself, my talents, my intellectual gifts. I rocked to music, devoured books, baked, painted, danced, smoked. I was so happening. And then I had one child and another and another. And now all I do from morning till night is direct them and clean up their cereal bowls. Go get your glasses. Go get your folder. Go get the letter for me to sign. Go get your shoes. Go get your bag, your lunch money, your coat, your sister, your clarinet. Or: put your shoes away. Put your bowl away. Put the cereal box away. Throw away that wrapper. Close the pantry door. Pick up the straw off the floor. Close the dishwasher. Clothes go in the hamper, not right outside. Make your bed. Fold your couch blanket. Give Riot some water. The tissues from your nose, do they belong on the table or in the garbage? The empty cups, the paper cups, the empty boxes, the open jar of peanut butter, when when when when when will it ever stop?"

Evelyn sat smiling lightly. "I agree with everything you say, Larissa. My back is bent because there's always something on the floor I need to pick up. I was, I am, just like you. I can't believe I'm doing this instead of reading, or writing, or being on the stage. Do you remember how much I loved the stage? It was my life! And now this is what I do while the kids run off to their friends. I bend down and down." Evelyn nodded. "Larissa, I know. But this I also know. When you spend your day, each and every day, all the time, picking up after other people, and not just other people, but your children, your flesh and blood children, you bend, you sigh, you pick up the toy they dropped, the milk cover, the money they had to take with them on a trip and didn't, when you do all those things for them, day in and day out, that's when you find the Divine inside yourself. You know why? Because it's only the Divine in you that would do it. Do you know what I mean? You do it because that is what Love looks like, bent at the basin on the floor, washing their feet."

Larissa nodded. "You are so right, Ev," she said. "That's so smart. That's exactly how it is, how I feel. Now look. I'm sorry I have to run. But I must get to the store, or otherwise, those children I love so dearly and that husband so hungry will have nothing to eat. Look at the time.

It's nearly noon. You don't mind, do you?" She was so late! *Kai had been waiting since eleven!*

"*Women are saved through childbirth,*" Evelyn said to her as a goodbye.

To begin, to end, all the traffic in between.

Larissa now knows what the lie is: that the sun always goes down. Not here. Not this sun. It is never going down.

Her eyes see something close to her, and she tries to focus. She is having a hard time focusing. She squints and gleans through the fog of her blurred vision a shape in front of her, supine, on its side, so familiar, yet alien, close, yet supernaturally distant.

She shakes her head, blinks and blinks again.

To her uncomprehending gaze, the shape in front of her is morphing into what looks like *Kai.*

But that can't be! She has been crawling away from him for hours! The horse is just over there, a few feet away. She is far away from Kai. This is an illusion. It *can't* be.

And yet. Here he is. Was her desperate attempt to crawl away to get to the horse just an illusion? He is just as she had left him. Except swollen, nearly unrecognizable.

If he is right here, it means that she is right there, too. It means she hasn't moved in all this time. A bubble on her skin bursts, starts to leak weak clear fluid, viscous lighthued blood. Another bubble bursts. And another.

She is just where she had left herself. She is in exactly the same place.

Lowering her head, Larissa bends to Kai, slumps next to his body in the sand. She is so tired. She is going to rest for a few minutes before she begins again.

Minutes pass.

Or is it hours?

Maybe no time at all passes since the sun doesn't move.

Maybe there is no more time.

A thought flashes by her. What if I can't get out of this? What if no one comes and I can't get on the horse? What if this is already out of my hands? She pushes it out of her head. Ezra was right. Matter could not contemplate its own extinction, could not conceive of itself not being. Atoms could not swirl and contemplate the end of their own electrical charge, could not betray or be betrayed. Could not abandon, or be abandoned. Atoms could not love . . . or be loved.

The soul could. And her soul kept searching for the faithless horse in the blinding white. If only she could get on it, all would be well. Paradise was lost, but it could be regained. What did Father Emilio say? *We have the power in us to begin the world anew.* She would get herself to a hospital and when she was better, she would fly to Manila and go back to San Agustin, work at the orphanage, do her obediences, pay her penance, take care of Nalini, and if Che hadn't come back yet, they would take what was left of Jared's money and fly back to the U.S., stopping off for a few days in Hong Kong because Larissa had never seen Hong Kong and always wanted to, and then they would go and visit Summit, such a nice town to raise a family. Larissa could show the young girl where she had once lived, introduce her to the husband and children she had left behind.

Epilogue

Benevolence, Goodness, Kindness, Mercy, Humility. There it was. Humility. Che couldn't believe how well she remembered the layout of the streets, their familiar names. She walked faster and faster through the old neighborhood, passing the market that still sold the shoes and pears side by side. She reveled in the pressed-together streets, in the bustle of the afternoon. Faster and faster until she started to run, her small bag on her back—well, she didn't have a lot left.

Moonwalk, such a nice name for a town. Everything about it pleased her today, the closeness of the buildings, the smells of fish and smoke, the briny muddy bay. She couldn't believe she was *finally* back. She had written Father Emilio a few months ago when she knew for certain she was going to be released from that fuckhole of a medium security prison for women in Mindanao, and he was good enough to write back. He even sent her a parcel, a care package of dried crackers and cookies and potato chips. He sent her a Bible and a few pictures of her unbelievable baby, a big girl now.

But then he wrote Che a letter about Larissa that was so painful that Che had to put thinking about it away, the way she put thinking about Lorenzo away, or about being away for six years from the one thing she wanted most in the world. To be a mother.

Though the photo Father Emilio included of Jared's growing family comforted Che a tiny bit. His very pregnant Slovakian wife. In his arms a new baby. His three children with Larissa all grown by his side. Emily, 22, looking just like her mother. Asher, 21, with a guitar in his hands, shaggy-haired, scruffy, leather-jacketed, smiling. And Michelangelo, a lanky teenager, taller than his dad, and with a floppy head of curly blond hair. The girls must love him, Che thought as she prayed in the prison chapel for her dearest poorest Larissa.

She almost ran past San Agustin in her teary reverie.

"Che!" Father Emilio came down the church steps to greet her, open door behind him. He was older and grayer, and his back was more stooped than Che remembered. That was because he was always bending to bless the old people in their beds, to bless the heads of the orphans. He embraced her, held her to him for a moment. "You came back."

"Yes, Father." She kissed his hands, bent her head to be blessed by him.

"You've had a safe journey down from the islands, I hope?"

Che shrugged. "I got sick. Caught some viral thing. I'm better now."

"You do look very thin."

"Nothing a little rice pudding, some *pandesal*, some *halo-halo* won't cure."

The priest took her by the arm. "Come," he said. "No use standing on the street when there's someone who's waited so long to see you."

"I'm scared, Father," Che said, pulling her arm away. "She doesn't know who I am. She'll be angry. I know I would be."

"Would you? If your mother came back, is that what you'd be?"

"She won't understand," Che whispered. "She's so little. I can't explain to her what I've done, why I've been gone . . ."

He took her arm again. "Come," he said. "No use standing here when there's someone who's waited so long to see you."

With trembling hands, Che fumbled inside her bag. "Wait, let me find the thing I brought her. Maybe I could give her a gift first? I got her a dress, a pretty floral one. I don't even know her size, but . . ."

"Come, Che." The priest squeezed her hand. "You can give it to her later."

They walked through the long darkened corridor, just as Che remembered it, and walked out through the double glass doors into an interior sunlit courtyard. A small group of children played in the far corner. One tiny black-haired girl in an oversized gray smock was the ringleader. She was bossy and loud, schooling one confused boy on how to play hopscotch. "No, Sammy, no, no, no, no, no. You're not doing it right," she said imperiously to the befuddled child. "Are boys even capable of playing this game? Watch me. You throw the marker onto a square, but when you hop, you can't hop *onto* that square. That's the point of the game. Otherwise you lose. Now, let's try it again. I will throw it on square three, and then you hop. But not on square three. Got it?" The girl's back was to the adults watching her.

Father Emilio called out across the yard. "Nalini," he softly said. Che leaned on his arm for support. Her legs were giving out.

The girl turned around.

For a moment she was motionless.

The small centavo fell from her hands.

"Mama!" she cried. She ran across the stone yard, ran with all her might, and jumped into Che's arms.

"Oh, Mama . . ." She hugged Che around the neck, wrapping herself around her mother. For a few moments no one spoke, no one made a sound except the chirping birds on the stone ledges.

"I knew you'd come back," Nalini whispered. "I knew it. I told everybody. Didn't I, Papa Emilio?"

"You did, Nalini." He patted her back. "You most certainly did."

Che was crying and couldn't speak.

"Don't cry, Mama." Nalini covered Che's face with kisses. She touched her mother's streaked face, her short hair, she wiped her mother's cheeks, and kissed her face again.

"I can't believe how big you are, Nalini."

"I'm six," the girl said, a proud smile on her face.

"Yes, I know," Che said. "And you're playing hopscotch."

"Your friend Larissa showed me how. Oh no. Don't cry! Please. She came to live with us. She stayed a long time, but then had to leave. Papa Emilio said she would come back, but I didn't think so. Don't cry. Wait till you see us perform the Nativity play she wrote for us. It's so good. She built us a cave and sewed us costumes, and made us props and everything. I'm one of the Magi, Mama. I'm the one who brings myrrh, but I know everybody's lines. I could play any part. I know the whole play by heart. Larissa said when I grow up I should be a director."

"You definitely should, my love."

"We're putting it on again for the Christmas Festival next week. I'm so glad you'll be here to see it. Papa Emilio says next year if I'm good maybe I can be Mary. I'm going to try very hard to be good." She glanced at the priest sheepishly. With great fondness, he smiled at her.

"You are so busy," Che said, caressing her daughter's head. "When do you even find time to play hopscotch?"

The child giggled. "I find the time. I make time. I'm very good at it. Want to see?"

Reluctantly Che set her down. "I want to see everything."

Nalini took hold of Che's hand, looking up at her. Che brought her to a bench, sat down, and lifted Nalini to sit on her lap.

"I thought you wanted to see me play?"

"I do. In a minute." Che touched the girl's hair, her bare arms, her skinny legs, felt her through the fingertips, inhaled her, gazed at her with adoration. "I can't believe how big you are. How beautiful. What else can you do?"

"I can read! Wait till you hear me read Psalm 136."

"Praise for the Lord's everlasting mercy?" Che said. "You can sing that?"

"Well," Nalini said, "Papa Emilio says I memorized it, and maybe I did a little bit, but I can also read it. The Lord's mercy endures forever. And it's true. It does. Because He brought you back to me. Oh, Mama."

"Oh, Nalini."

They sat on the bench, wrapped around each other, in a disbelieving embrace. "Nobody believed me," Nalini said. "I told the other kids, I told Larissa, I told Papa Emilio. No one believed me. But I knew you'd come back."

"It was really hard, Nalini. So many times I thought I might not make it. I've had a rough few years."

Nalini patted her mother's face. "But now you're here. And that nice man, Larissa's uncle or brother or somebody, Mr. Jared, he left us money to go to America if we want to. He said we could stay in his house for as long as we want. Papa Emilio told me."

"Do you want to do that?"

Nalini clapped. "So much."

"Well, maybe we can go and visit him after we get settled. We have to figure out some things first. Like where we're going to live. Mama has to look for a job."

"But after," Nalini said, "we'll go and visit the nice man in his big house?"

"Yes, darling. We can do that." It was pleasant out, hot, humid, not much of a breeze, no storms, nothing but twinkling sunshine.

They got up. Nalini was still in Che's arms. "You're nearly my size."

"No. I'm still your little baby." She kissed her mother and wriggled down. "What does my name mean, Mama? It's not Filipino. My friends keep asking me."

"It's Indian," Che replied. "It means the most beautiful one."

Nalini giggled. "Wait till I tell them. They'll be so jealous. Come," she said. "I want to introduce you. You want to play hopscotch with us? I can teach you. I'm a very good teacher."

"Let's go play," Che said. "I know how. Me and Larissa used to play a long time ago"—Che lowered her head—"when we were kids."

"Please don't cry," Nalini said, taking hold of Che's hand and pulling her mother to her waiting friends. "Come, Mama."

∾⚭∾

My dear Che,

It is with a heavy heart I write you these words.

About a year ago, a man from Australia got in touch with me. His name was Billy-O. He said he found my name and San Agustin's phone number in the letters that were sent to his friend Kai by a woman named Larissa.

Billy-O told me that Kai and Larissa went into the outback on two of his Walers to mark the trails. They never returned. Billy-O and three of his wranglers searched for them in the desert. It took them over three weeks to find their bodies. They lay close together, almost in an embrace, he said.

Billy-O didn't know what to do. He lived in a tiny town with no mortuary or funeral home and had no money to bury either of them. He barely knew Kai, and Larissa not at all. No one knew who she was or where she came from or even what her last name was. One day she appeared in Kai's life, and then just as suddenly vanished, and he with her.

Wedge-tailed eagles and black kites had scattered what remained of their clothes and left nothing but their bones behind. So Billy-O, after careful consideration, decided to also leave their bones behind.

He fashioned a cross out of wood and stuck it in the sand next to the small shallow grave he had dug for them. The cross was a marker. If Jared Stark wanted to bring his former wife's body back home to be buried, I was sure Billy-O could take him to her.

You can imagine how difficult it was for me to make that call to America. Though I'm sure nowhere near as difficult as it was for Jared to receive such a call. But I had to speak to him. I didn't want to take the choice away from him and her children.

When I told him about Larissa, he wept.

He thanked me for contacting him and said he needed a few days to think.

After a week, he called me back. He said he really struggled with what to do. He said Larissa just couldn't help herself. On and on she found interminable ways to continue to break his heart. But in the end Jared decided not to impose his will on her will, even in death. Especially in death. No matter what he wanted, he chose to give her what she wanted. She didn't want to come home. She refused to return, found bliss in the other world where few dared to tread. Even when wounded, she rejected all rescue, all call for redemption. She wanted freedom to be, to live unbound, without a past and without regret. So Jared let her be, and left her in the Mungo wilderness, cast out into the open and beholden to no one.

My prayers are with you, Che. Come home. Nalini is waiting.

As ever,

Father Emilio